THE LONESOME ERA

JON ALLEN

IRON CIRCUS COMICS
™

strange and amazing

inquiry@ironcircus.com

www.ironcircus.com

creator
Jon Allen

publisher, editor
C. Spike Trotman

assistant editor
Andrea Purcell

book designer
Matt Sheridan

proofreader
Abby Lehrke

print technician
Rhiannon Rasmussen-Silverstein

published by
Iron Circus Comics
329 West 18th Street, Suite 604
Chicago, IL 60616
ironcircus.com

first edition: October 2019

print book ISBN: 978-1-945820-38-0

1 2 3 4 5 6 7 8 9 10

printed in China

THE LONESOME ERA

Names: Allen, Jon (Cartoonist), creator. | Spike, 1978- editor, publisher. | Sheridan, Matt, 1978- designer.
Title: The Lonesome Era / creator, Jon Allen ; publisher, editor, C. Spike Trotman ; book designer, Matt Sheridan ; proofreader, Abby Lehrke ; print technician, Rhiannon Rasmussen-Silverstein.
Description: First edition. | Chicago, IL : Iron Circus Comics, 2019. | Interest age level: 15 and up. | Summary: "Cute animal characters tell the coming-of-age tale of an awkward, unreciprocated queer crush in Rust Belt America."--Provided by publisher.
Identifiers: ISBN 9781945820380
Subjects: LCSH: Gay teenagers--Comic books, strips, etc. | Infatuation--Comic books, strips, etc. | CYAC: Gay teenagers--Cartoons and comics. | Infatuation--Cartoons and comics. | LCGFT: Bildungsromans. | Graphic novels.
Classification: LCC PZ7.7.A375 Lo 2019 | DDC 741.5973 [Fic]--dc23

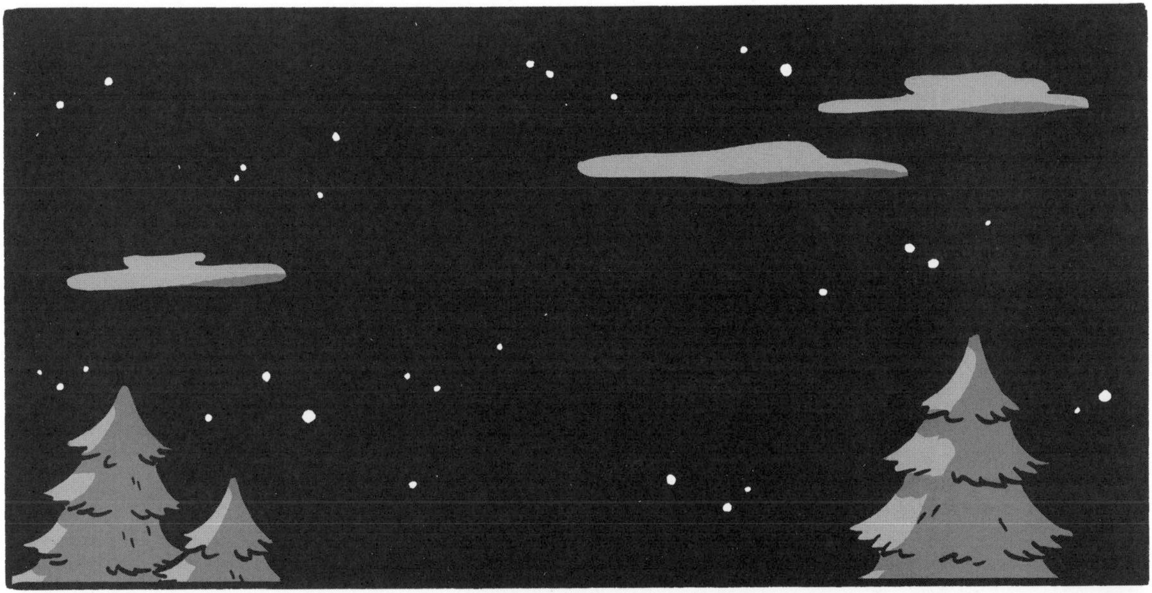

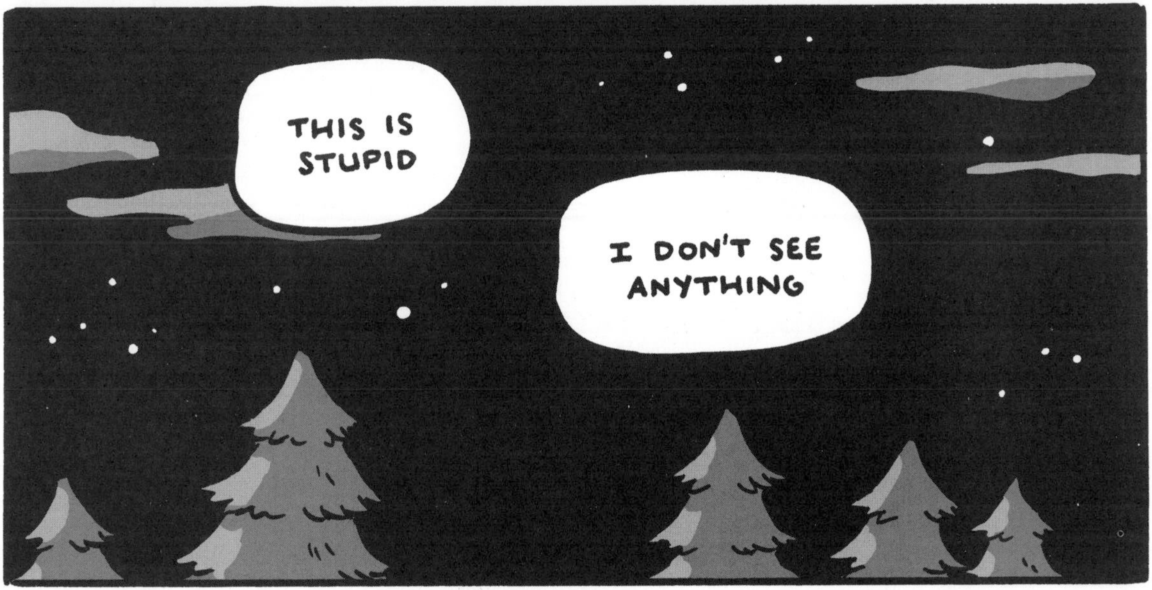
THIS IS STUPID
I DON'T SEE ANYTHING

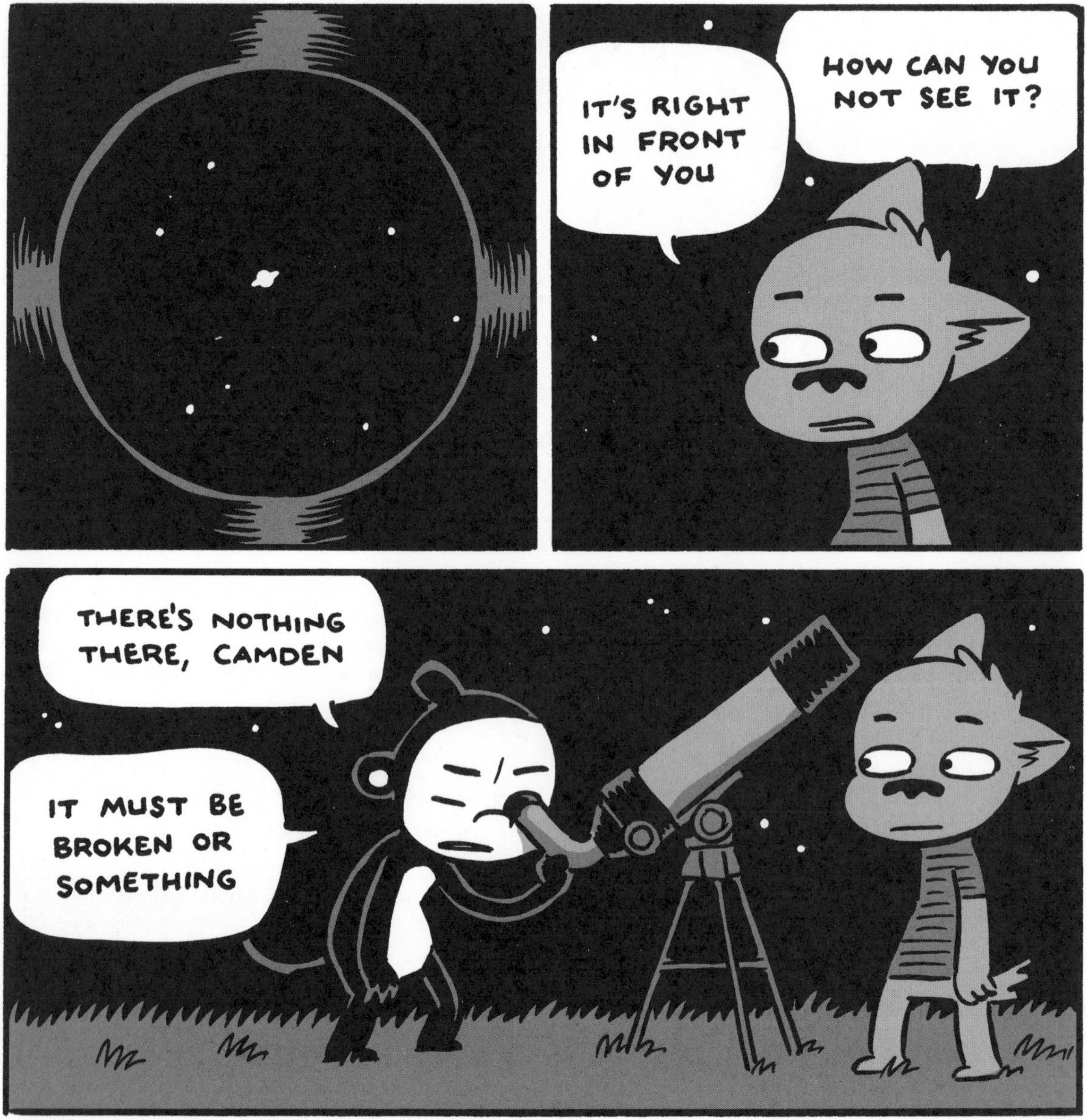
IT'S RIGHT IN FRONT OF YOU
HOW CAN YOU NOT SEE IT?
THERE'S NOTHING THERE, CAMDEN
IT MUST BE BROKEN OR SOMETHING

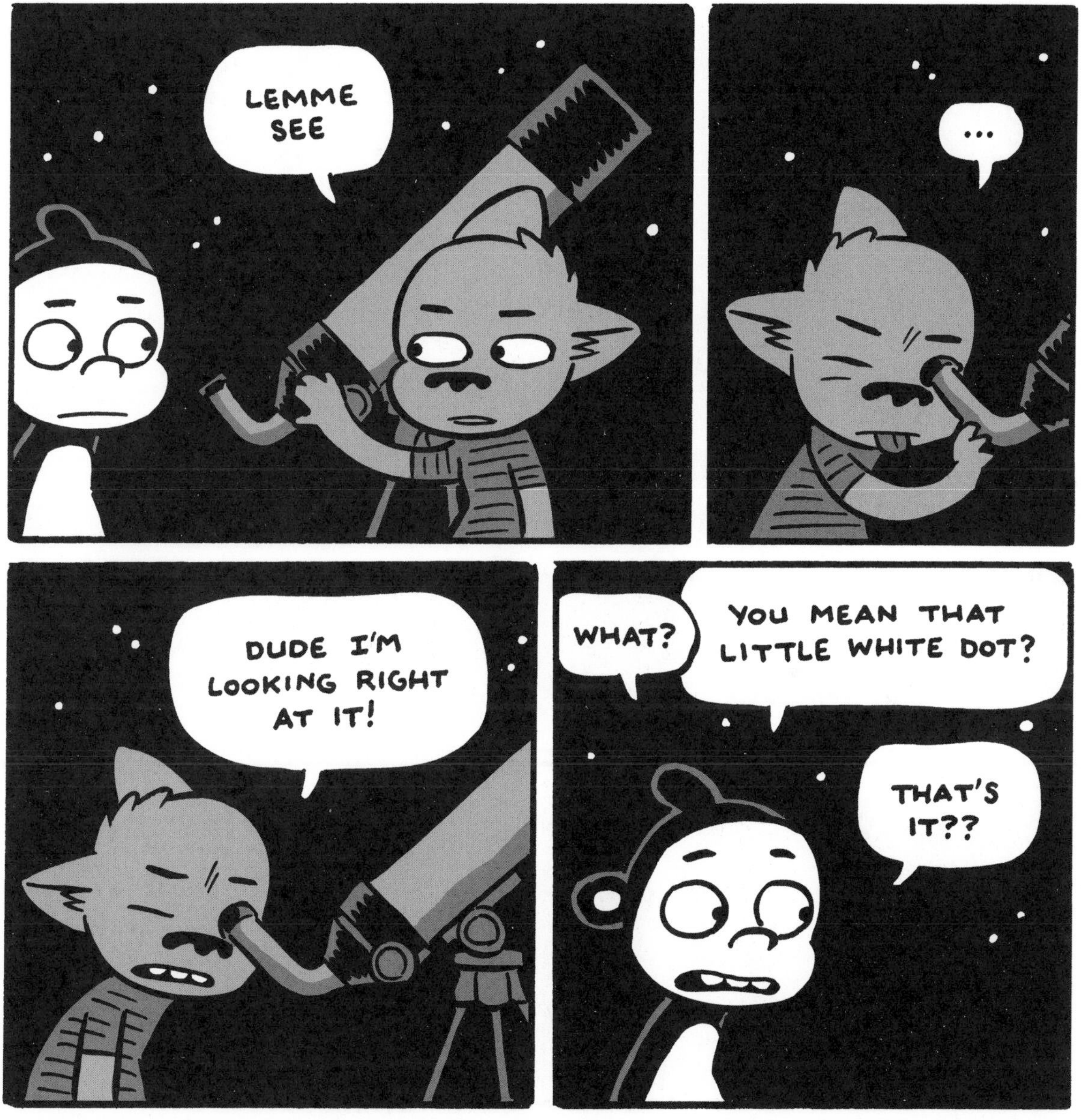
LEMME SEE
...
DUDE I'M LOOKING RIGHT AT IT!
WHAT?
YOU MEAN THAT LITTLE WHITE DOT?
THAT'S IT??

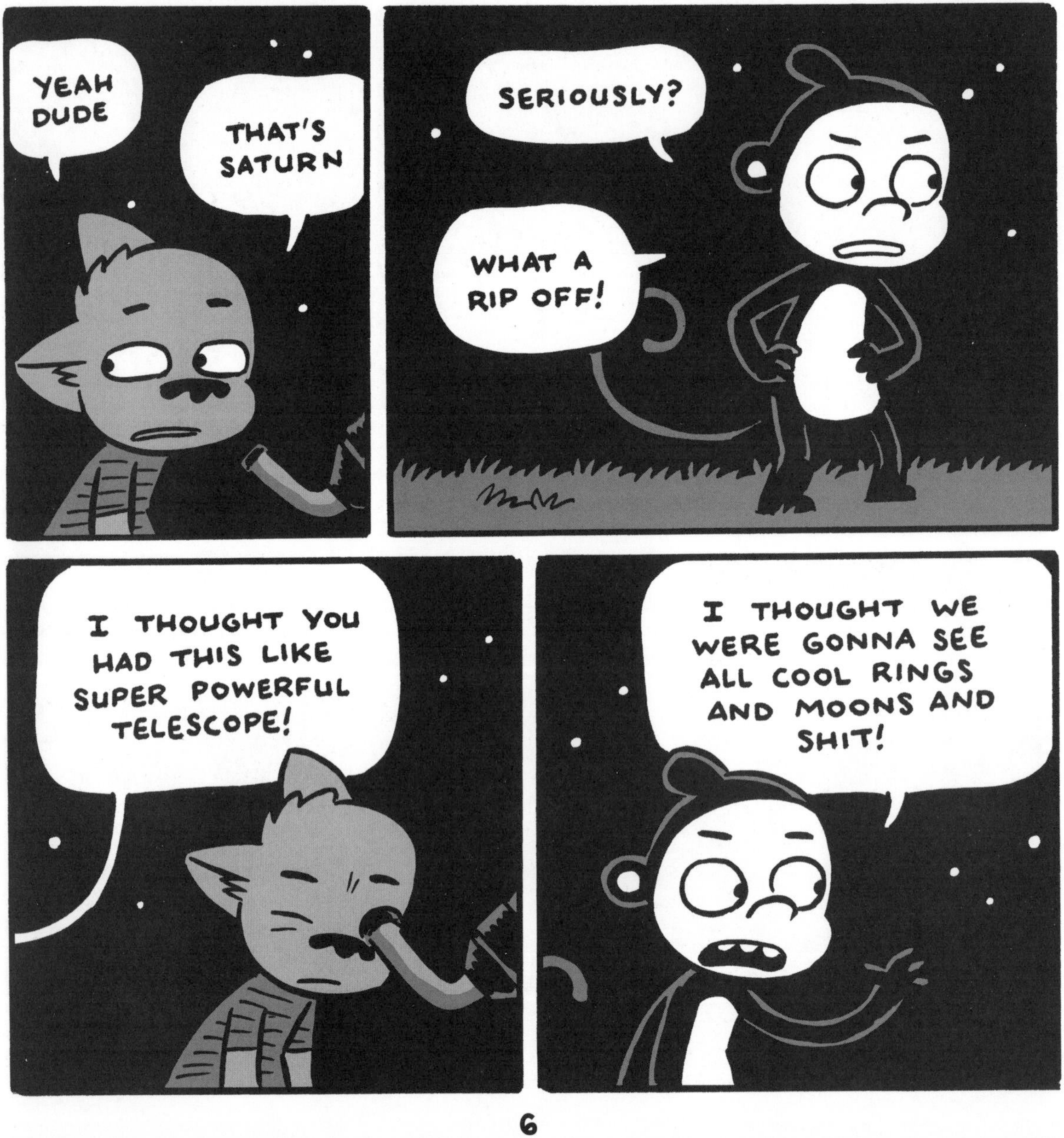
YEAH DUDE
THAT'S SATURN
SERIOUSLY?
WHAT A RIP OFF!
I THOUGHT YOU HAD THIS LIKE SUPER POWERFUL TELESCOPE!
I THOUGHT WE WERE GONNA SEE ALL COOL RINGS AND MOONS AND SHIT!

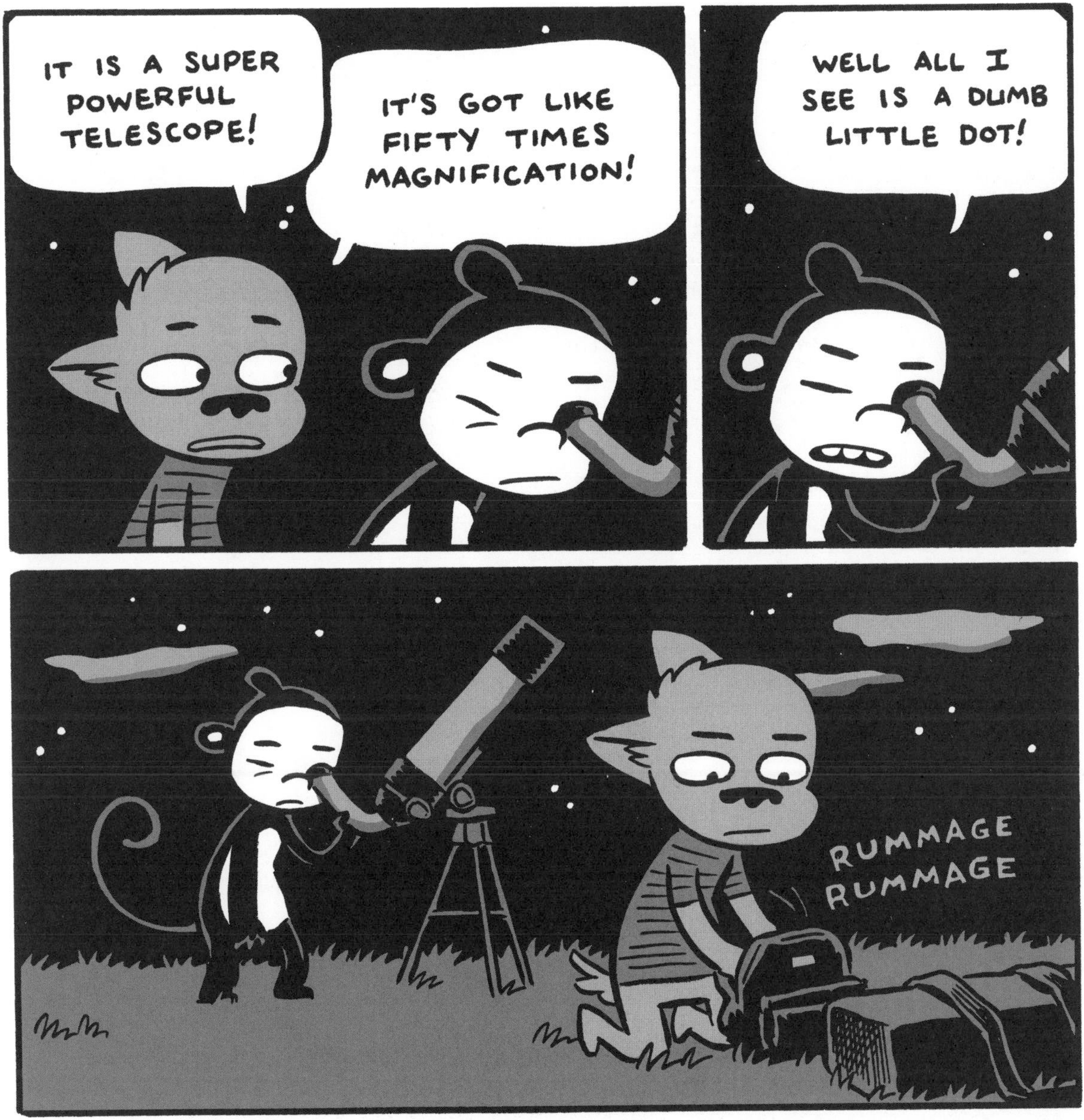
IT IS A SUPER POWERFUL TELESCOPE!
IT'S GOT LIKE FIFTY TIMES MAGNIFICATION!
WELL ALL I SEE IS A DUMB LITTLE DOT!
RUMMAGE RUMMAGE

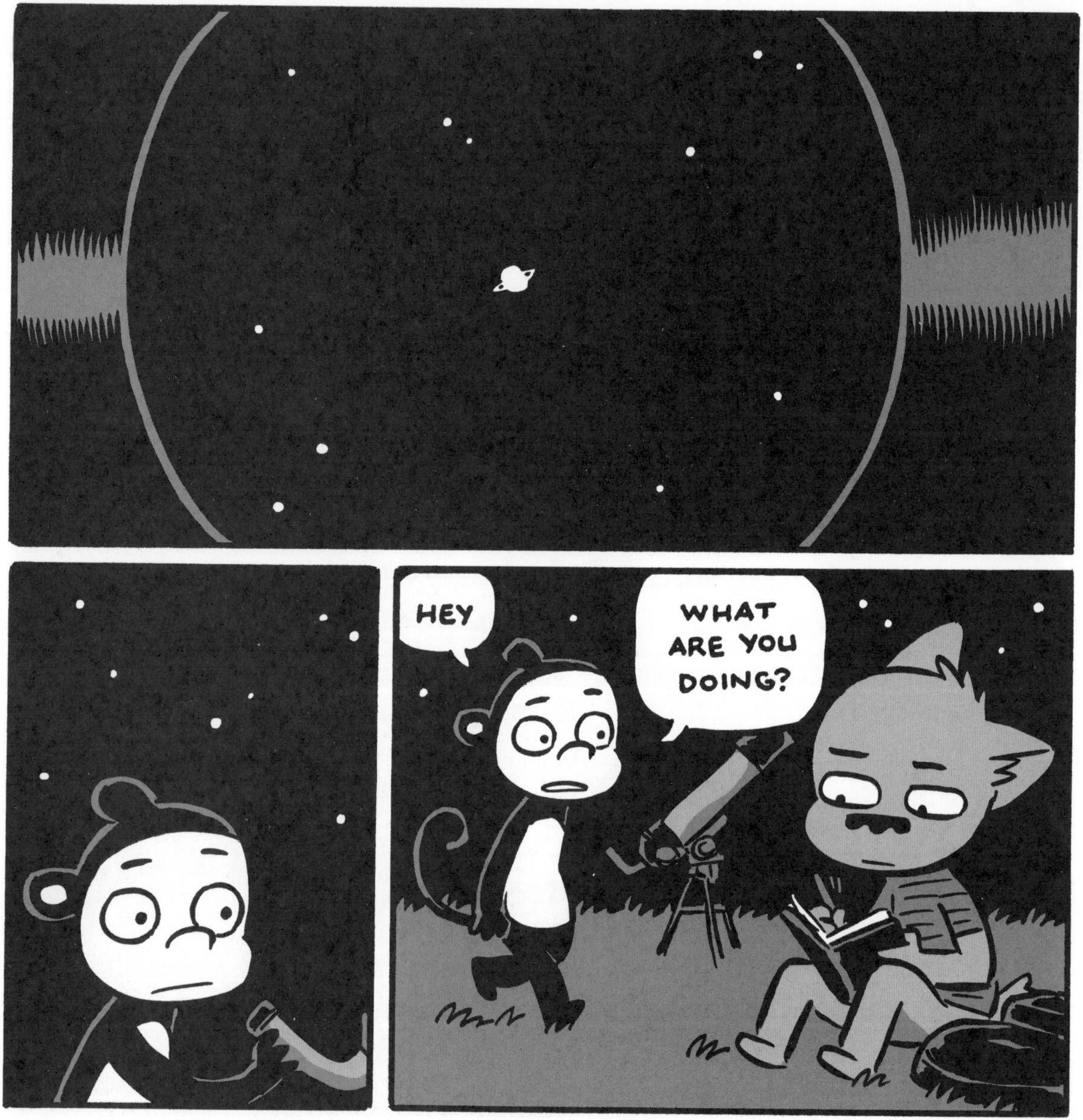
HEY
WHAT ARE YOU DOING?

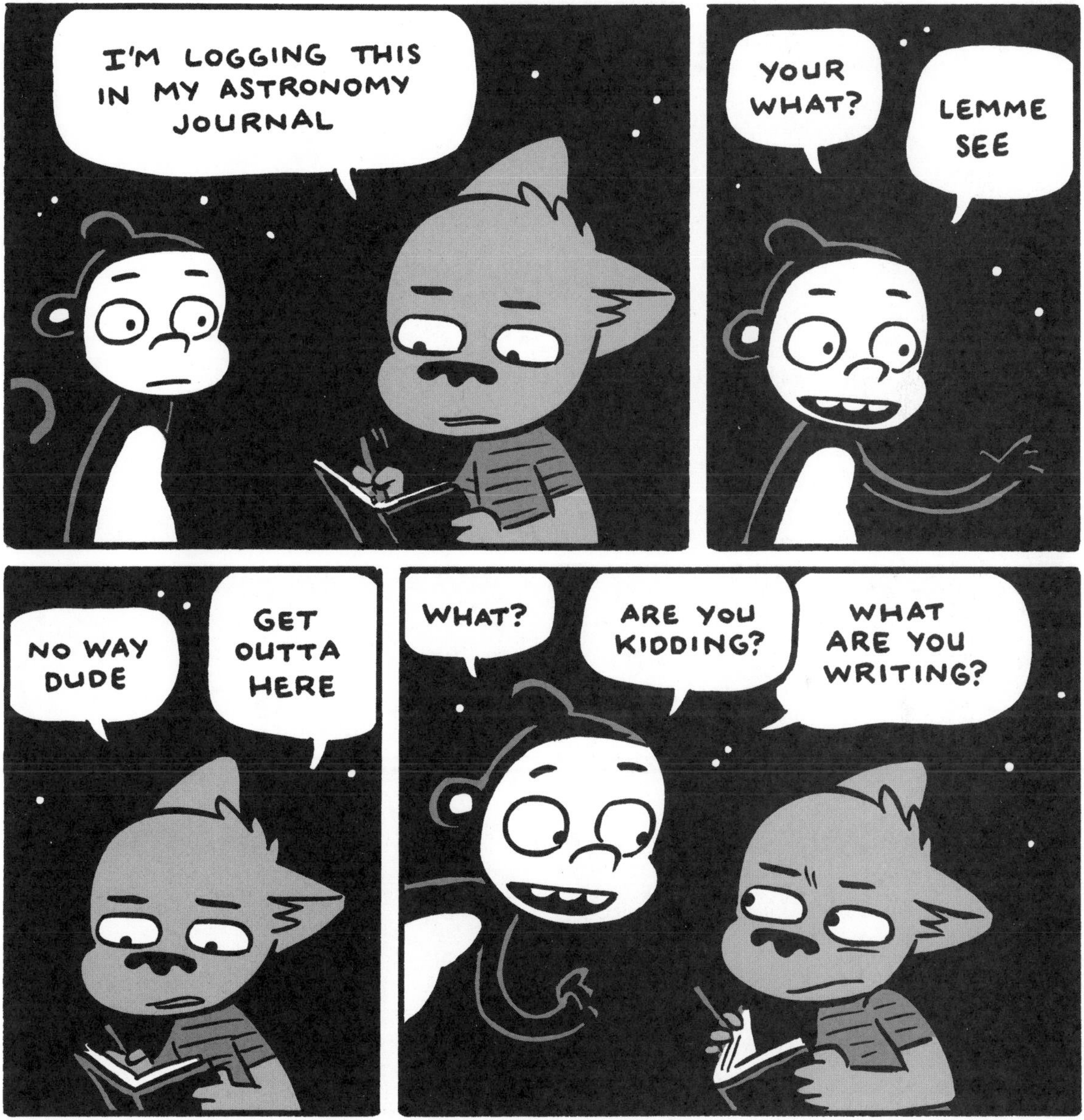
I'M LOGGING THIS IN MY ASTRONOMY JOURNAL
YOUR WHAT?
LEMME SEE
NO WAY DUDE
GET OUTTA HERE
WHAT?
ARE YOU KIDDING?
WHAT ARE YOU WRITING?

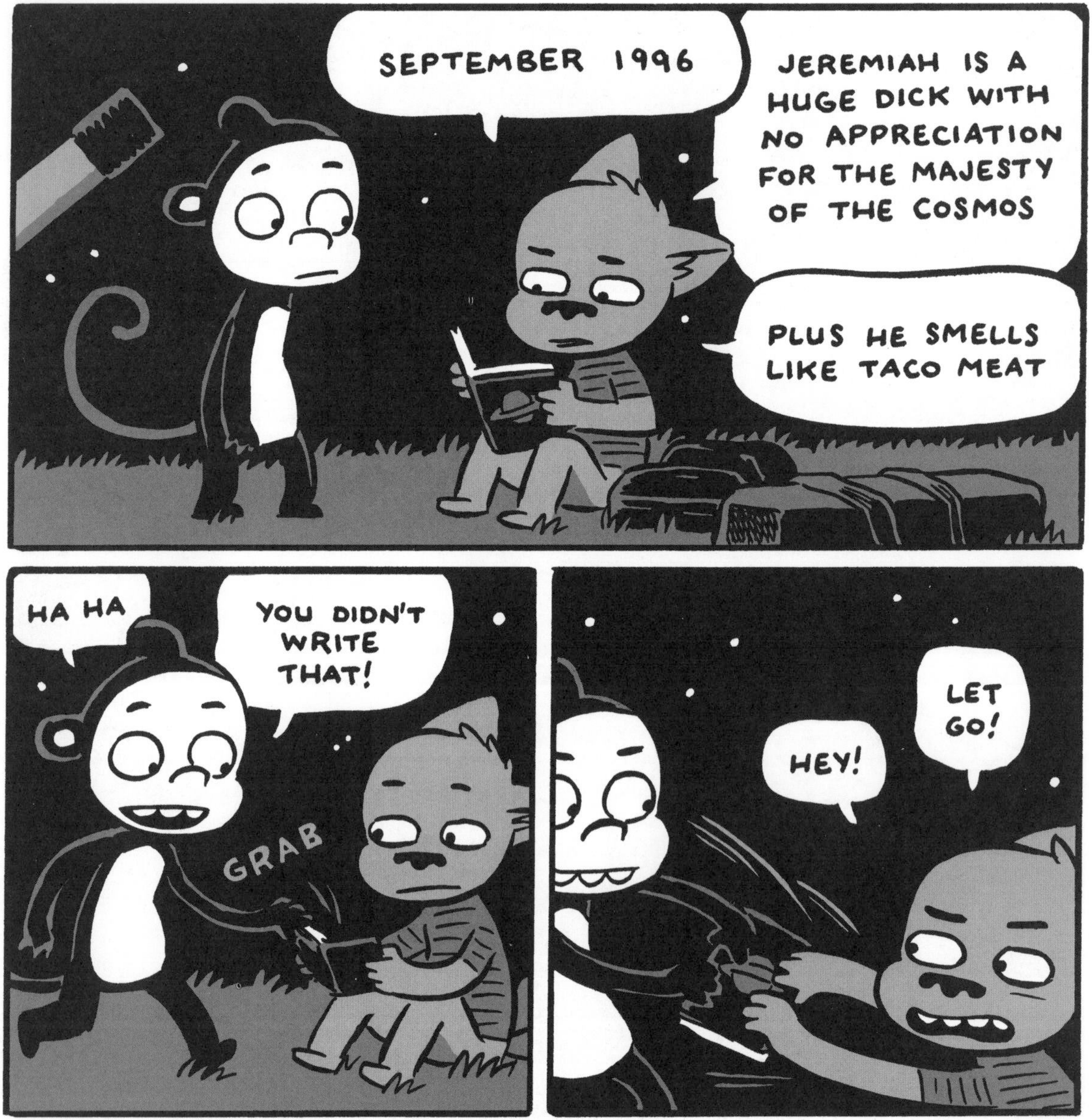
SEPTEMBER 1996
JEREMIAH IS A HUGE DICK WITH NO APPRECIATION FOR THE MAJESTY OF THE COSMOS
PLUS HE SMELLS LIKE TACO MEAT
HA HA
YOU DIDN'T WRITE THAT!
GRAB
HEY!
LET GO!

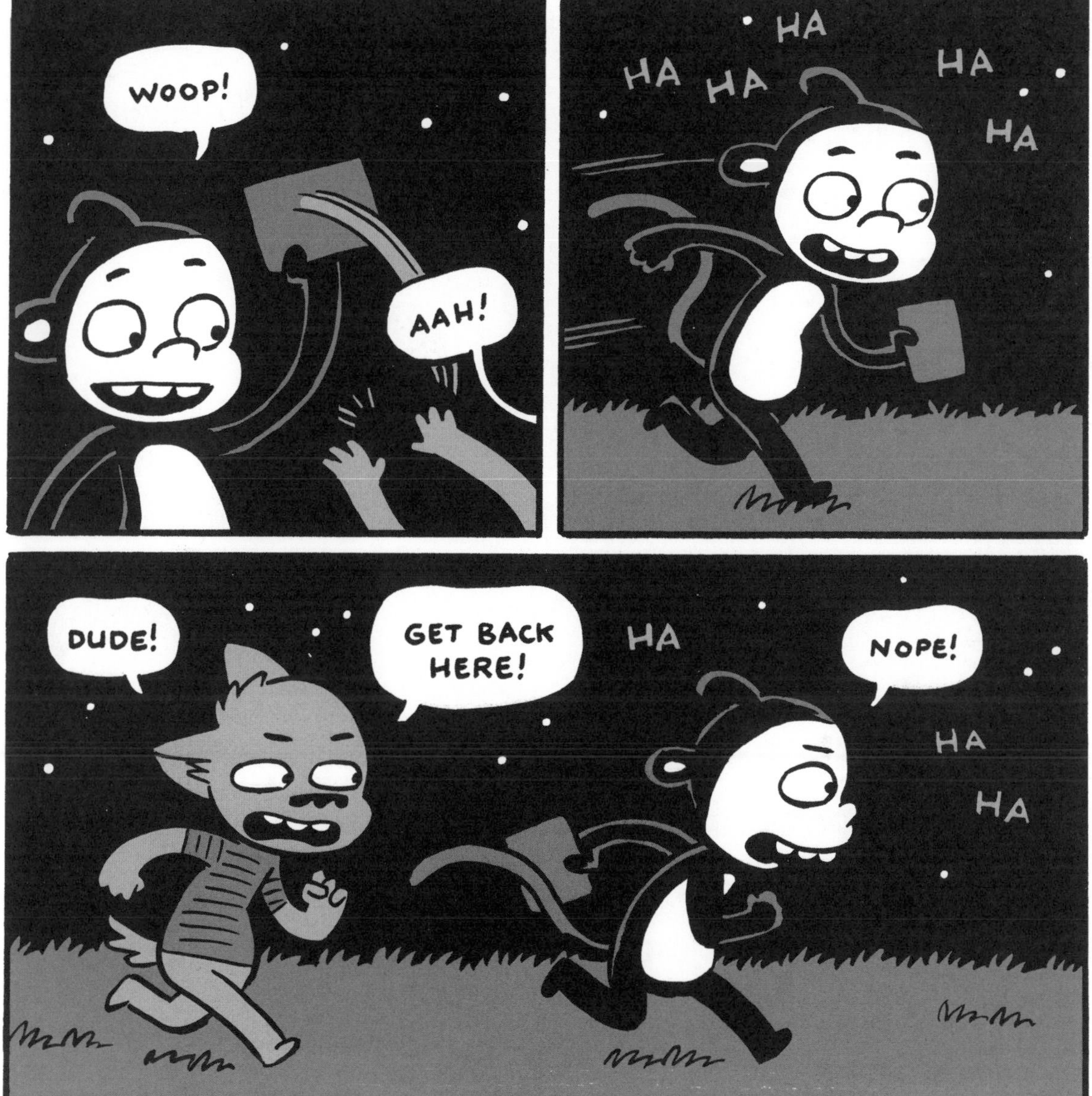
WOOP!
AAH!
HA
HA
HA
HA
HA
DUDE!
GET BACK HERE!
HA
NOPE!
HA
HA

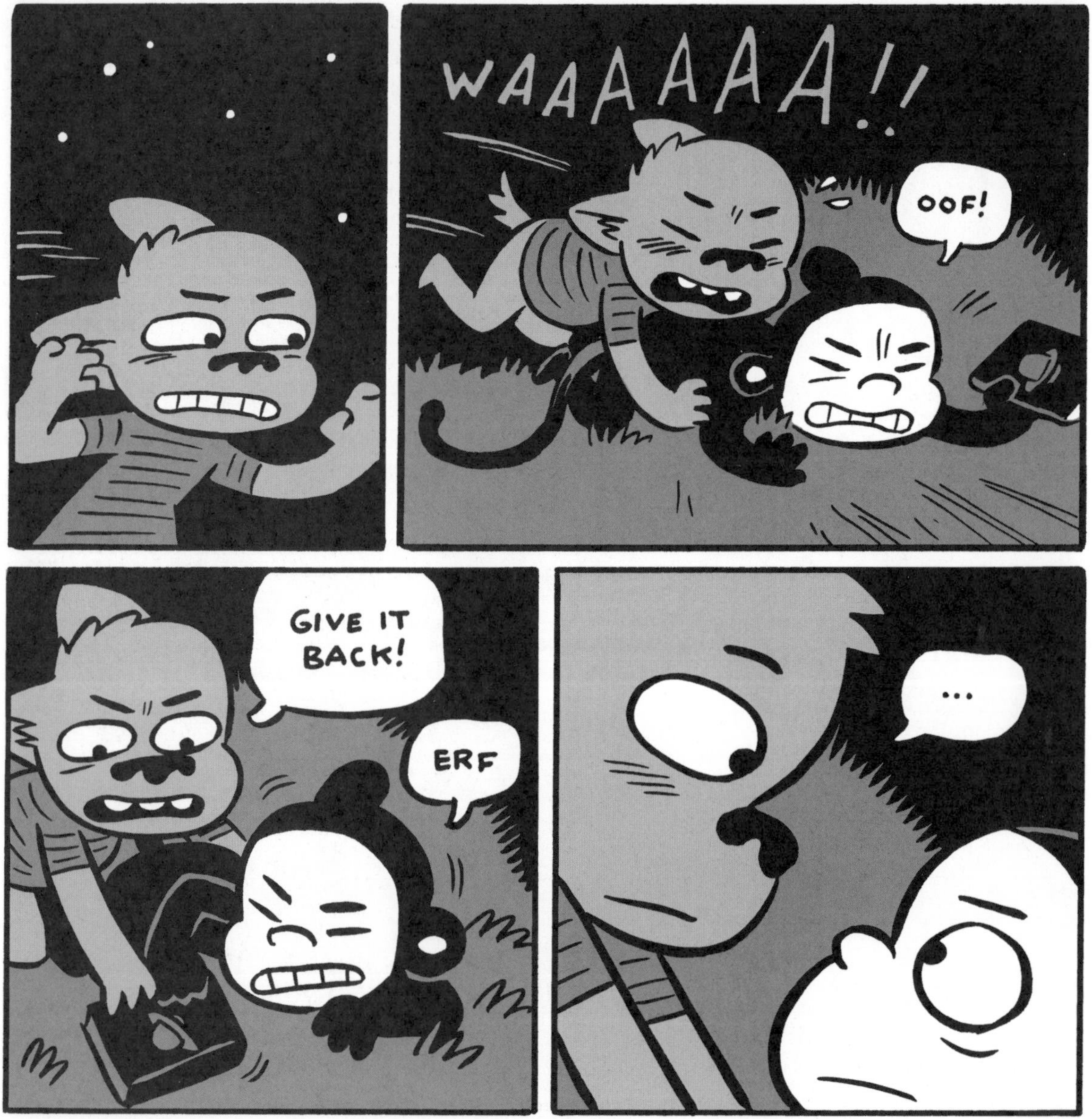
WAAAAAAA!!
OOF!
GIVE IT BACK!
ERF
...

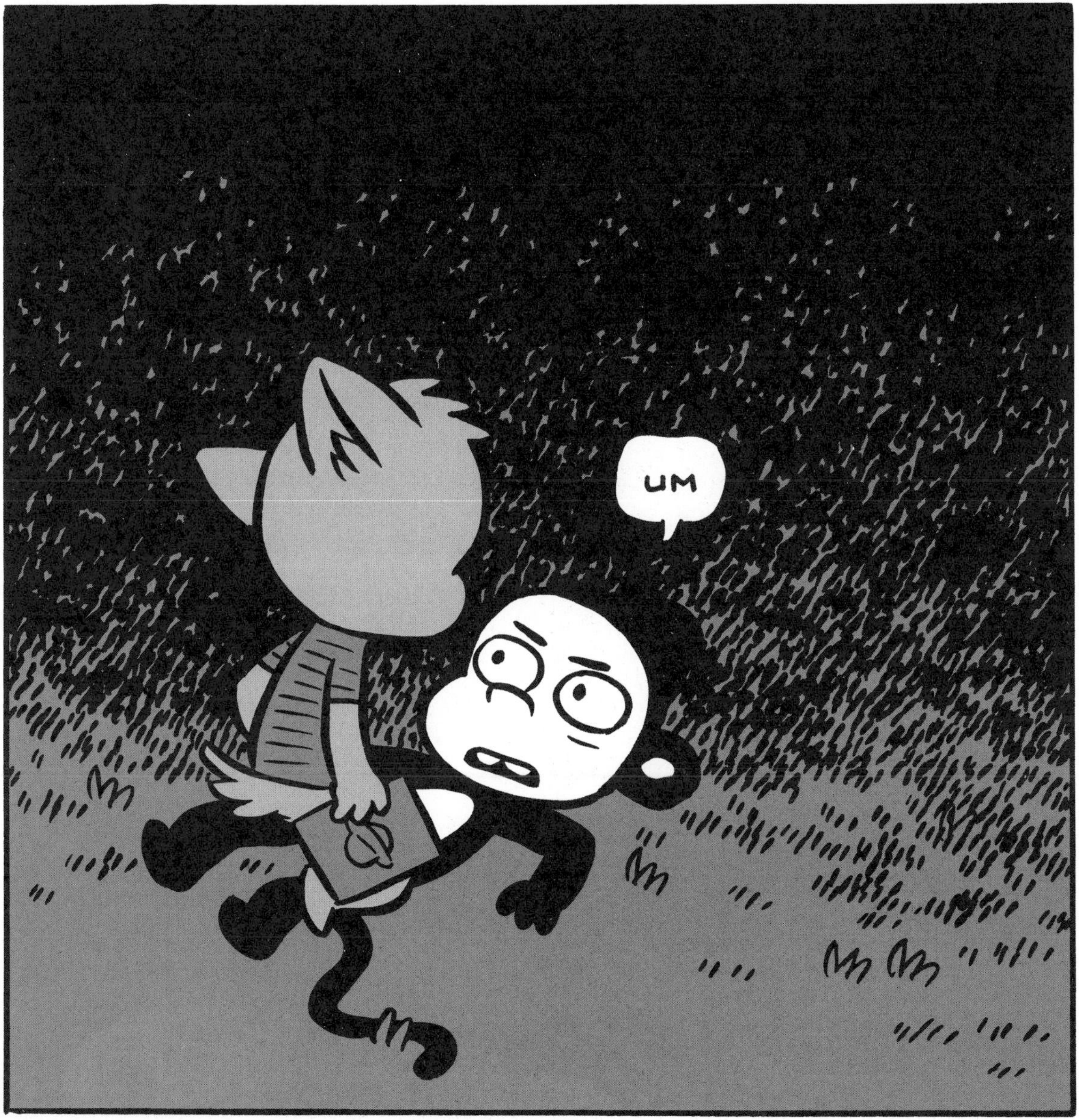
UM

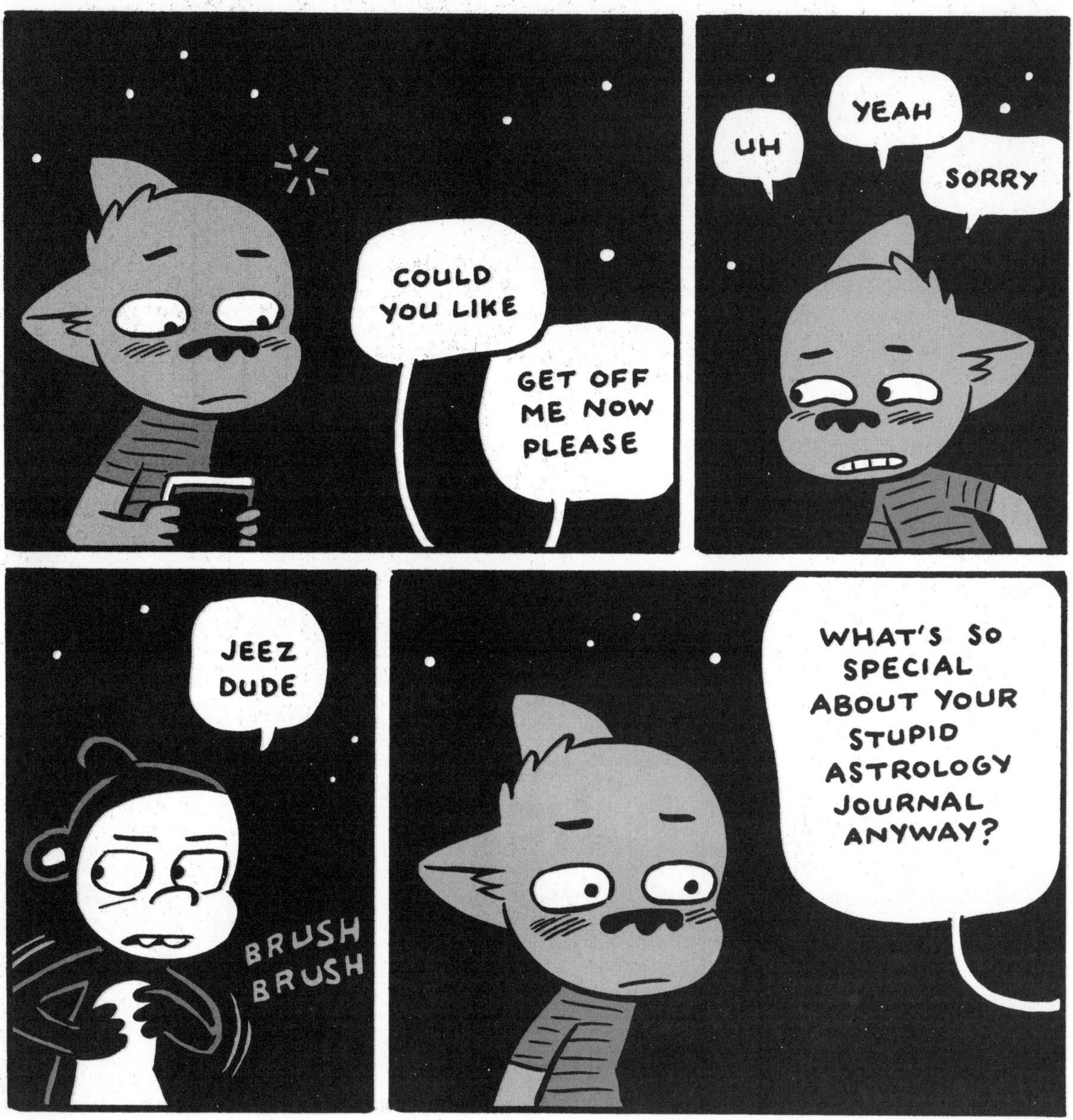
COULD YOU LIKE
GET OFF ME NOW PLEASE
UH
YEAH
SORRY
JEEZ DUDE
BRUSH BRUSH
WHAT'S SO SPECIAL ABOUT YOUR STUPID ASTROLOGY JOURNAL ANYWAY?

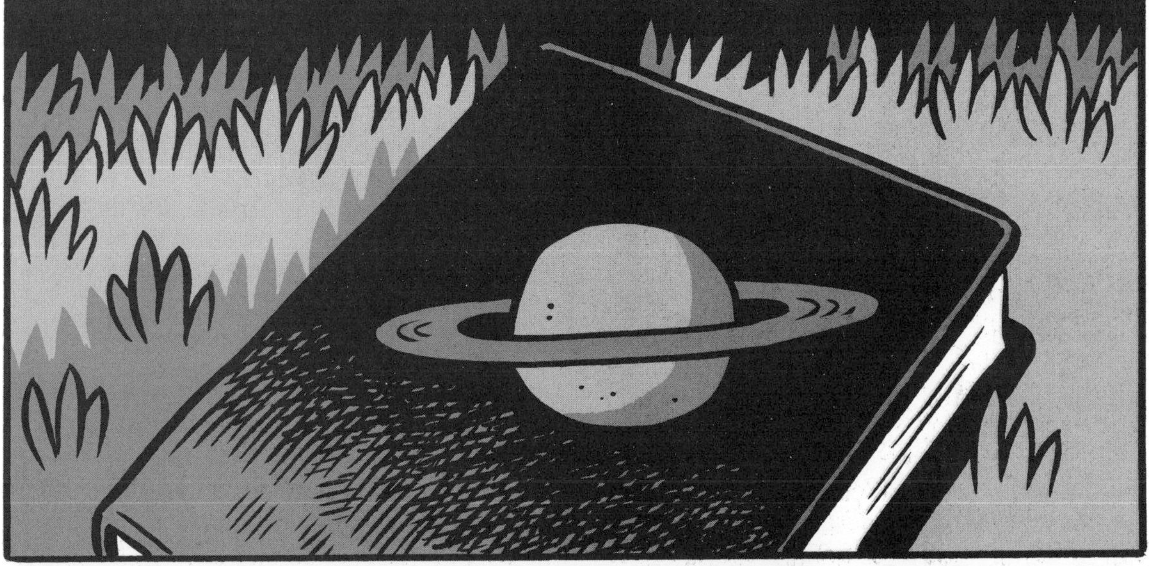

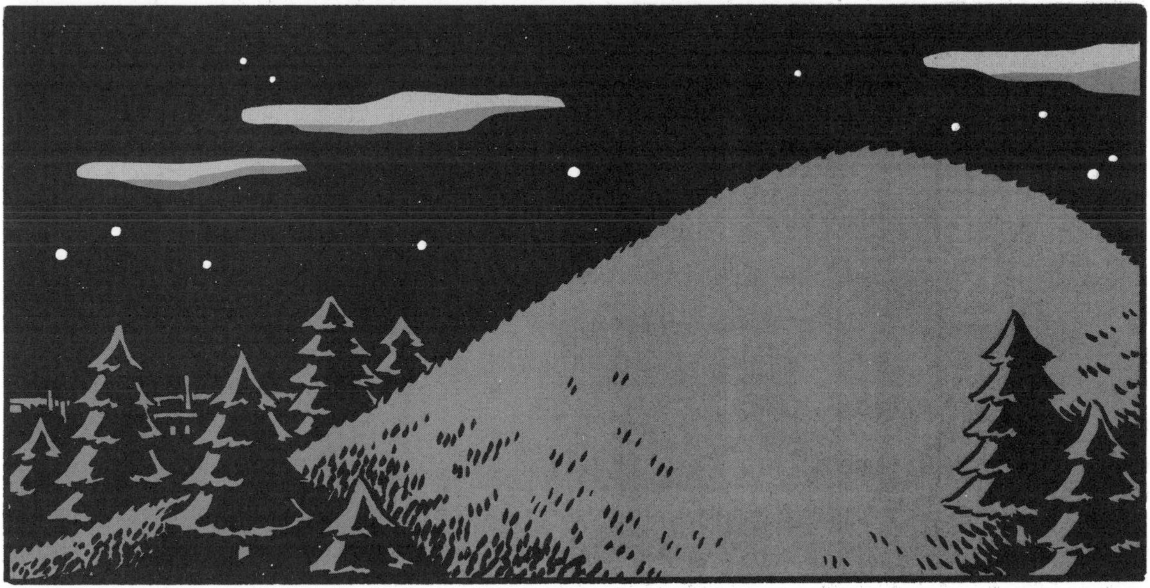

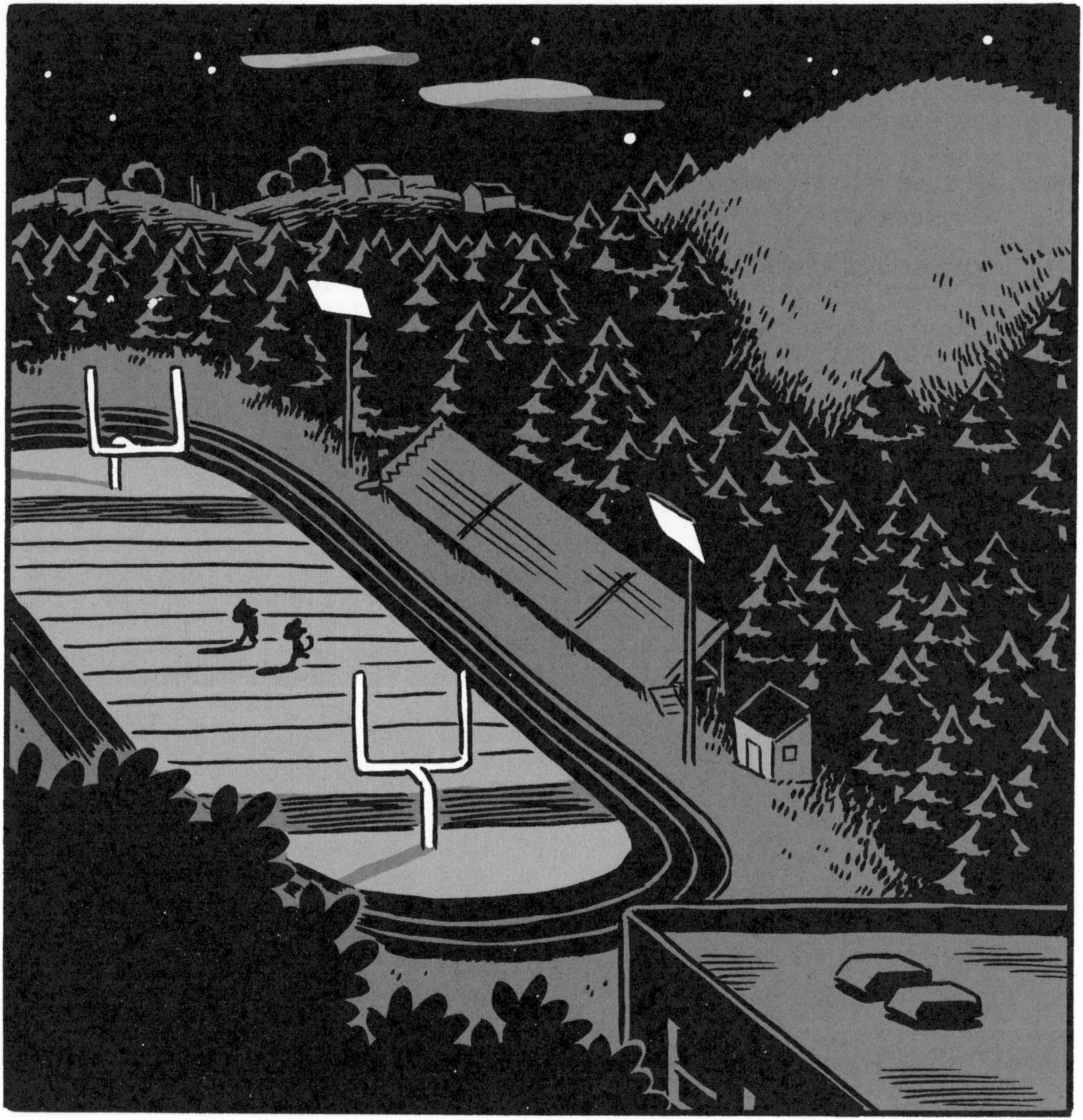

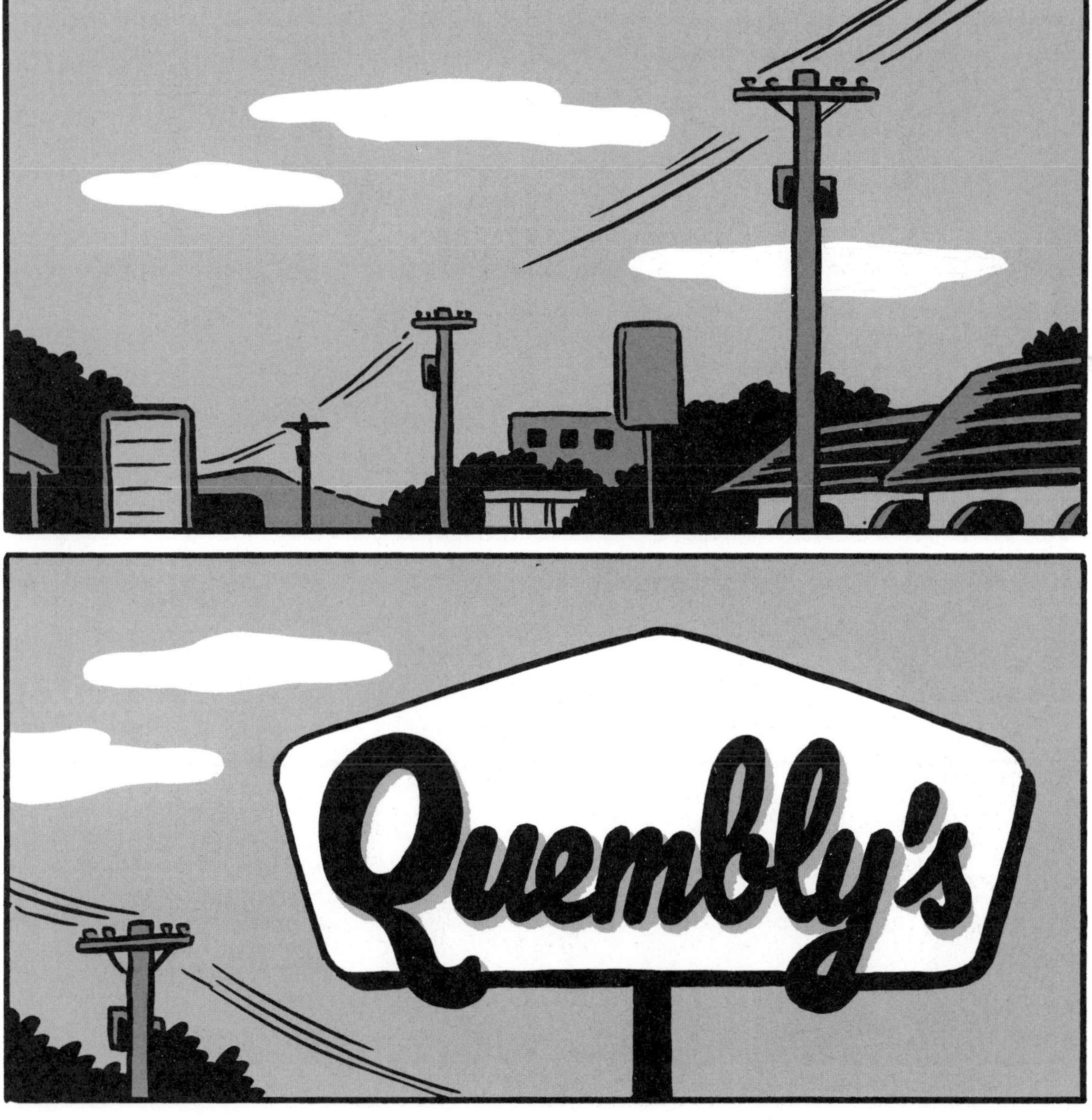
Quembly's

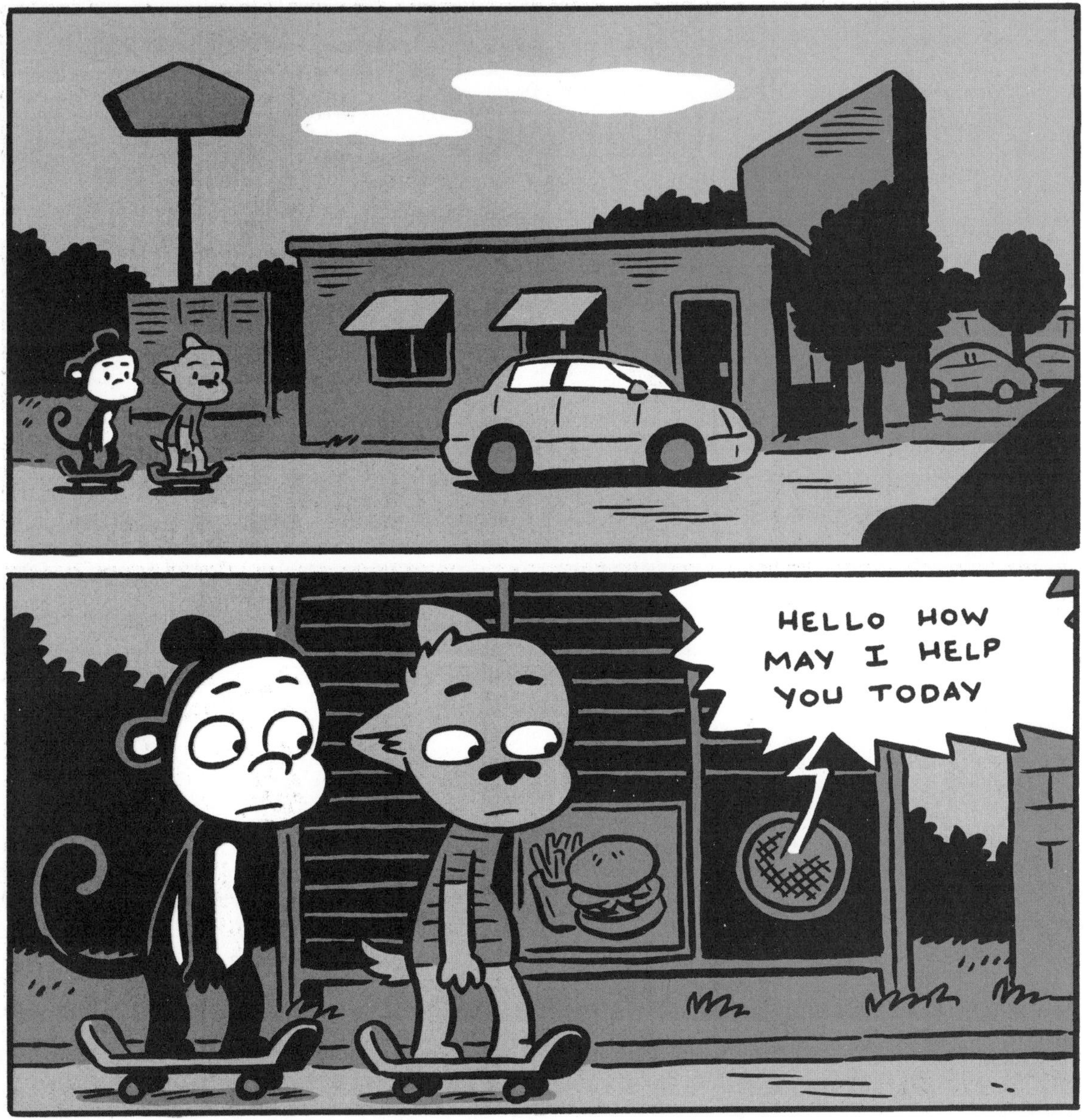
HELLO HOW MAY I HELP YOU TODAY

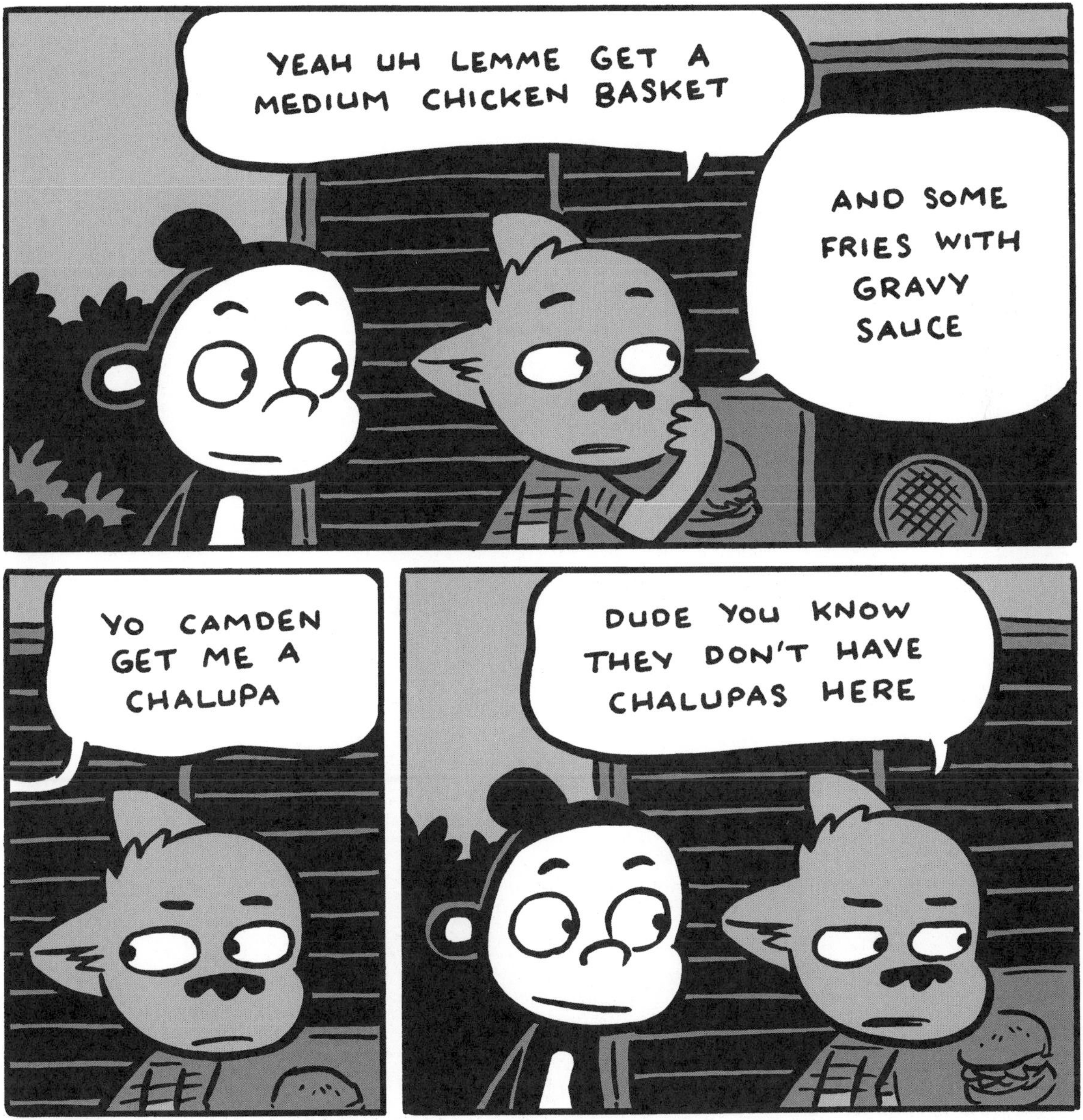
YEAH UH LEMME GET A MEDIUM CHICKEN BASKET
AND SOME FRIES WITH GRAVY SAUCE
YO CAMDEN GET ME A CHALUPA
DUDE YOU KNOW THEY DON'T HAVE CHALUPAS HERE

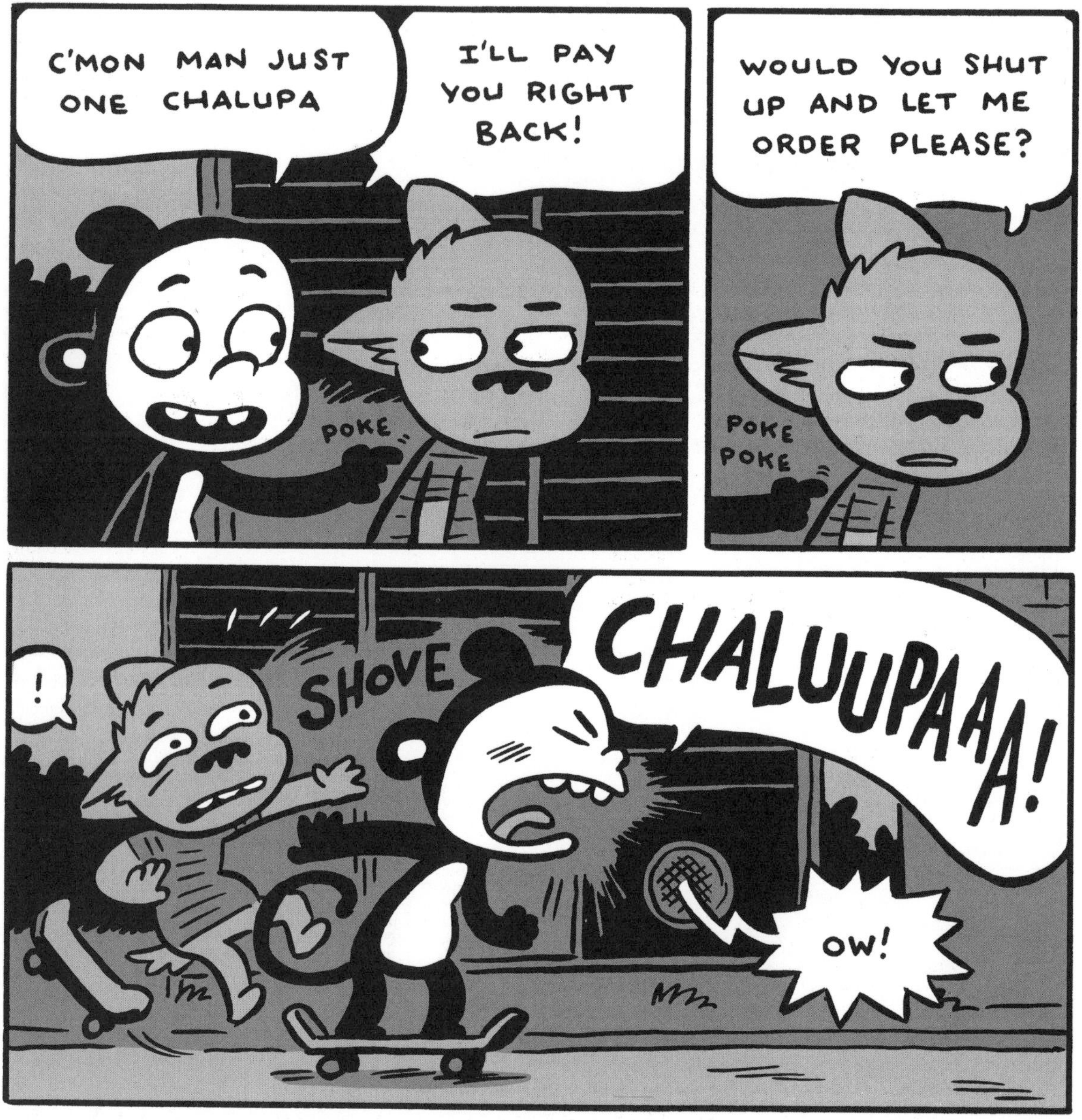
C'MON MAN JUST ONE CHALUPA
I'LL PAY YOU RIGHT BACK!
POKE
WOULD YOU SHUT UP AND LET ME ORDER PLEASE?
POKE POKE
!
SHOVE
CHALUUPAAAA!
OW!

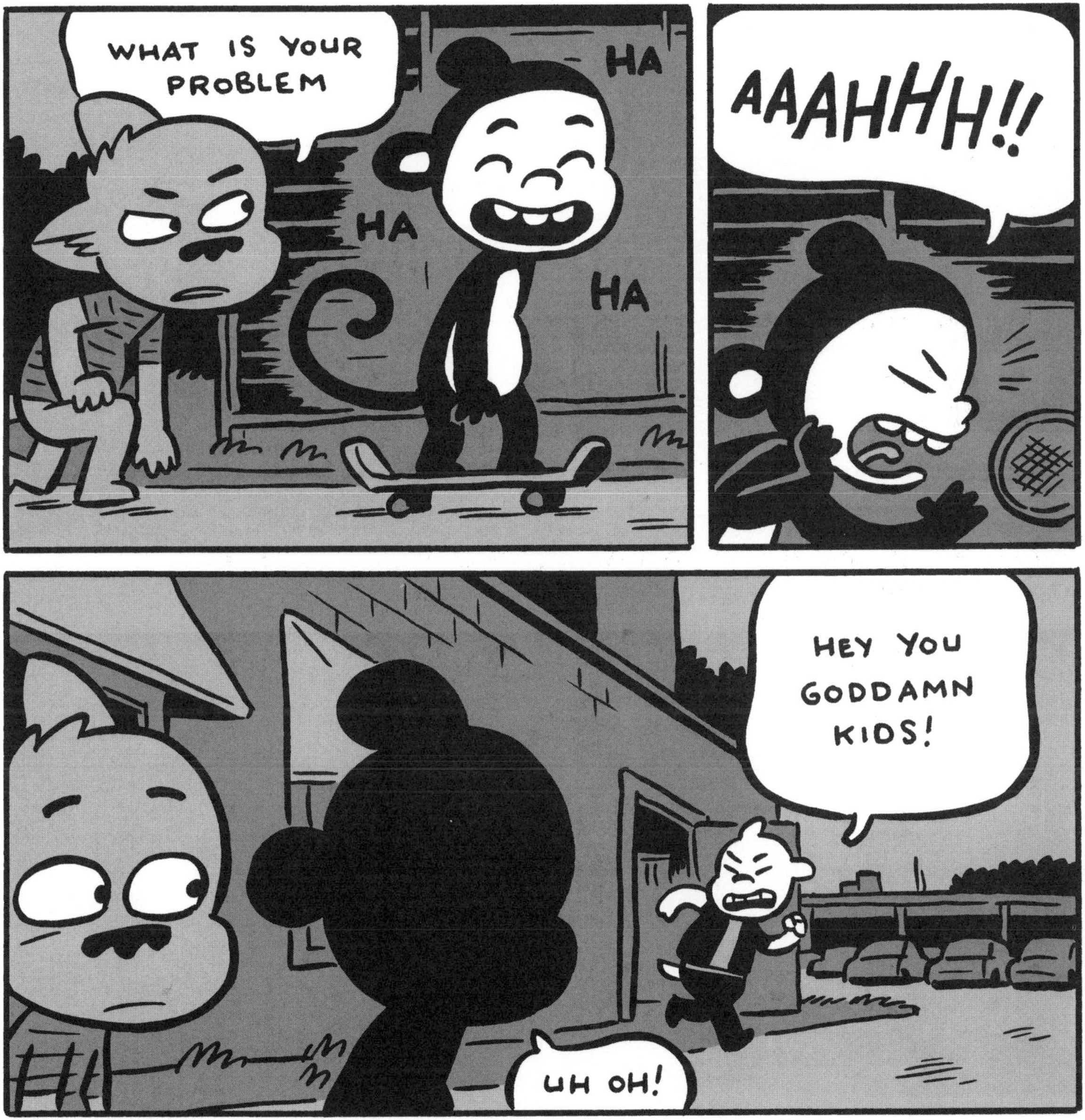
WHAT IS YOUR PROBLEM
HA
HA
HA
AAAHHHH!!
HEY YOU GODDAMN KIDS!
UH OH!

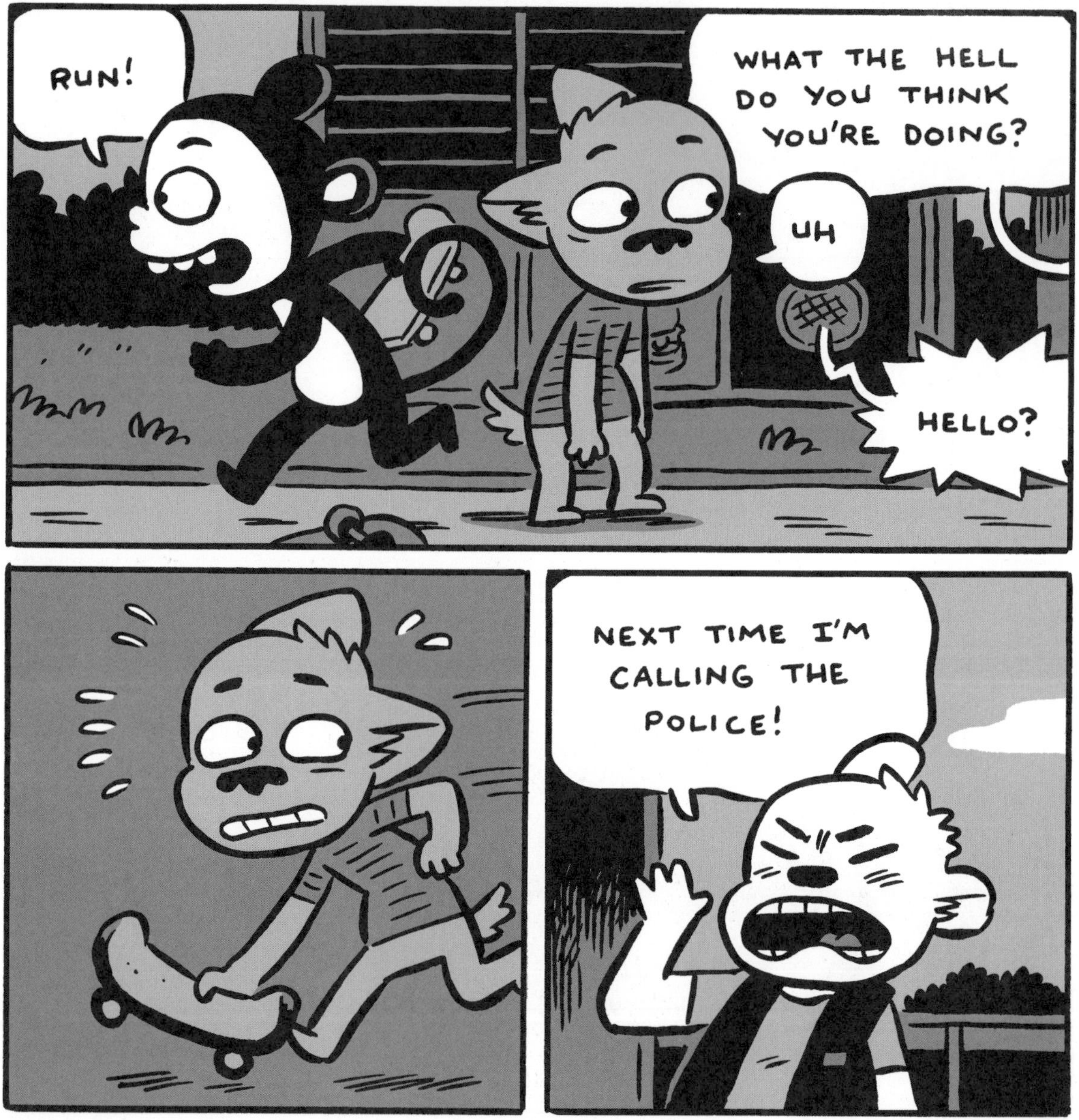
RUN!
WHAT THE HELL DO YOU THINK YOU'RE DOING?
UH
HELLO?
NEXT TIME I'M CALLING THE POLICE!

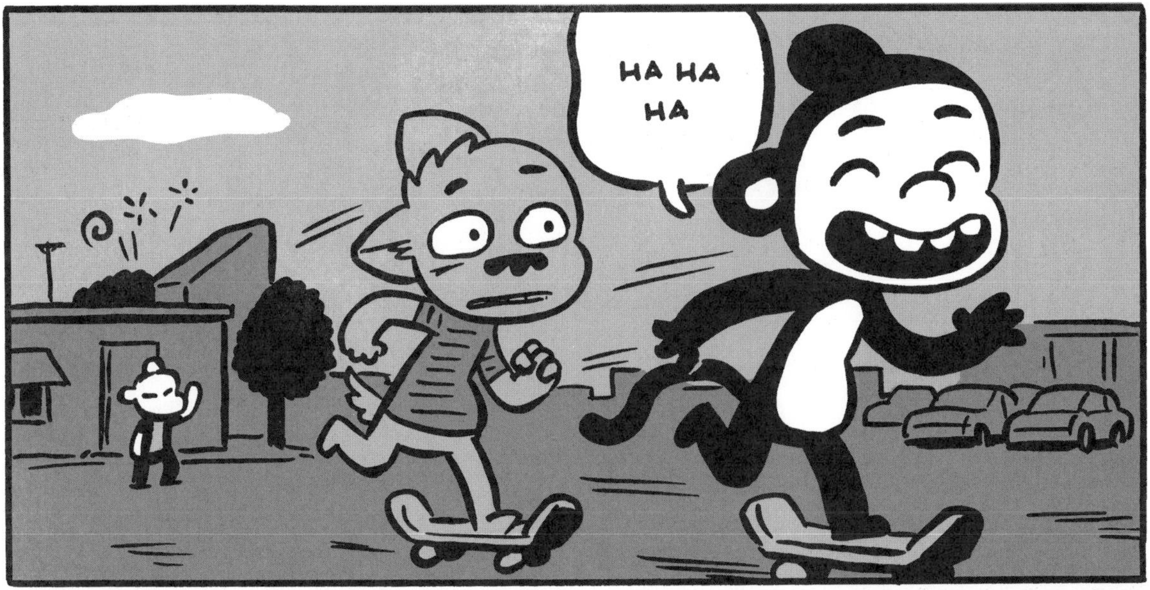
HA HA HA HA

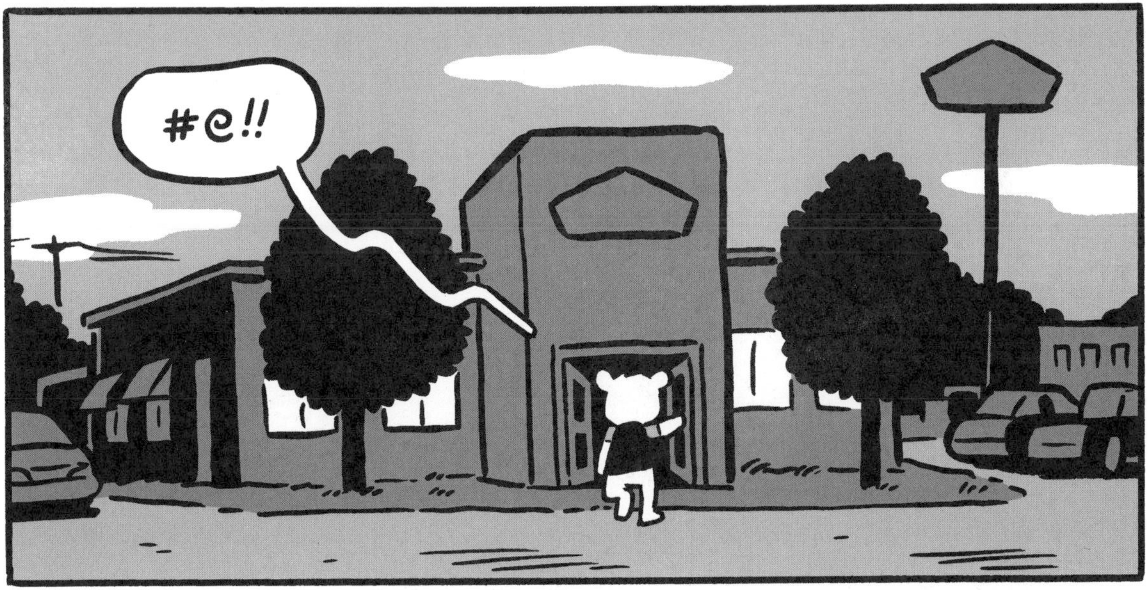
#@!!

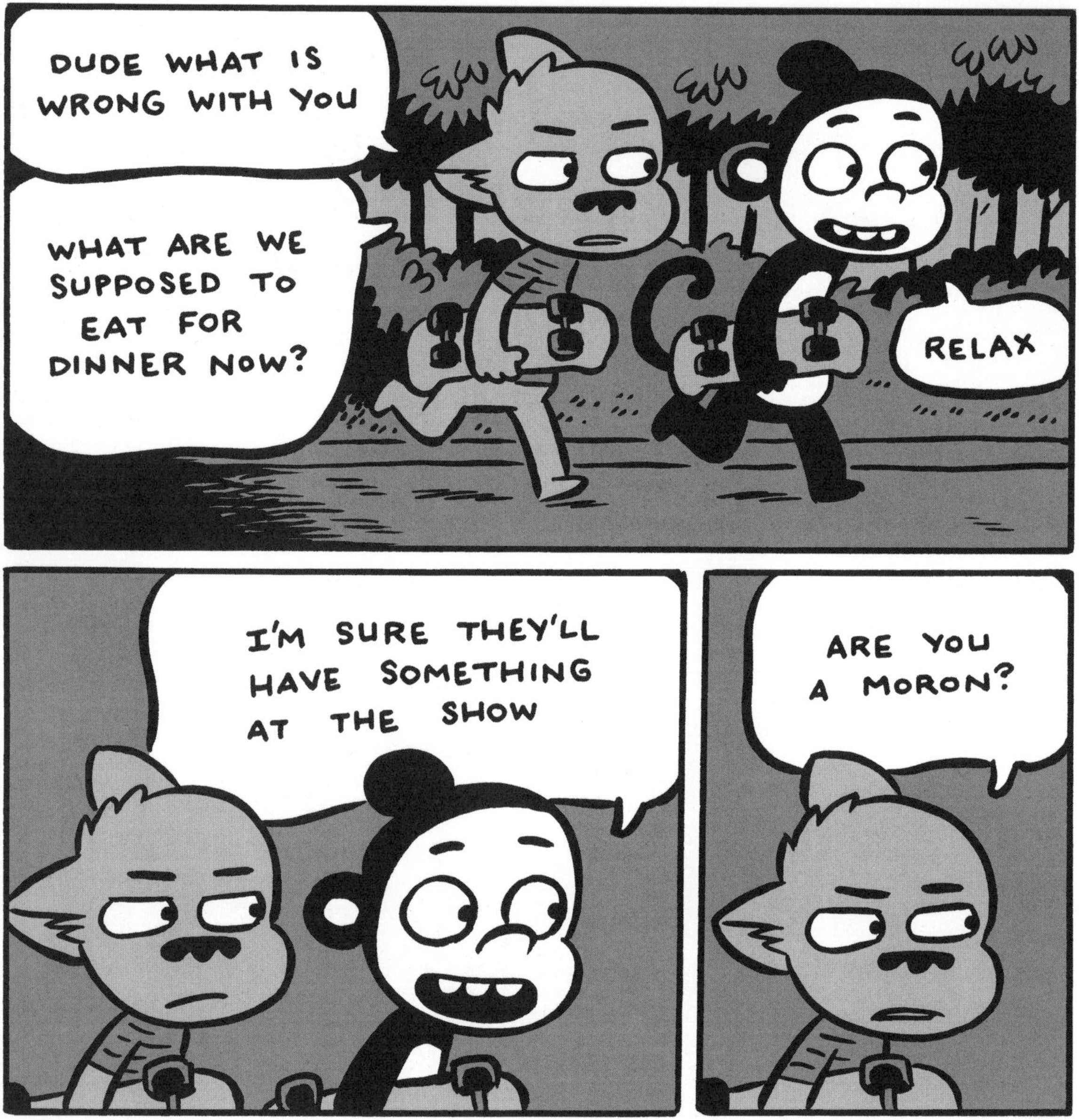
DUDE WHAT IS WRONG WITH YOU
WHAT ARE WE SUPPOSED TO EAT FOR DINNER NOW?
RELAX
I'M SURE THEY'LL HAVE SOMETHING AT THE SHOW
ARE YOU A MORON?

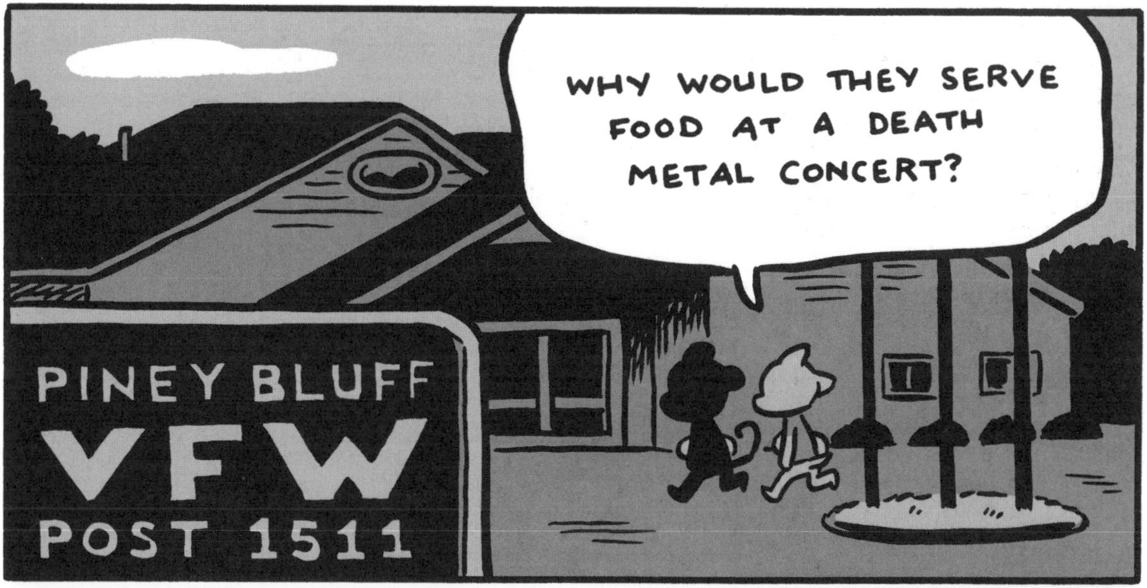
WHY WOULD THEY SERVE FOOD AT A DEATH METAL CONCERT?
PINEY BLUFF
VFW
POST 1511

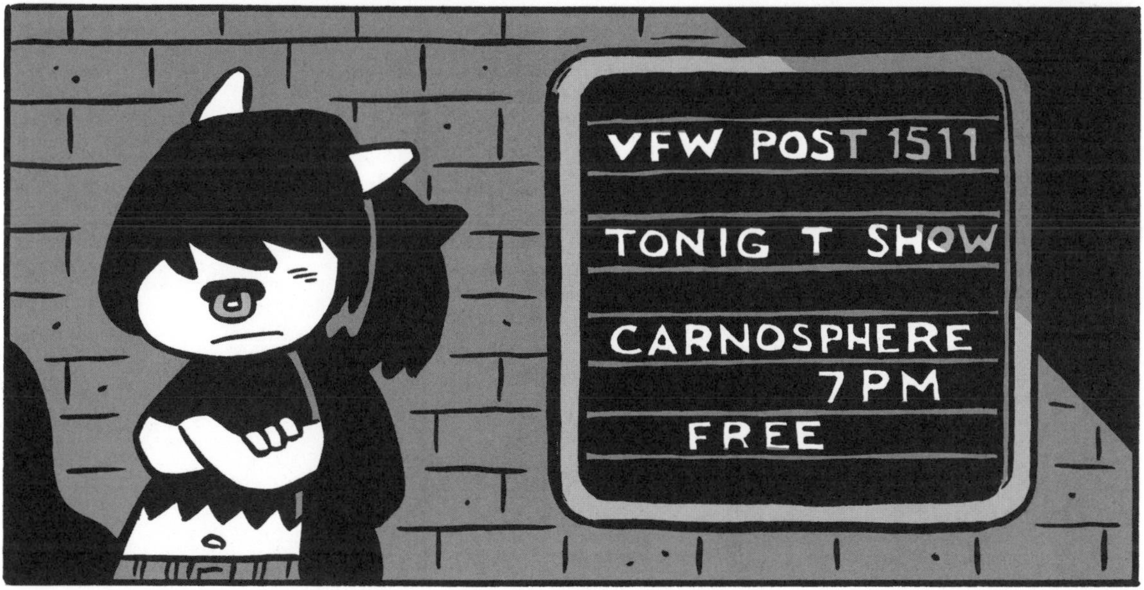
VFW POST 1511
TONIG T SHOW
CARNOSPHERE
7PM
FREE

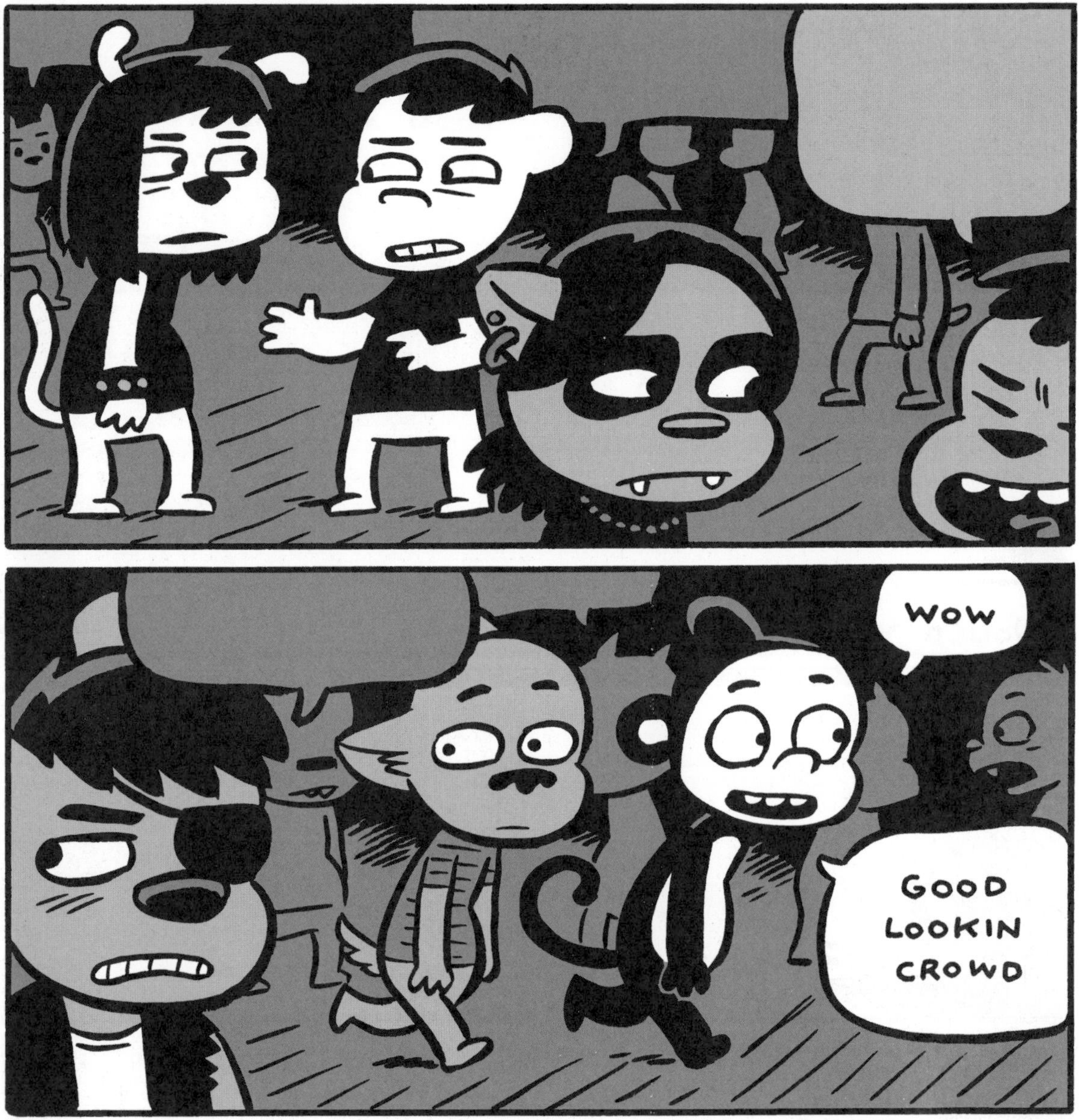
WOW
GOOD LOOKIN CROWD

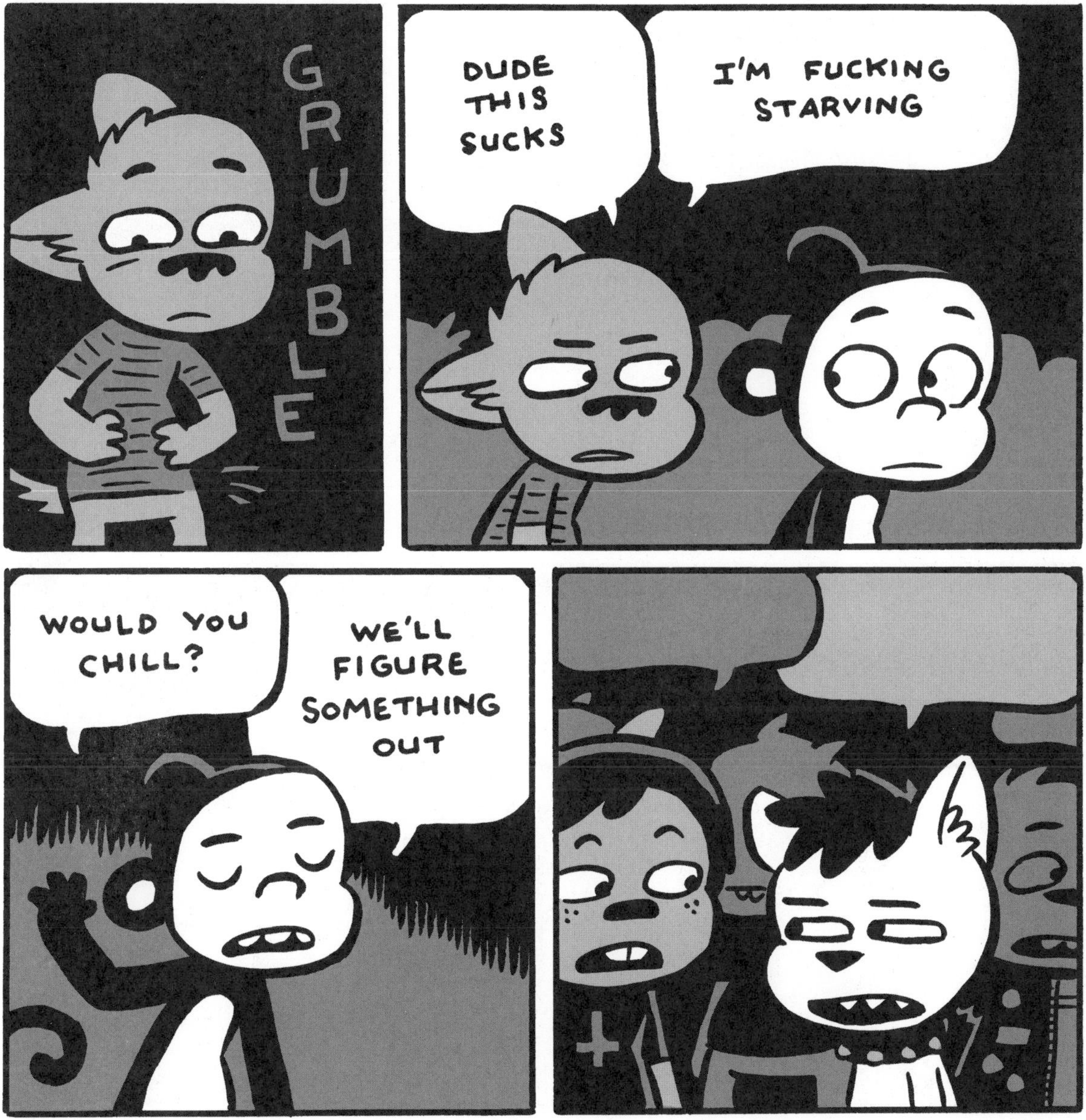
GRUMBLE
DUDE THIS SUCKS
I'M FUCKING STARVING
WOULD YOU CHILL?
WE'LL FIGURE SOMETHING OUT

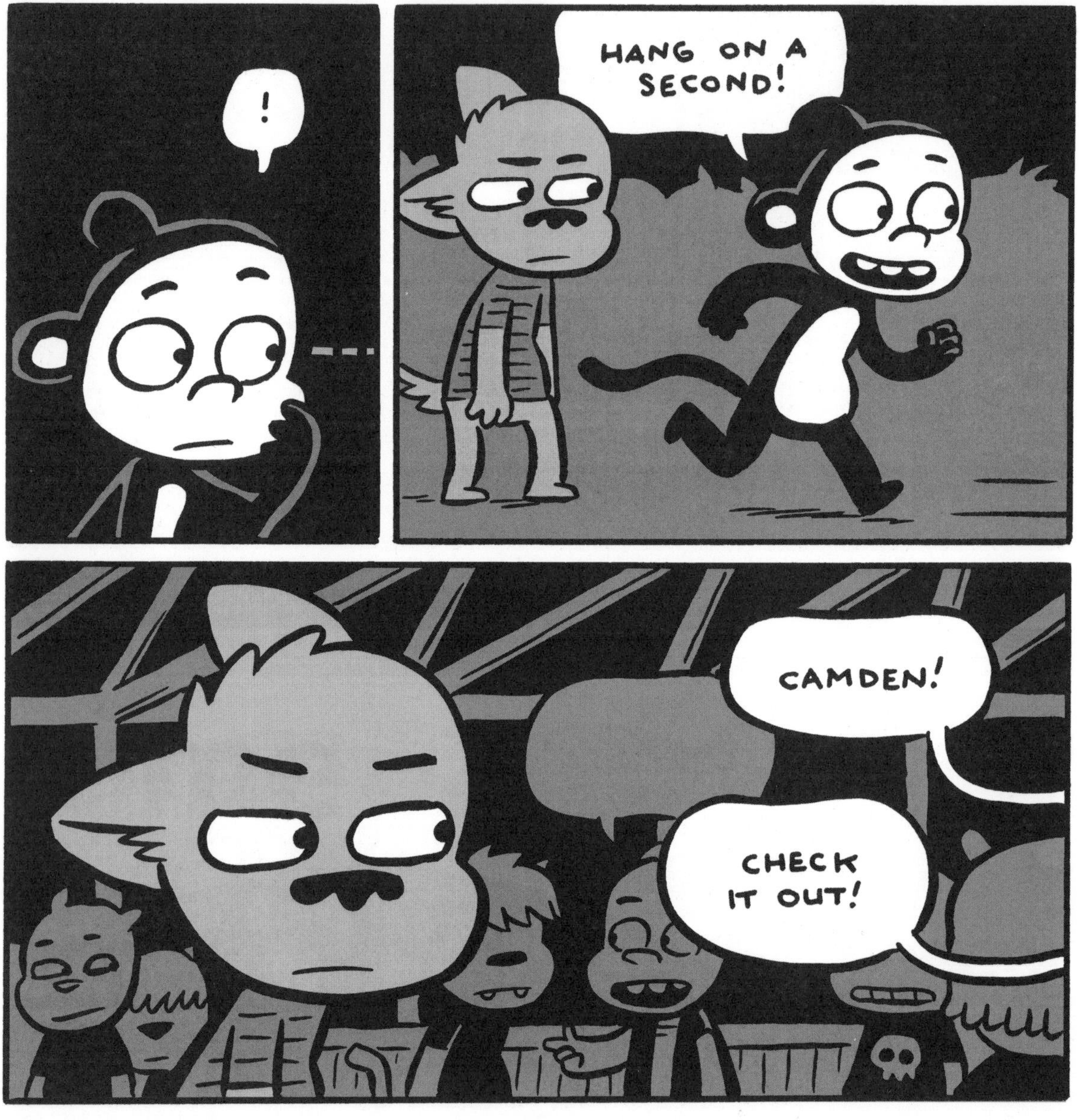
!
HANG ON A SECOND!
CAMDEN!
CHECK IT OUT!

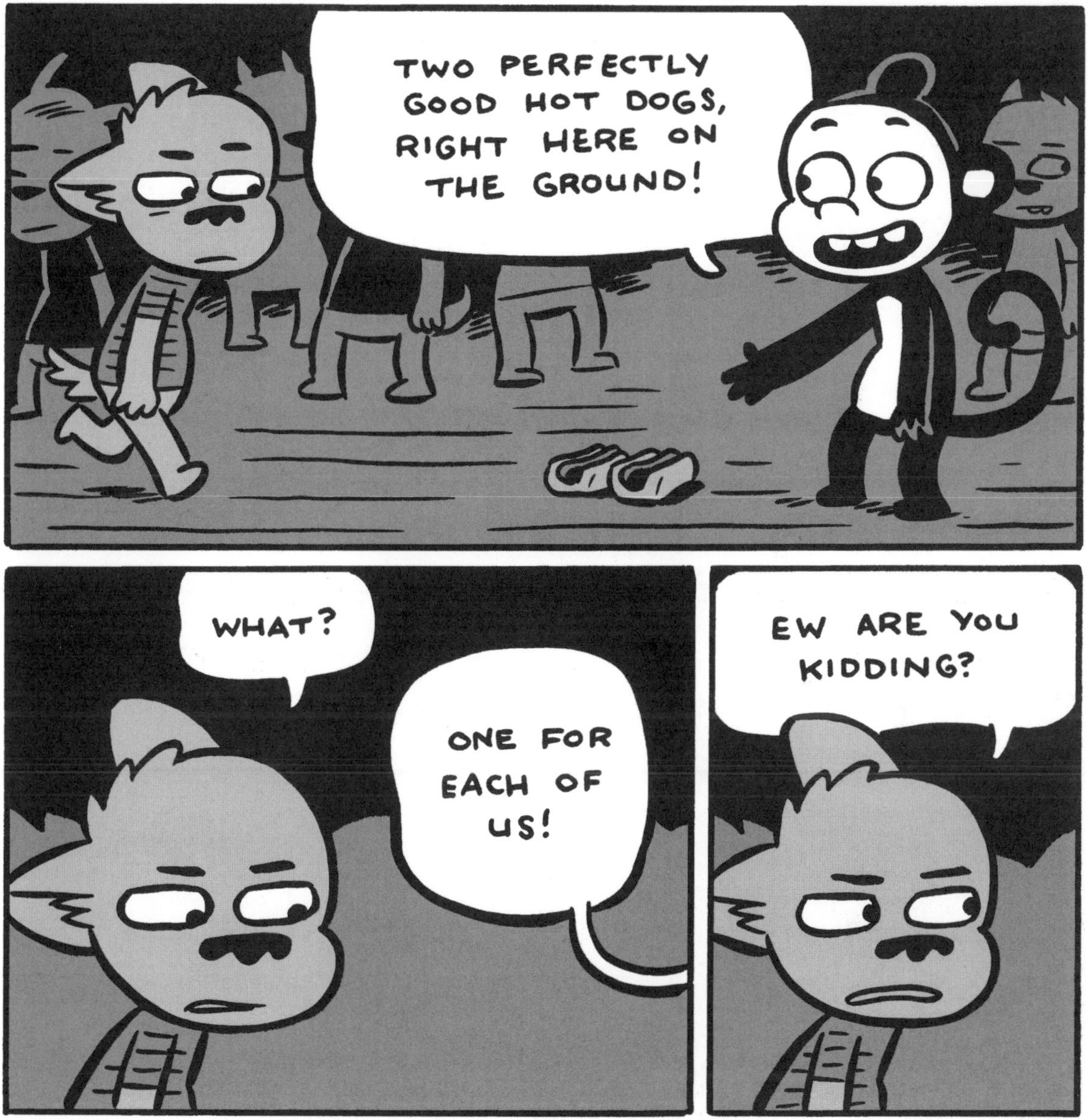
TWO PERFECTLY GOOD HOT DOGS, RIGHT HERE ON THE GROUND!
WHAT?
ONE FOR EACH OF US!
EW ARE YOU KIDDING?

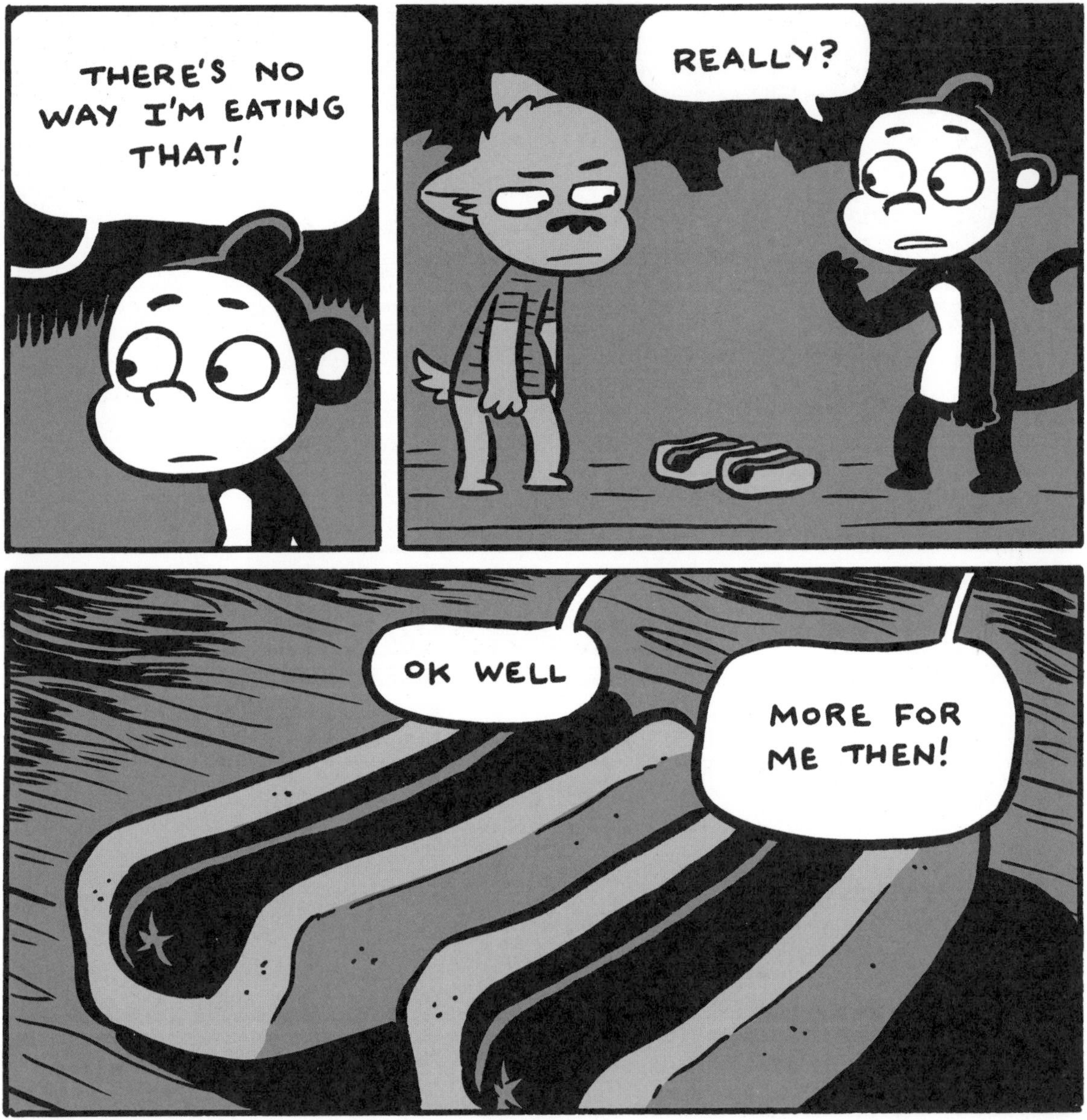
THERE'S NO WAY I'M EATING THAT!
REALLY?
OK WELL
MORE FOR ME THEN!

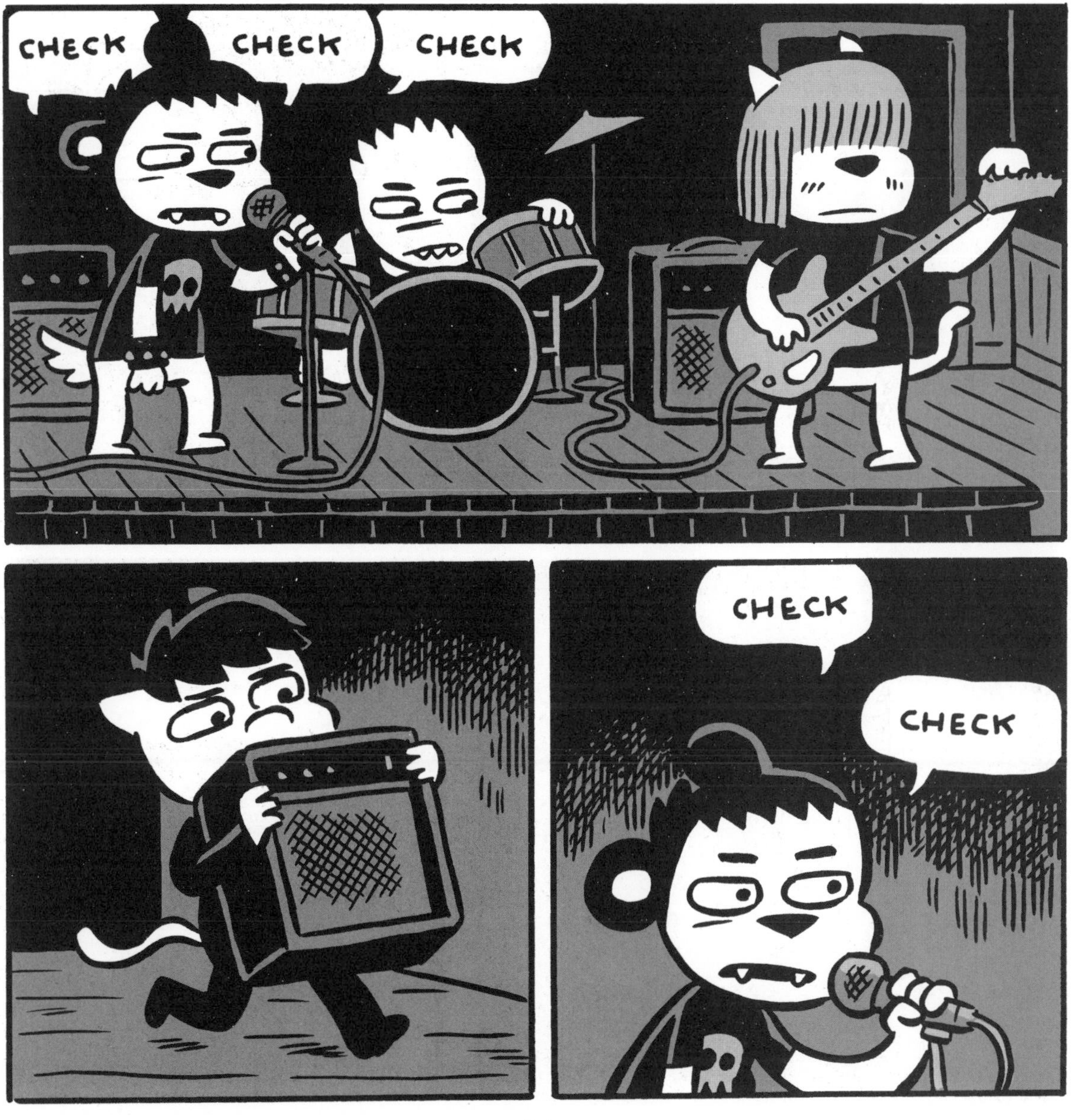
CHECK
CHECK
CHECK
CHECK
CHECK

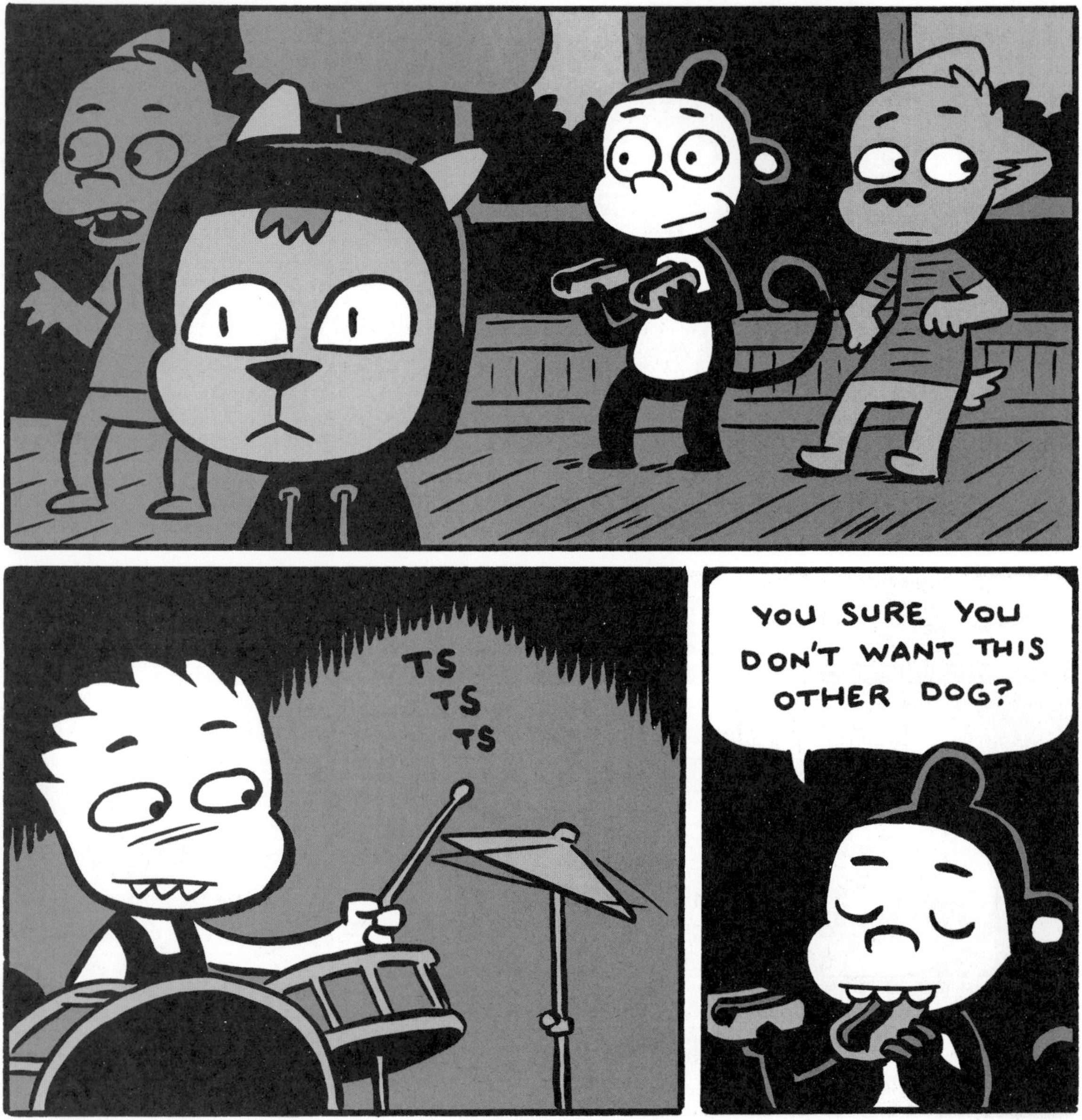
TS
TS
TS
YOU SURE YOU DON'T WANT THIS OTHER DOG?

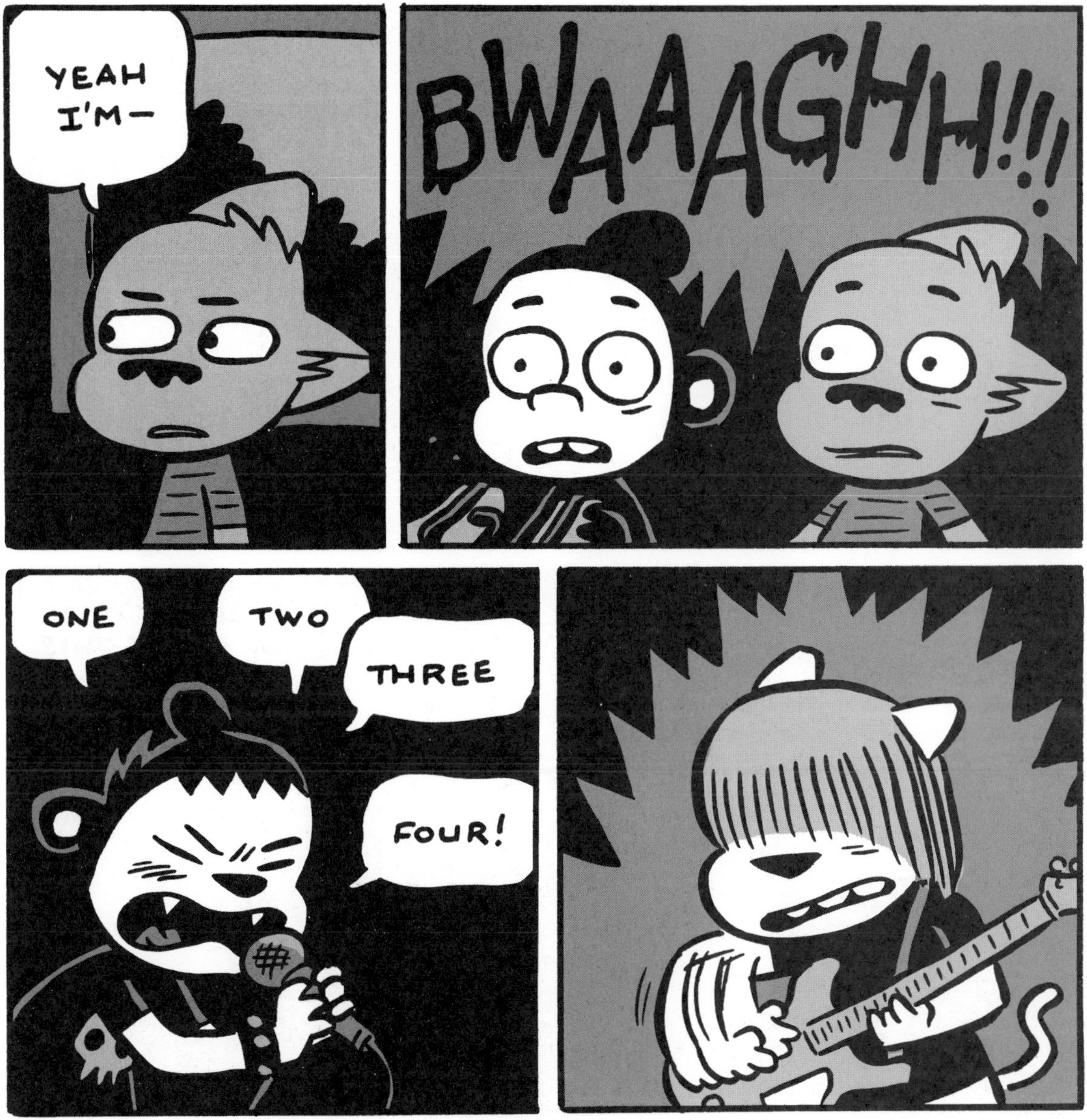
YEAH I'M—
BWAAAGHH!!!
ONE
TWO
THREE
FOUR!

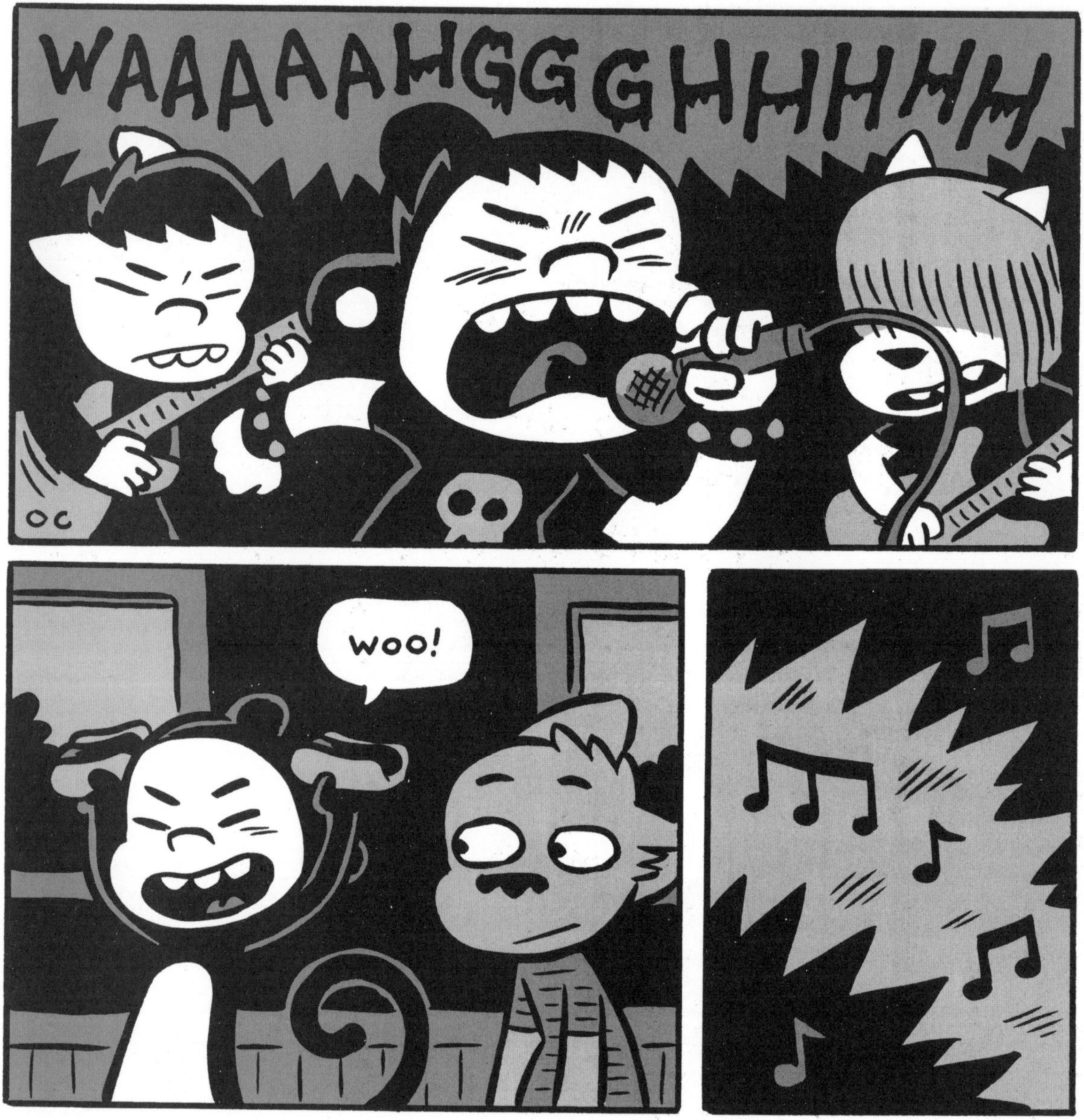
WAAAAAHGGGHHHHHH
OC
woo!

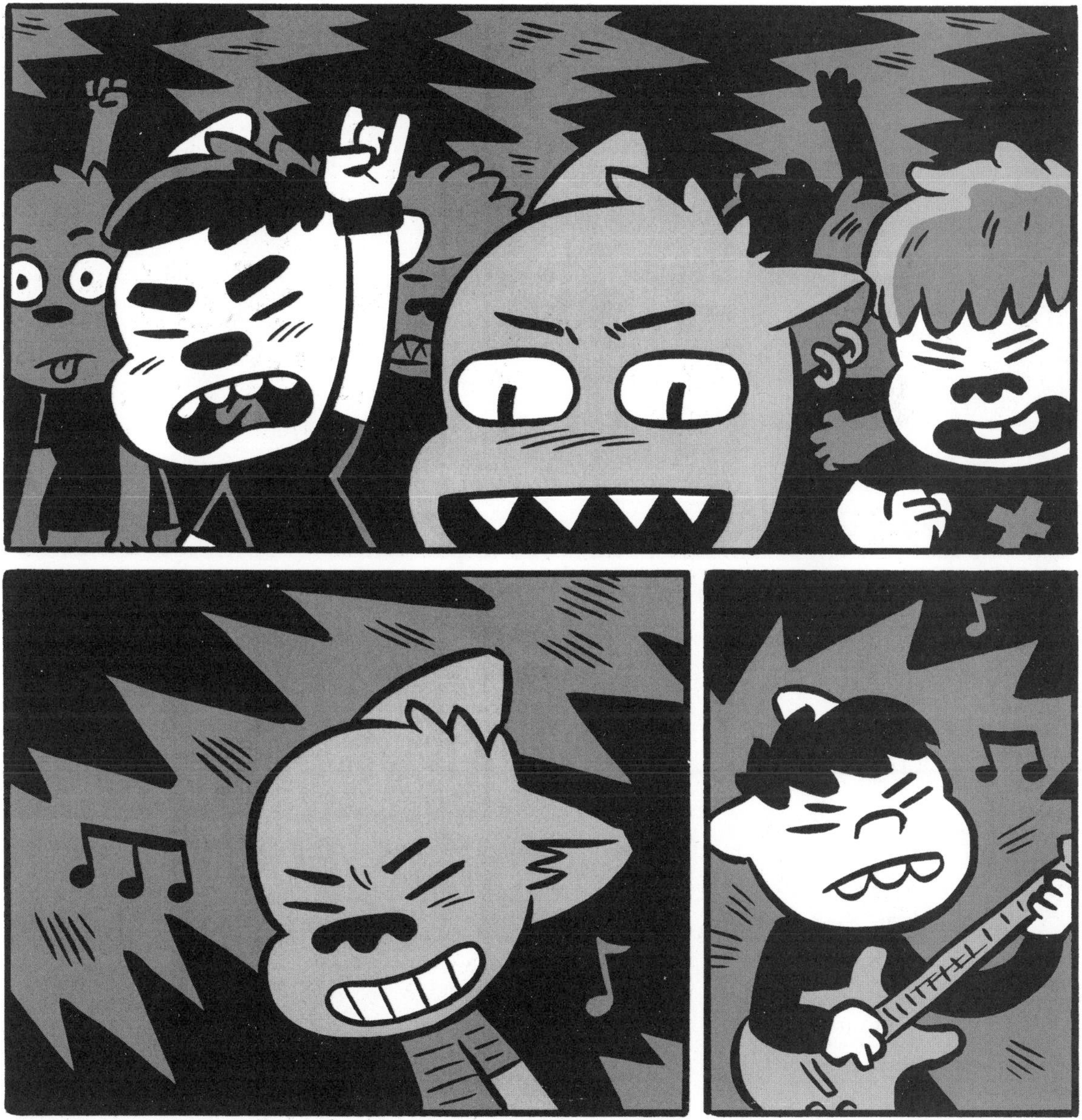

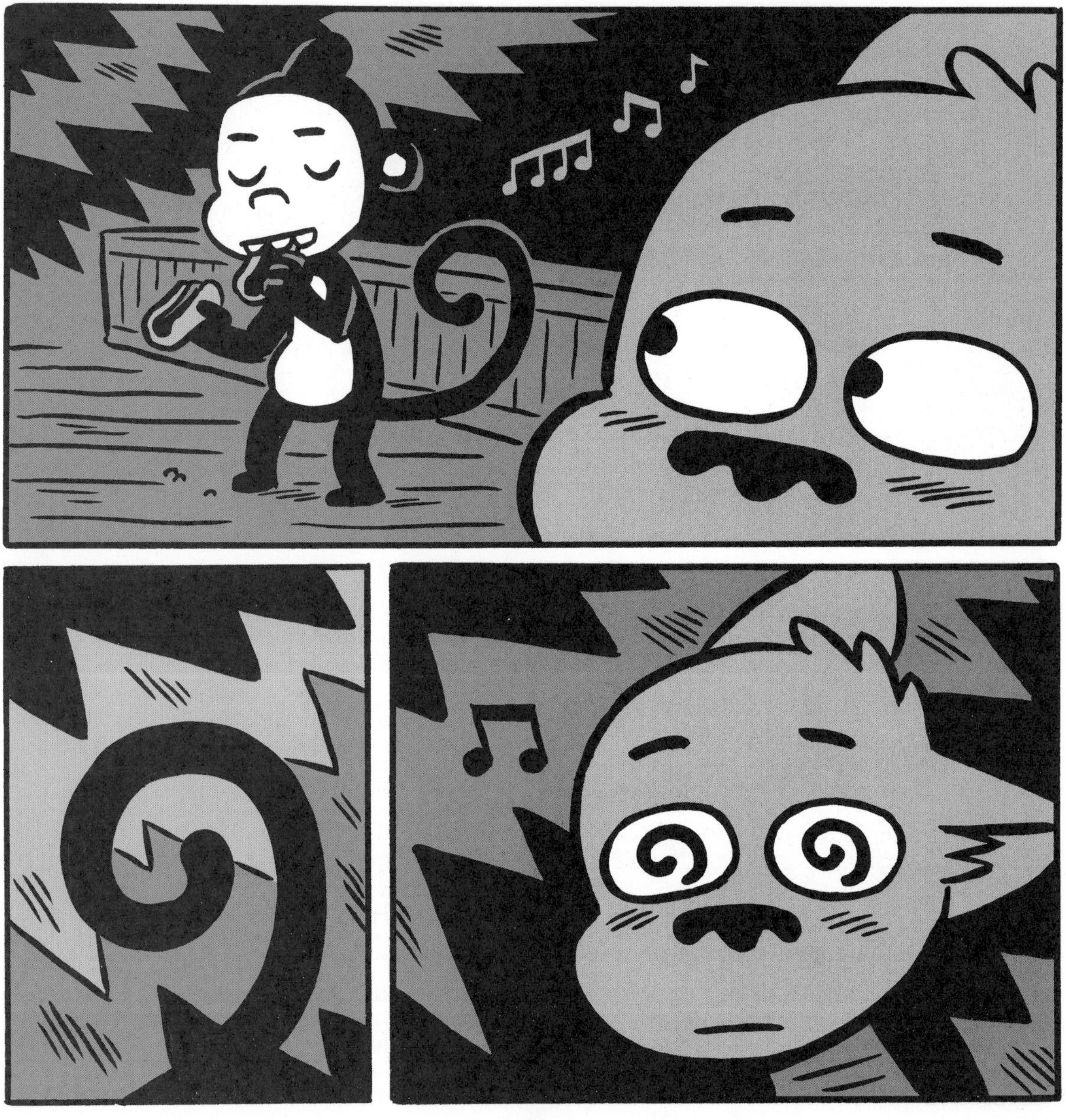

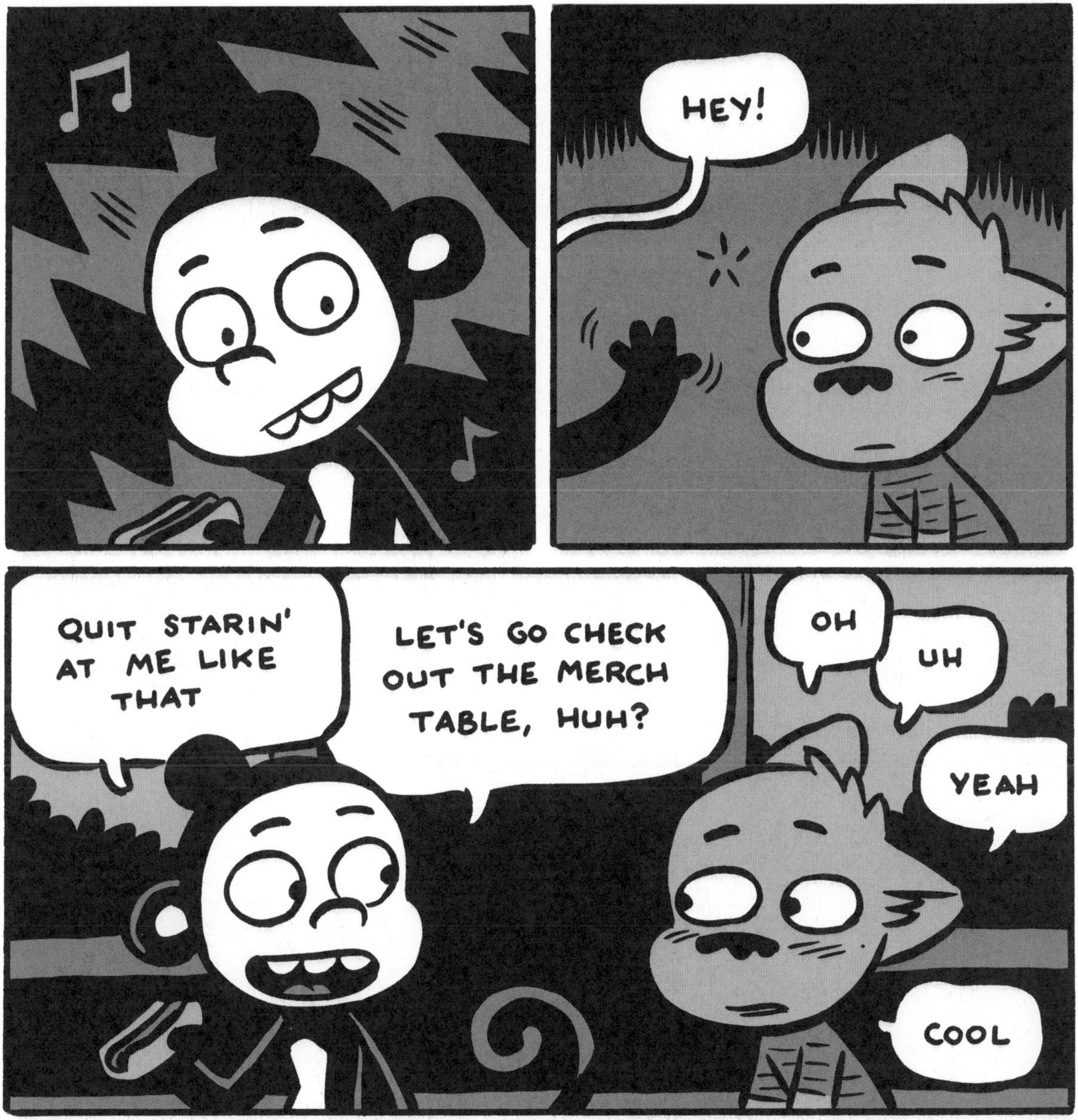
HEY!
QUIT STARIN' AT ME LIKE THAT
LET'S GO CHECK OUT THE MERCH TABLE, HUH?
OH
UH
YEAH
COOL

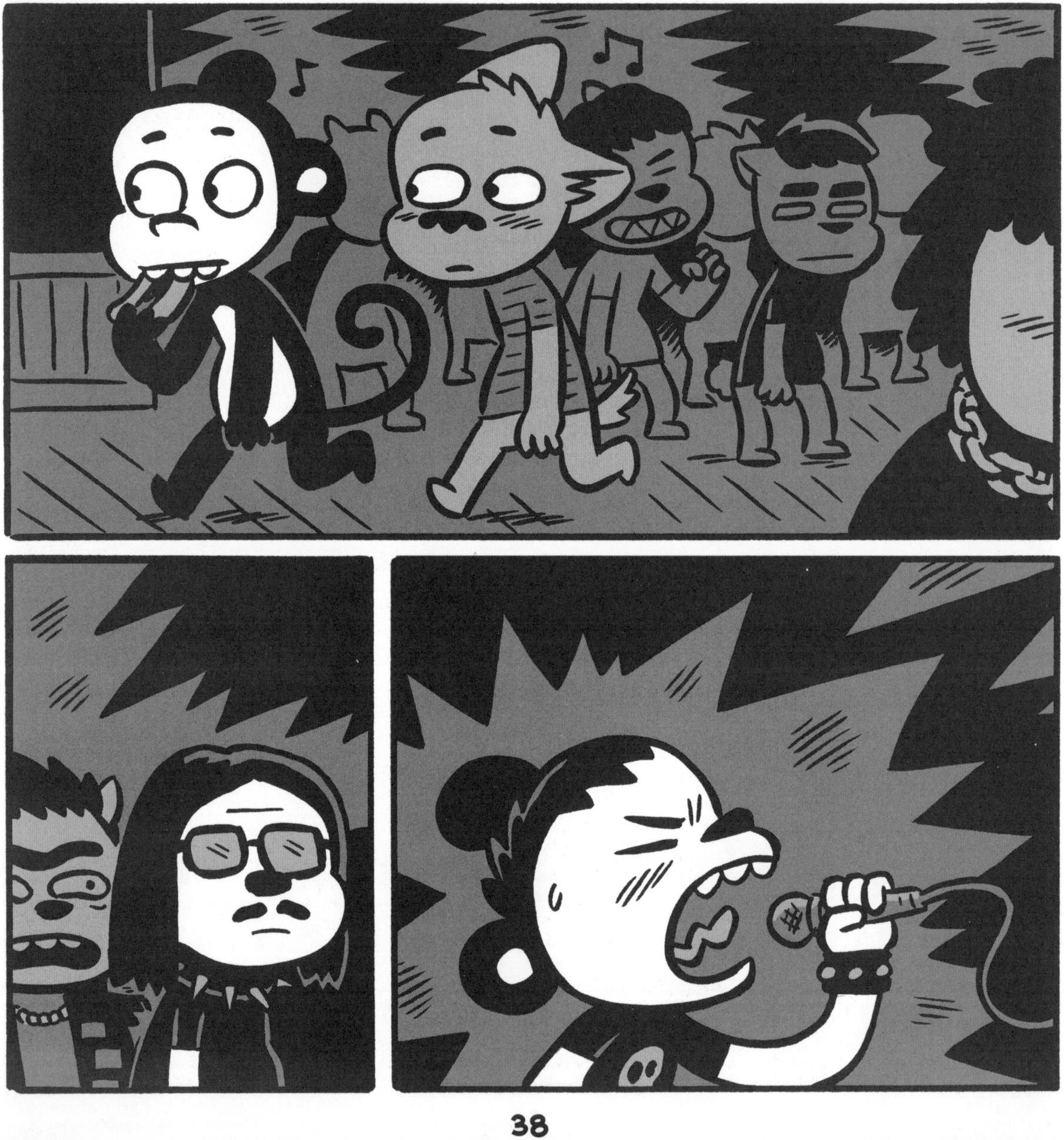

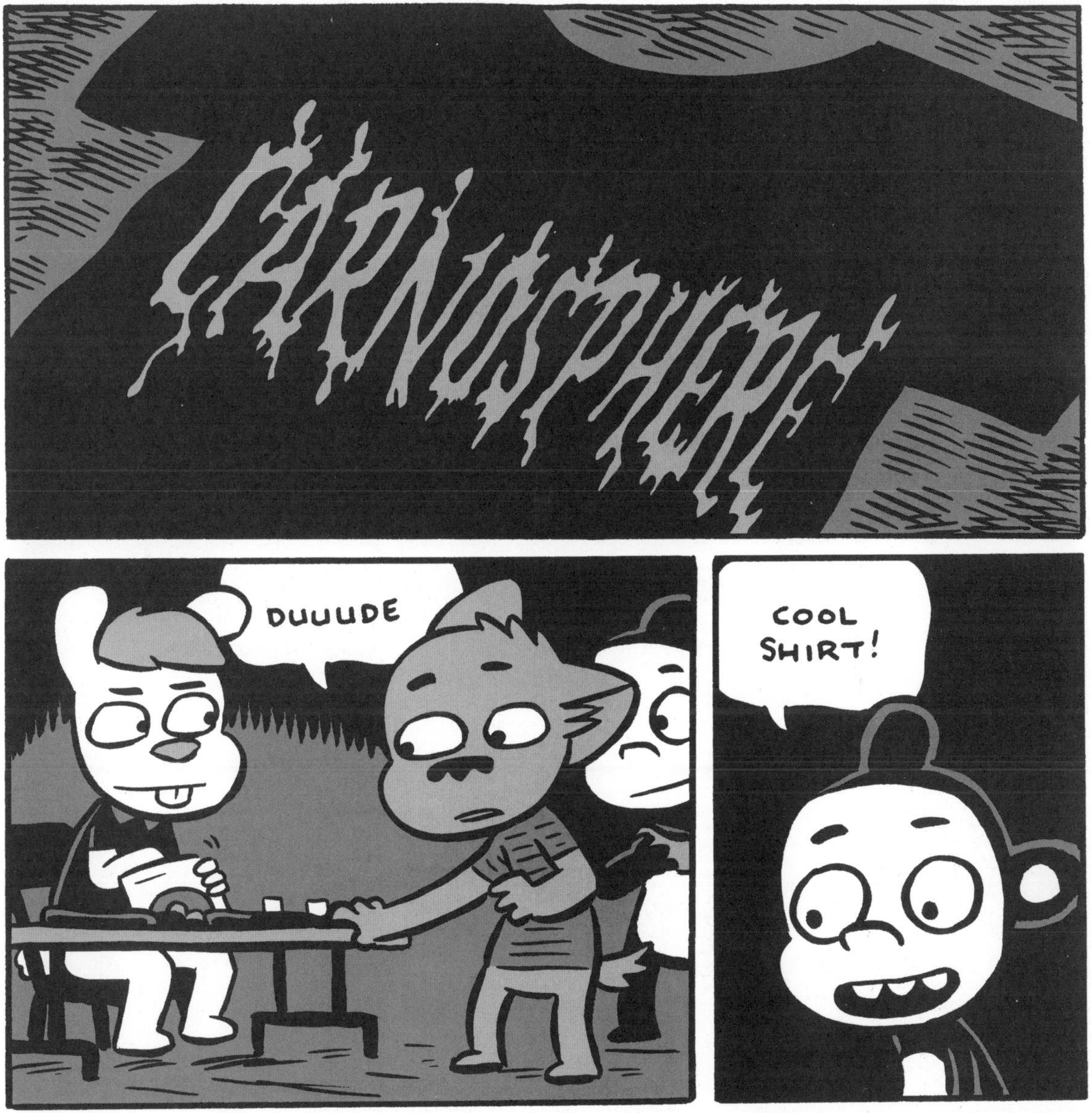
CARNOSPHERE
DUUUDE
COOL SHIRT!

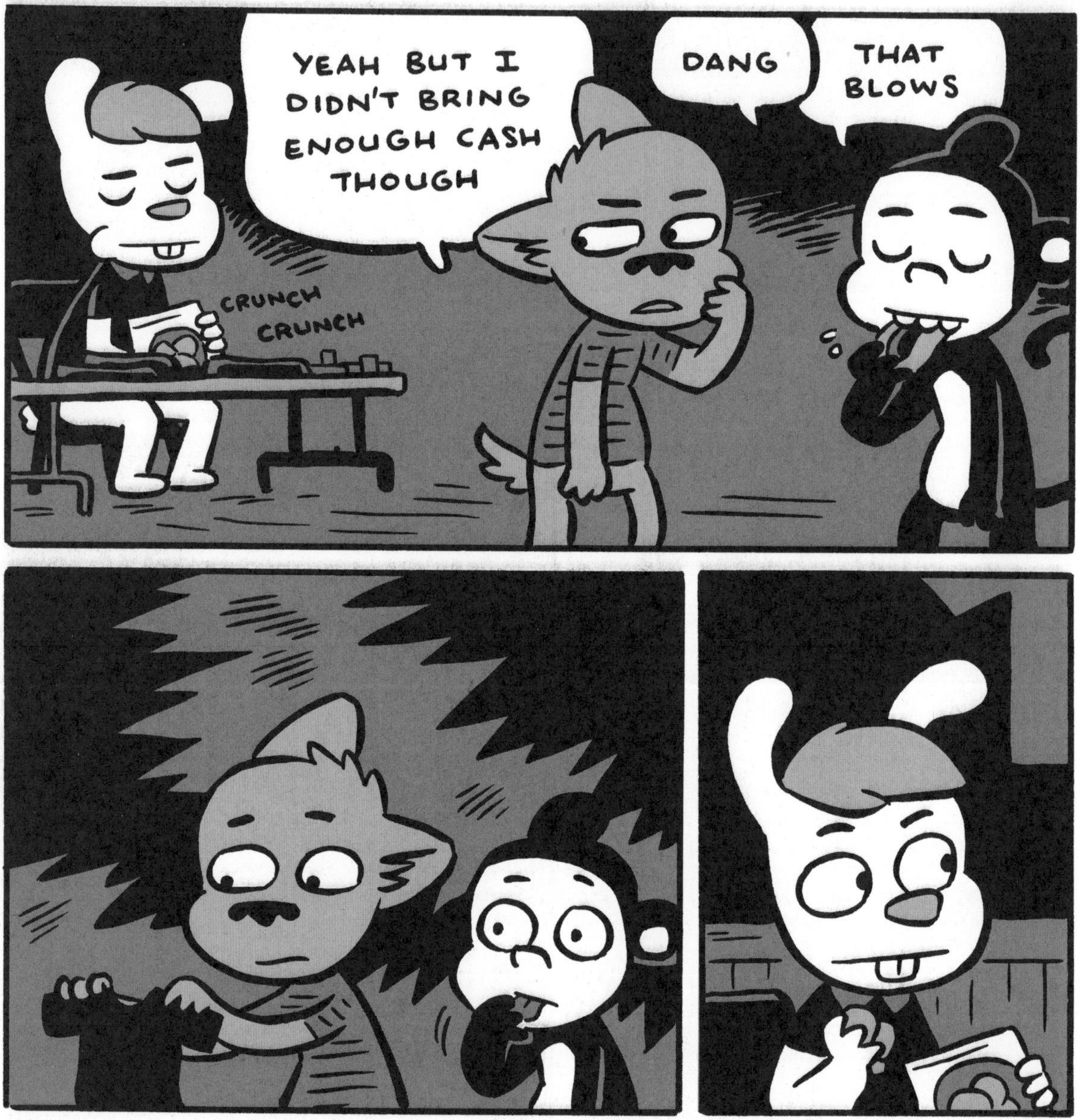
YEAH BUT I DIDN'T BRING ENOUGH CASH THOUGH
DANG
THAT BLOWS
CRUNCH
CRUNCH

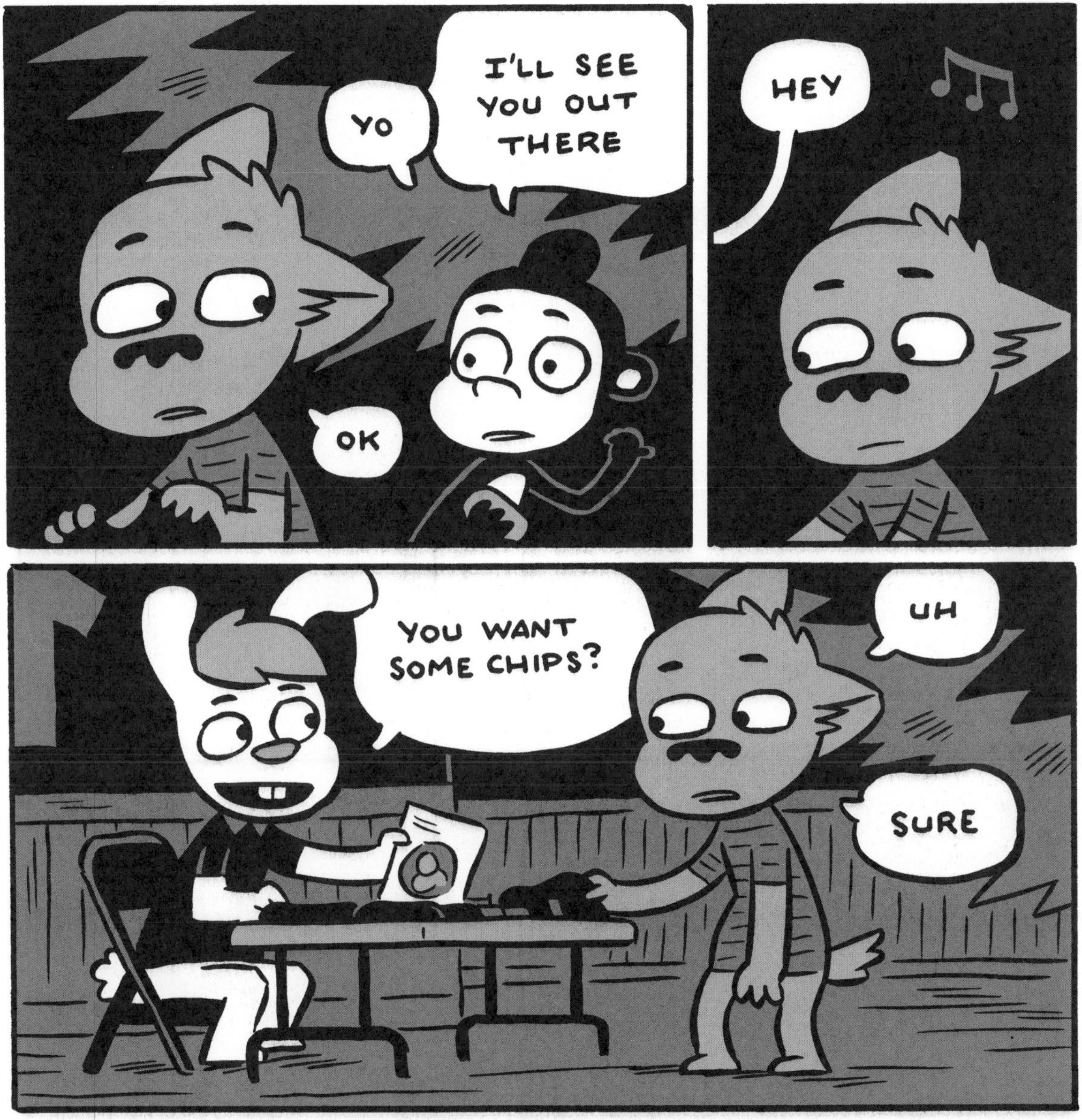
YO
I'LL SEE YOU OUT THERE
OK
HEY
YOU WANT SOME CHIPS?
UH
SURE

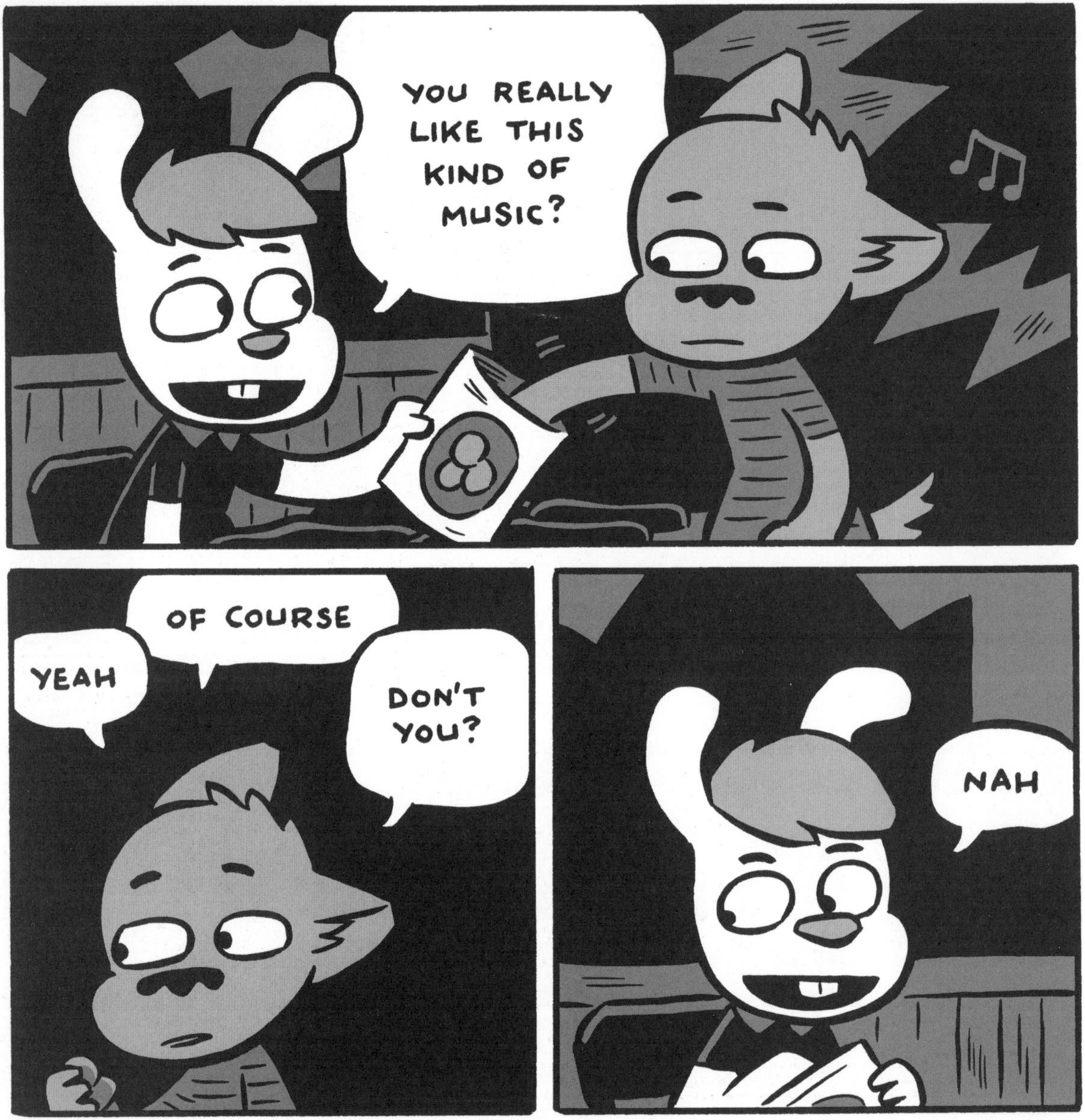
YOU REALLY LIKE THIS KIND OF MUSIC?
OF COURSE
YEAH
DON'T YOU?
NAH

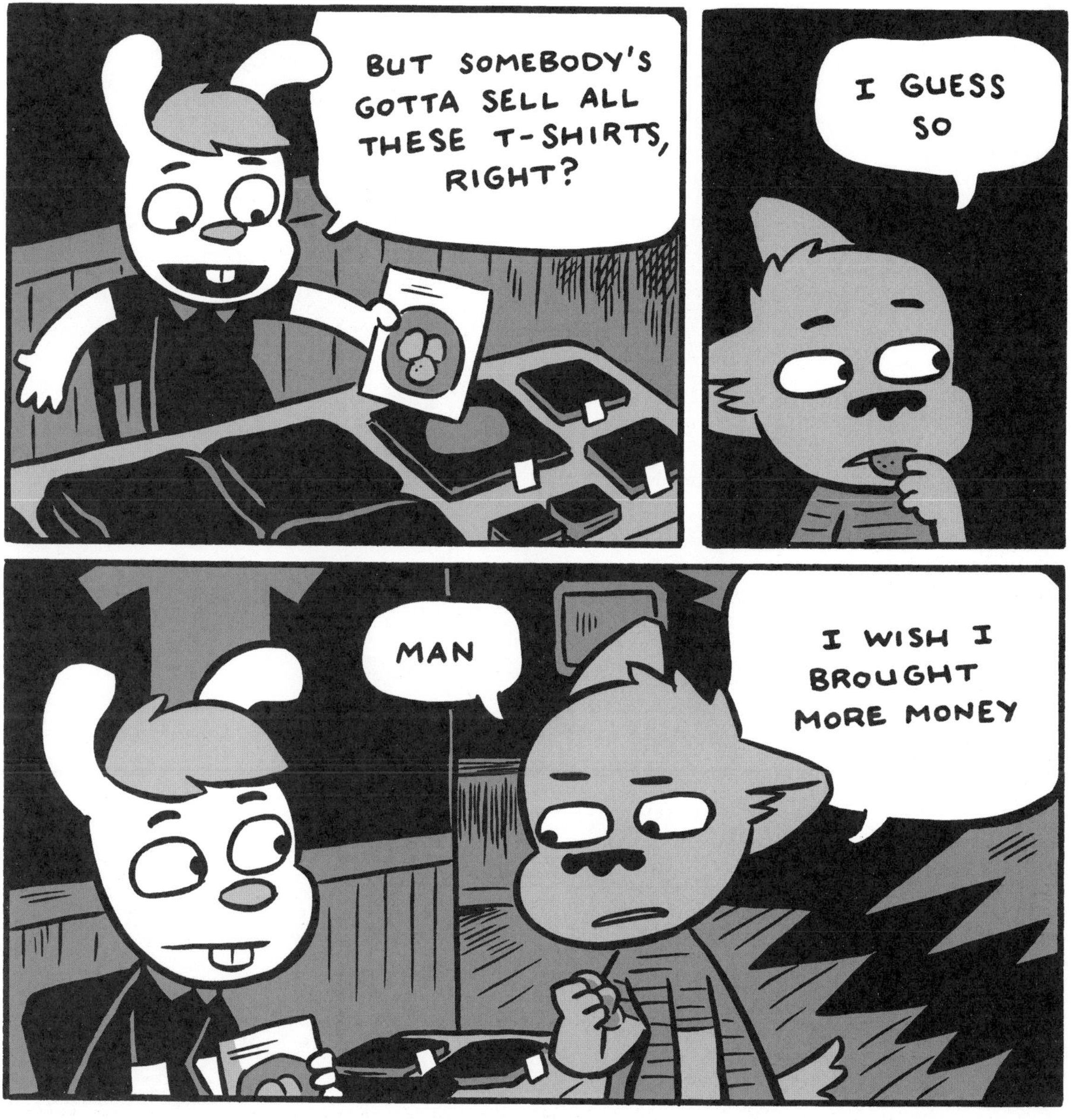
BUT SOMEBODY'S GOTTA SELL ALL THESE T-SHIRTS, RIGHT?
I GUESS SO
MAN
I WISH I BROUGHT MORE MONEY

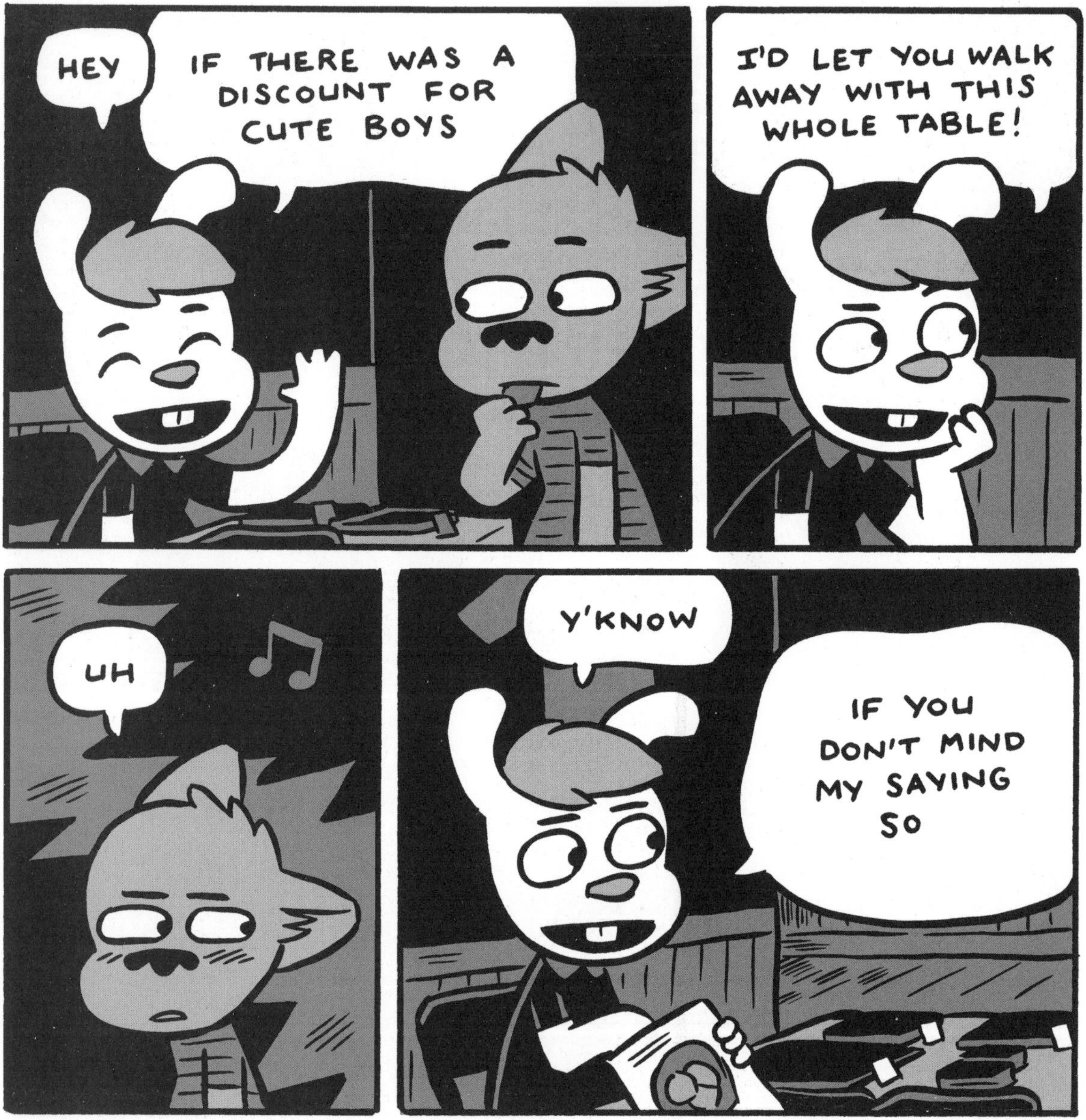
HEY
IF THERE WAS A DISCOUNT FOR CUTE BOYS
I'D LET YOU WALK AWAY WITH THIS WHOLE TABLE!
UH
Y'KNOW
IF YOU DON'T MIND MY SAYING SO

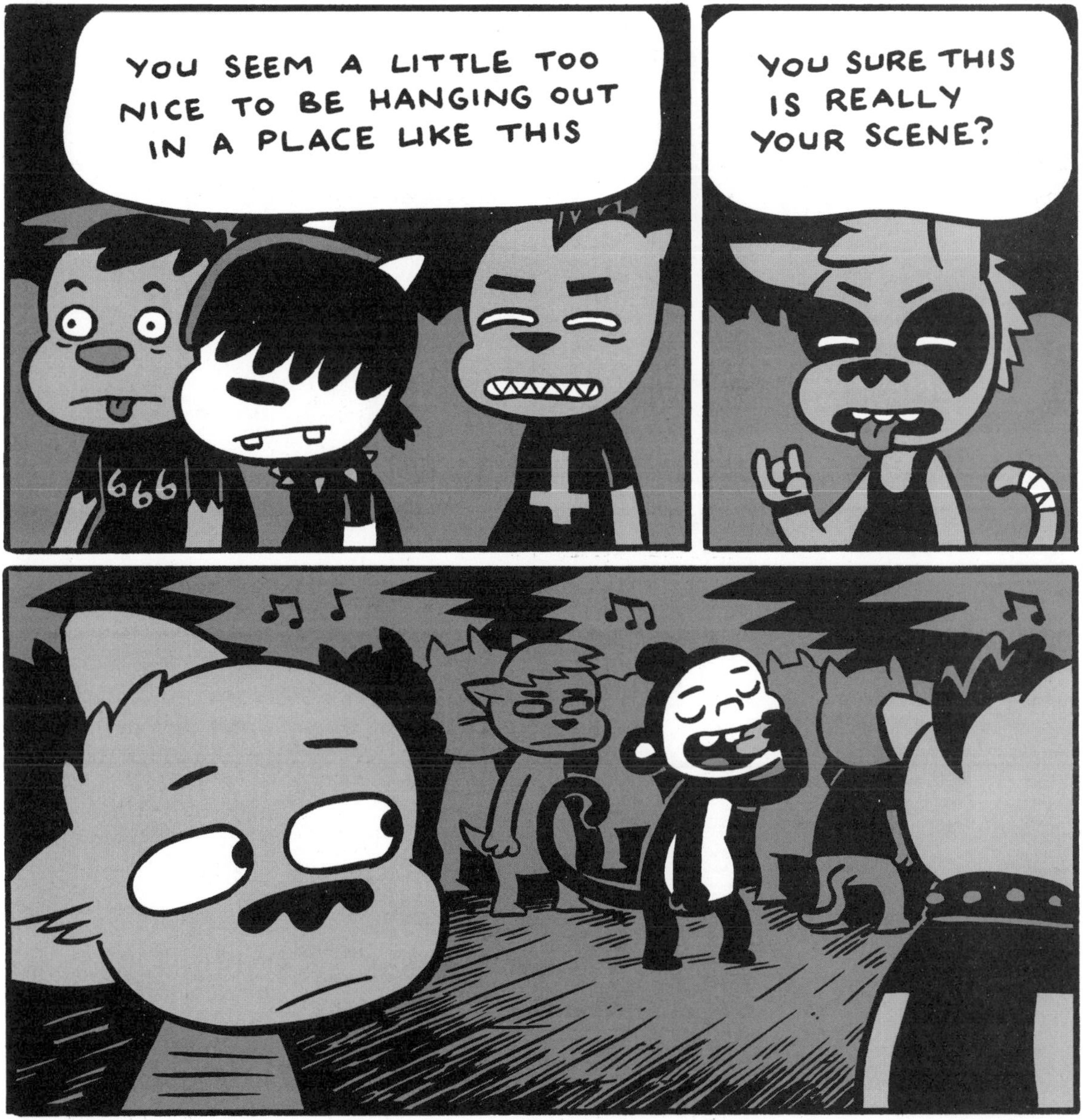
YOU SEEM A LITTLE TOO NICE TO BE HANGING OUT IN A PLACE LIKE THIS
666
YOU SURE THIS IS REALLY YOUR SCENE?

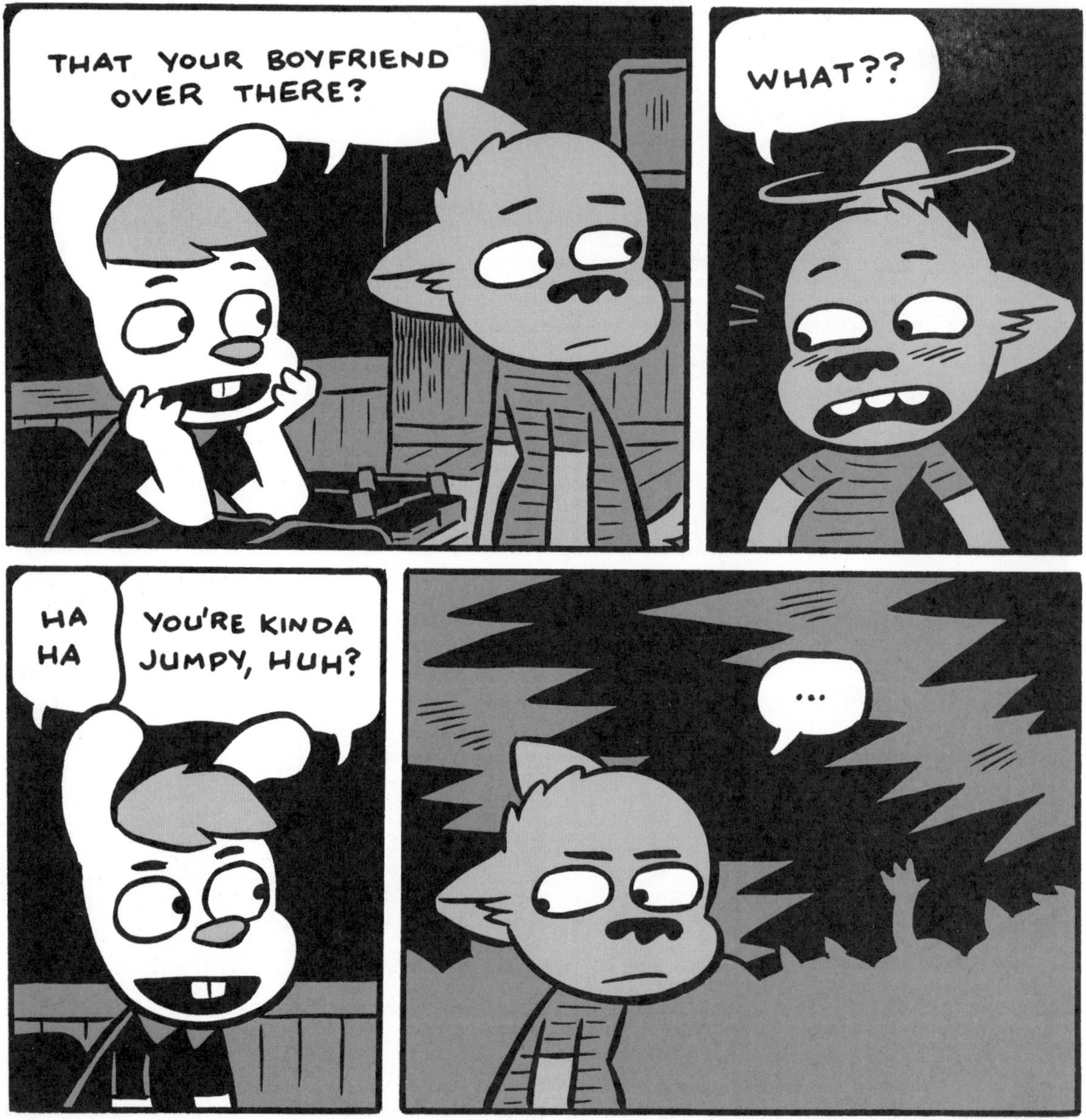
THAT YOUR BOYFRIEND OVER THERE?
WHAT??
HA HA
YOU'RE KINDA JUMPY, HUH?
...

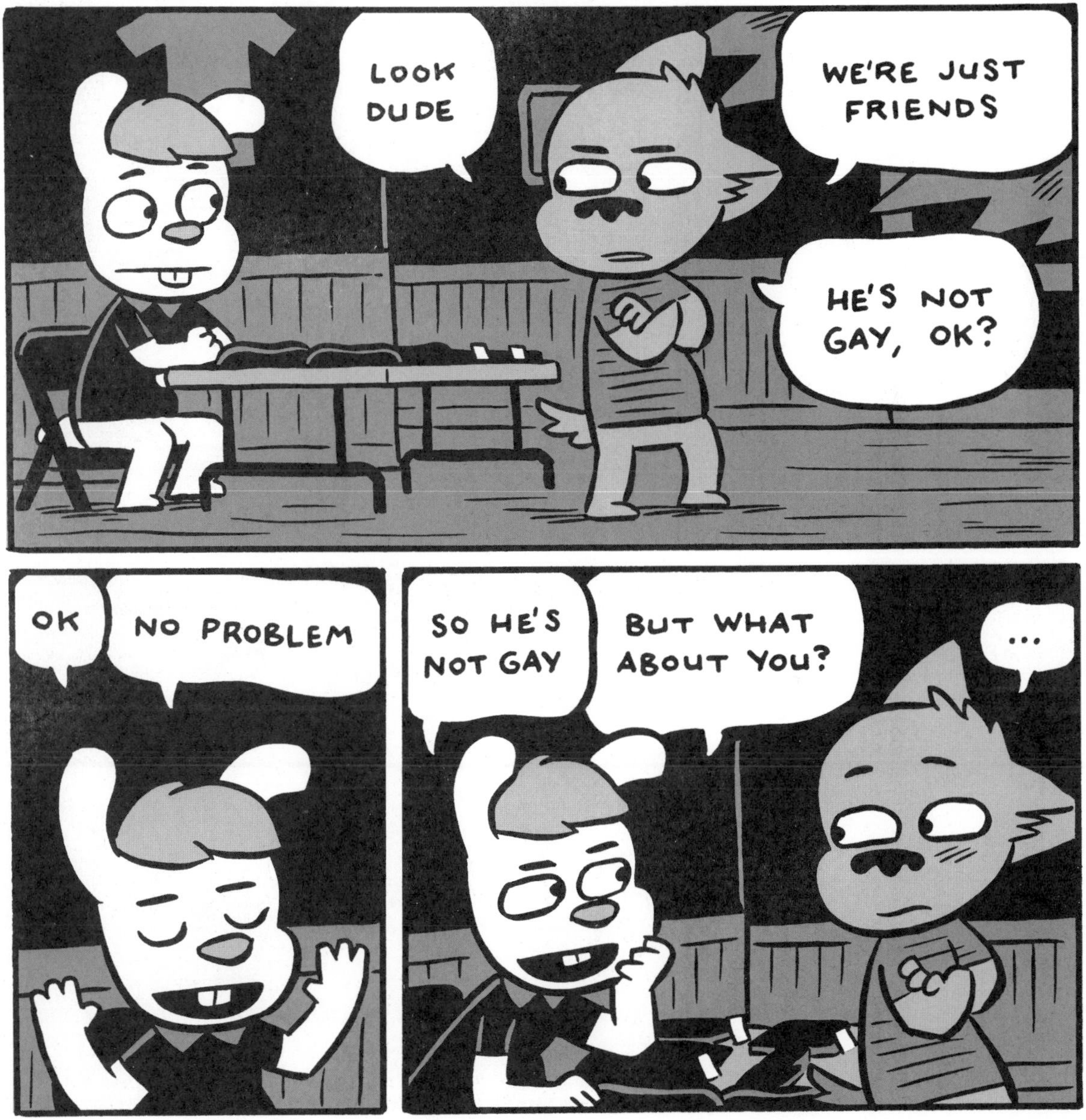
LOOK DUDE
WE'RE JUST FRIENDS
HE'S NOT GAY, OK?
OK
NO PROBLEM
SO HE'S NOT GAY
BUT WHAT ABOUT YOU?
...

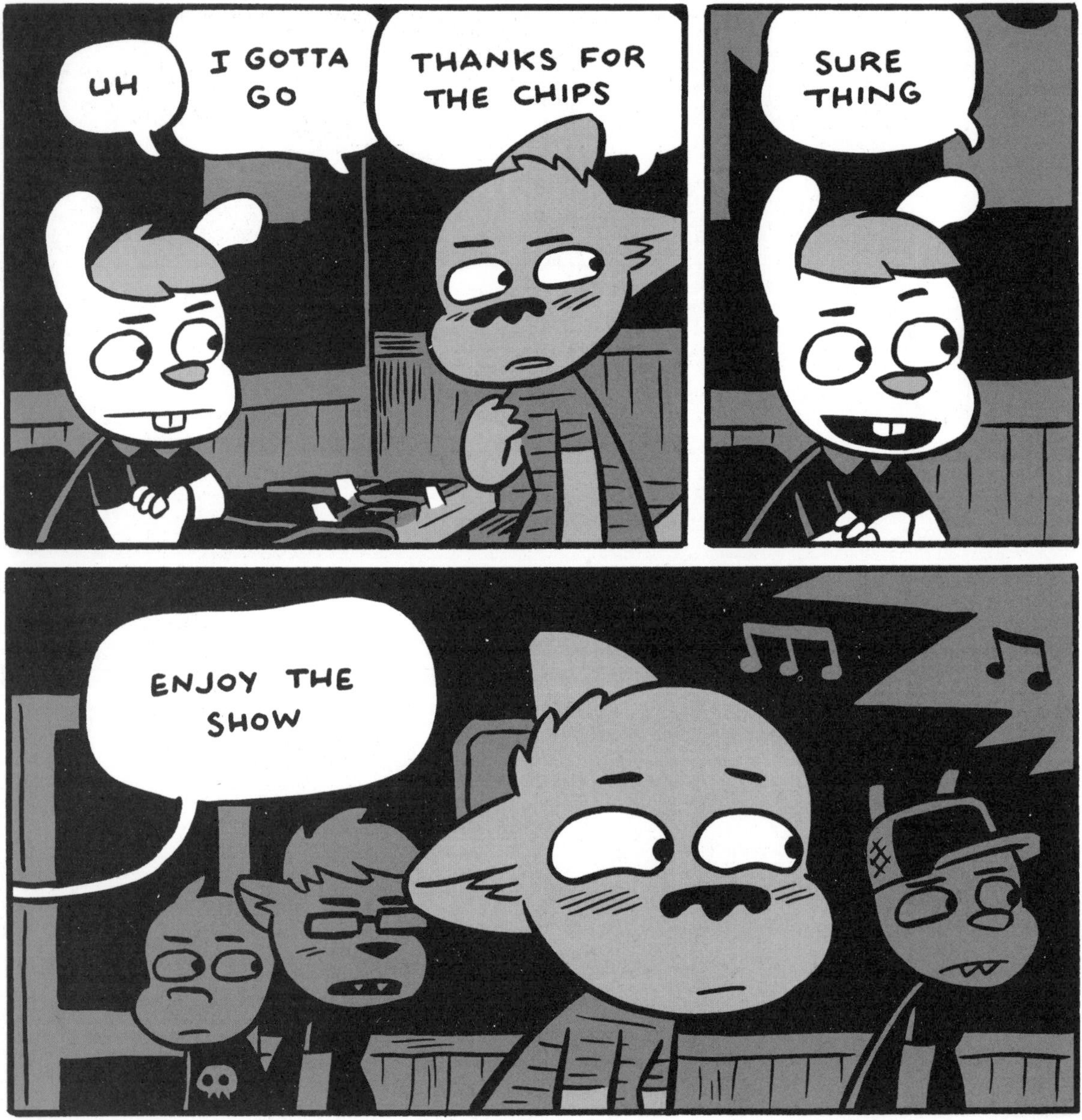
UH
I GOTTA GO
THANKS FOR THE CHIPS
SURE THING
ENJOY THE SHOW

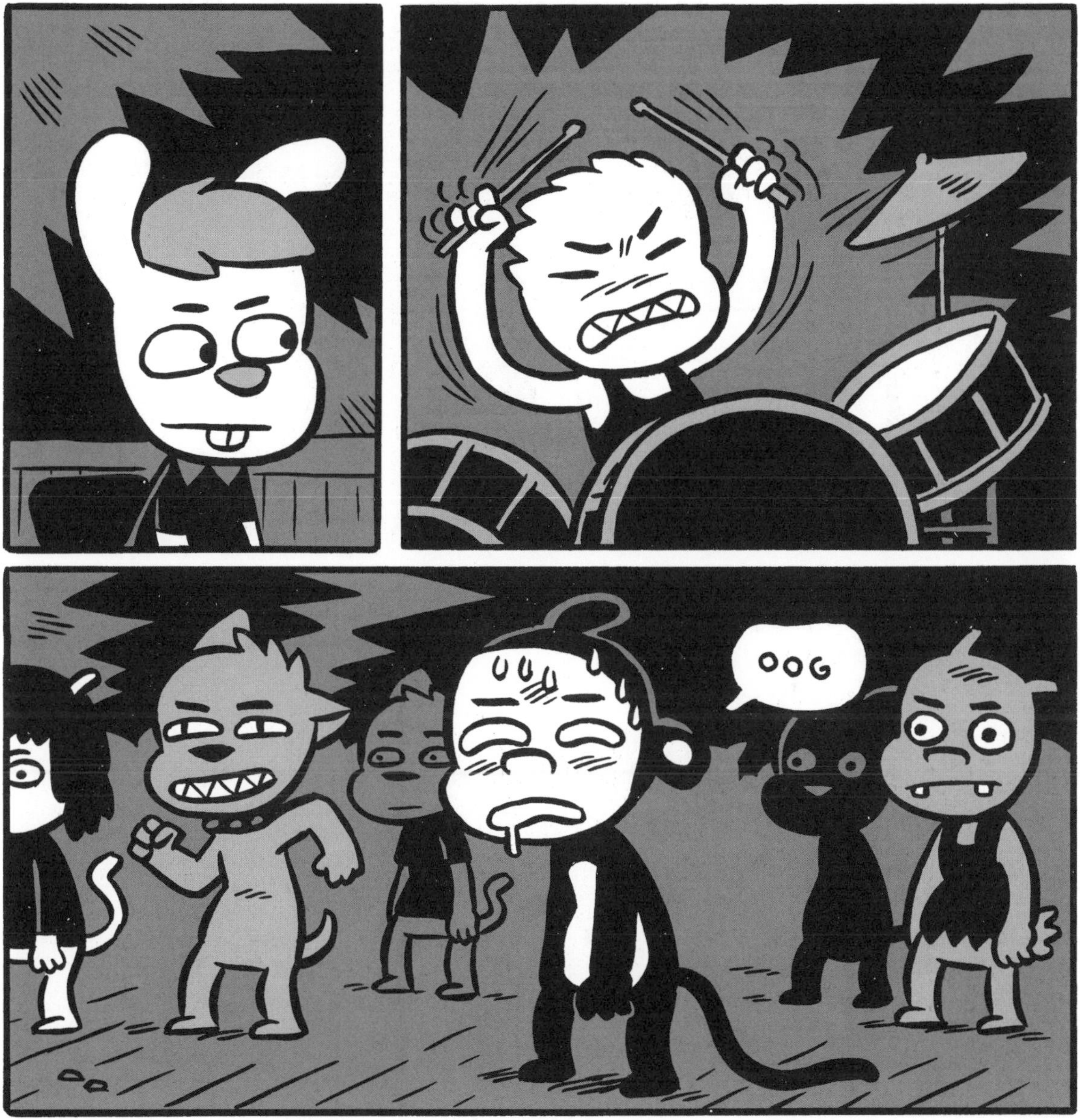
OOG

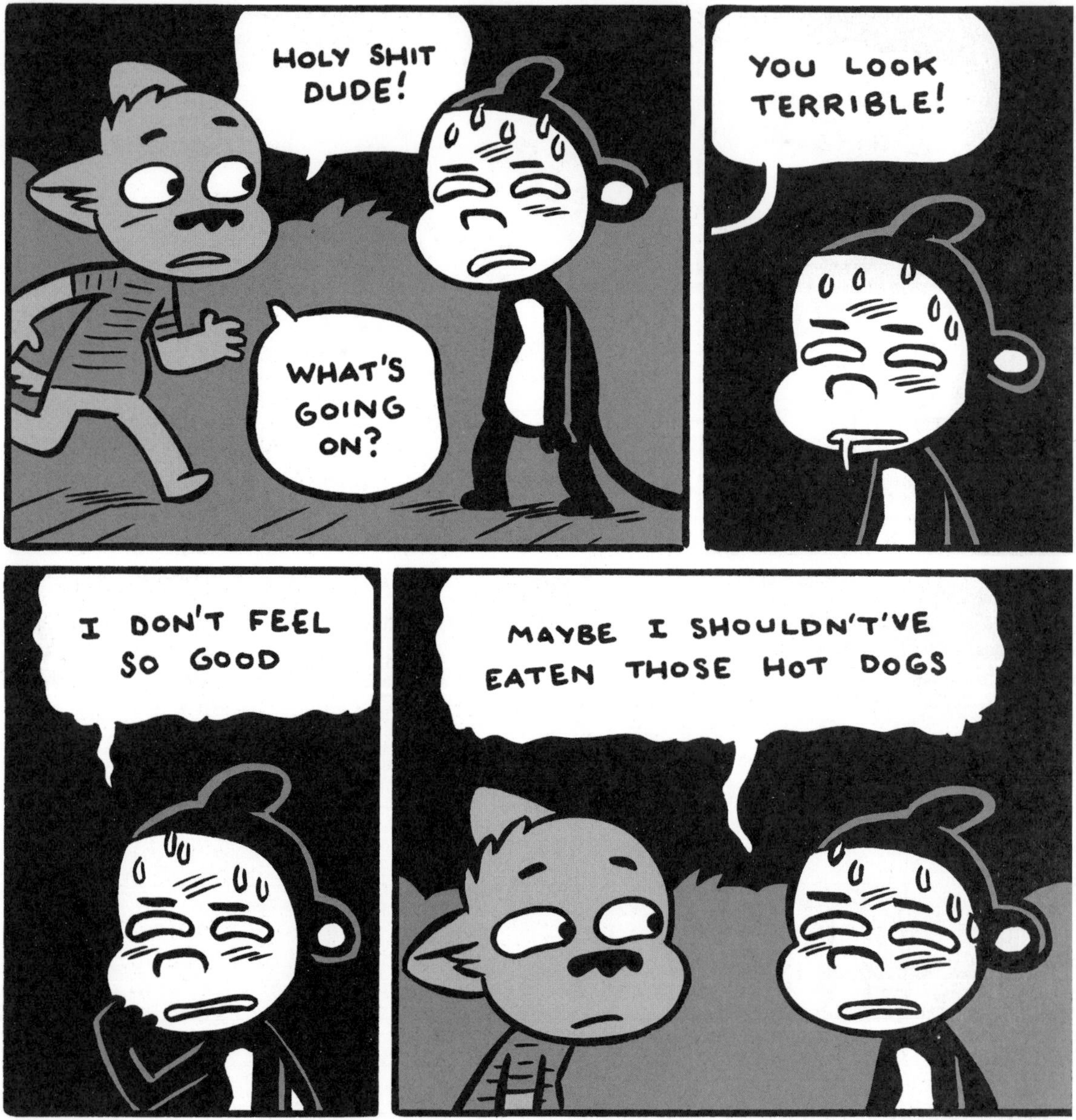
HOLY SHIT DUDE!
WHAT'S GOING ON?
YOU LOOK TERRIBLE!
I DON'T FEEL SO GOOD
MAYBE I SHOULDN'T'VE EATEN THOSE HOT DOGS

THINK I'M GONNA PUKE
OH MAN
JEEZ
UH
WE SHOULD GET YOU HOME
NO DUDE
NO
I
I JUST GOT AN IDEA

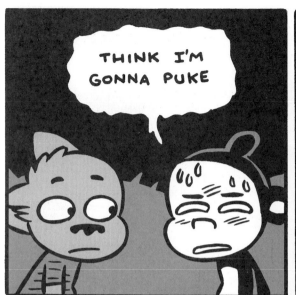

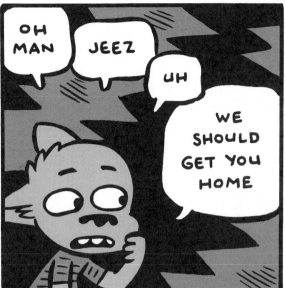

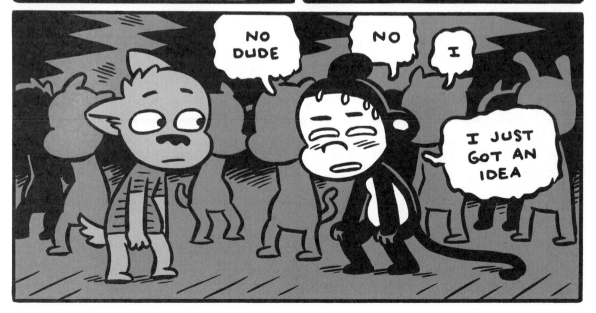

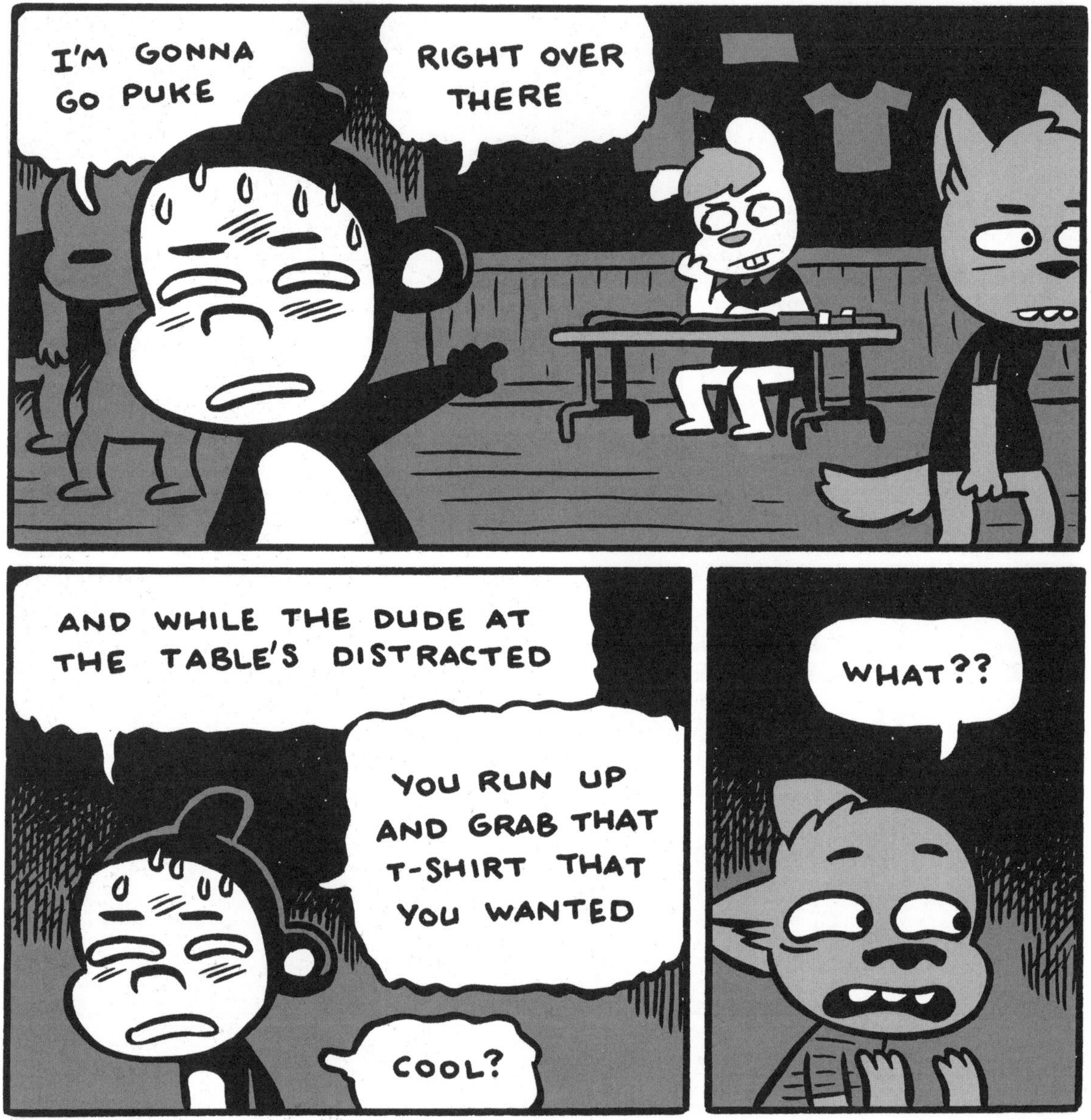
I'M GONNA GO PUKE
RIGHT OVER THERE
AND WHILE THE DUDE AT THE TABLE'S DISTRACTED
YOU RUN UP AND GRAB THAT T-SHIRT THAT YOU WANTED
COOL?
WHAT??

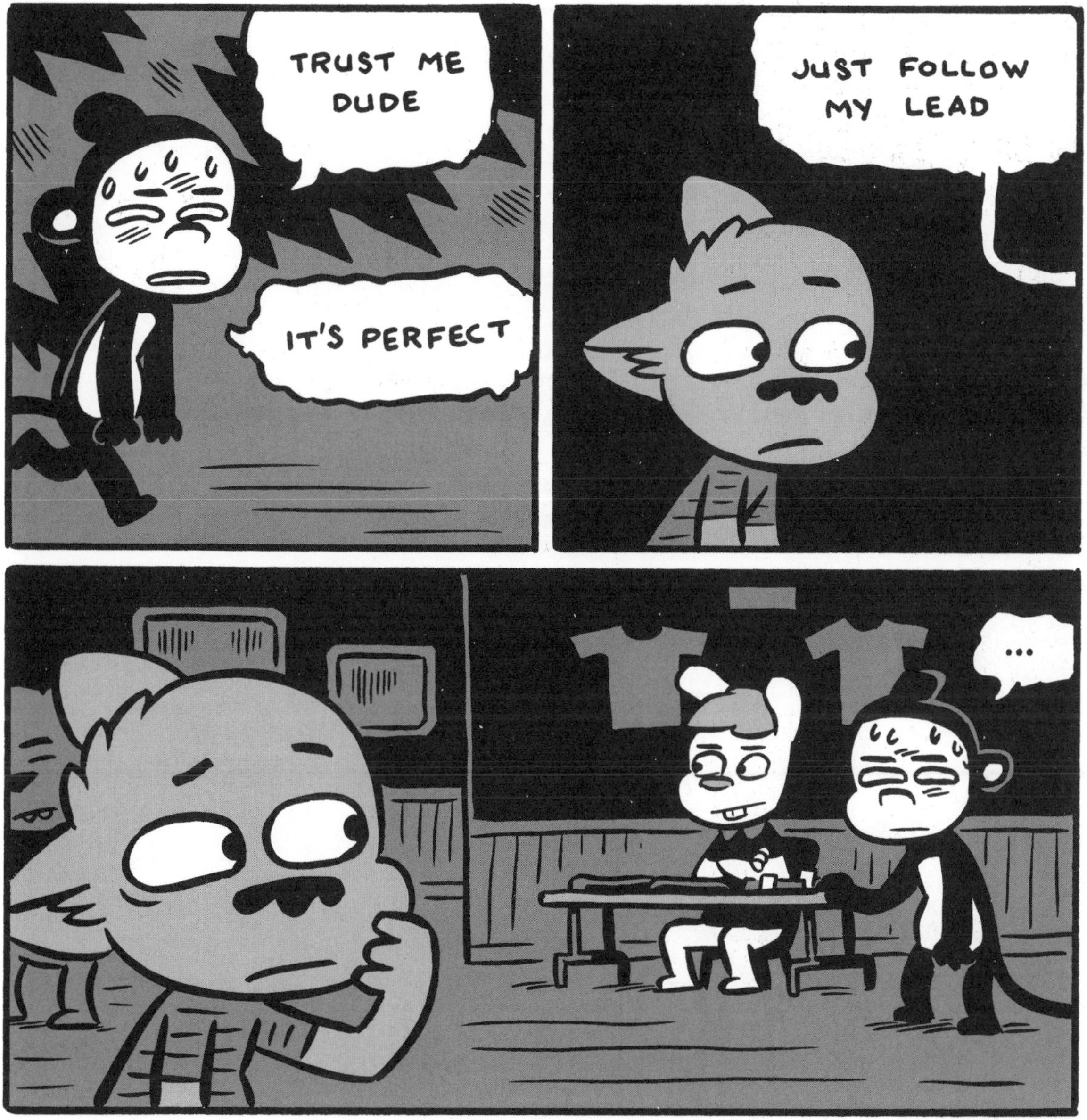
TRUST ME DUDE
IT'S PERFECT
JUST FOLLOW MY LEAD
...

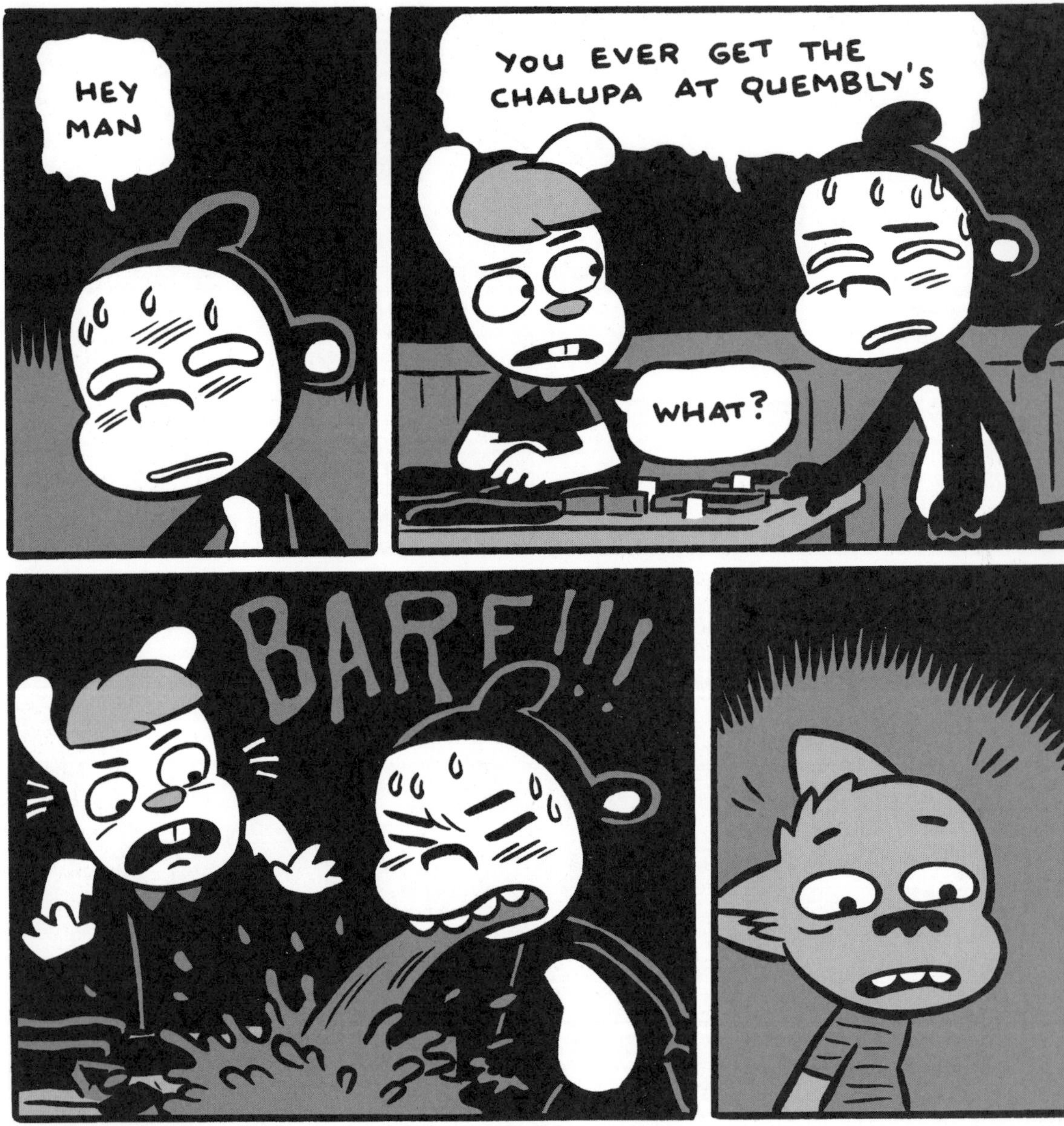

HEY MAN
YOU EVER GET THE CHALUPA AT QUEMBLY'S
WHAT?
BARF!!!

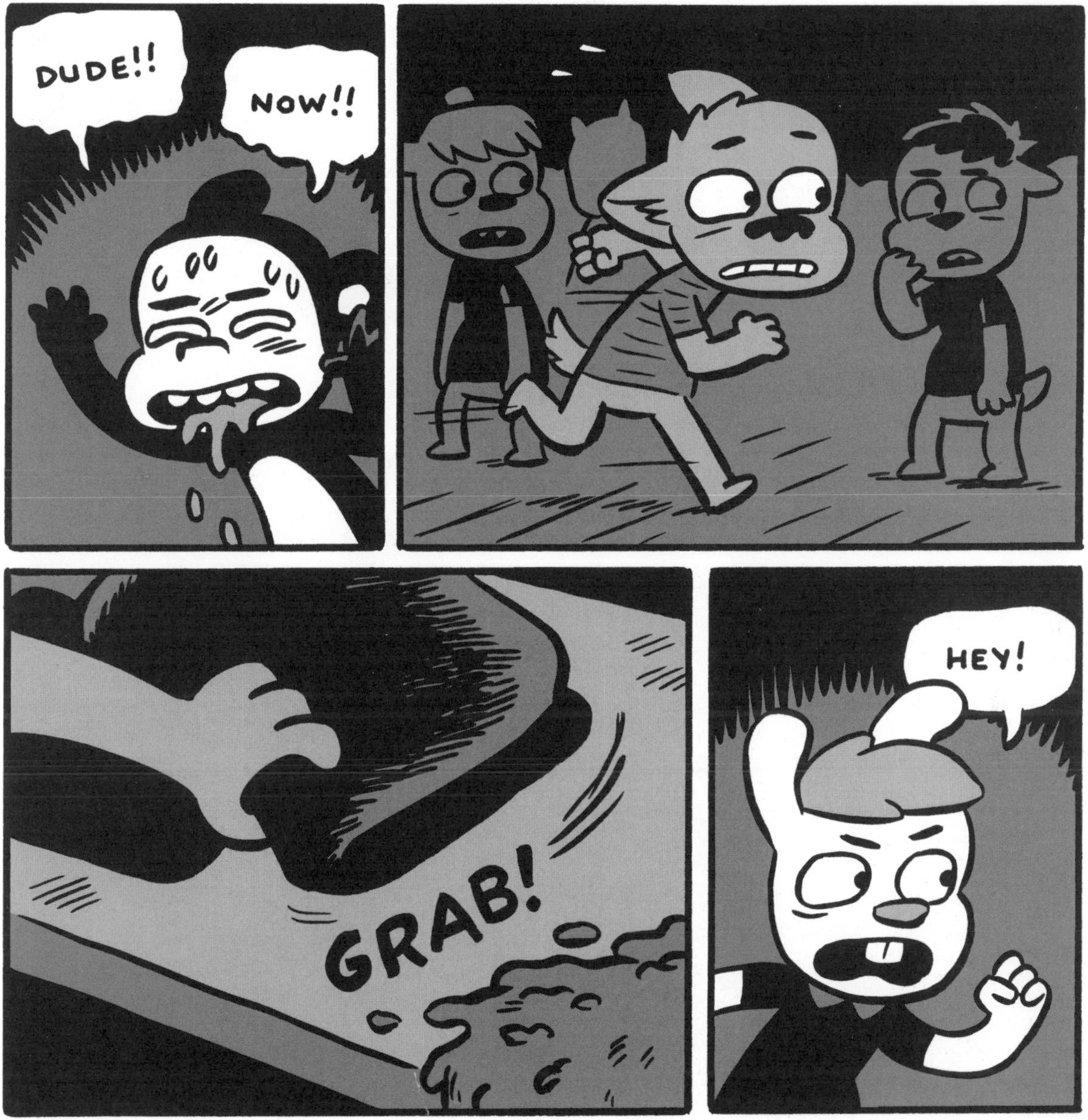
DUDE!!
NOW!!
GRAB!
HEY!

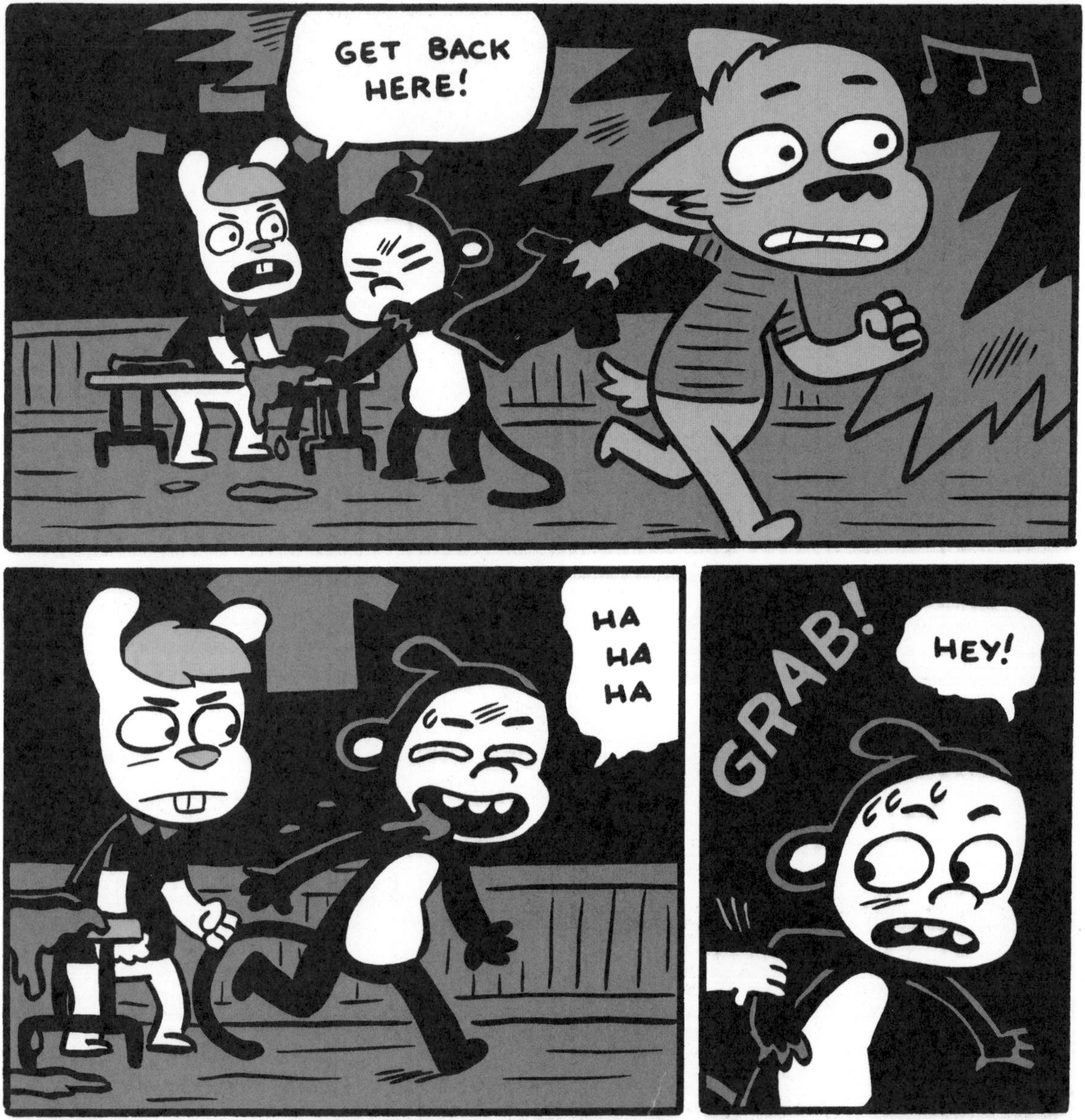
GET BACK HERE!
HA HA HA
GRAB!
HEY!

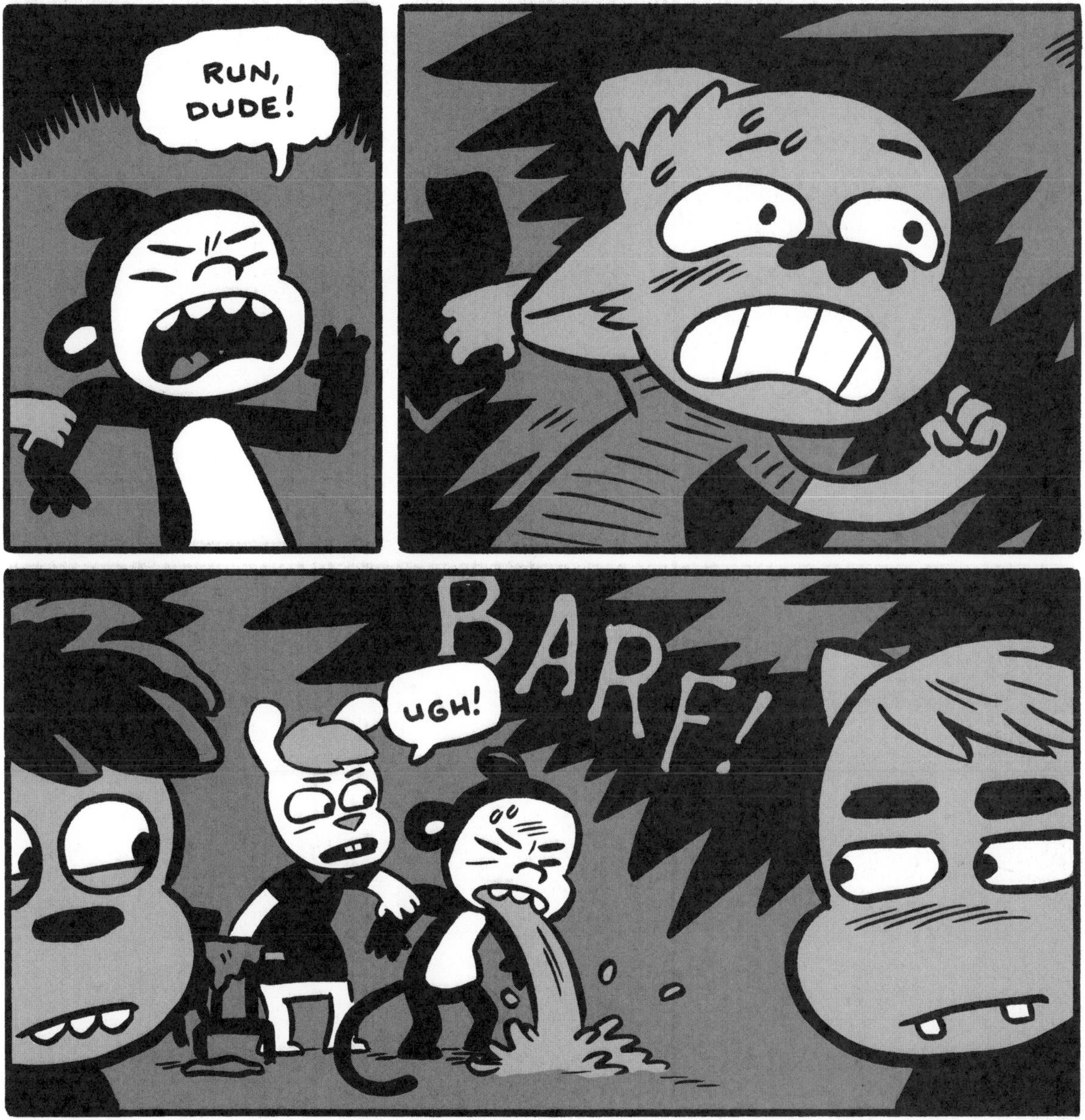
RUN, DUDE!
BARF!
UGH!

OH SHIT
OH SHIT
OH SHIT

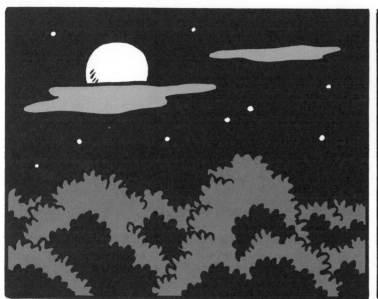

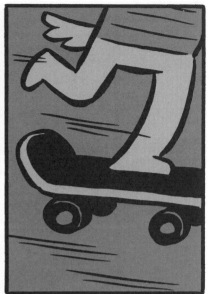

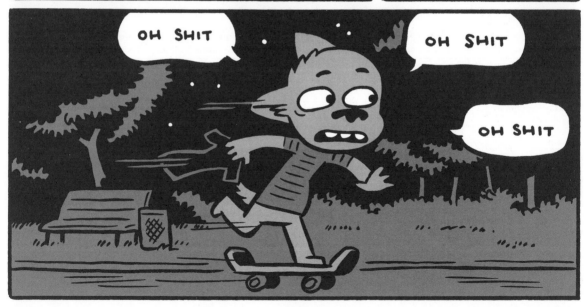

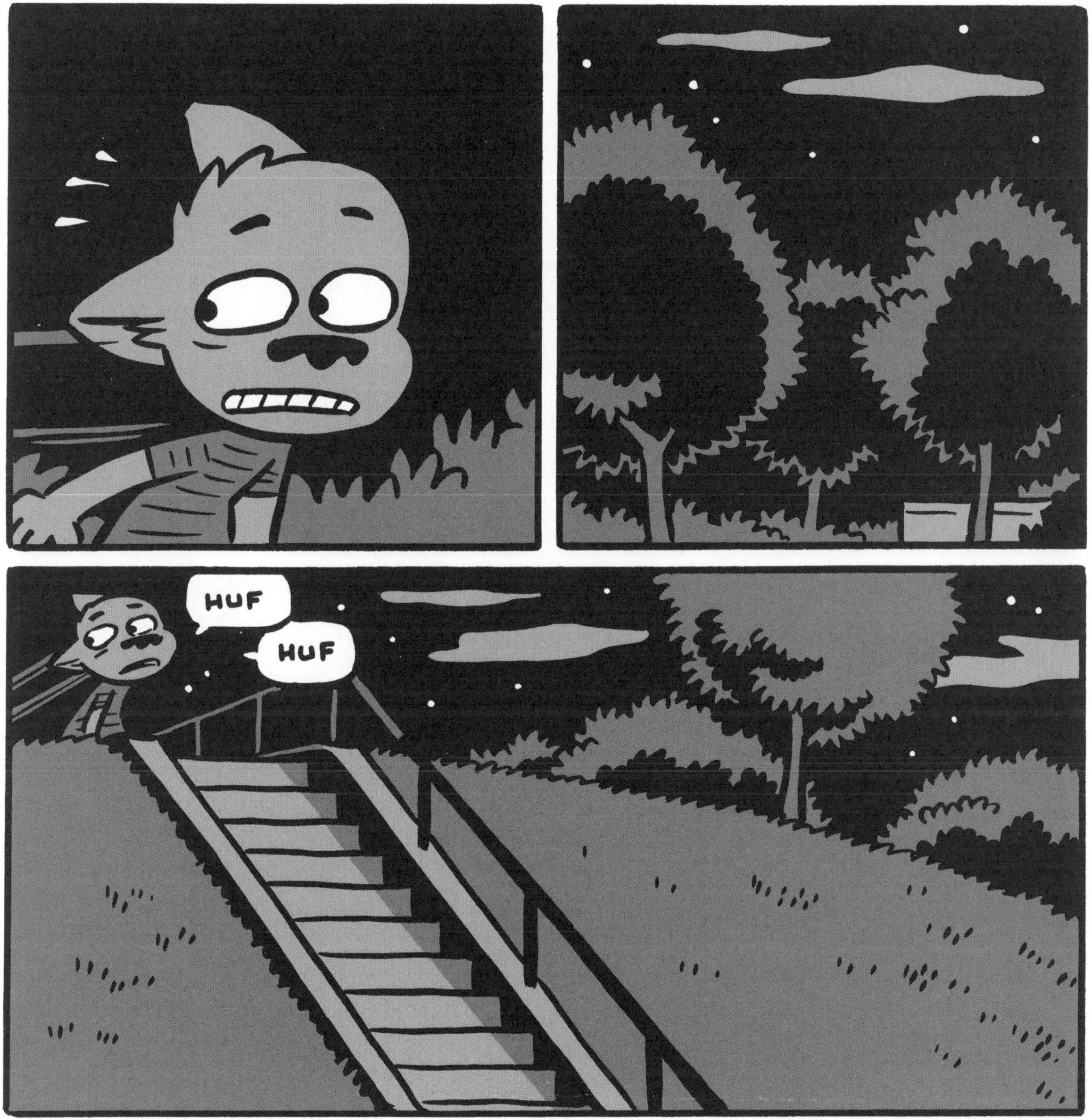
HUF
HUF

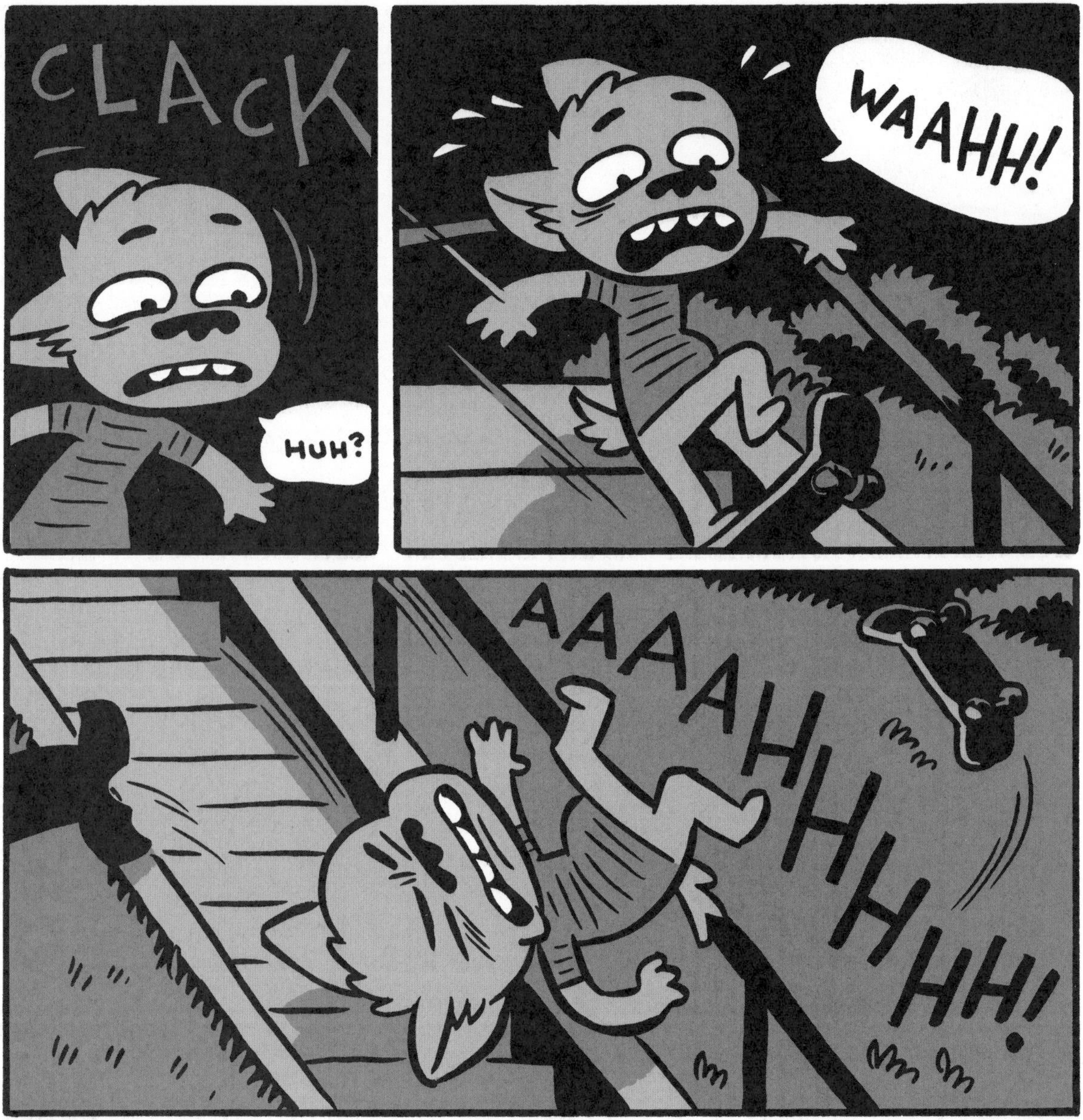
CLACK
HUH?
WAAHH!
AAAAHHHHHHH!

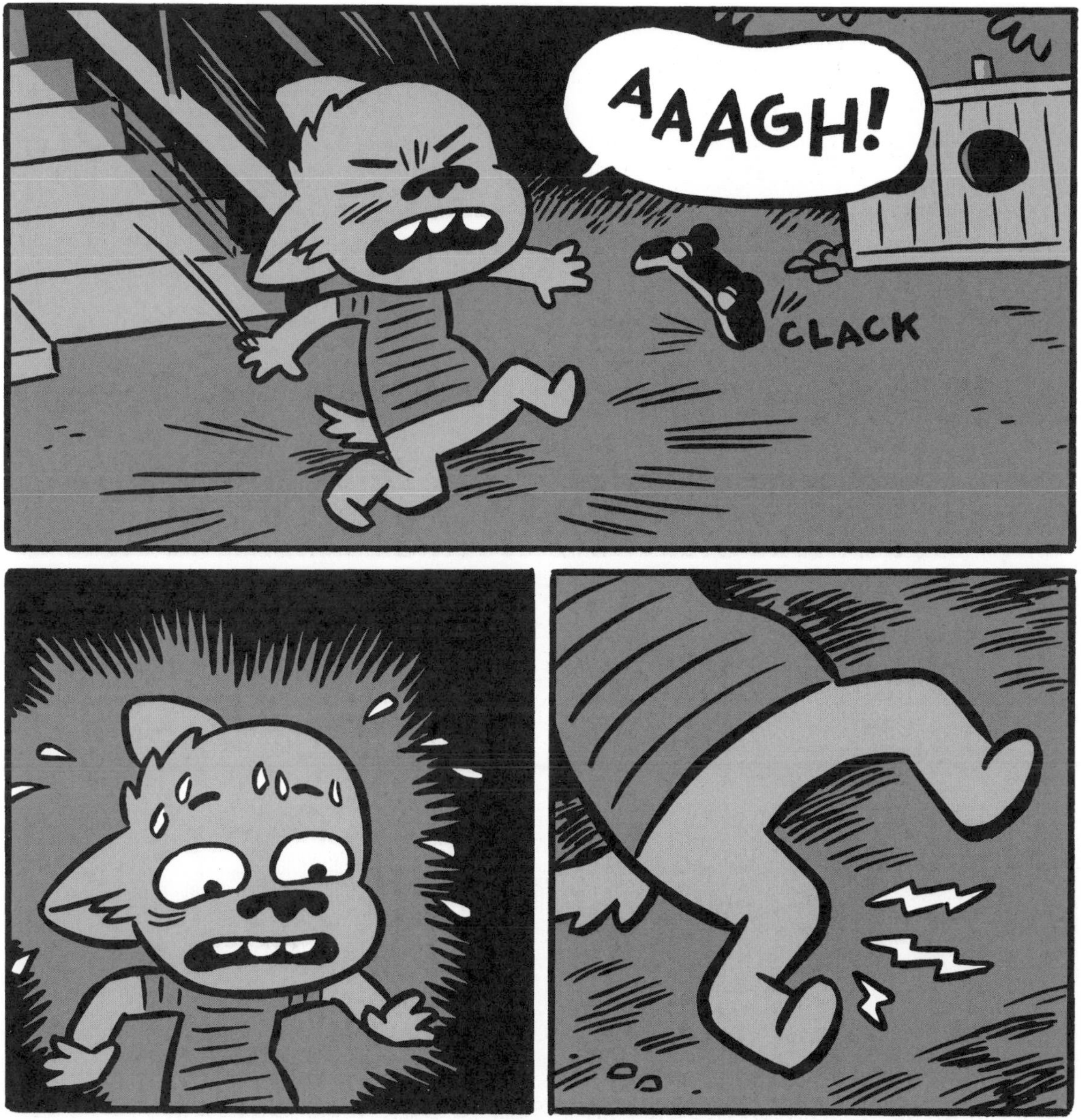
AAAGH!
CLACK

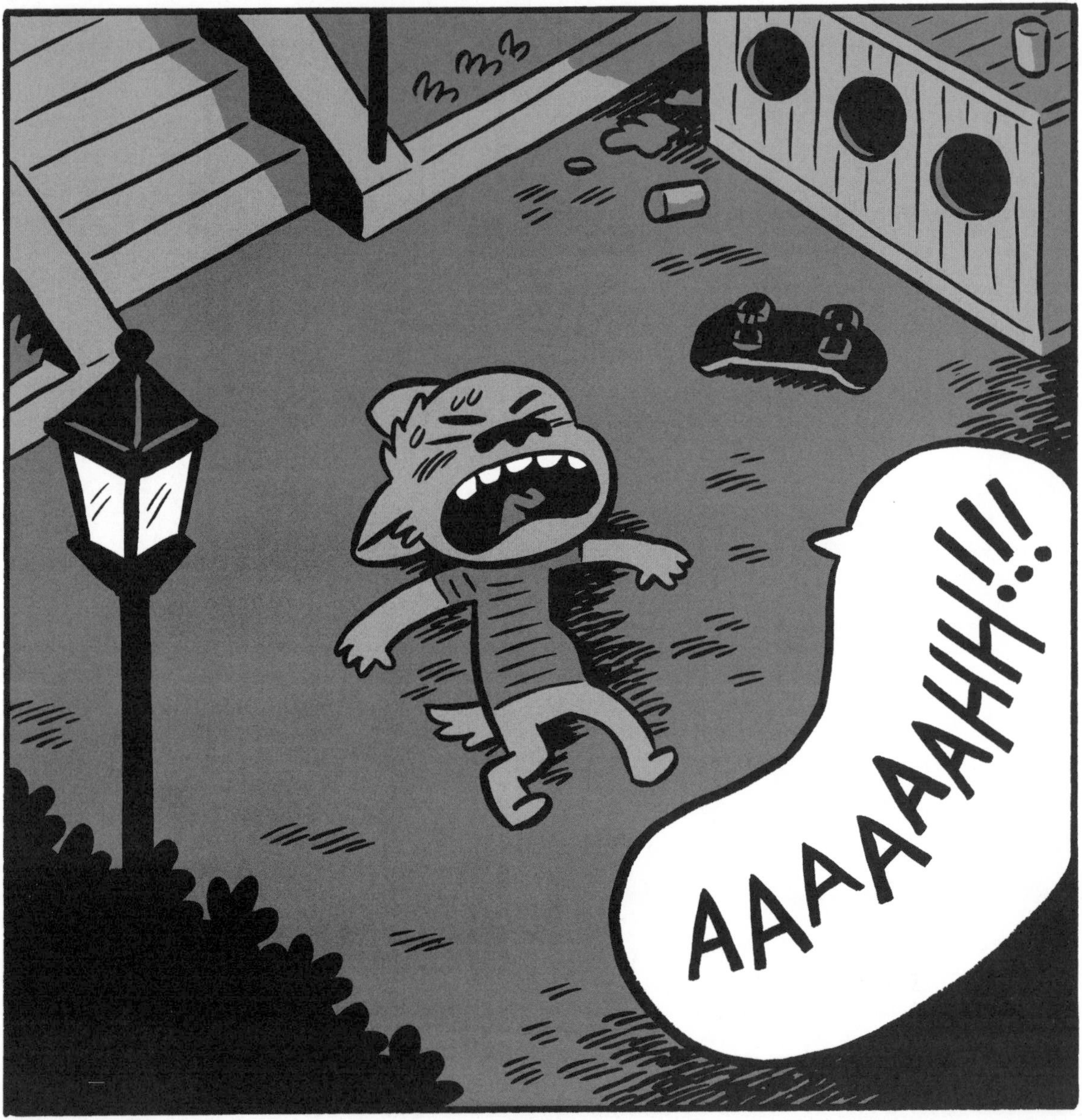
AAAAAAHH!!!

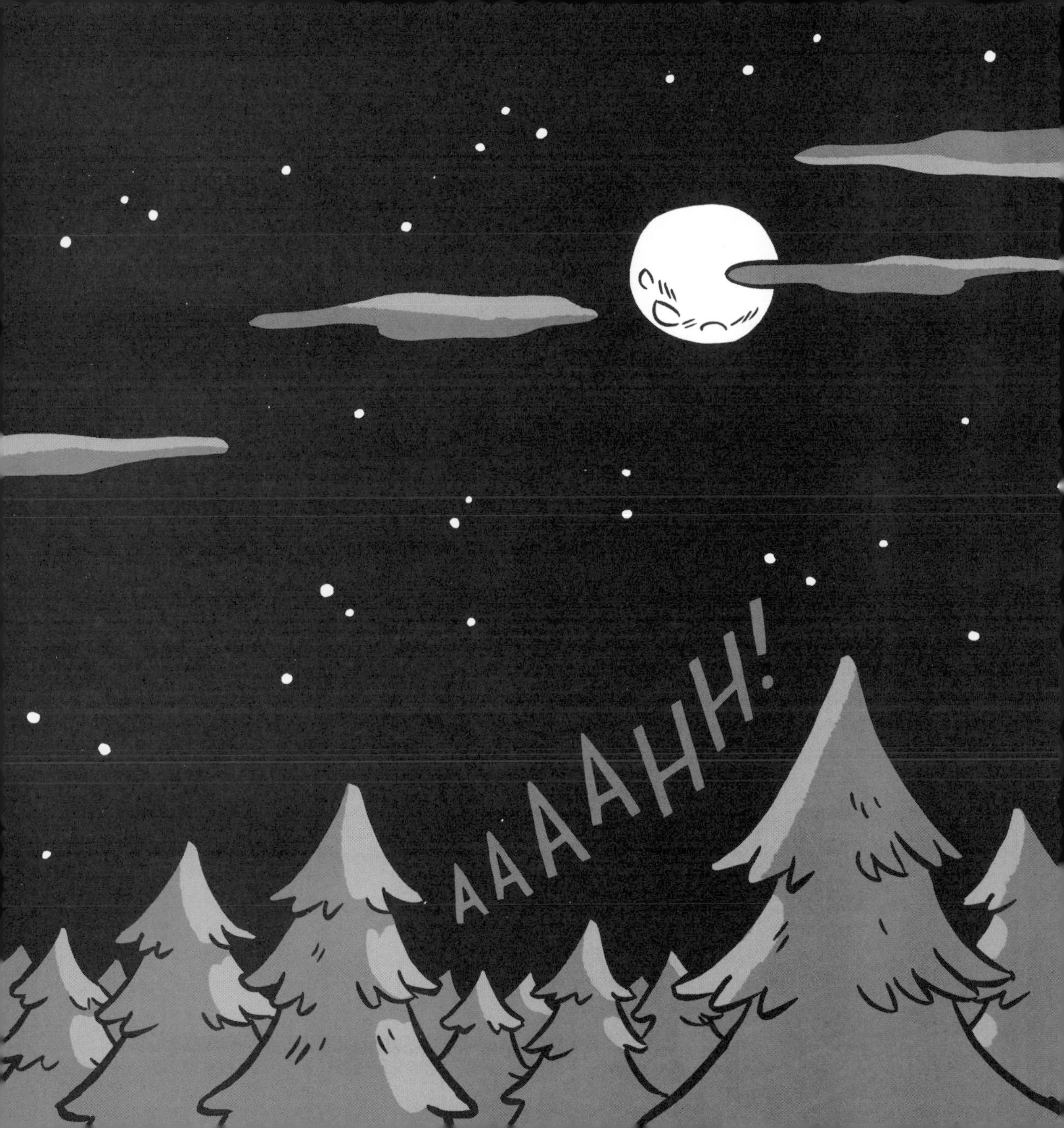
AAAAHH!

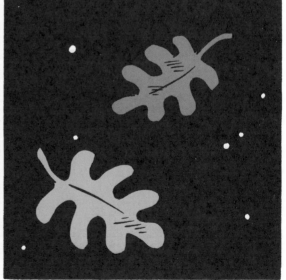

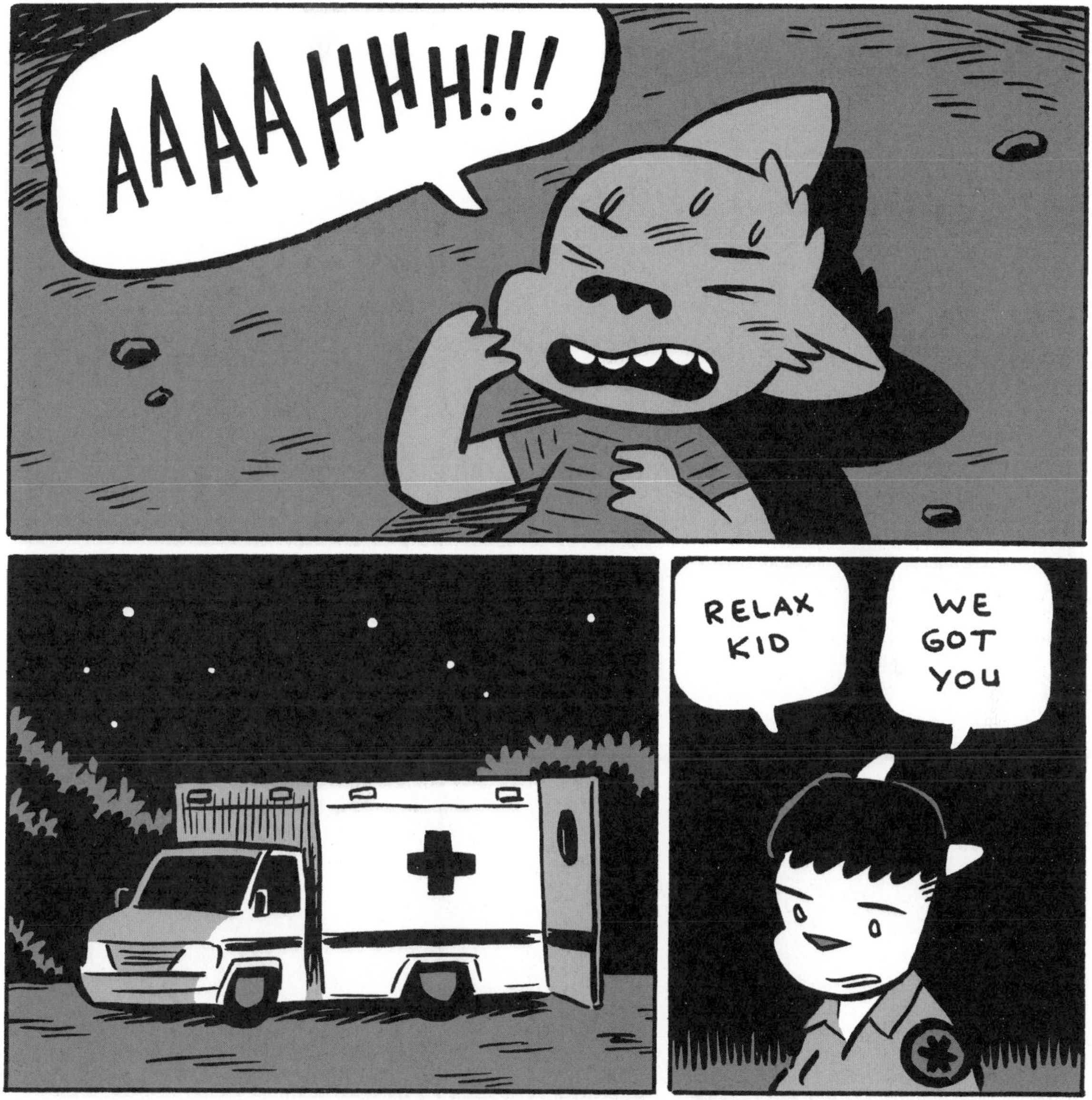
AAAAHHHH!!!
RELAX KID
WE GOT YOU

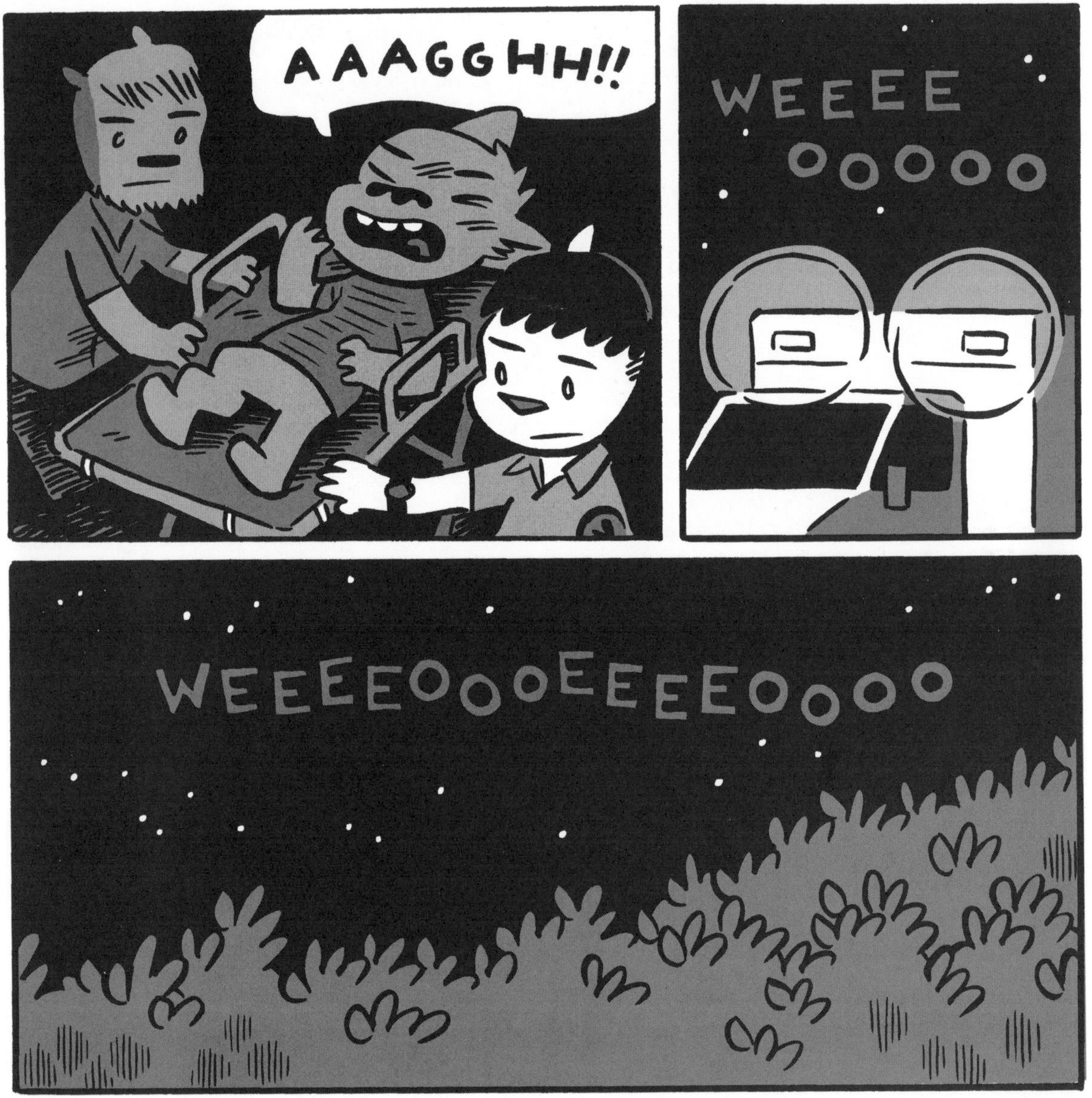
AAAGGHH!!
WEEEE
OOOOO
WEEEEOOOEEEEOOOO

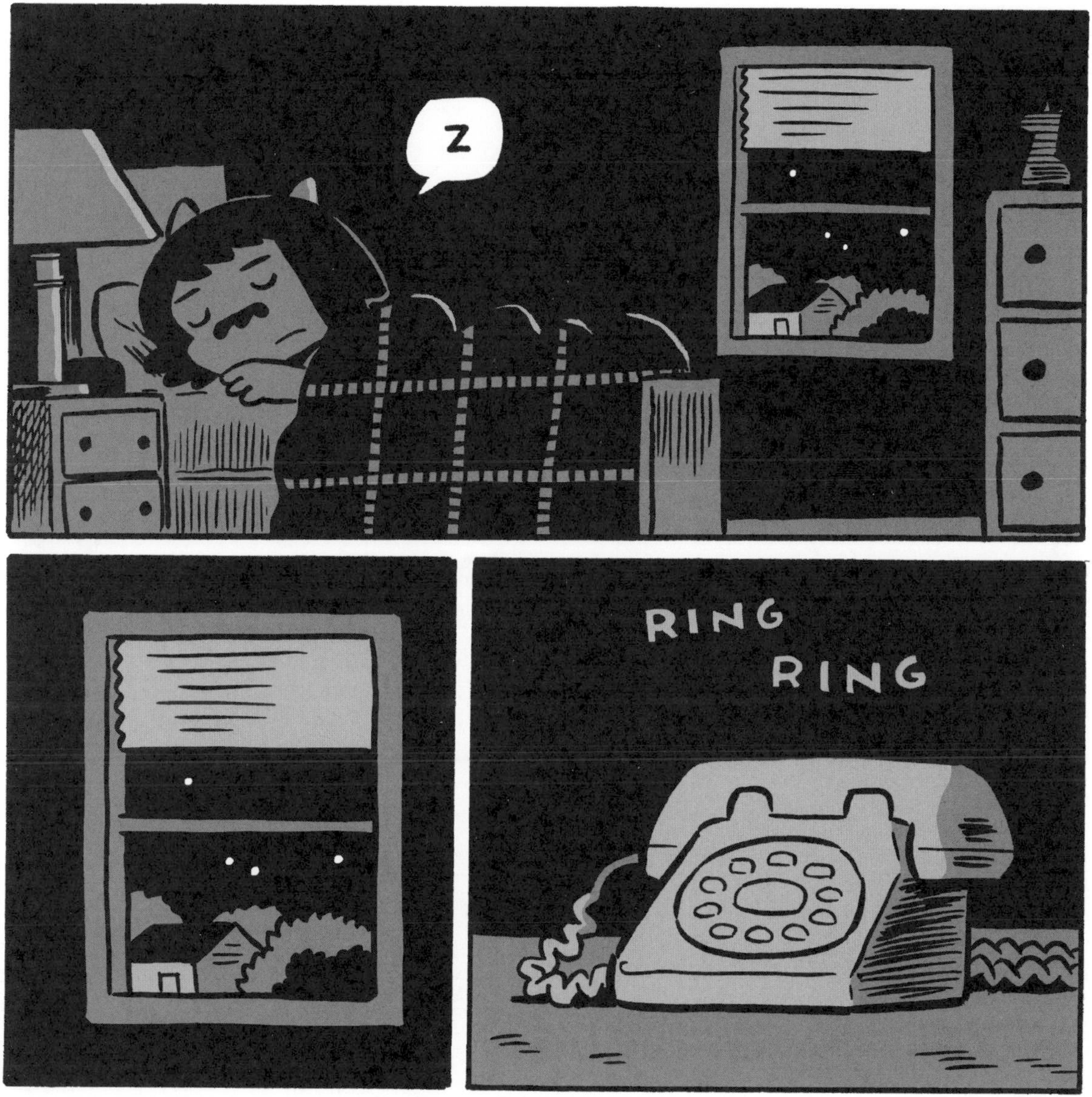
Z
RING
RING

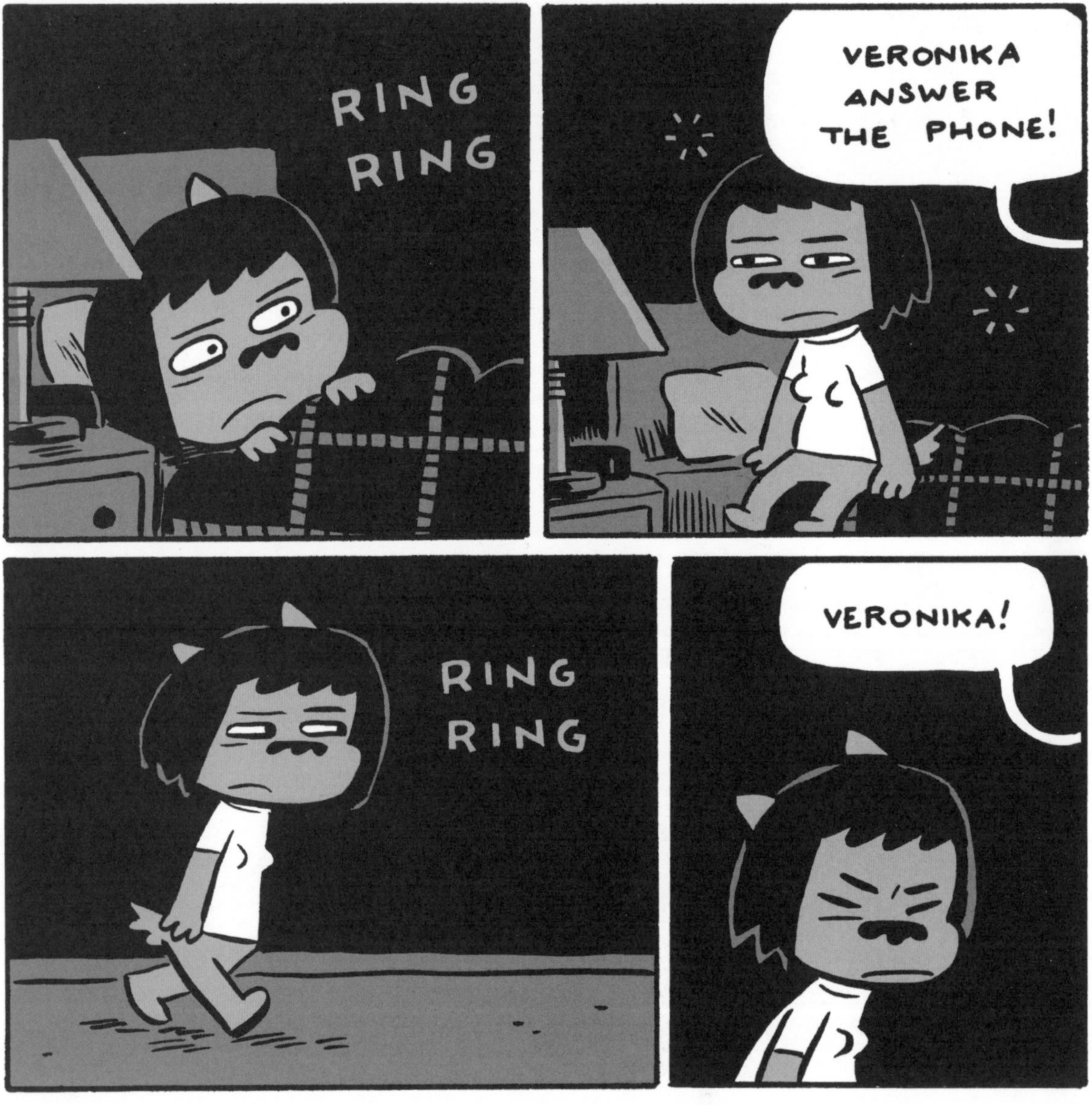
RING RING
VERONIKA ANSWER THE PHONE!
RING RING
VERONIKA!

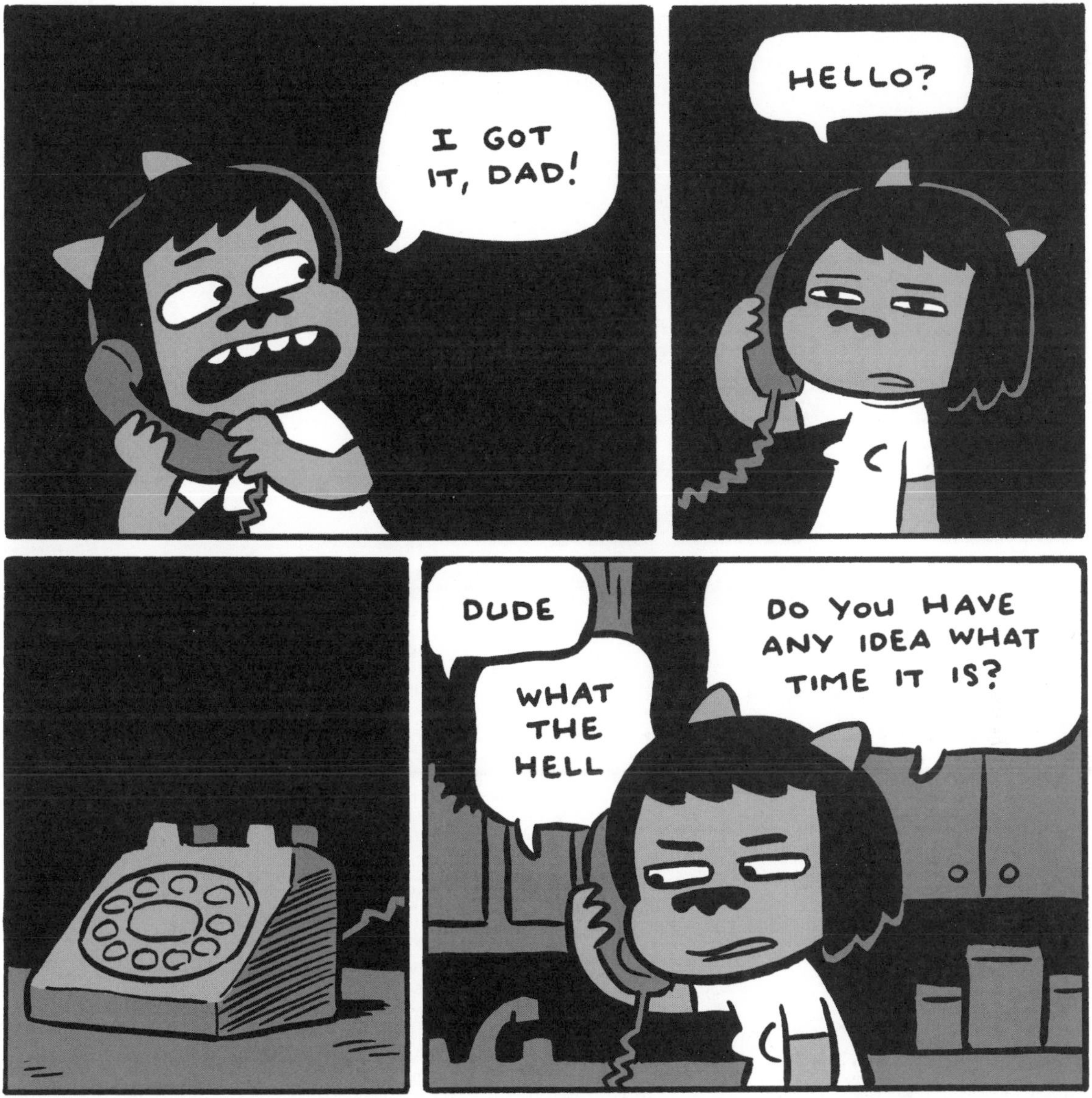
I GOT IT, DAD!
HELLO?
DUDE
WHAT THE HELL
DO YOU HAVE ANY IDEA WHAT TIME IT IS?

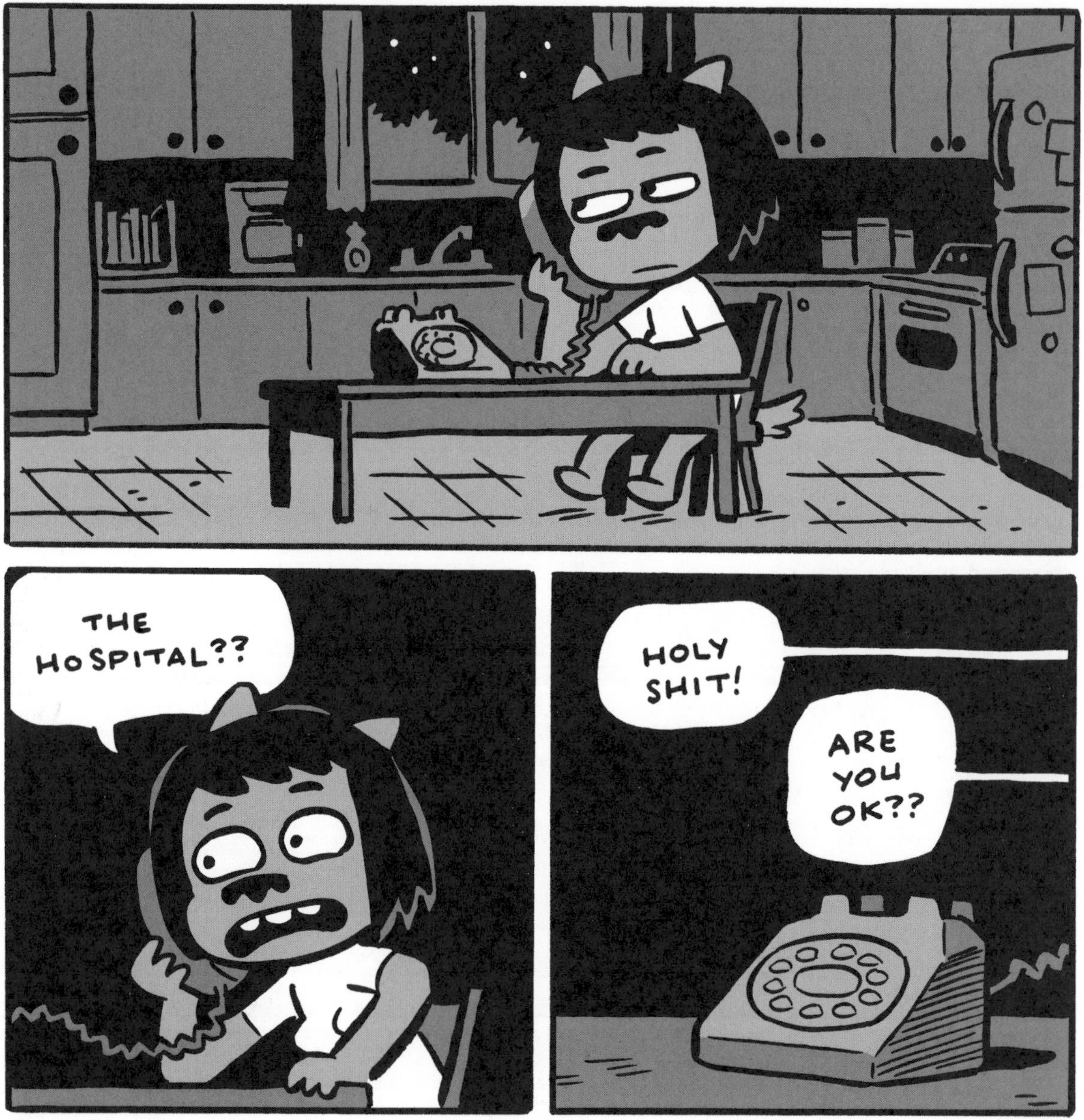
THE HOSPITAL??
HOLY SHIT!
ARE YOU OK??

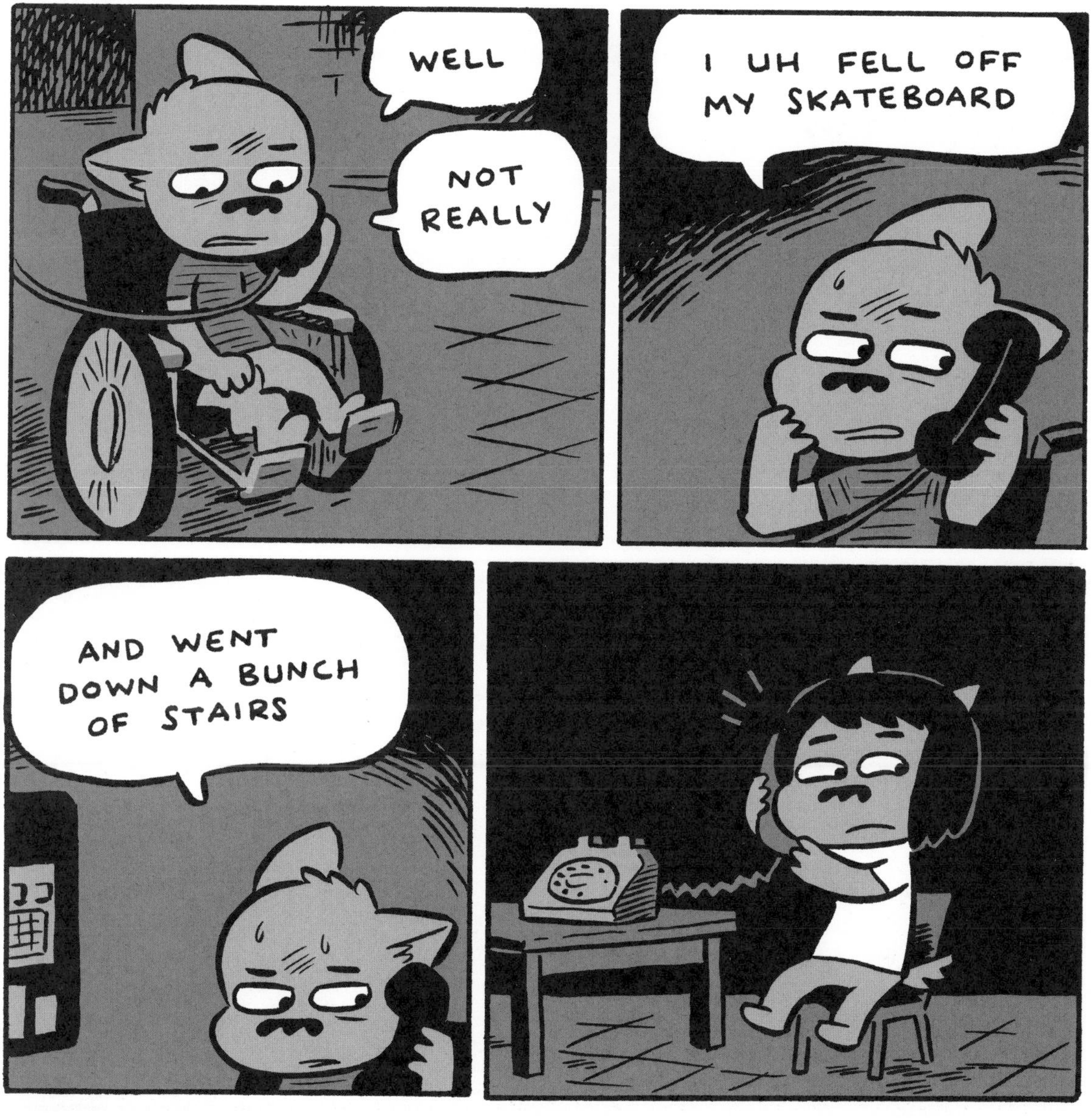
WELL
NOT REALLY
I UH FELL OFF MY SKATEBOARD
AND WENT DOWN A BUNCH OF STAIRS

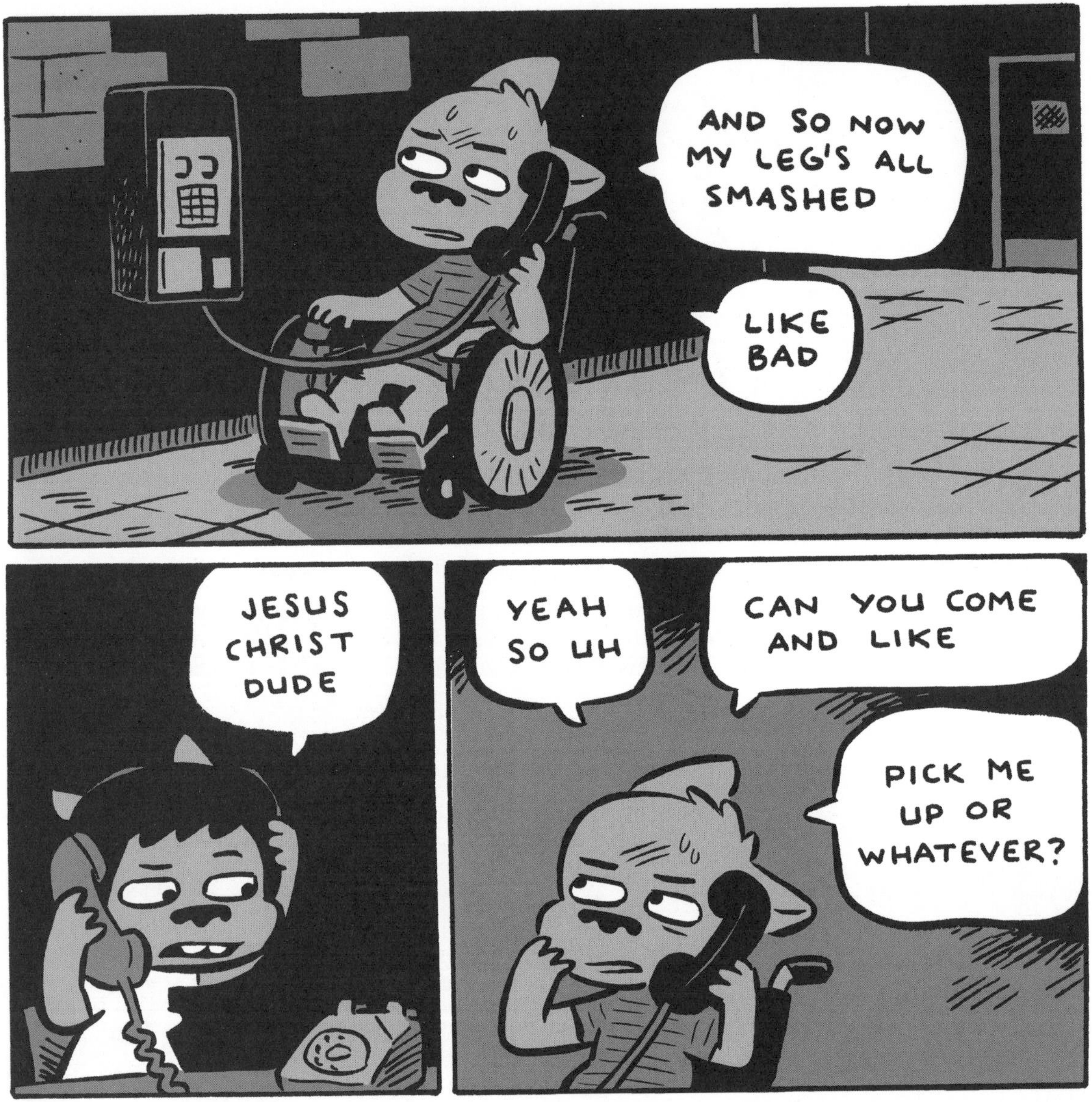
AND SO NOW MY LEG'S ALL SMASHED
LIKE BAD
JESUS CHRIST DUDE
YEAH SO UH
CAN YOU COME AND LIKE
PICK ME UP OR WHATEVER?

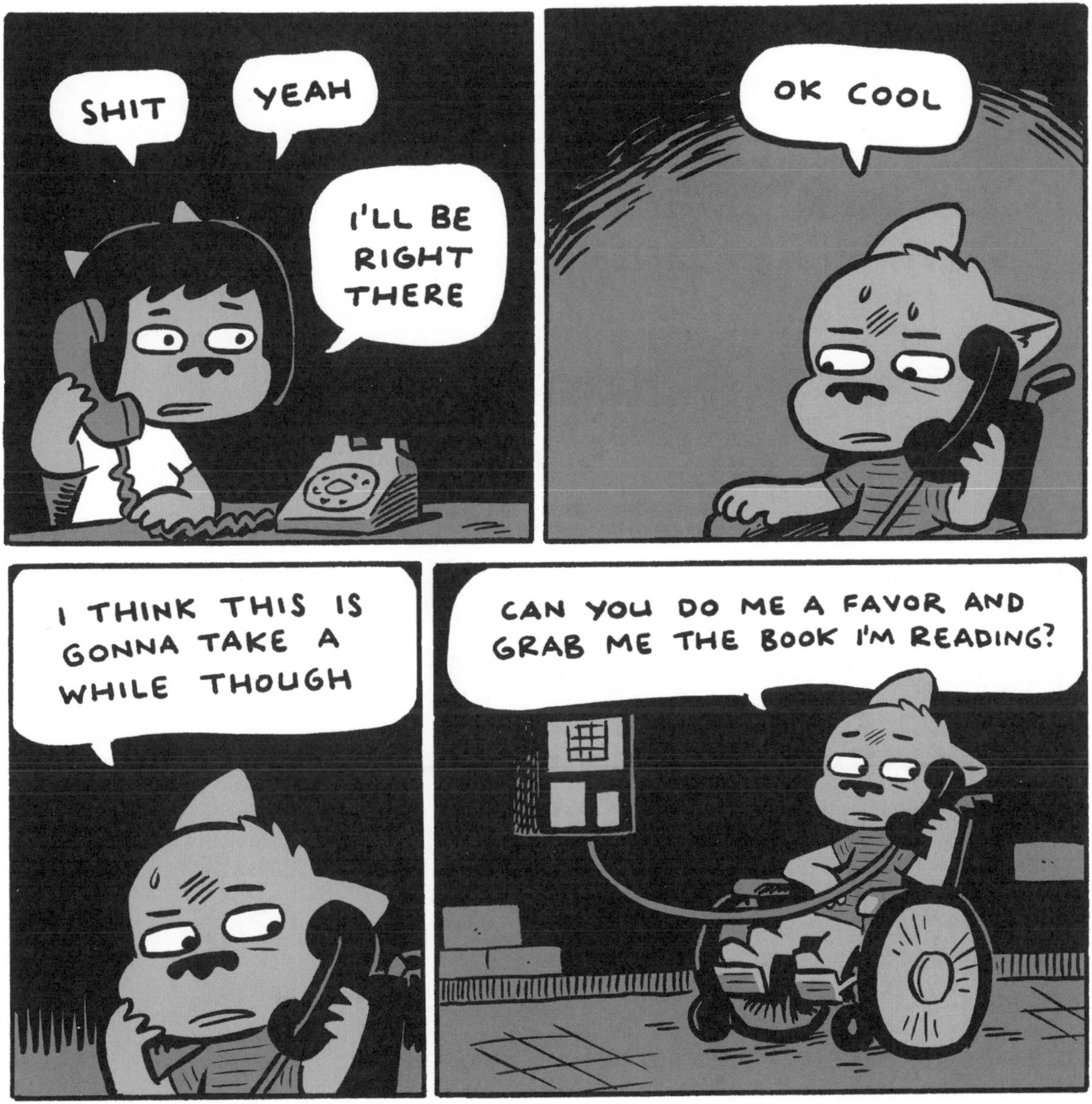
SHIT
YEAH
I'LL BE RIGHT THERE
OK COOL
I THINK THIS IS GONNA TAKE A WHILE THOUGH
CAN YOU DO ME A FAVOR AND GRAB ME THE BOOK I'M READING?

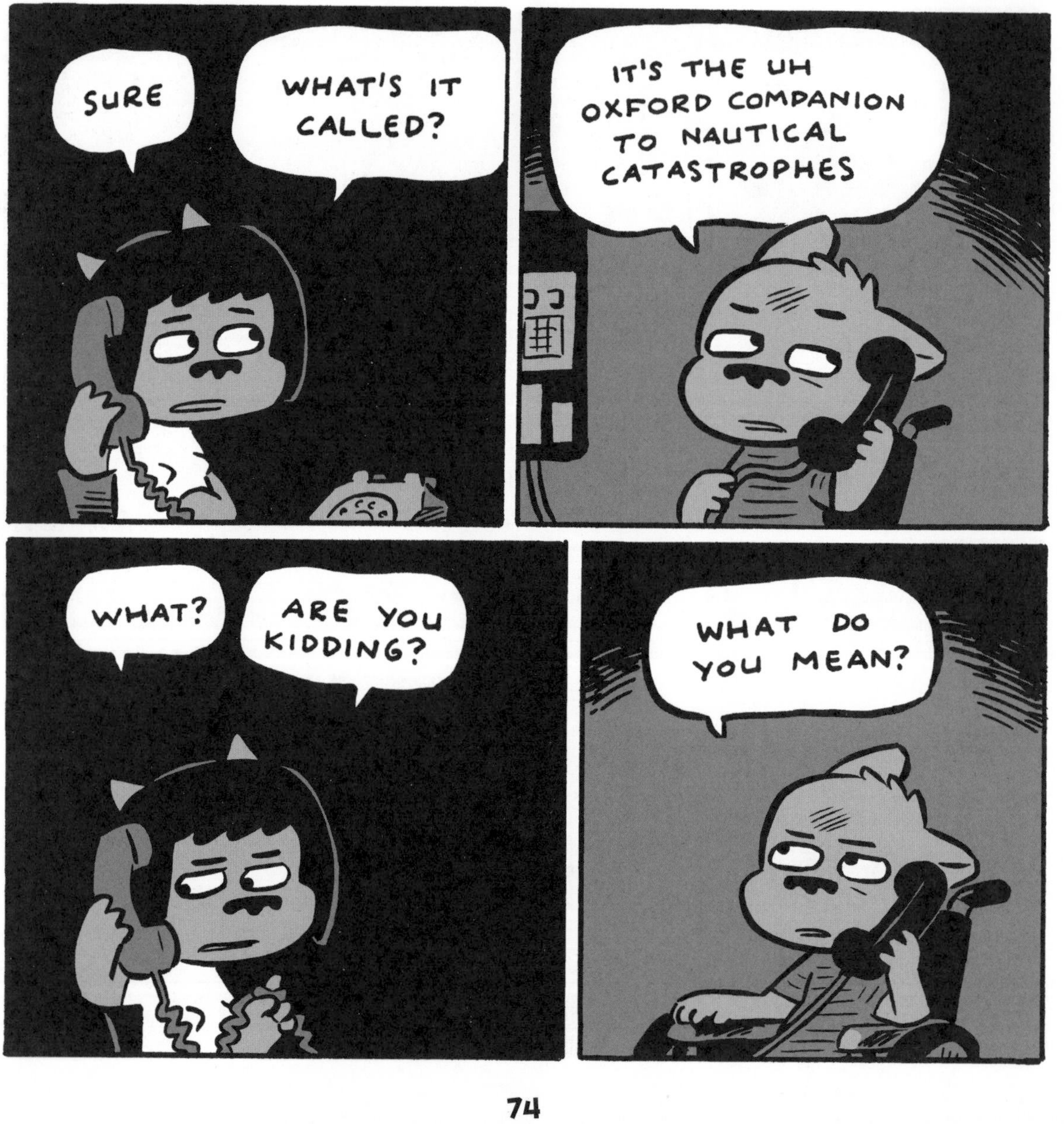
SURE
WHAT'S IT CALLED?
IT'S THE UH OXFORD COMPANION TO NAUTICAL CATASTROPHES
WHAT?
ARE YOU KIDDING?
WHAT DO YOU MEAN?

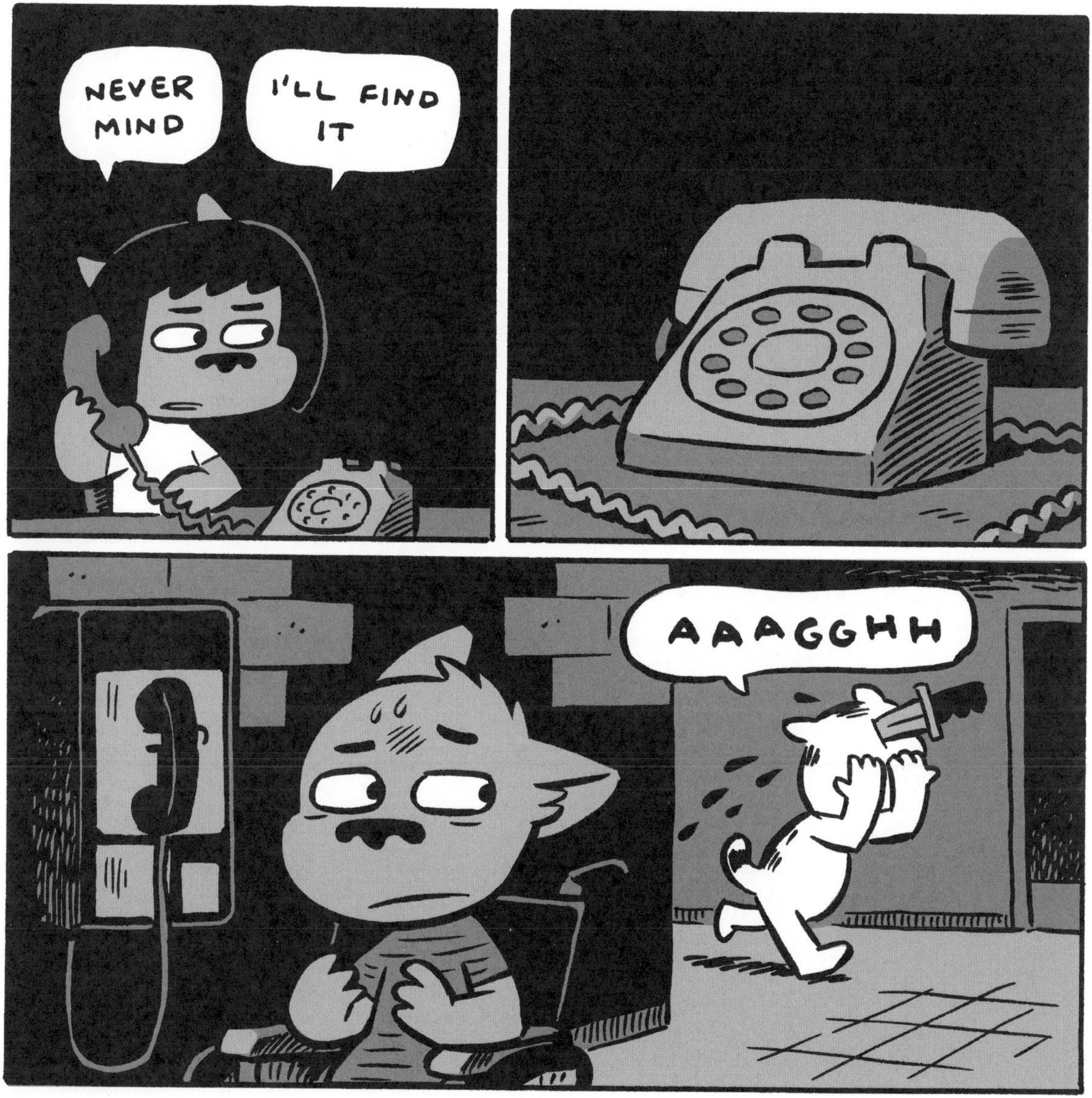
NEVER MIND
I'LL FIND IT
AAAGGHH

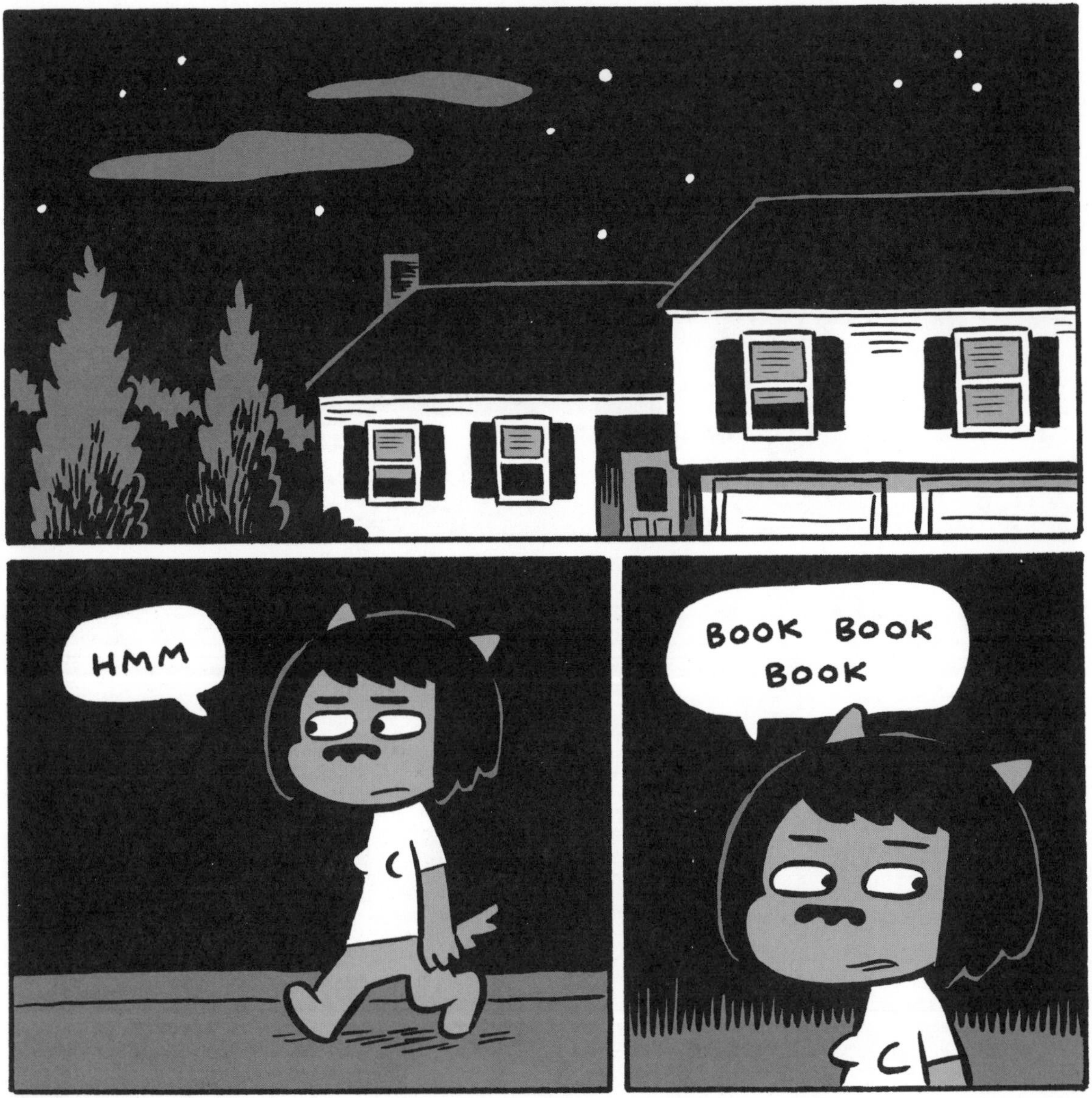
HMM
BOOK BOOK BOOK

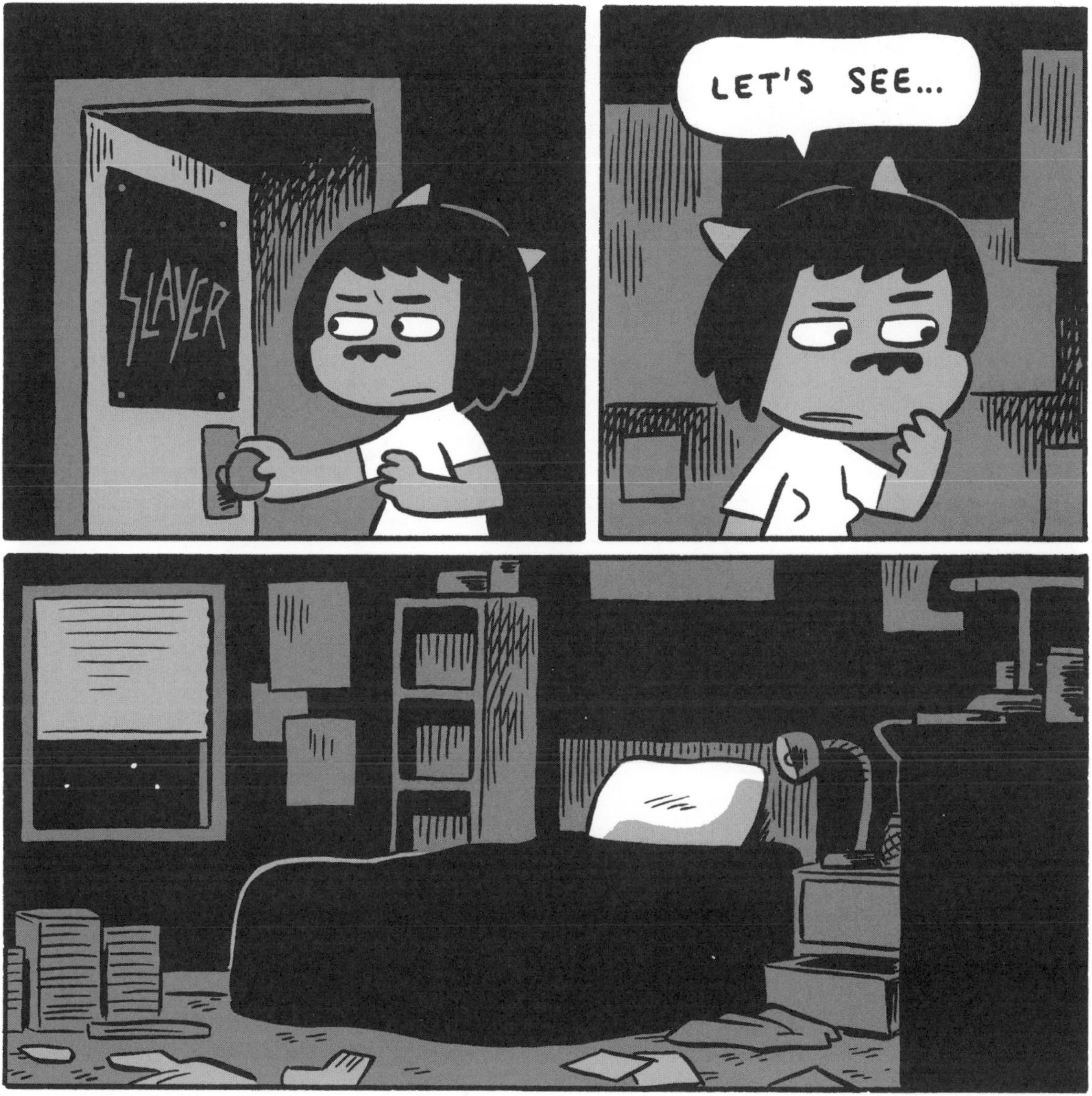
SLAYER
LET'S SEE...

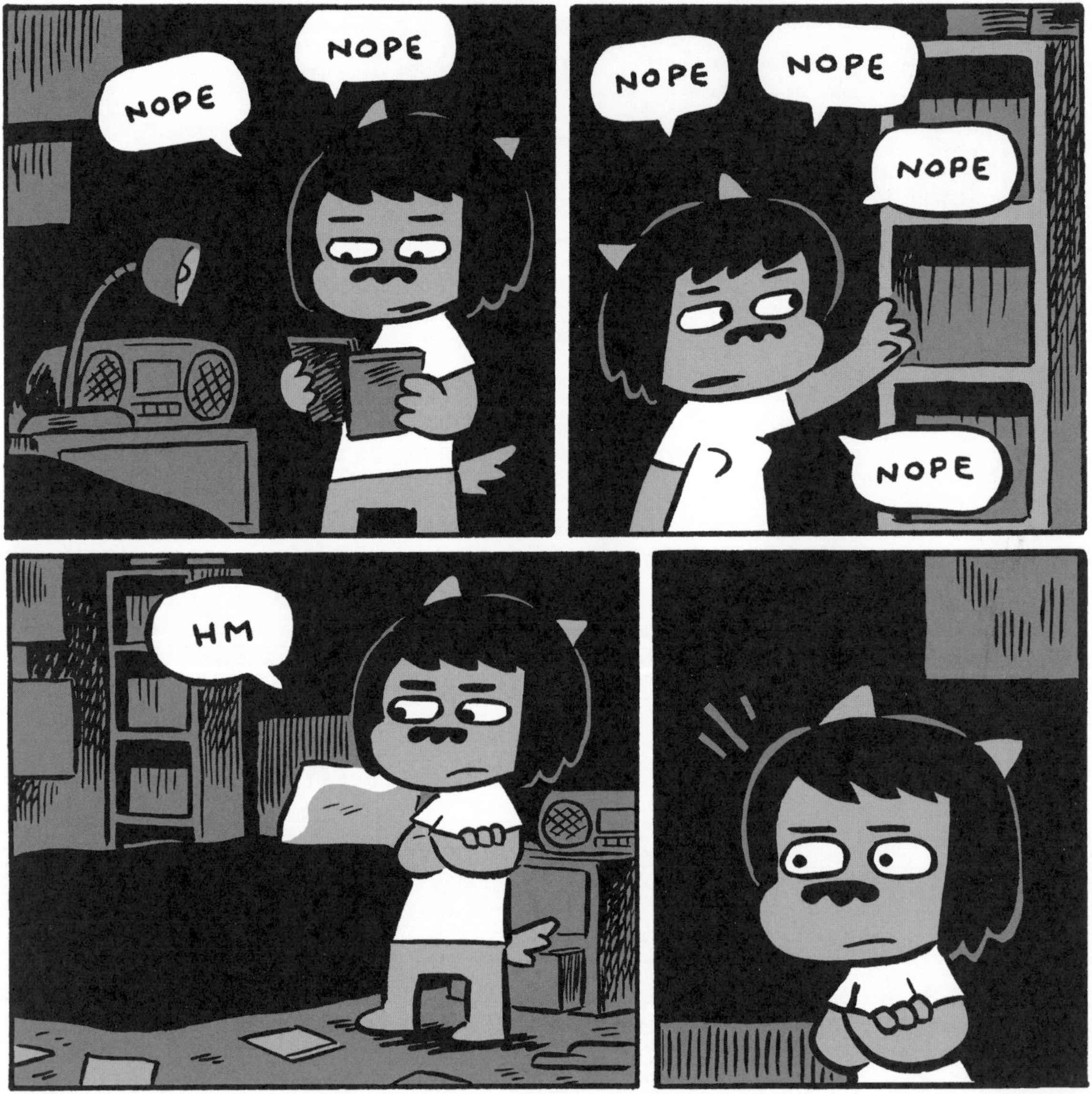
NOPE
NOPE
NOPE
NOPE
NOPE
NOPE
HM

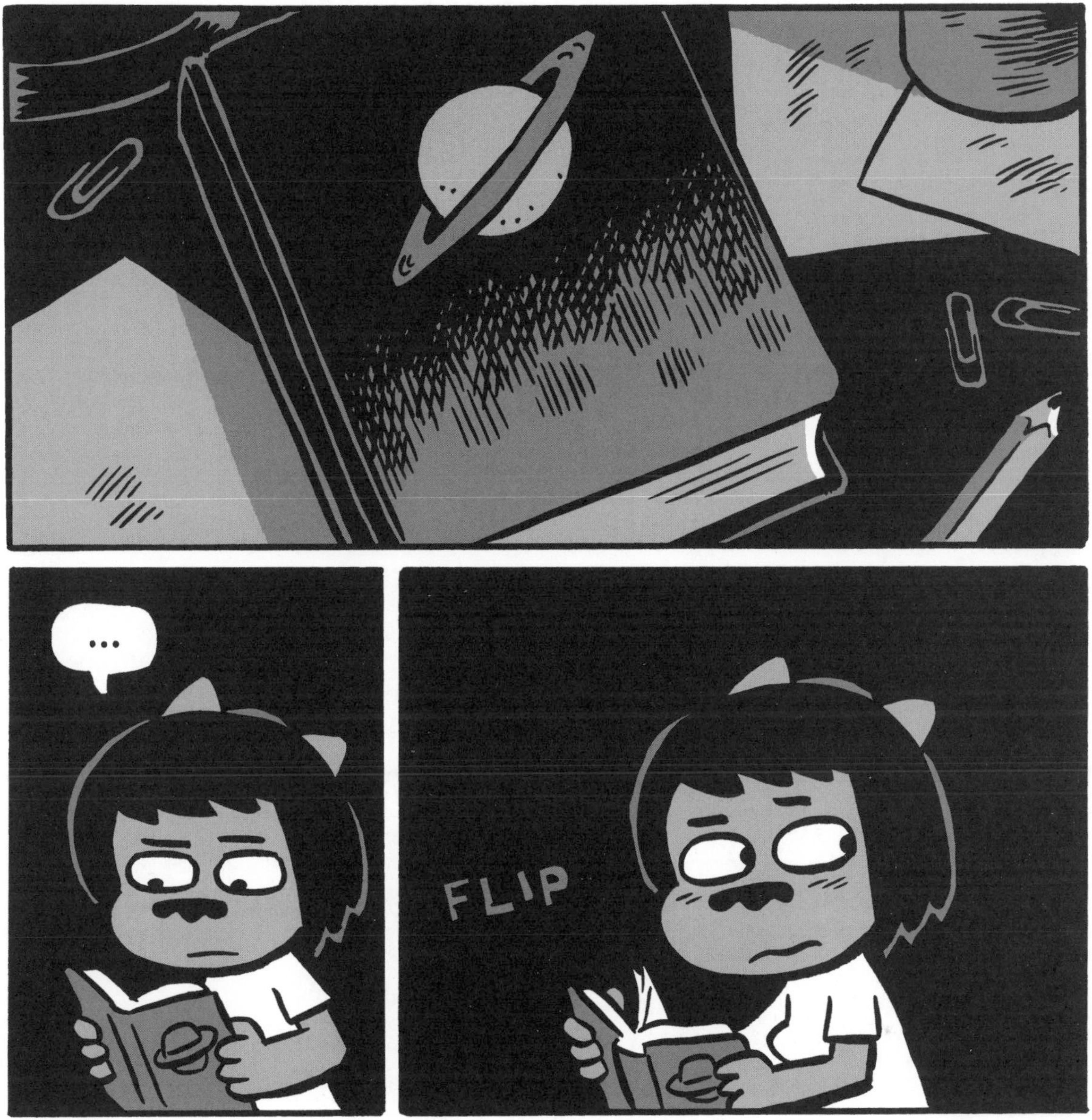
...
FLIP

April 15, 1998
Clear night tonight. New moon. On nights like this you can even see the Milky Way from up here. It's hard to believe how big the universe is when I'm stuck down here in this boring little town. I wish I could fly away and live on another planet. I wish I could take Jeremiah with me...

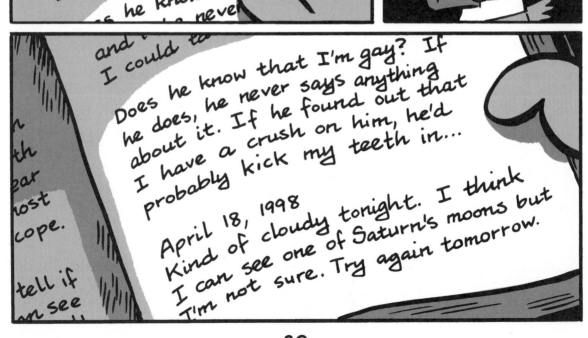

Does he know that I'm gay? If he does, he never says anything about it. If he found out that I have a crush on him, he'd probably kick my teeth in...

April 18, 1998
Kind of cloudy tonight. I think I can see one of Saturn's moons but I'm not sure. Try again tomorrow.

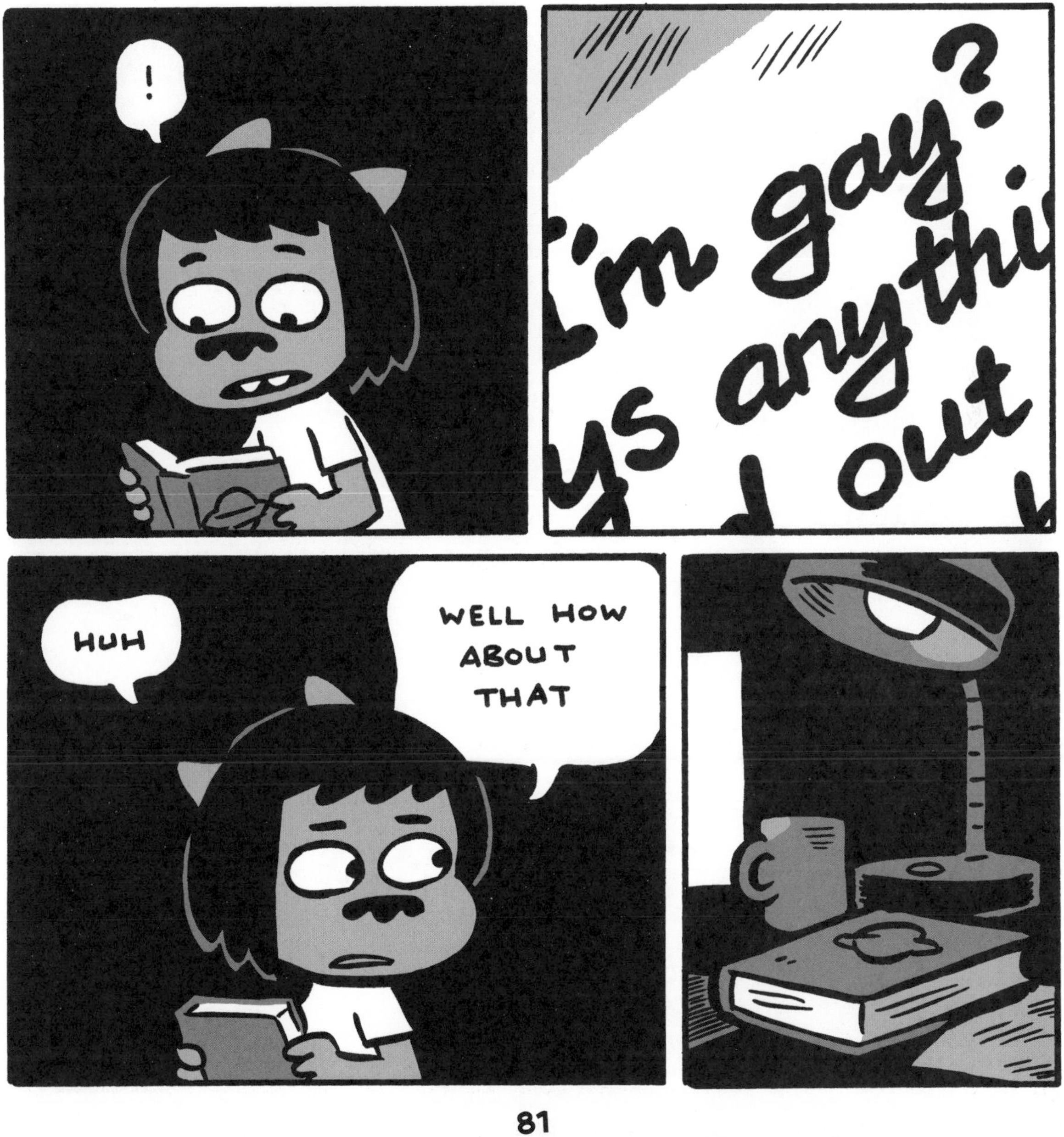
!
'm gay?
ys anythi
out
HUH
WELL HOW ABOUT THAT

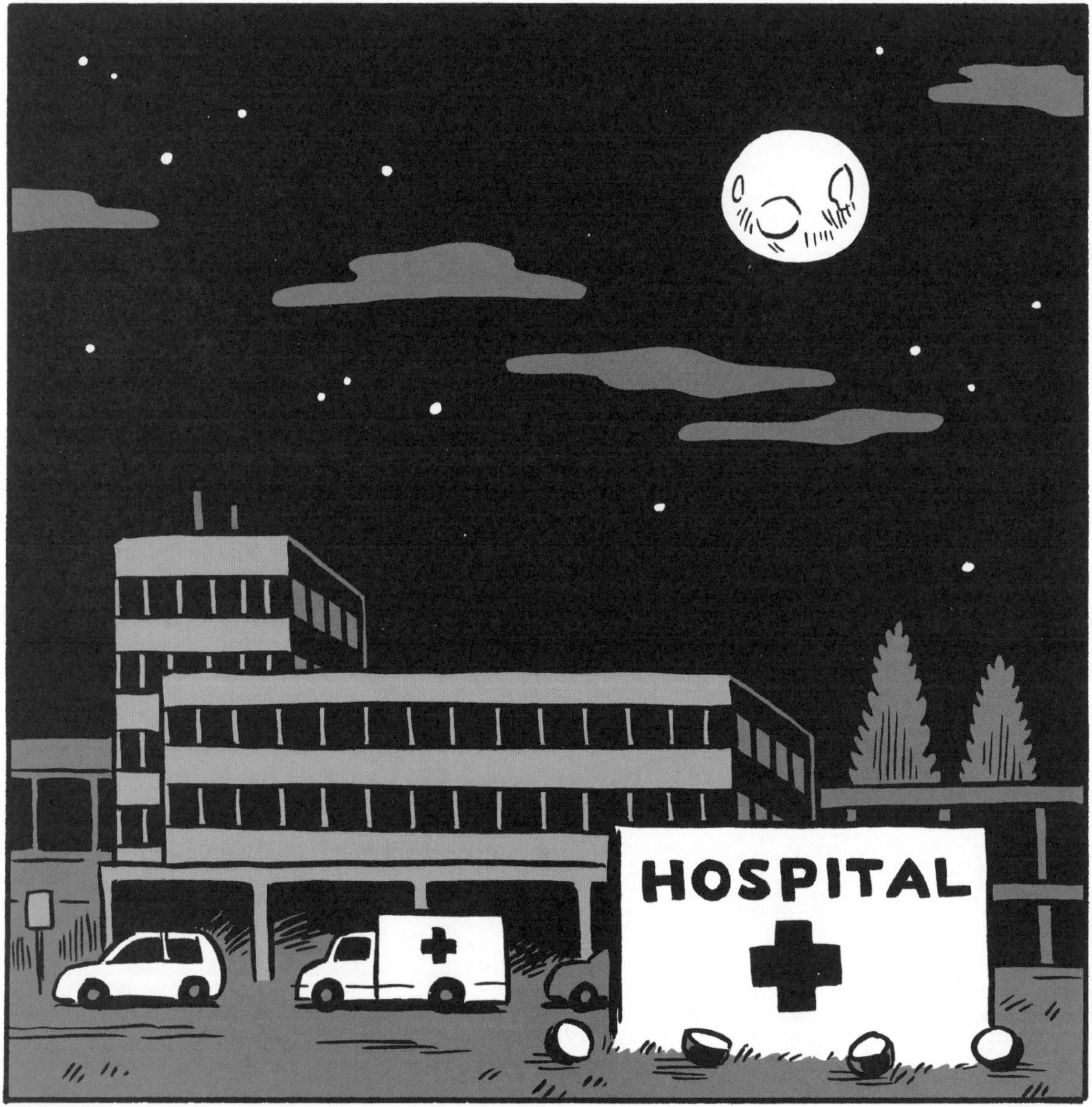
HOSPITAL

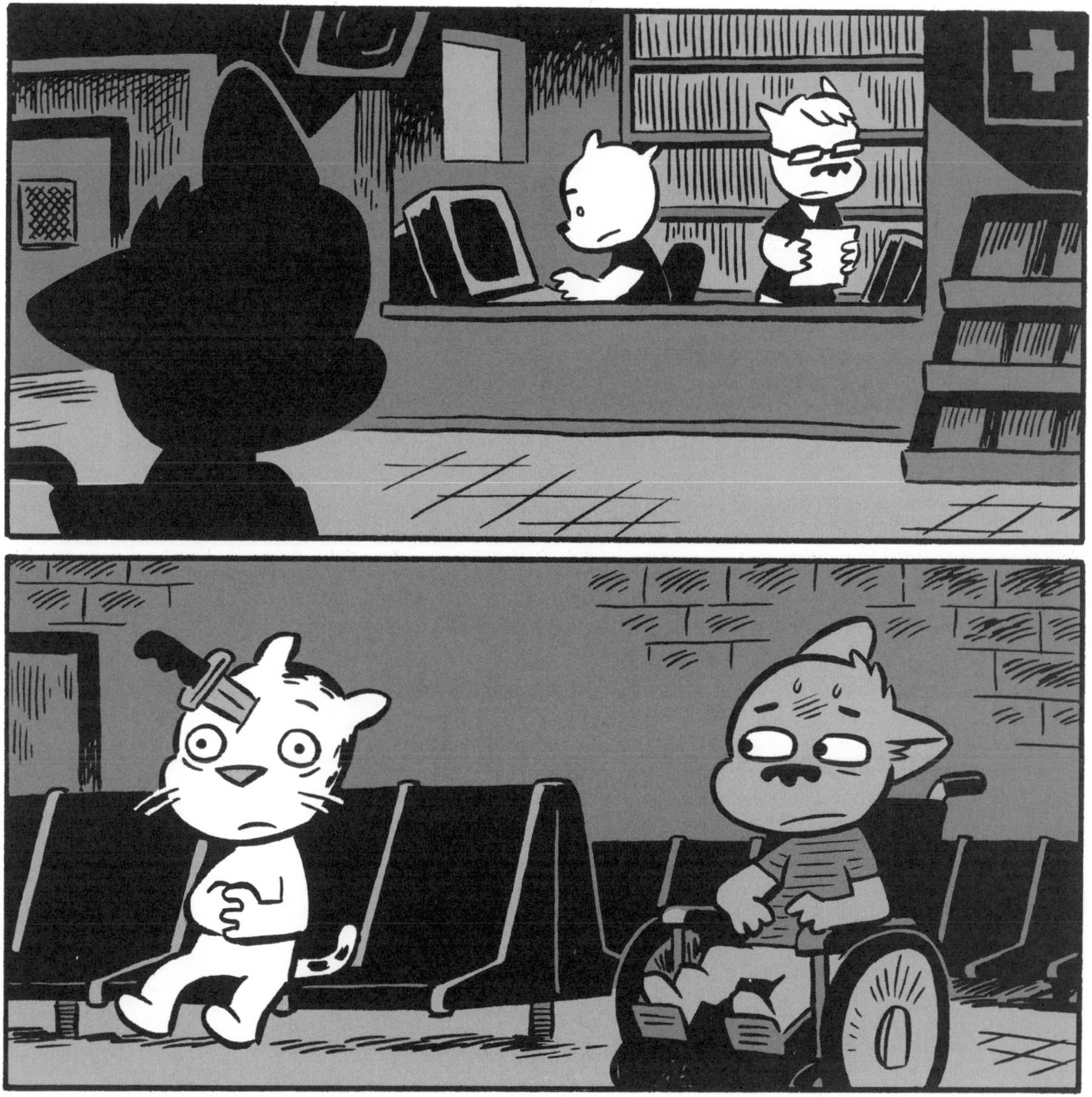

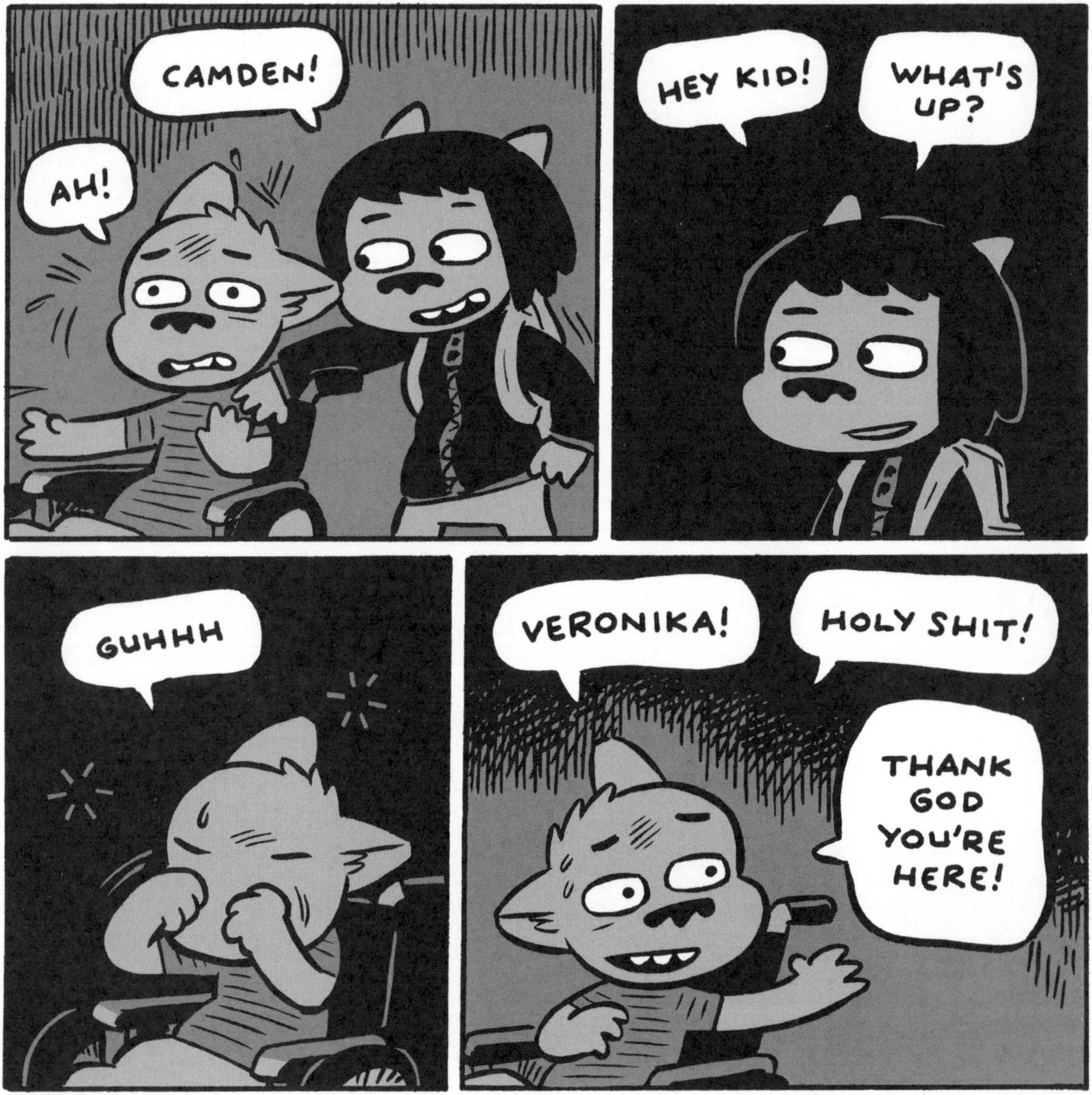
CAMDEN!
AH!
HEY KID!
WHAT'S UP?
GUHHH
VERONIKA!
HOLY SHIT!
THANK GOD YOU'RE HERE!

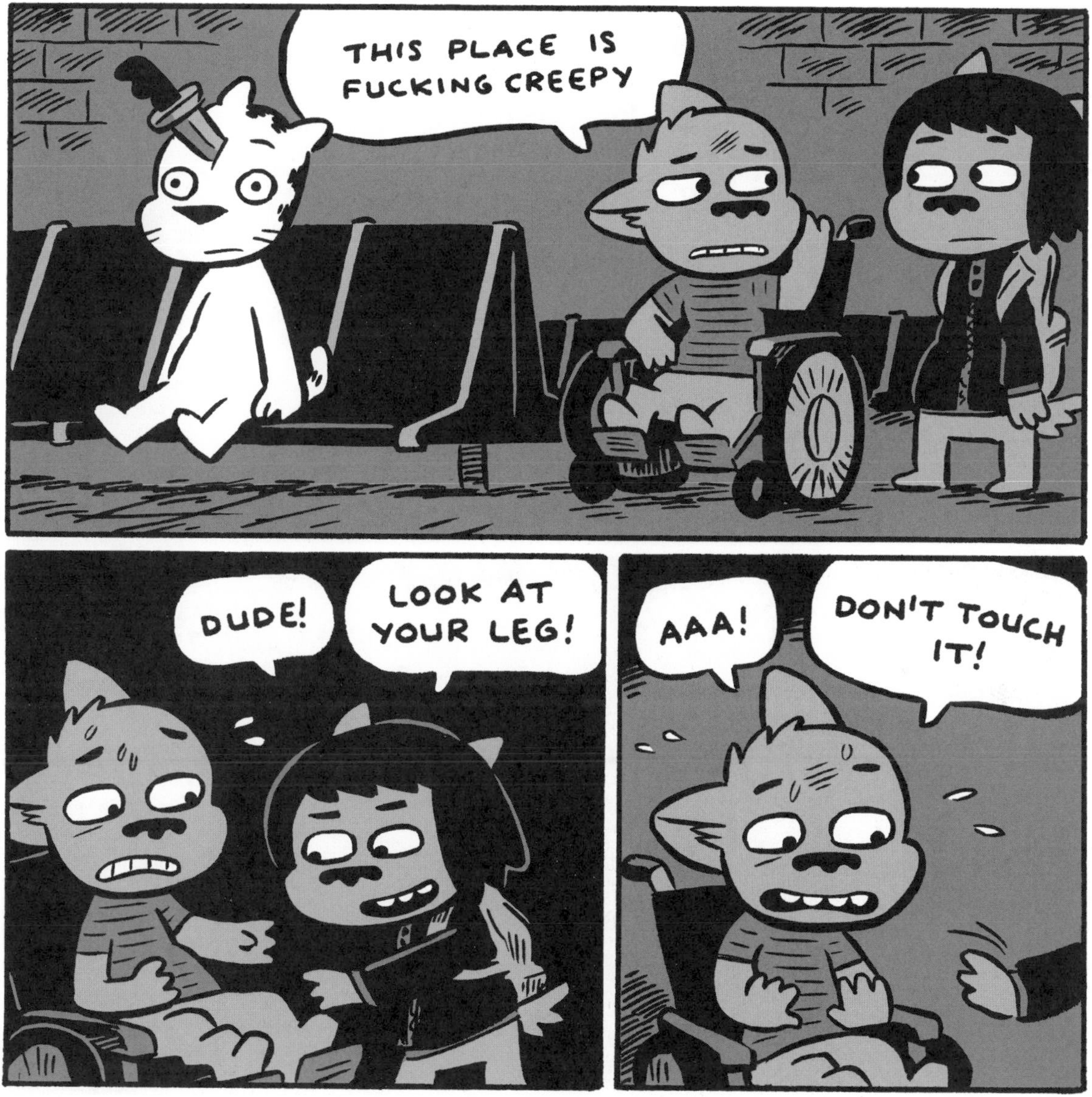
THIS PLACE IS FUCKING CREEPY
DUDE!
LOOK AT YOUR LEG!
AAA!
DON'T TOUCH IT!

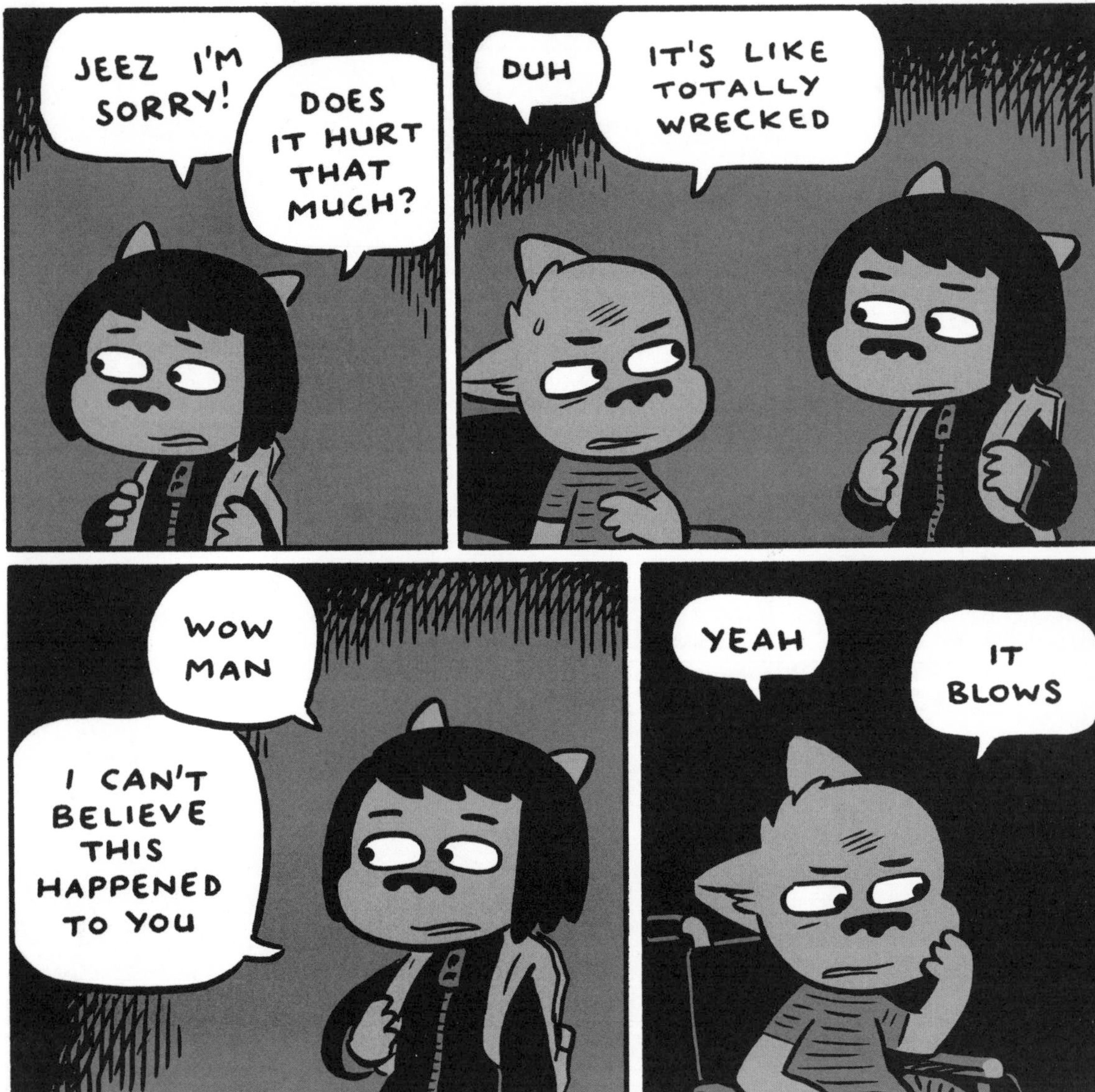
JEEZ I'M SORRY!
DOES IT HURT THAT MUCH?
DUH
IT'S LIKE TOTALLY WRECKED
WOW MAN
I CAN'T BELIEVE THIS HAPPENED TO YOU
YEAH
IT BLOWS

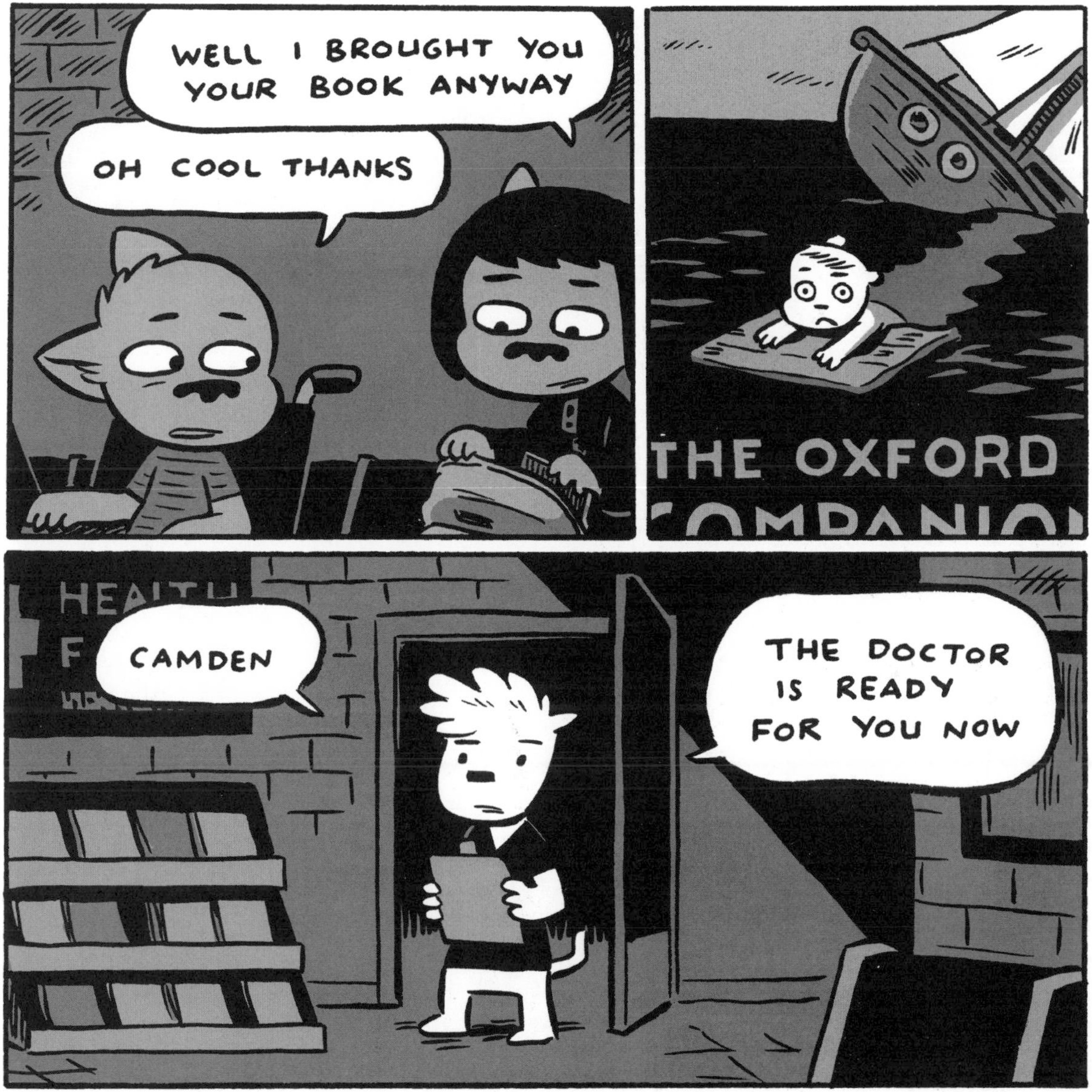
WELL I BROUGHT YOU YOUR BOOK ANYWAY
OH COOL THANKS
THE OXFORD
CAMDEN
THE DOCTOR IS READY FOR YOU NOW

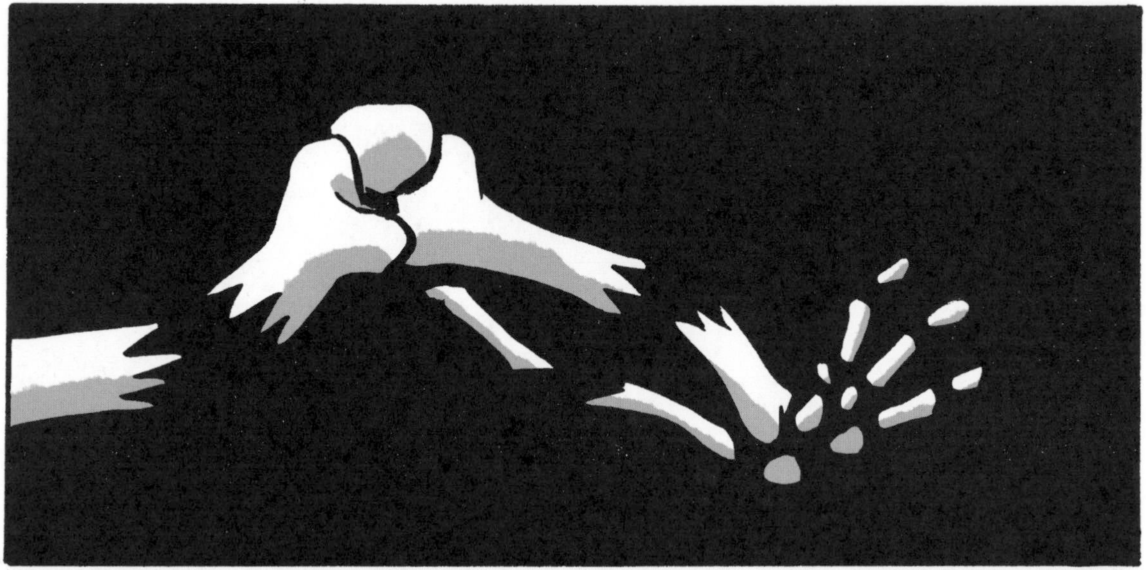

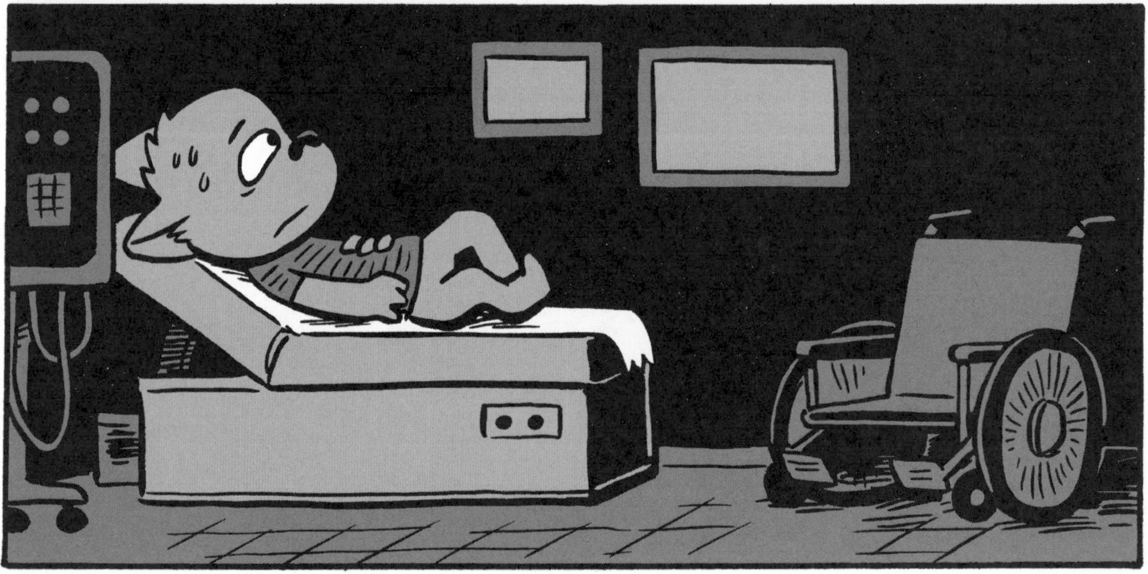

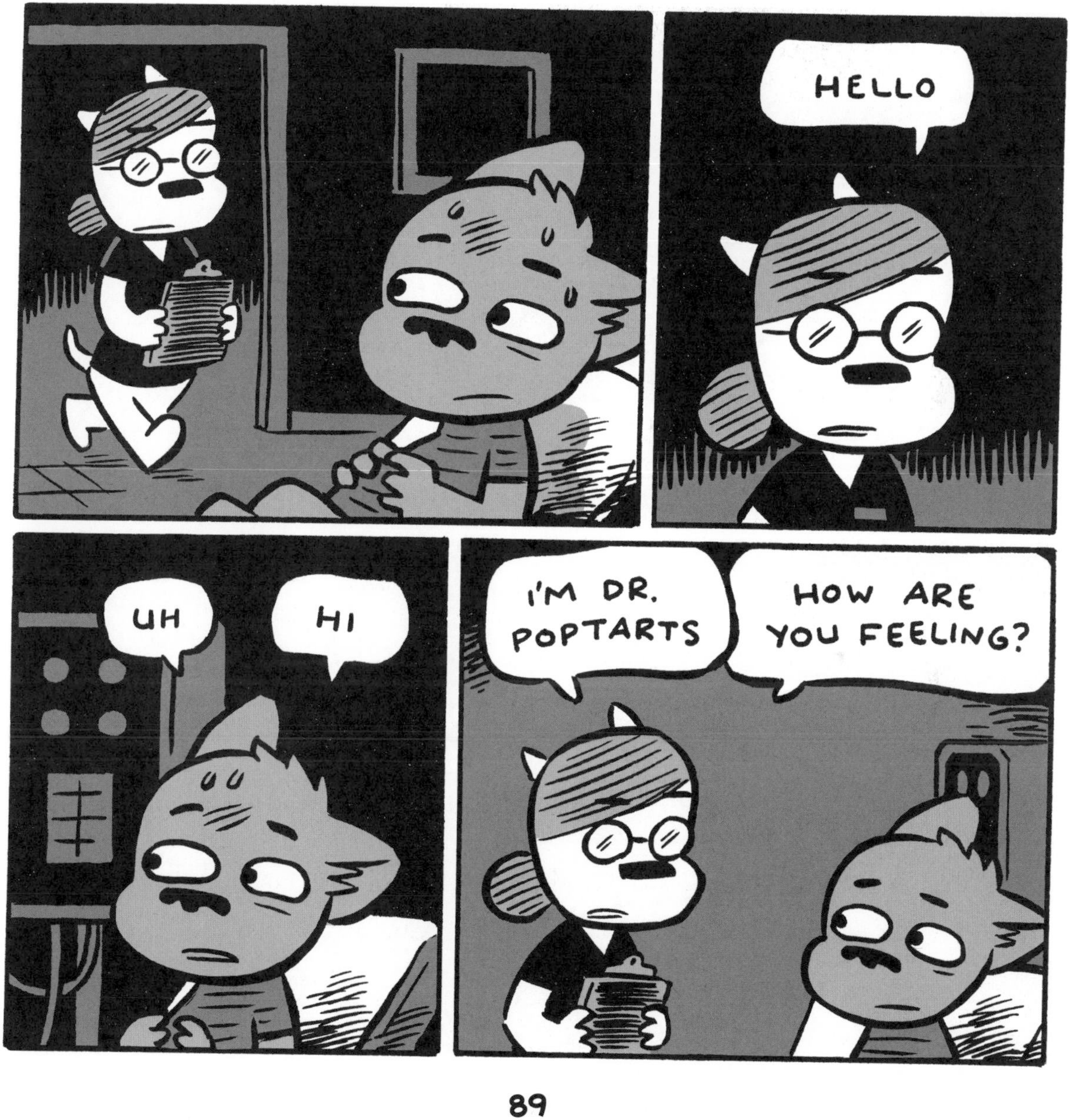
HELLO
UH
HI
I'M DR. POPTARTS
HOW ARE YOU FEELING?

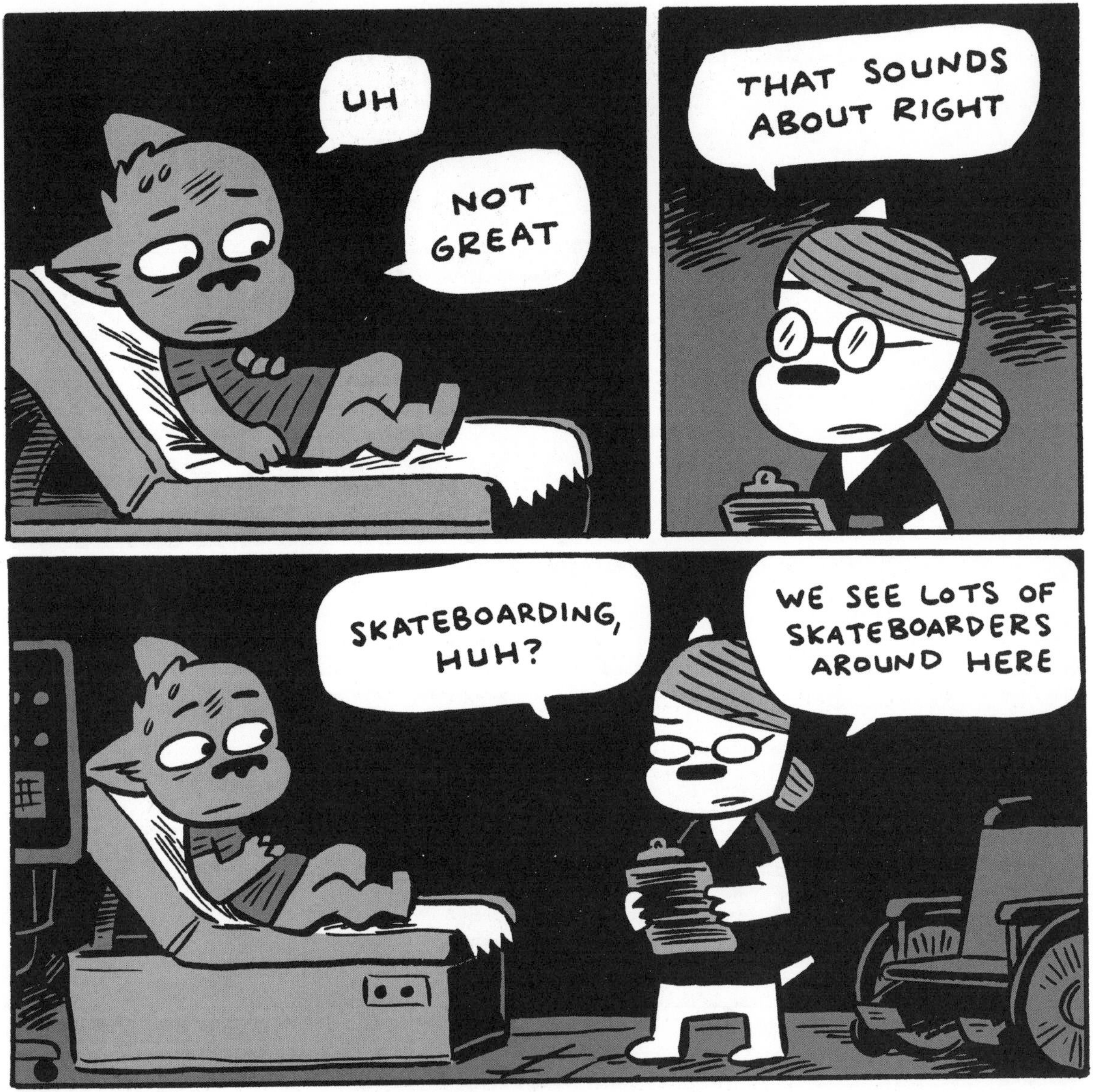
UH
NOT GREAT
THAT SOUNDS ABOUT RIGHT
SKATEBOARDING, HUH?
WE SEE LOTS OF SKATEBOARDERS AROUND HERE

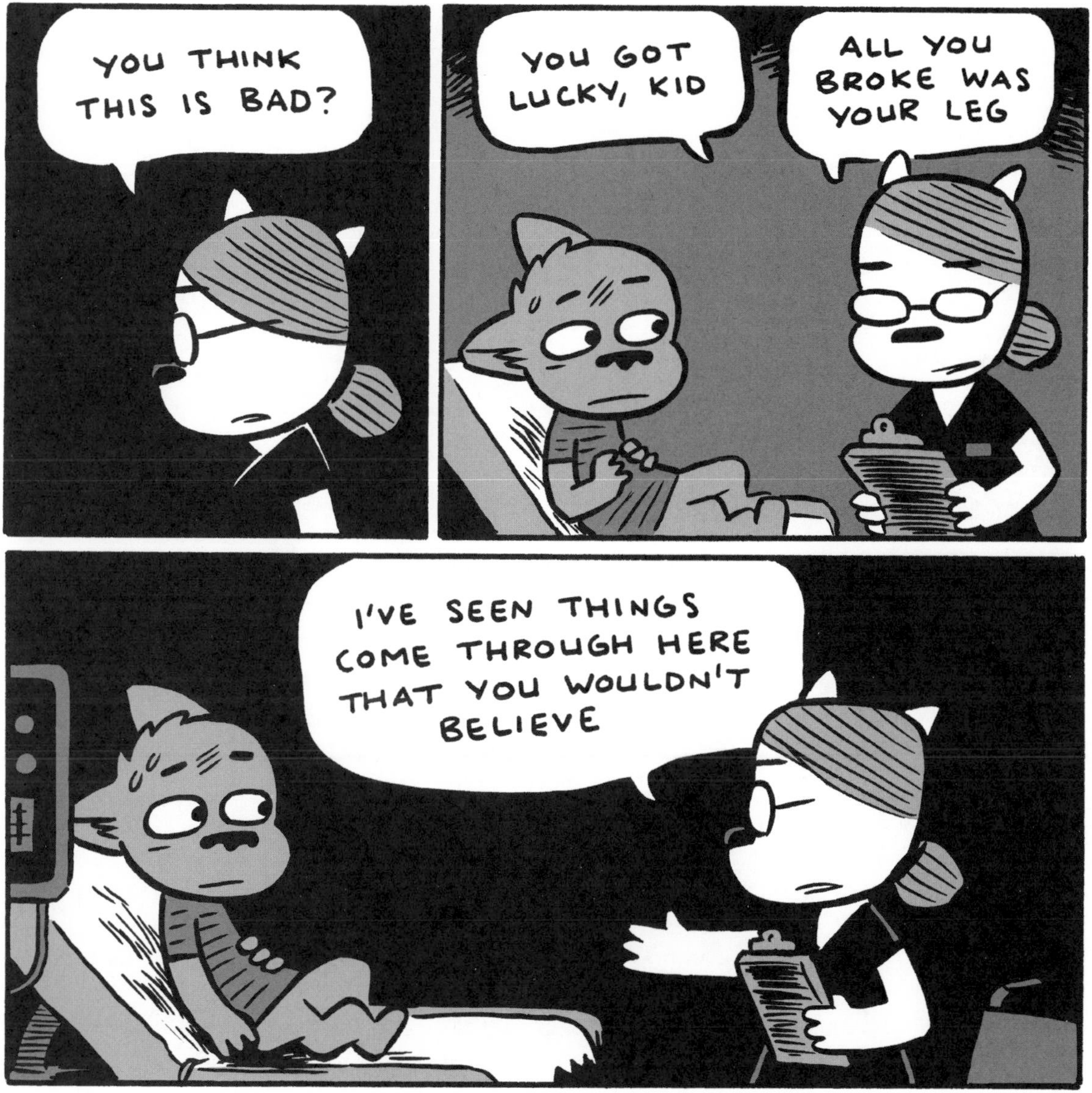
YOU THINK THIS IS BAD?
YOU GOT LUCKY, KID
ALL YOU BROKE WAS YOUR LEG
I'VE SEEN THINGS COME THROUGH HERE THAT YOU WOULDN'T BELIEVE

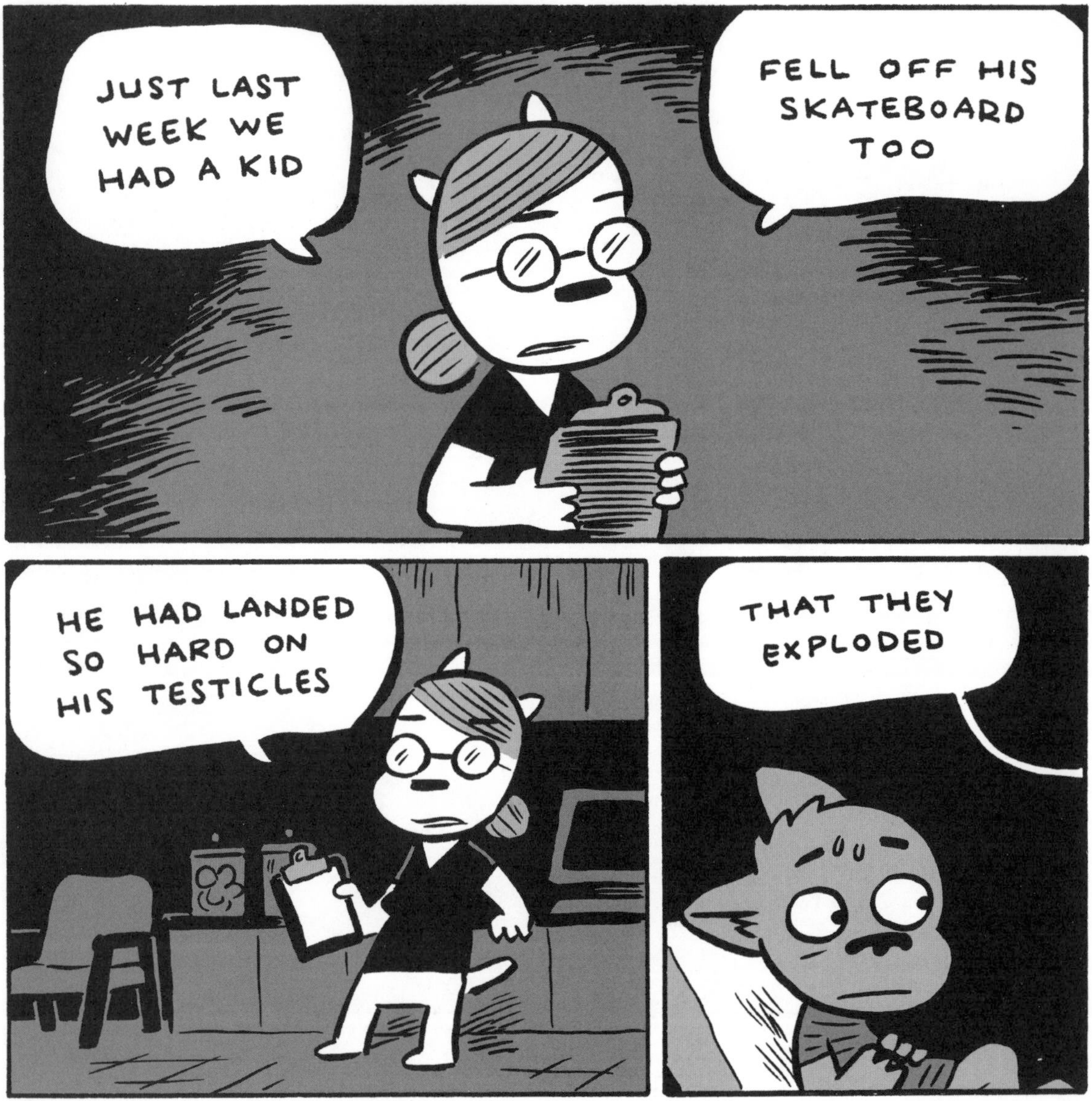
JUST LAST WEEK WE HAD A KID
FELL OFF HIS SKATEBOARD TOO
HE HAD LANDED SO HARD ON HIS TESTICLES
THAT THEY EXPLODED

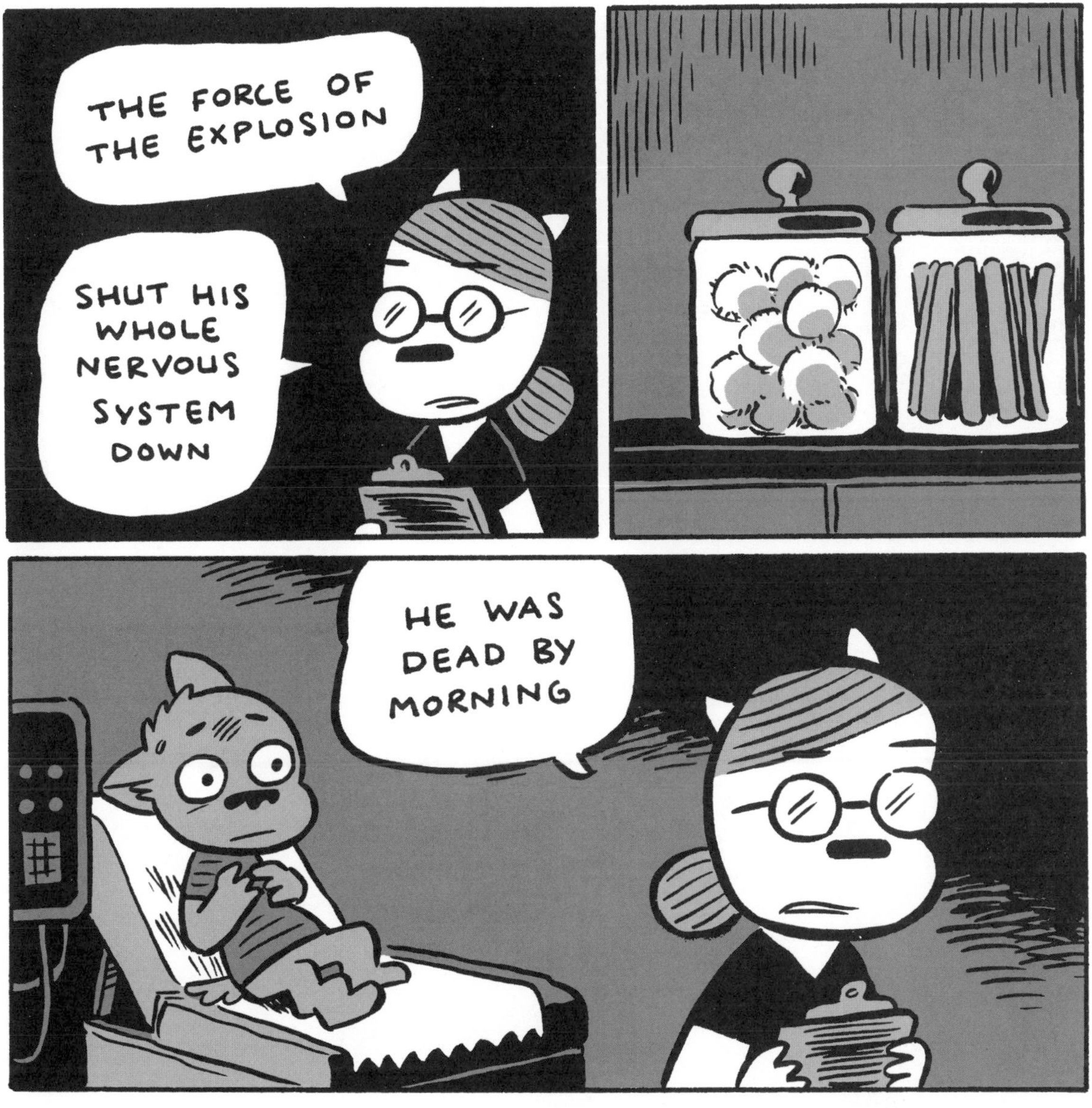
THE FORCE OF THE EXPLOSION
SHUT HIS WHOLE NERVOUS SYSTEM DOWN
HE WAS DEAD BY MORNING

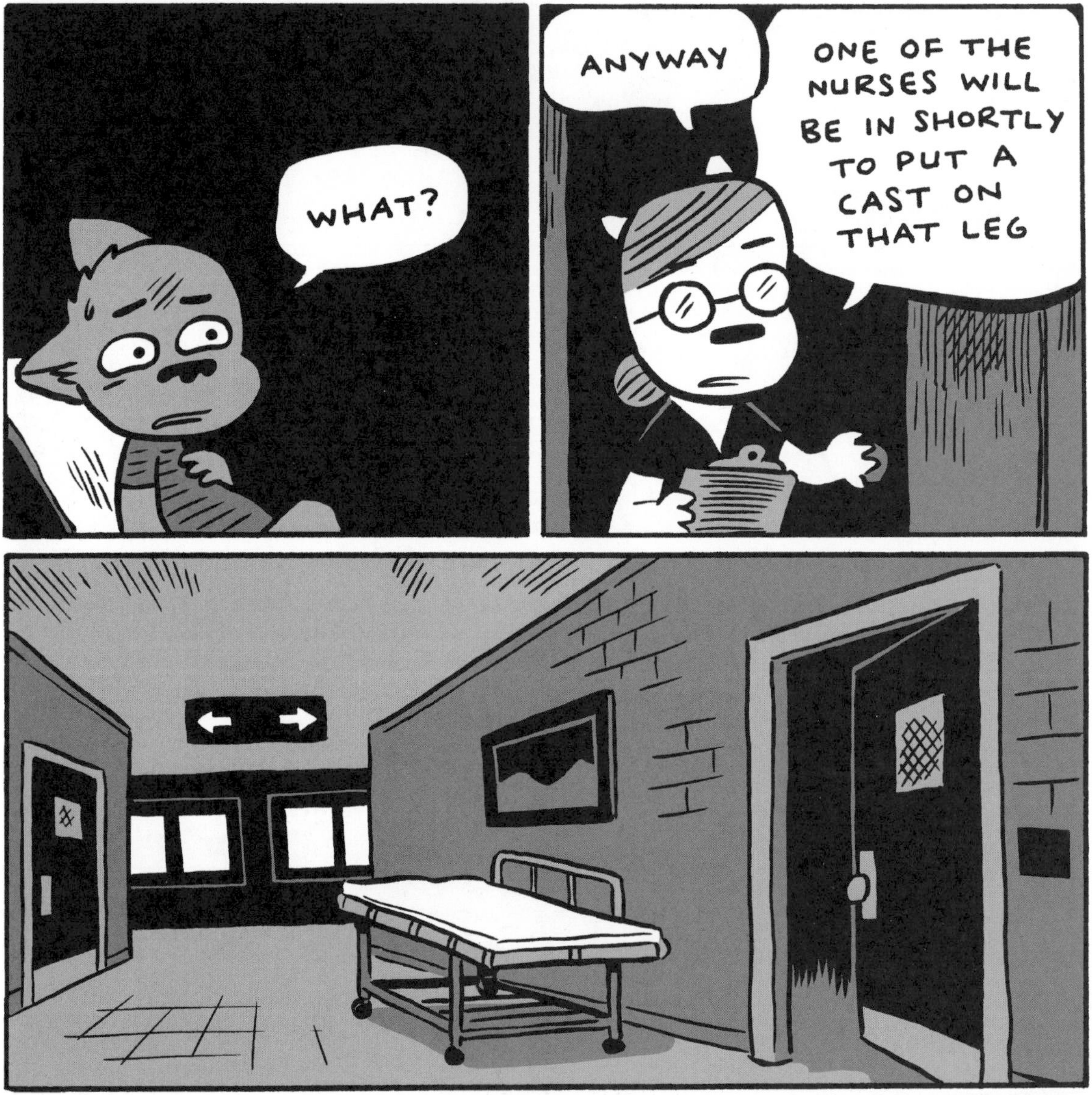
WHAT?
ANYWAY
ONE OF THE NURSES WILL BE IN SHORTLY TO PUT A CAST ON THAT LEG

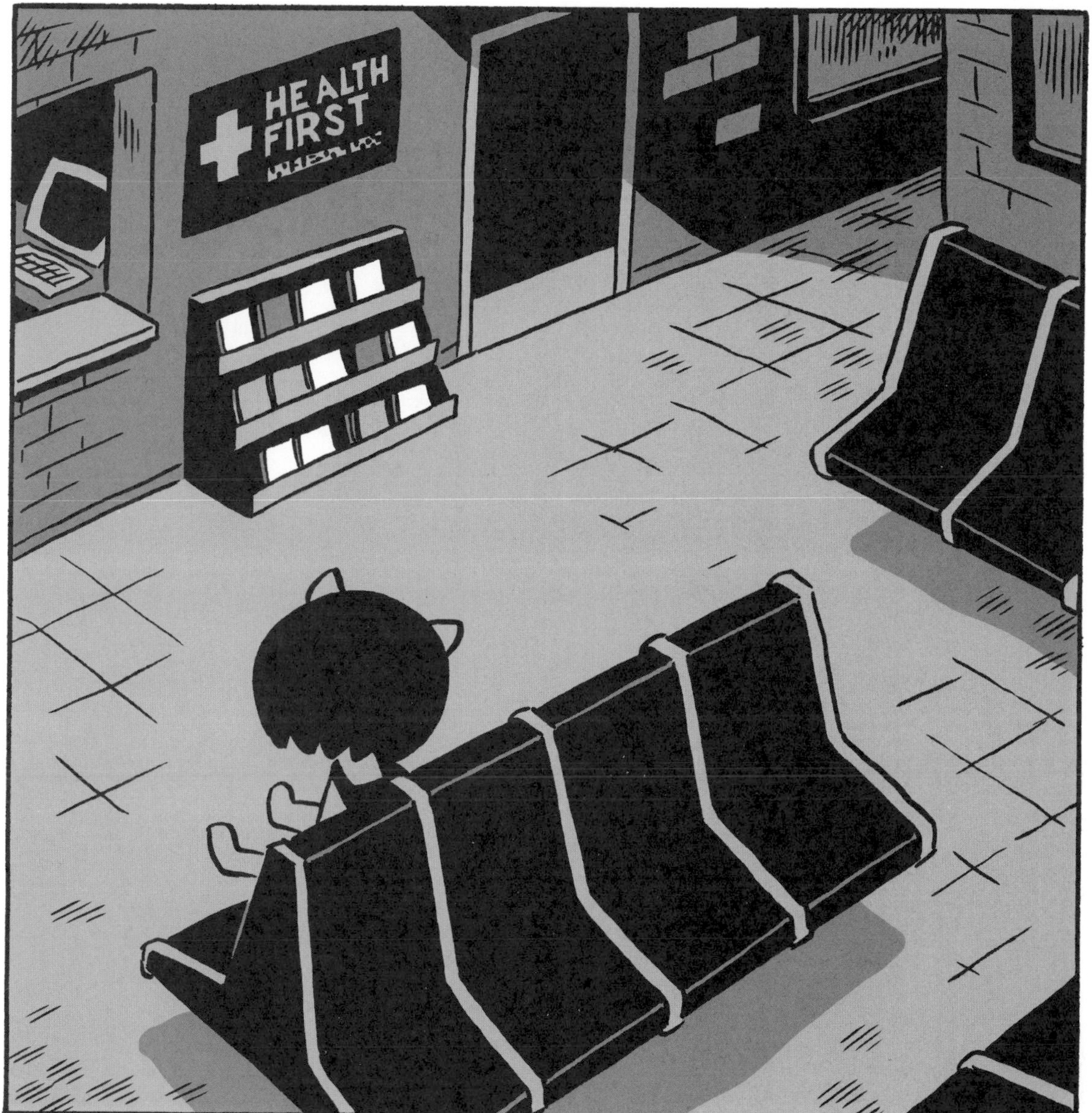
HEALTH
FIRST

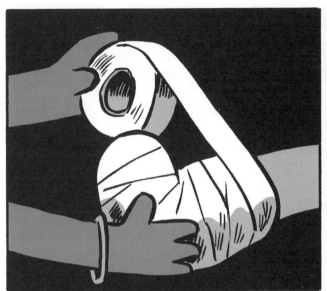

BEEP
BEEP
BEEP

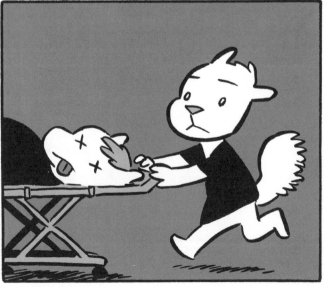

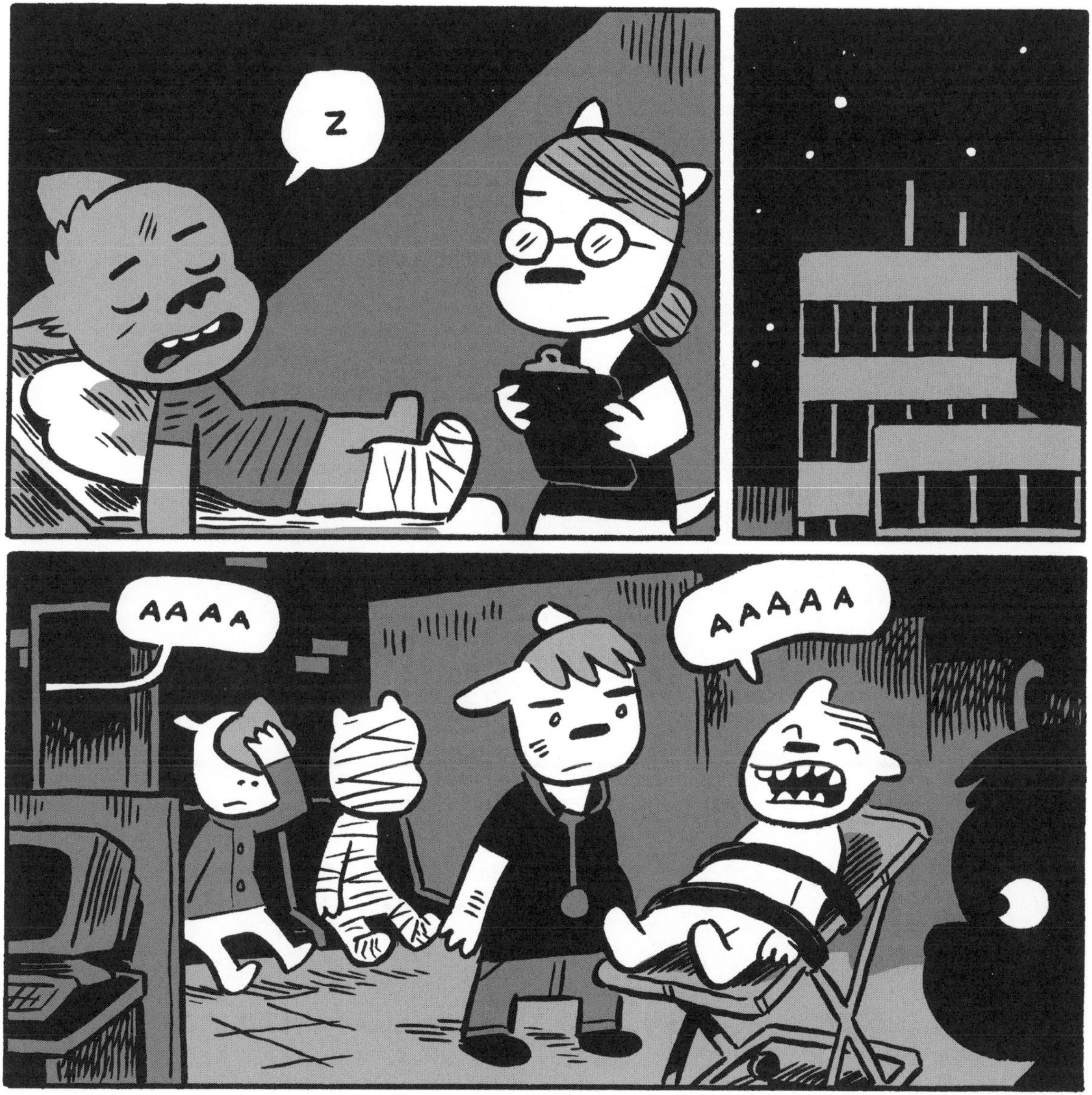
Z
AAAA
AAAAA

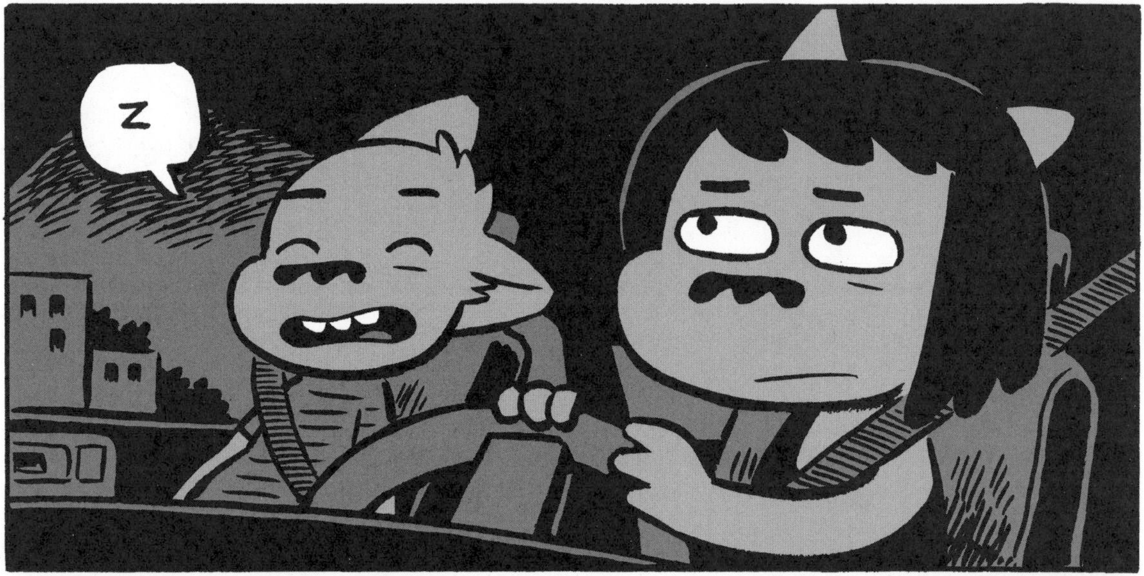
Z

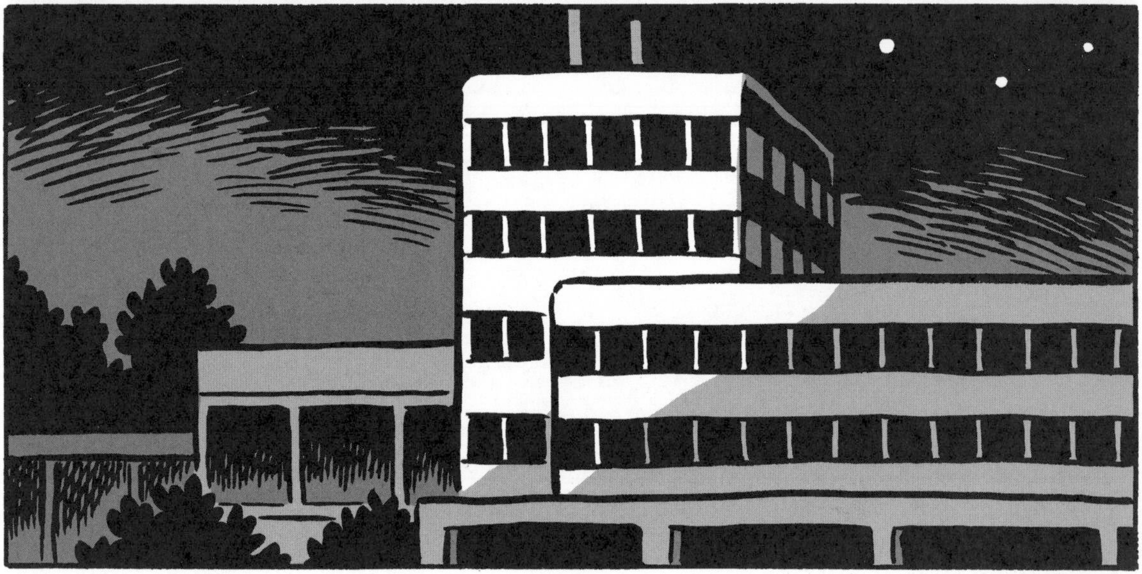

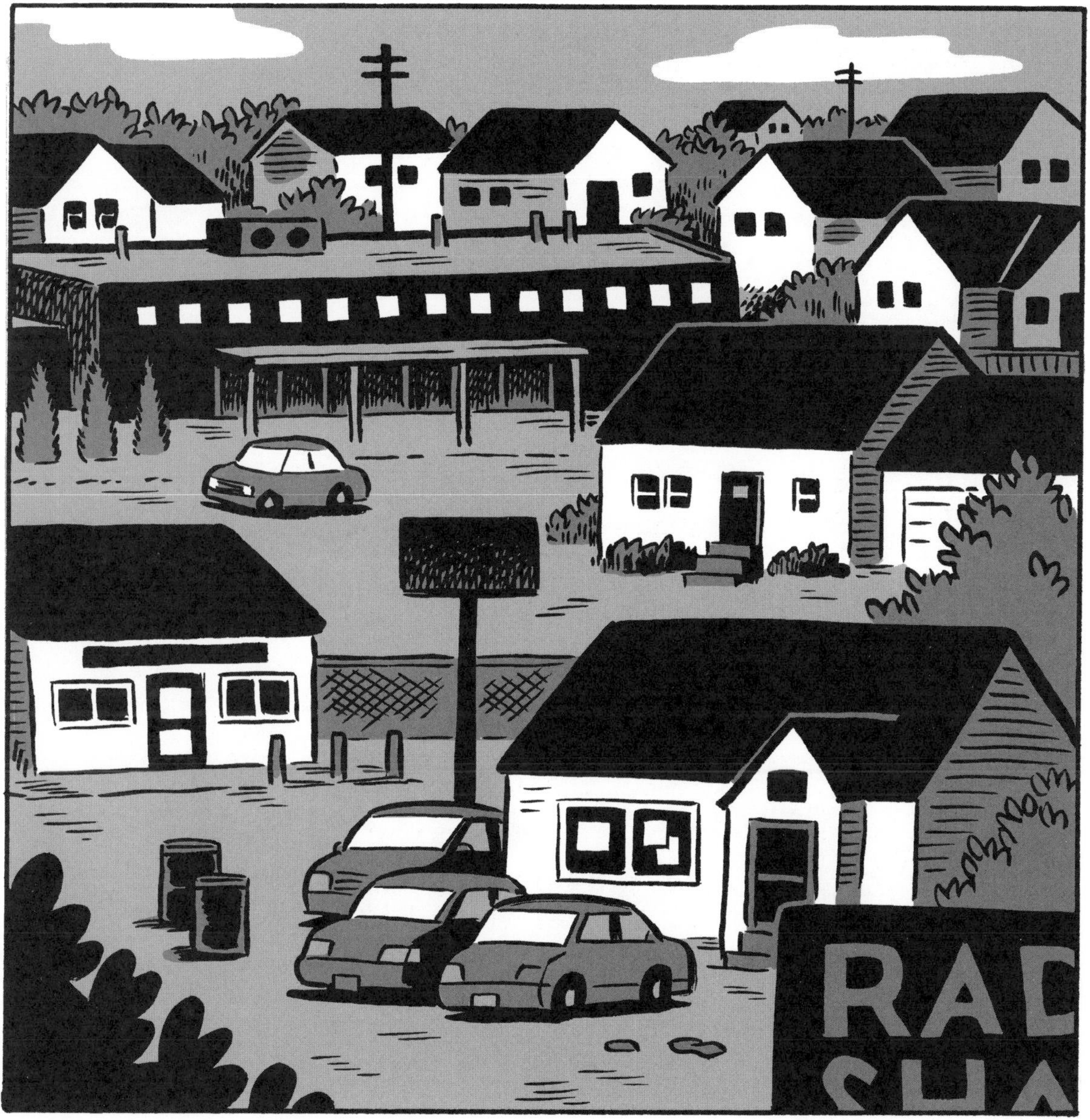
RAD

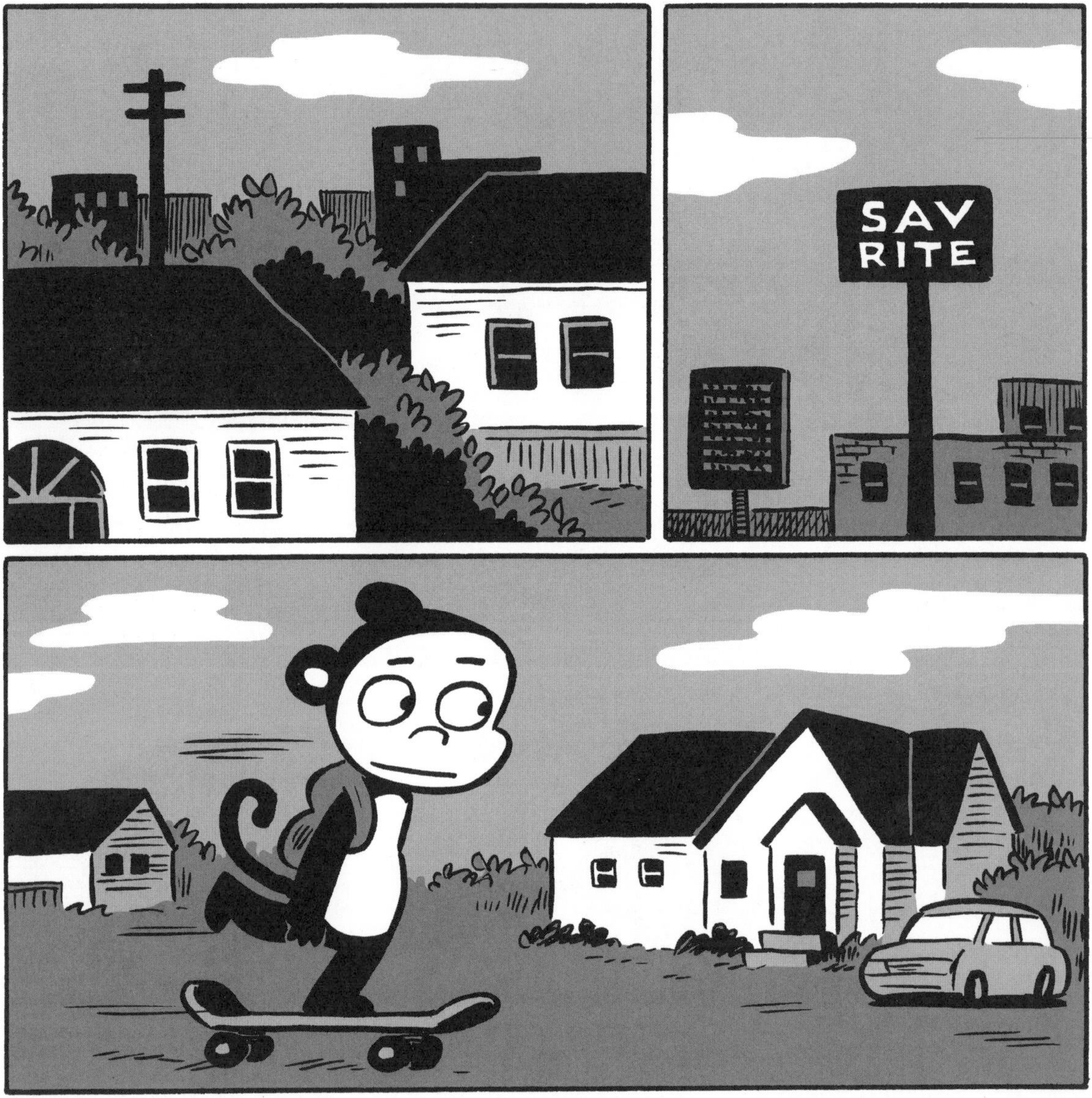
SAV
RITE

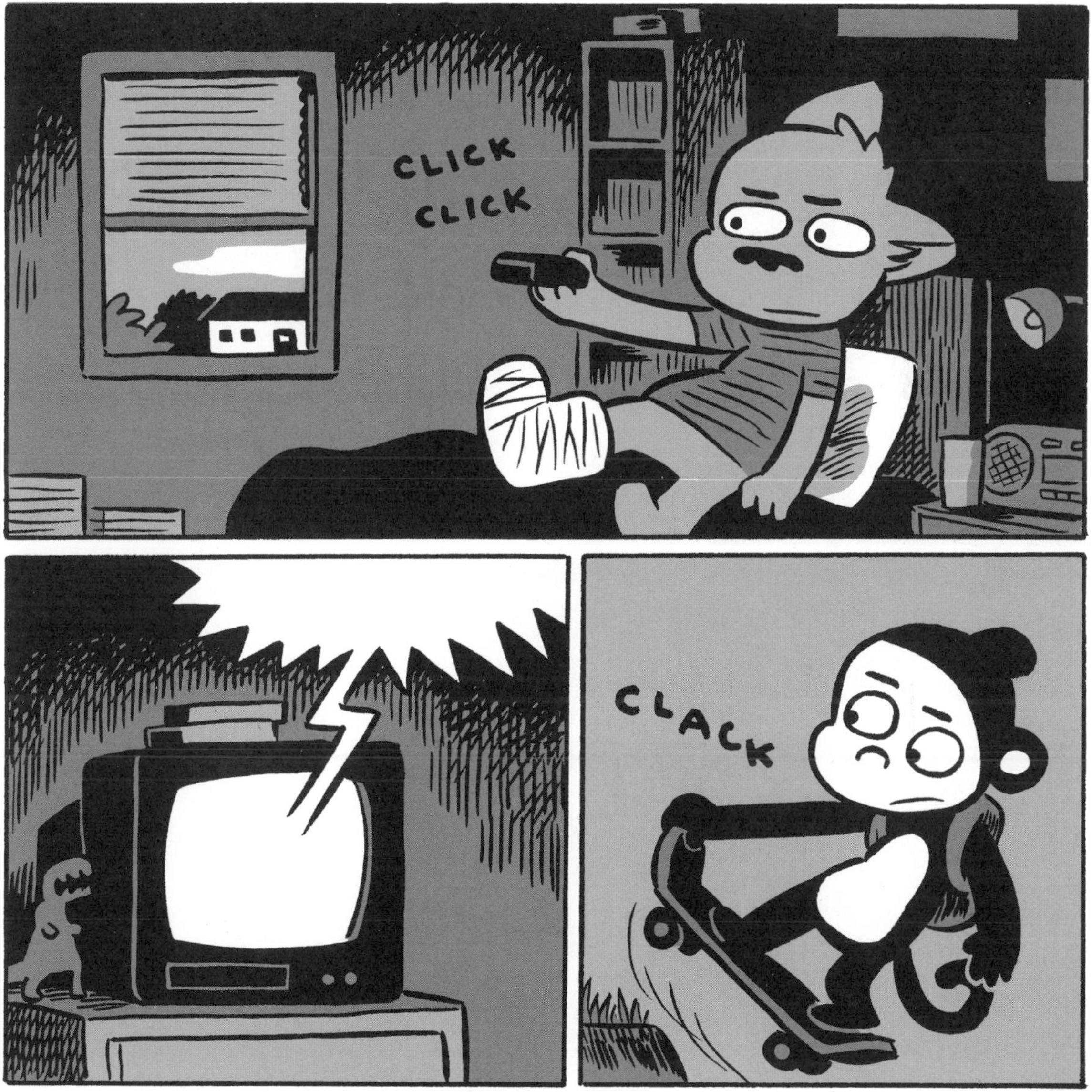
CLICK
CLICK
CLACK

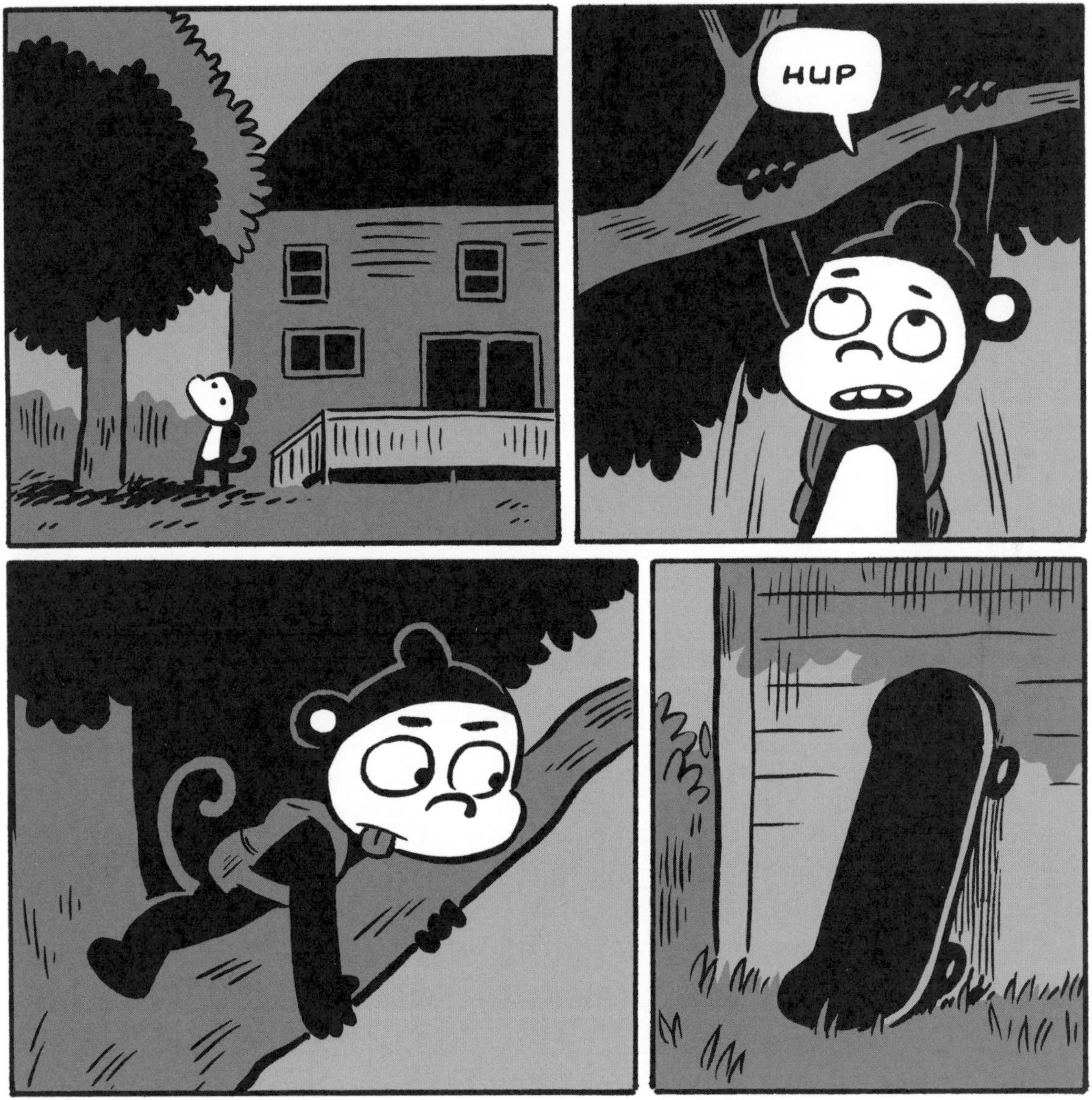
HUP

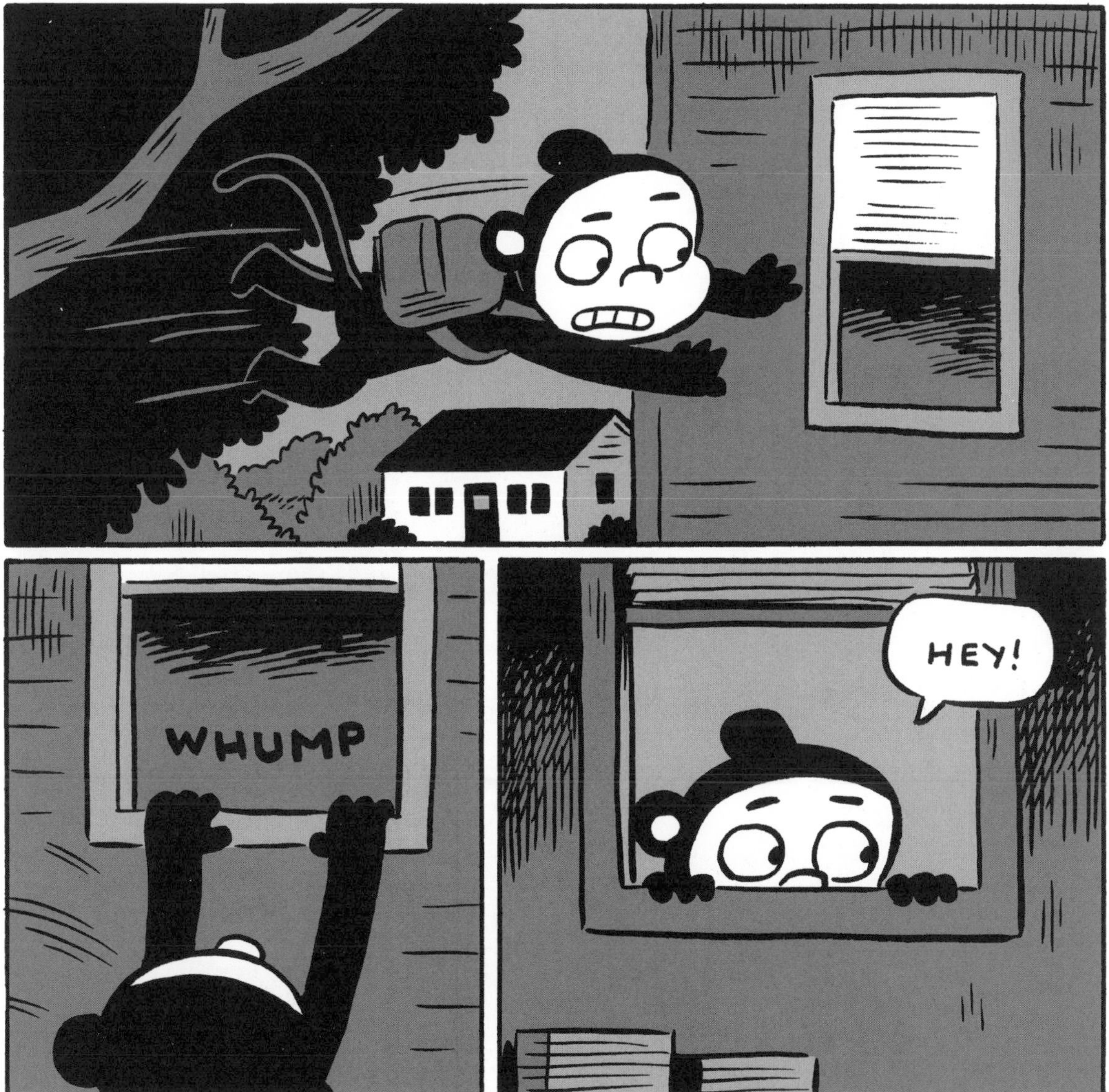
WHUMP
HEY!

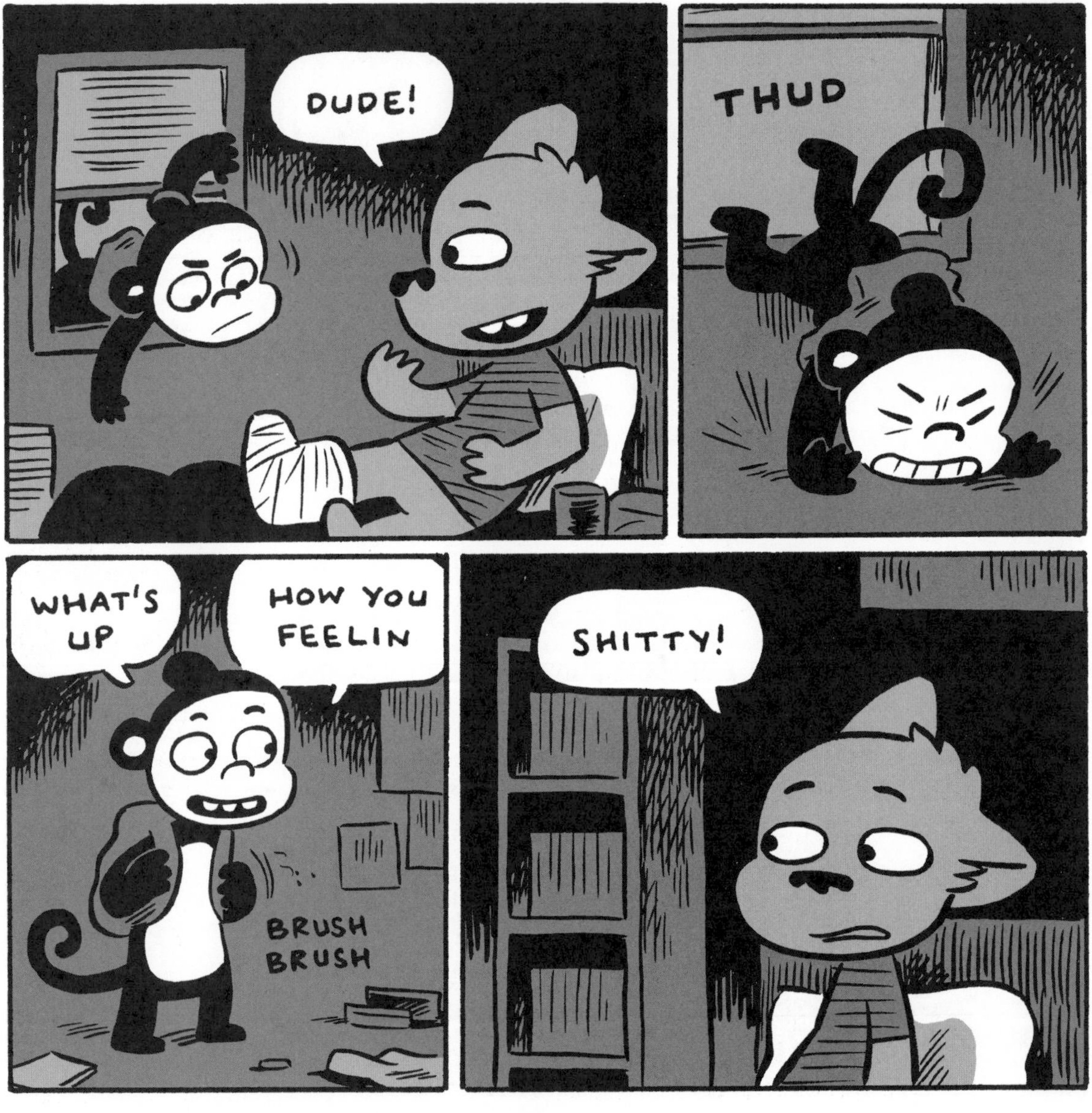
DUDE!
THUD
WHAT'S UP
HOW YOU FEELIN
BRUSH BRUSH
SHITTY!

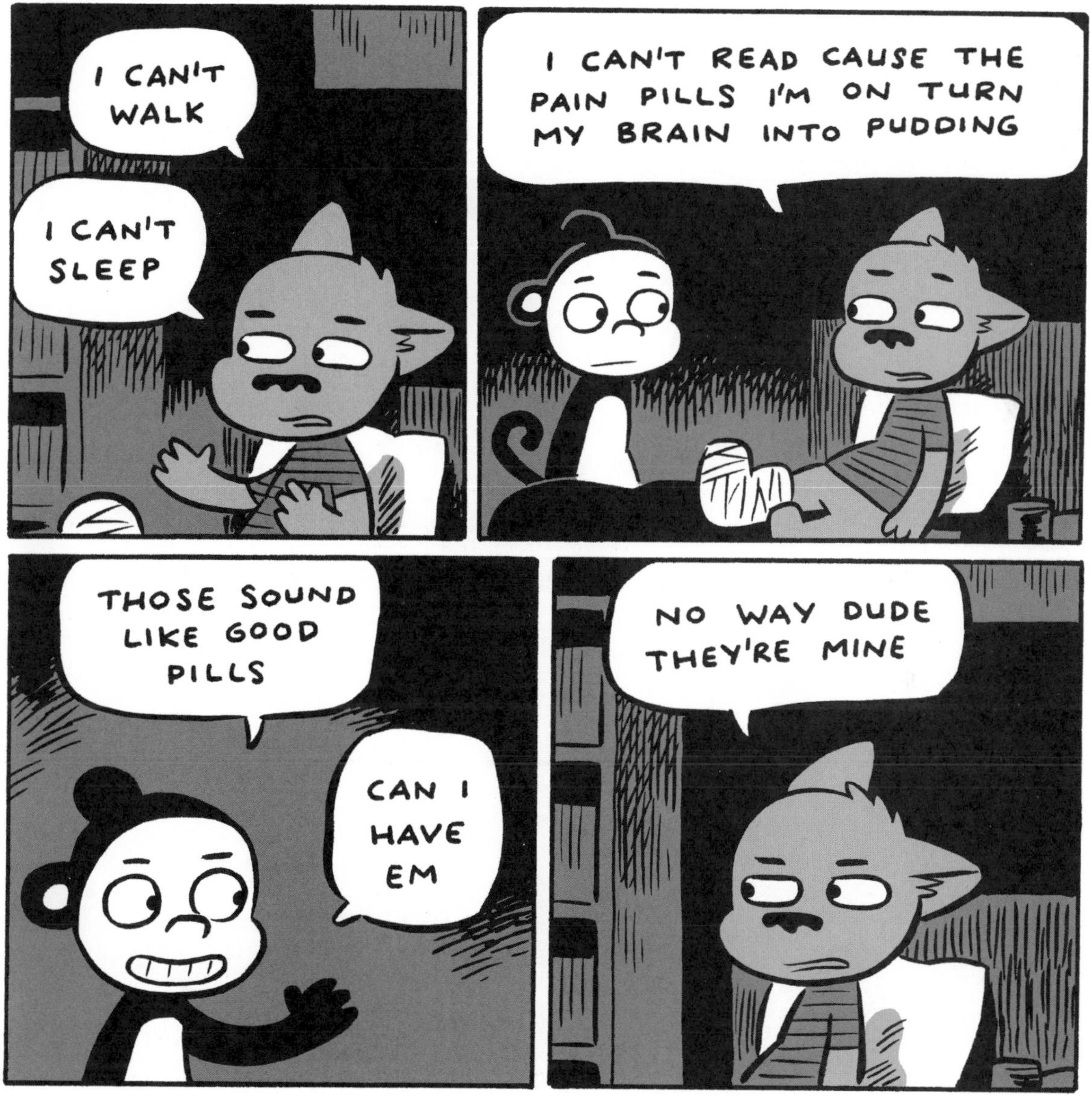
I CAN'T WALK
I CAN'T SLEEP
I CAN'T READ CAUSE THE PAIN PILLS I'M ON TURN MY BRAIN INTO PUDDING
THOSE SOUND LIKE GOOD PILLS
CAN I HAVE EM
NO WAY DUDE THEY'RE MINE

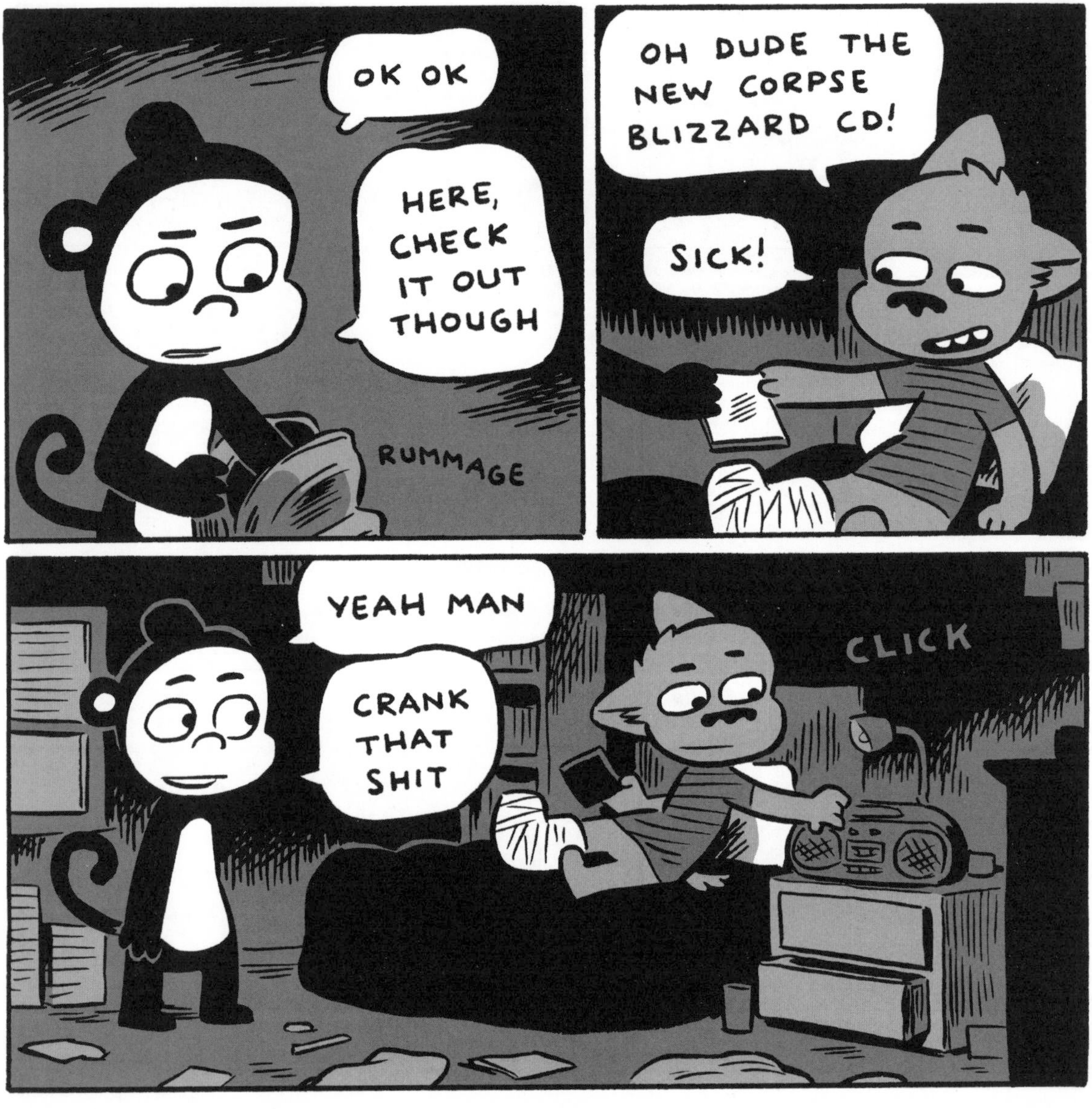
OK OK
HERE, CHECK IT OUT THOUGH
RUMMAGE
OH DUDE THE NEW CORPSE BLIZZARD CD!
SICK!
YEAH MAN
CRANK THAT SHIT
CLICK

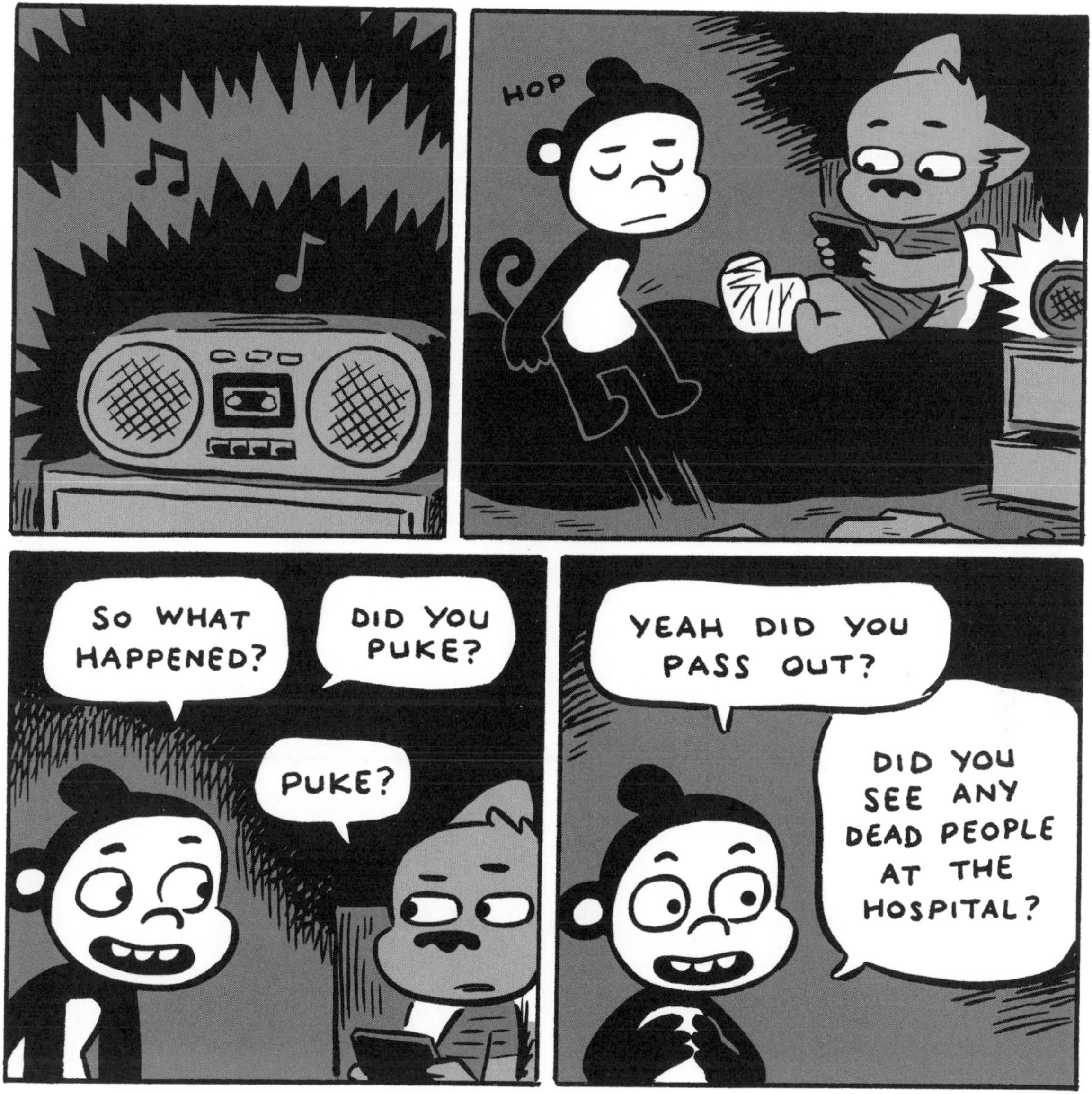
HOP
SO WHAT HAPPENED?
DID YOU PUKE?
PUKE?
YEAH DID YOU PASS OUT?
DID YOU SEE ANY DEAD PEOPLE AT THE HOSPITAL?

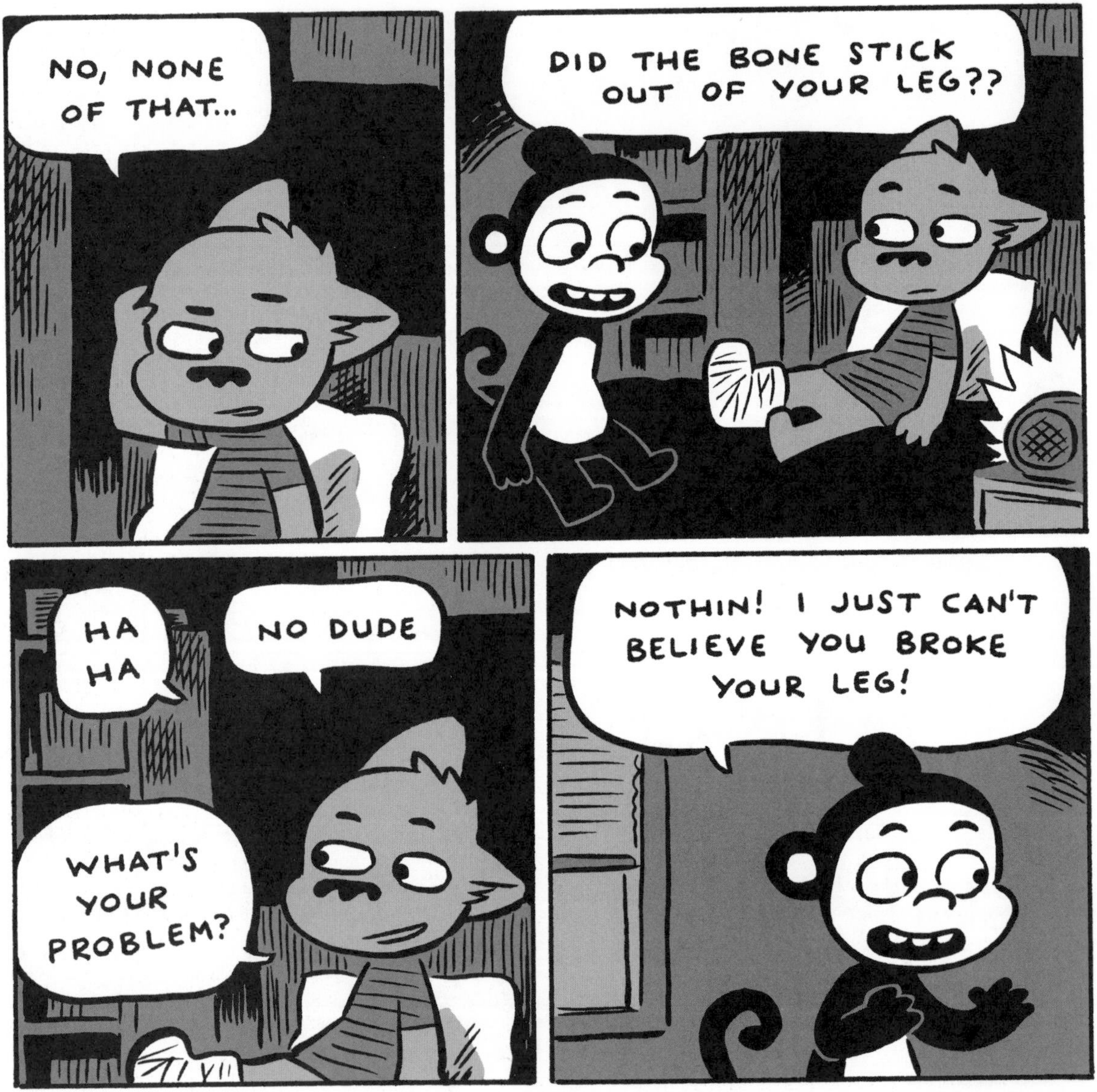
NO, NONE OF THAT...
DID THE BONE STICK OUT OF YOUR LEG??
HA HA
NO DUDE
WHAT'S YOUR PROBLEM?
NOTHIN! I JUST CAN'T BELIEVE YOU BROKE YOUR LEG!

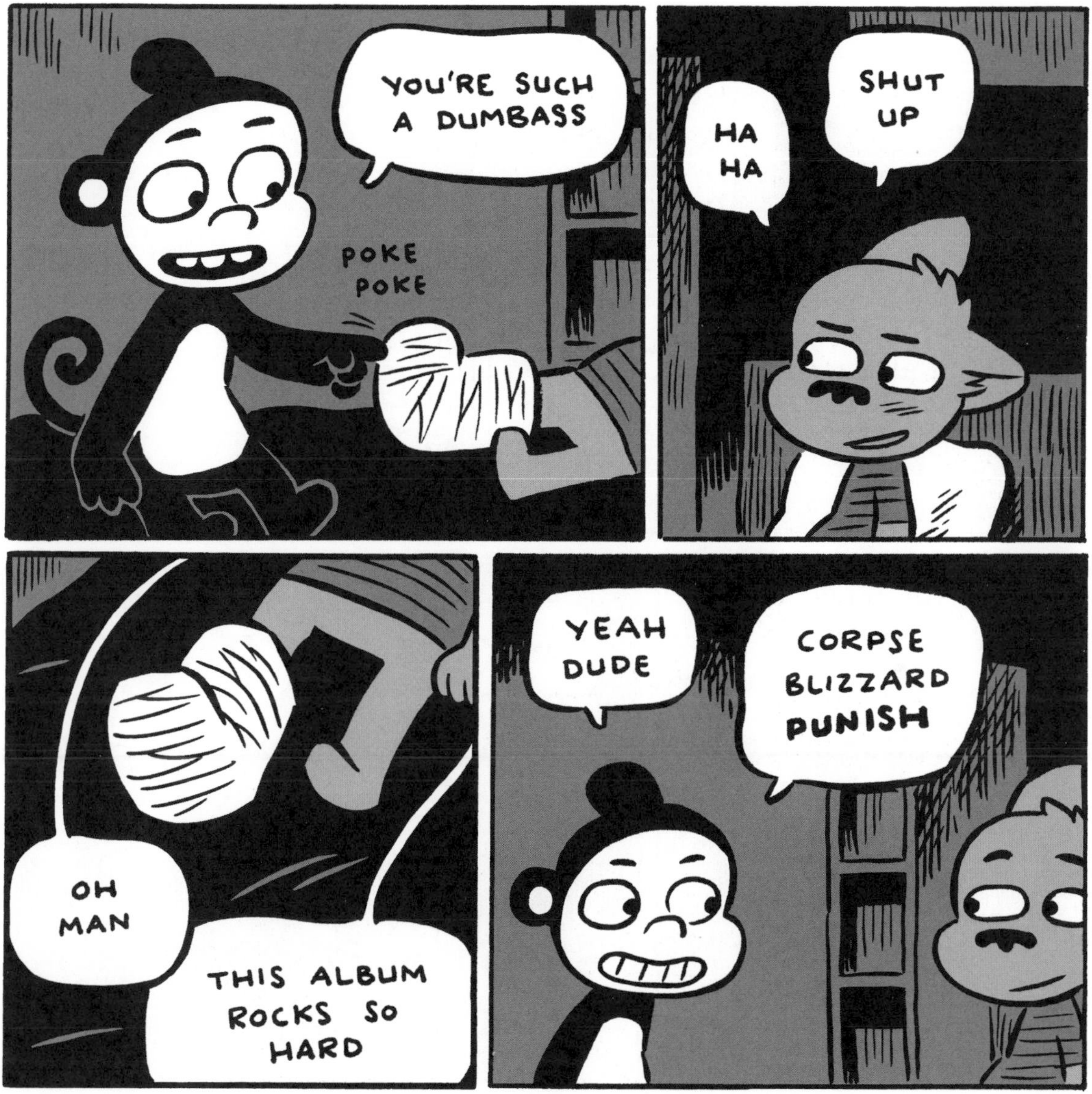
YOU'RE SUCH A DUMBASS
POKE POKE
HA HA
SHUT UP
OH MAN
THIS ALBUM ROCKS SO HARD
YEAH DUDE
CORPSE BLIZZARD **PUNISH**

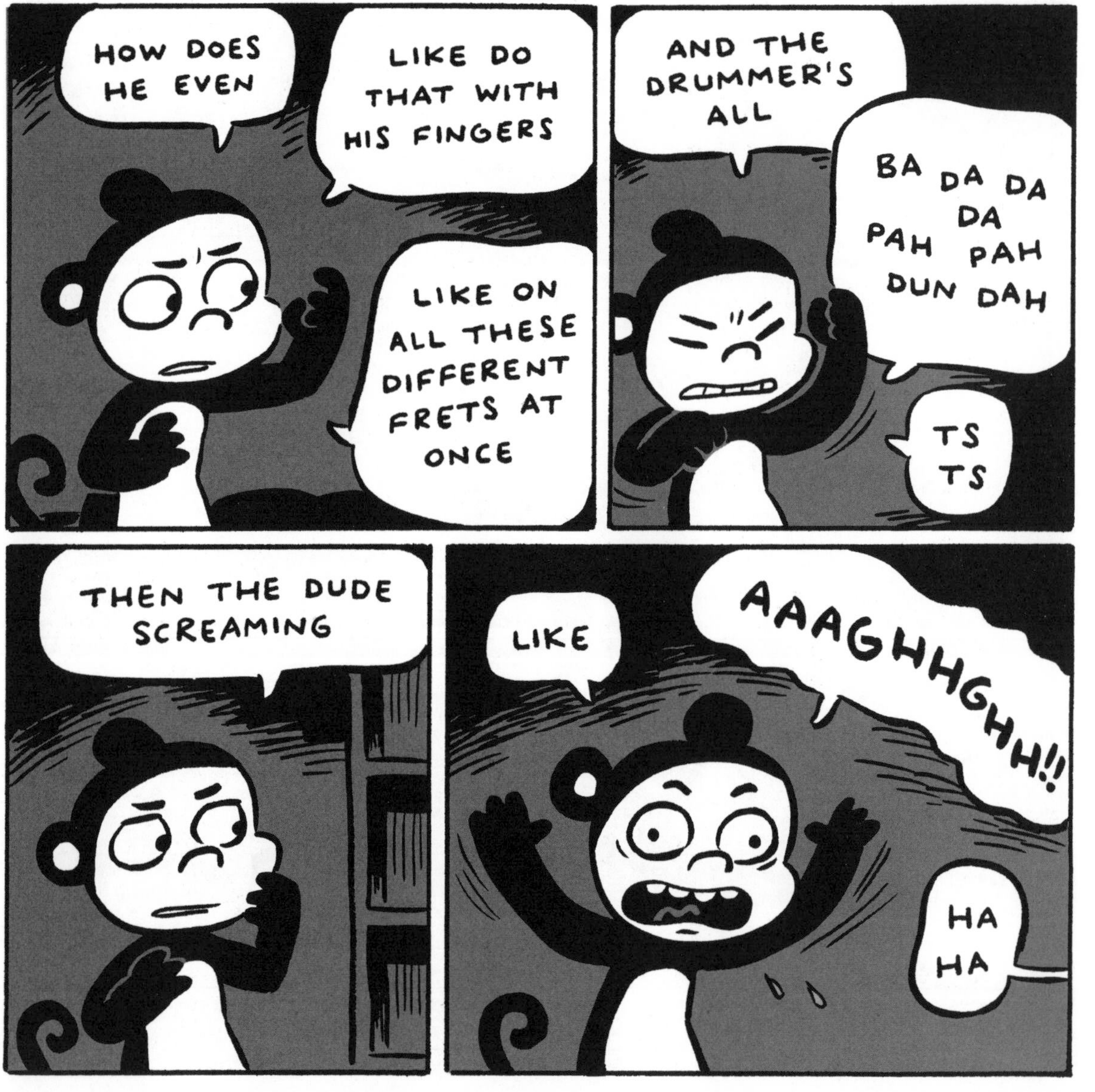
HOW DOES HE EVEN
LIKE DO THAT WITH HIS FINGERS
LIKE ON ALL THESE DIFFERENT FRETS AT ONCE
AND THE DRUMMER'S ALL
BA DA DA DA PAH PAH DUN DAH
TS TS
THEN THE DUDE SCREAMING
LIKE
AAAGHHGHH!!
HA HA

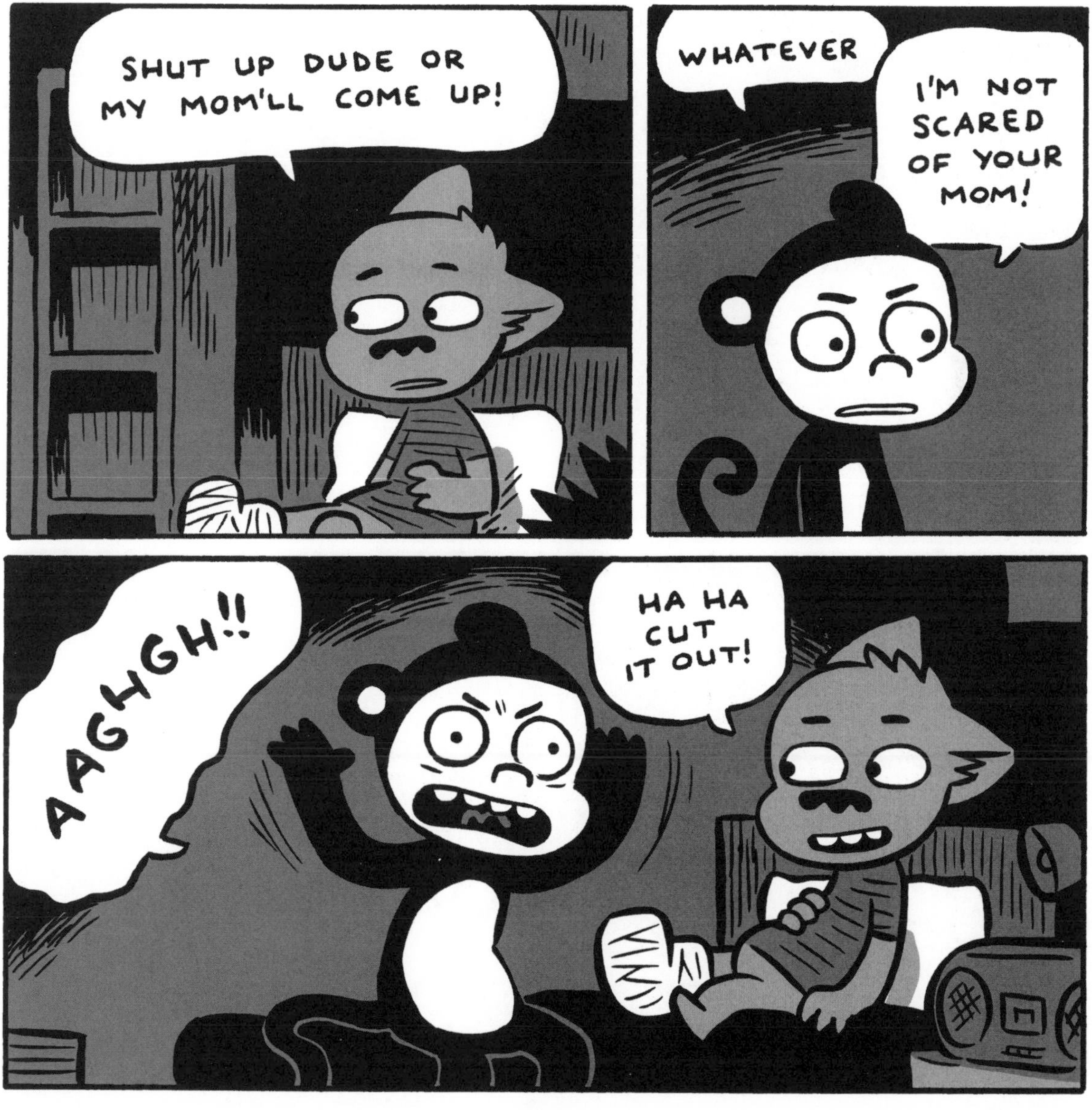
SHUT UP DUDE OR MY MOM'LL COME UP!
WHATEVER
I'M NOT SCARED OF YOUR MOM!
AAGHGH!!
HA HA CUT IT OUT!

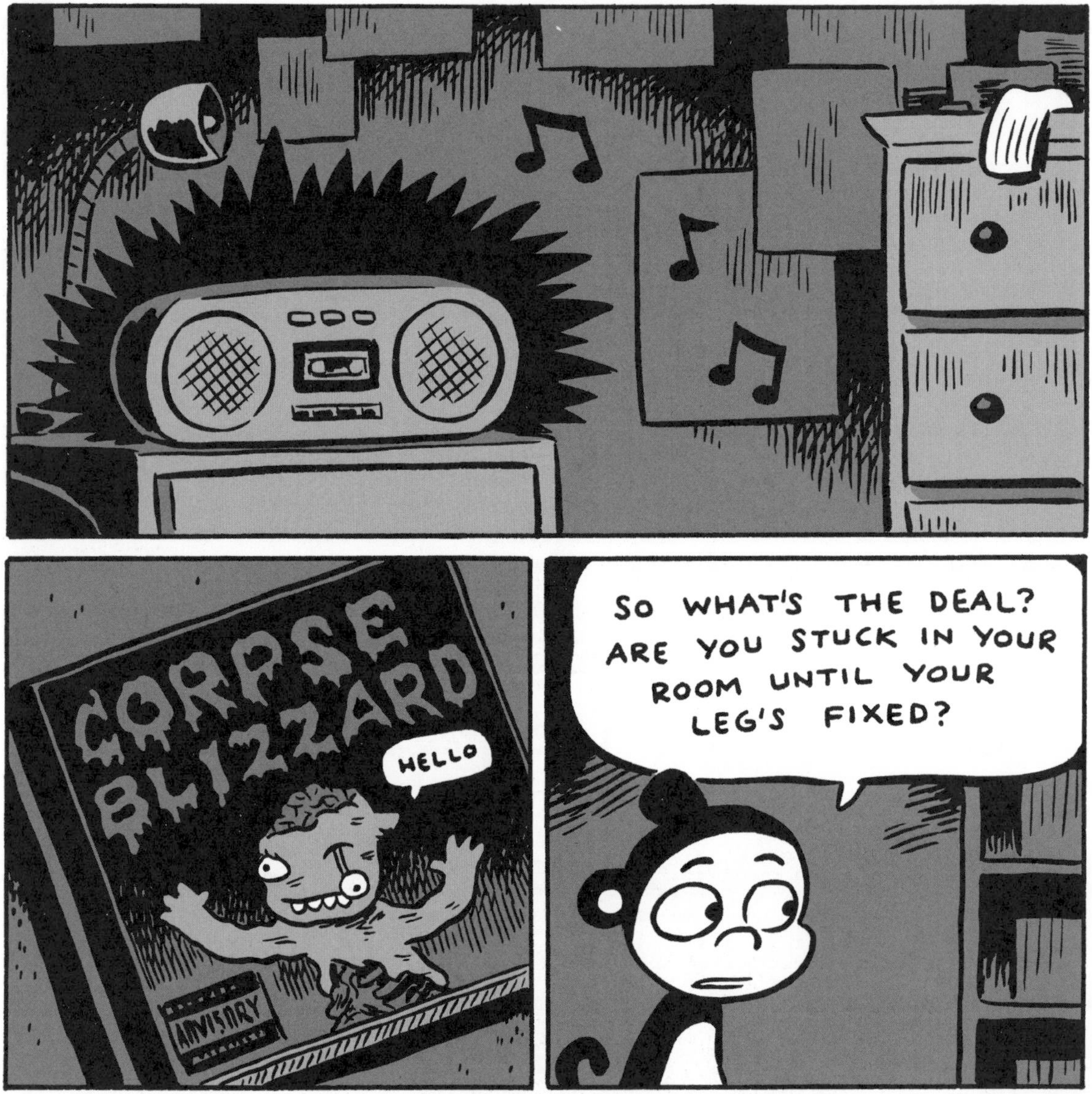
CORPSE BLIZZARD
HELLO
SO WHAT'S THE DEAL? ARE YOU STUCK IN YOUR ROOM UNTIL YOUR LEG'S FIXED?

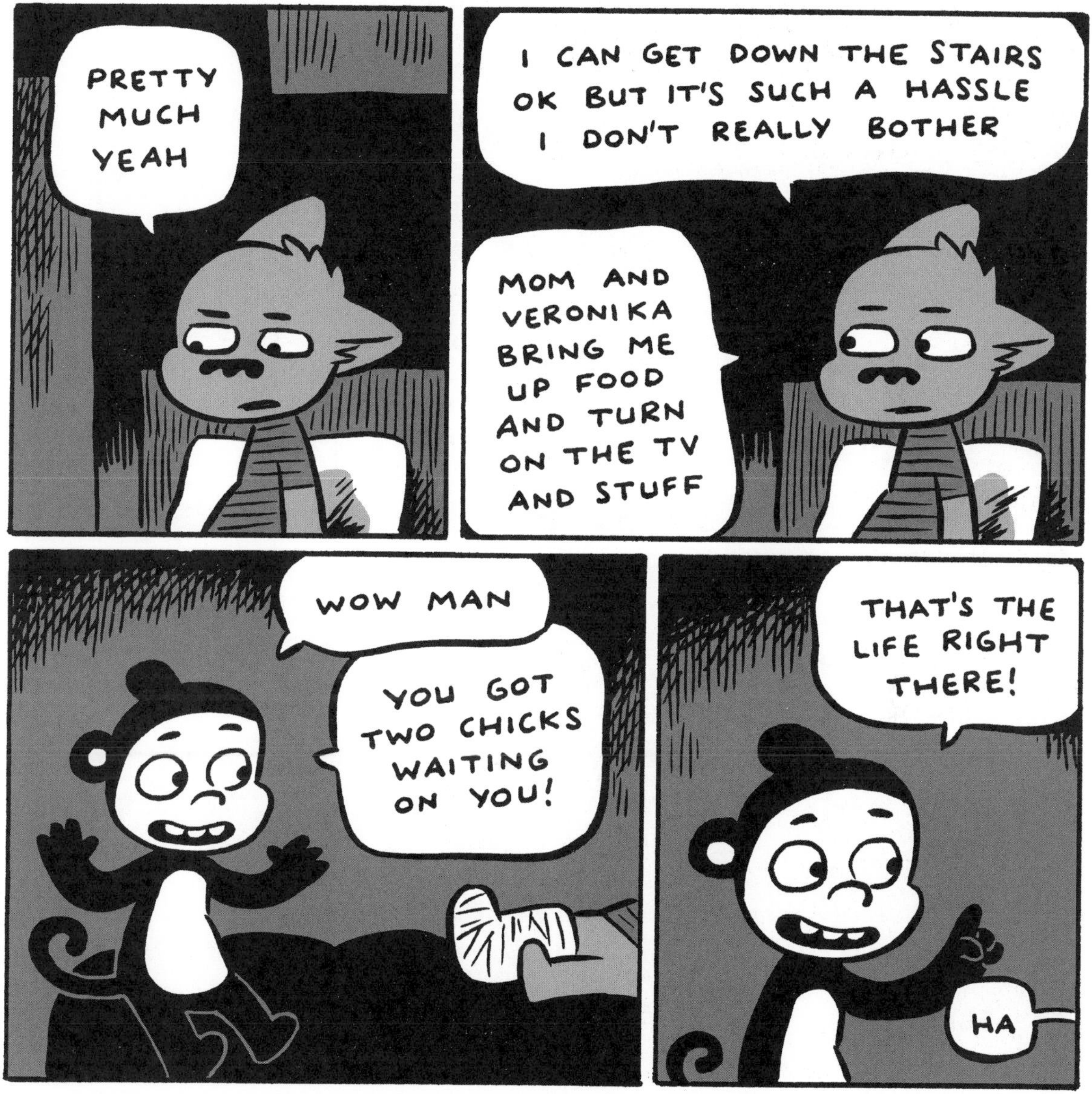
PRETTY MUCH YEAH
I CAN GET DOWN THE STAIRS OK BUT IT'S SUCH A HASSLE I DON'T REALLY BOTHER
MOM AND VERONIKA BRING ME UP FOOD AND TURN ON THE TV AND STUFF
WOW MAN
YOU GOT TWO CHICKS WAITING ON YOU!
THAT'S THE LIFE RIGHT THERE!
HA

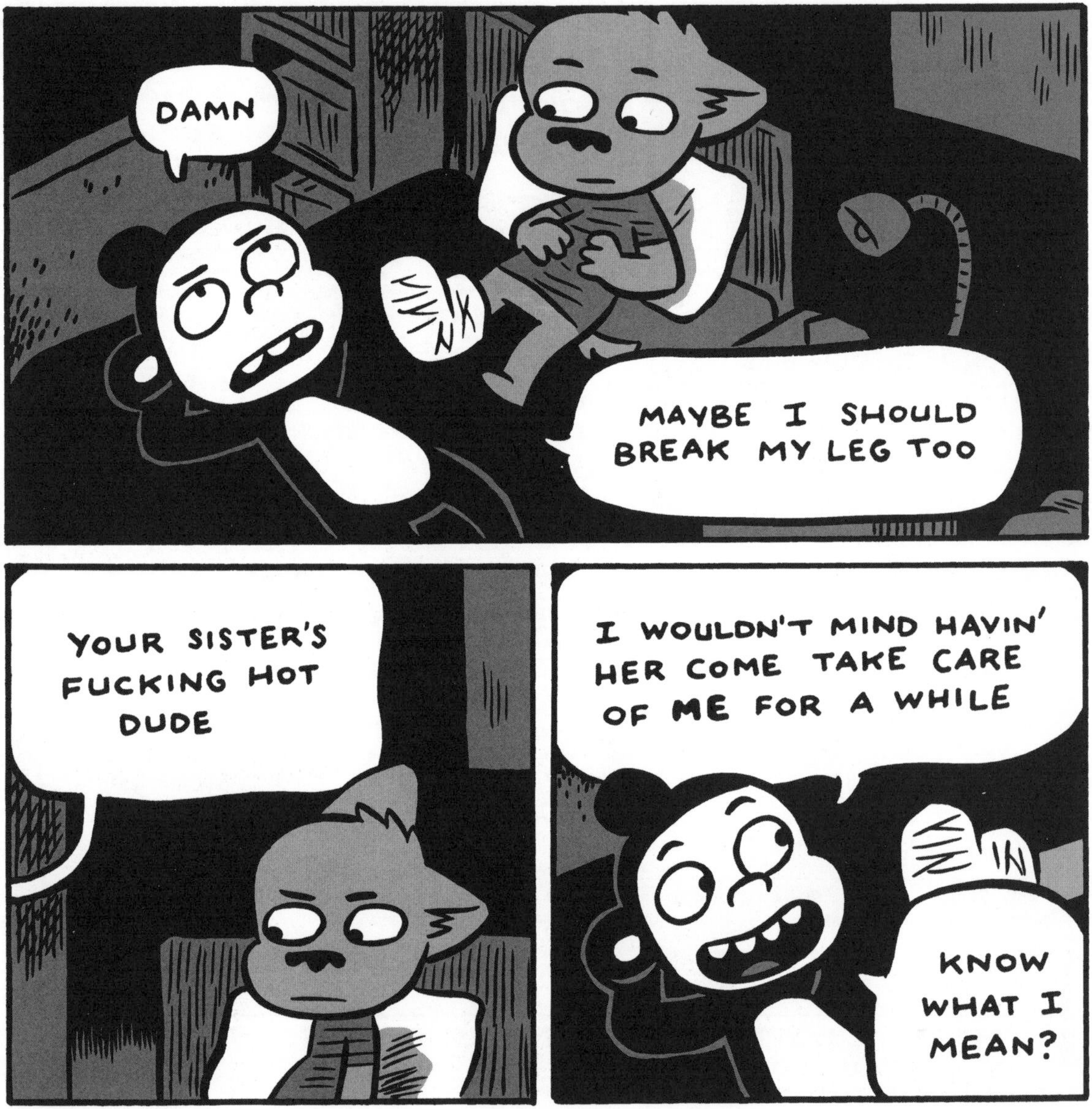
DAMN
MAYBE I SHOULD BREAK MY LEG TOO
YOUR SISTER'S FUCKING HOT DUDE
I WOULDN'T MIND HAVIN' HER COME TAKE CARE OF ME FOR A WHILE
KNOW WHAT I MEAN?

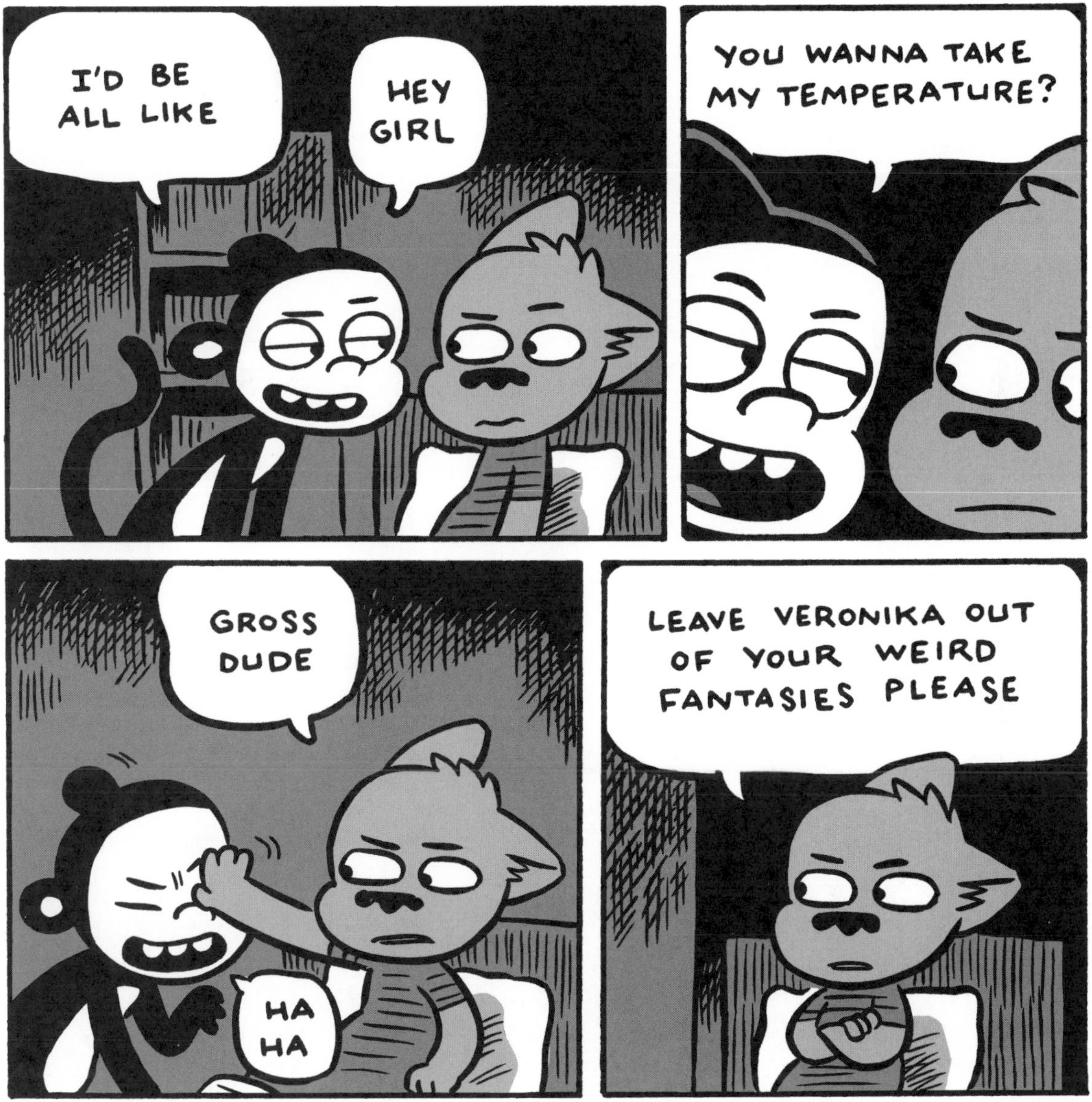
I'D BE ALL LIKE
HEY GIRL
YOU WANNA TAKE MY TEMPERATURE?
GROSS DUDE
HA HA
LEAVE VERONIKA OUT OF YOUR WEIRD FANTASIES PLEASE

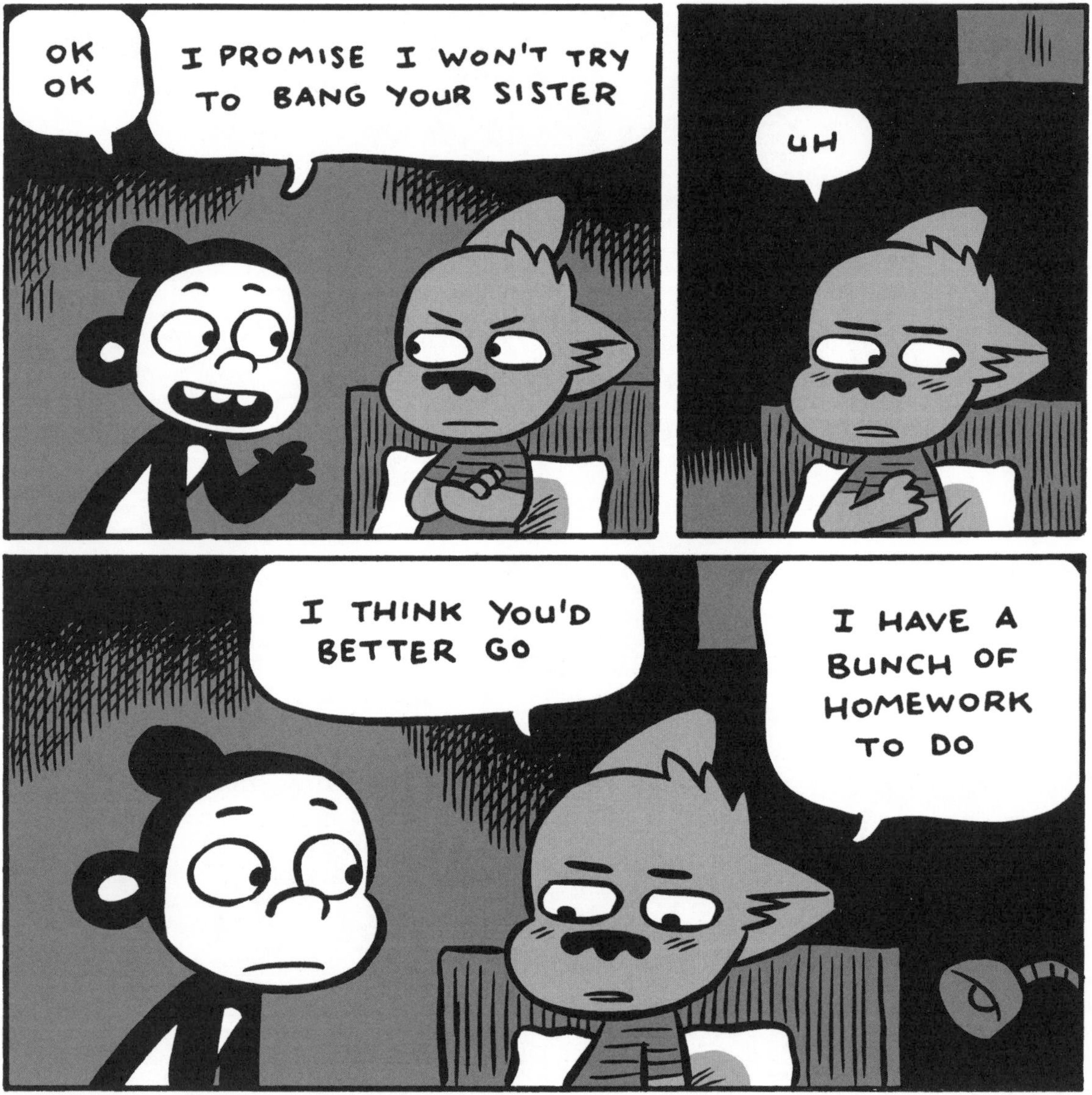

OK
OK
I PROMISE I WON'T TRY TO BANG YOUR SISTER
UH
I THINK YOU'D BETTER GO
I HAVE A BUNCH OF HOMEWORK TO DO

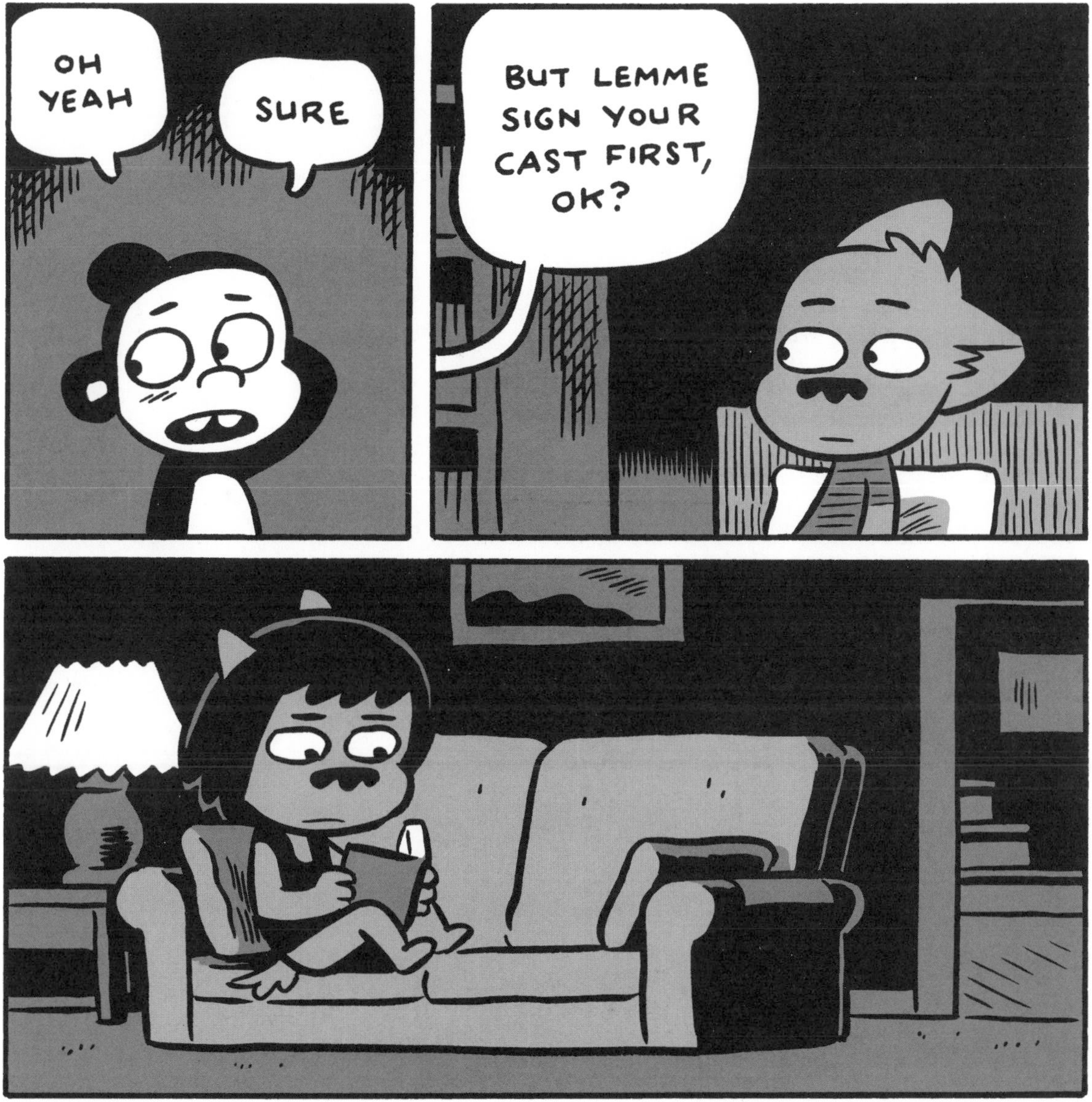
OH YEAH
SURE
BUT LEMME SIGN YOUR CAST FIRST, OK?

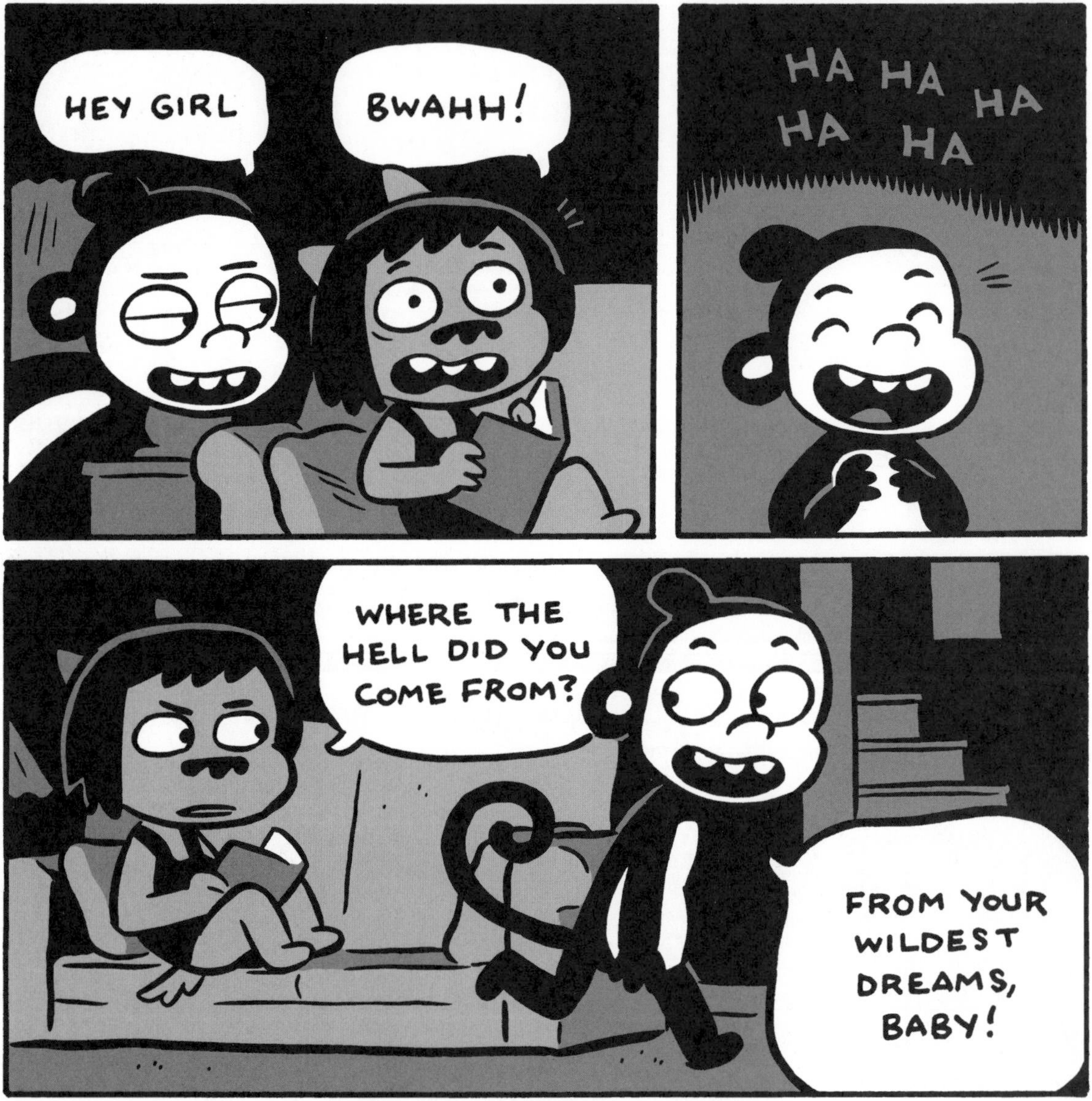
HEY GIRL
BWAHH!
HA HA HA HA HA
WHERE THE HELL DID YOU COME FROM?
FROM YOUR WILDEST DREAMS, BABY!

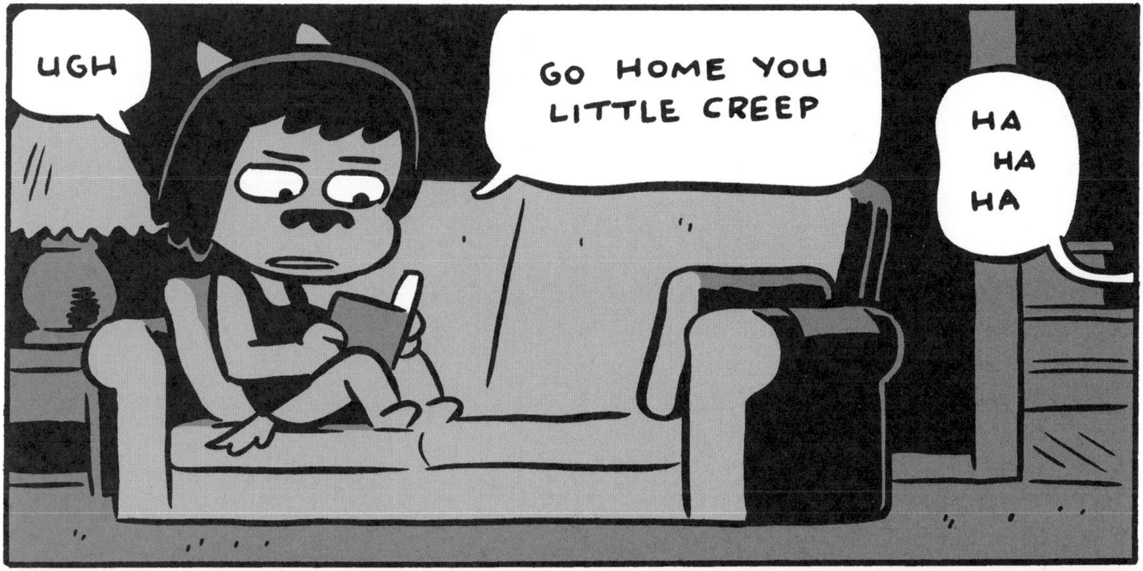
UGH
GO HOME YOU LITTLE CREEP
HA HA HA

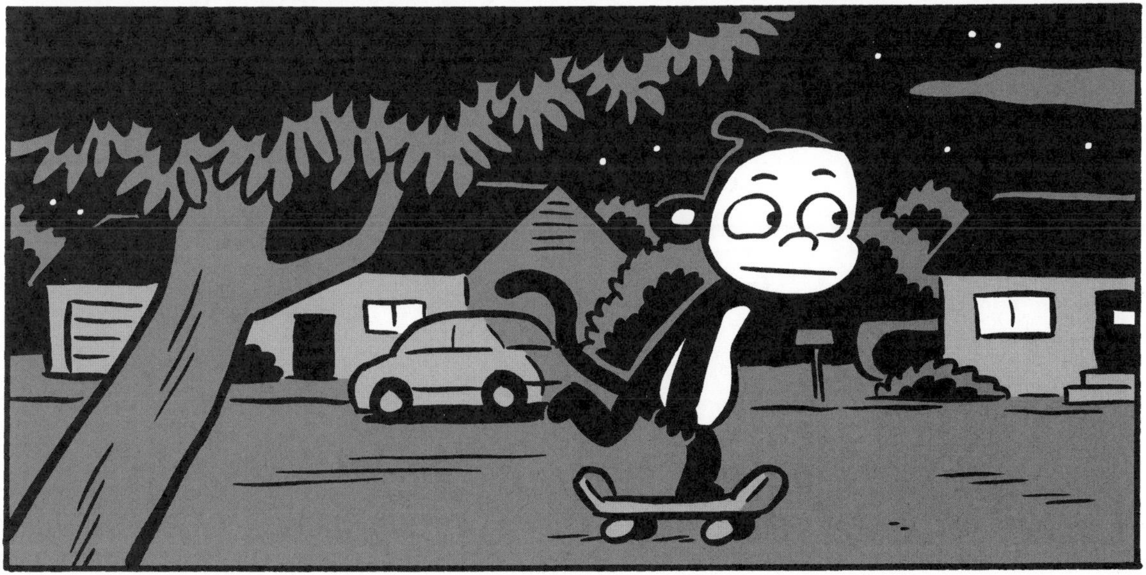

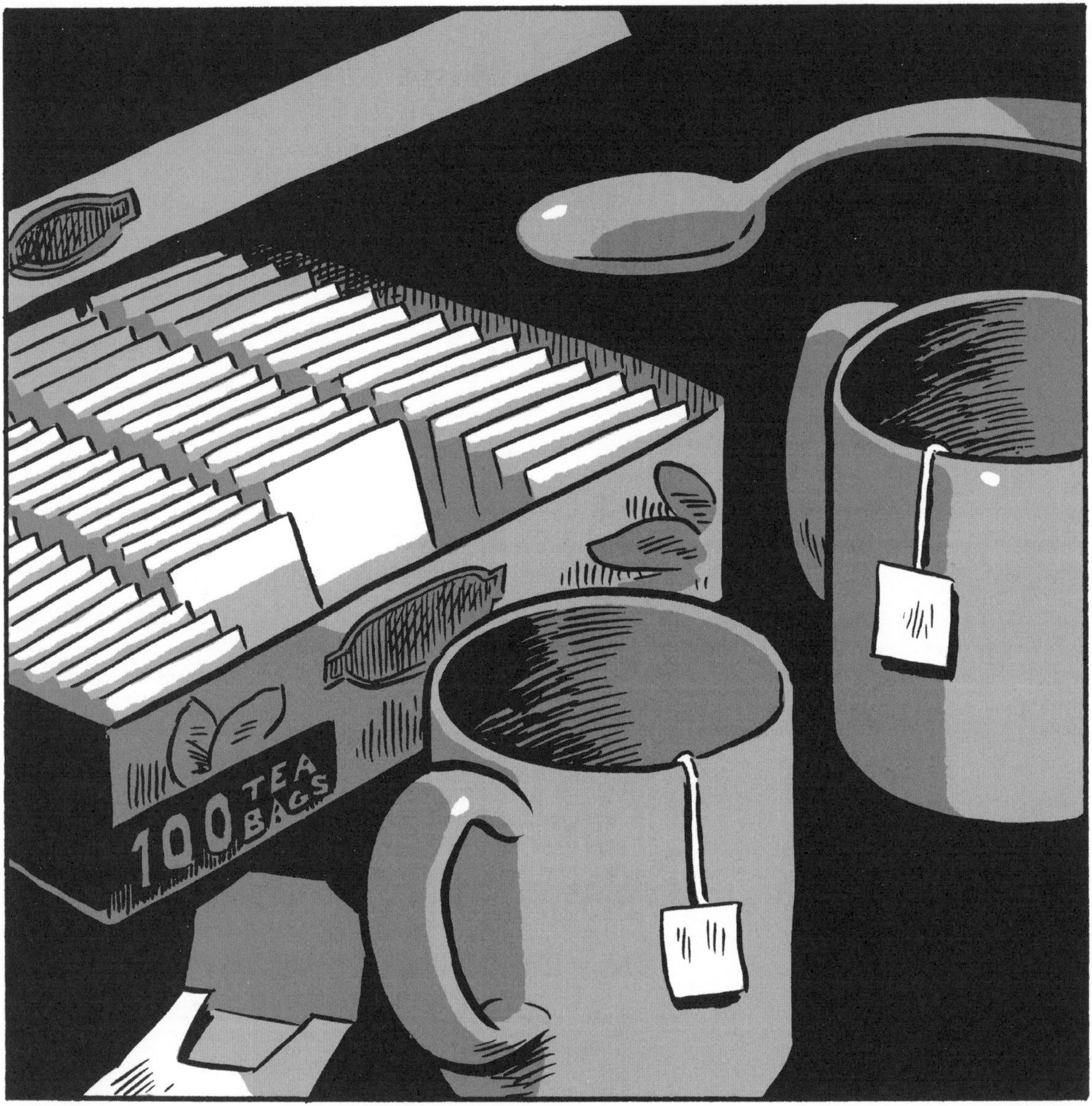
100 TEA BAGS

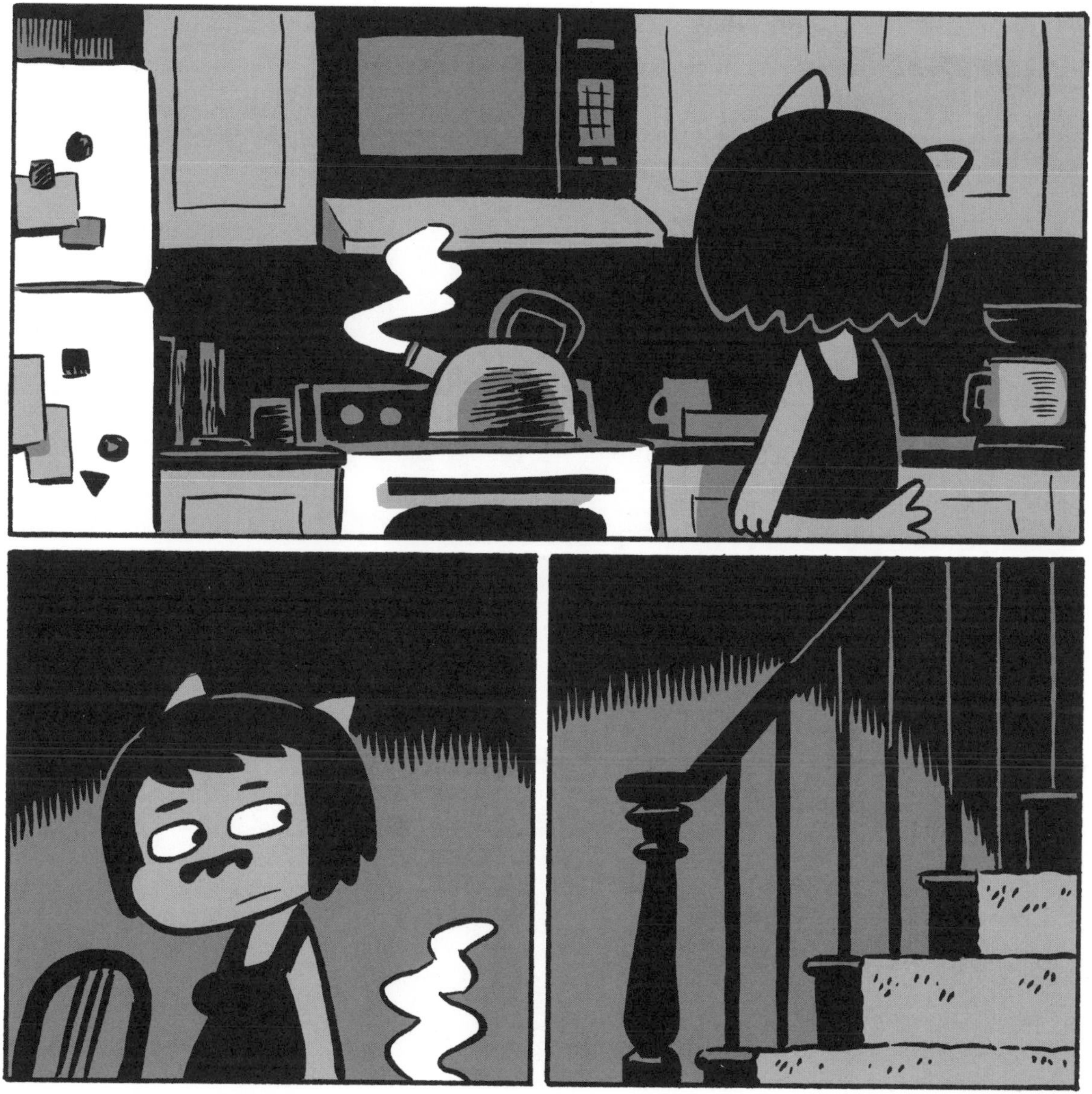

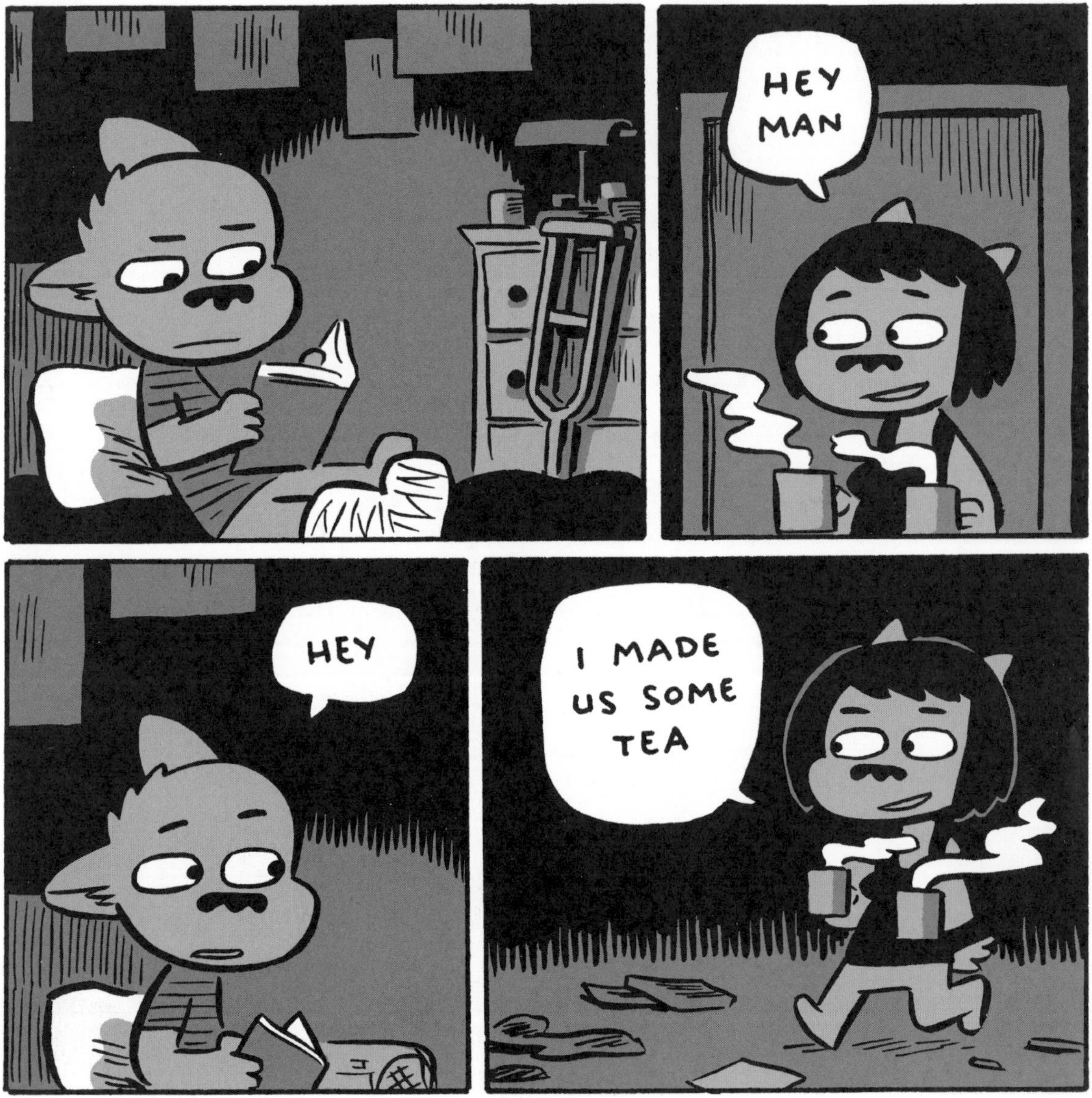
HEY MAN
HEY
I MADE US SOME TEA

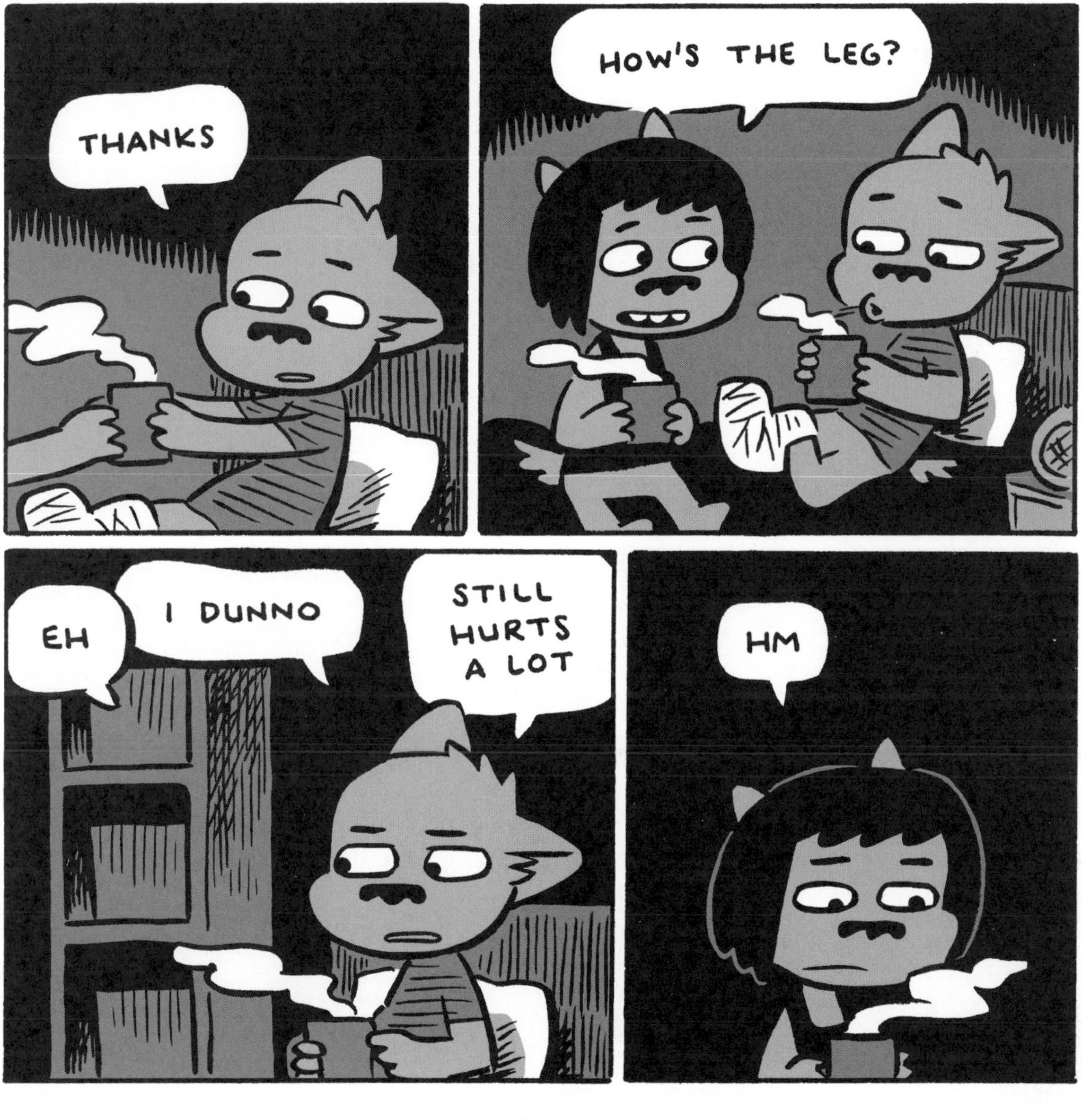
THANKS
HOW'S THE LEG?
EH
I DUNNO
STILL HURTS A LOT
HM

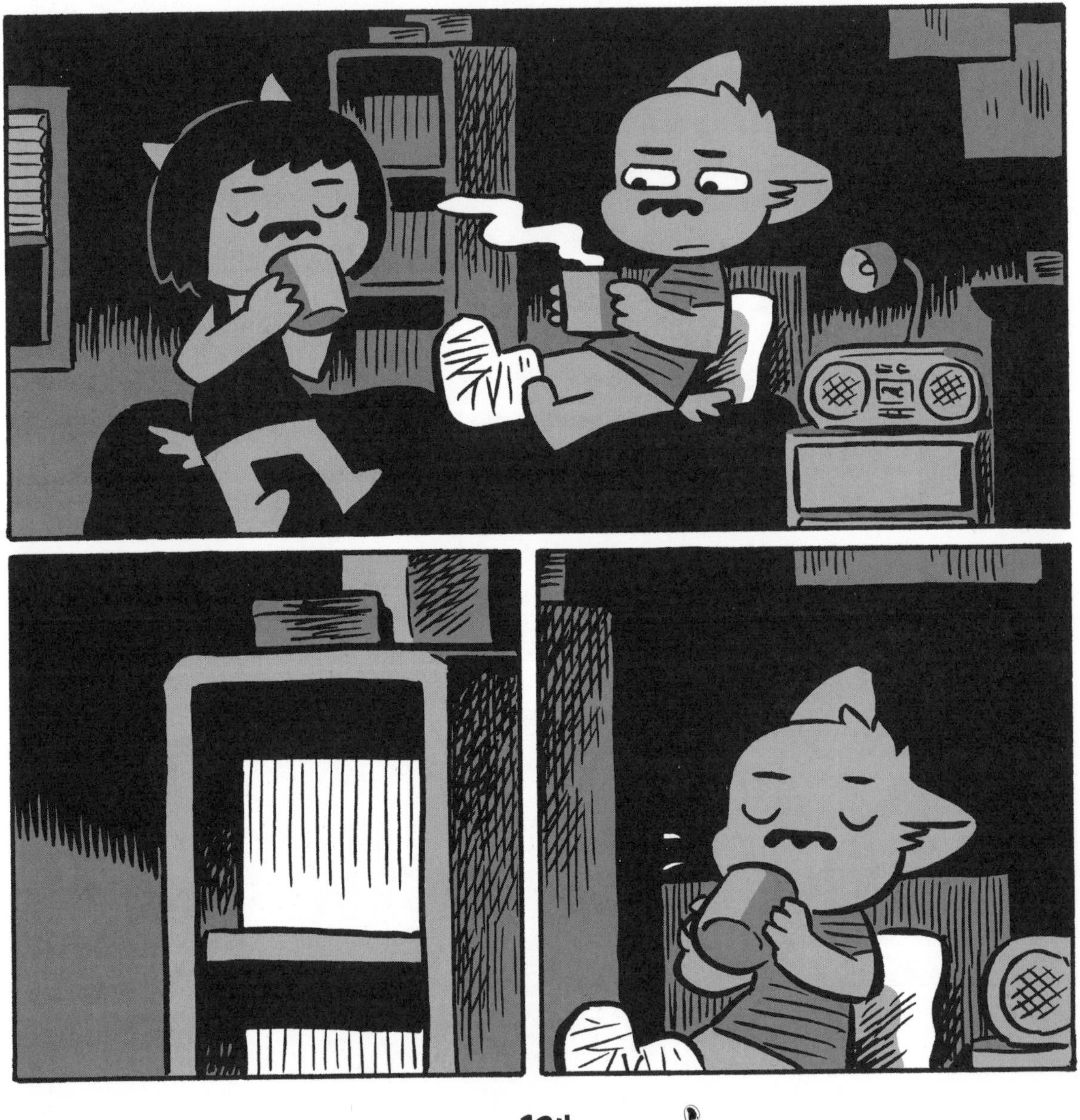

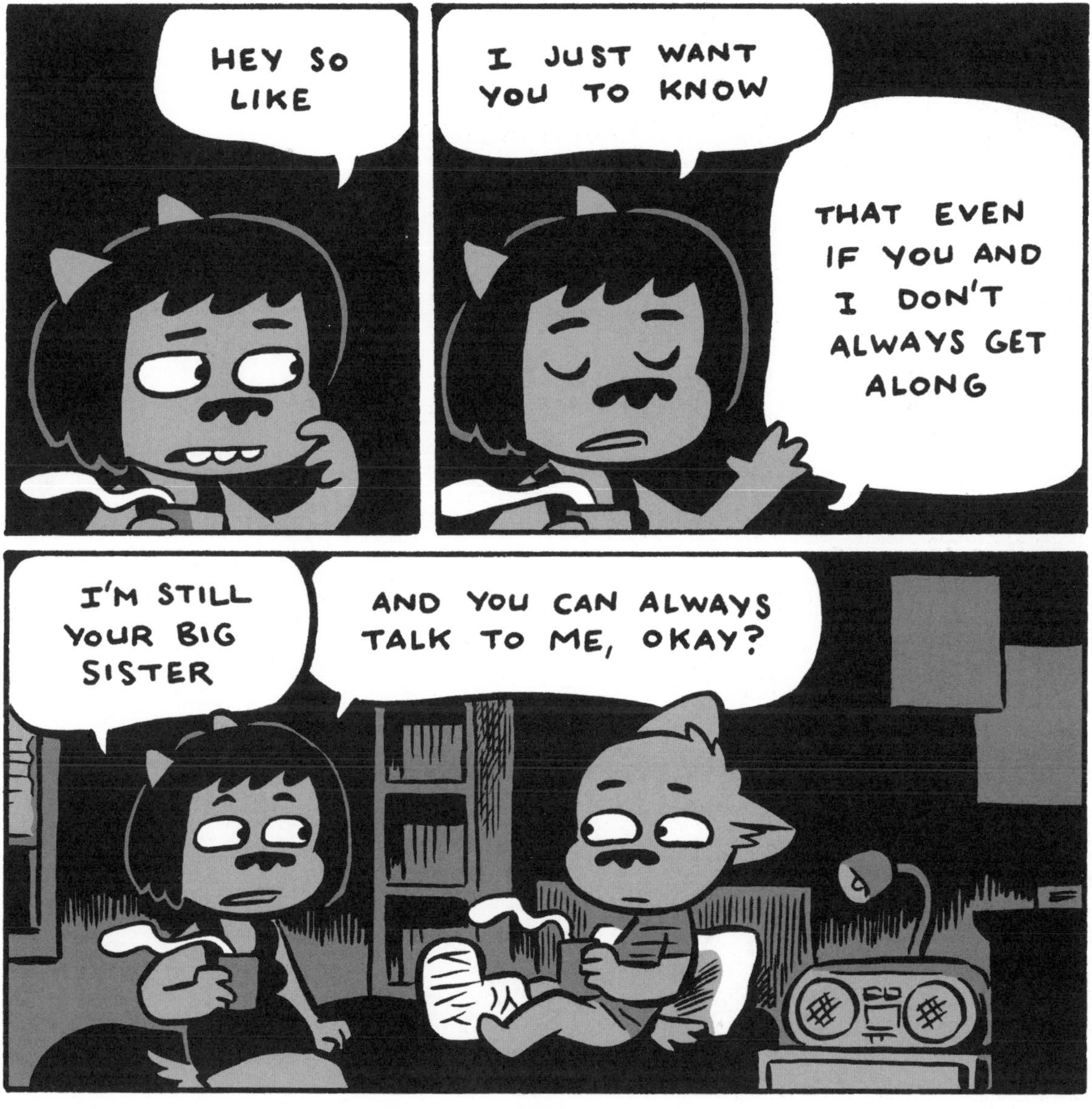
HEY SO LIKE
I JUST WANT YOU TO KNOW
THAT EVEN IF YOU AND I DON'T ALWAYS GET ALONG
I'M STILL YOUR BIG SISTER
AND YOU CAN ALWAYS TALK TO ME, OKAY?

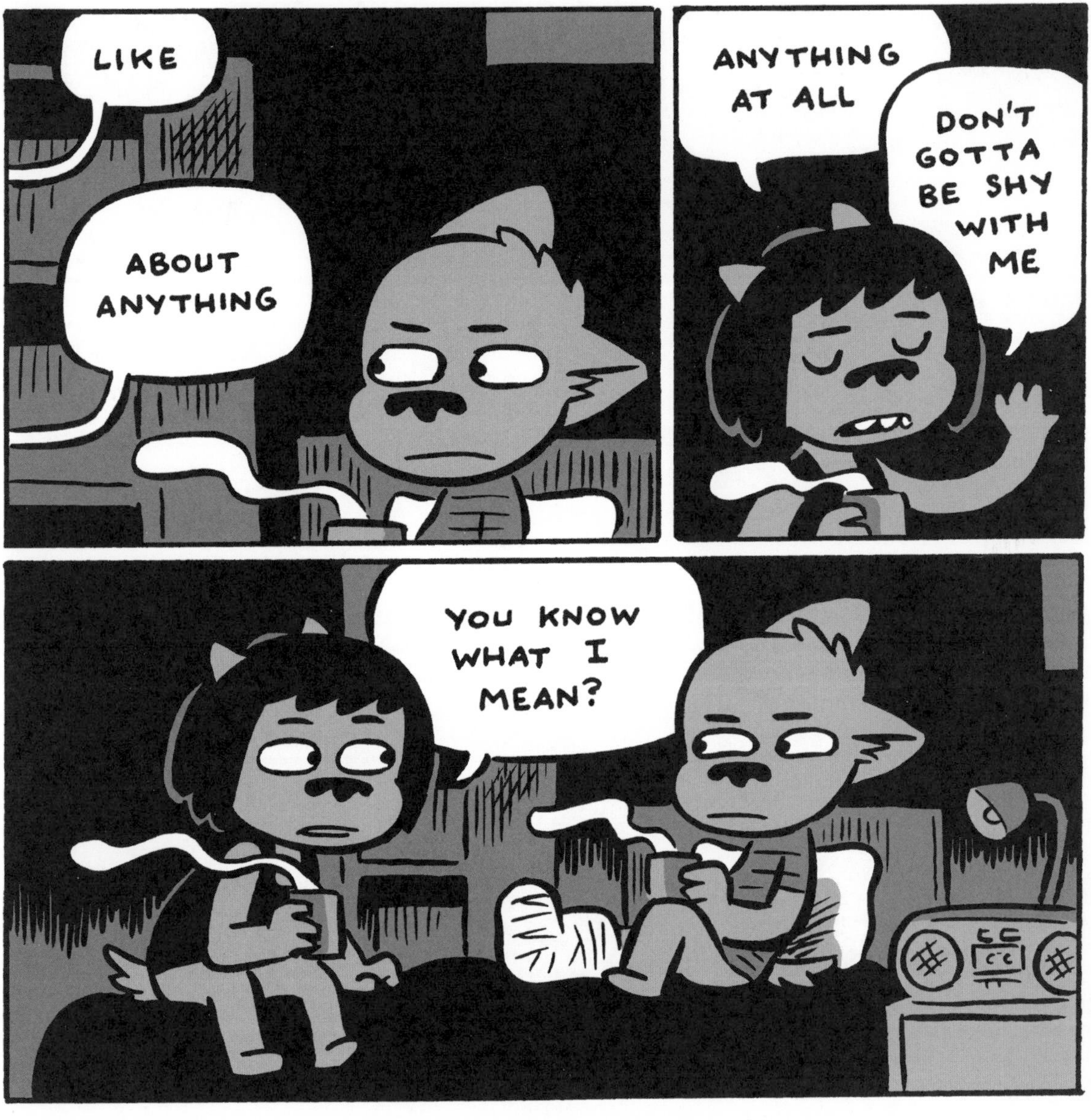
LIKE
ABOUT ANYTHING
ANYTHING AT ALL
DON'T GOTTA BE SHY WITH ME
YOU KNOW WHAT I MEAN?

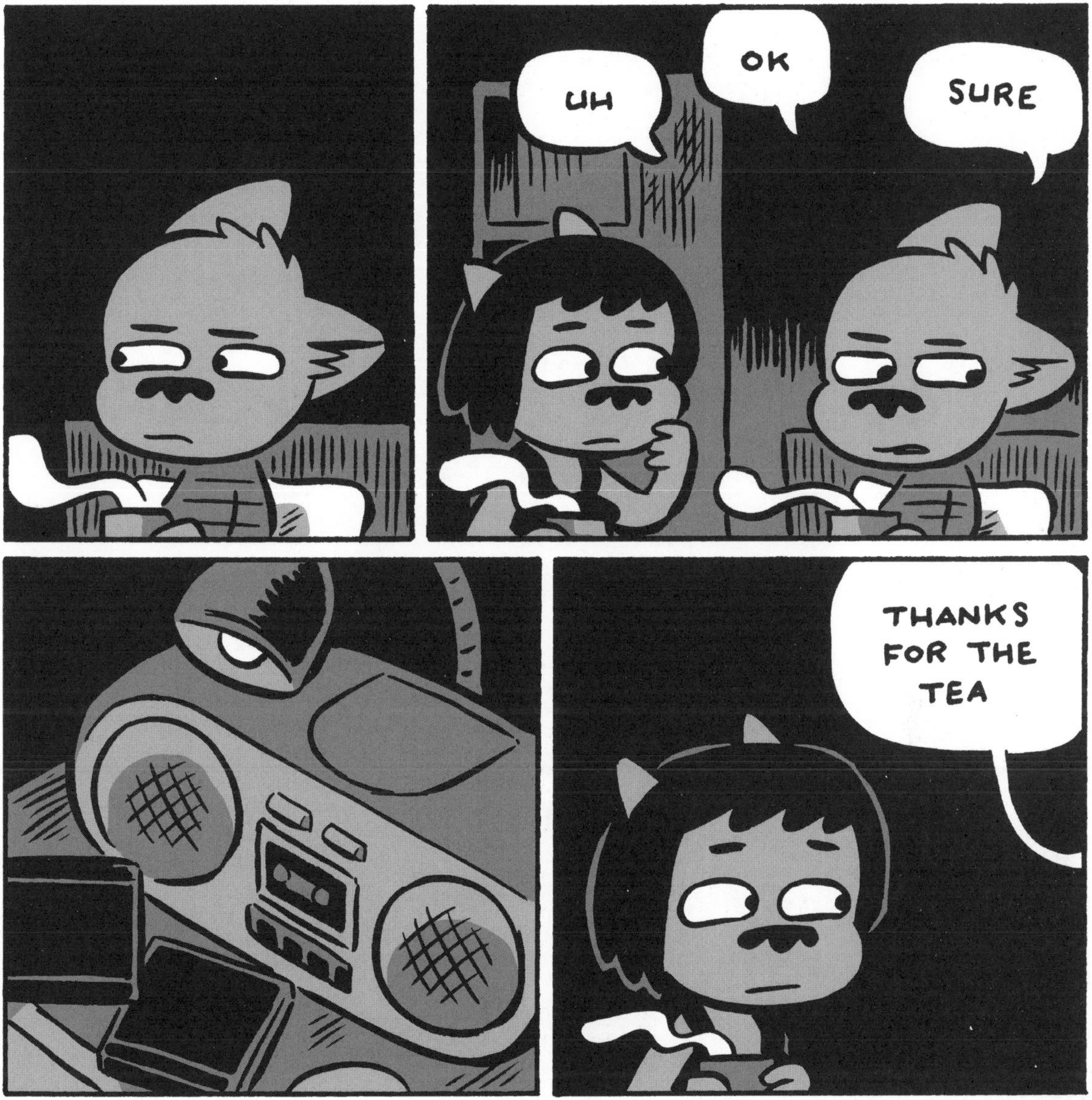
UH
OK
SURE
THANKS FOR THE TEA

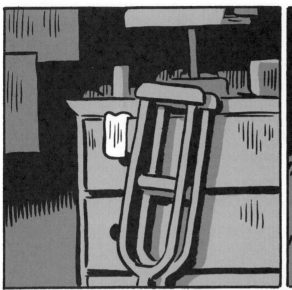

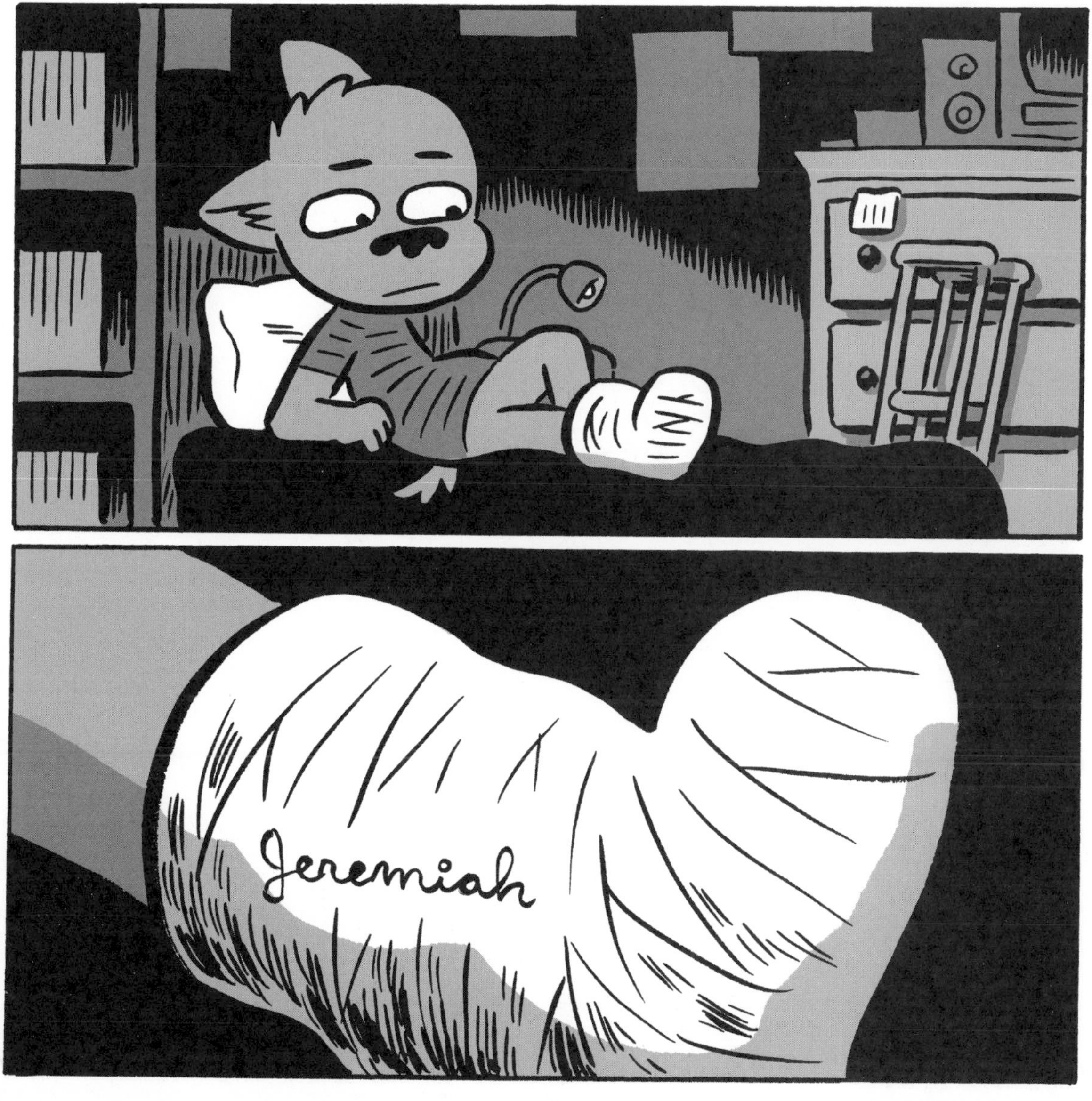
Jeremiah

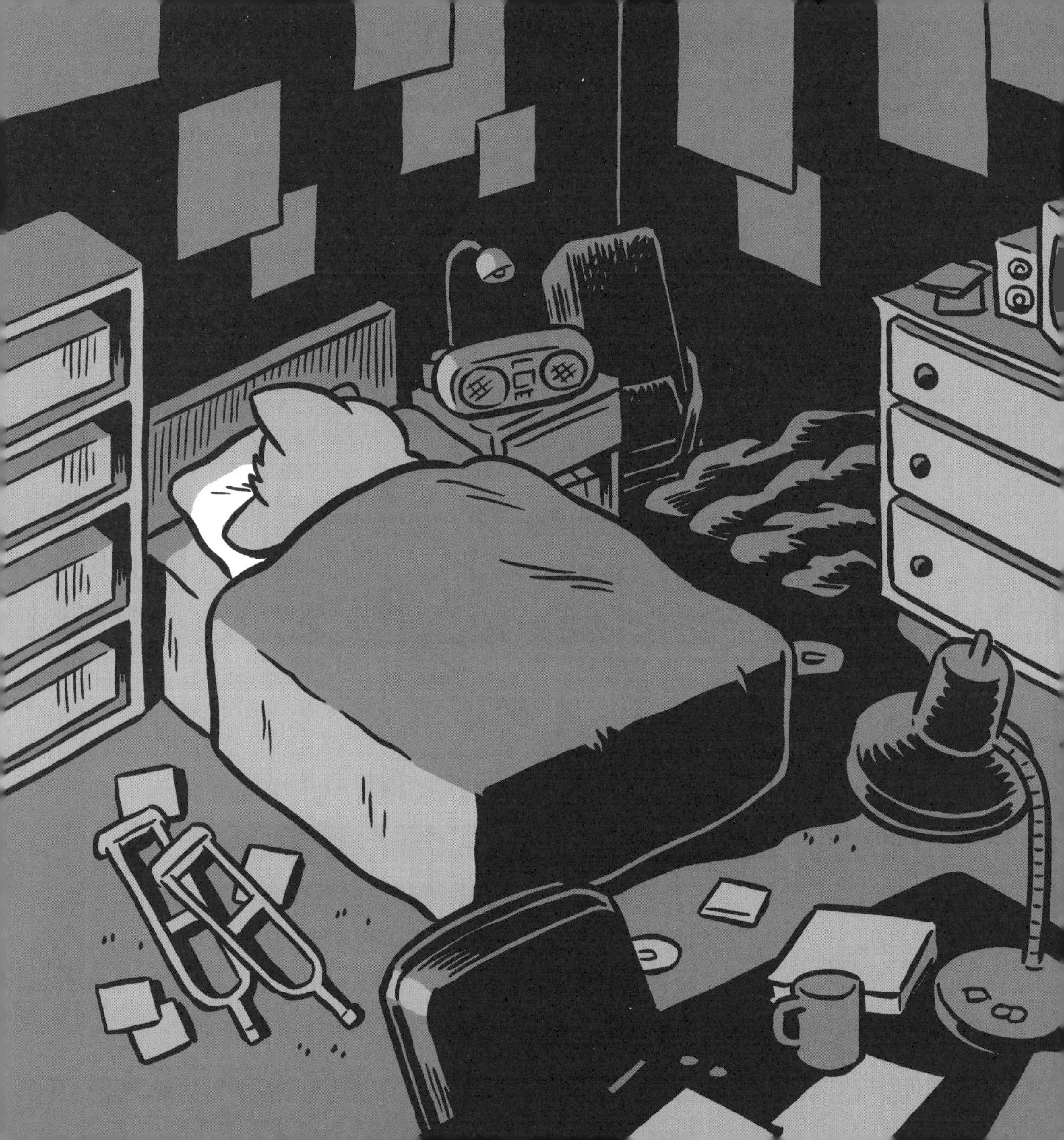

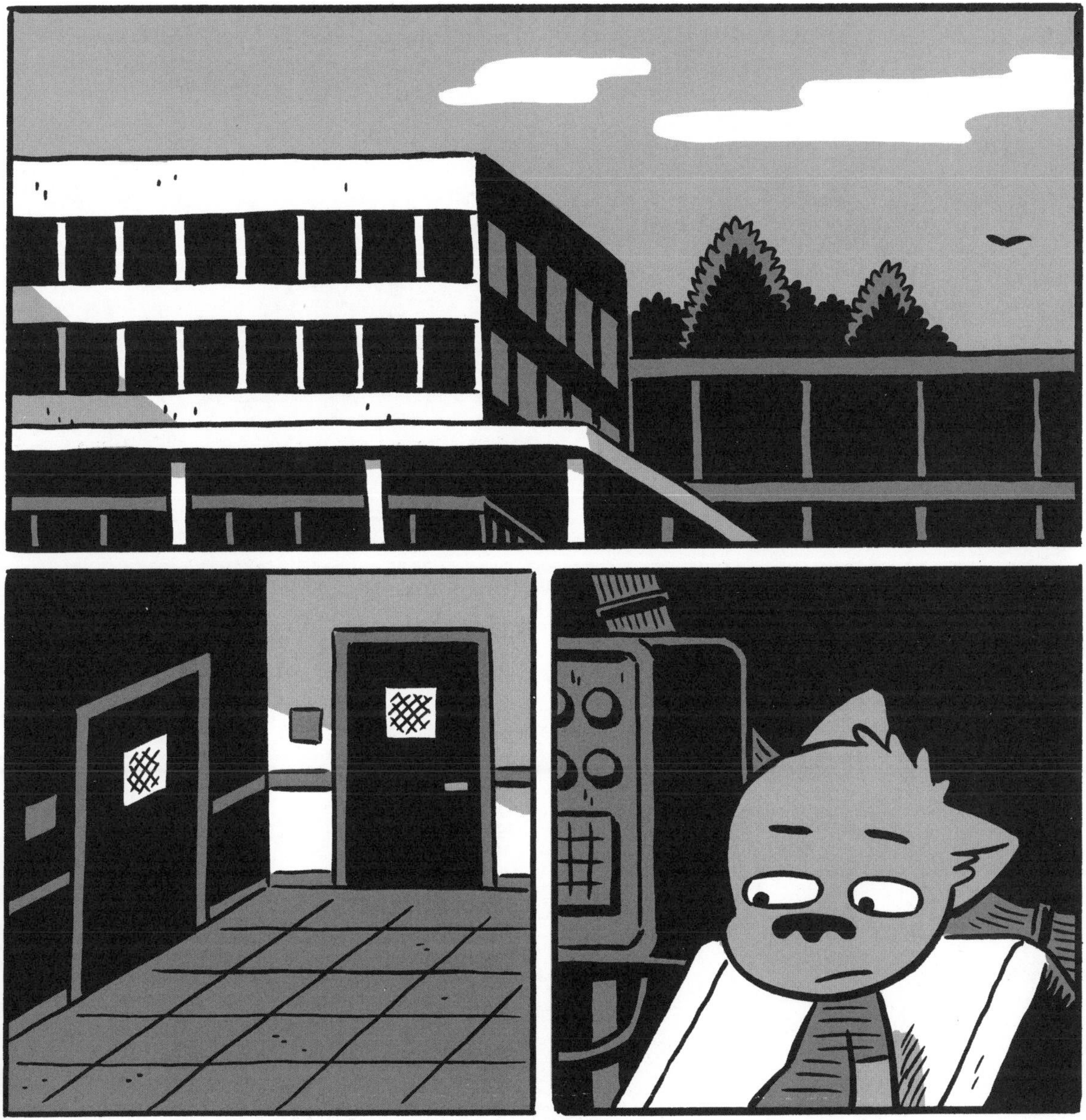

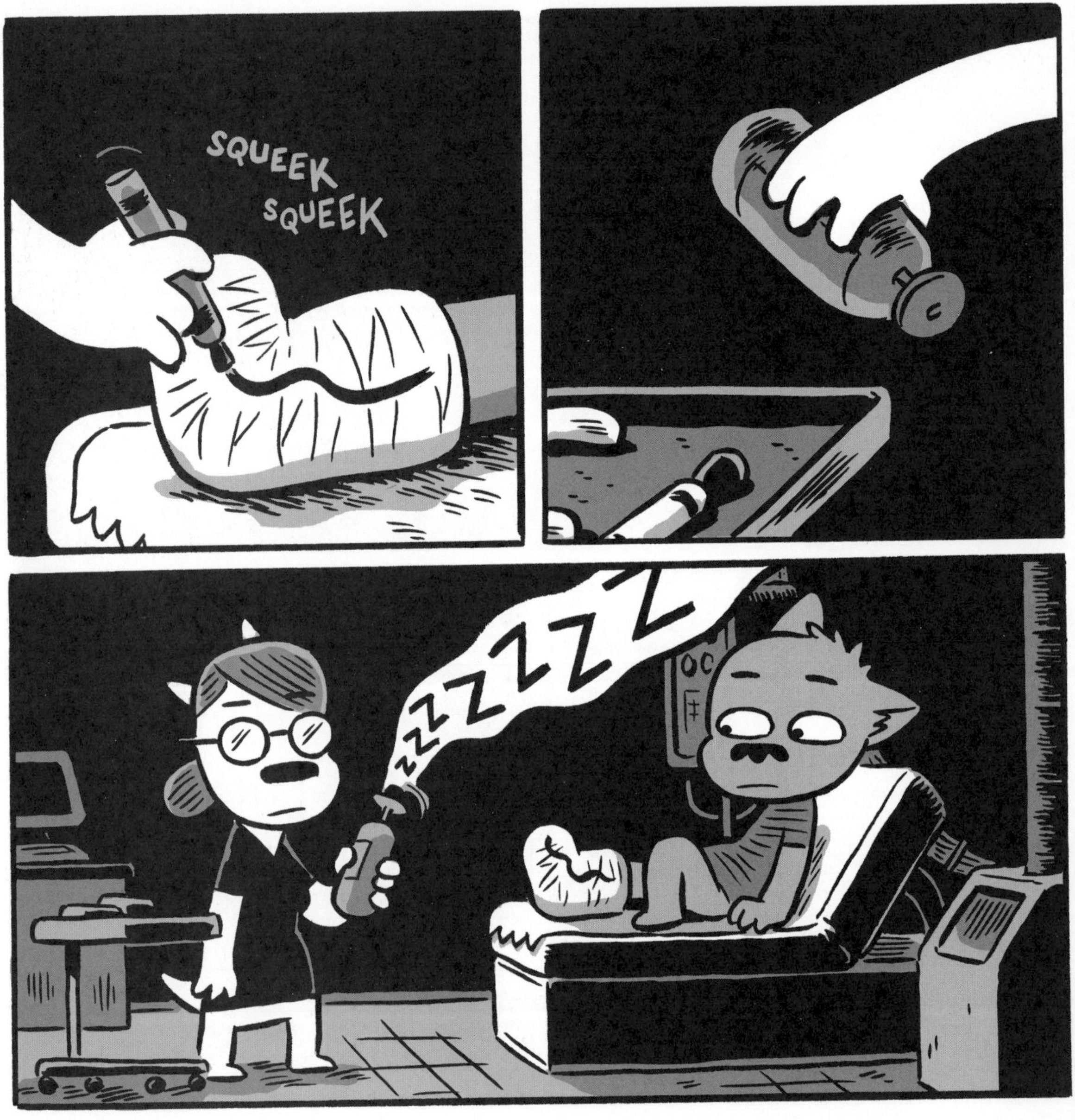
SQUEEK
SQUEEK
ZZZZZZZZZZ

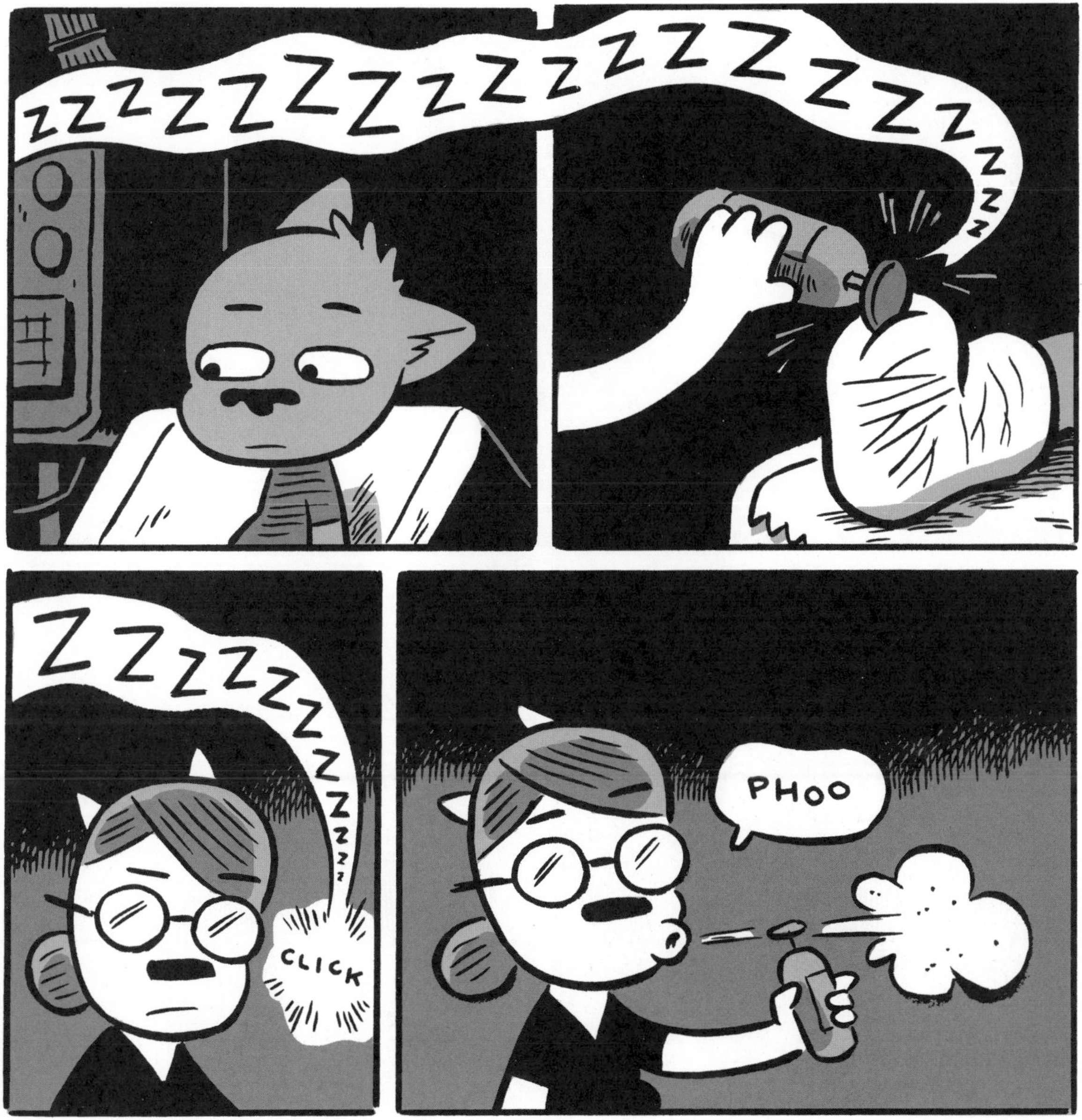
ZZZZZZZZZZZZZZZZZZZZZZ
ZZZZZZZZZZZ
CLICK
PHOO

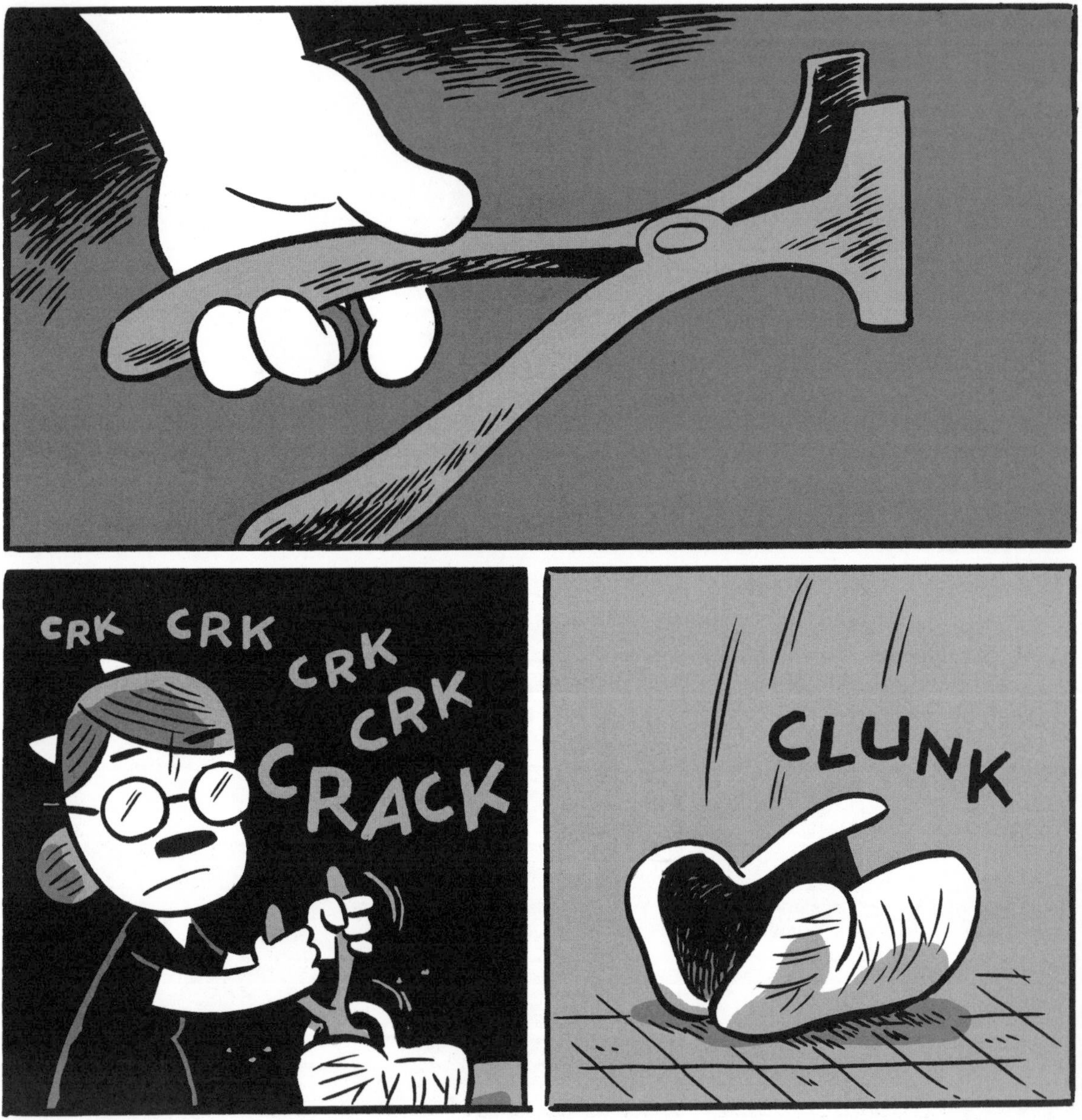
CRK CRK
CRK
CRK
CRACK
CLUNK

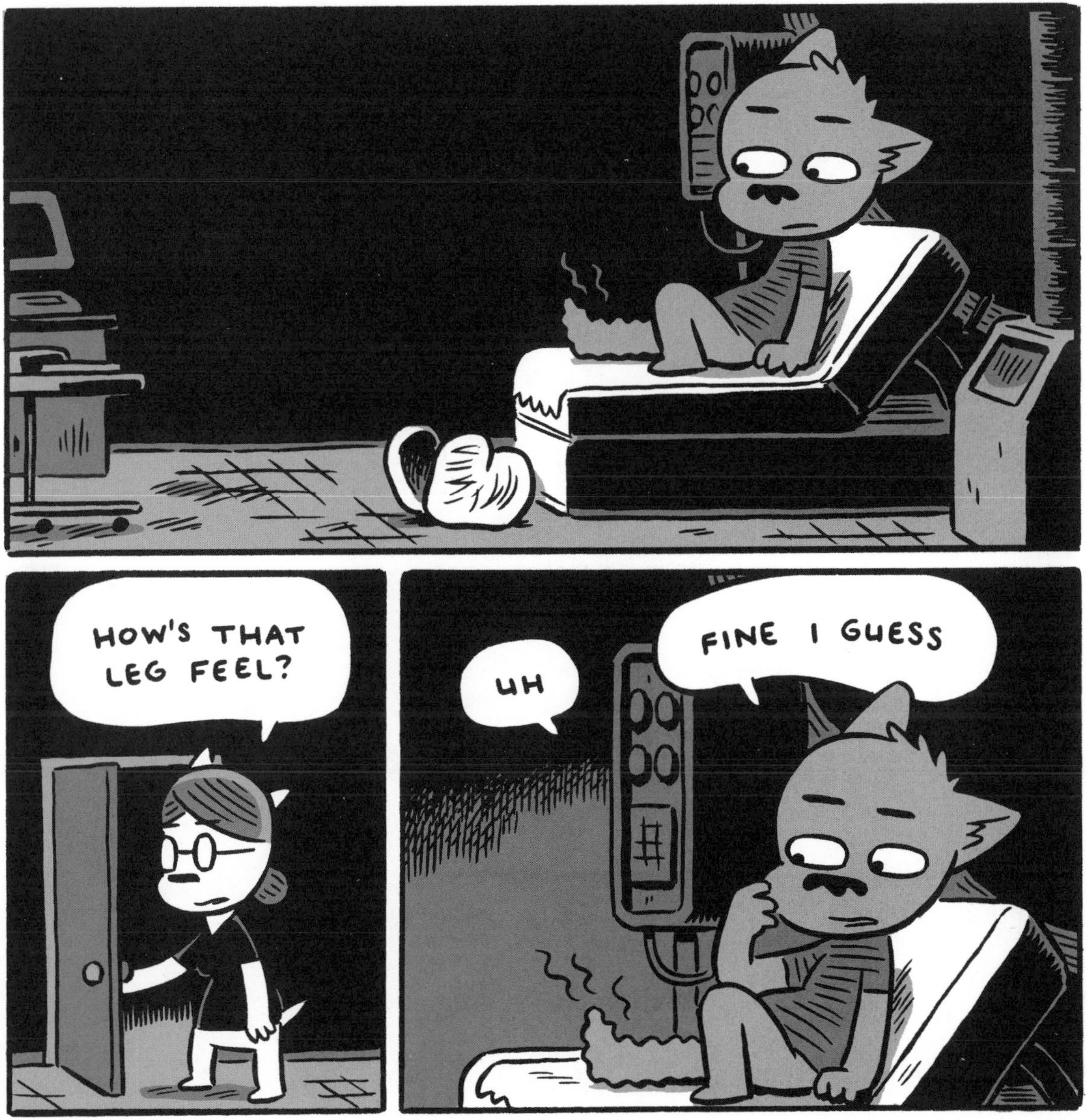
HOW'S THAT LEG FEEL?
UH
FINE I GUESS

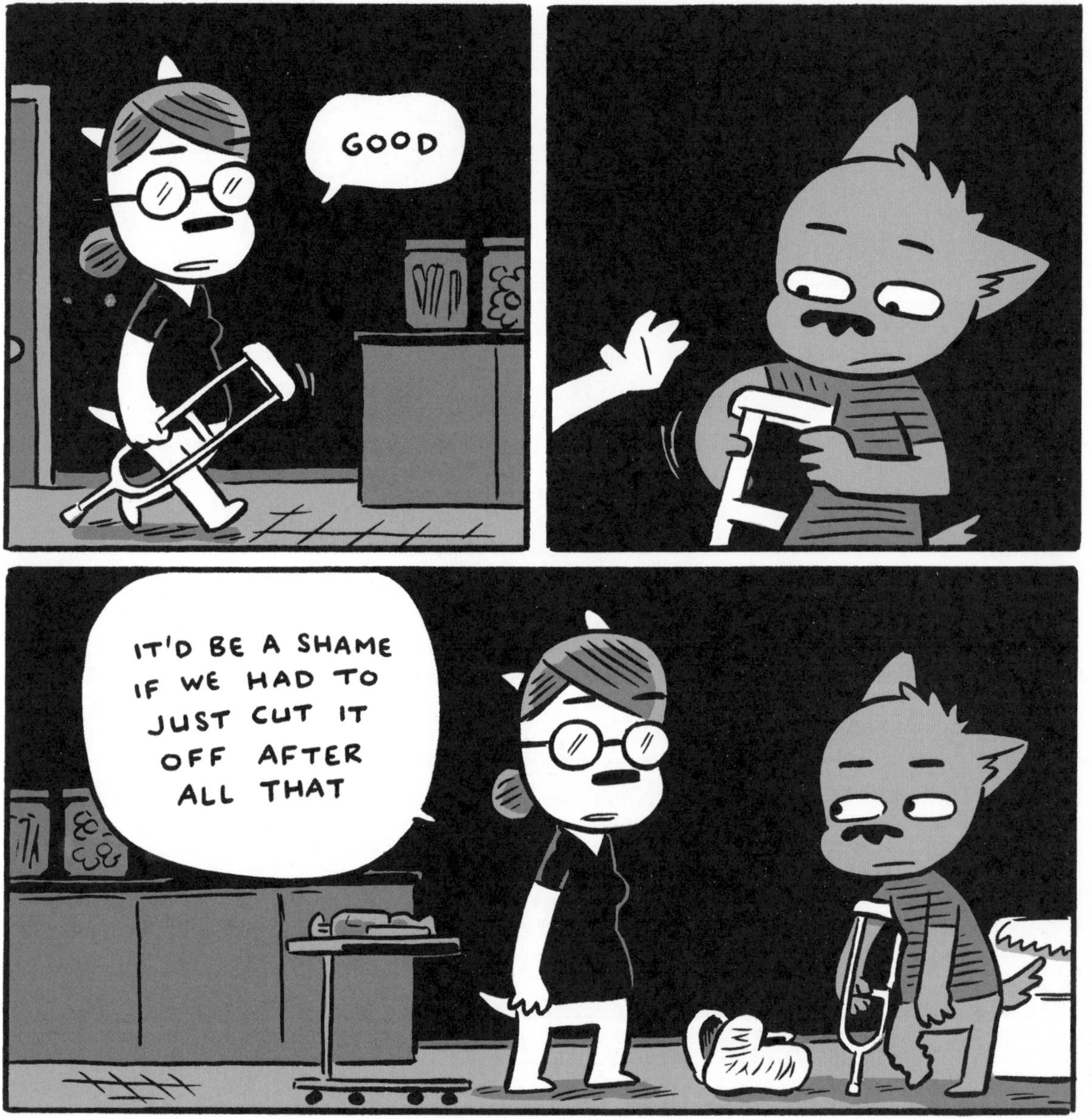
GOOD
IT'D BE A SHAME IF WE HAD TO JUST CUT IT OFF AFTER ALL THAT

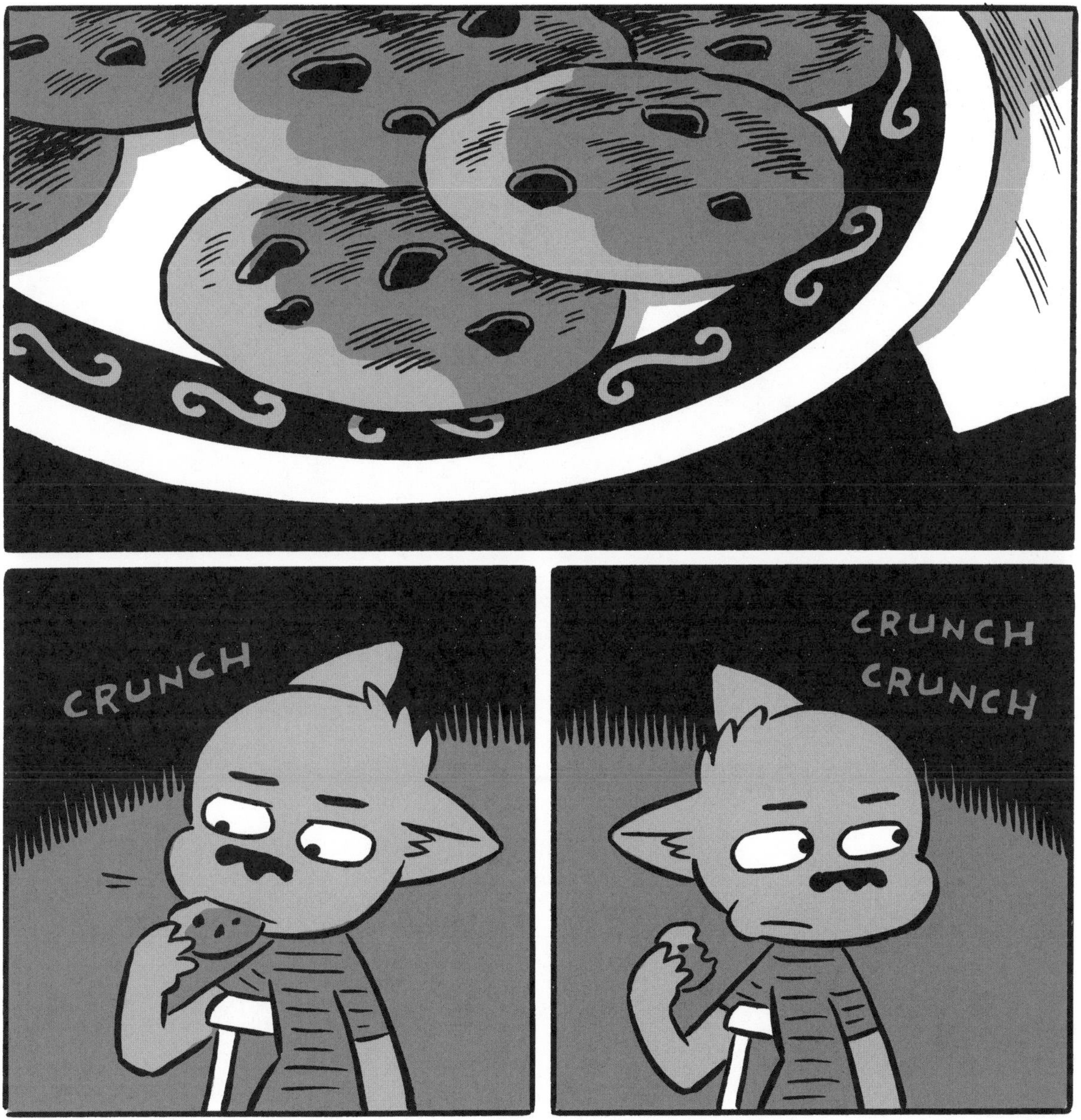
CRUNCH
CRUNCH
CRUNCH

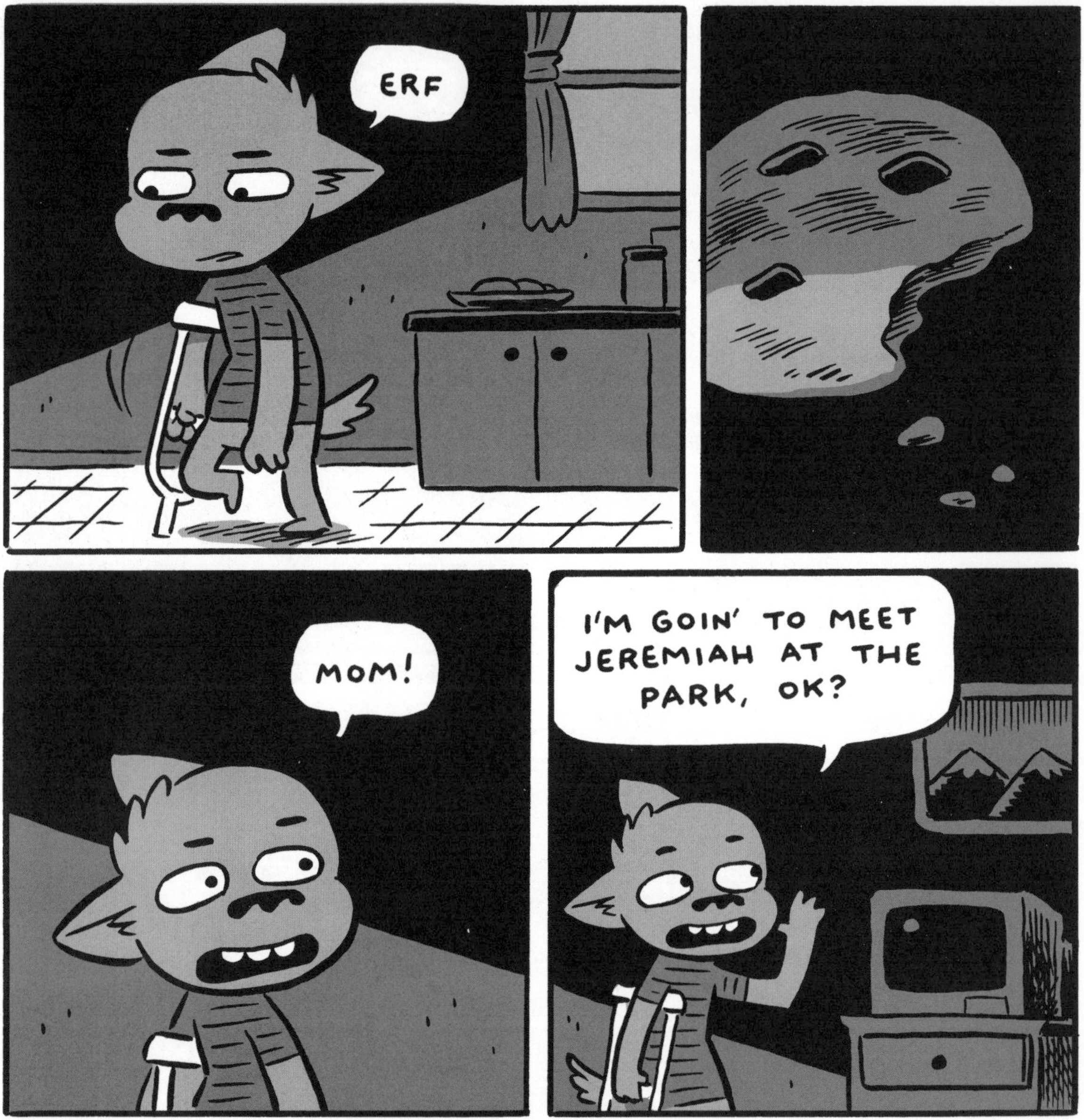

ERF
MOM!
I'M GOIN' TO MEET JEREMIAH AT THE PARK, OK?

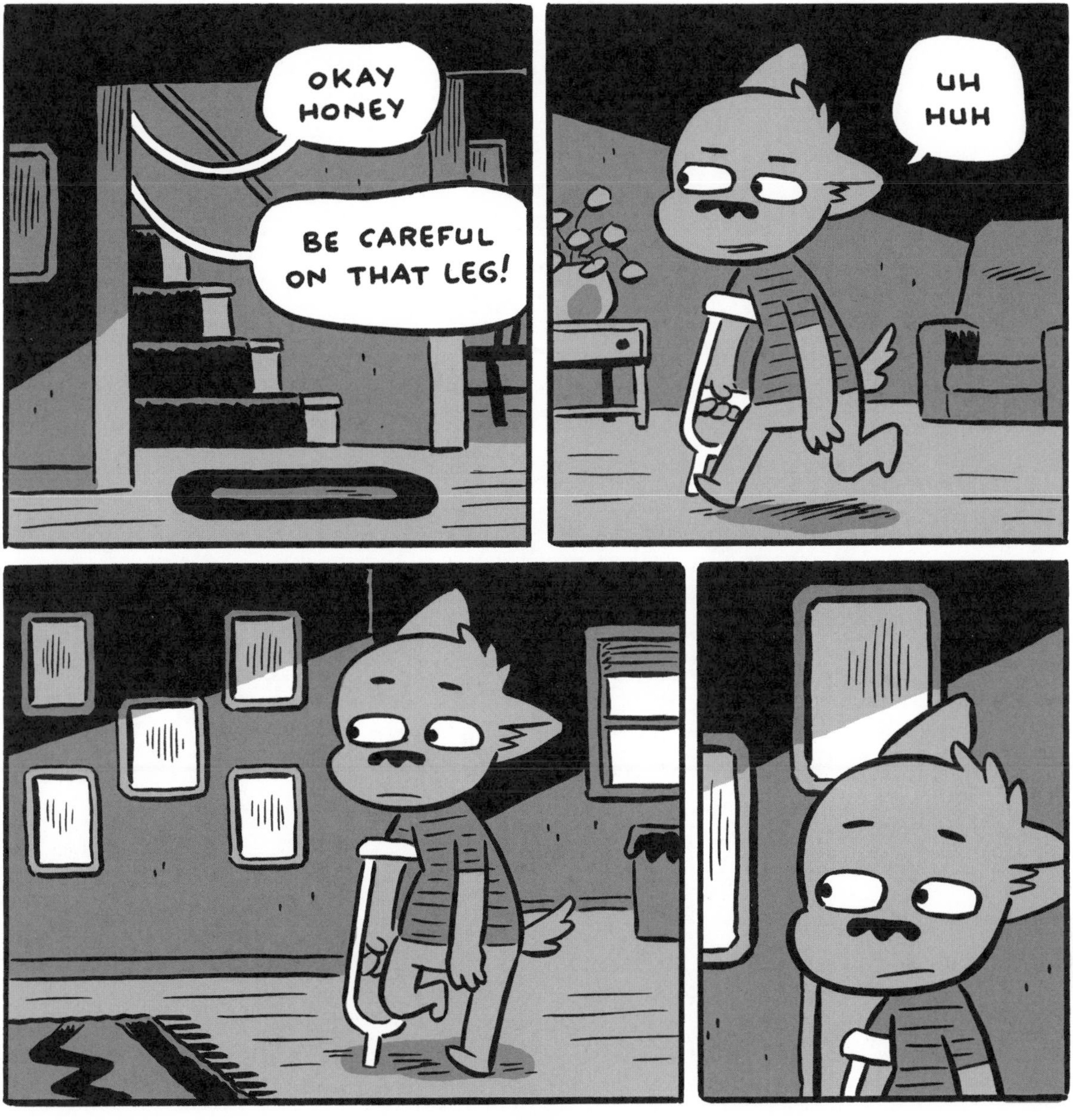
OKAY HONEY
BE CAREFUL ON THAT LEG!
UH HUH

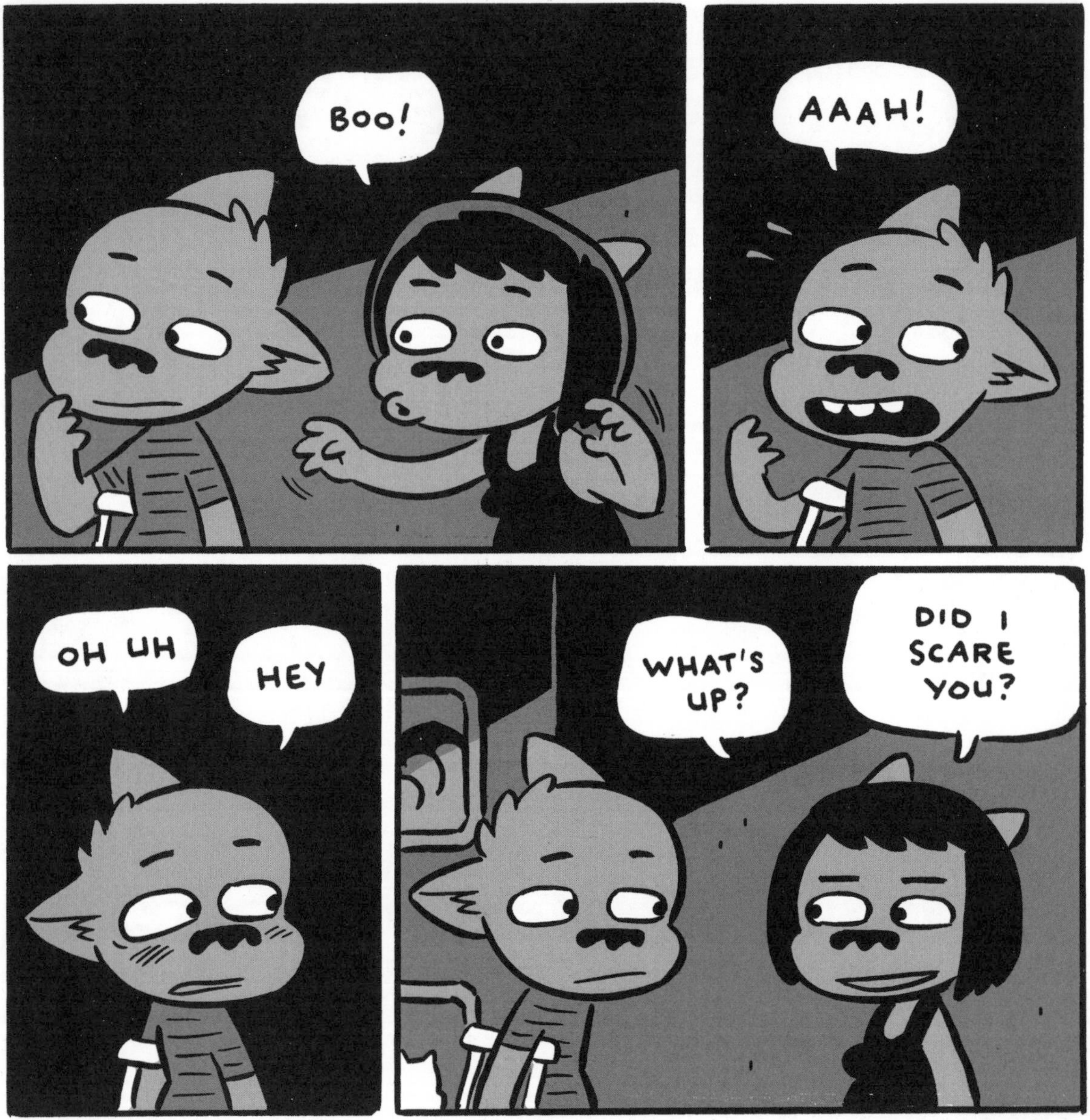
BOO!
AAAH!
OH UH
HEY
WHAT'S UP?
DID I SCARE YOU?

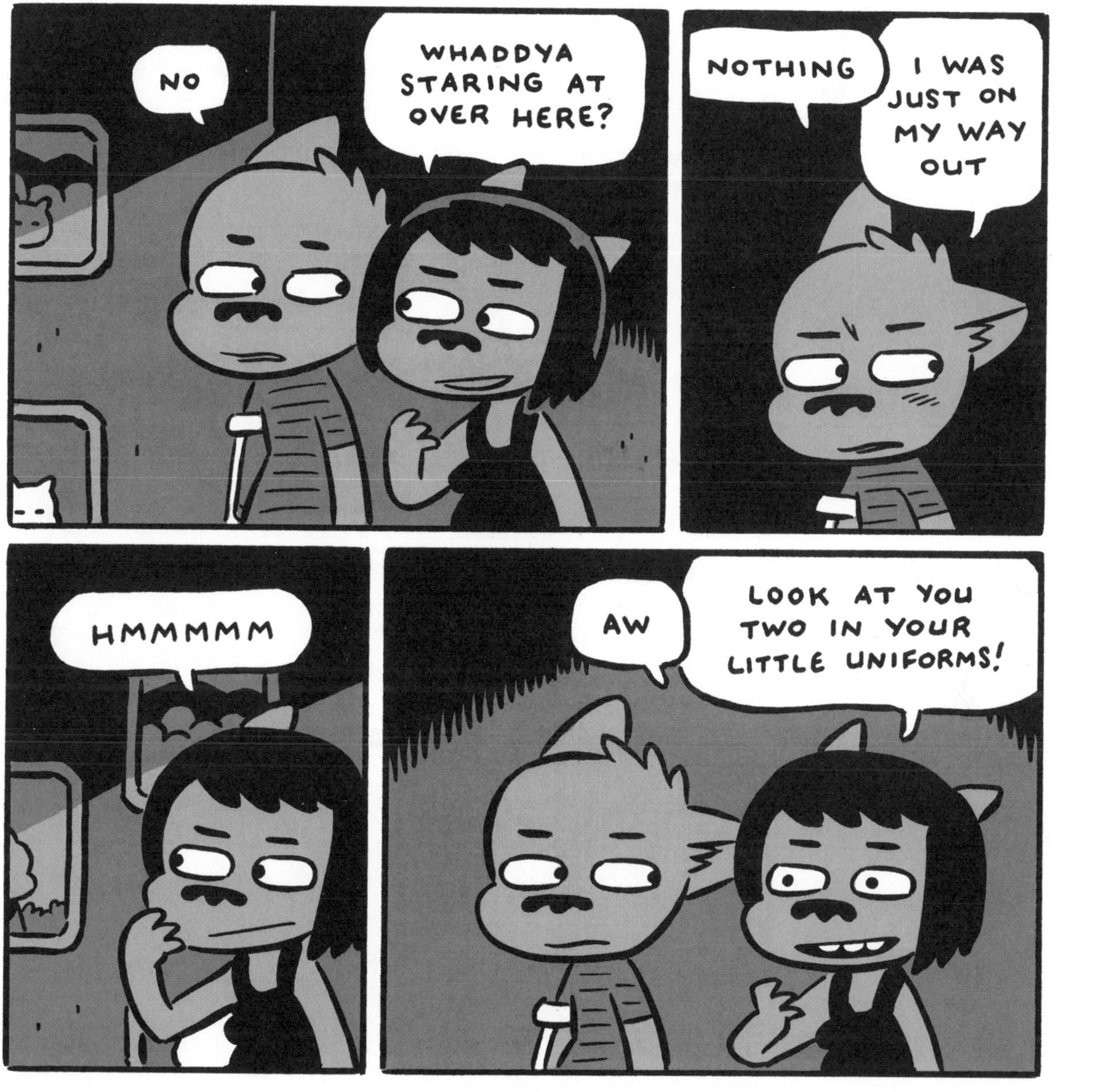
NO
WHADDYA STARING AT OVER HERE?
NOTHING
I WAS JUST ON MY WAY OUT
HMMMMM
AW
LOOK AT YOU TWO IN YOUR LITTLE UNIFORMS!

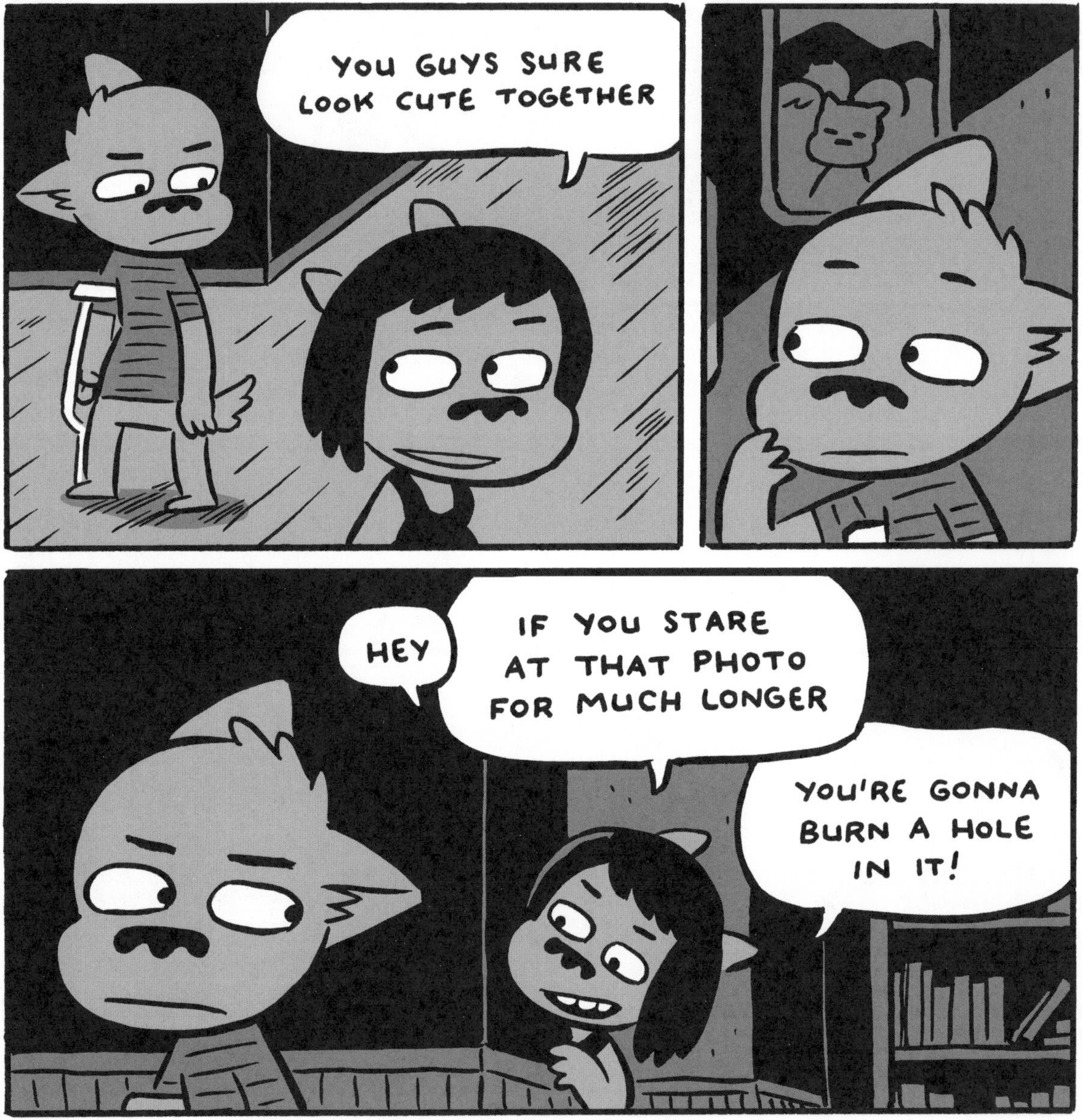
YOU GUYS SURE LOOK CUTE TOGETHER
HEY
IF YOU STARE AT THAT PHOTO FOR MUCH LONGER
YOU'RE GONNA BURN A HOLE IN IT!

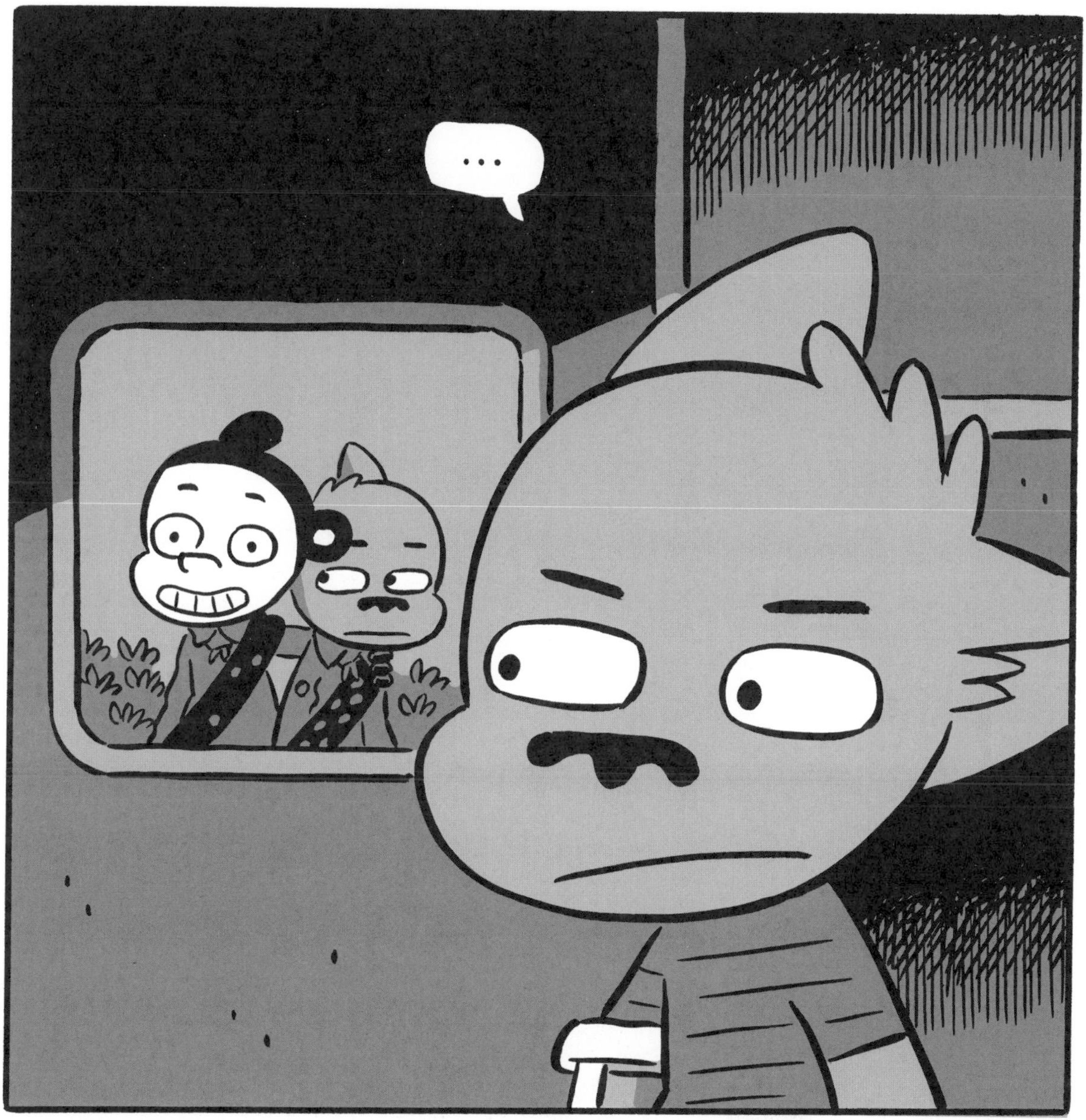
...

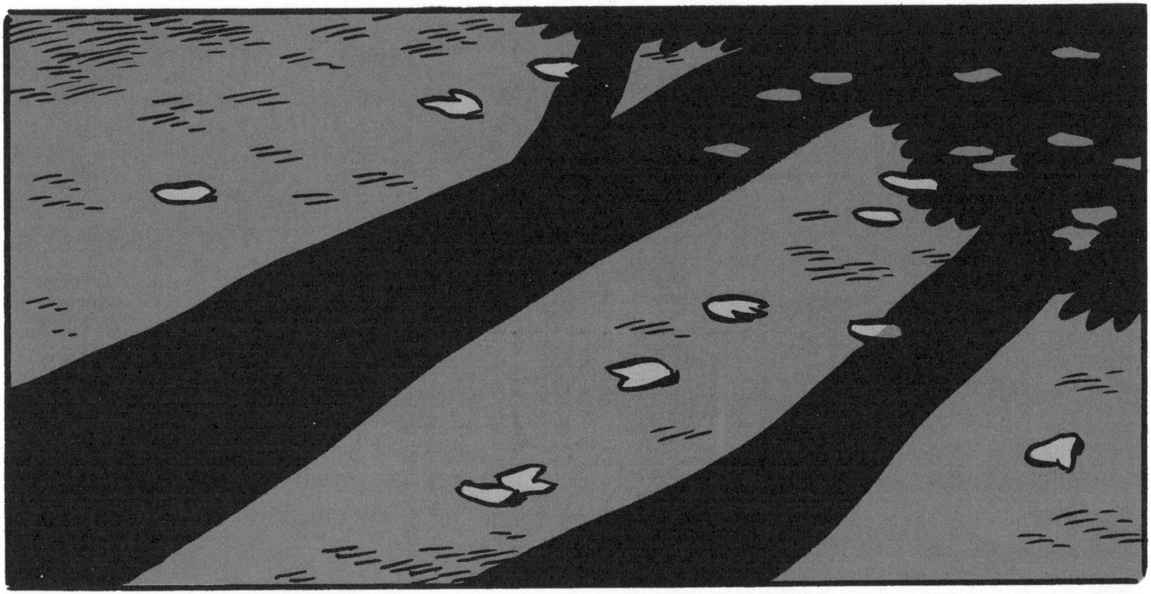

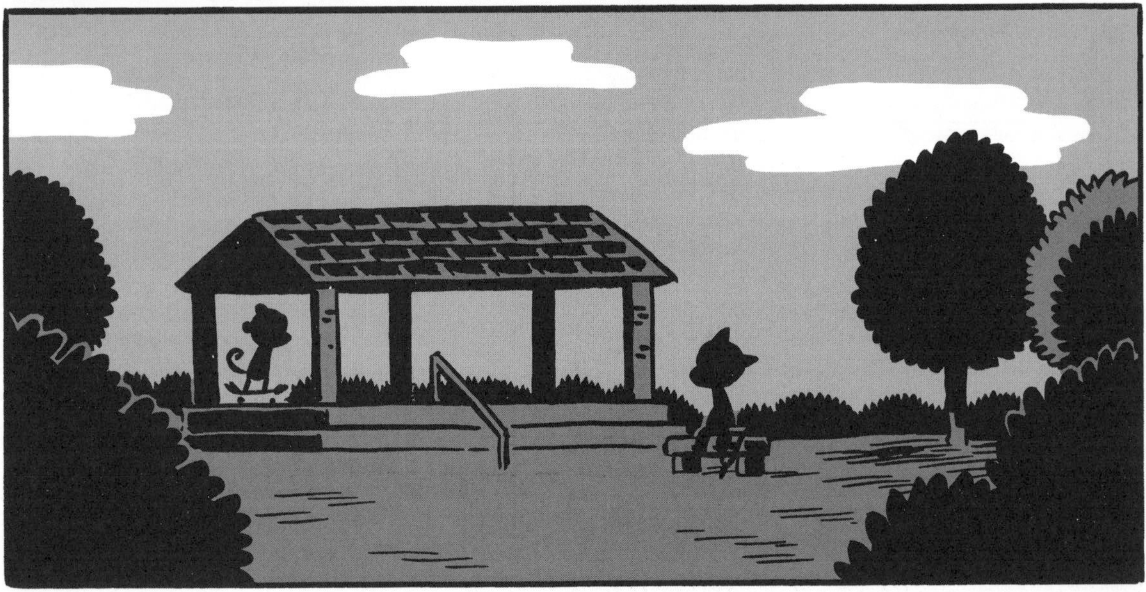

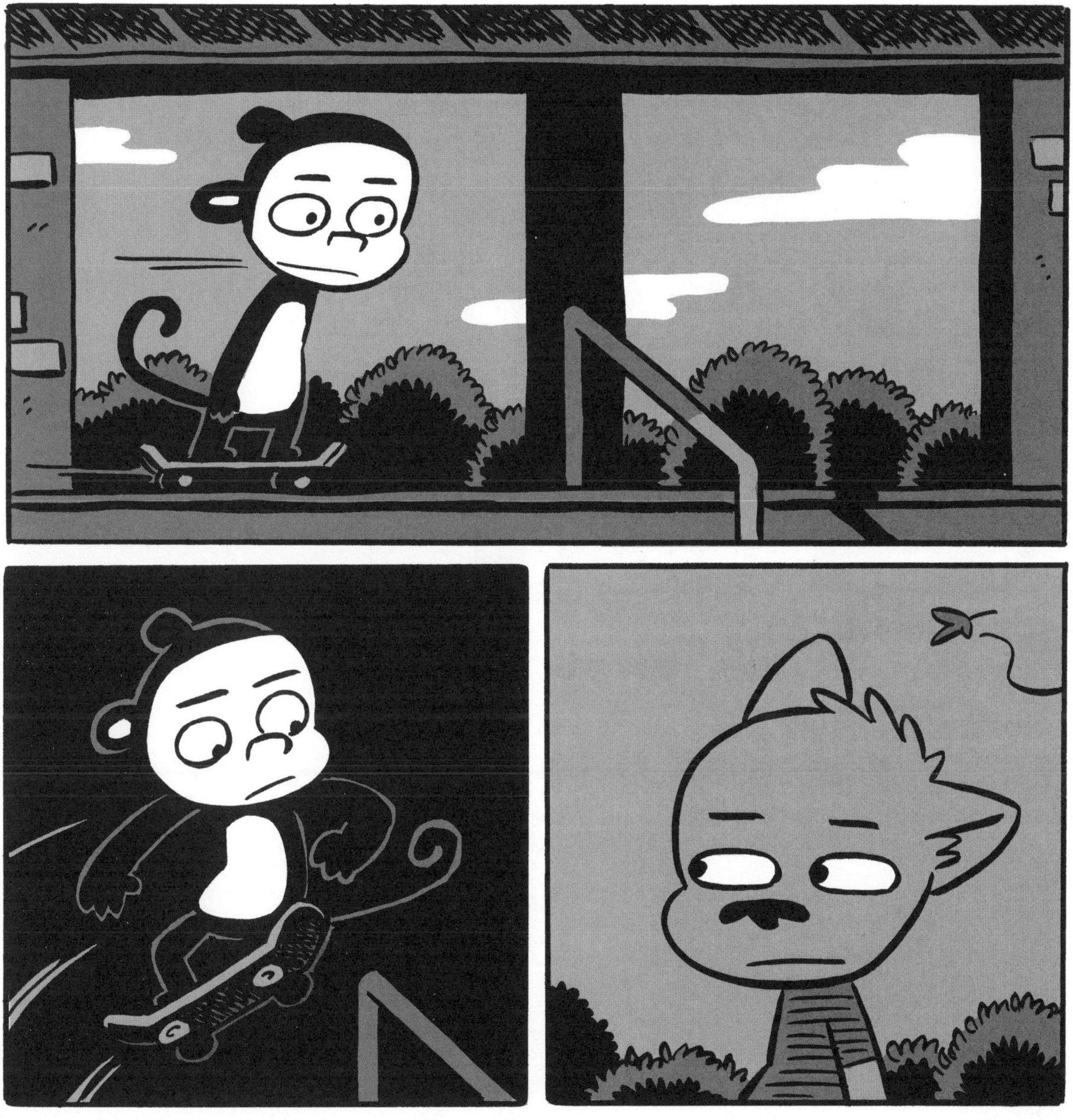

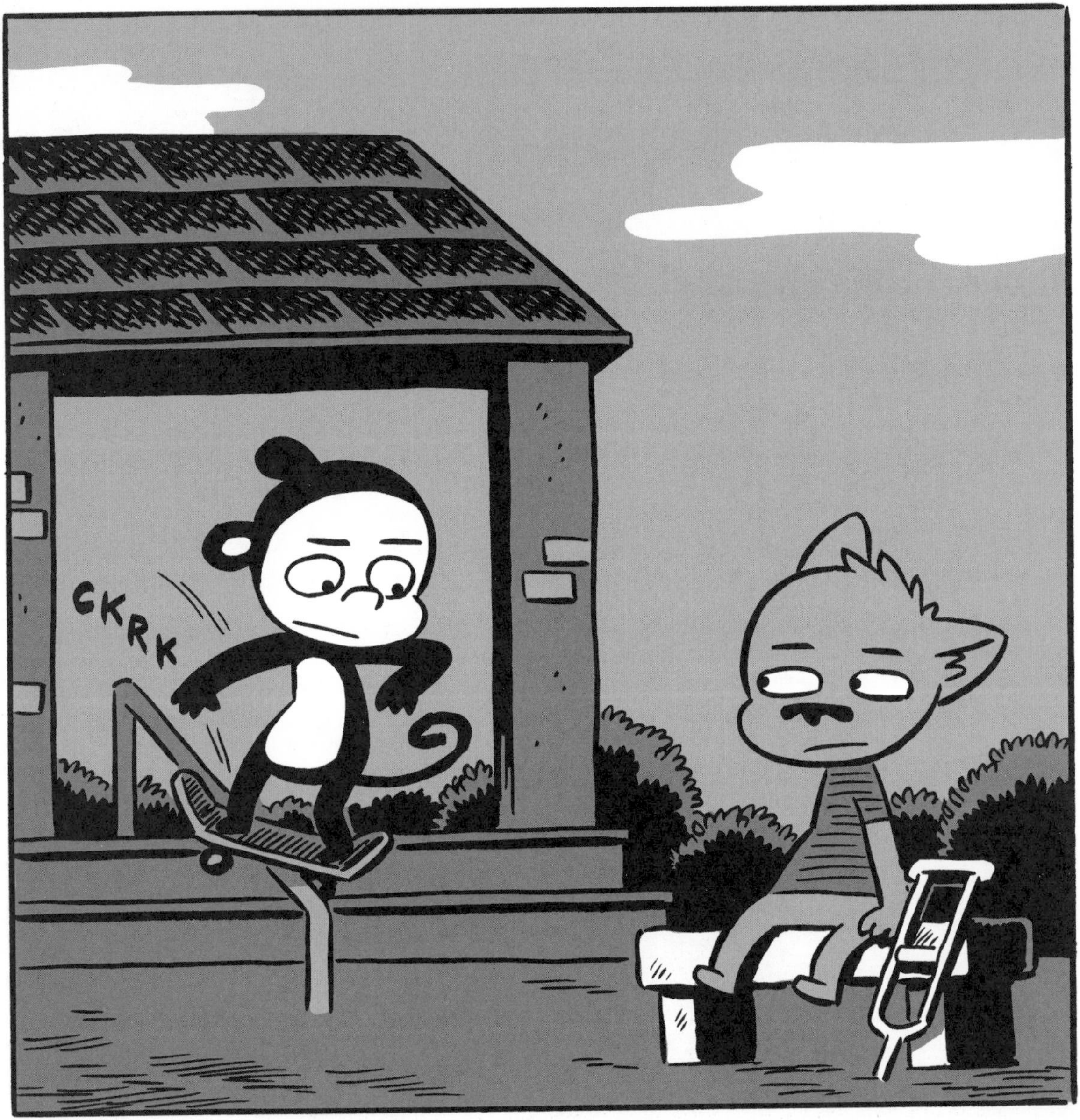
CKRK

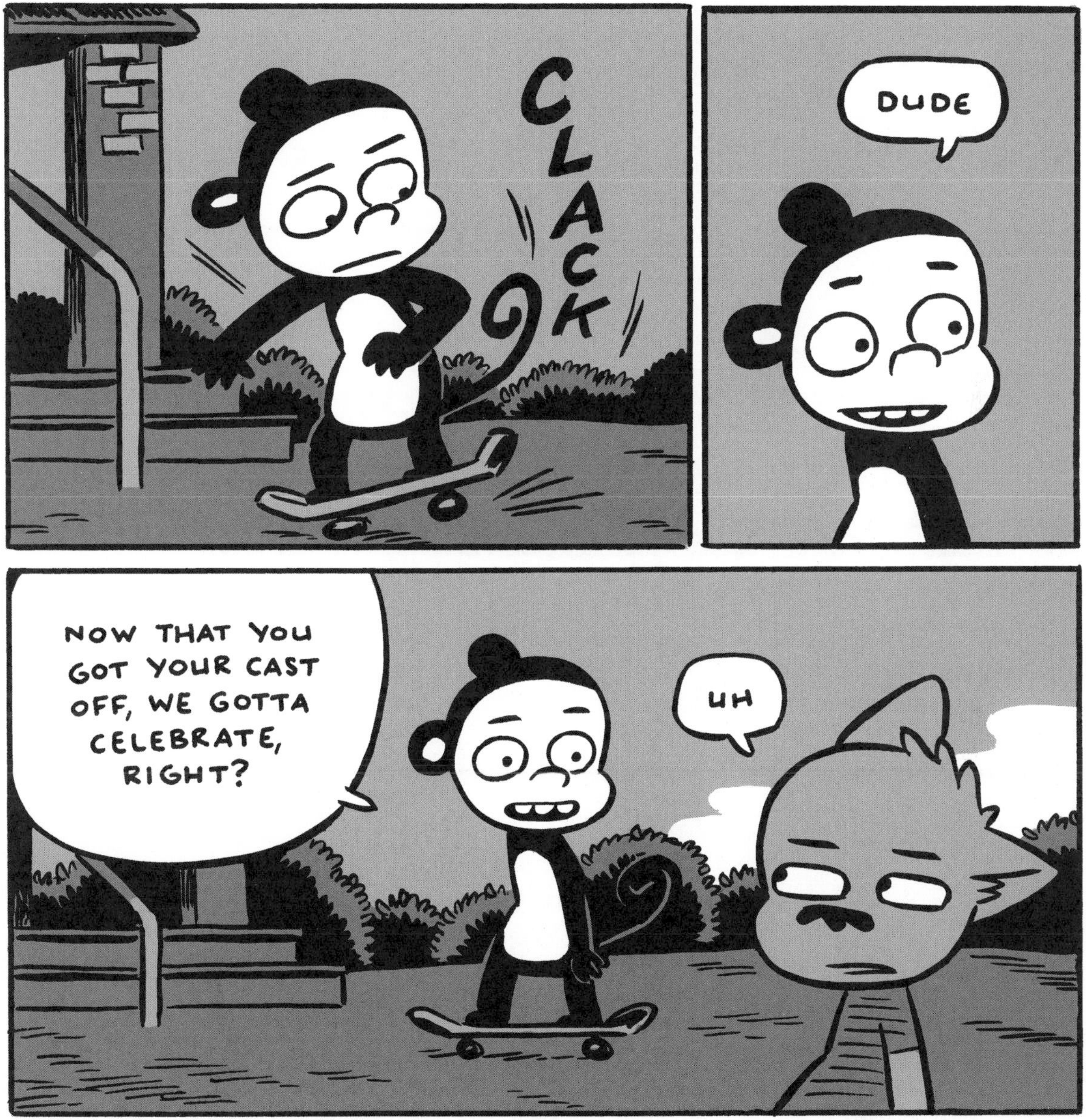
CLACK
DUDE
NOW THAT YOU GOT YOUR CAST OFF, WE GOTTA CELEBRATE, RIGHT?
UH

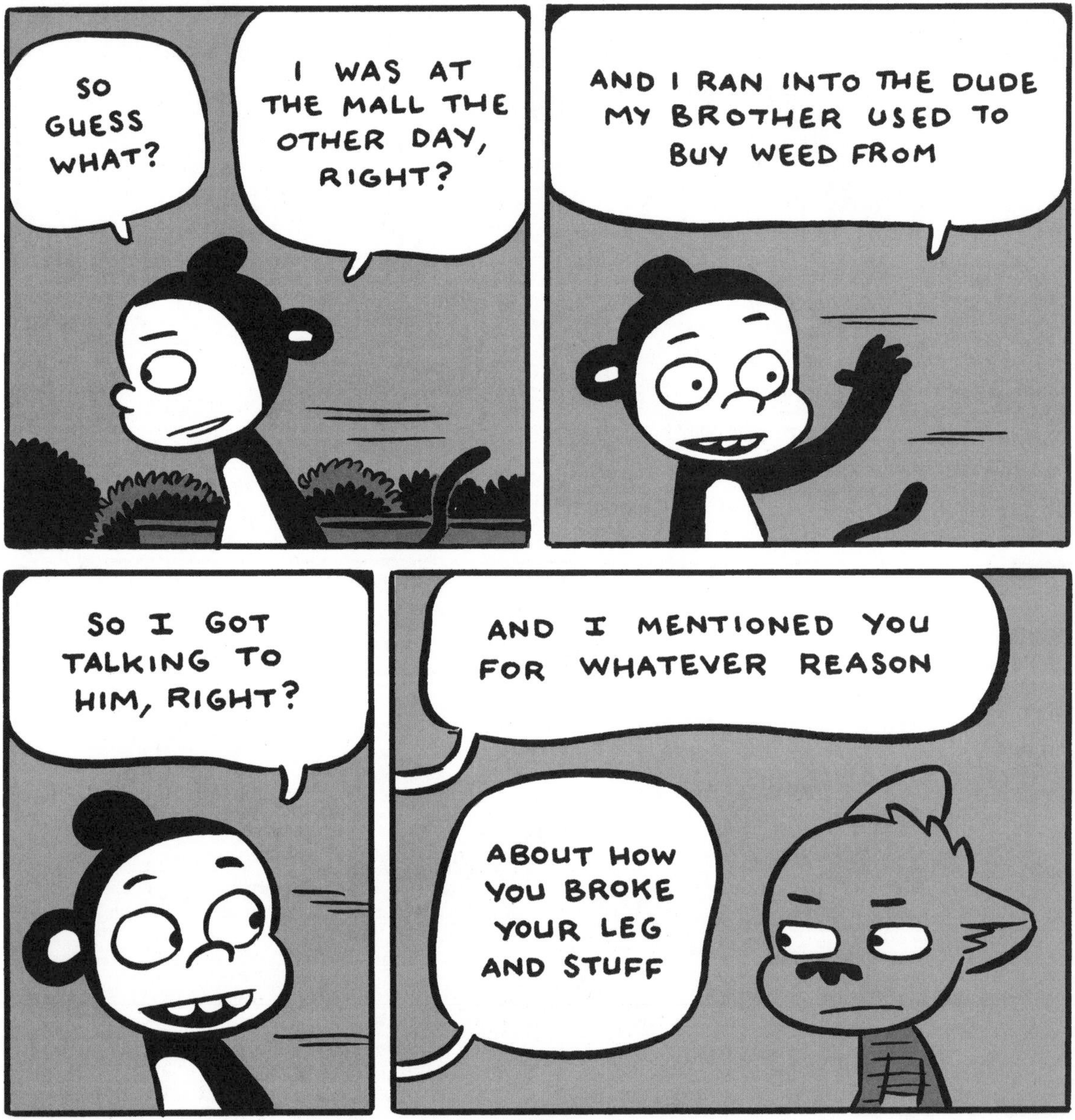
SO GUESS WHAT?
I WAS AT THE MALL THE OTHER DAY, RIGHT?
AND I RAN INTO THE DUDE MY BROTHER USED TO BUY WEED FROM
SO I GOT TALKING TO HIM, RIGHT?
AND I MENTIONED YOU FOR WHATEVER REASON
ABOUT HOW YOU BROKE YOUR LEG AND STUFF

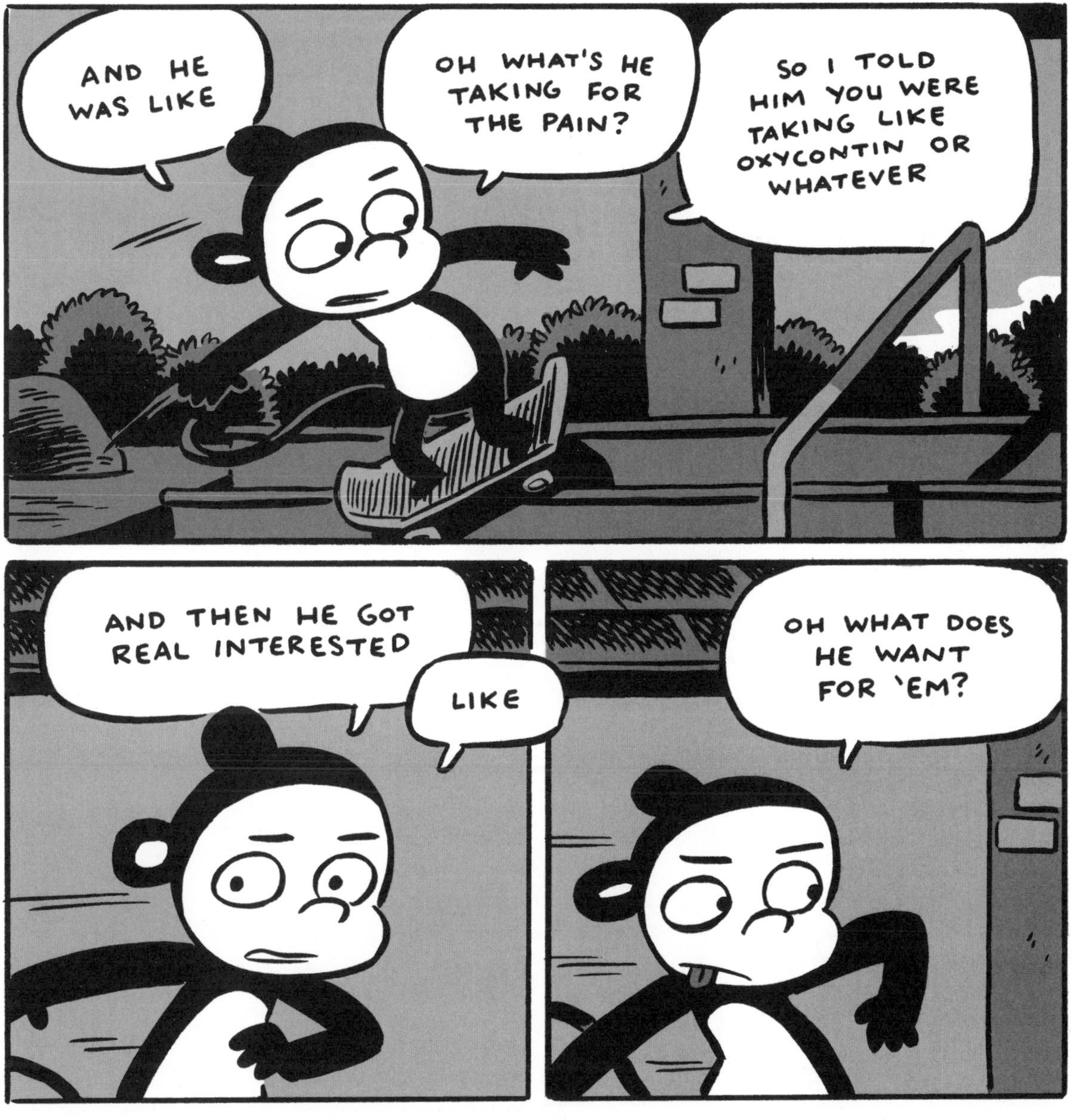
AND HE WAS LIKE
OH WHAT'S HE TAKING FOR THE PAIN?
SO I TOLD HIM YOU WERE TAKING LIKE OXYCONTIN OR WHATEVER
AND THEN HE GOT REAL INTERESTED
LIKE
OH WHAT DOES HE WANT FOR 'EM?

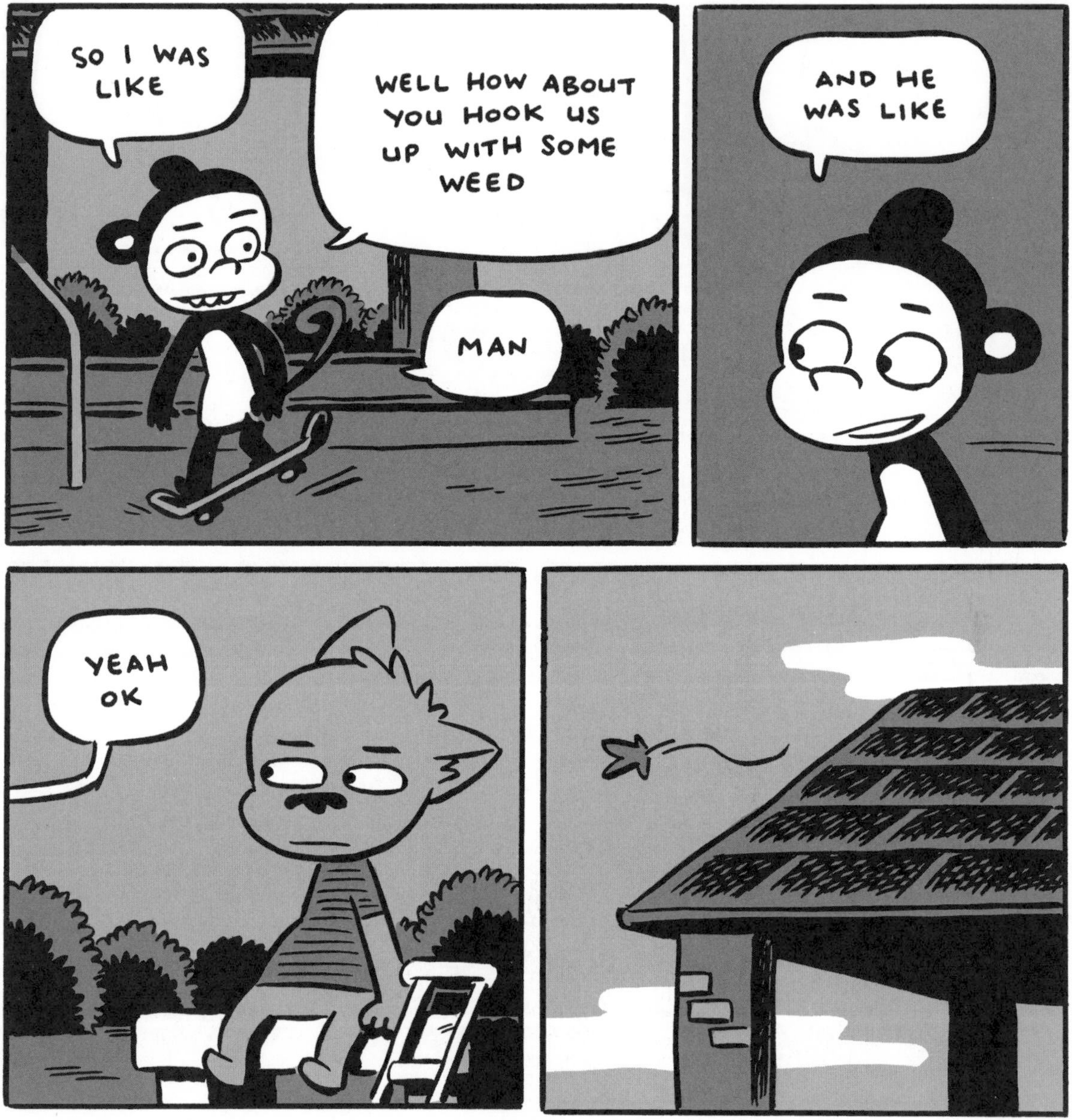
SO I WAS LIKE
WELL HOW ABOUT YOU HOOK US UP WITH SOME WEED
MAN
AND HE WAS LIKE
YEAH OK

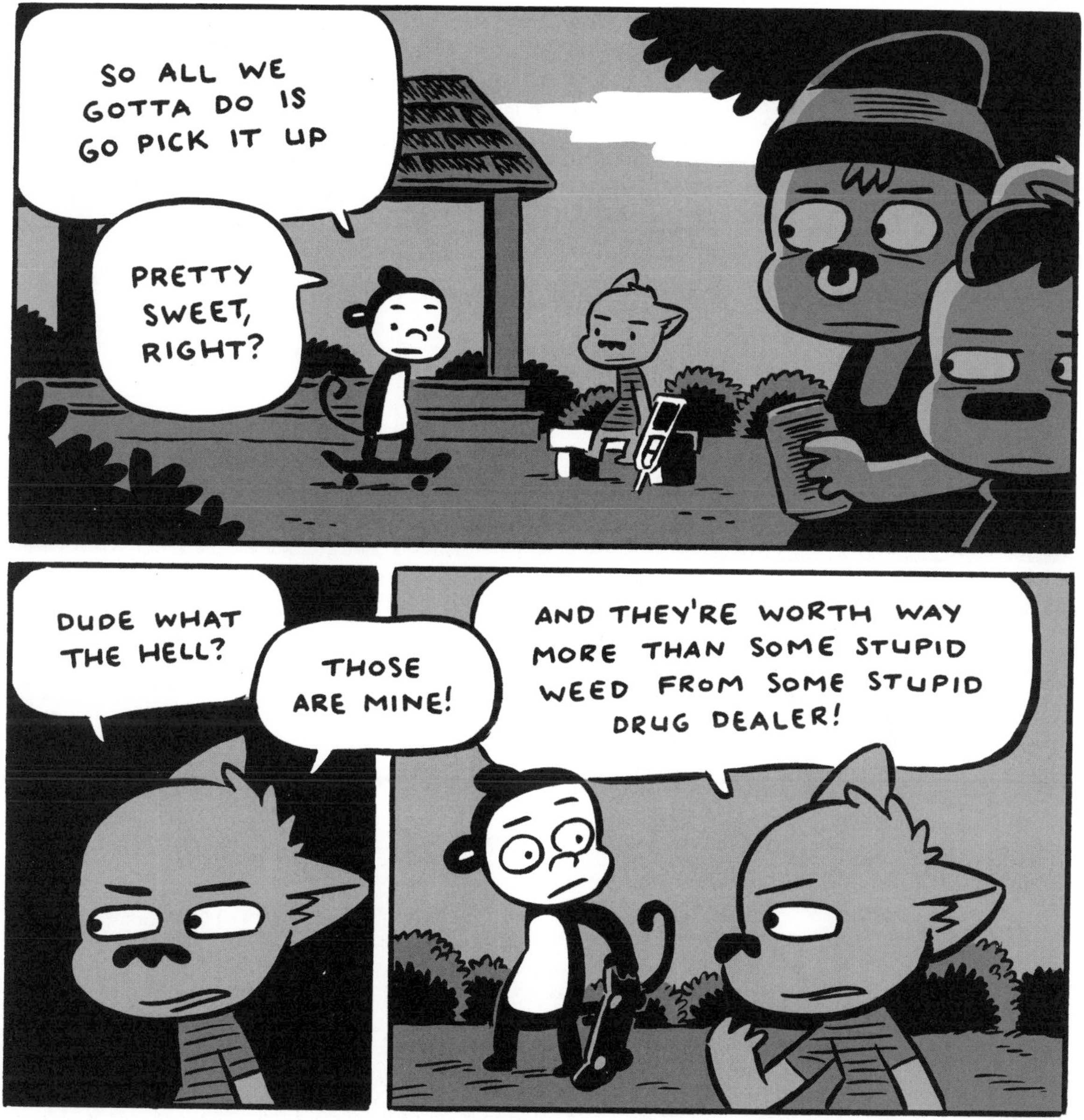

SO ALL WE GOTTA DO IS GO PICK IT UP
PRETTY SWEET, RIGHT?
DUDE WHAT THE HELL?
THOSE ARE MINE!
AND THEY'RE WORTH WAY MORE THAN SOME STUPID WEED FROM SOME STUPID DRUG DEALER!

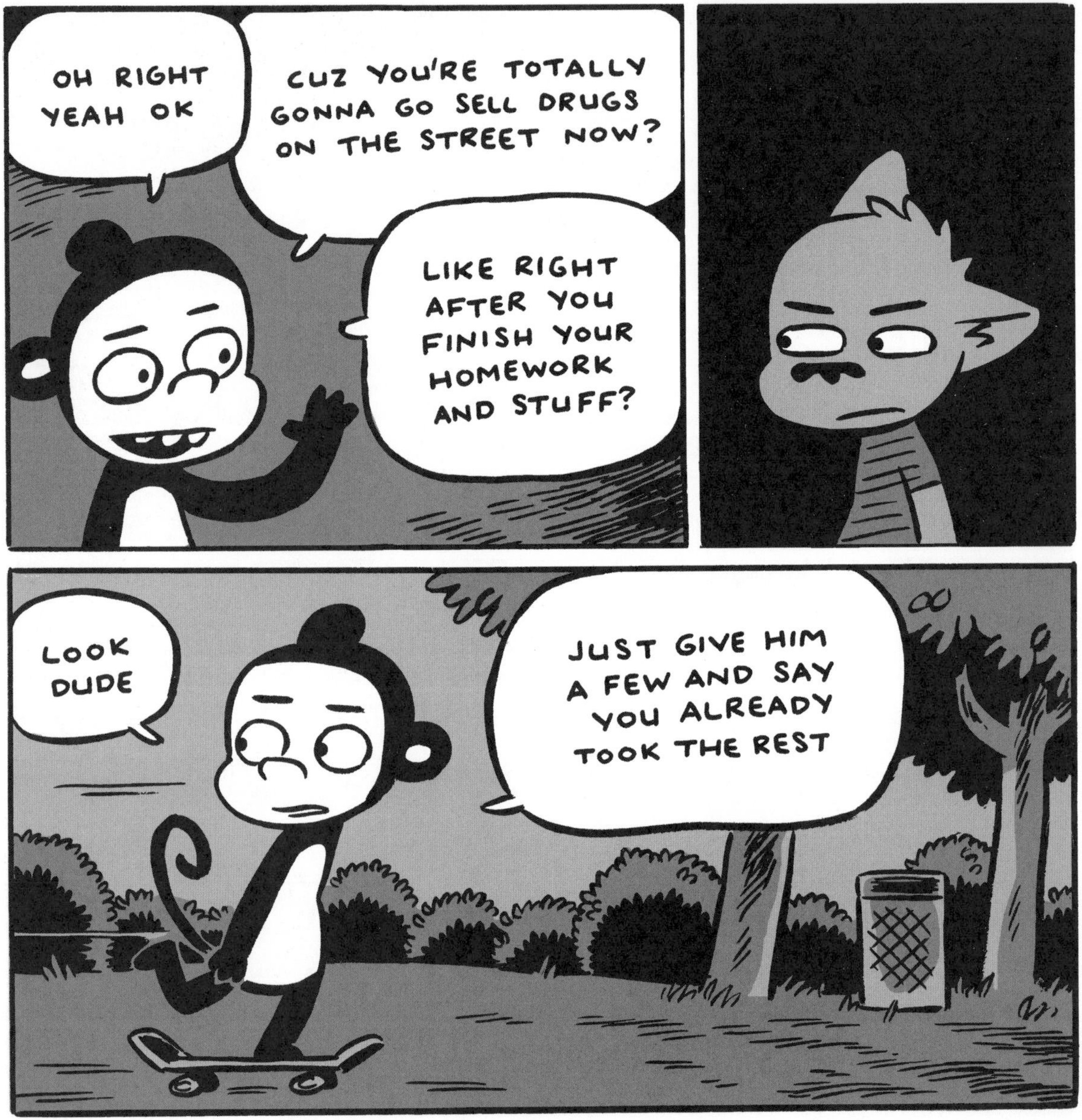
OH RIGHT YEAH OK
CUZ YOU'RE TOTALLY GONNA GO SELL DRUGS ON THE STREET NOW?
LIKE RIGHT AFTER YOU FINISH YOUR HOMEWORK AND STUFF?
LOOK DUDE
JUST GIVE HIM A FEW AND SAY YOU ALREADY TOOK THE REST

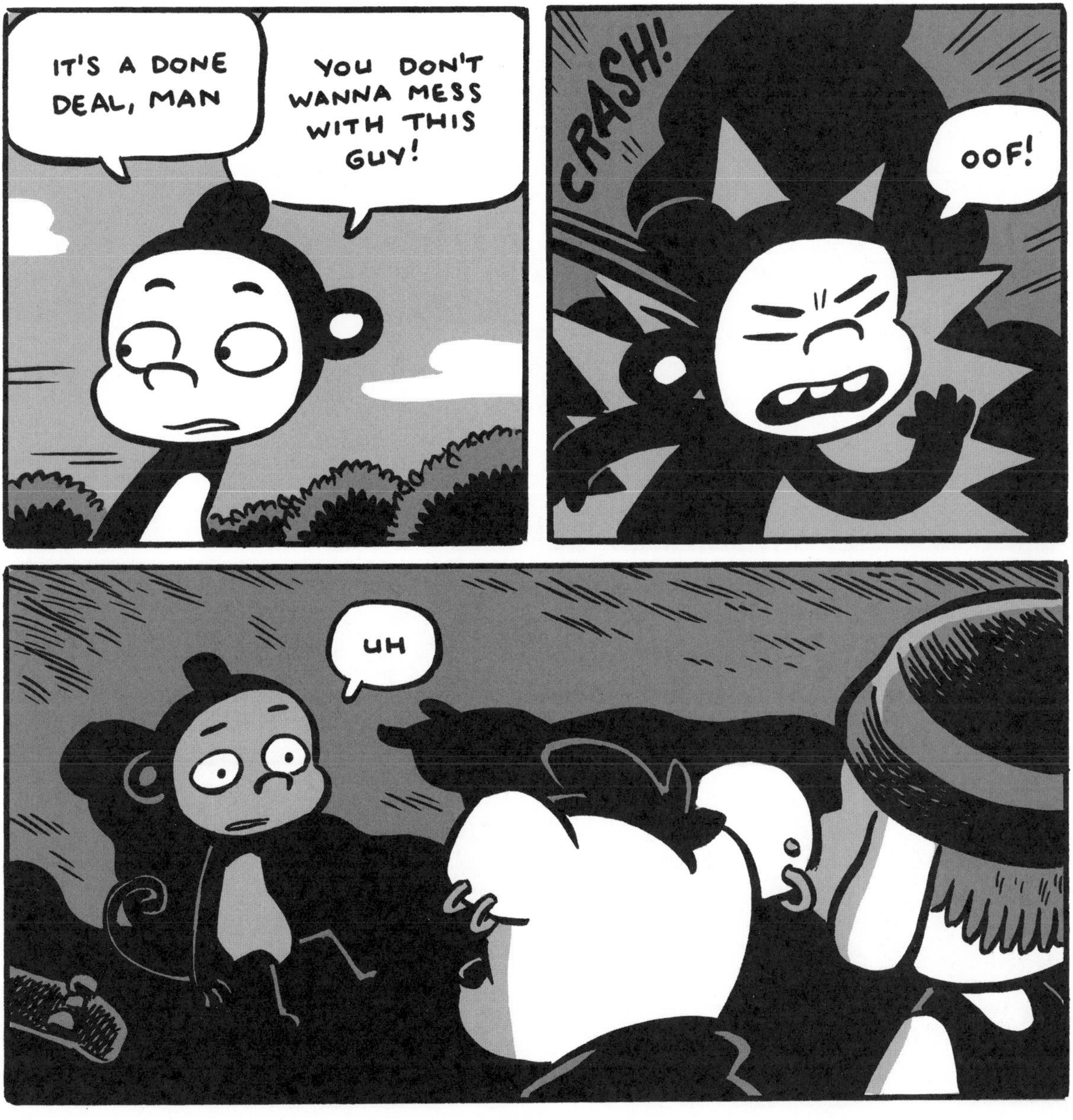
IT'S A DONE DEAL, MAN
YOU DON'T WANNA MESS WITH THIS GUY!
CRASH!
OOF!
UH

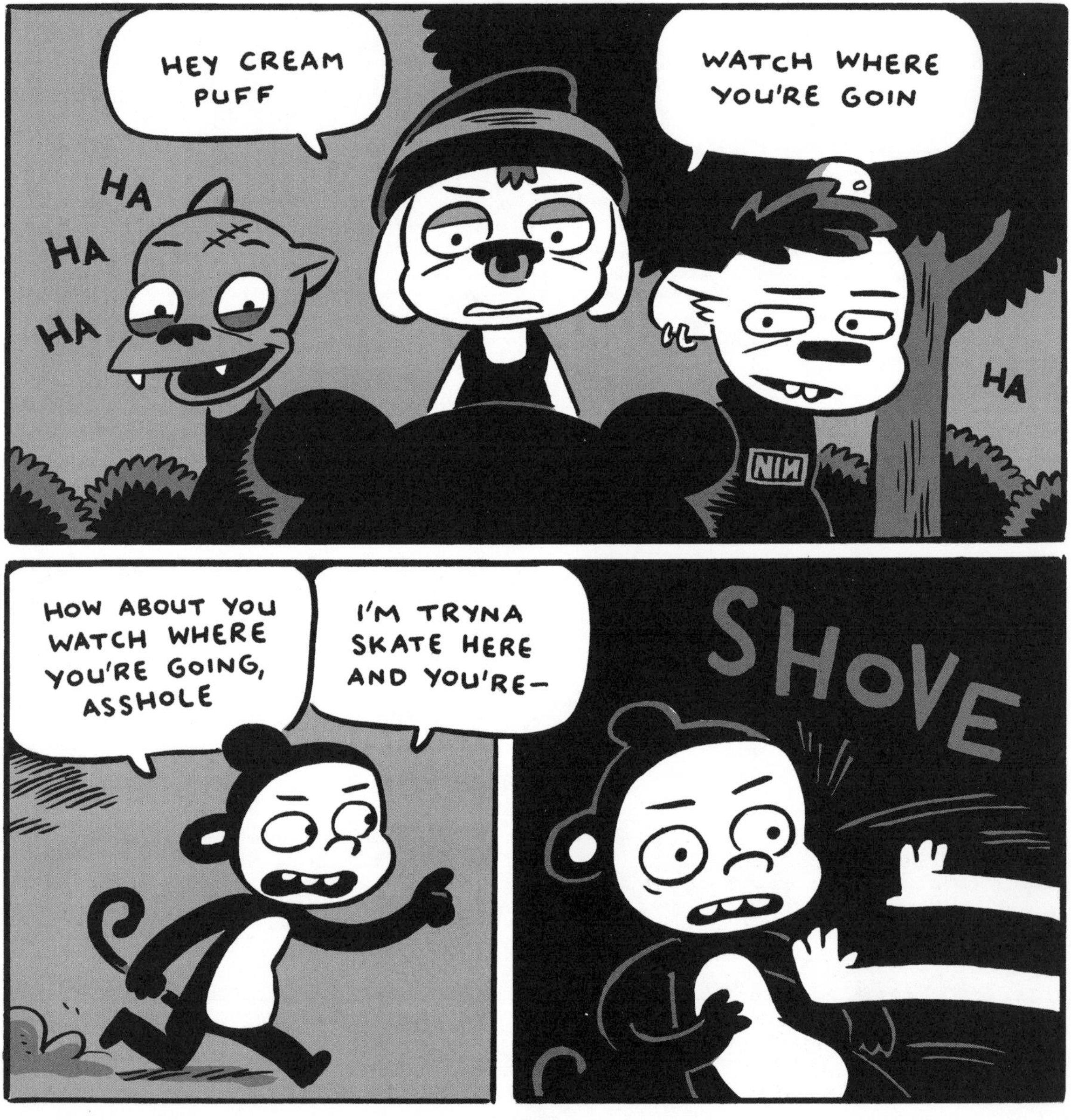
HEY CREAM PUFF
HA
HA
HA
WATCH WHERE YOU'RE GOIN
HA
HOW ABOUT YOU WATCH WHERE YOU'RE GOING, ASSHOLE
I'M TRYNA SKATE HERE AND YOU'RE—
SHOVE

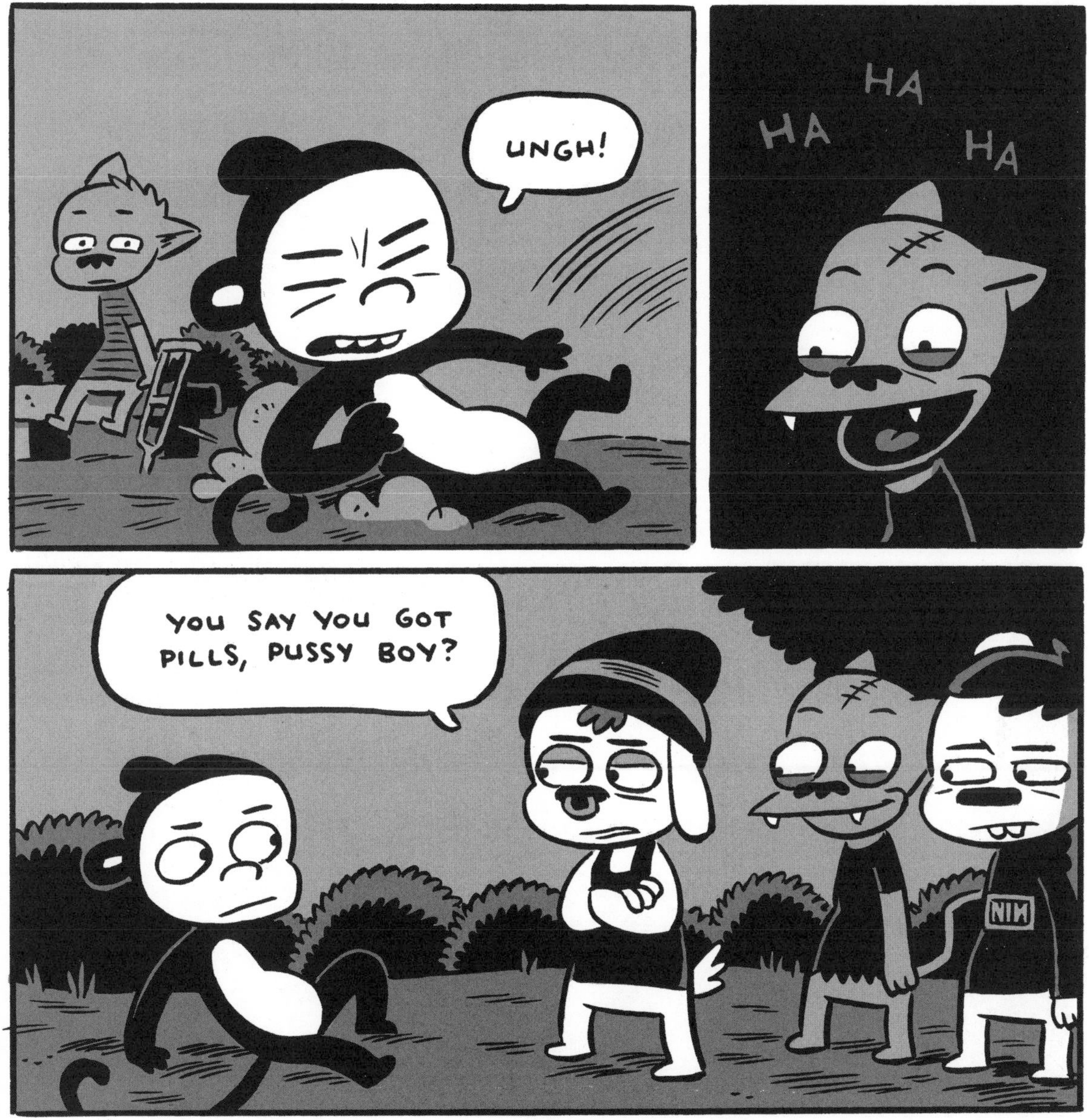
UNGH!
HA HA HA HA
YOU SAY YOU GOT PILLS, PUSSY BOY?
NIN

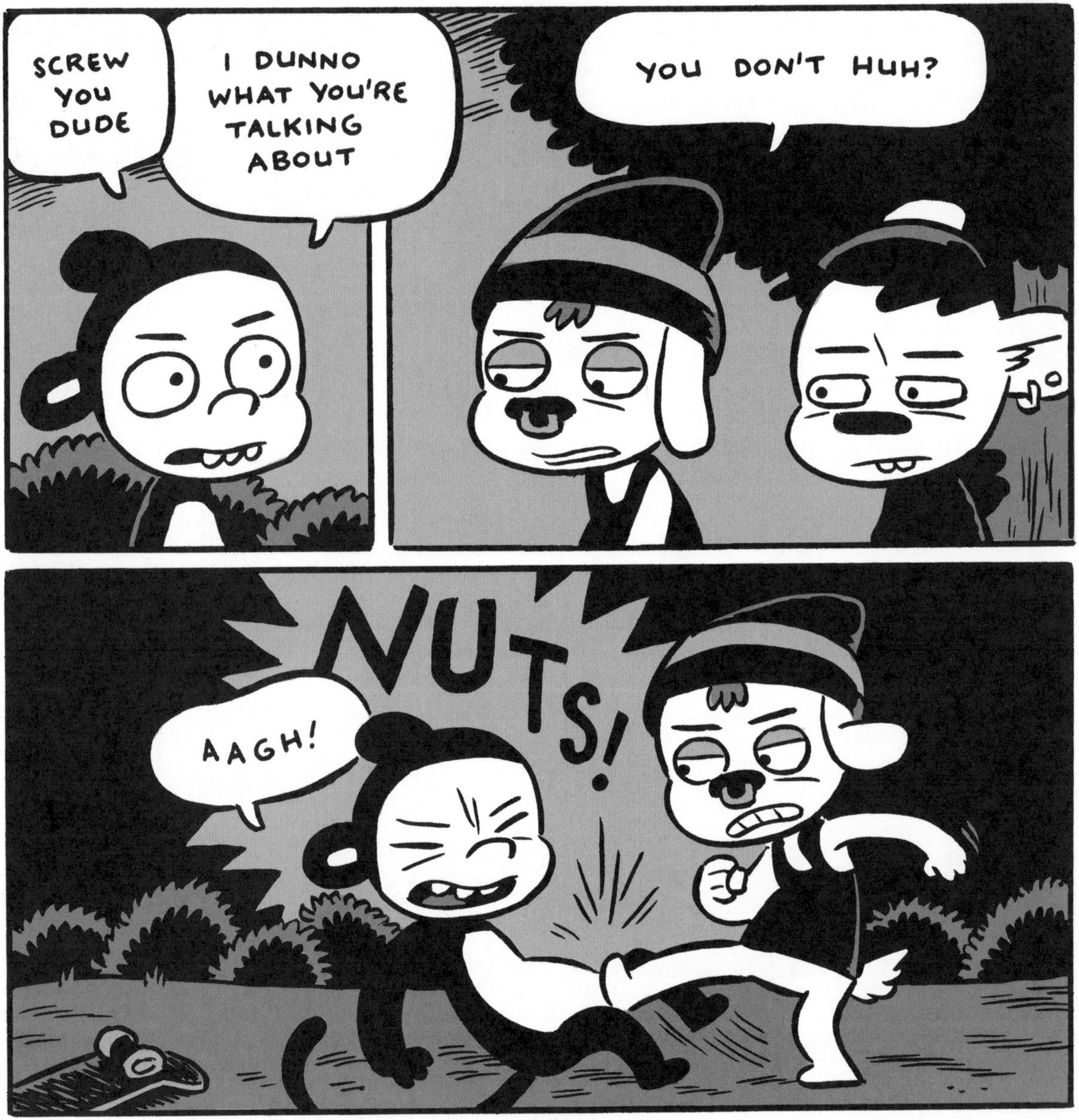
SCREW YOU DUDE
I DUNNO WHAT YOU'RE TALKING ABOUT
YOU DON'T HUH?
NUTS!
AAGH!

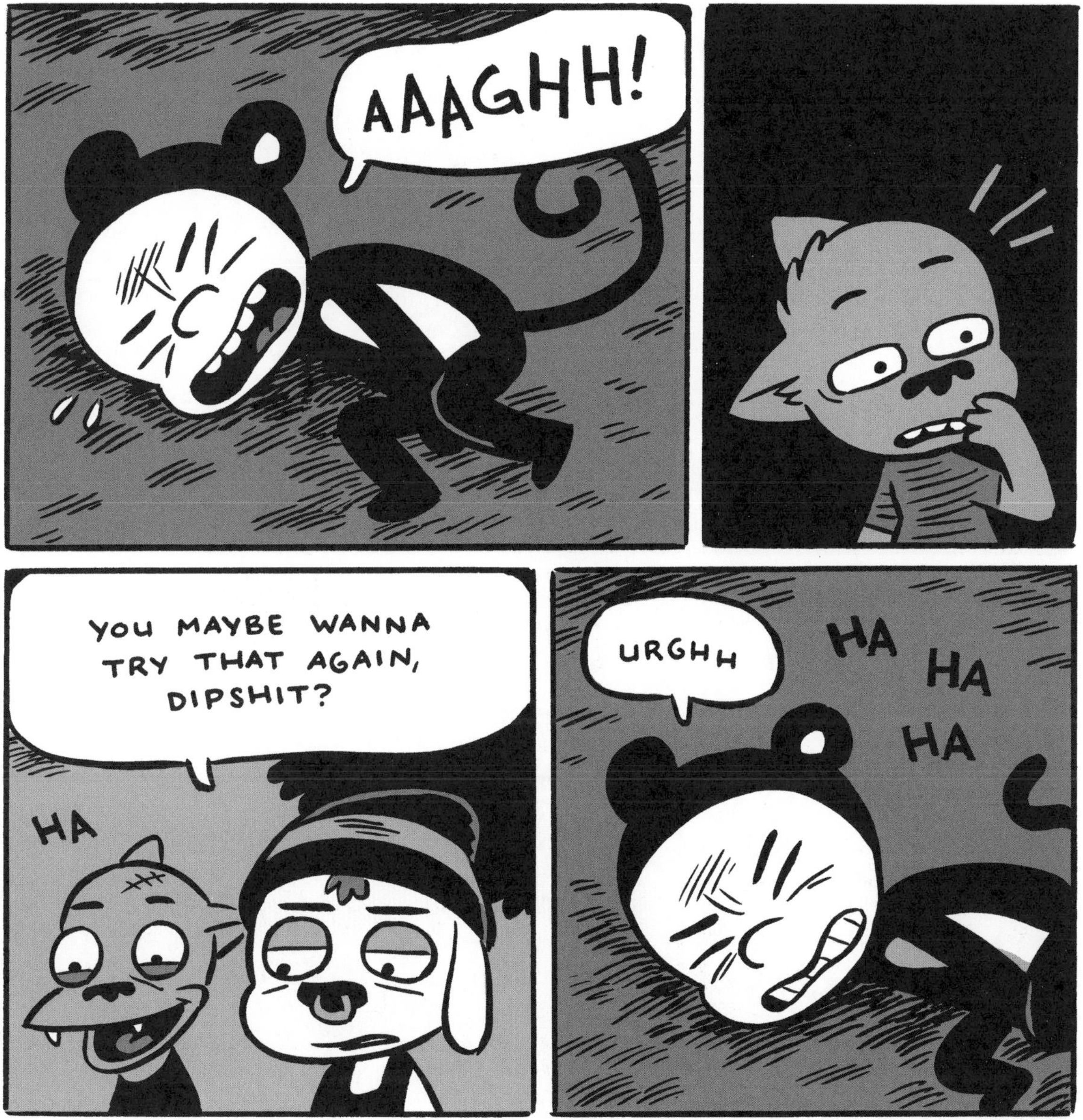
AAAGHH!
YOU MAYBE WANNA TRY THAT AGAIN, DIPSHIT?
HA
URGHH
HA HA HA

HA HA HA
THE PILLS
FORK 'EM OVER
OK
OK
SHIT
I DON'T HAVE 'EM ON ME, OK?
WE GOTTA GO GET 'EM

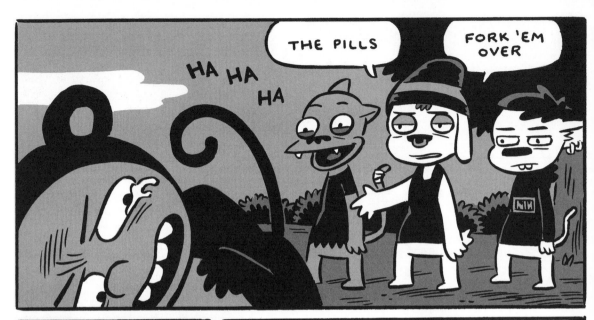

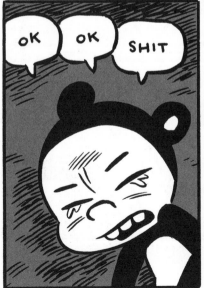

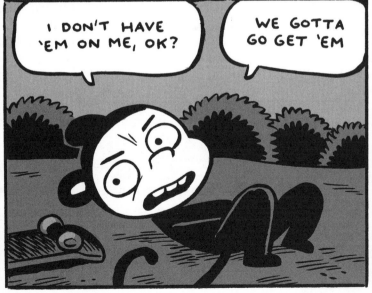

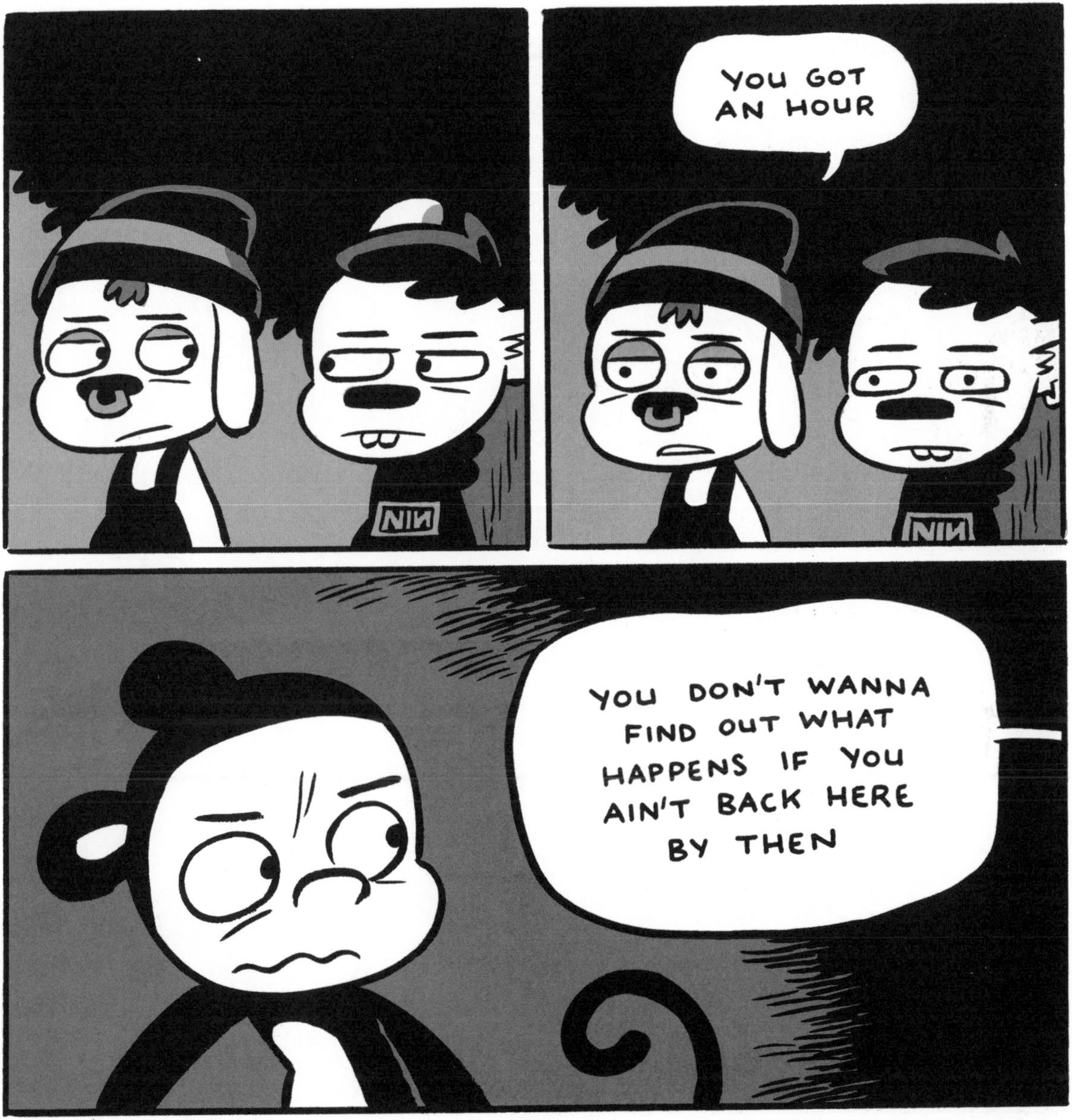
YOU GOT AN HOUR
NIN
YOU DON'T WANNA FIND OUT WHAT HAPPENS IF YOU AIN'T BACK HERE BY THEN

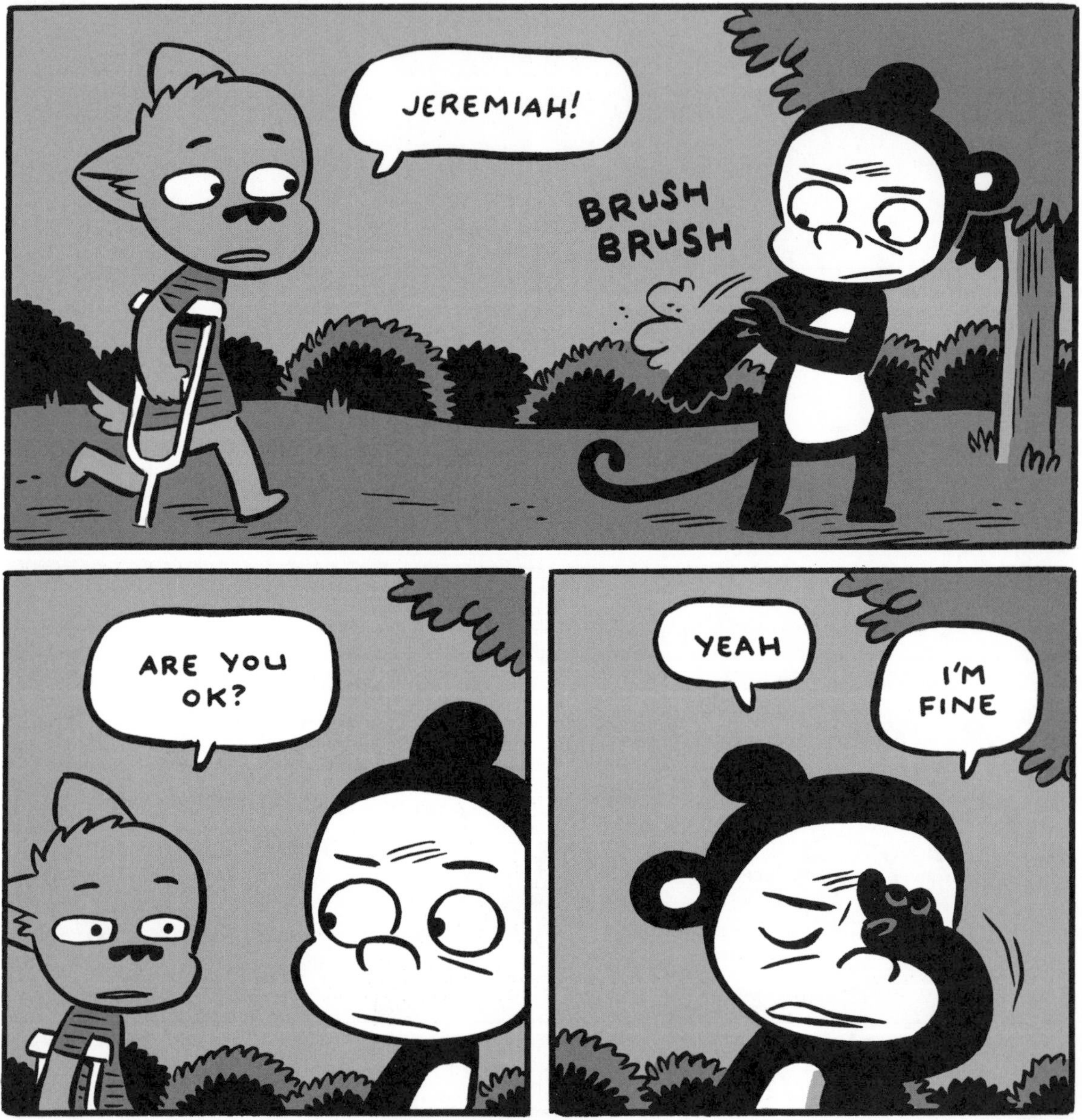
JEREMIAH!
BRUSH BRUSH
ARE YOU OK?
YEAH
I'M FINE

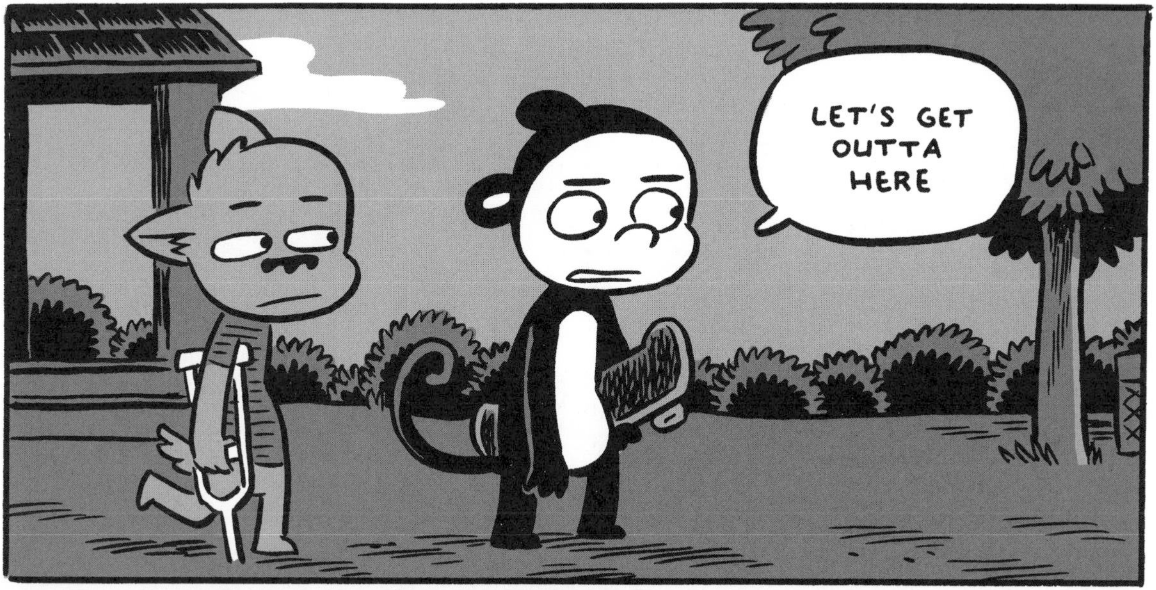
LET'S GET OUTTA HERE

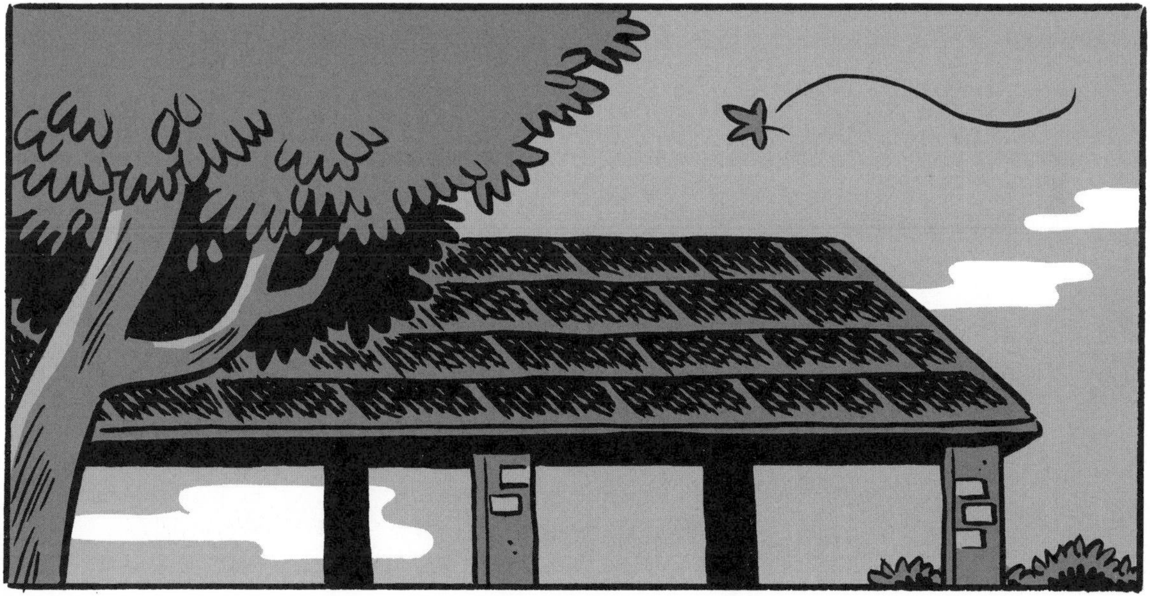

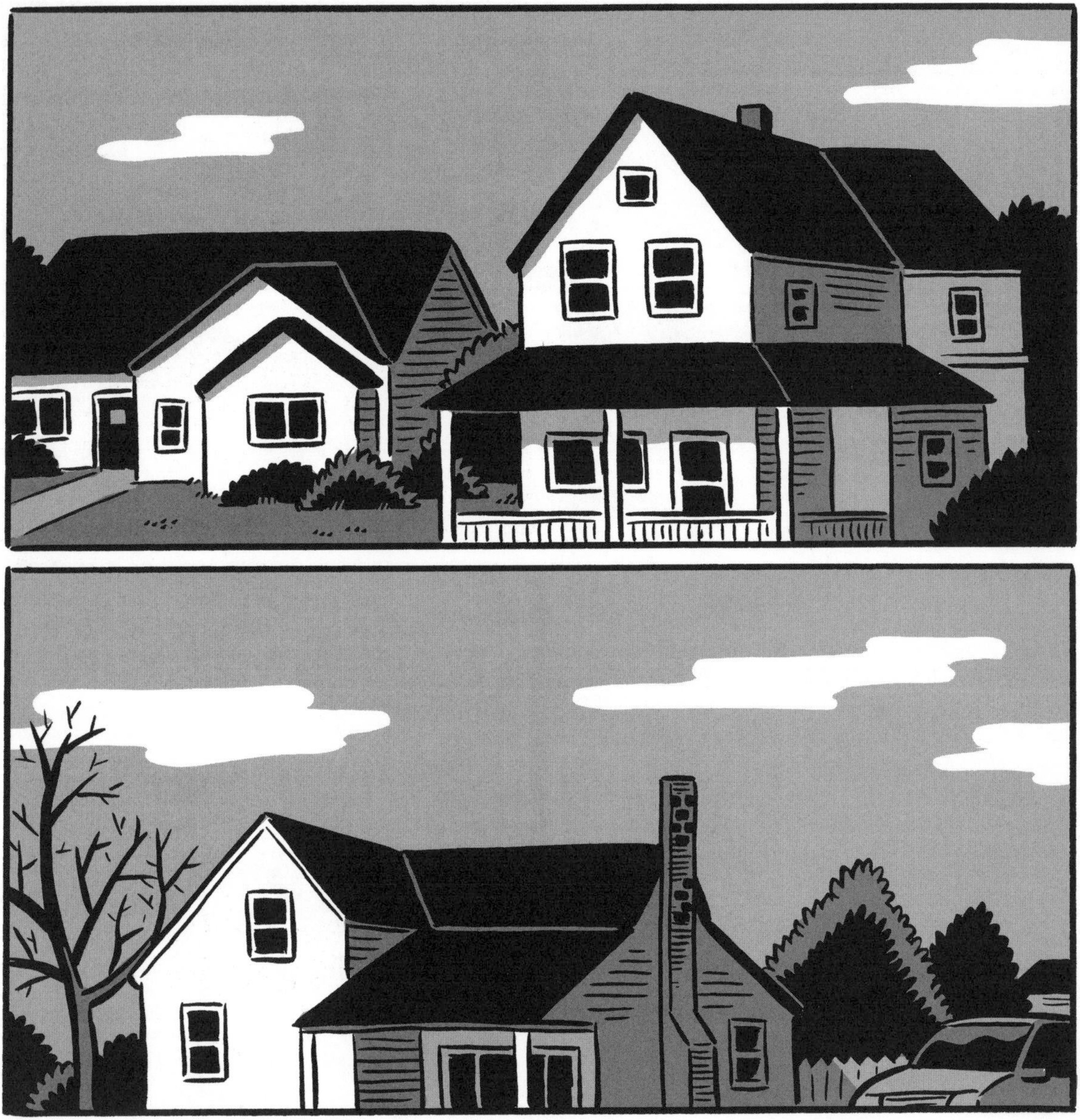

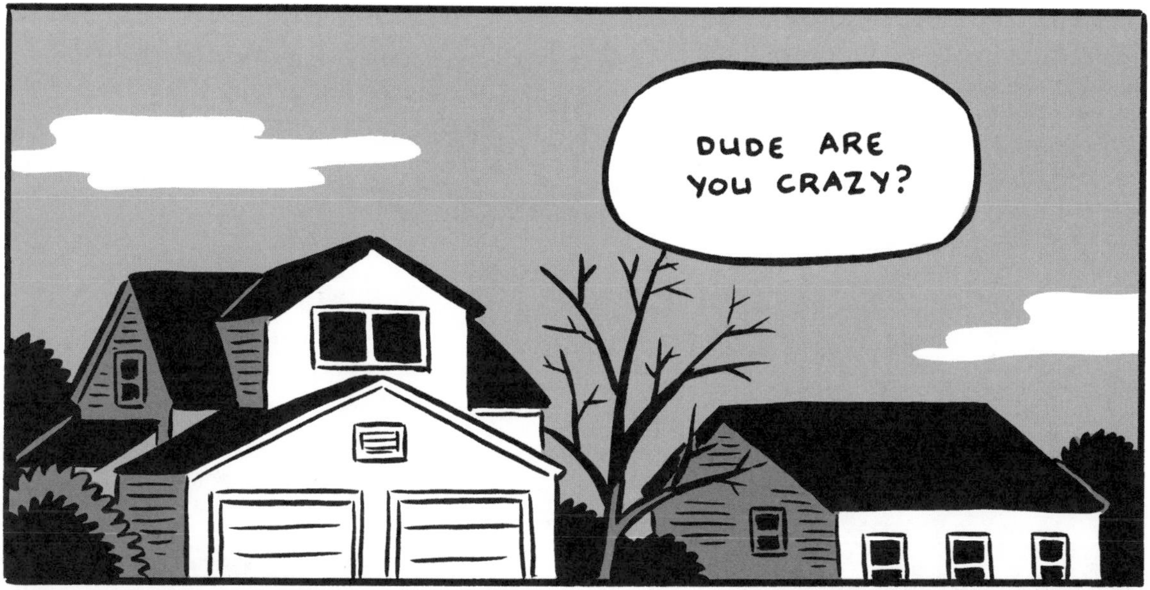
DUDE ARE YOU CRAZY?

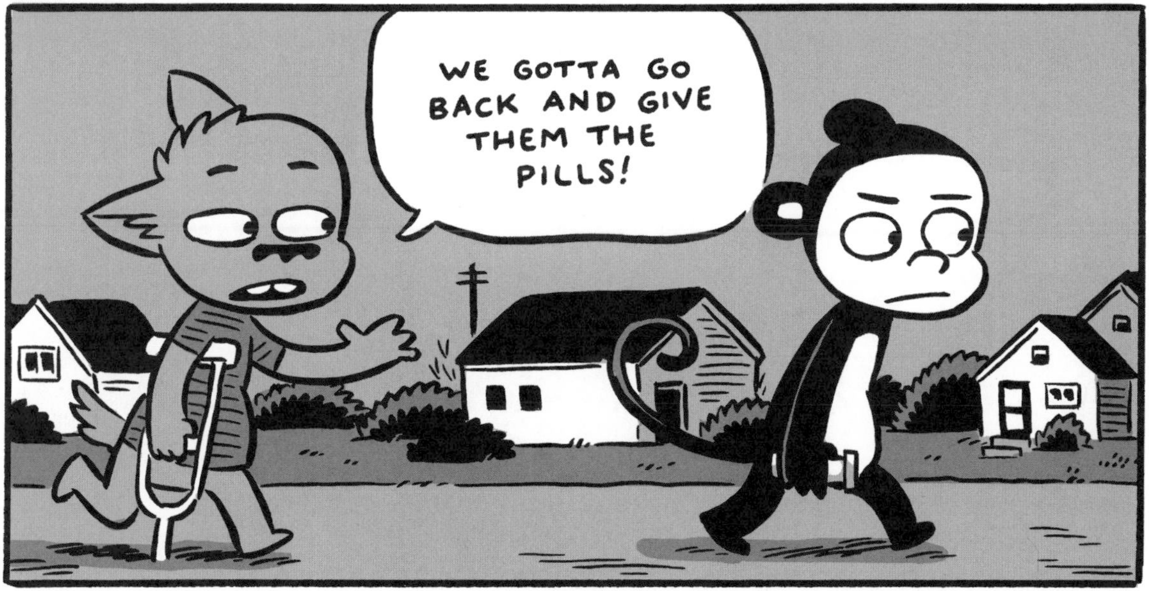
WE GOTTA GO BACK AND GIVE THEM THE PILLS!

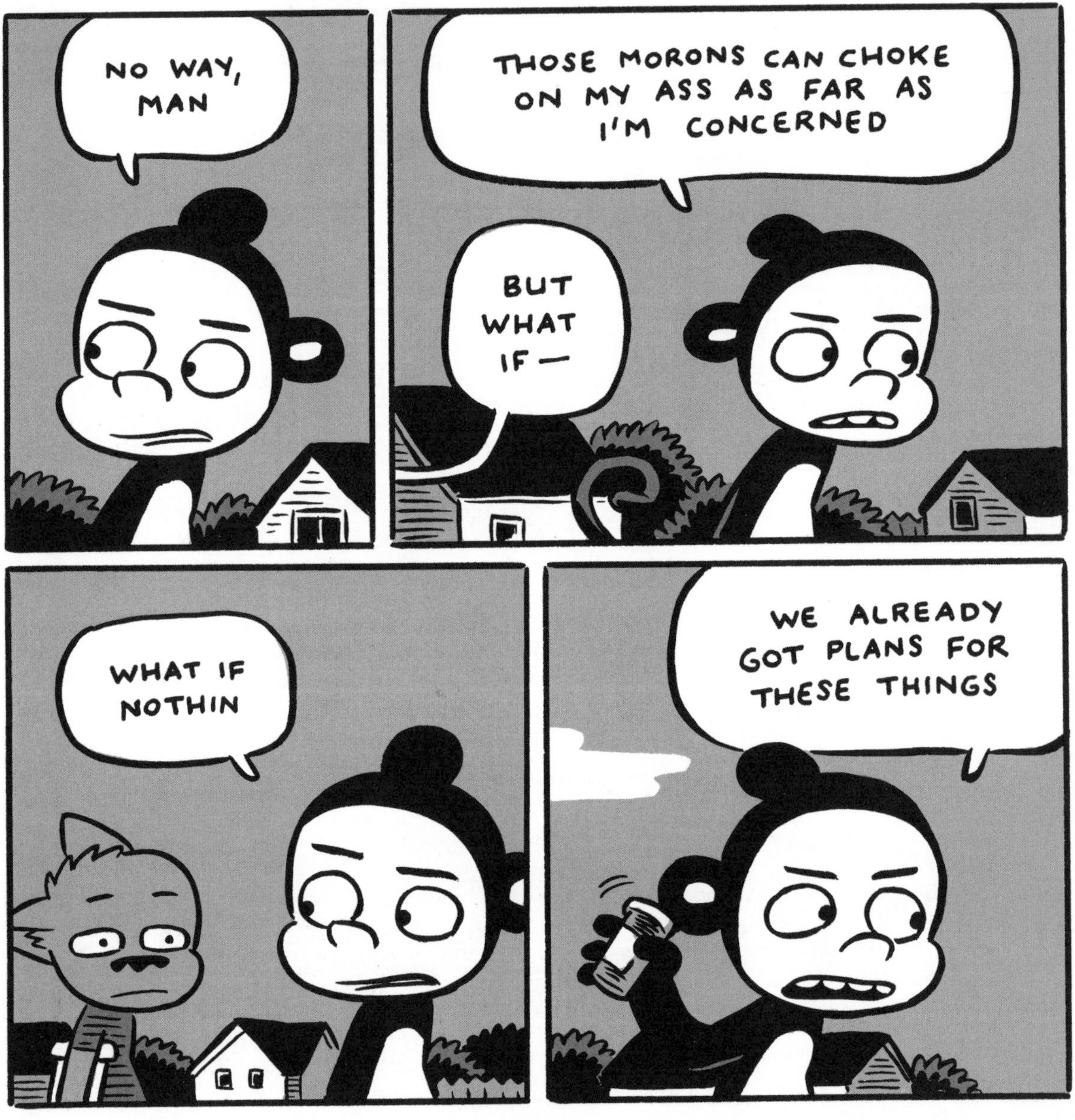
NO WAY, MAN
THOSE MORONS CAN CHOKE ON MY ASS AS FAR AS I'M CONCERNED
BUT WHAT IF—
WHAT IF NOTHIN
WE ALREADY GOT PLANS FOR THESE THINGS

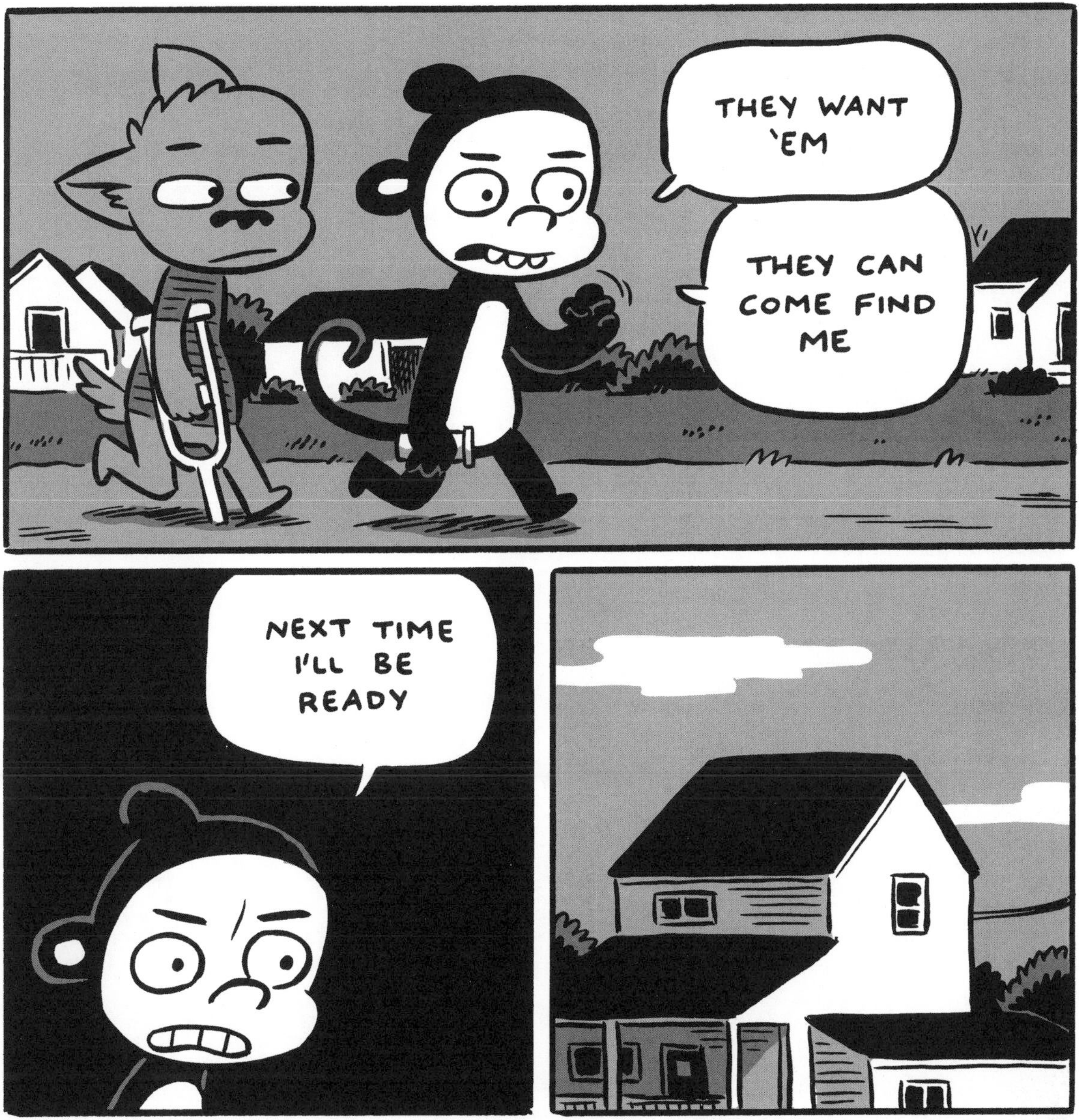
THEY WANT 'EM
THEY CAN COME FIND ME
NEXT TIME I'LL BE READY

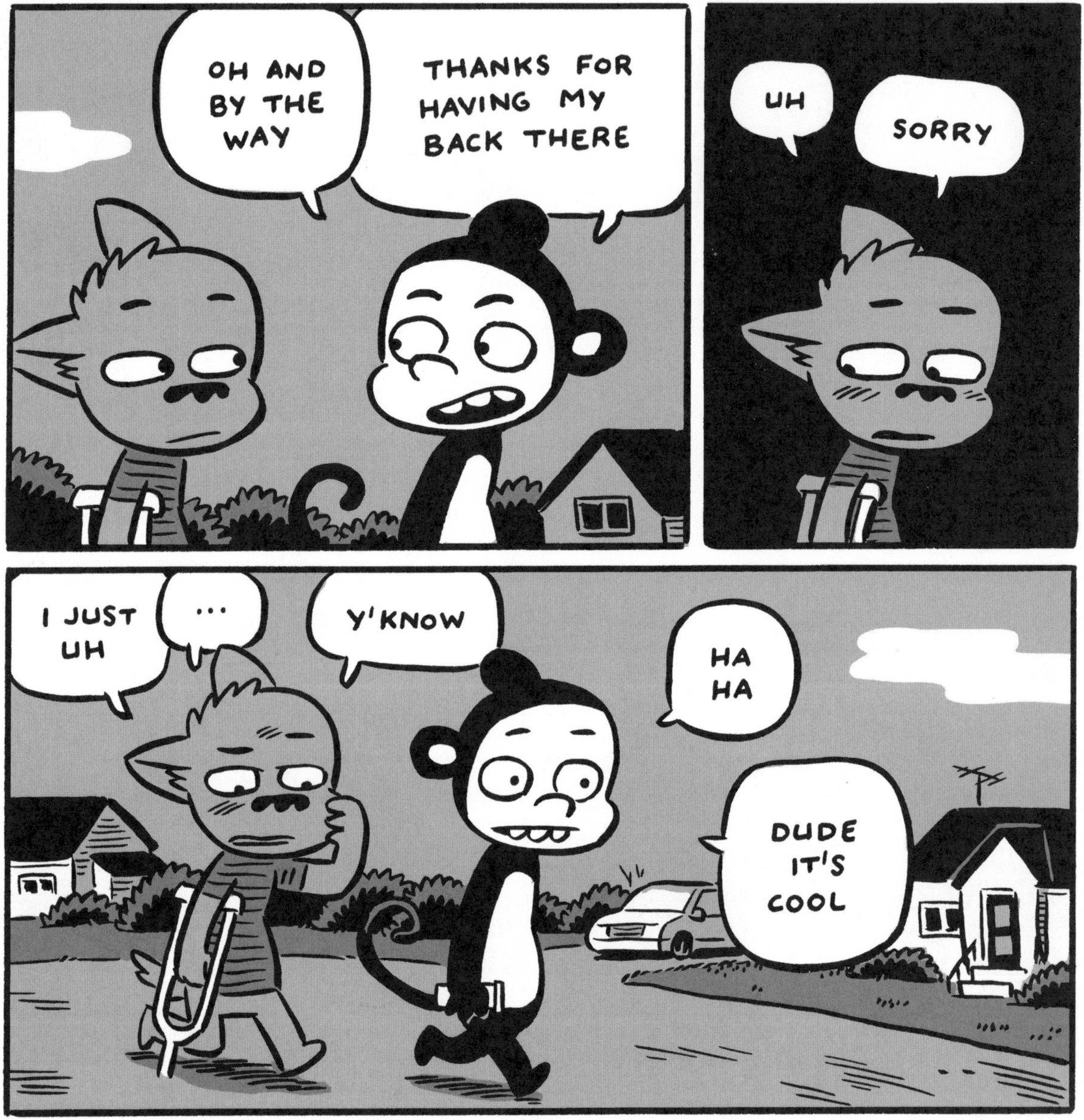
OH AND BY THE WAY
THANKS FOR HAVING MY BACK THERE
UH
SORRY
I JUST UH
...
Y'KNOW
HA HA
DUDE IT'S COOL

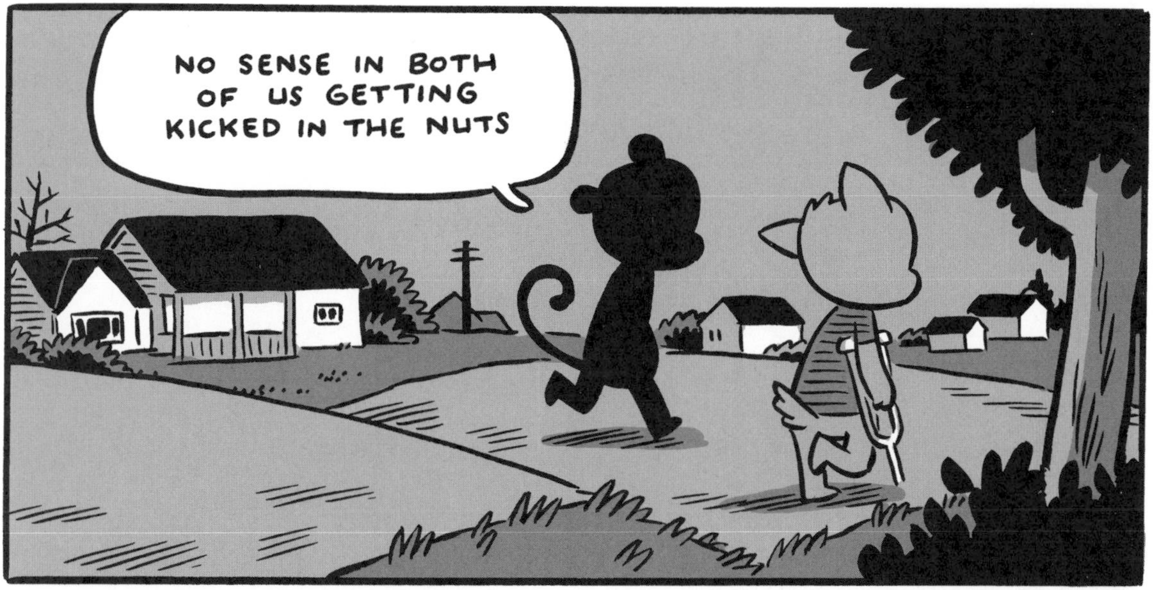
NO SENSE IN BOTH OF US GETTING KICKED IN THE NUTS

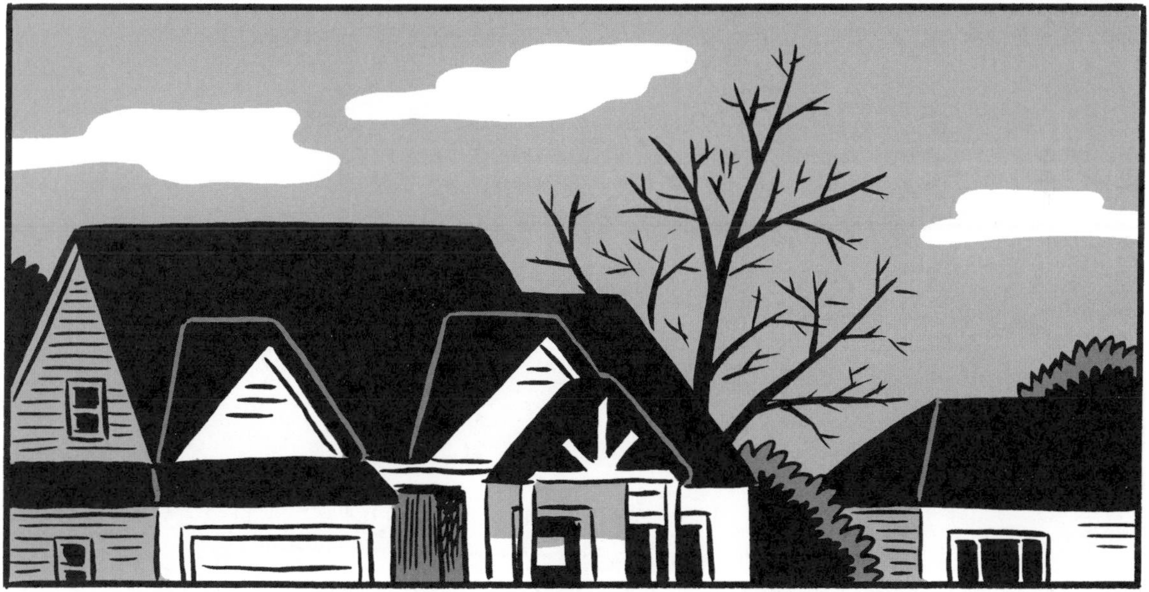

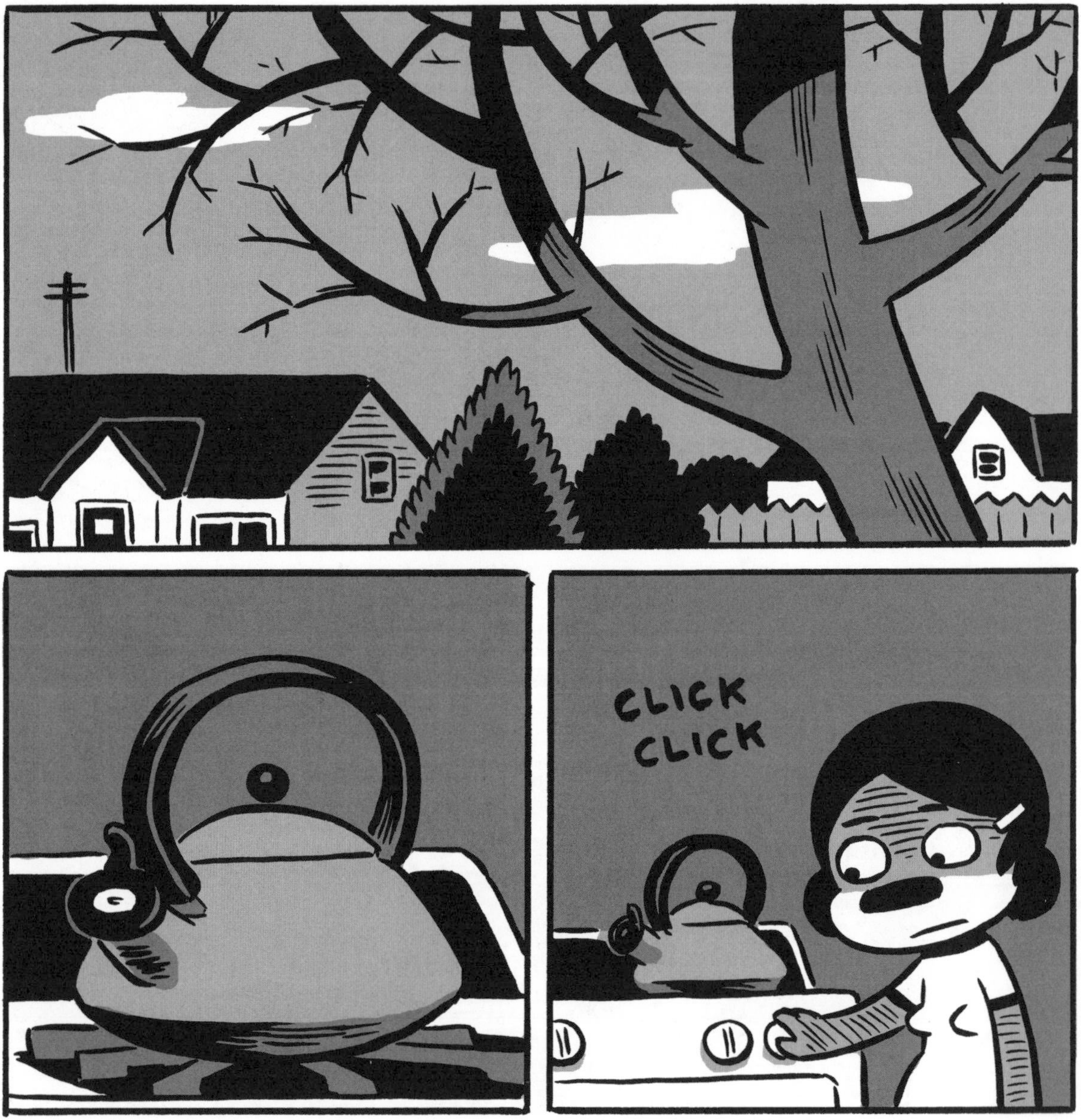
CLICK
CLICK

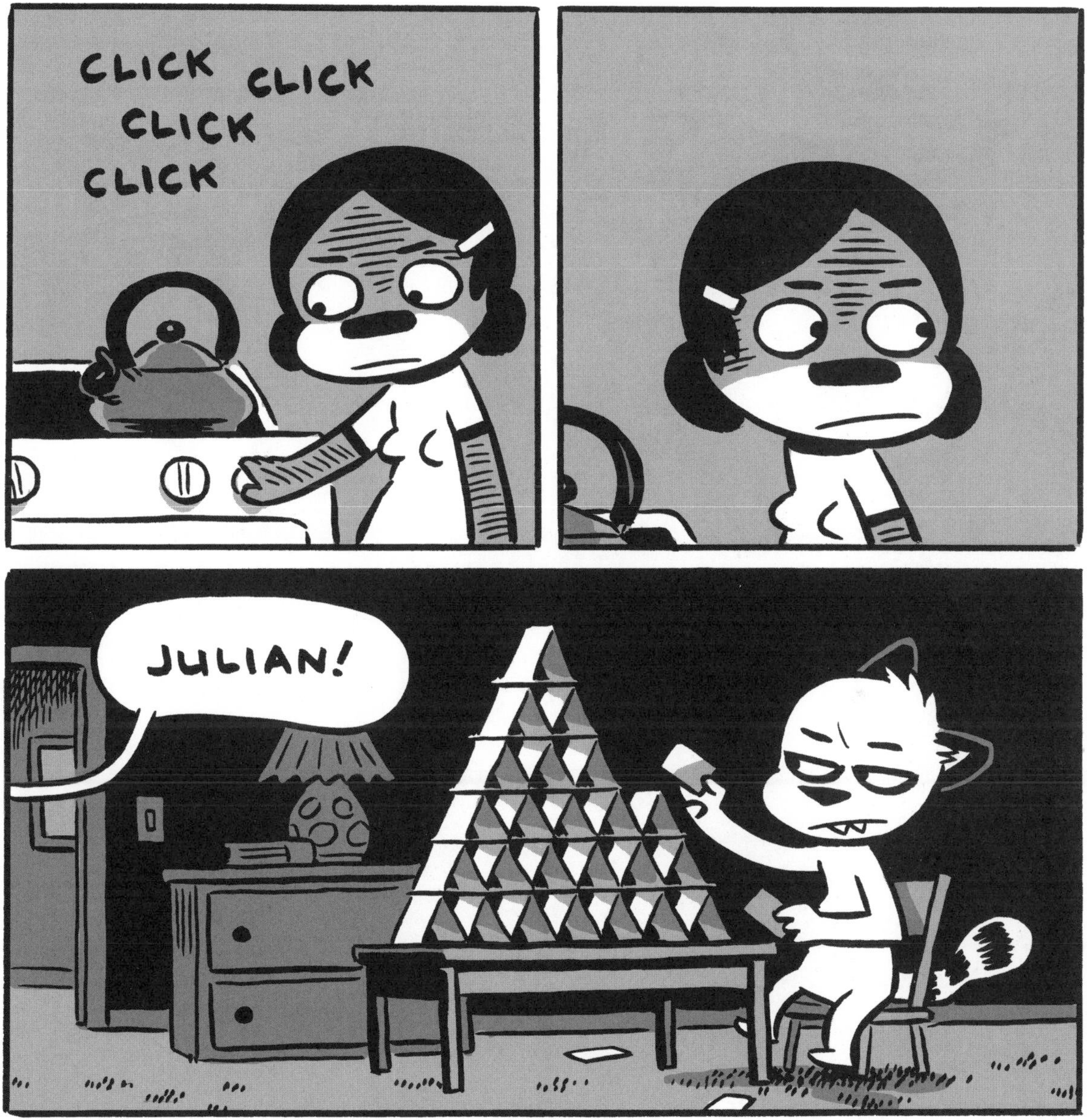
CLICK
CLICK
CLICK
CLICK
JULIAN!

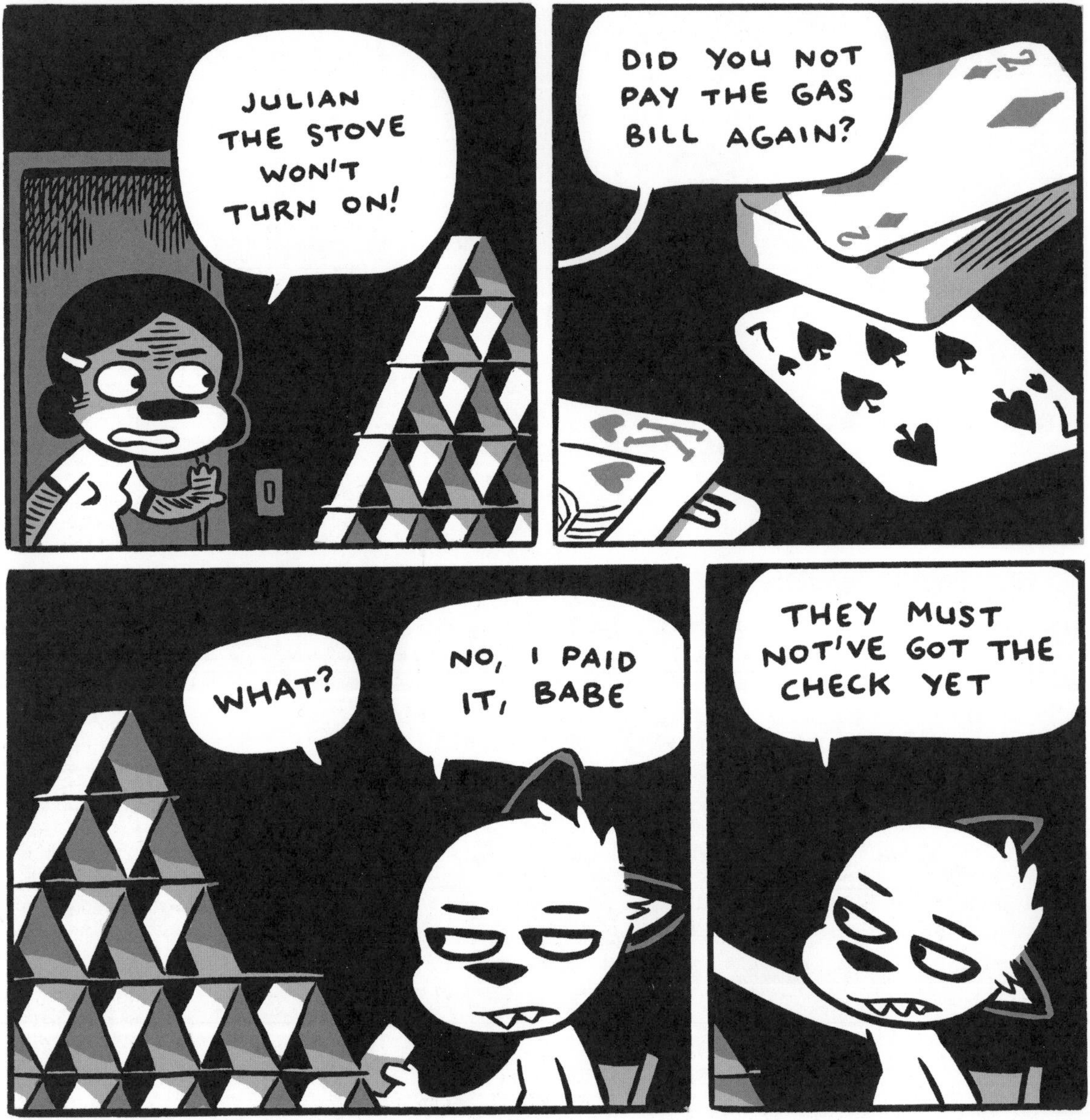
JULIAN THE STOVE WON'T TURN ON!
DID YOU NOT PAY THE GAS BILL AGAIN?
WHAT?
NO, I PAID IT, BABE
THEY MUST NOT'VE GOT THE CHECK YET

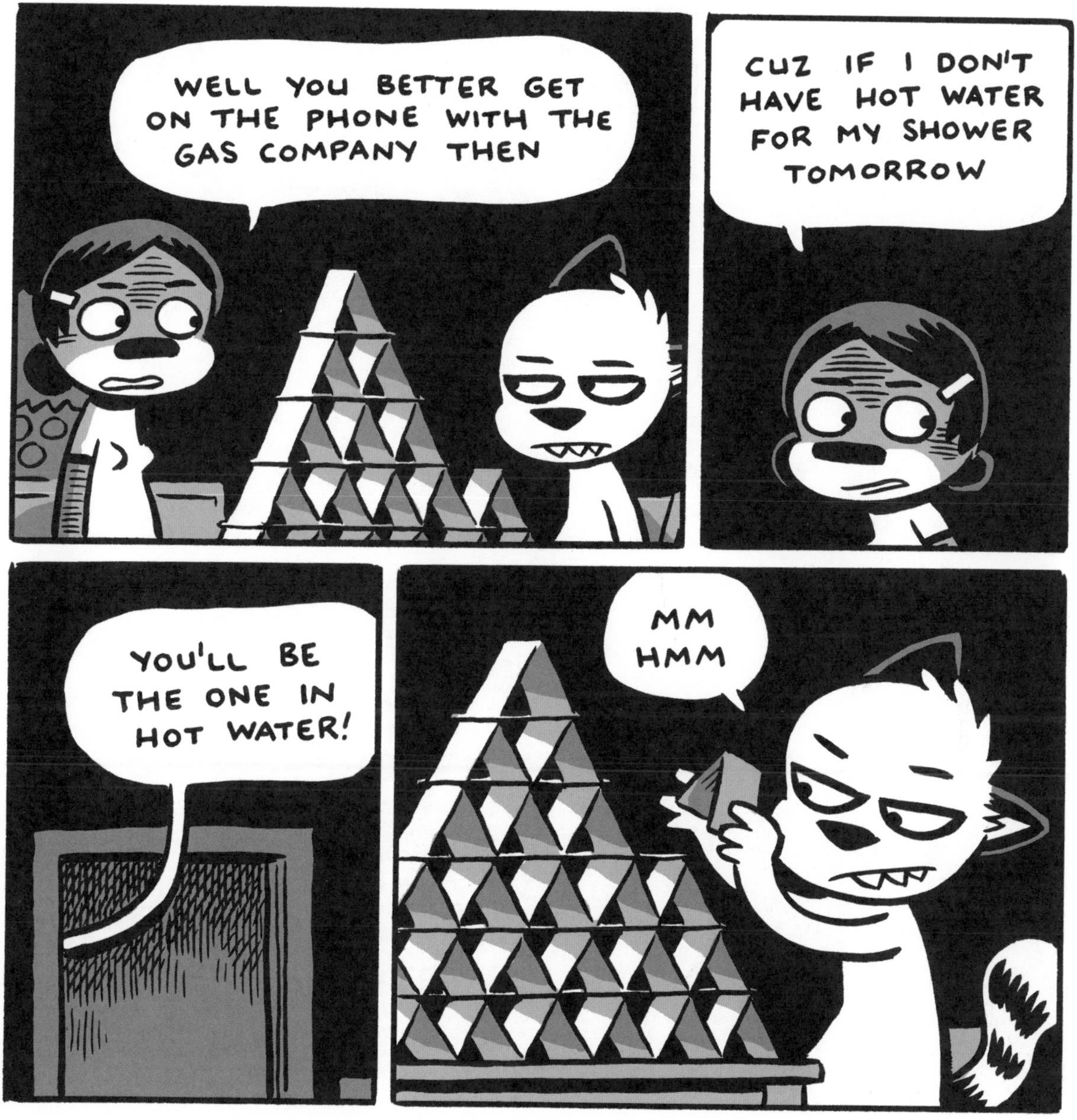
WELL YOU BETTER GET ON THE PHONE WITH THE GAS COMPANY THEN
CUZ IF I DON'T HAVE HOT WATER FOR MY SHOWER TOMORROW
YOU'LL BE THE ONE IN HOT WATER!
MM HMM

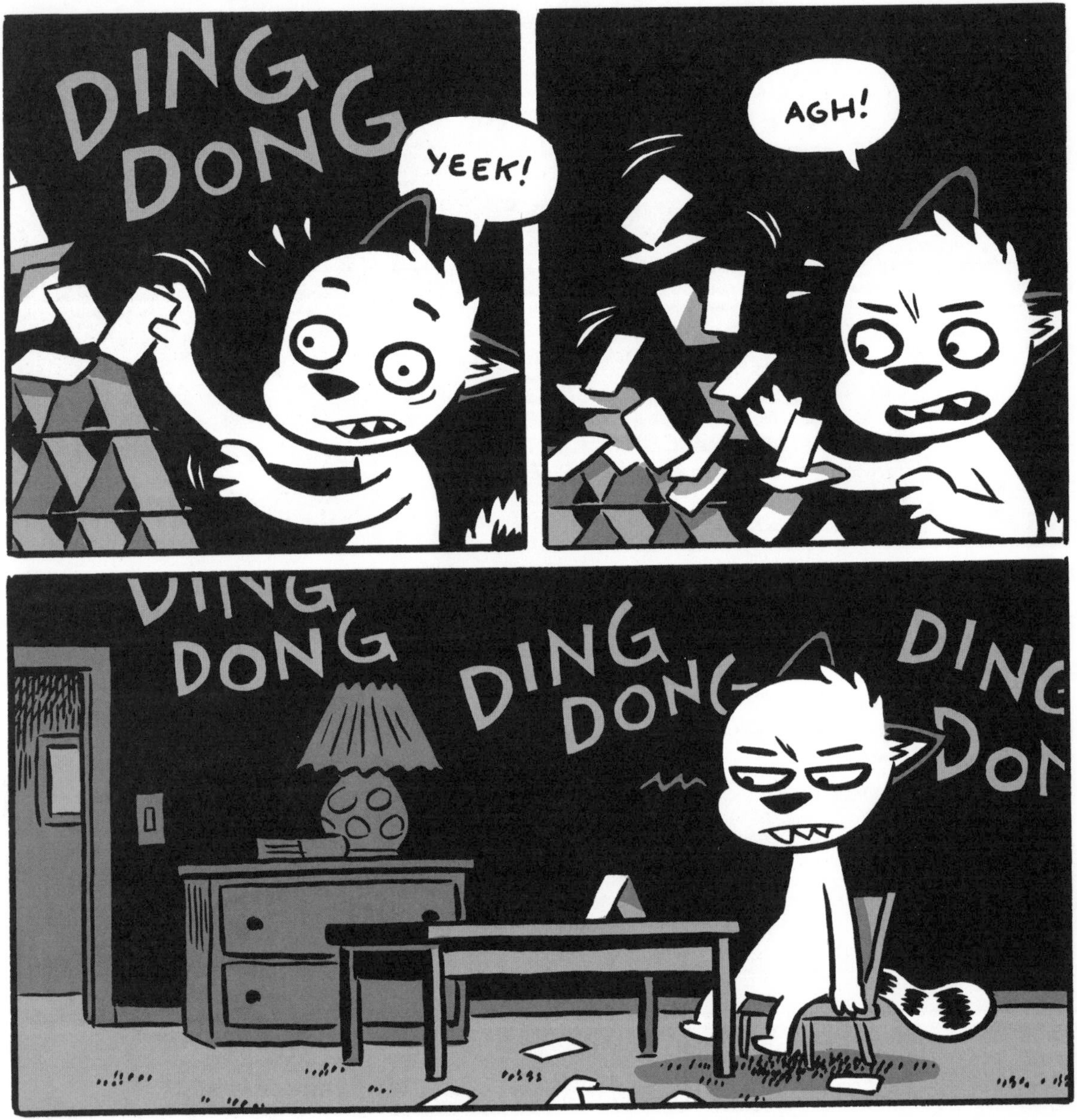
DING DONG
YEEK!
AGH!
DING DONG
DING DONG
DING DON

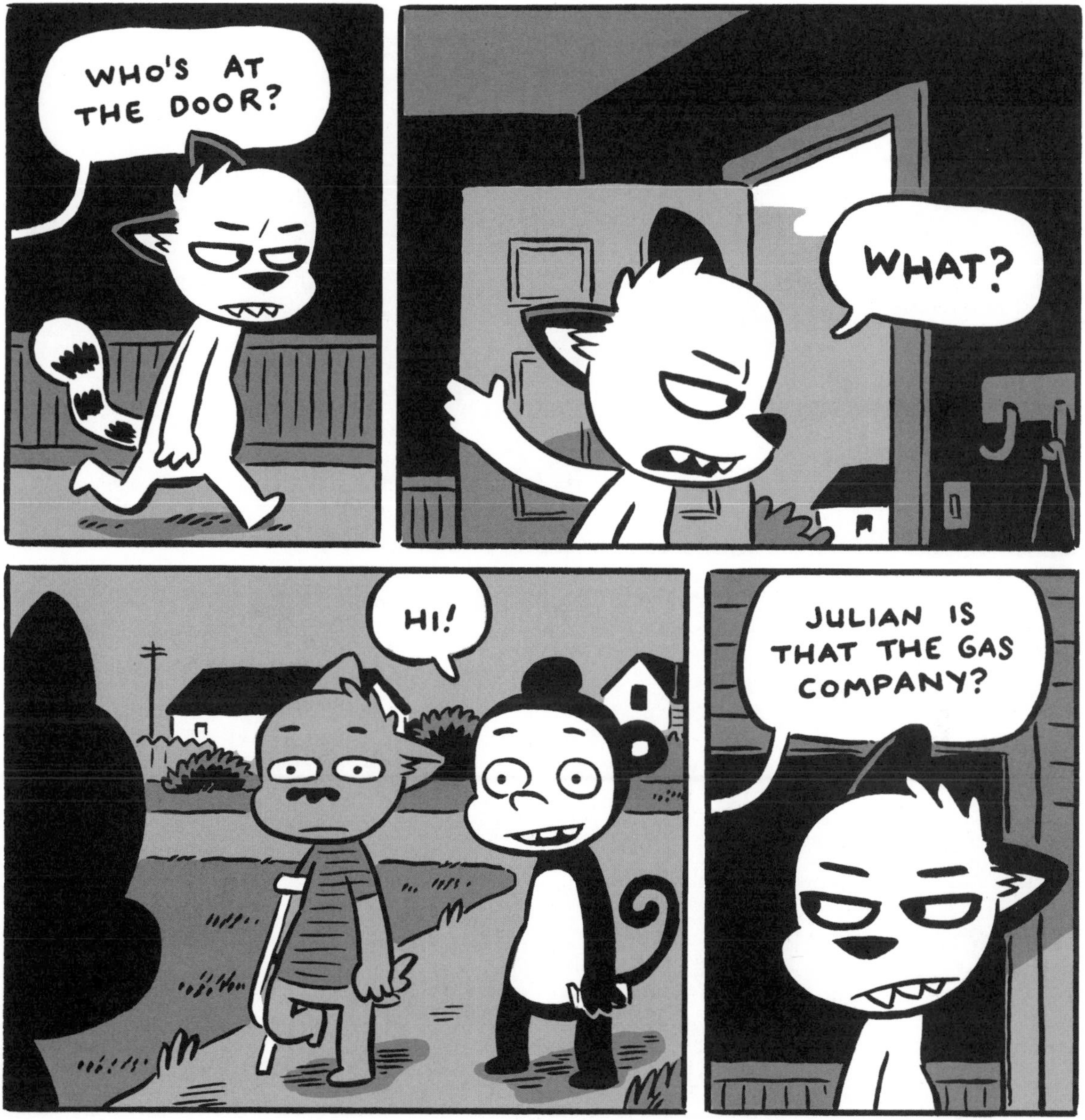
WHO'S AT THE DOOR?
WHAT?
HI!
JULIAN IS THAT THE GAS COMPANY?

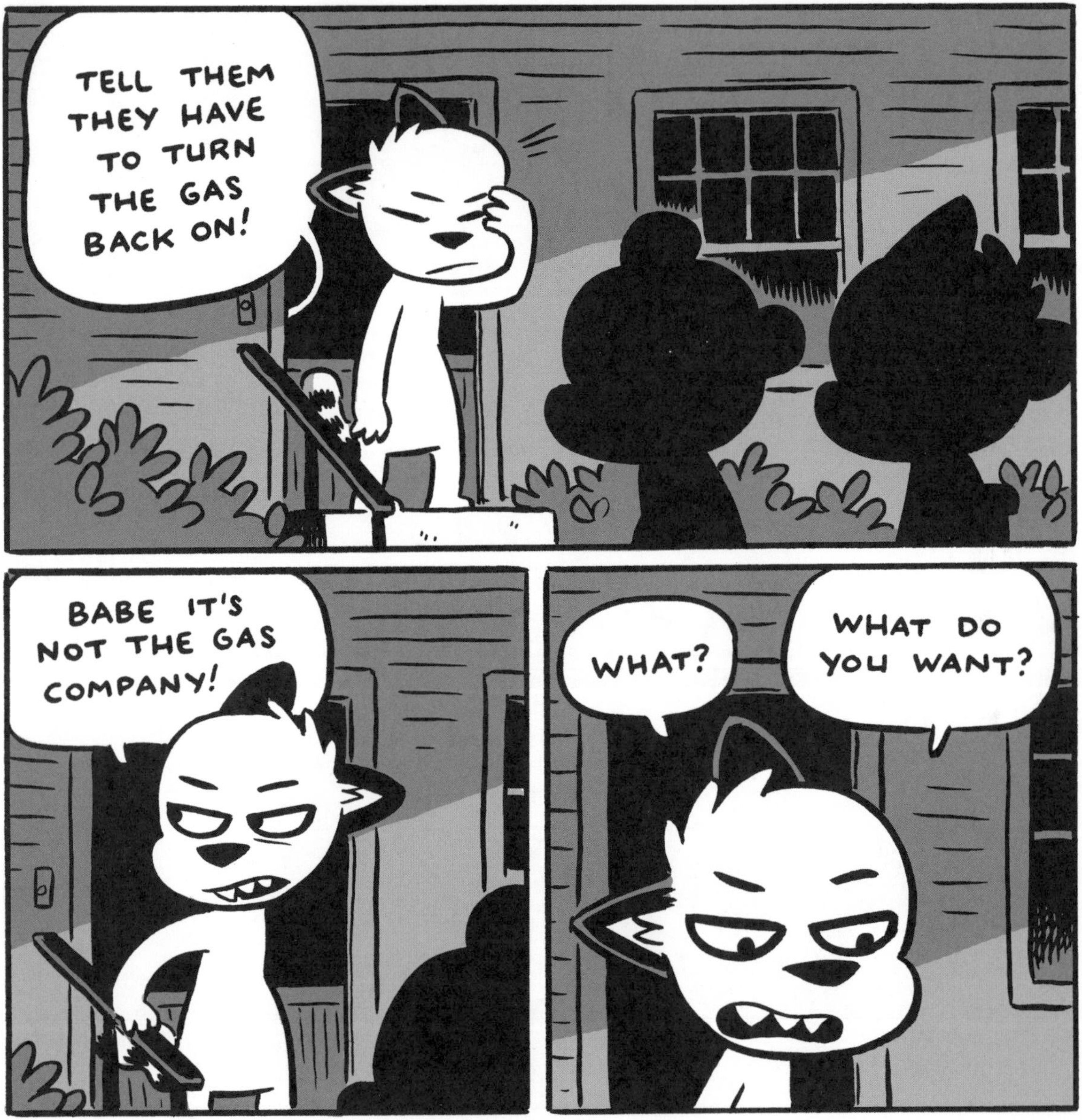
TELL THEM THEY HAVE TO TURN THE GAS BACK ON!
BABE IT'S NOT THE GAS COMPANY!
WHAT?
WHAT DO YOU WANT?

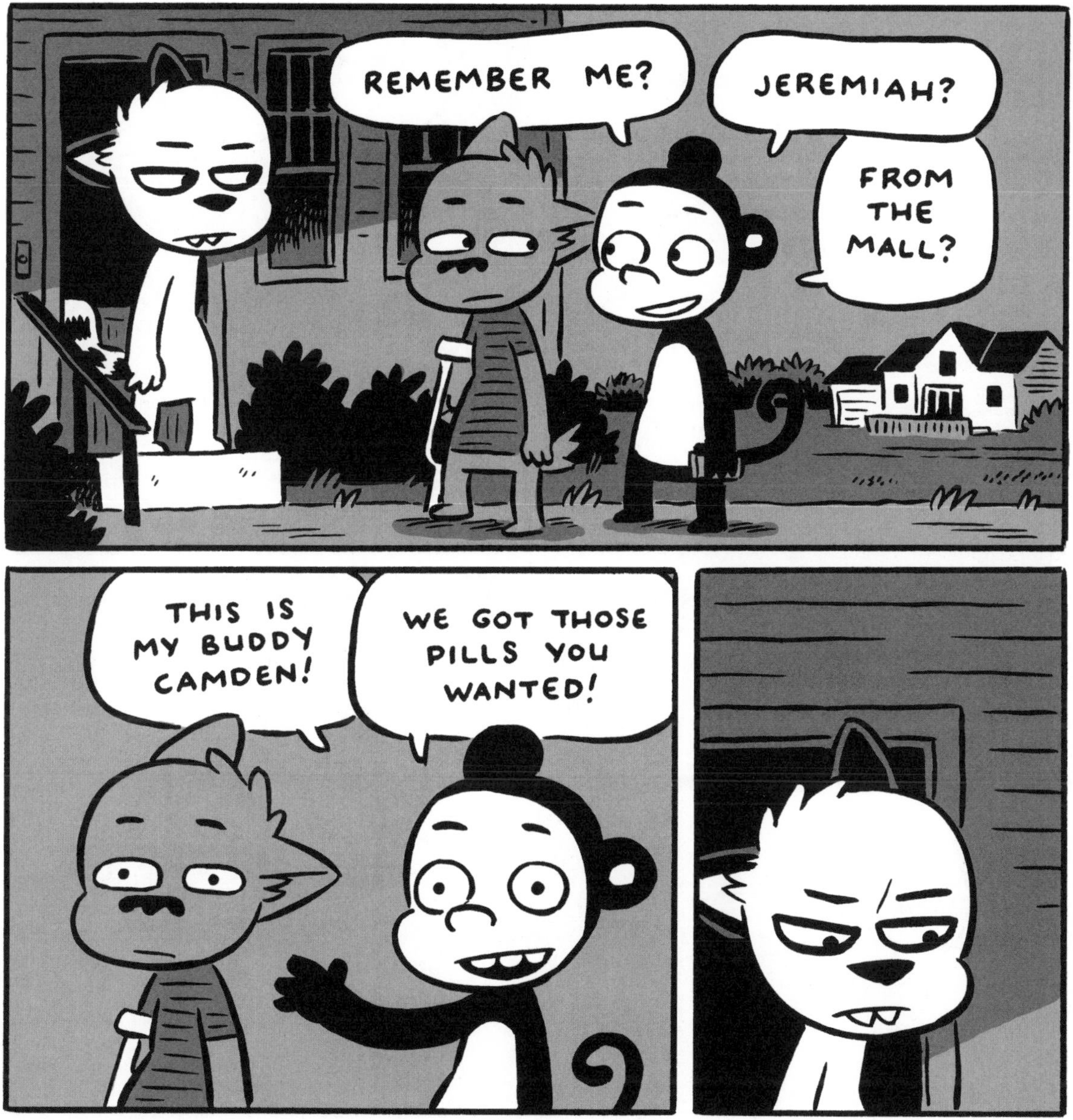
REMEMBER ME?
JEREMIAH?
FROM THE MALL?
THIS IS MY BUDDY CAMDEN!
WE GOT THOSE PILLS YOU WANTED!

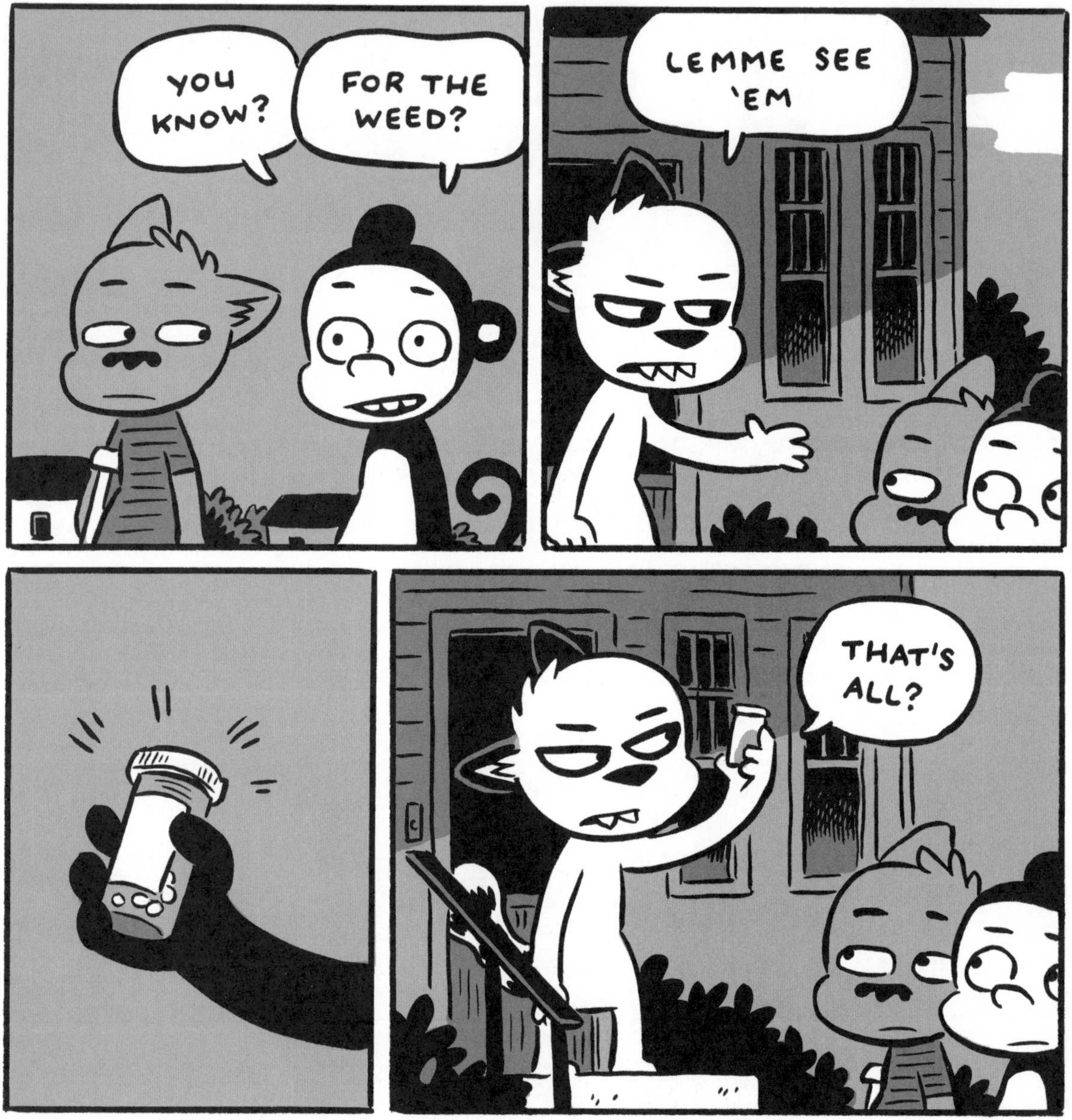
YOU KNOW?
FOR THE WEED?
LEMME SEE 'EM
THAT'S ALL?

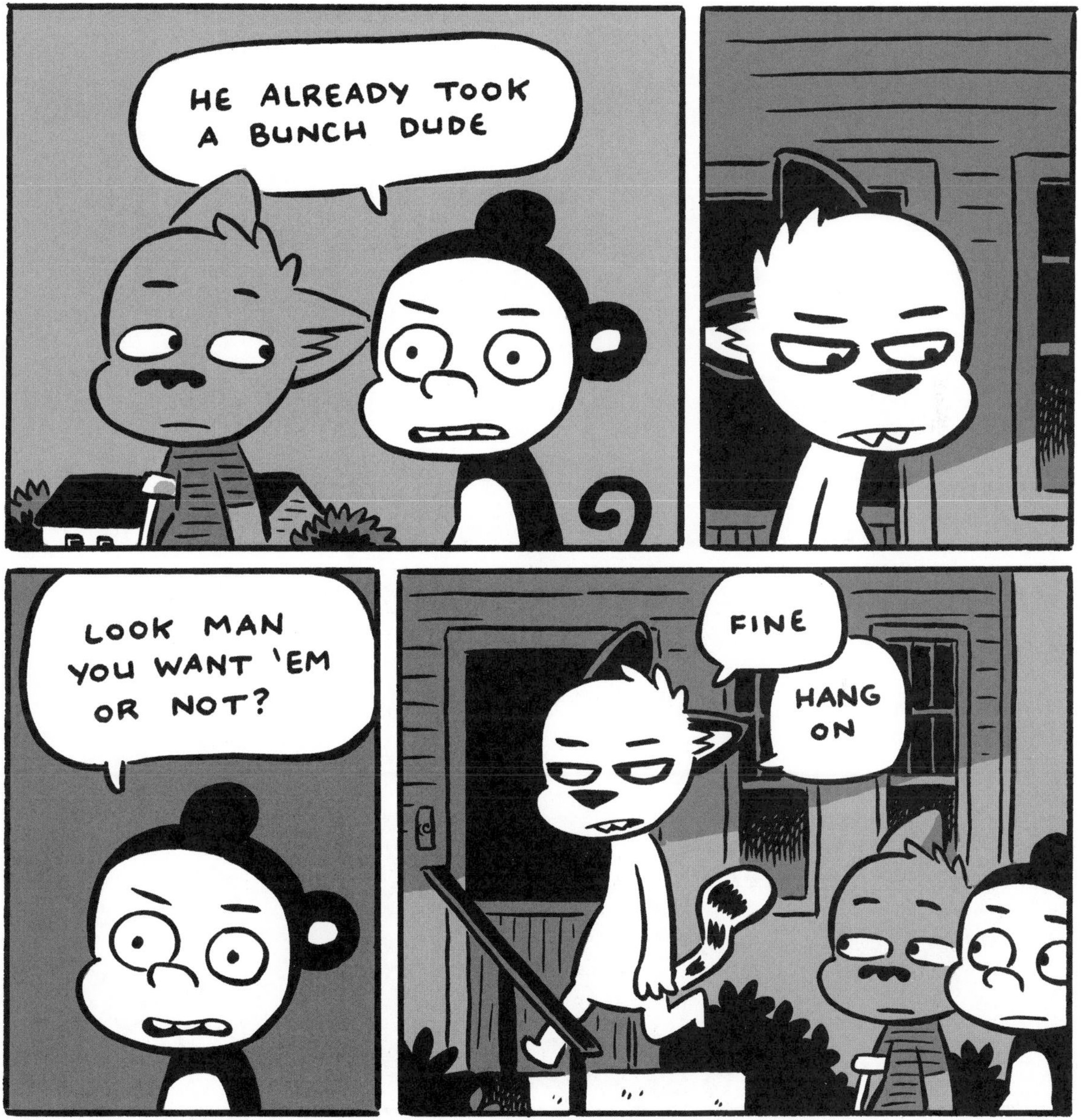
HE ALREADY TOOK A BUNCH DUDE
LOOK MAN YOU WANT 'EM OR NOT?
FINE
HANG ON

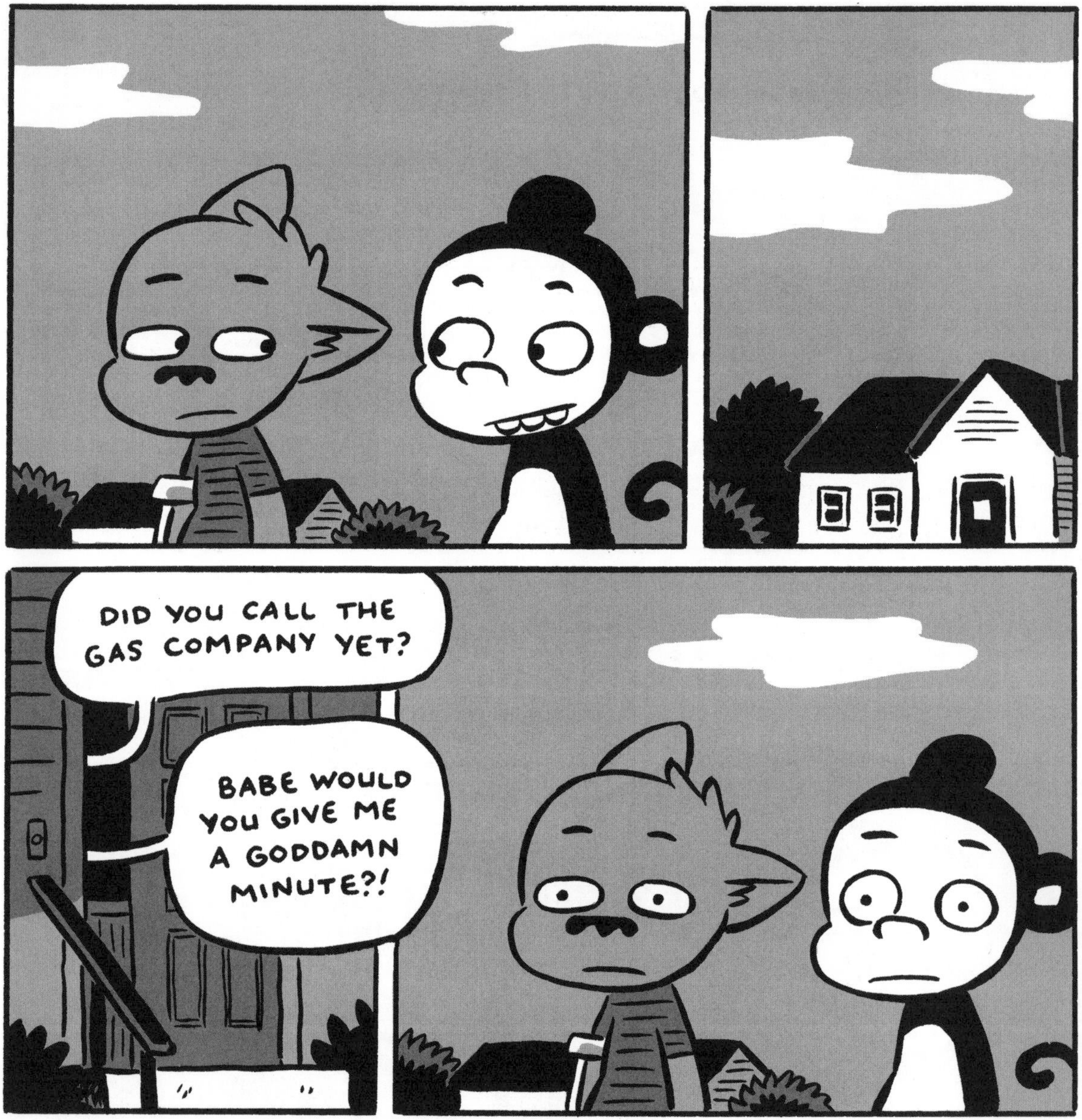
DID YOU CALL THE GAS COMPANY YET?
BABE WOULD YOU GIVE ME A GODDAMN MINUTE?!

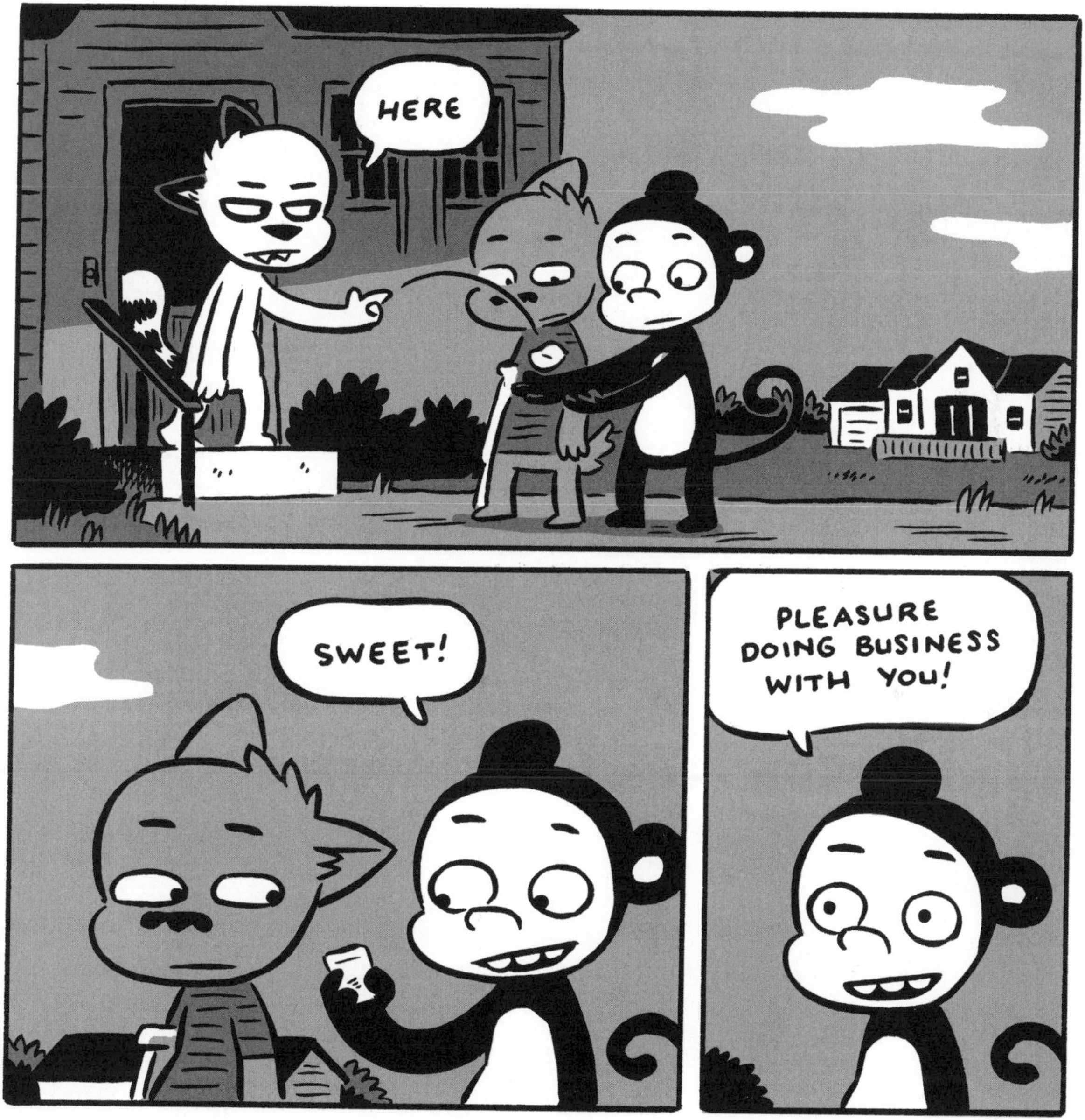
HERE
SWEET!
PLEASURE DOING BUSINESS WITH YOU!

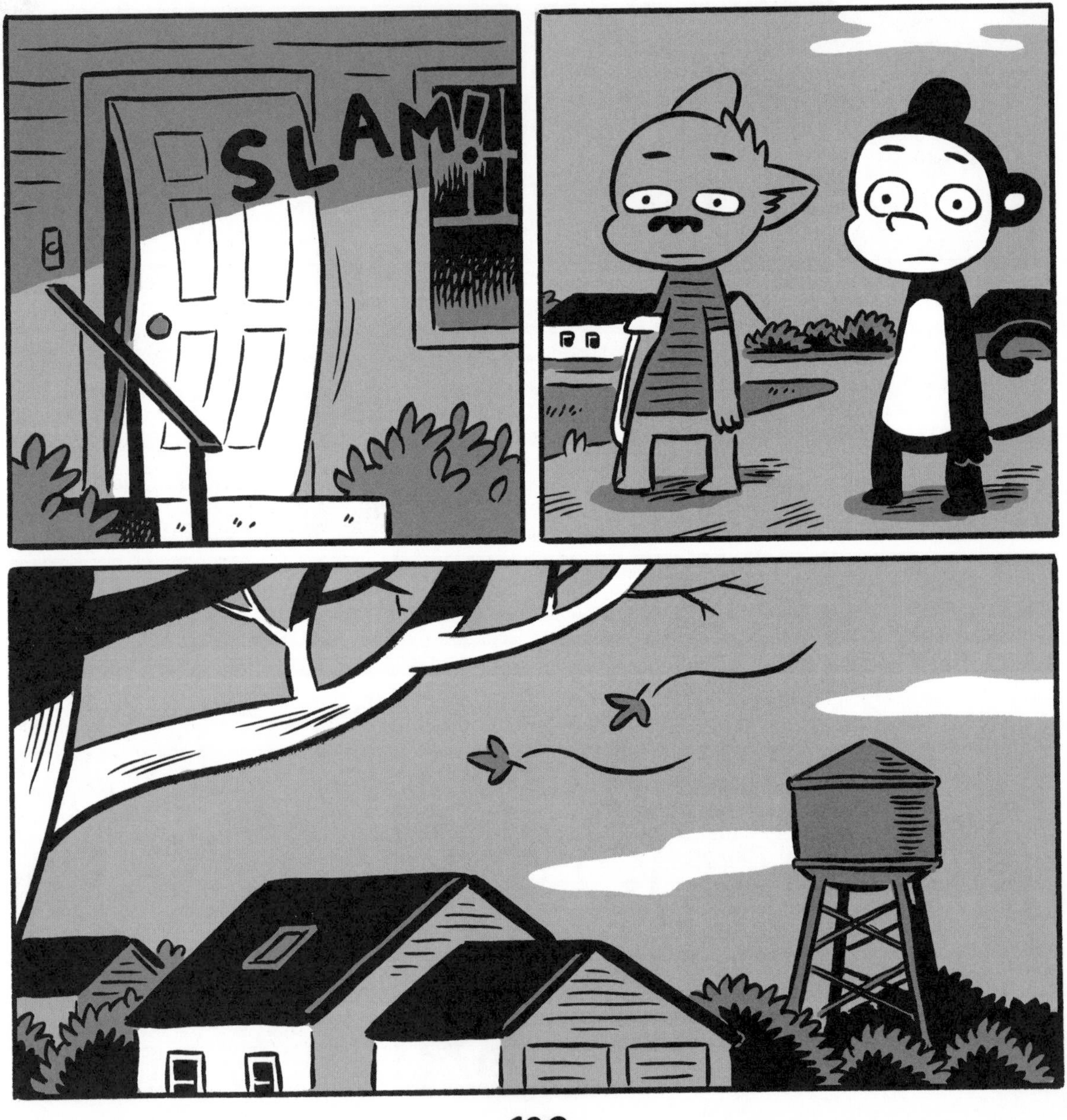
SLAM!

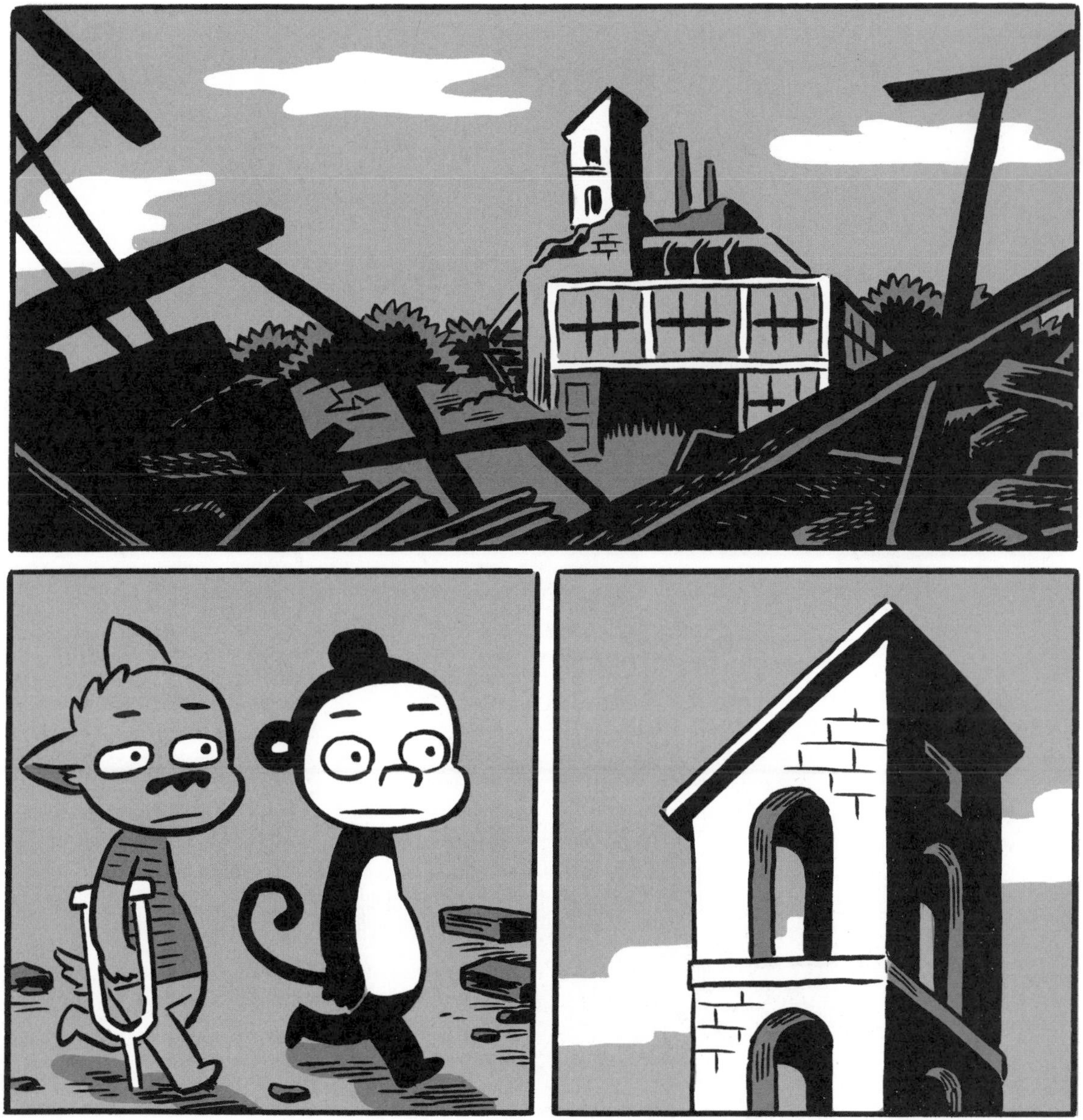

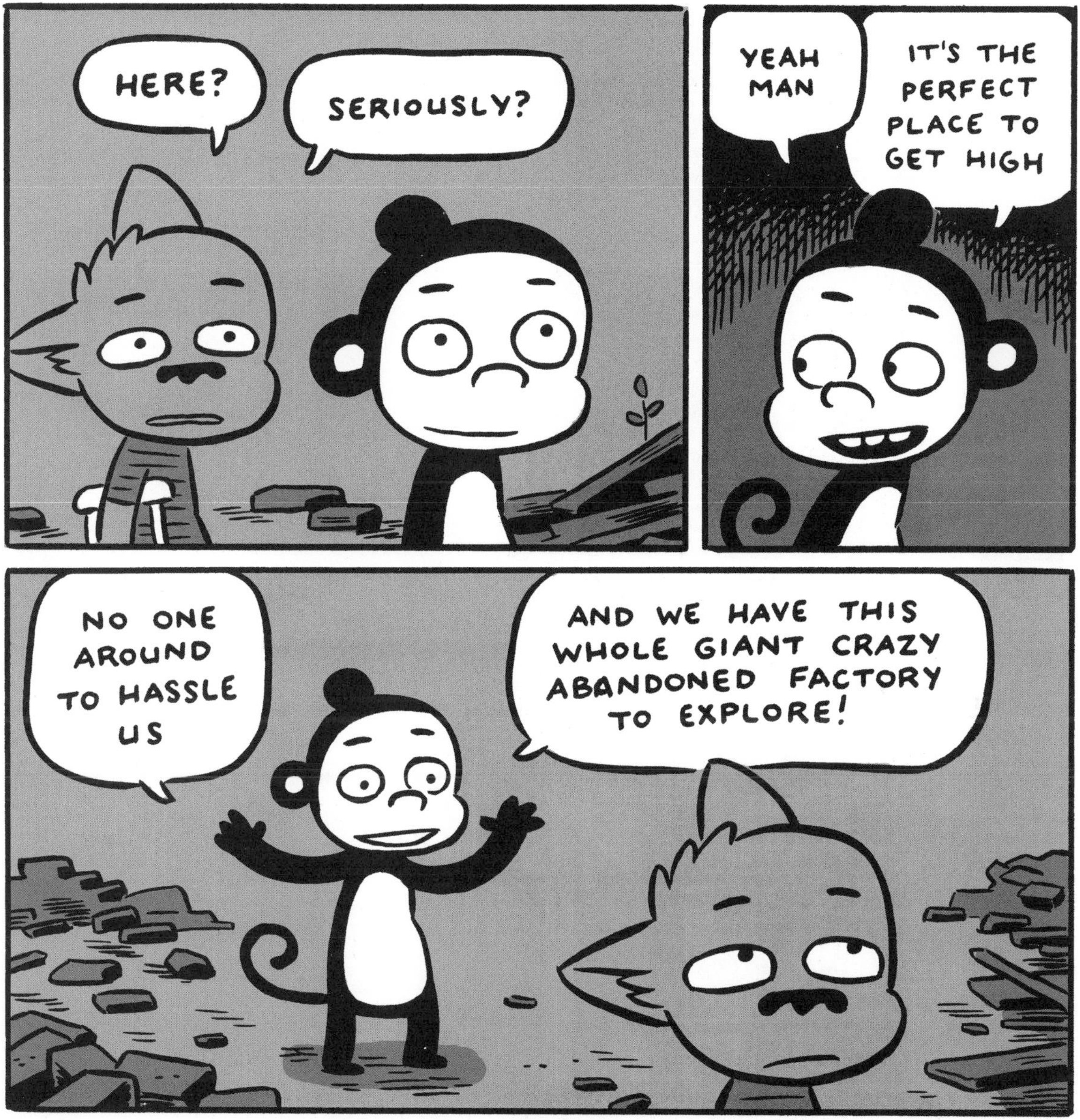
HERE?
SERIOUSLY?
YEAH MAN
IT'S THE PERFECT PLACE TO GET HIGH
NO ONE AROUND TO HASSLE US
AND WE HAVE THIS WHOLE GIANT CRAZY ABANDONED FACTORY TO EXPLORE!

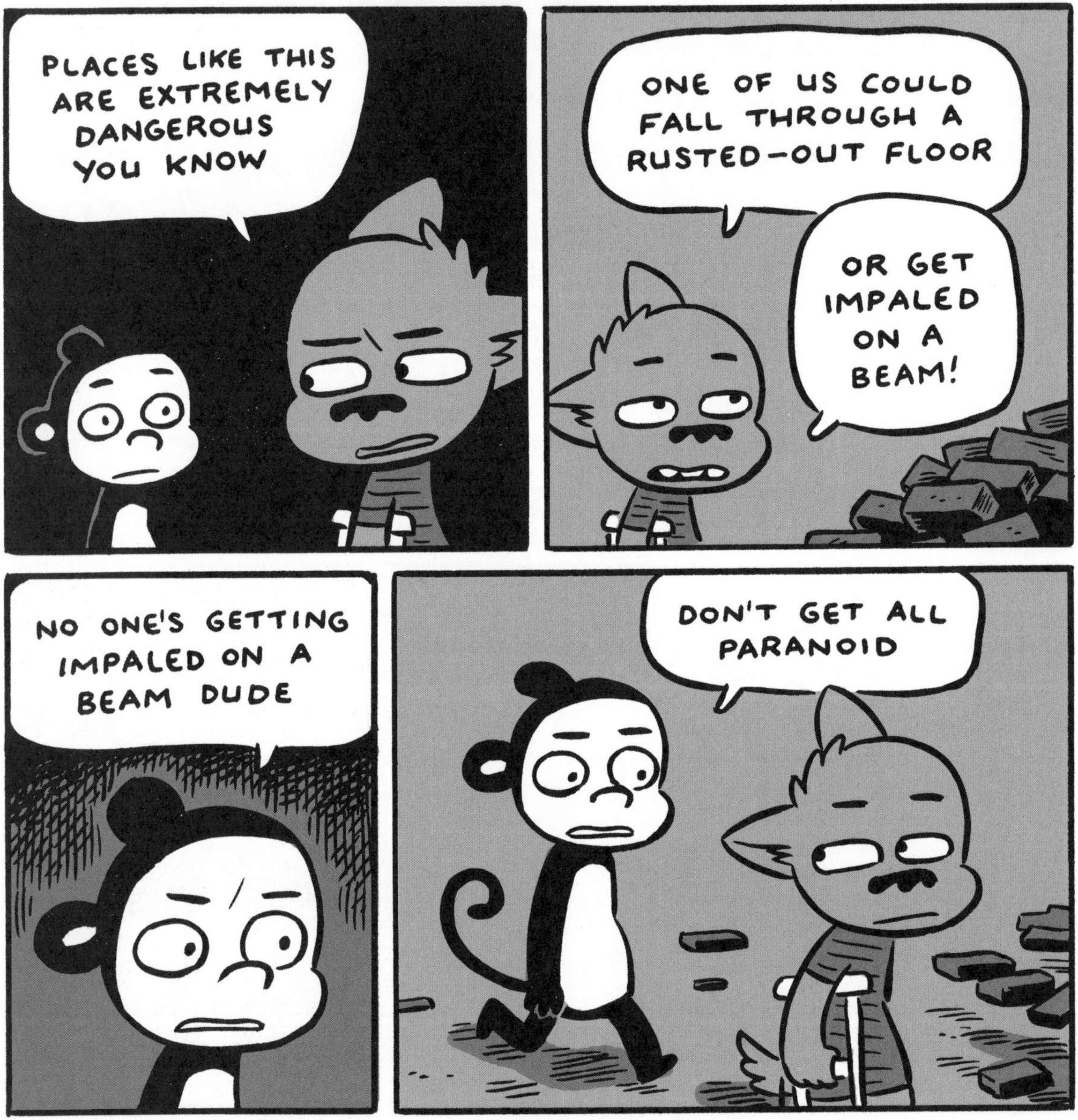
PLACES LIKE THIS ARE EXTREMELY DANGEROUS YOU KNOW
ONE OF US COULD FALL THROUGH A RUSTED-OUT FLOOR
OR GET IMPALED ON A BEAM!
NO ONE'S GETTING IMPALED ON A BEAM DUDE
DON'T GET ALL PARANOID

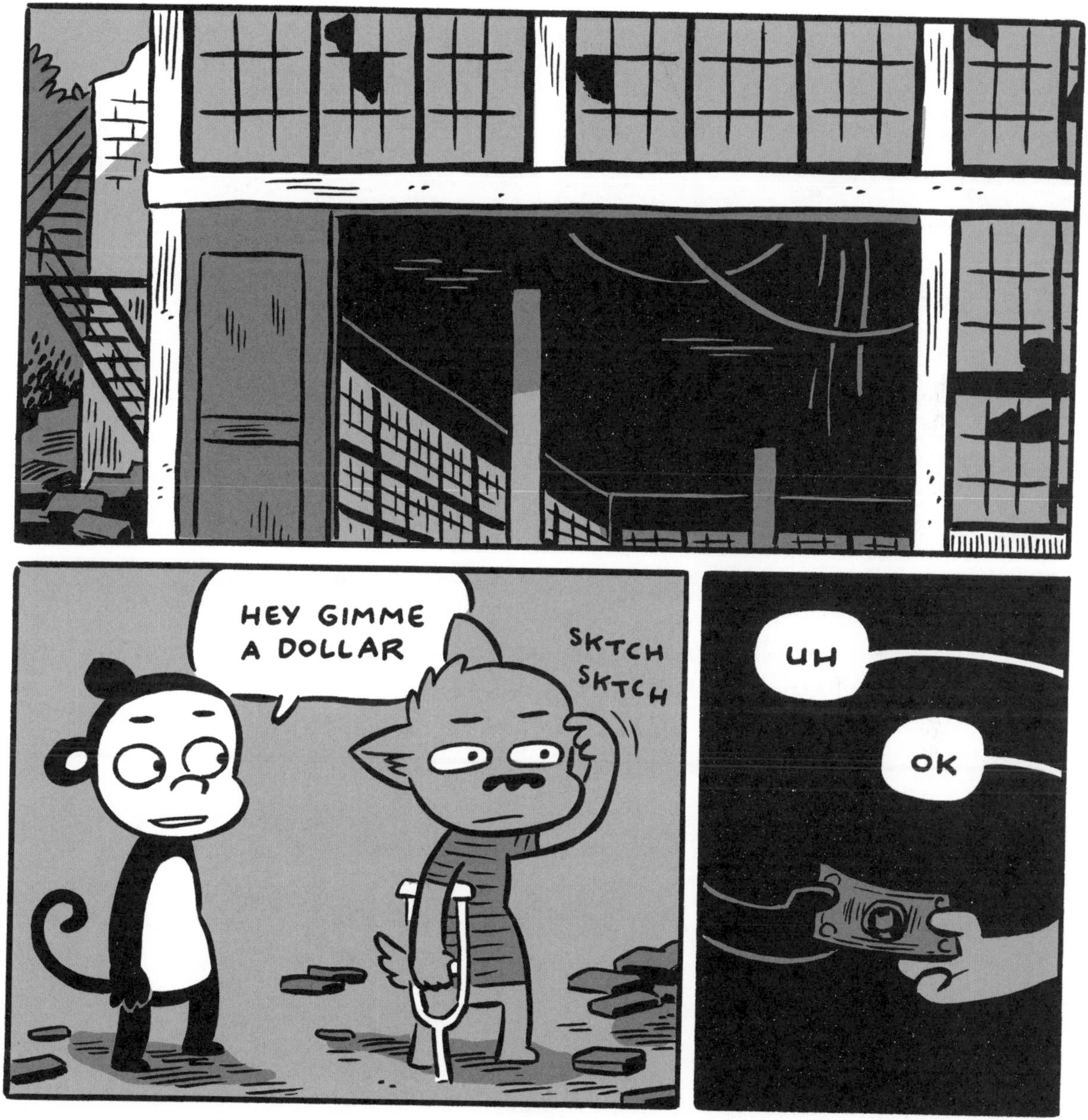
HEY GIMME A DOLLAR
SKTCH SKTCH
UH
OK

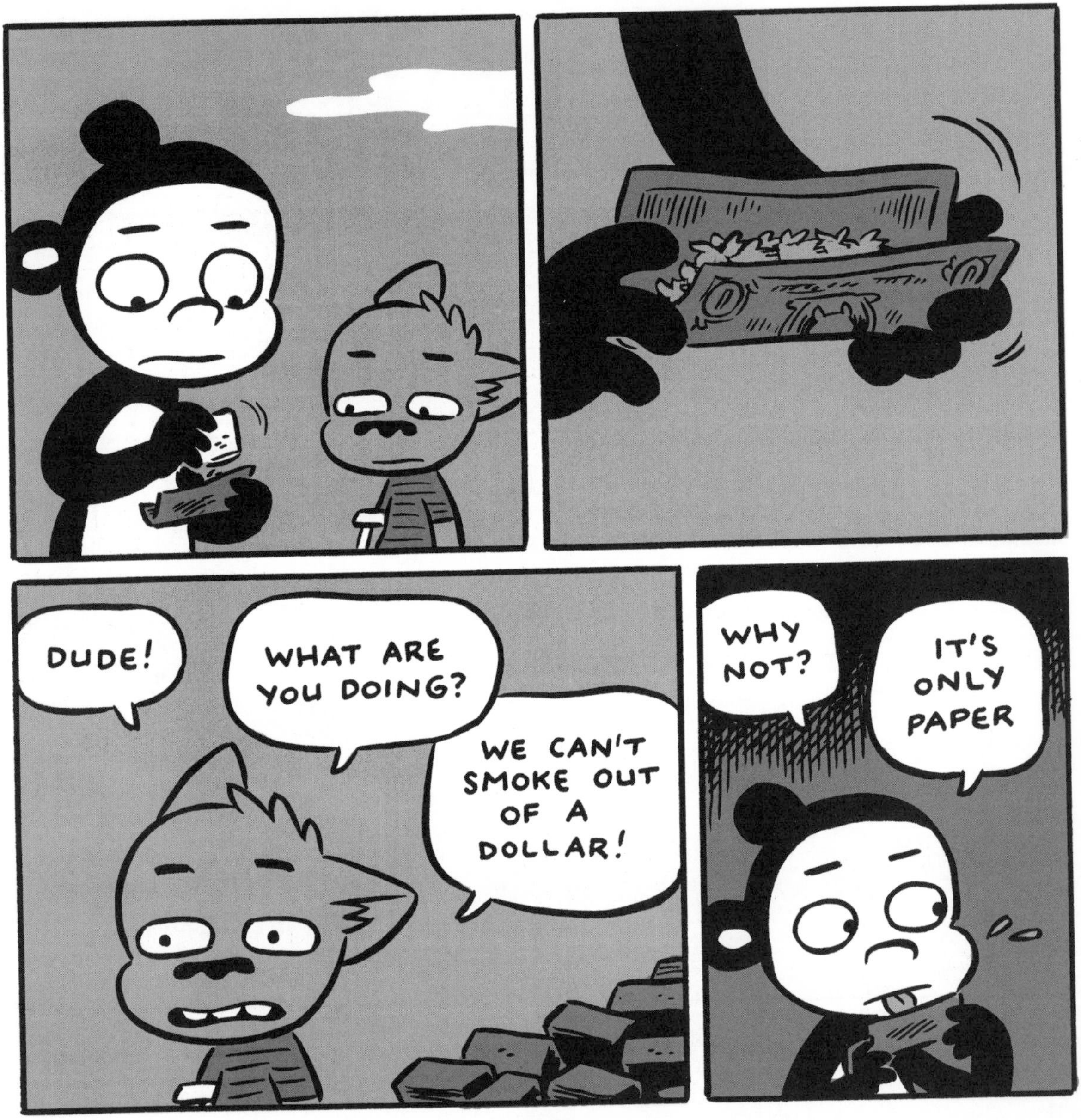
DUDE!
WHAT ARE YOU DOING?
WE CAN'T SMOKE OUT OF A DOLLAR!
WHY NOT?
IT'S ONLY PAPER

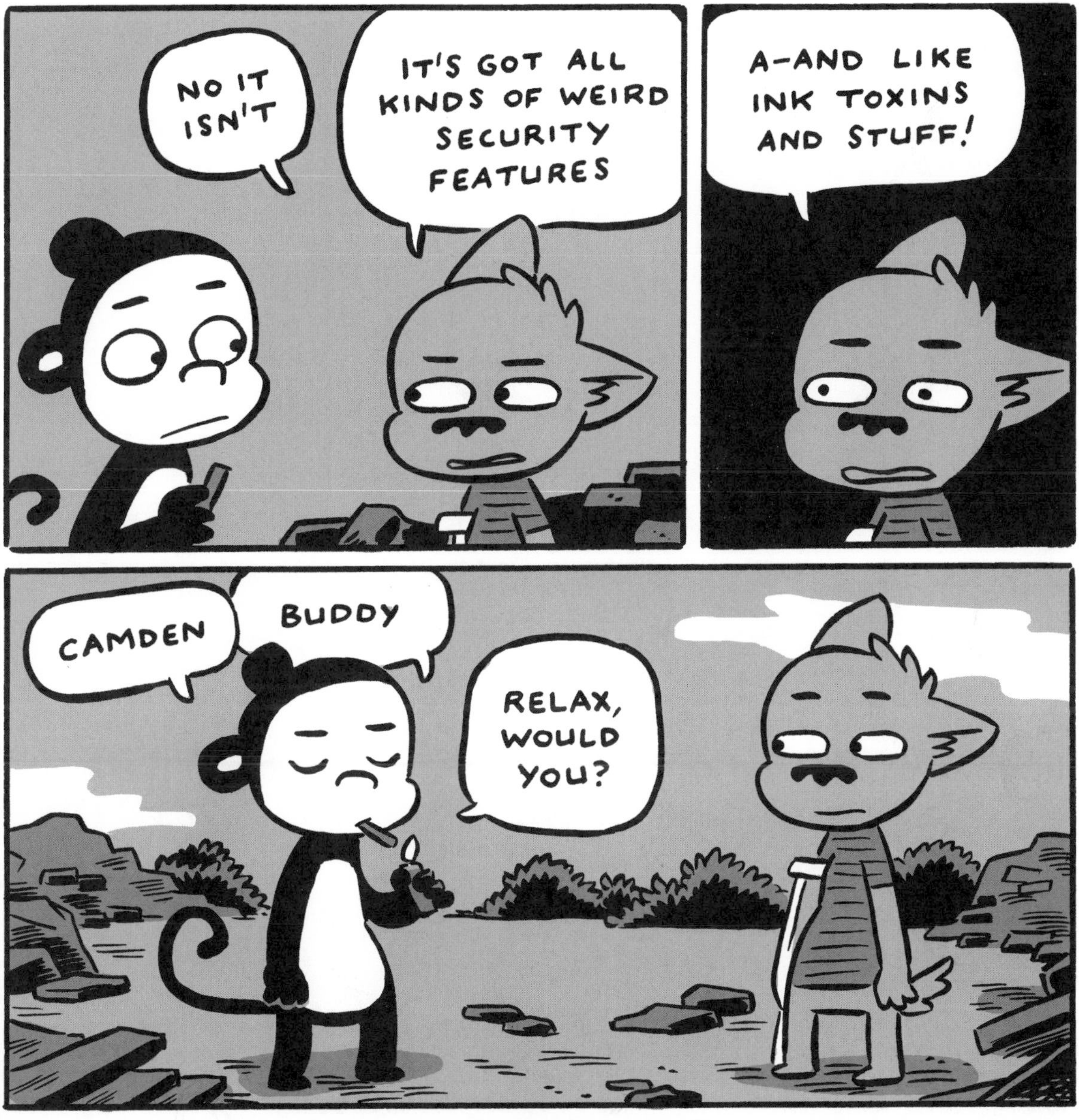
NO IT ISN'T
IT'S GOT ALL KINDS OF WEIRD SECURITY FEATURES
A-AND LIKE INK TOXINS AND STUFF!
CAMDEN
BUDDY
RELAX, WOULD YOU?

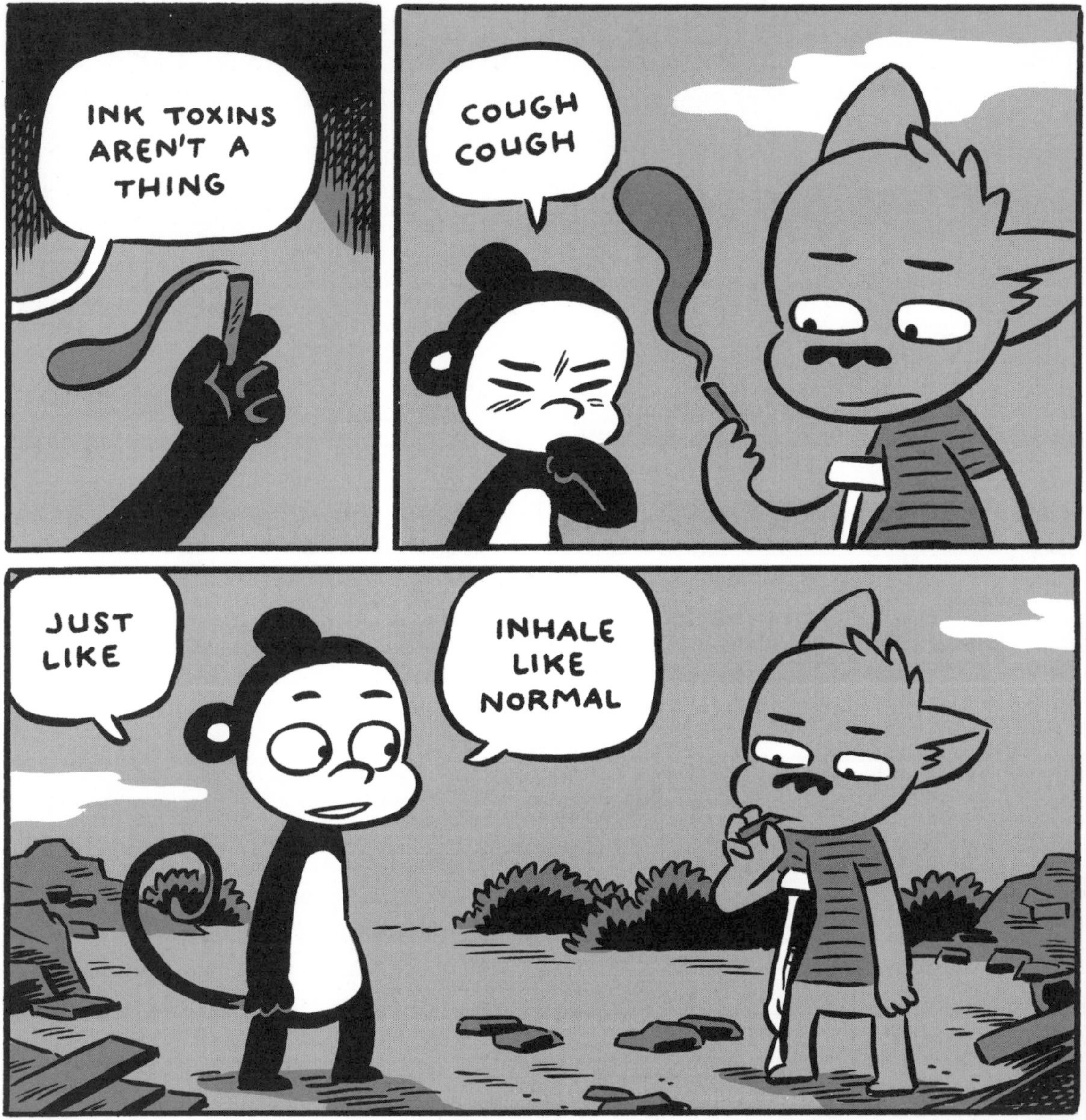
INK TOXINS AREN'T A THING
COUGH COUGH
JUST LIKE
INHALE LIKE NORMAL

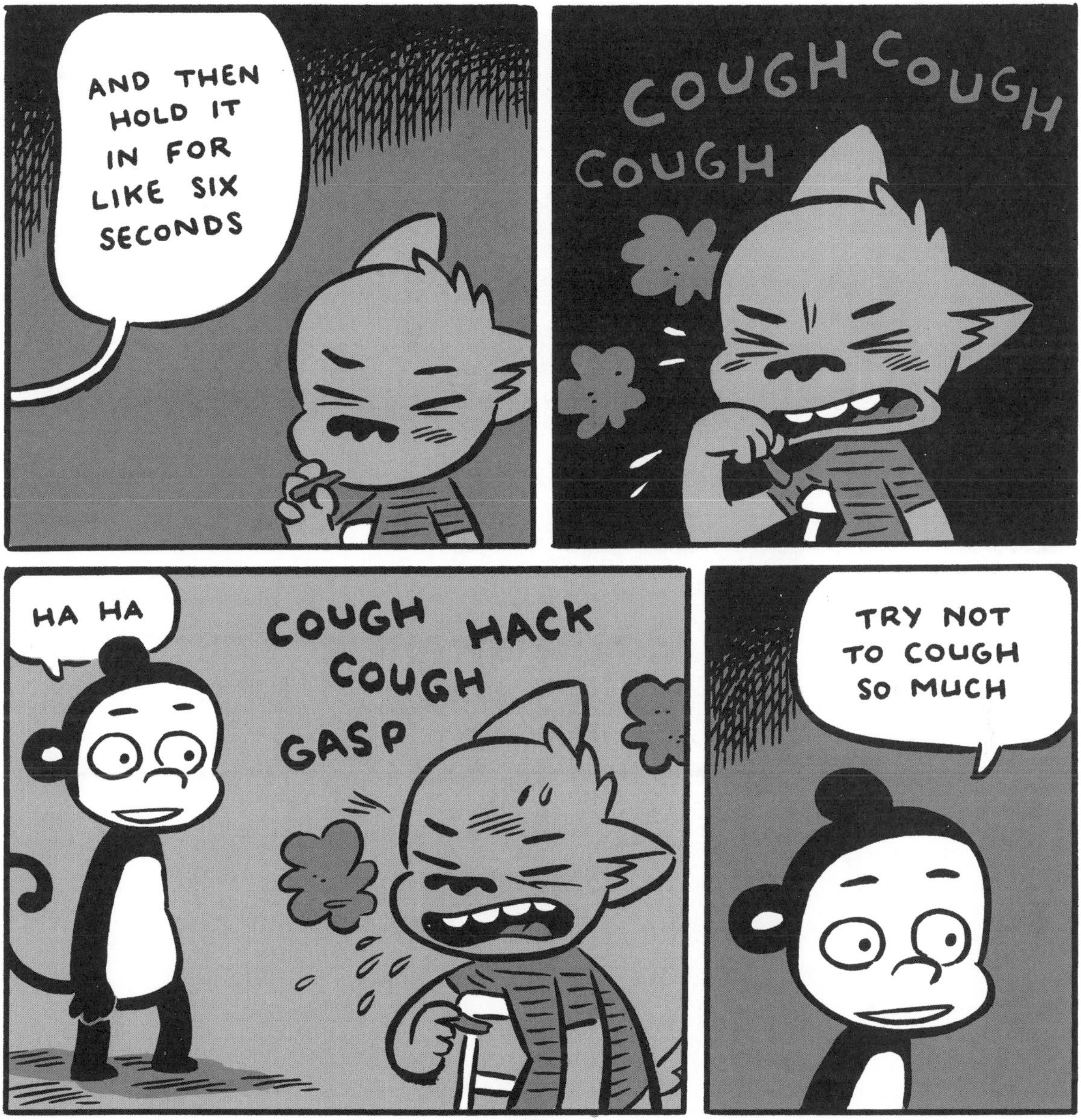
AND THEN HOLD IT IN FOR LIKE SIX SECONDS
COUGH COUGH COUGH
HA HA
COUGH HACK COUGH GASP
TRY NOT TO COUGH SO MUCH

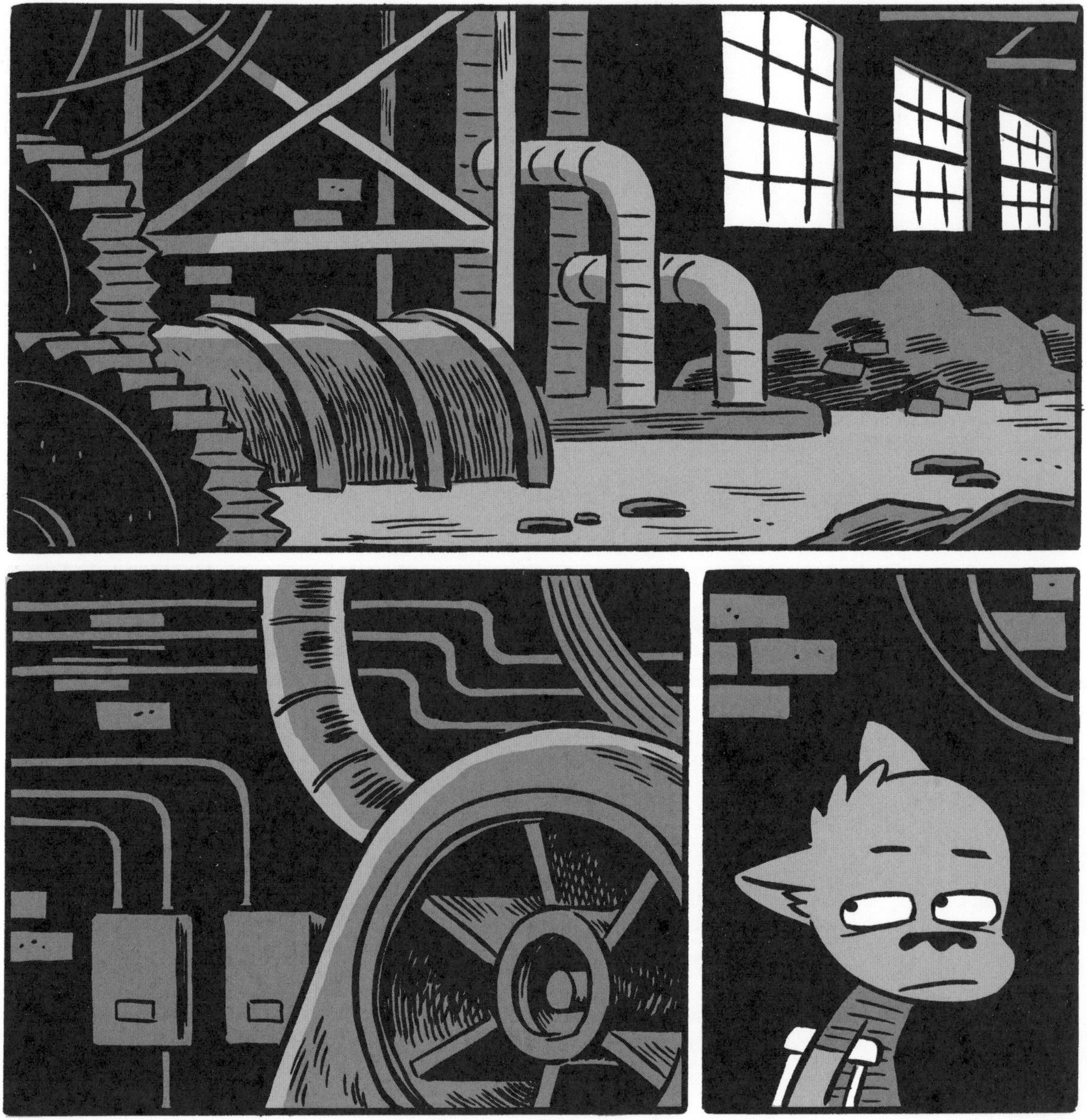

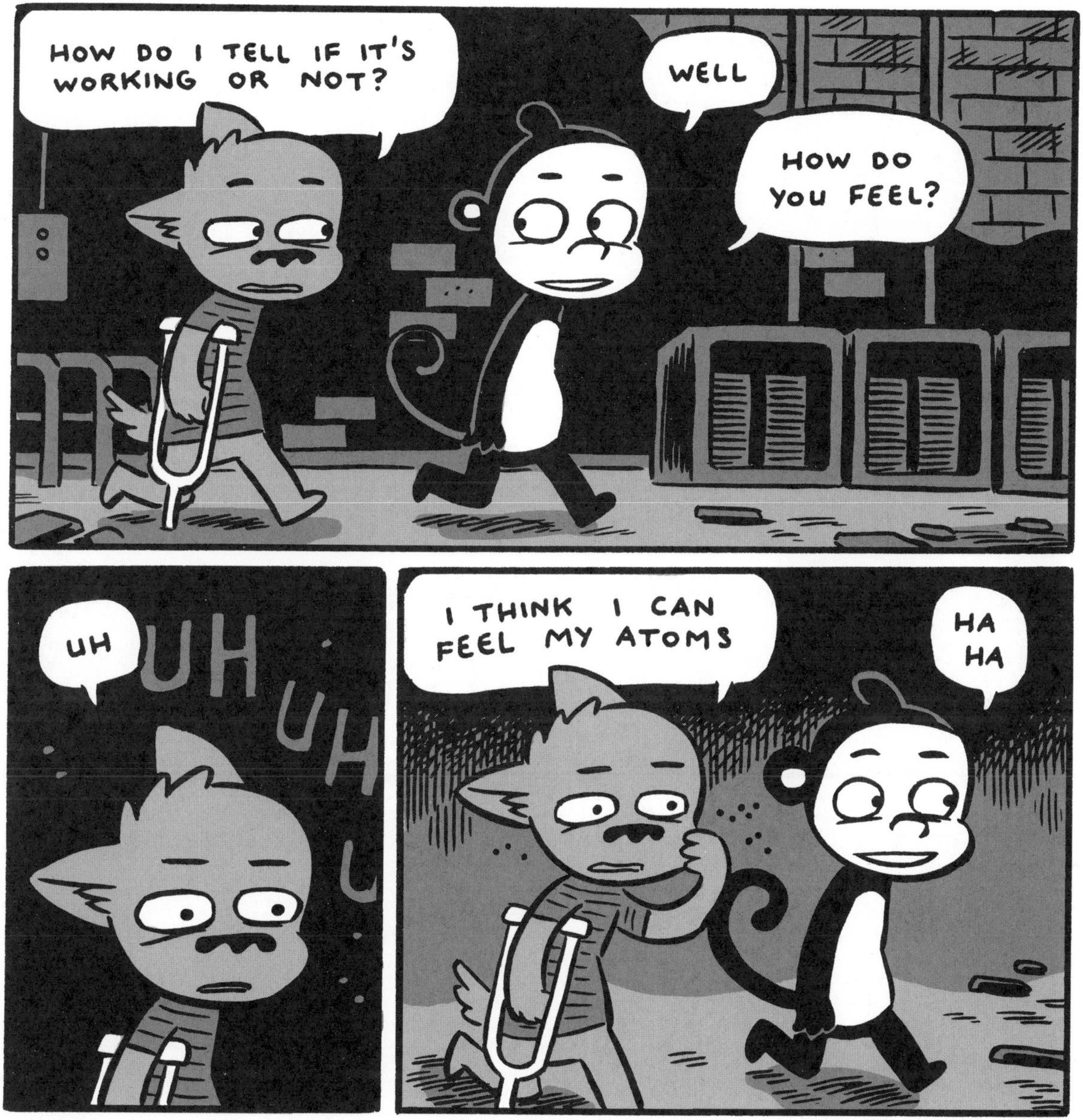
HOW DO I TELL IF IT'S WORKING OR NOT?
WELL
HOW DO YOU FEEL?
UH
UH UH UH U
I THINK I CAN FEEL MY ATOMS
HA HA

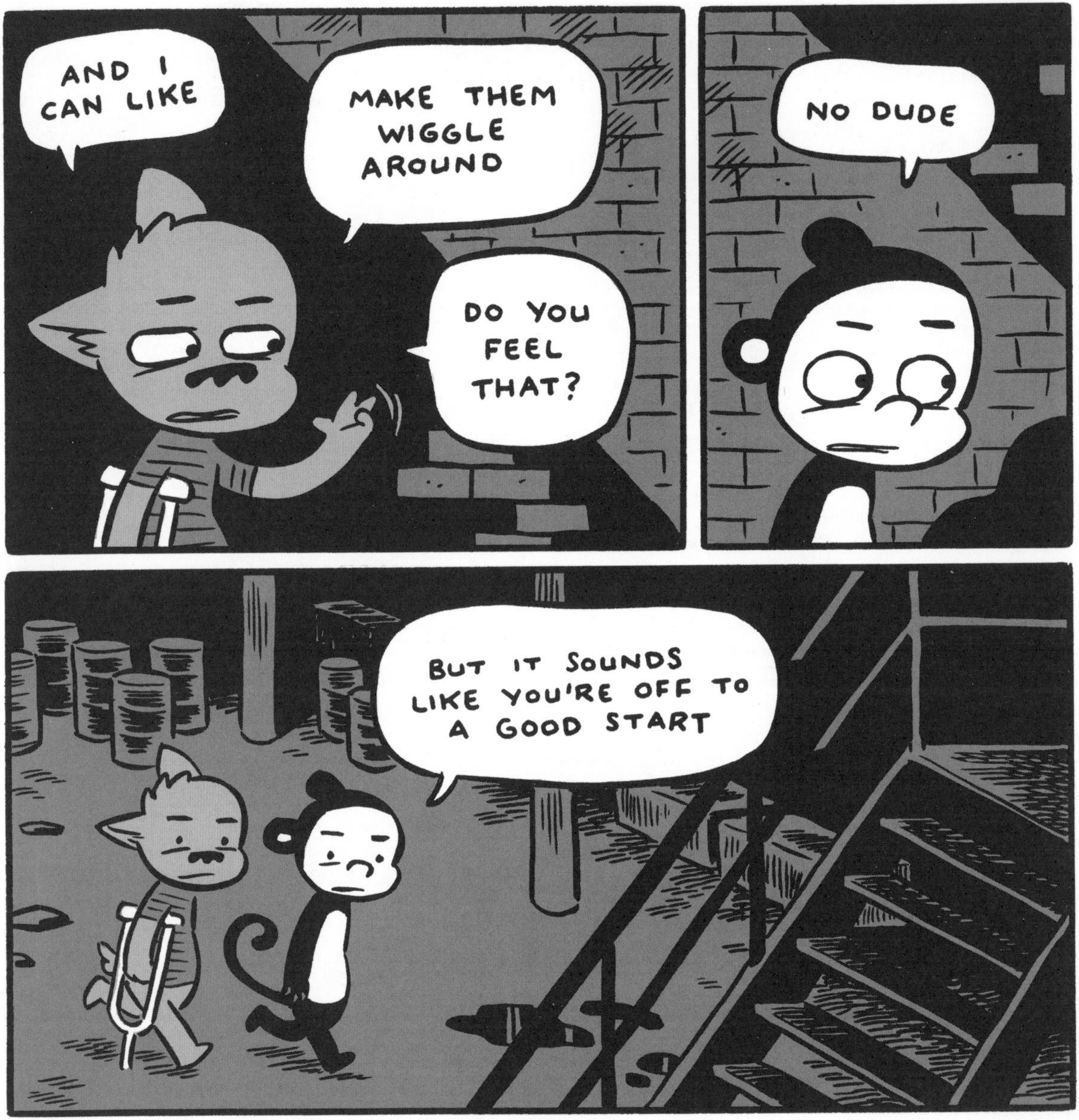
AND I CAN LIKE
MAKE THEM WIGGLE AROUND
DO YOU FEEL THAT?
NO DUDE
BUT IT SOUNDS LIKE YOU'RE OFF TO A GOOD START

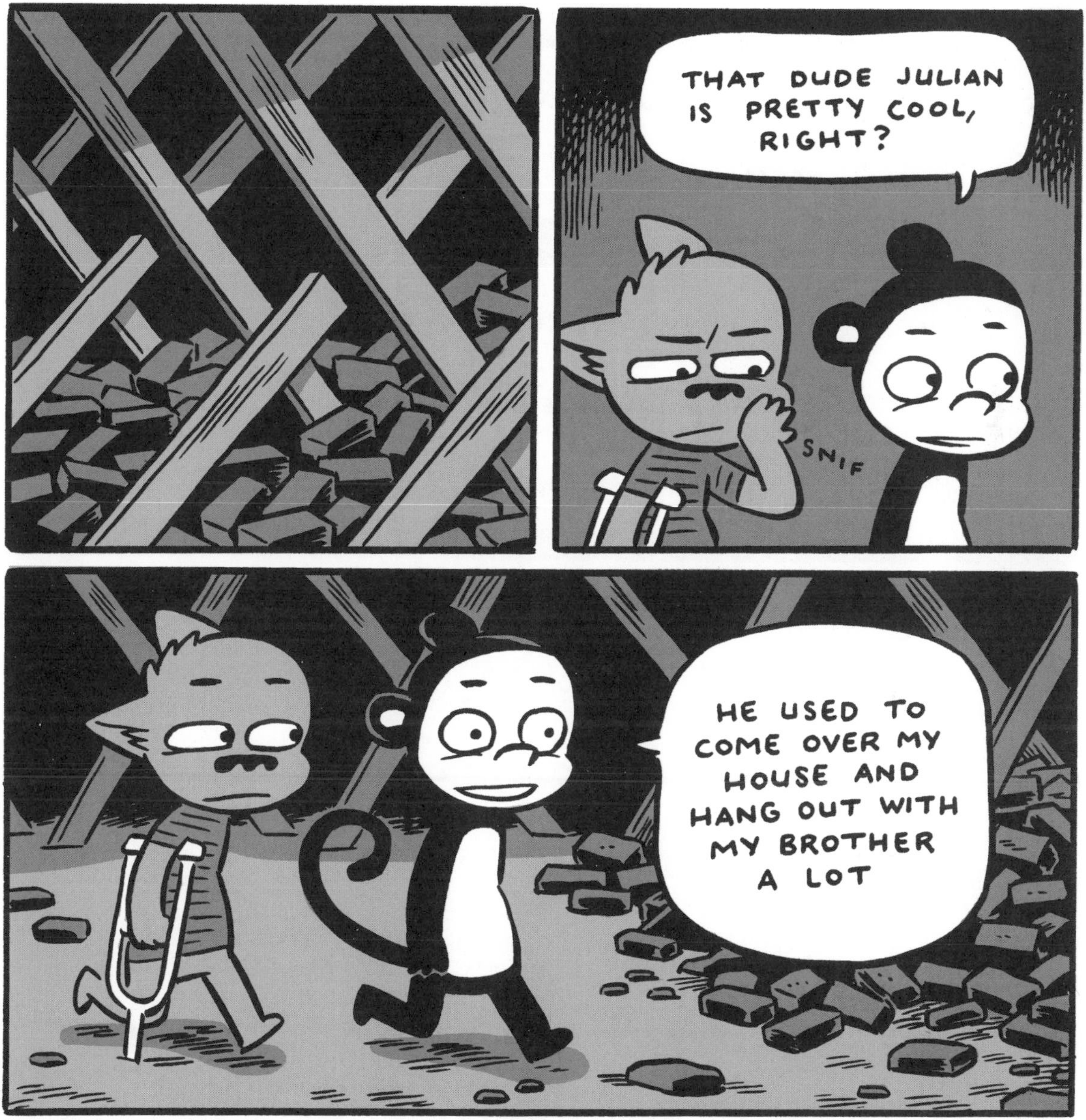
THAT DUDE JULIAN IS PRETTY COOL, RIGHT?
SNIF
HE USED TO COME OVER MY HOUSE AND HANG OUT WITH MY BROTHER A LOT

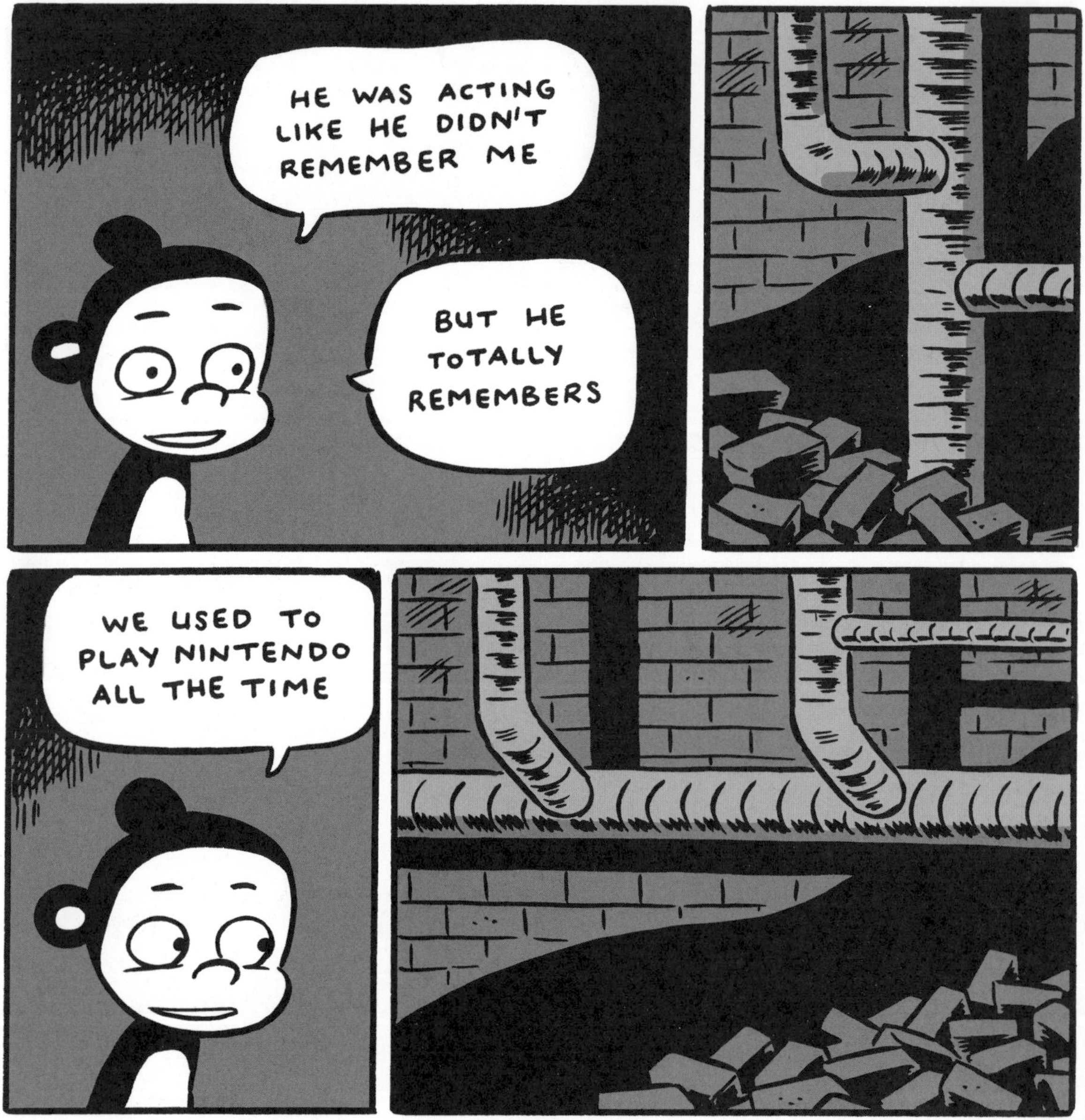
HE WAS ACTING LIKE HE DIDN'T REMEMBER ME
BUT HE TOTALLY REMEMBERS
WE USED TO PLAY NINTENDO ALL THE TIME

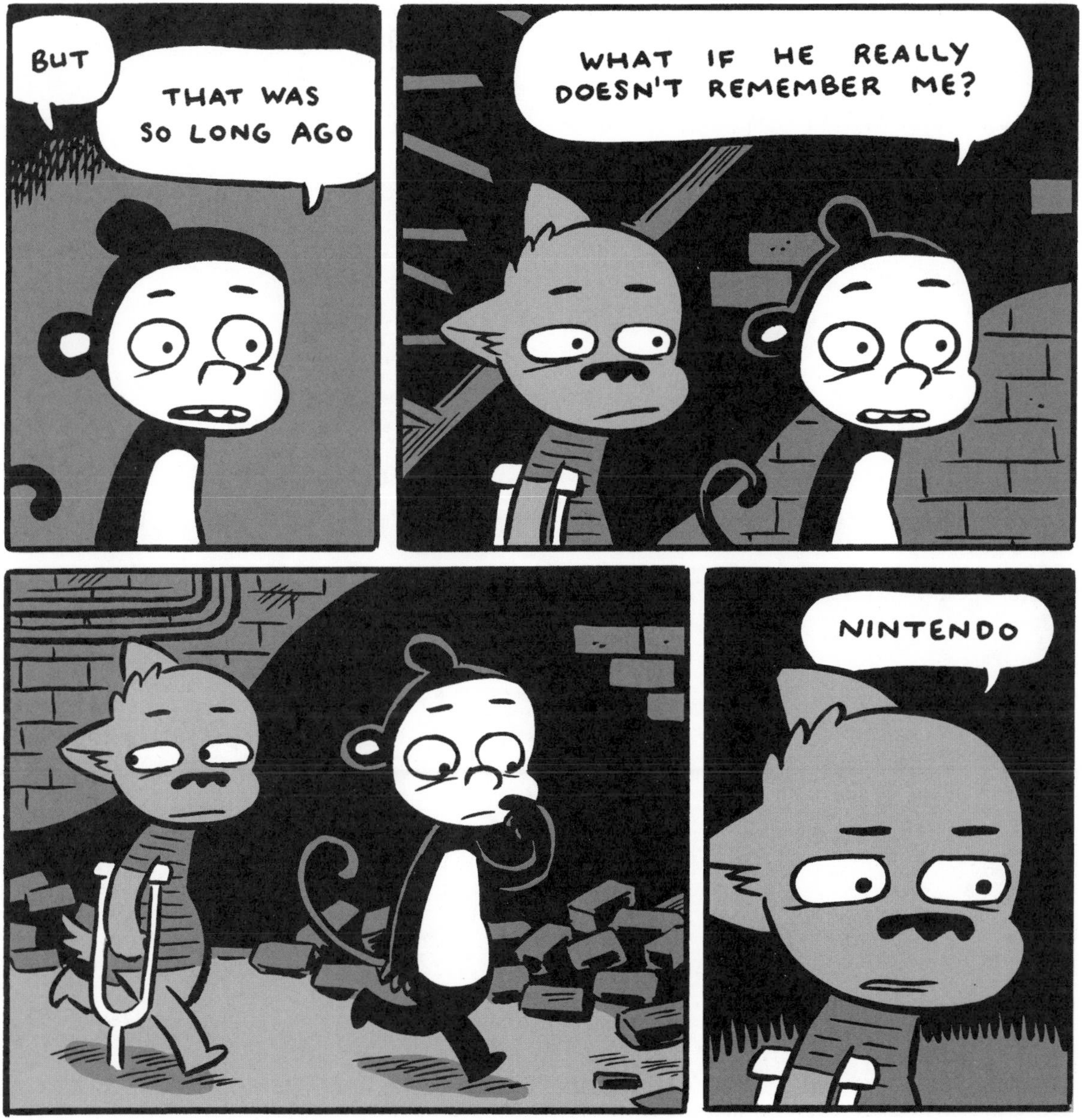
BUT
THAT WAS SO LONG AGO
WHAT IF HE REALLY DOESN'T REMEMBER ME?
NINTENDO

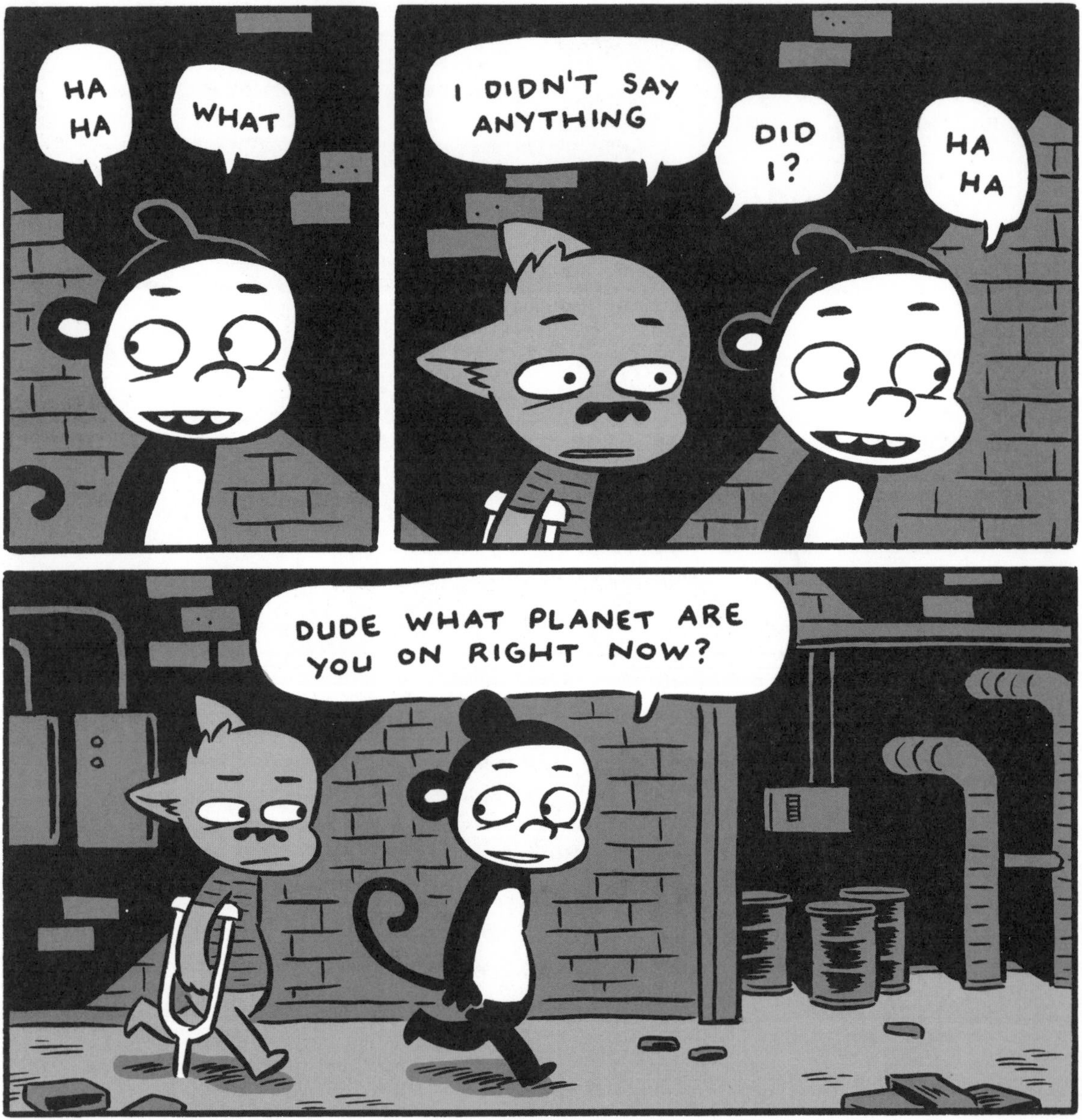
HA HA
WHAT
I DIDN'T SAY ANYTHING
DID I?
HA HA
DUDE WHAT PLANET ARE YOU ON RIGHT NOW?

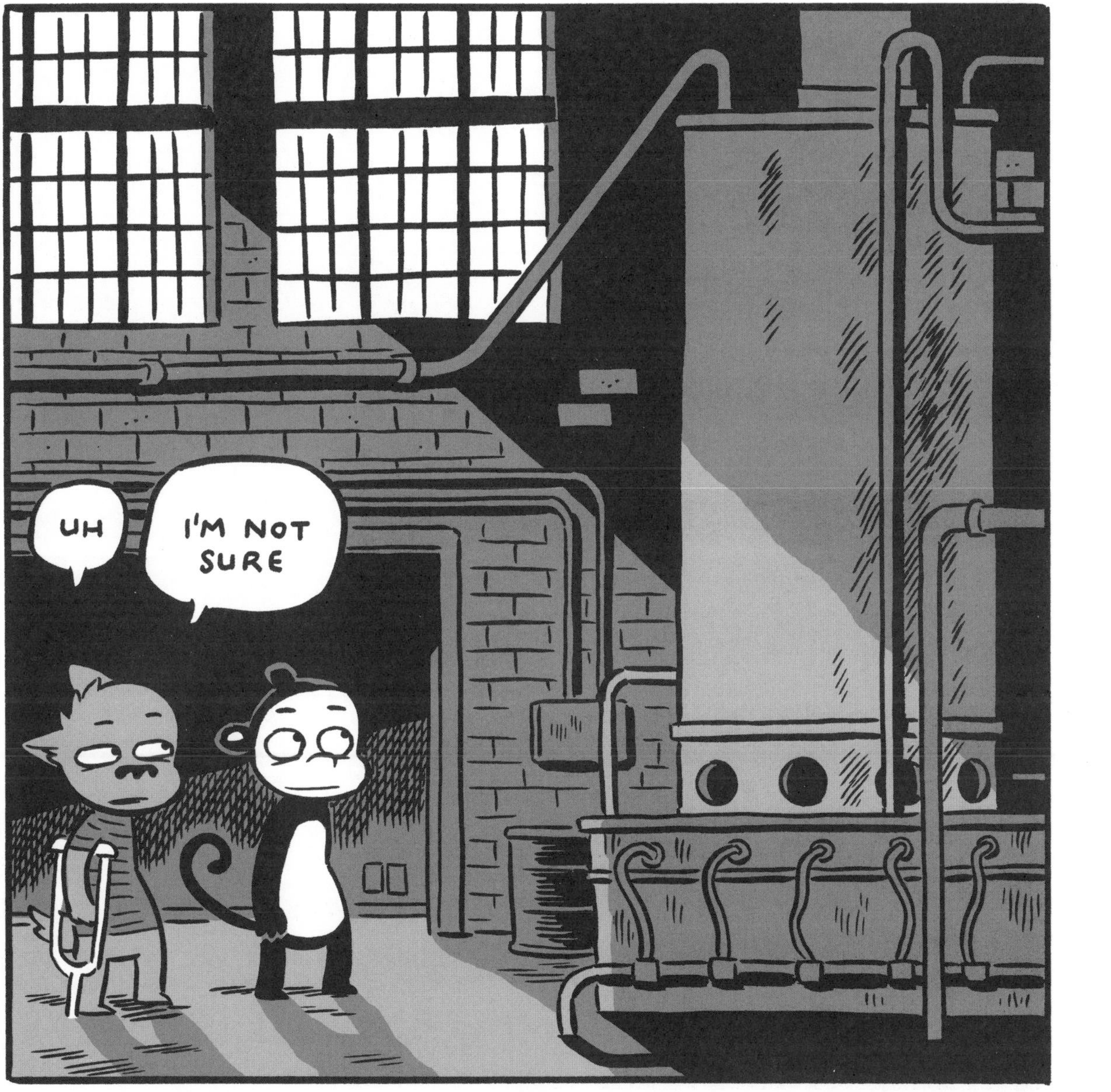
UH
I'M NOT SURE

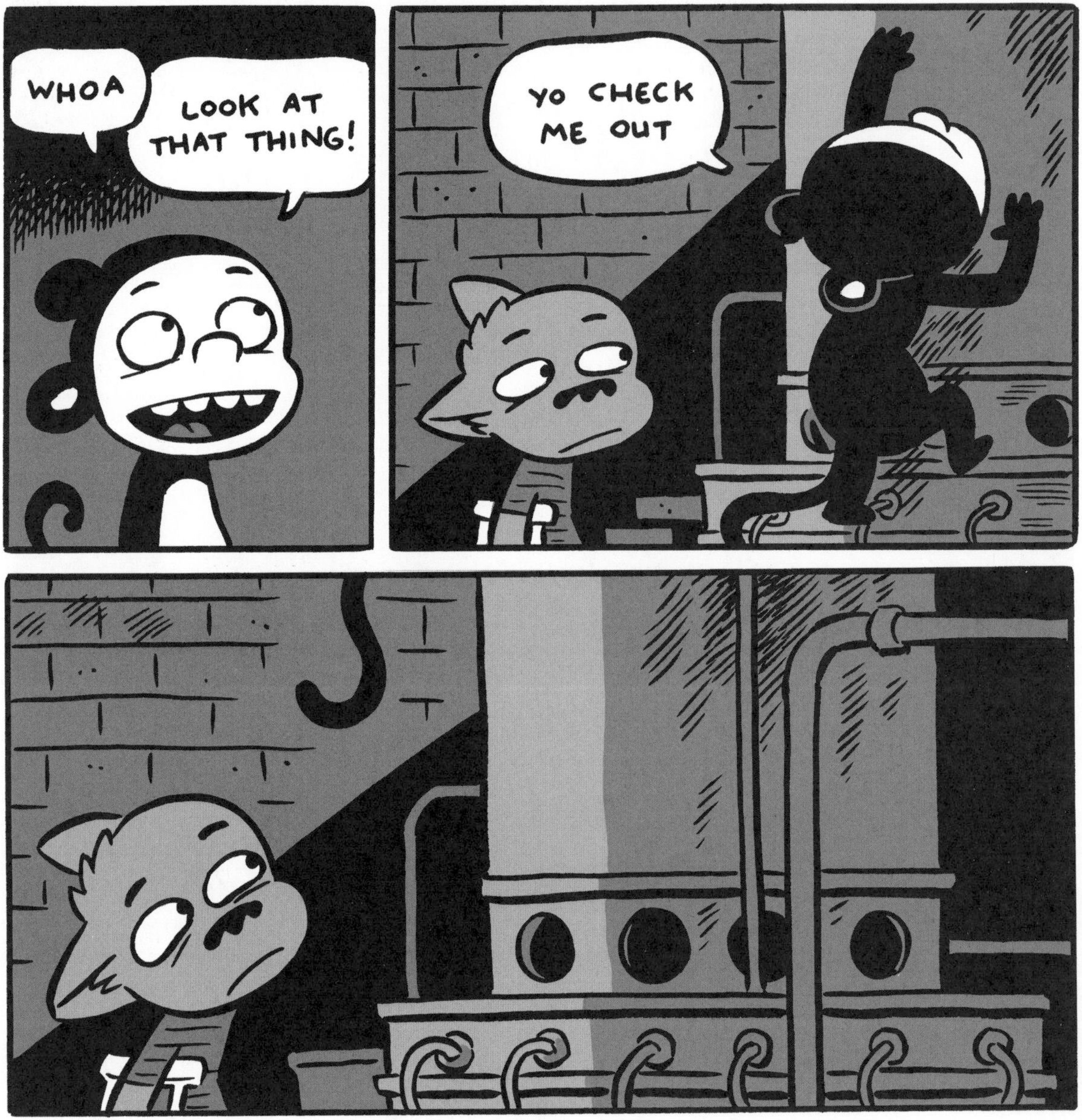
WHOA
LOOK AT THAT THING!
YO CHECK ME OUT

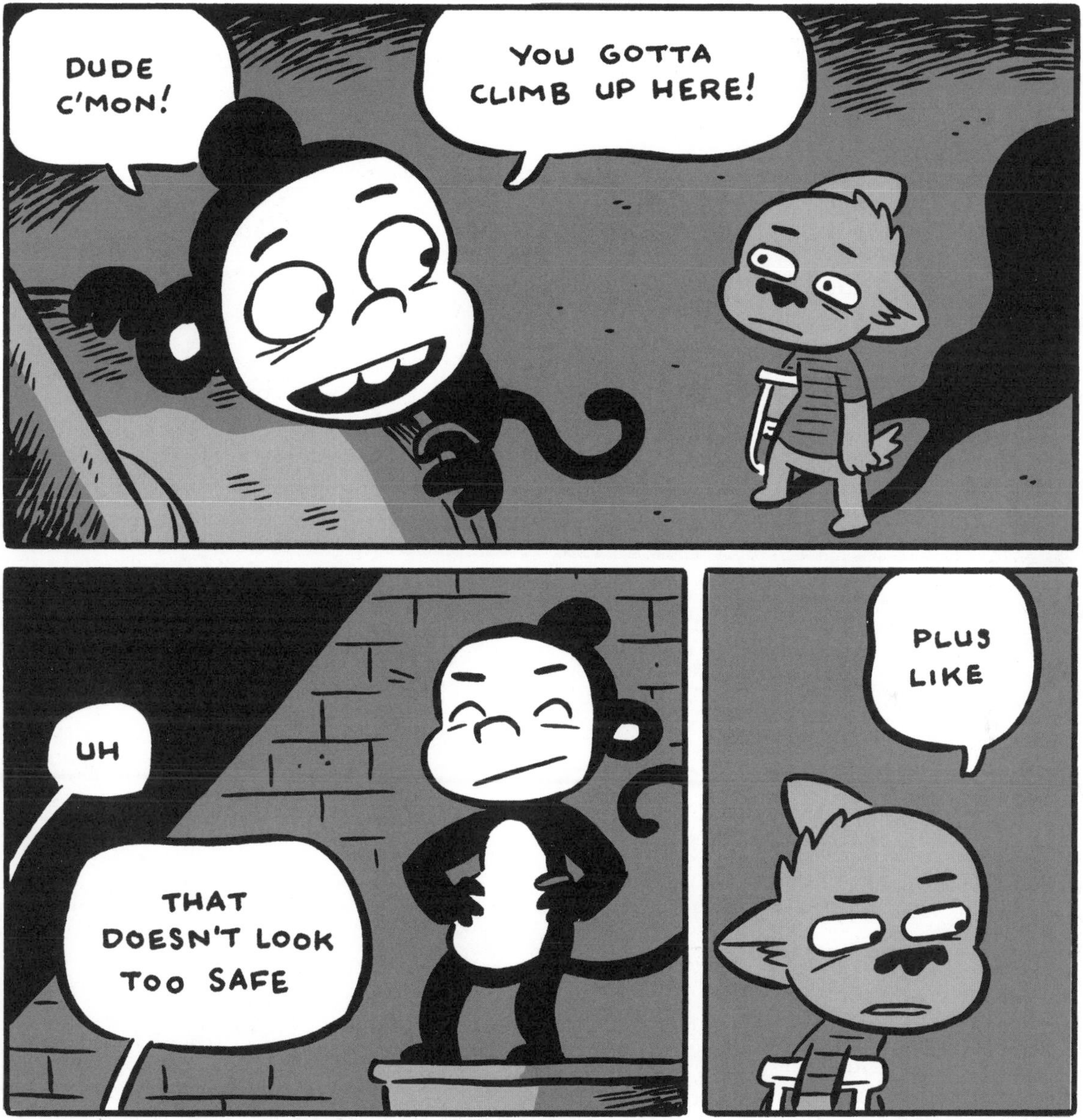
DUDE C'MON!
YOU GOTTA CLIMB UP HERE!
UH
THAT DOESN'T LOOK TOO SAFE
PLUS LIKE

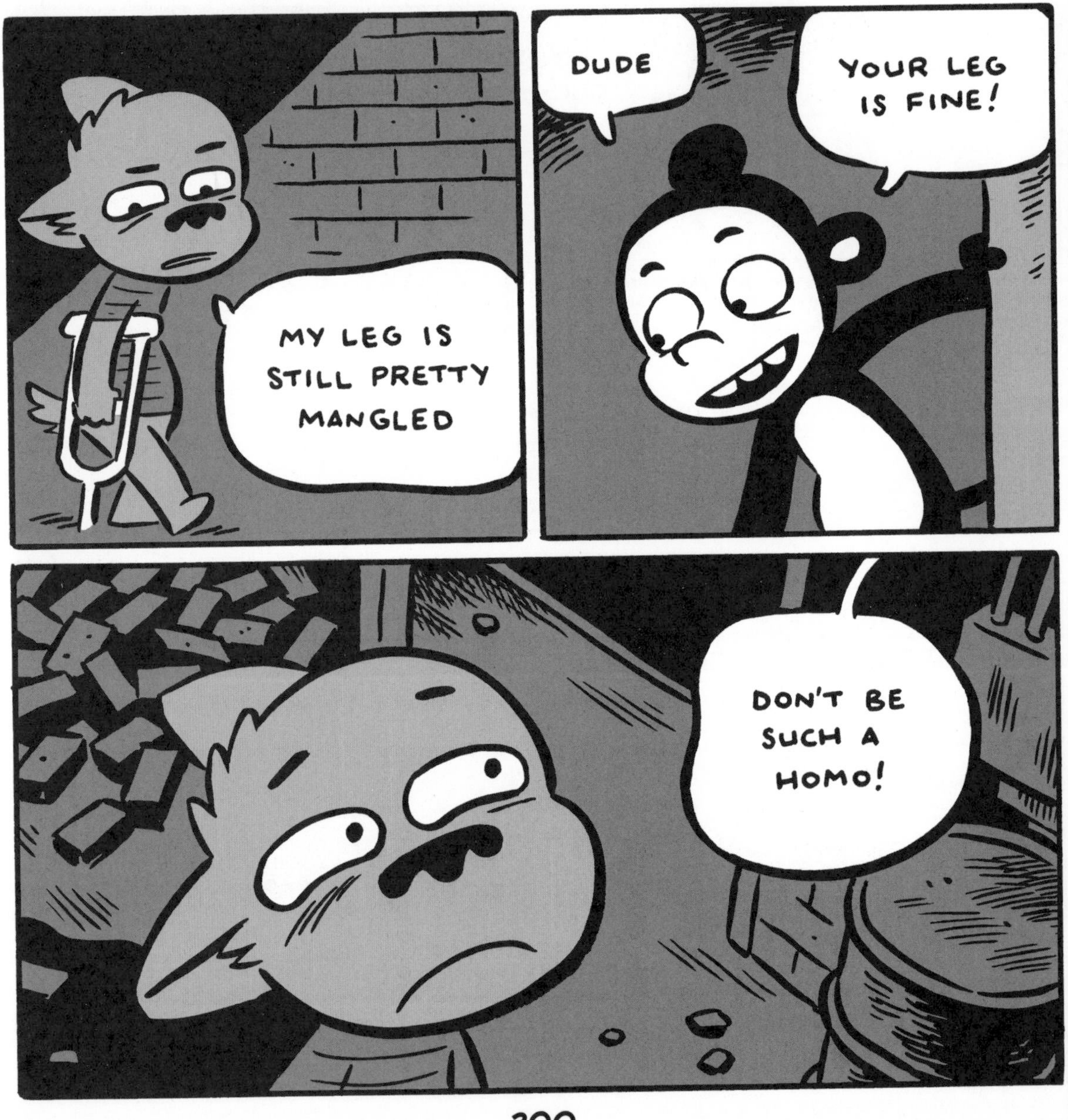
MY LEG IS STILL PRETTY MANGLED
DUDE
YOUR LEG IS FINE!
DON'T BE SUCH A HOMO!

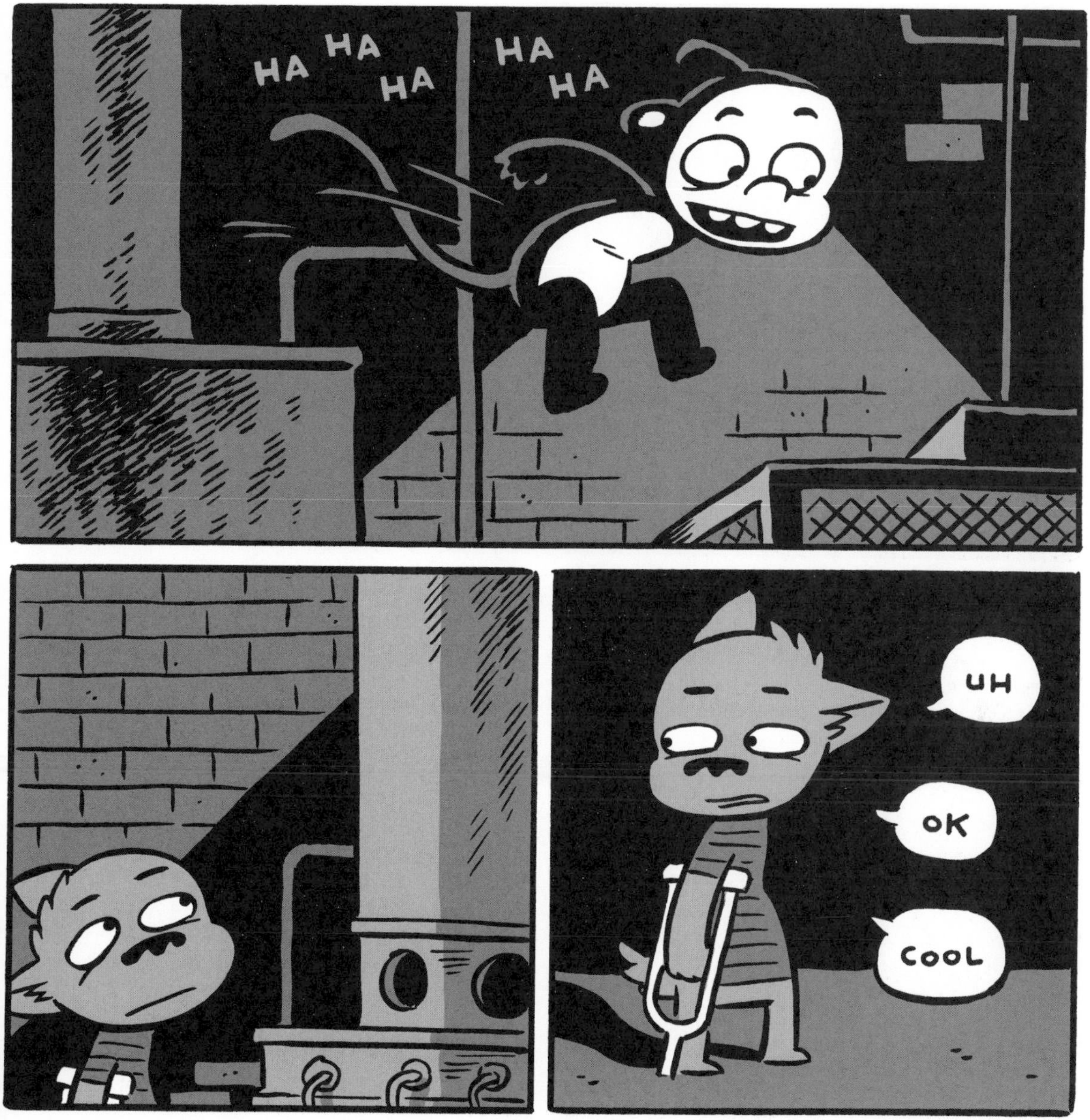
HA HA
HA
HA
HA
UH
OK
COOL

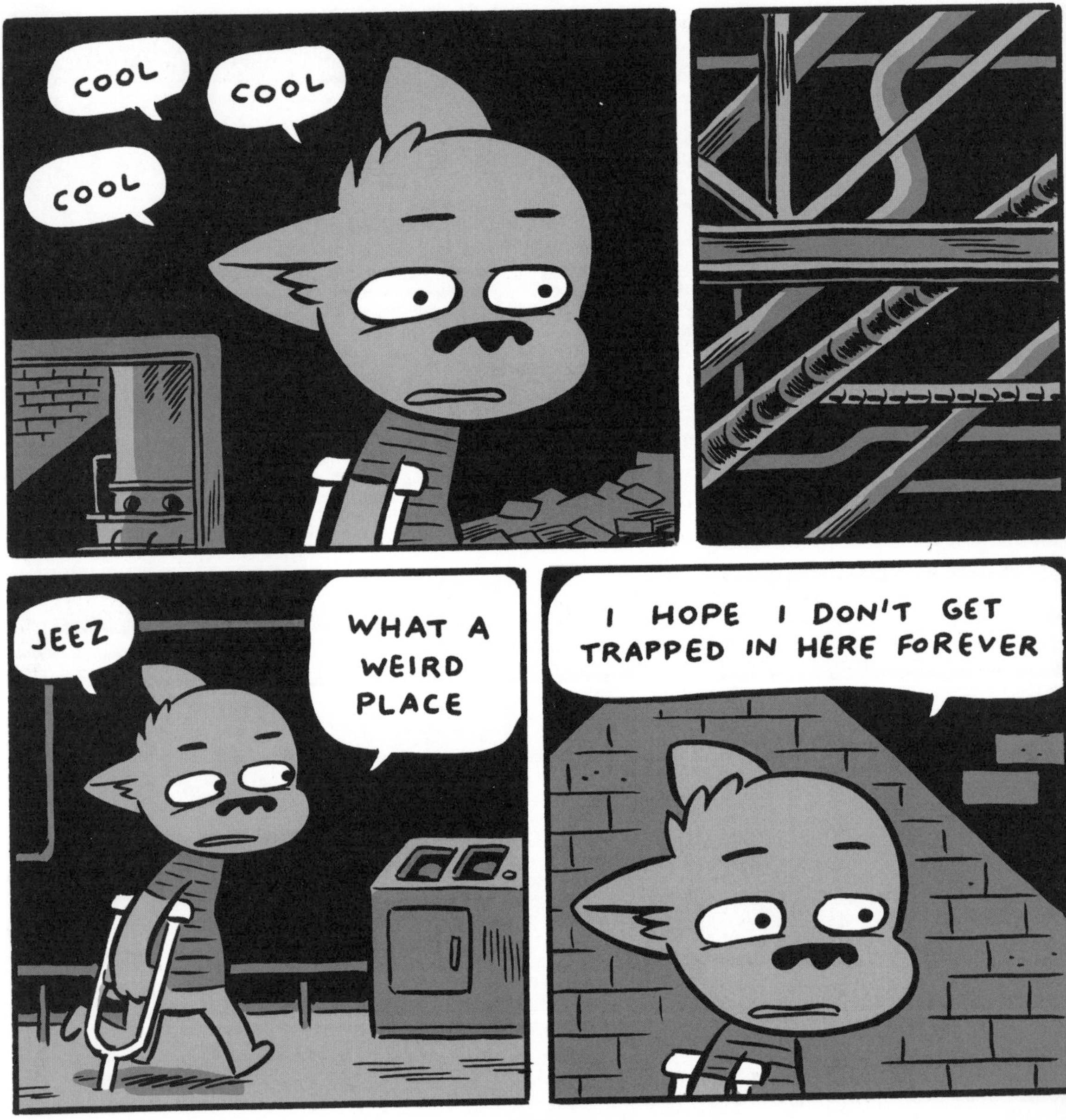
COOL
COOL
COOL
JEEZ
WHAT A WEIRD PLACE
I HOPE I DON'T GET TRAPPED IN HERE FOREVER

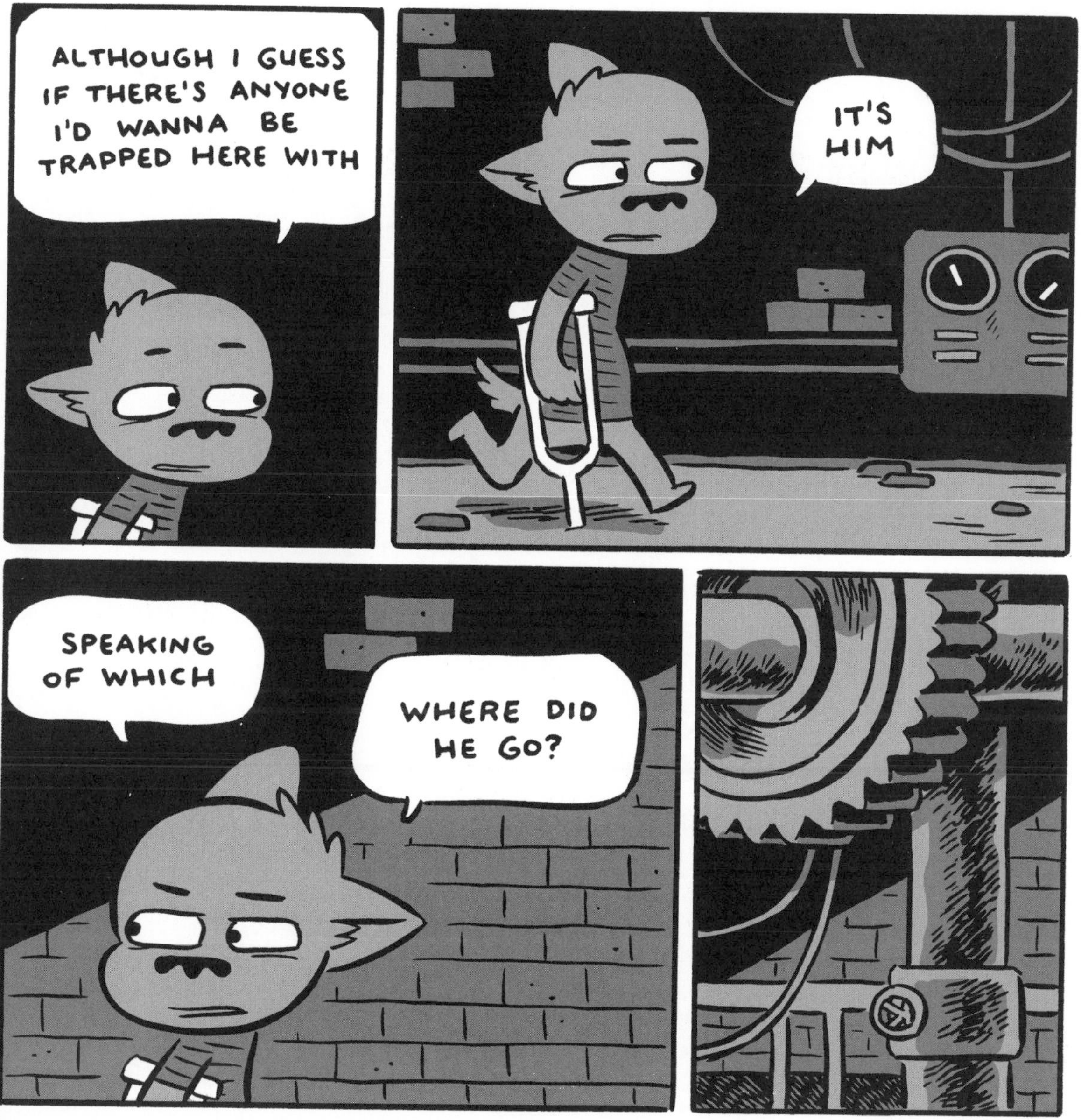
ALTHOUGH I GUESS IF THERE'S ANYONE I'D WANNA BE TRAPPED HERE WITH
IT'S HIM
SPEAKING OF WHICH
WHERE DID HE GO?

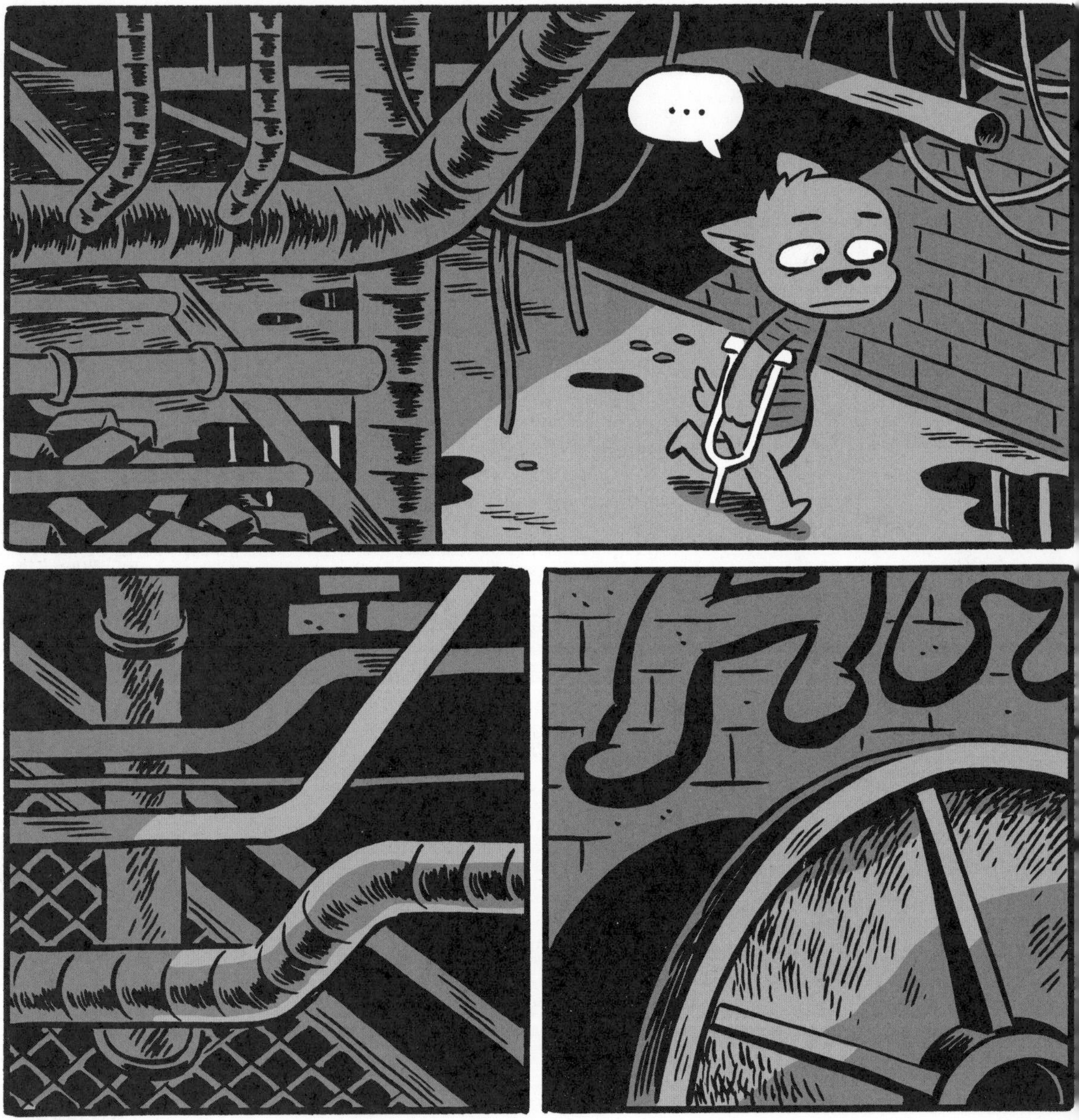
...

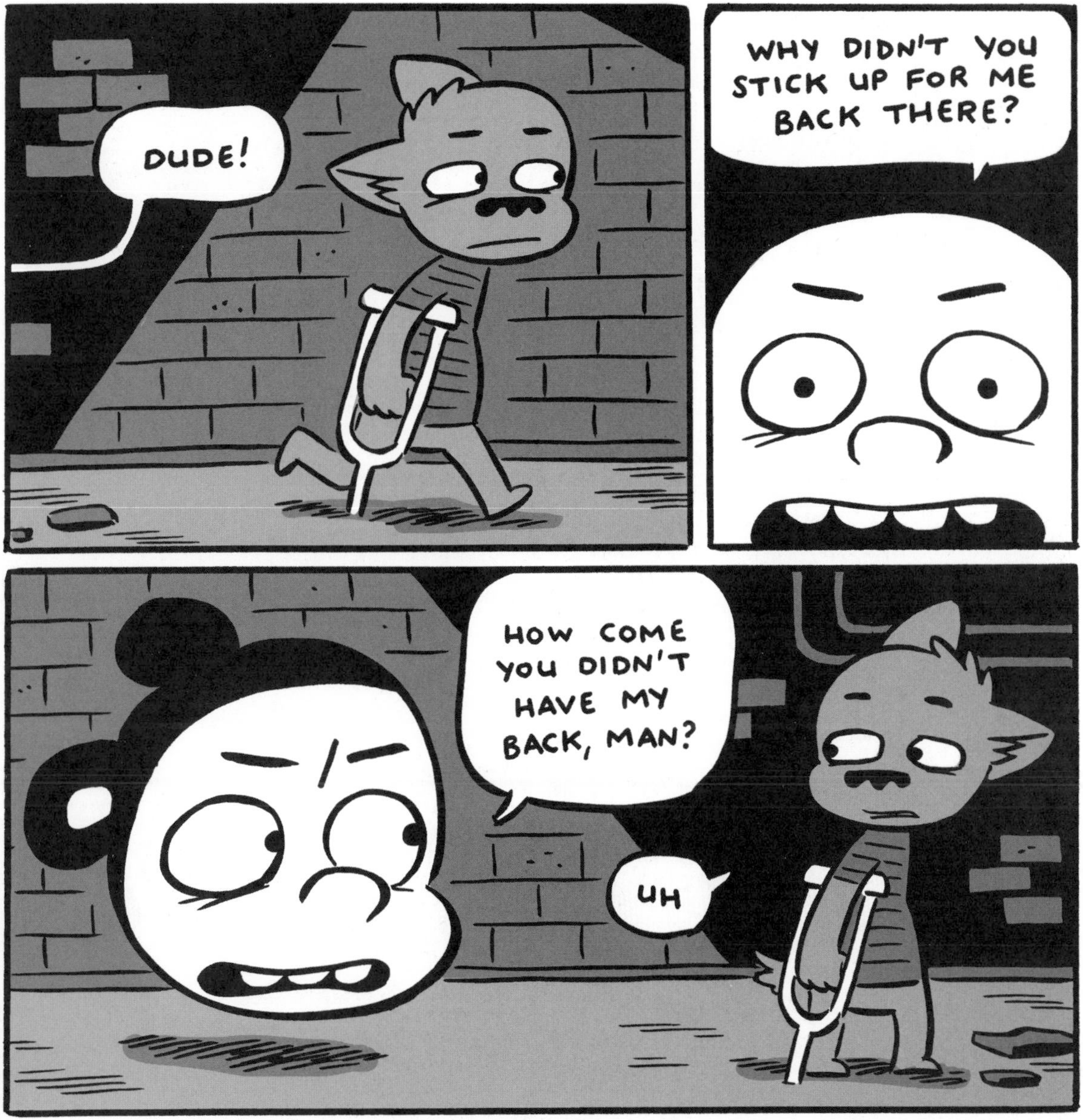
DUDE!
WHY DIDN'T YOU STICK UP FOR ME BACK THERE?
HOW COME YOU DIDN'T HAVE MY BACK, MAN?
UH

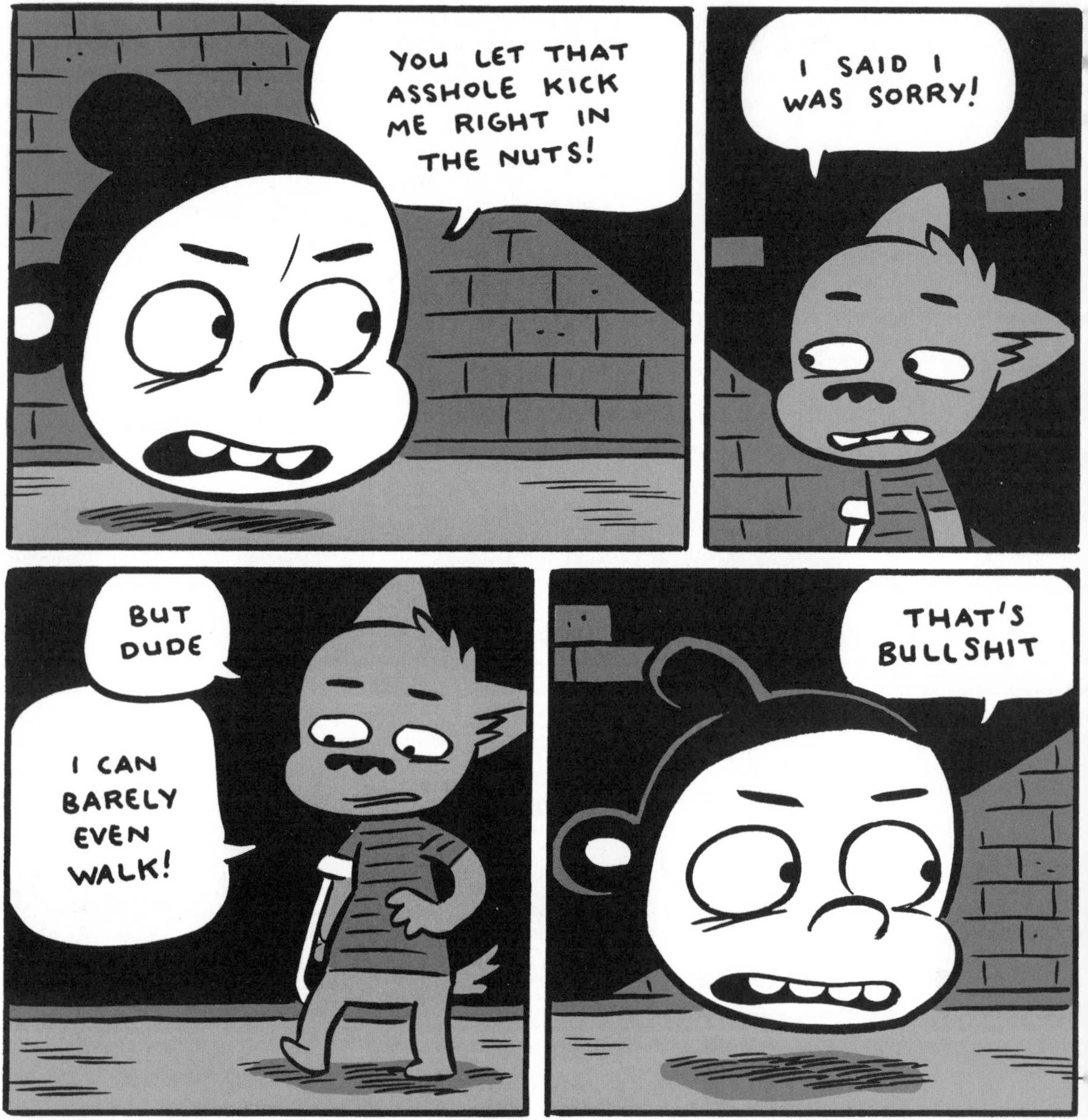
YOU LET THAT ASSHOLE KICK ME RIGHT IN THE NUTS!
I SAID I WAS SORRY!
BUT DUDE
I CAN BARELY EVEN WALK!
THAT'S BULLSHIT

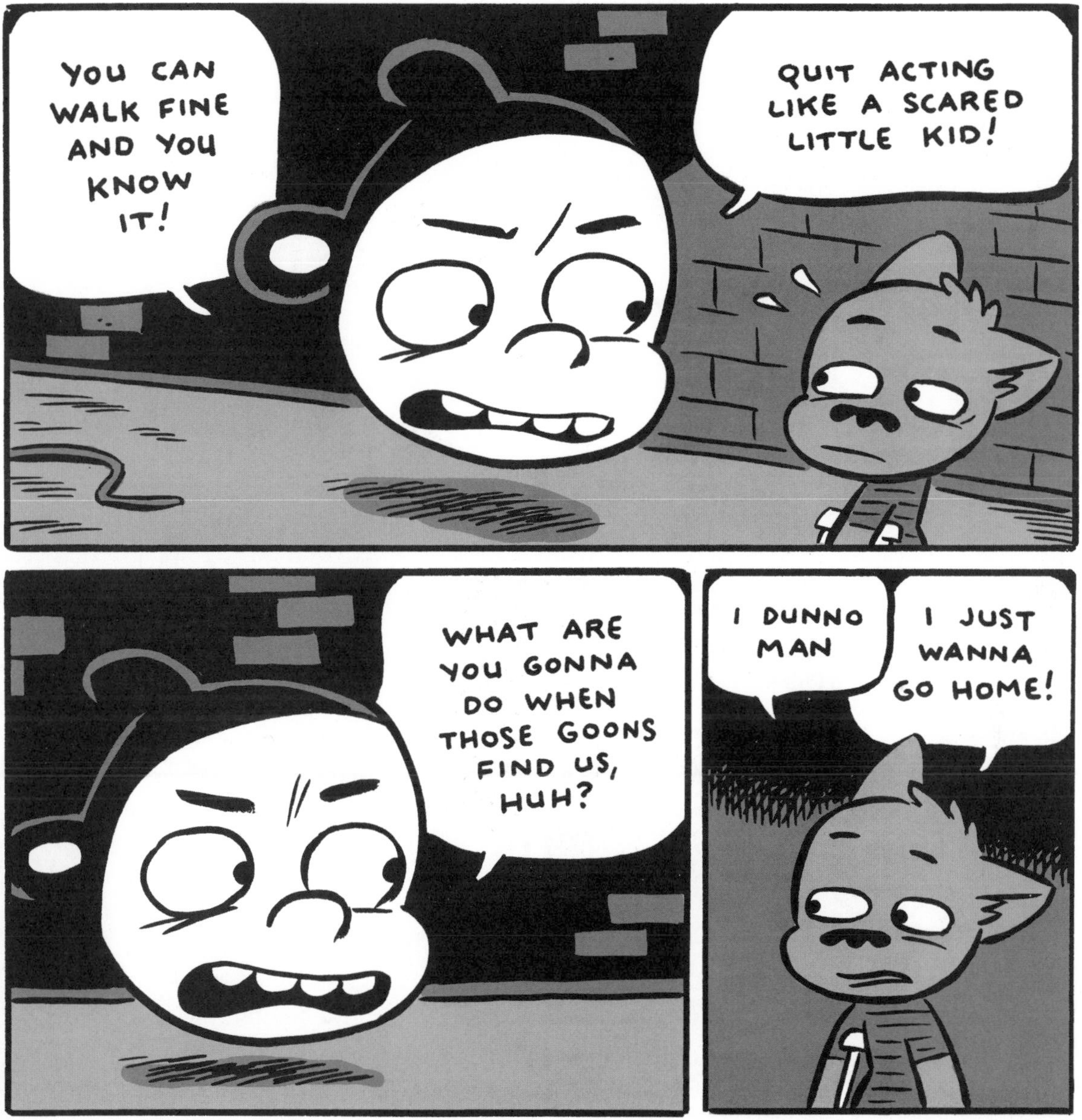
YOU CAN WALK FINE AND YOU KNOW IT!
QUIT ACTING LIKE A SCARED LITTLE KID!
WHAT ARE YOU GONNA DO WHEN THOSE GOONS FIND US, HUH?
I DUNNO MAN
I JUST WANNA GO HOME!

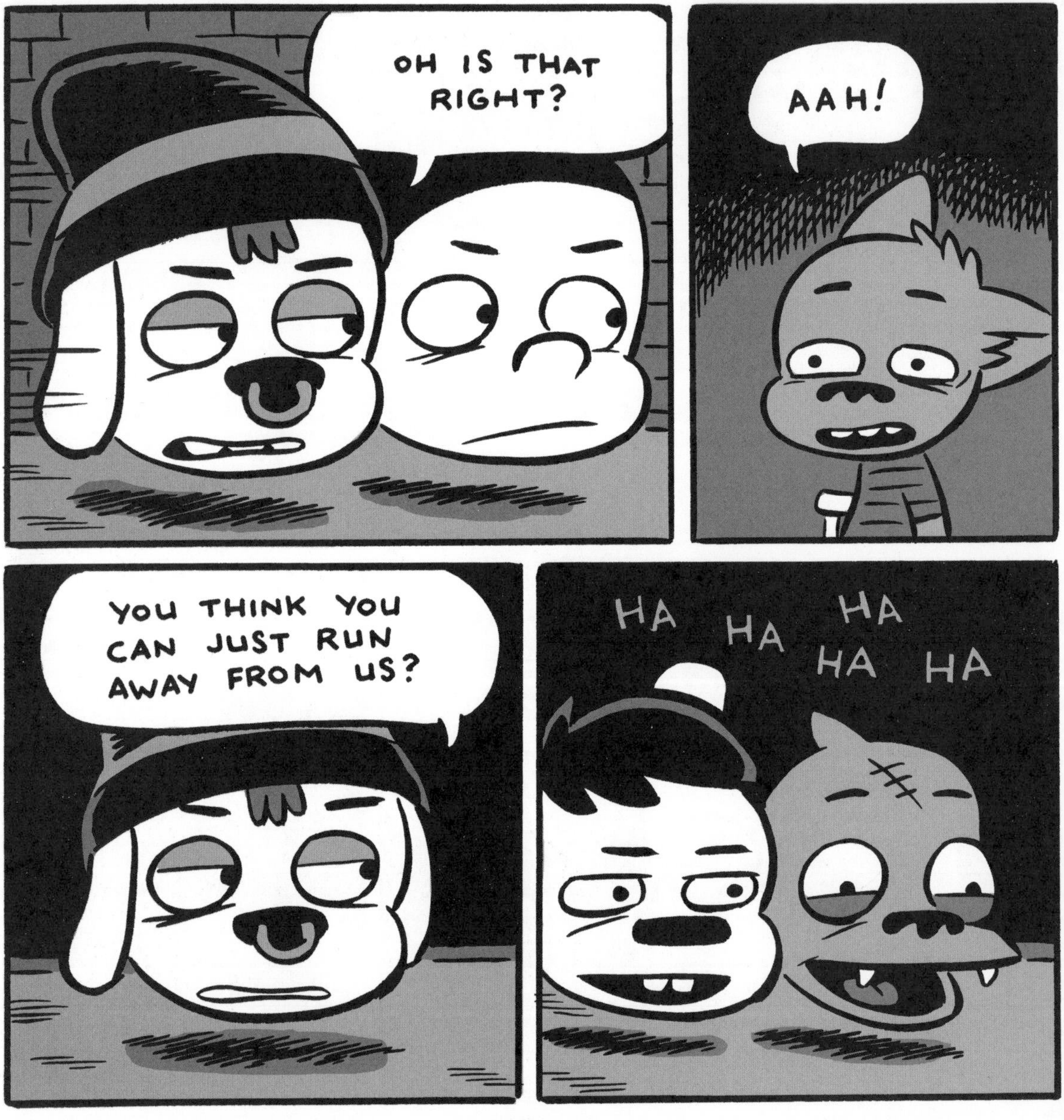
OH IS THAT RIGHT?
AAH!
YOU THINK YOU CAN JUST RUN AWAY FROM US?
HA HA HA HA HA

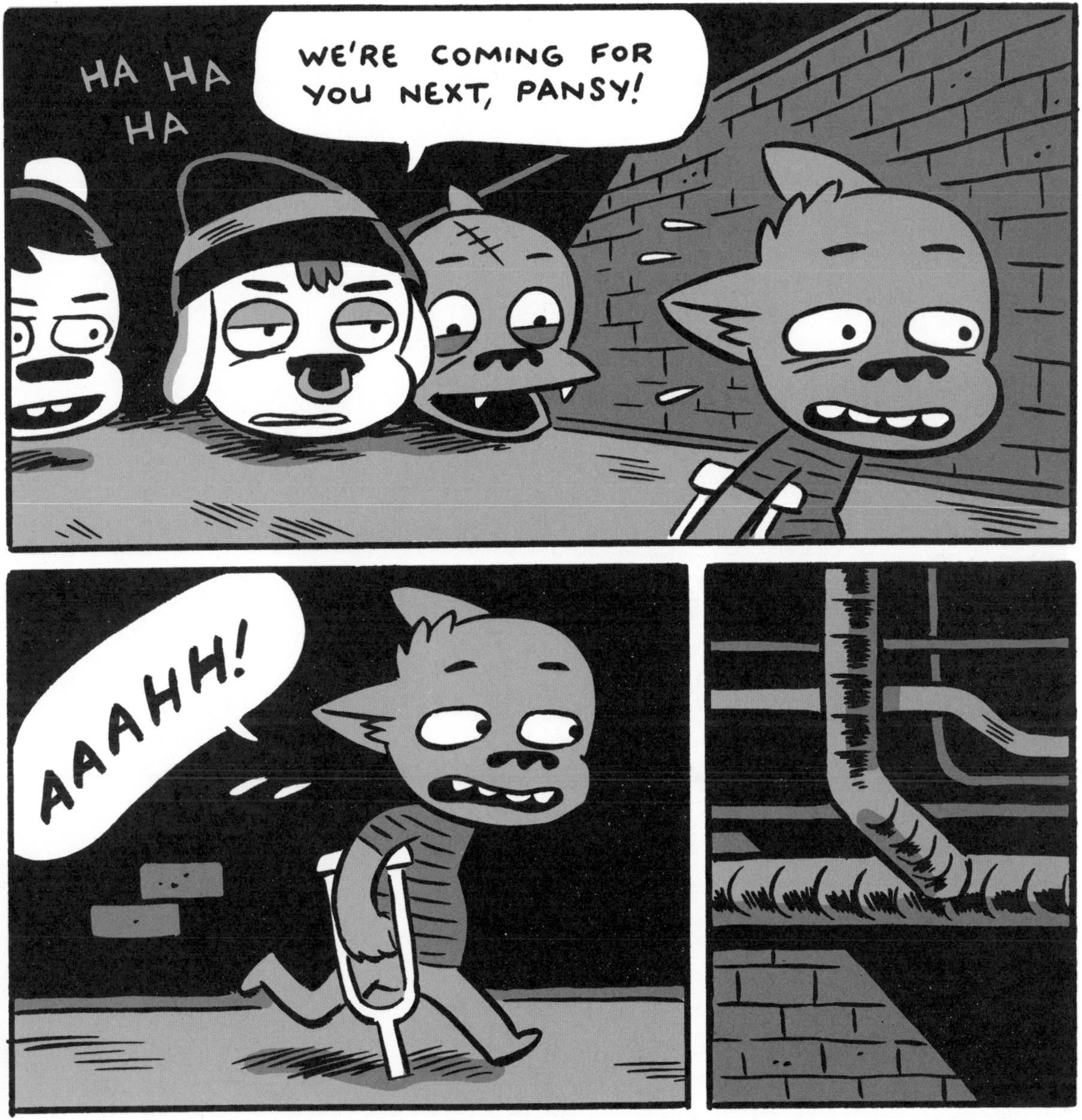
HA HA
HA
WE'RE COMING FOR YOU NEXT, PANSY!
AAAHH!

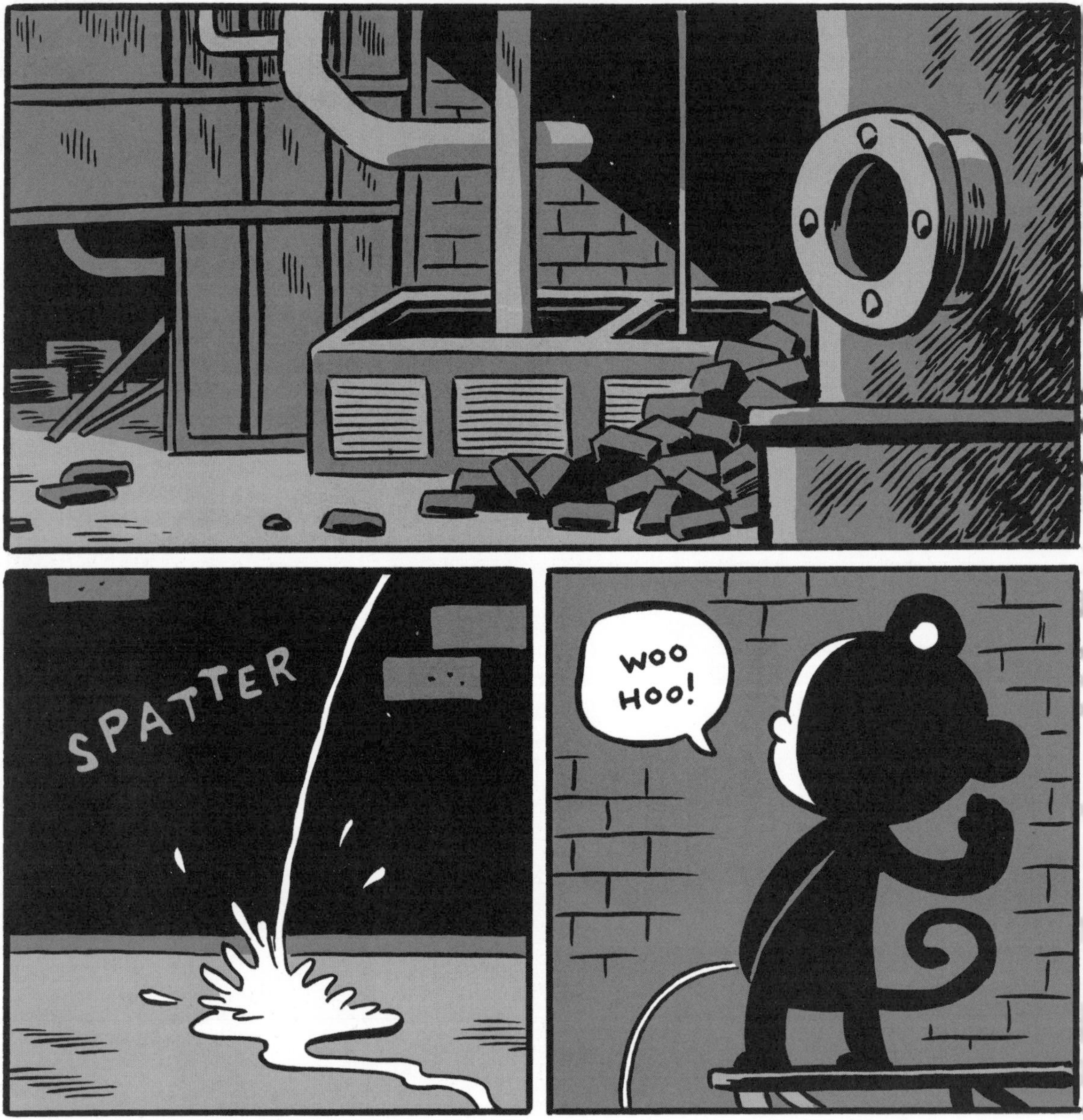
SPATTER
WOO HOO!

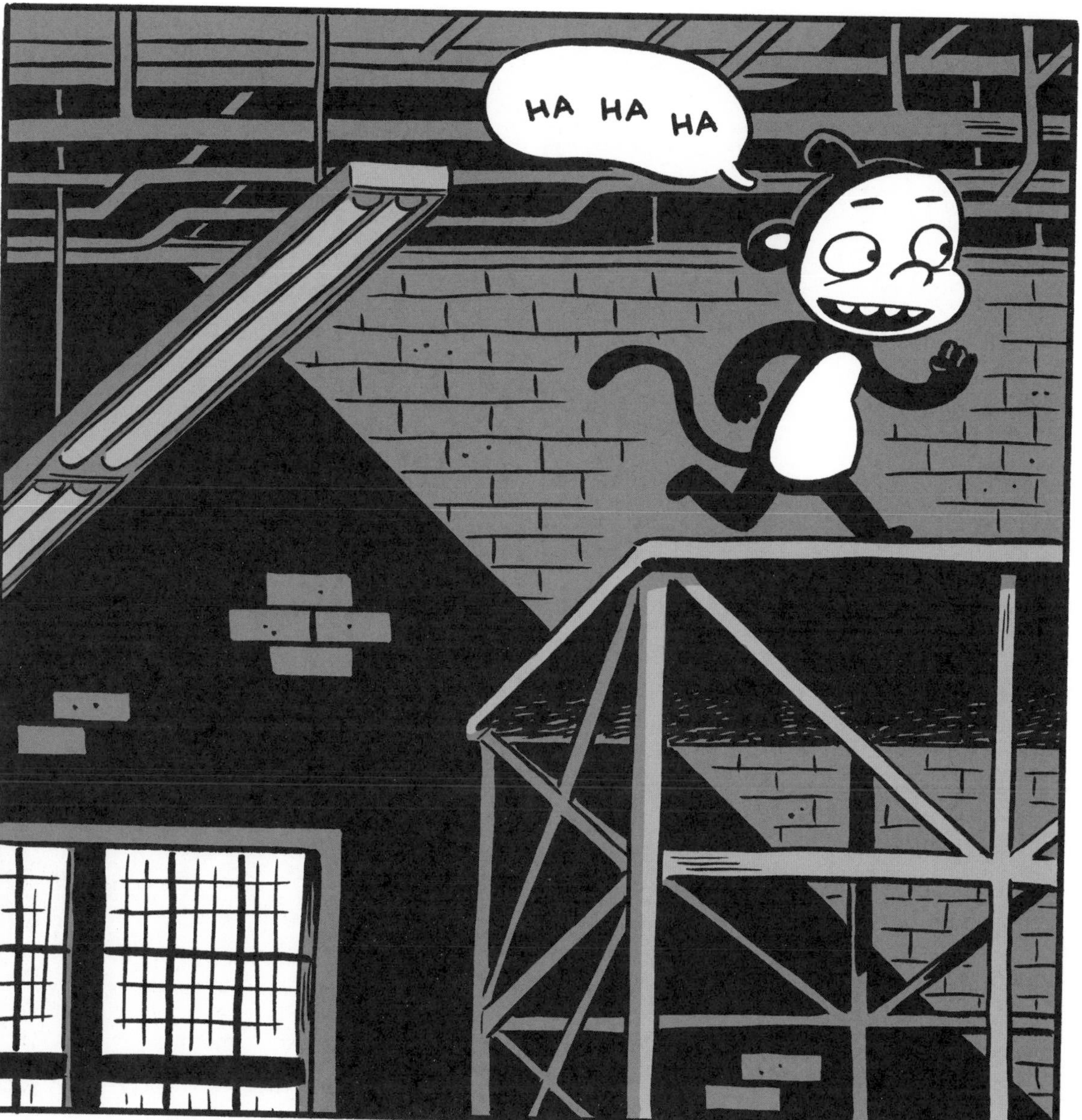
HA HA HA

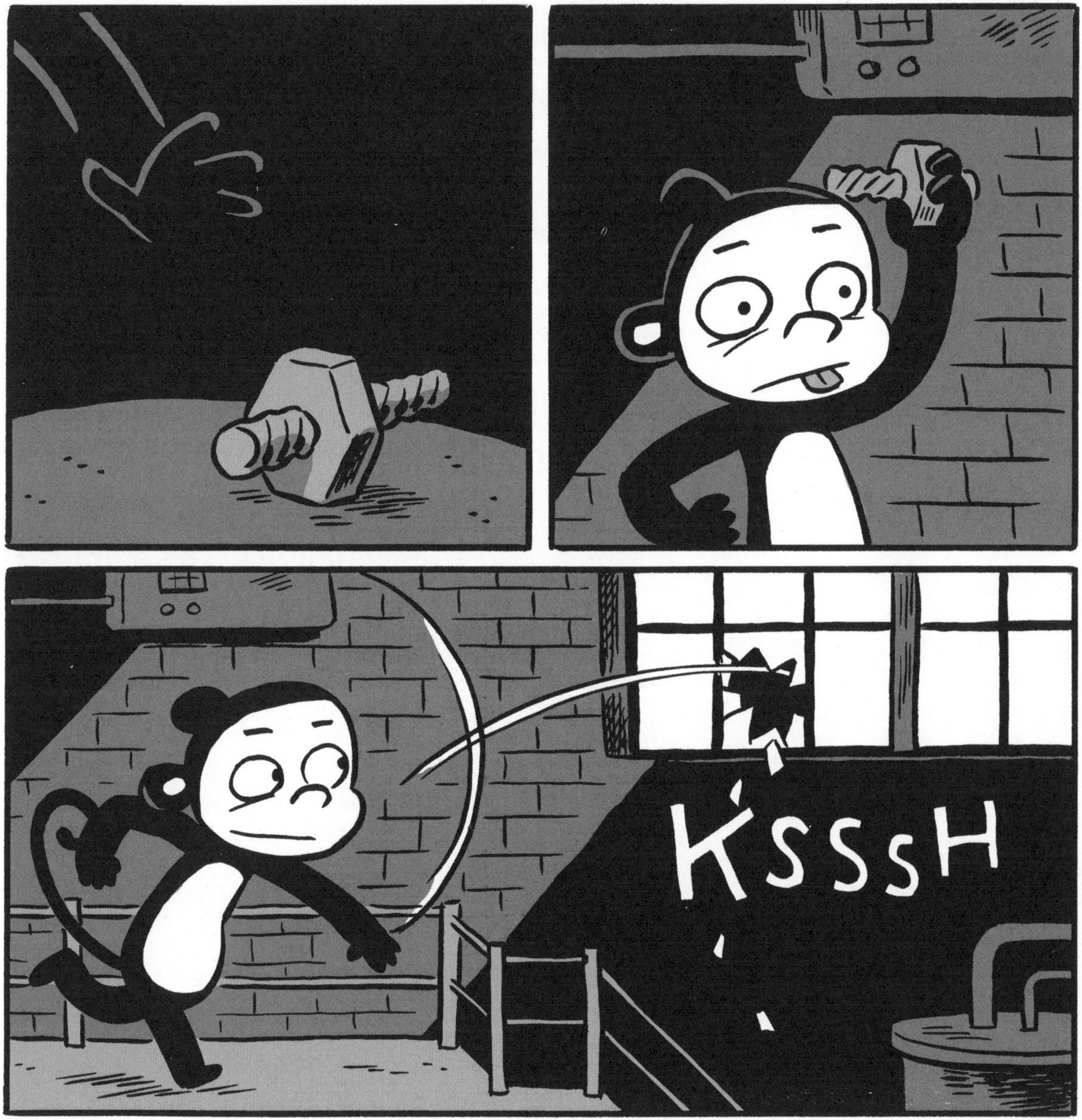
KSSSH

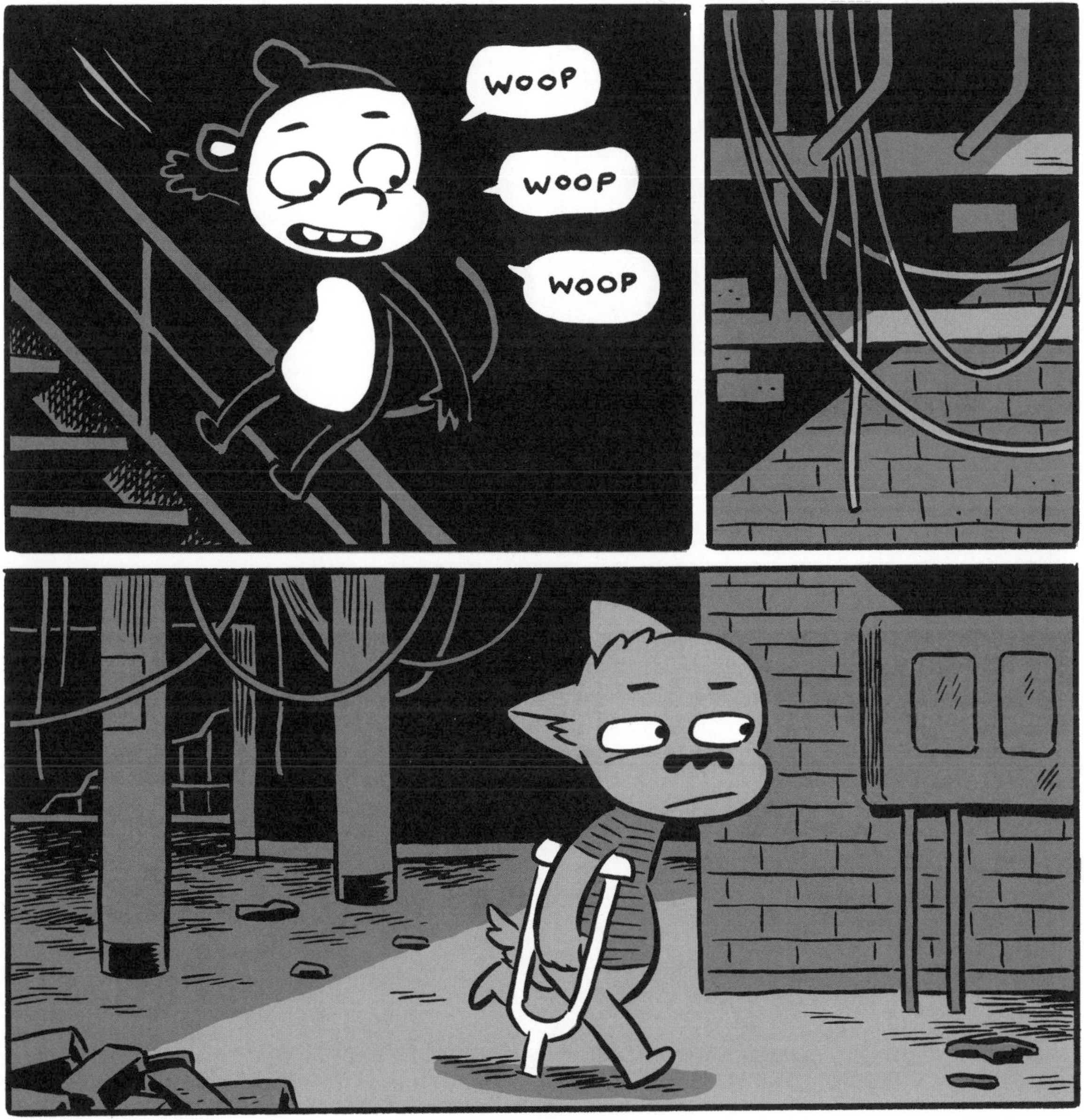
WOOP
WOOP
WOOP

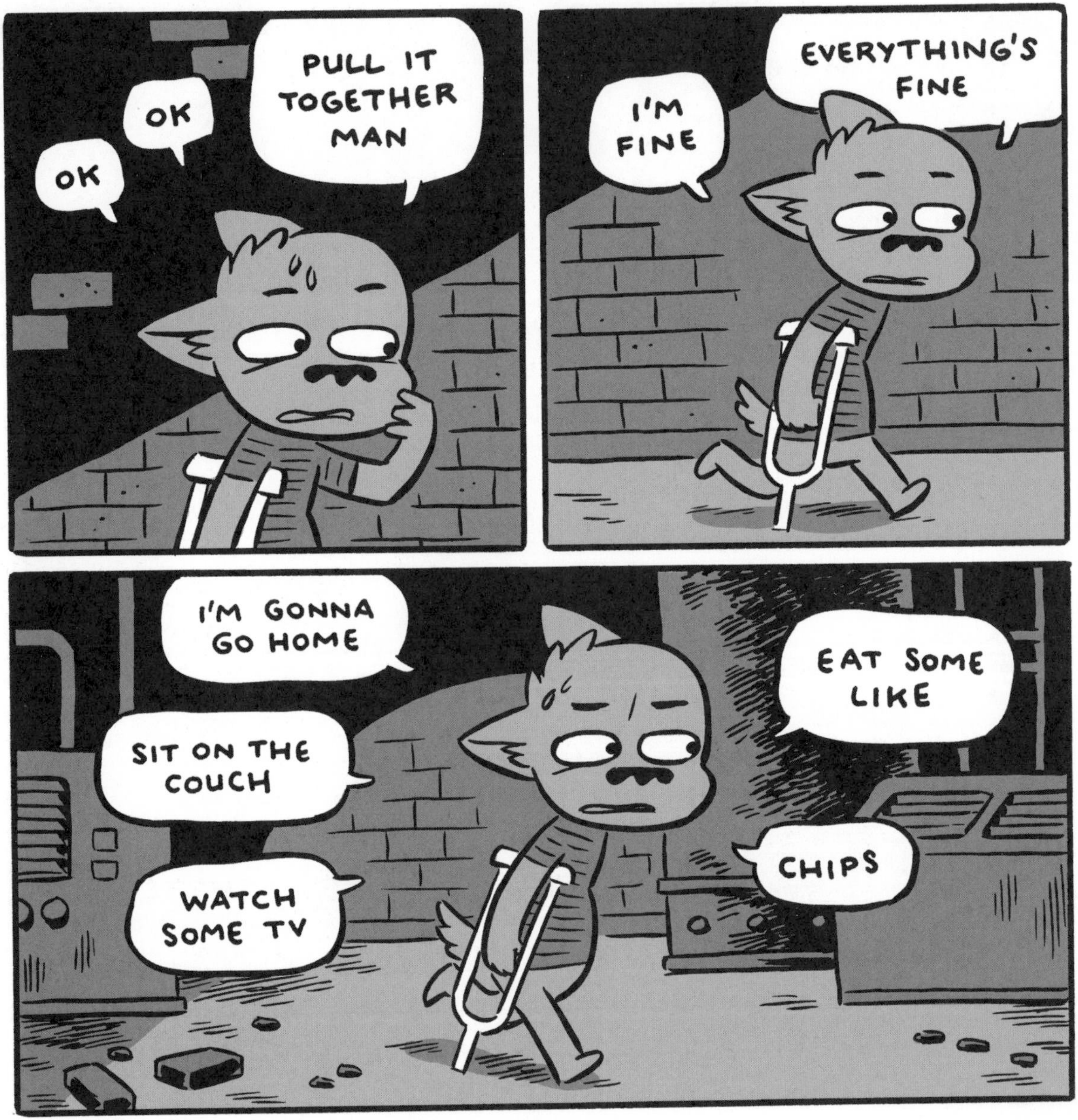
OK
OK
PULL IT TOGETHER MAN
I'M FINE
EVERYTHING'S FINE
I'M GONNA GO HOME
SIT ON THE COUCH
WATCH SOME TV
EAT SOME LIKE
CHIPS

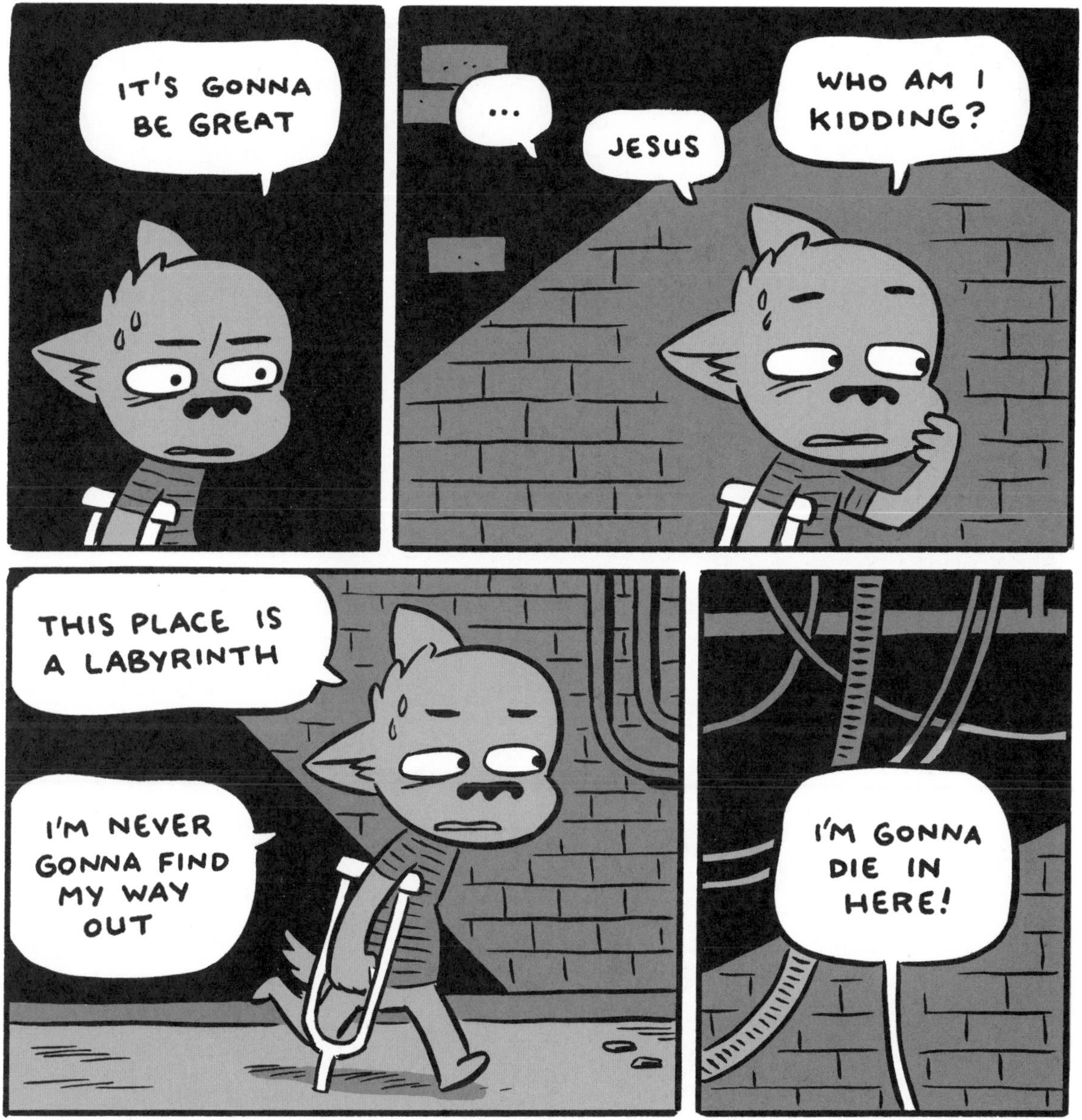
IT'S GONNA BE GREAT
...
JESUS
WHO AM I KIDDING?
THIS PLACE IS A LABYRINTH
I'M NEVER GONNA FIND MY WAY OUT
I'M GONNA DIE IN HERE!

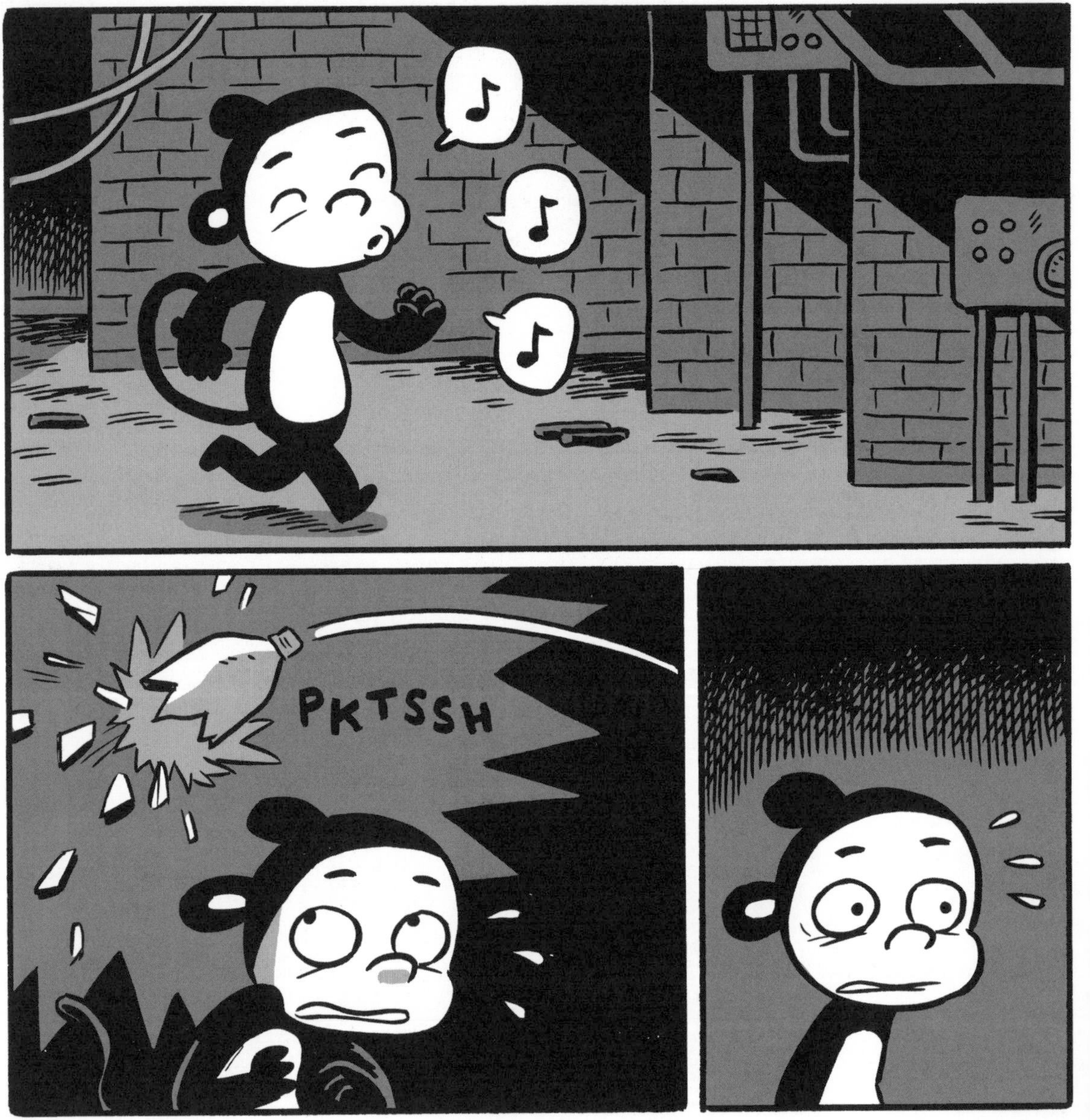
♪
♪
♪
PKTSSH

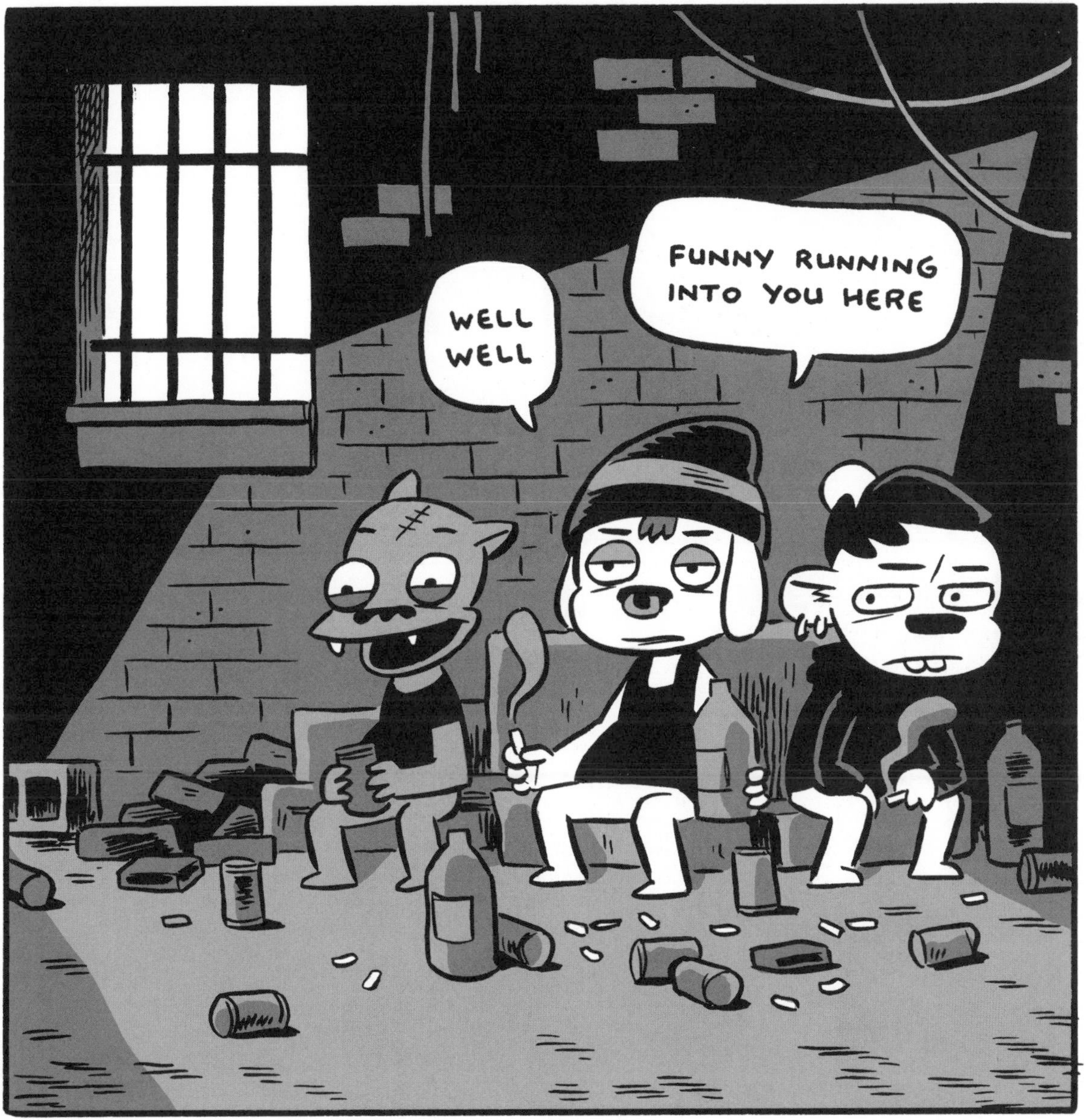
WELL WELL
FUNNY RUNNING INTO YOU HERE

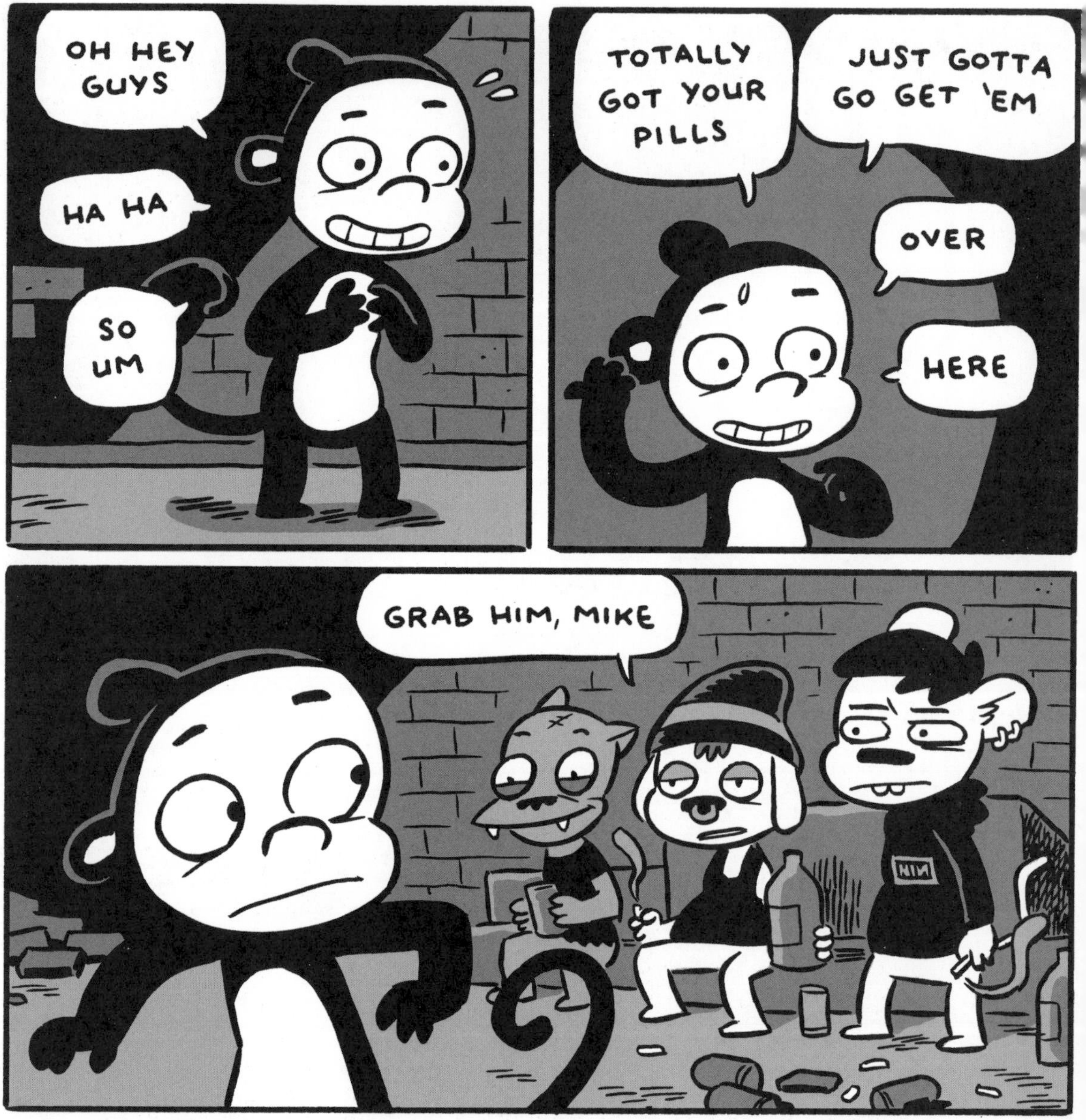
OH HEY GUYS
HA HA
SO UM
TOTALLY GOT YOUR PILLS
JUST GOTTA GO GET 'EM
OVER
HERE
GRAB HIM, MIKE
NIN

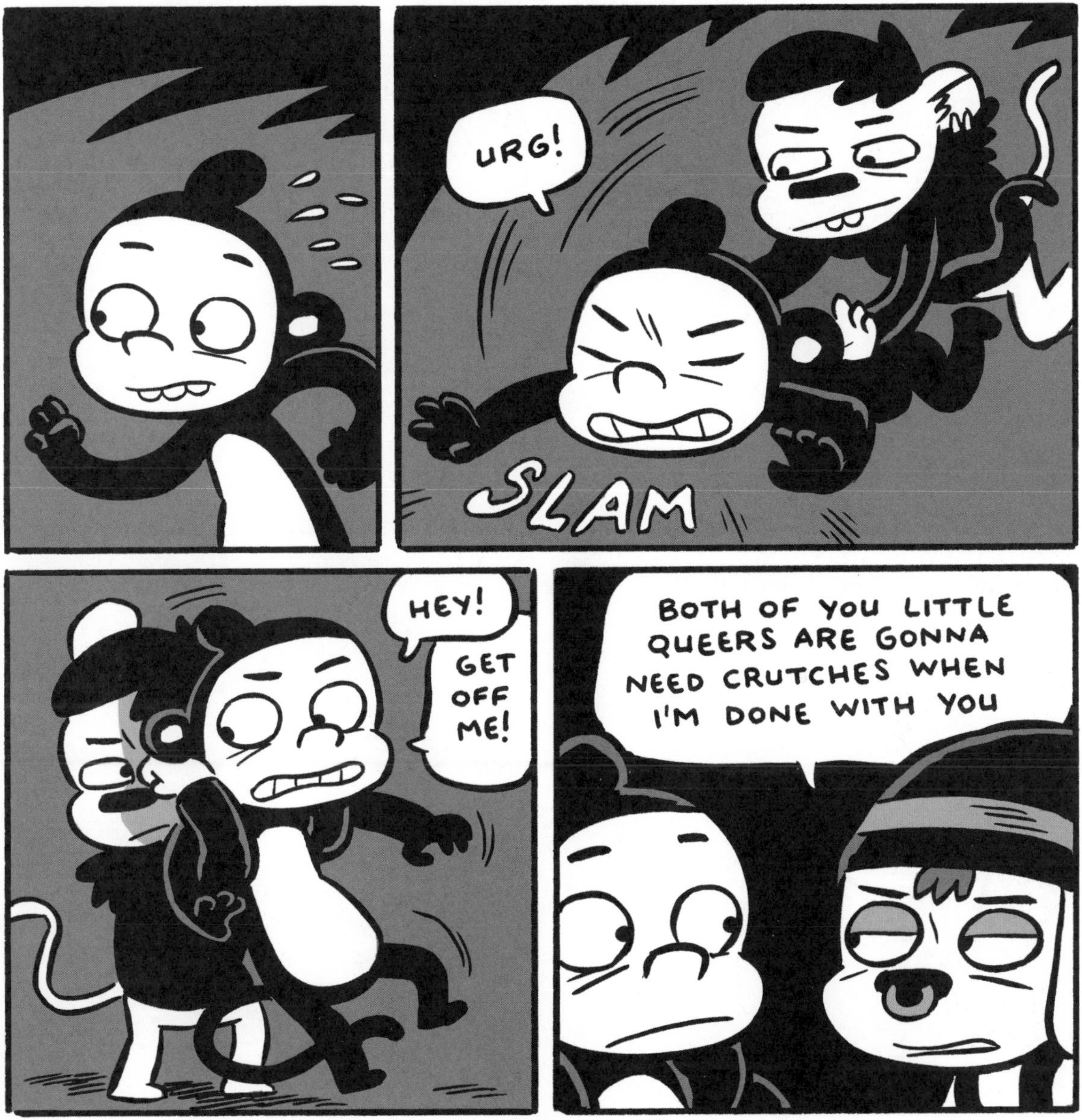
URG!
SLAM
HEY!
GET OFF ME!
BOTH OF YOU LITTLE QUEERS ARE GONNA NEED CRUTCHES WHEN I'M DONE WITH YOU

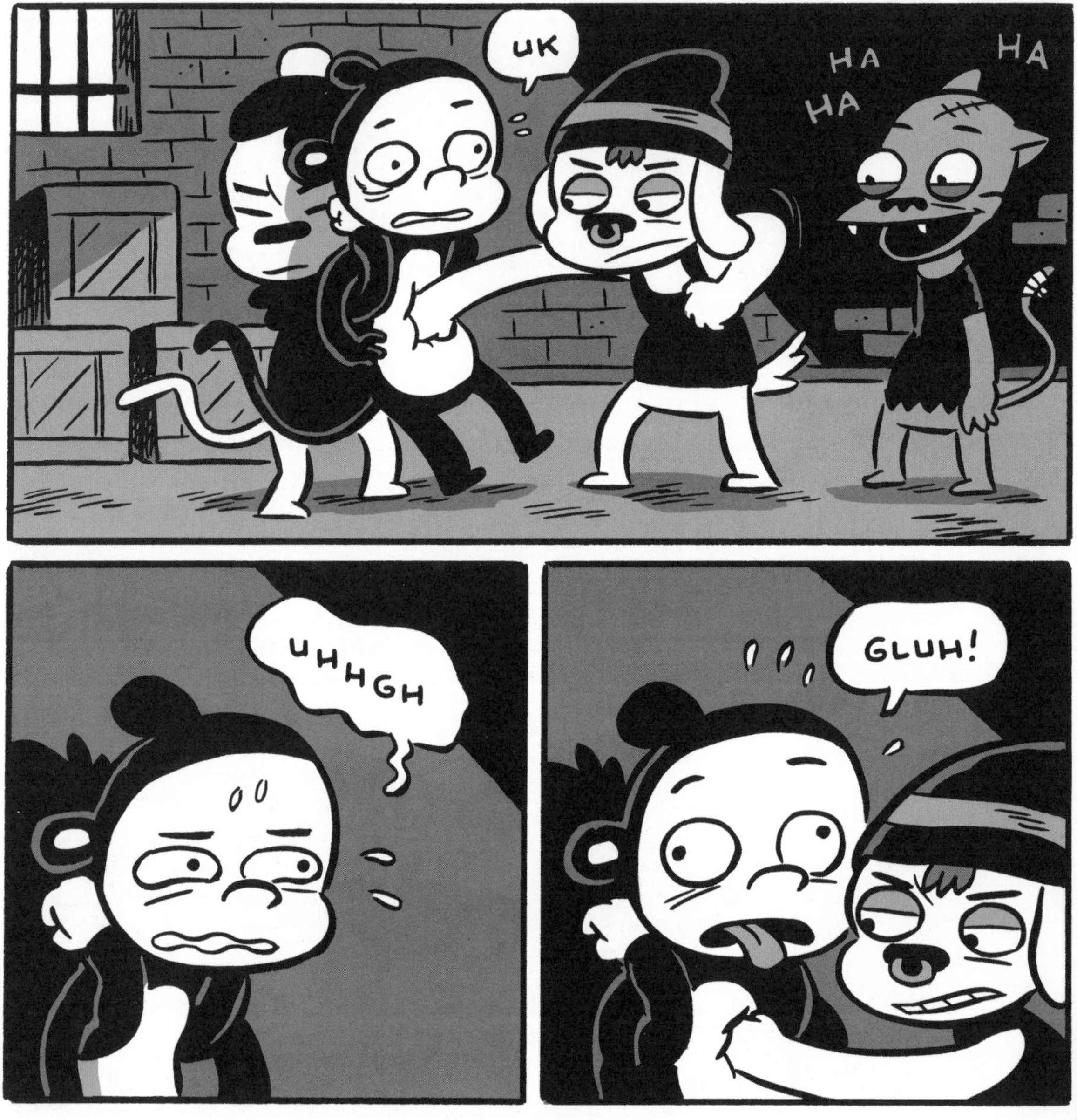
UK
HA
HA
HA
UHHGH
GLUH!

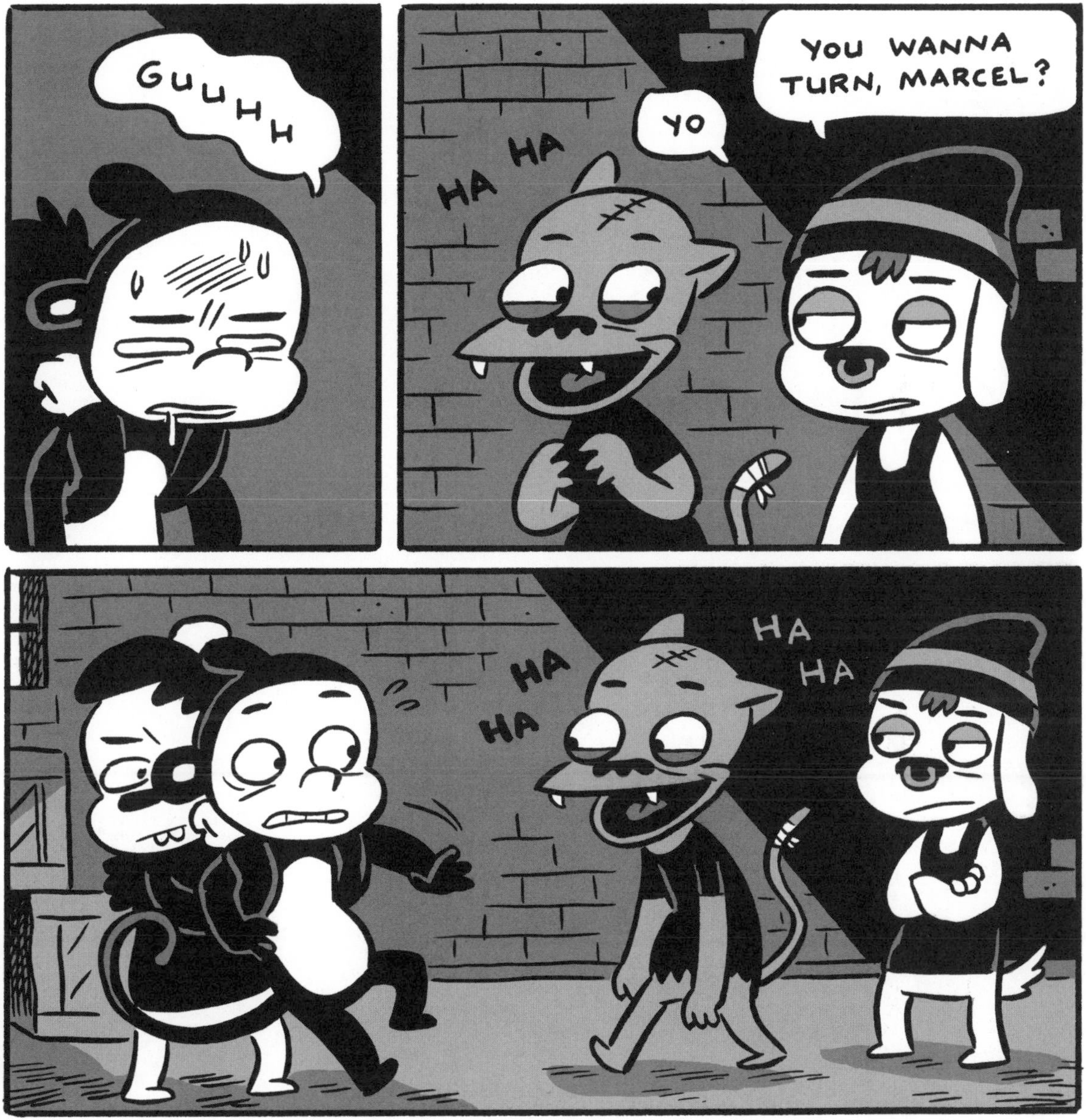
GUUHHH
HA HA
YO
YOU WANNA TURN, MARCEL?
HA HA
HA HA

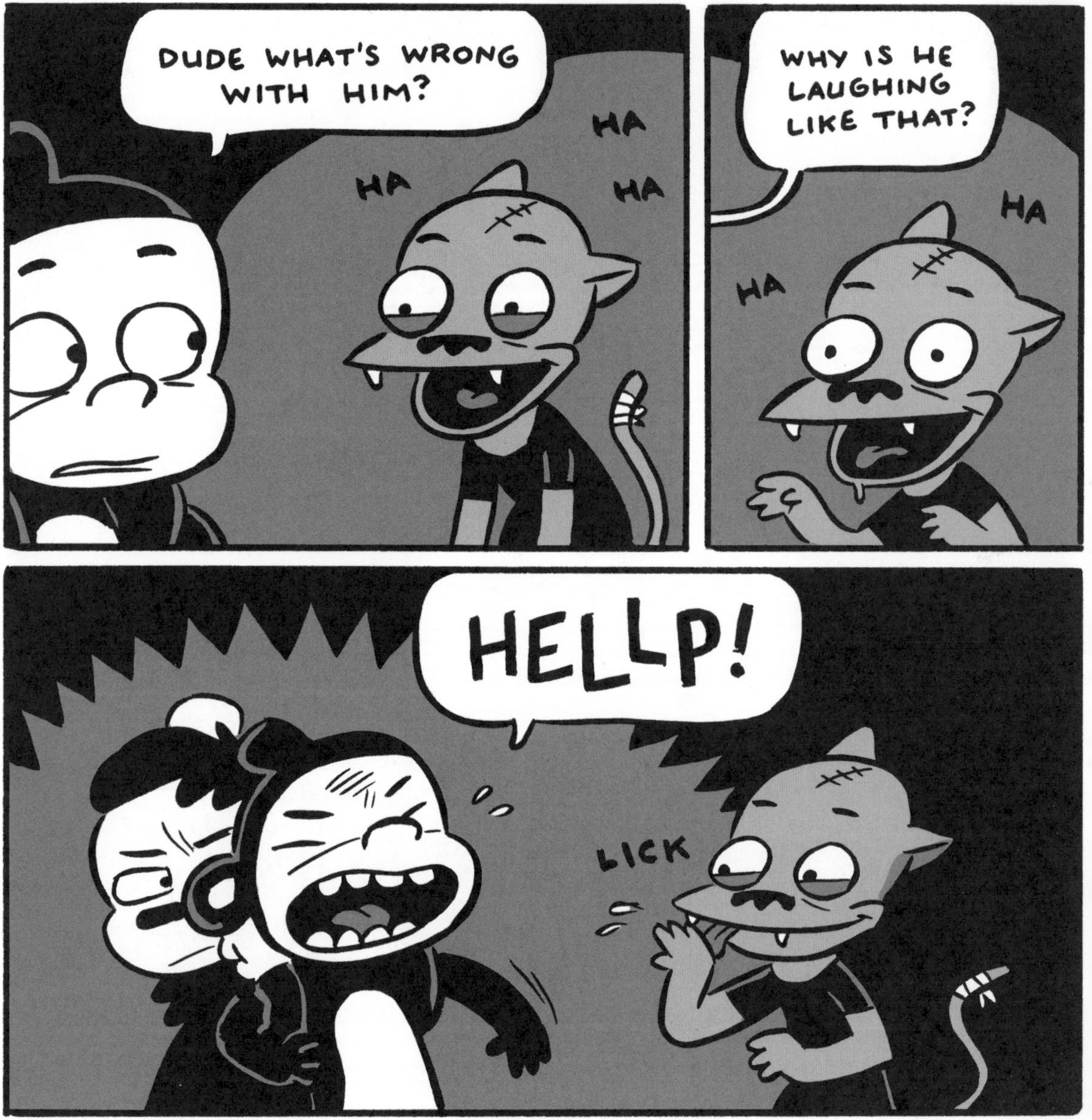
DUDE WHAT'S WRONG WITH HIM?
HA
HA
HA
WHY IS HE LAUGHING LIKE THAT?
HA
HA
HELLP!
LICK

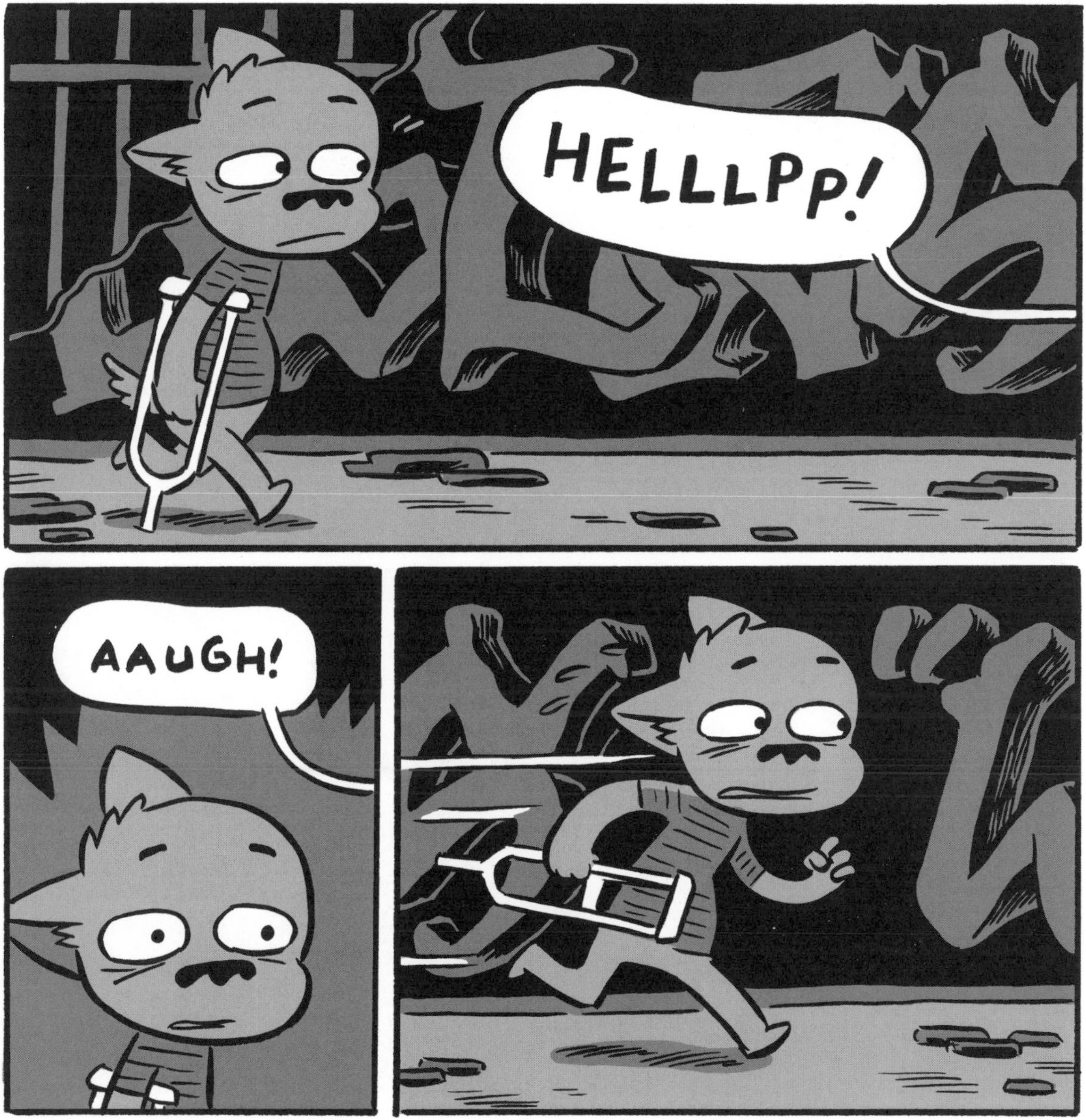
HELLLPP!
AAUGH!

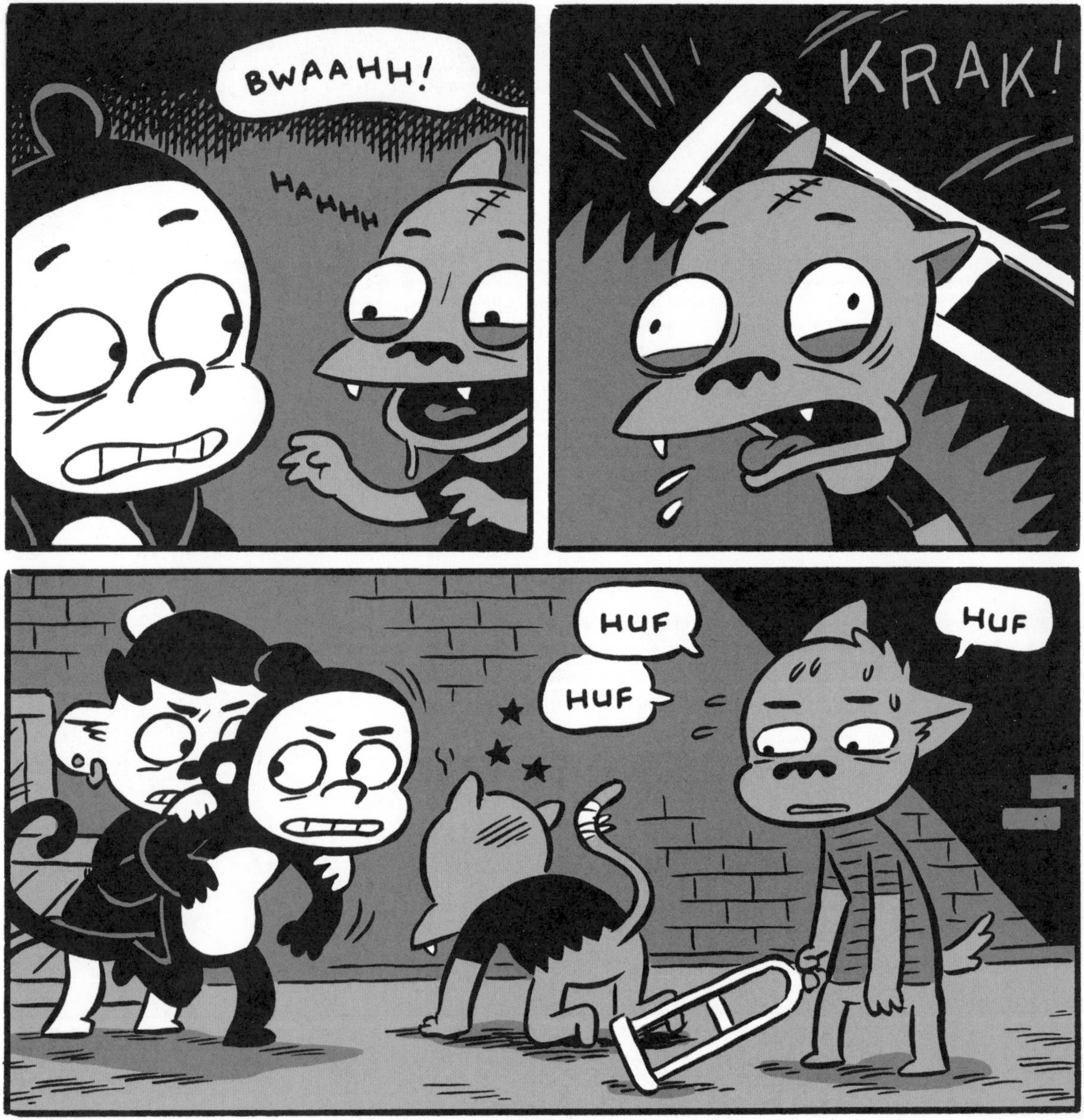
BWAAHH!
HAHHHH
KRAK!
HUF
HUF
HUF

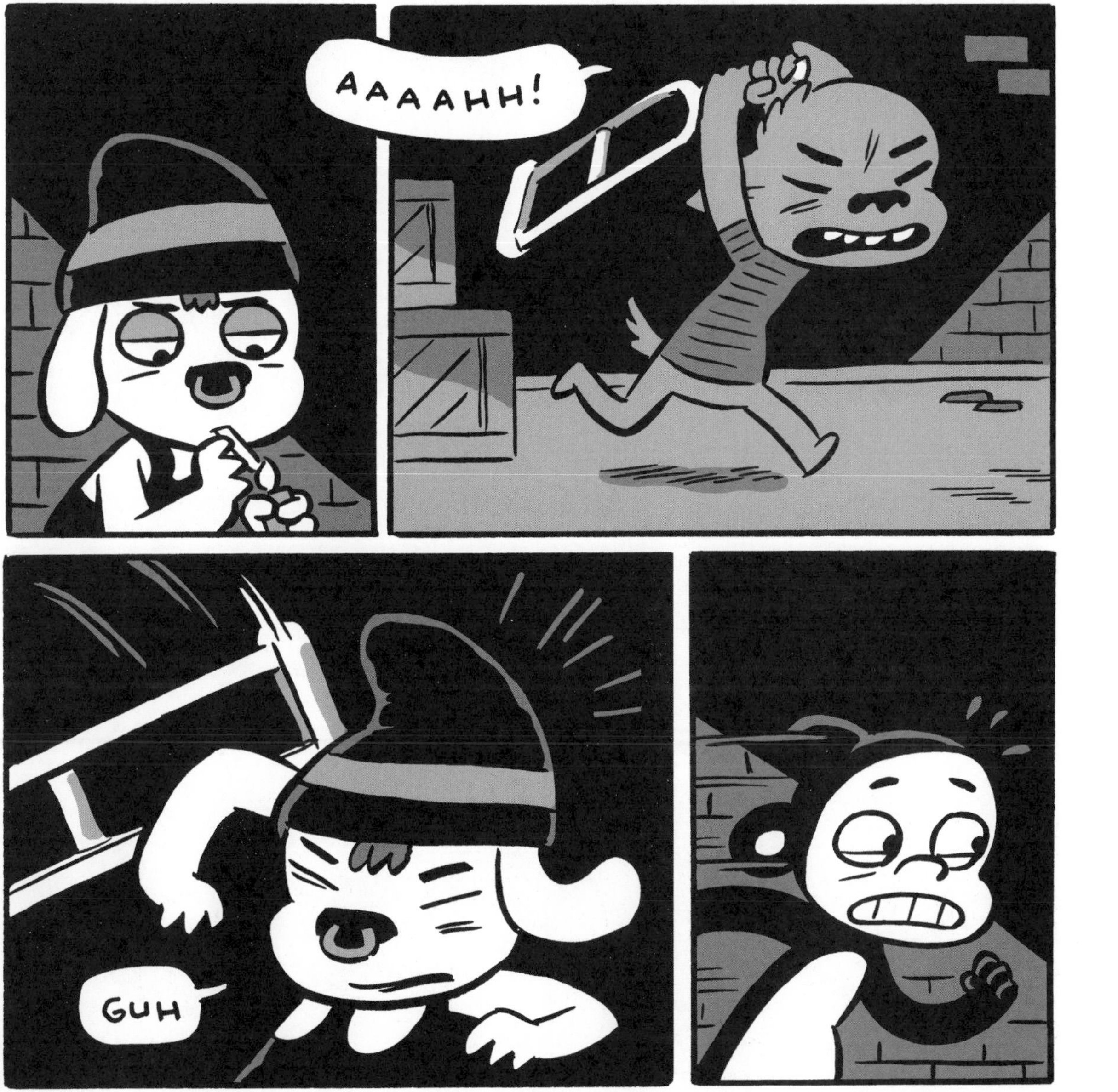
AAAAHH!
GUH

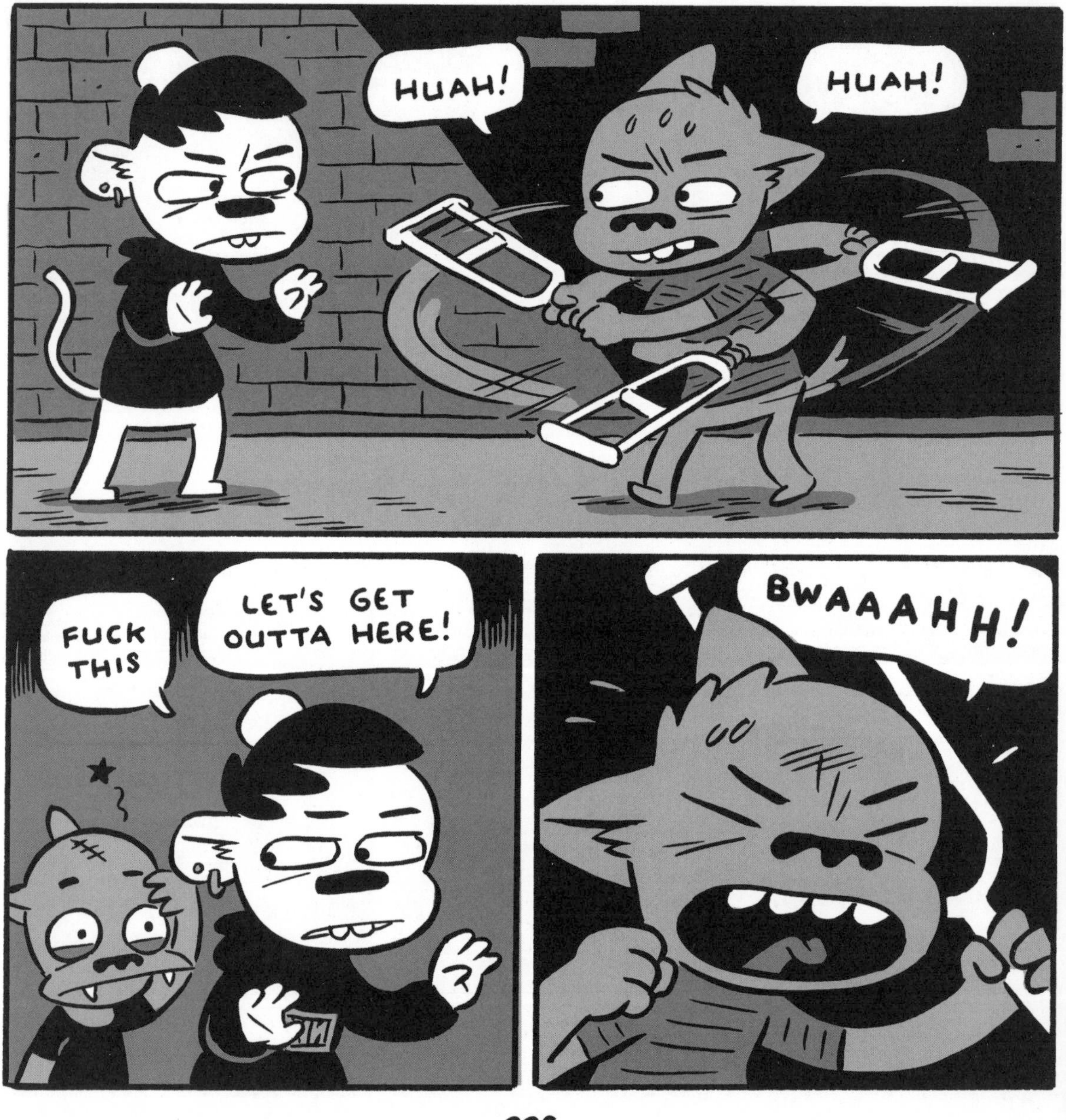
HUAH!
HUAH!
FUCK THIS
LET'S GET OUTTA HERE!
BWAAAAHH!

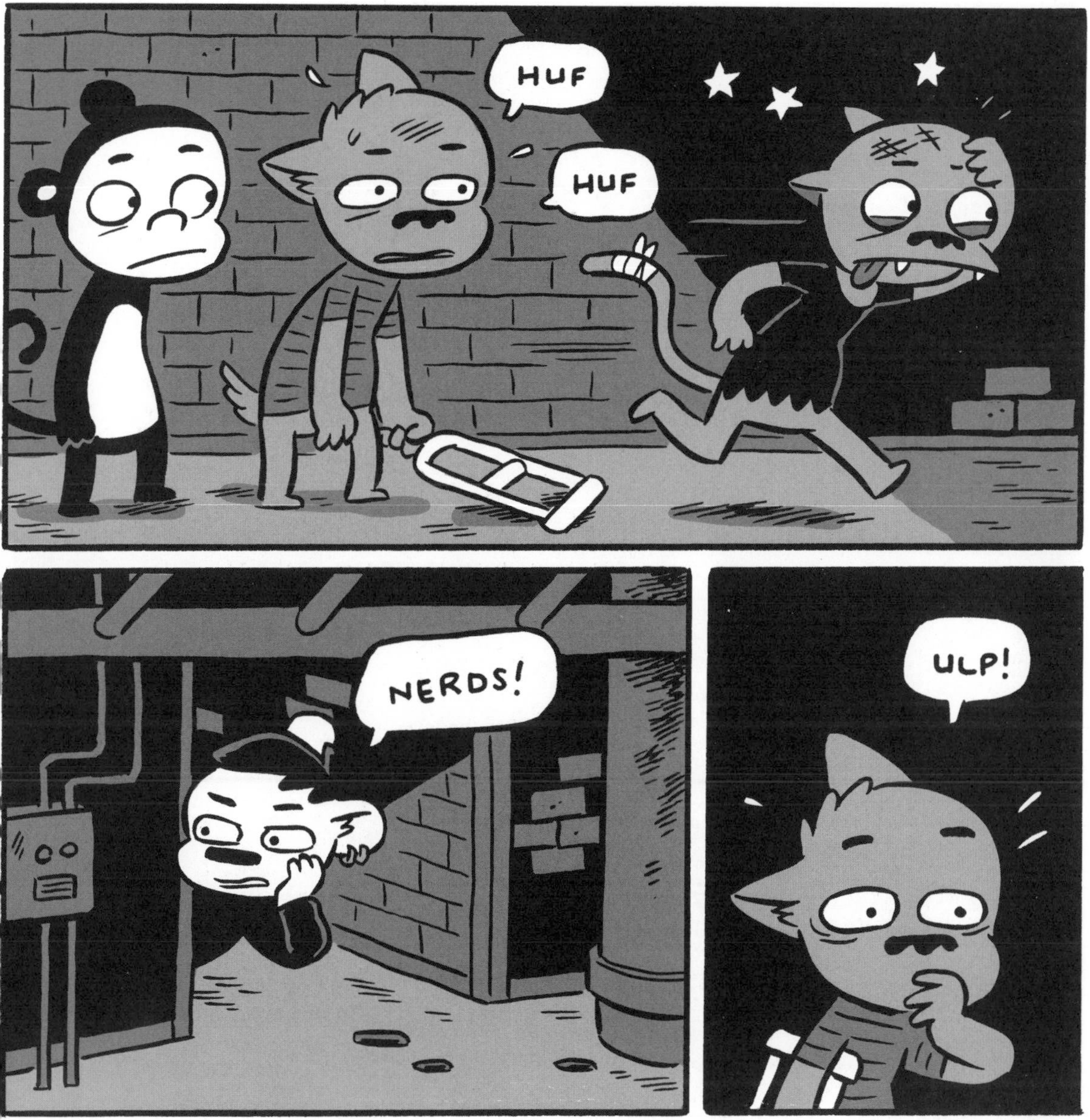
HUF
HUF
NERDS!
ULP!

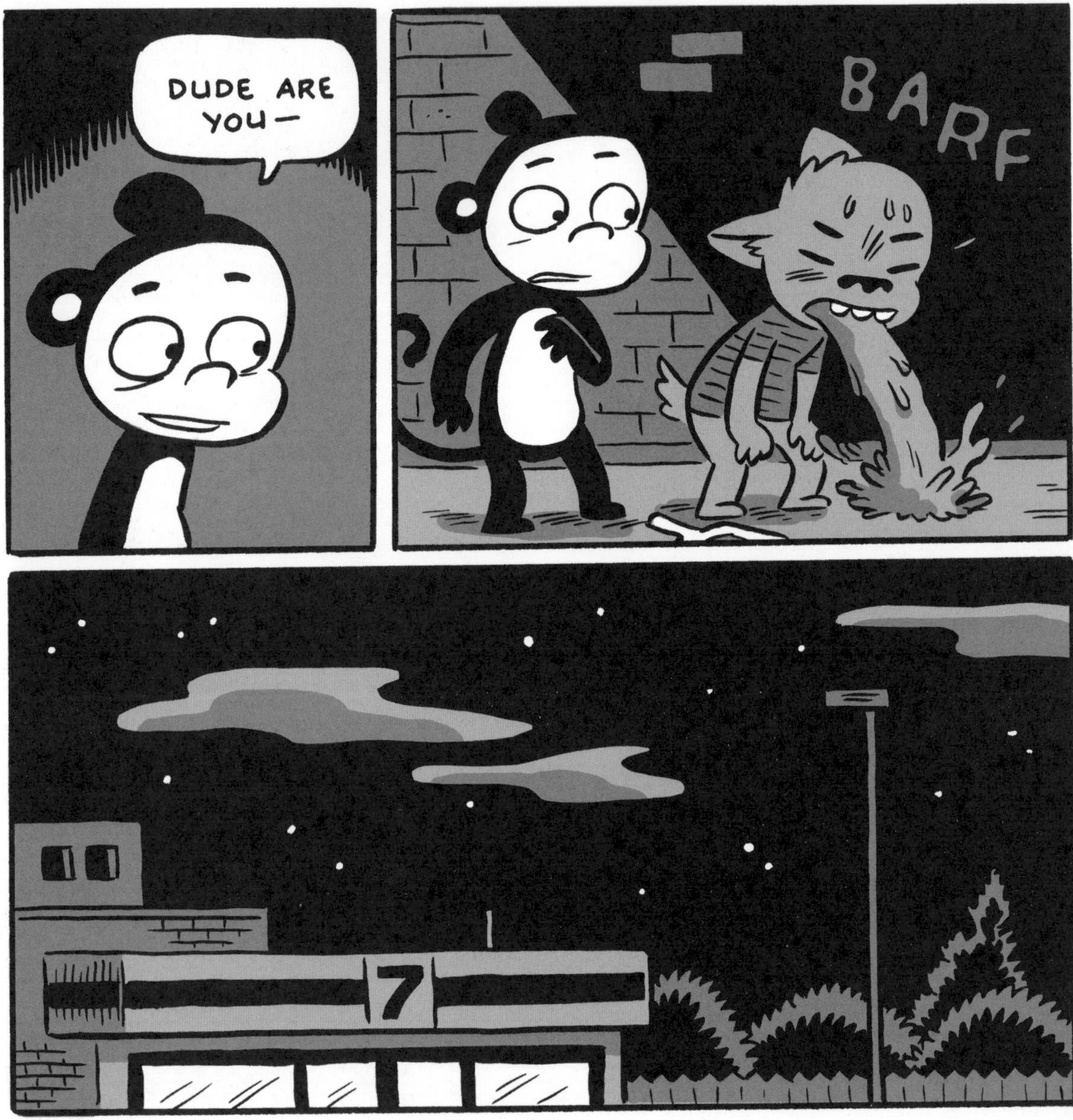
DUDE ARE YOU—
BARF
7

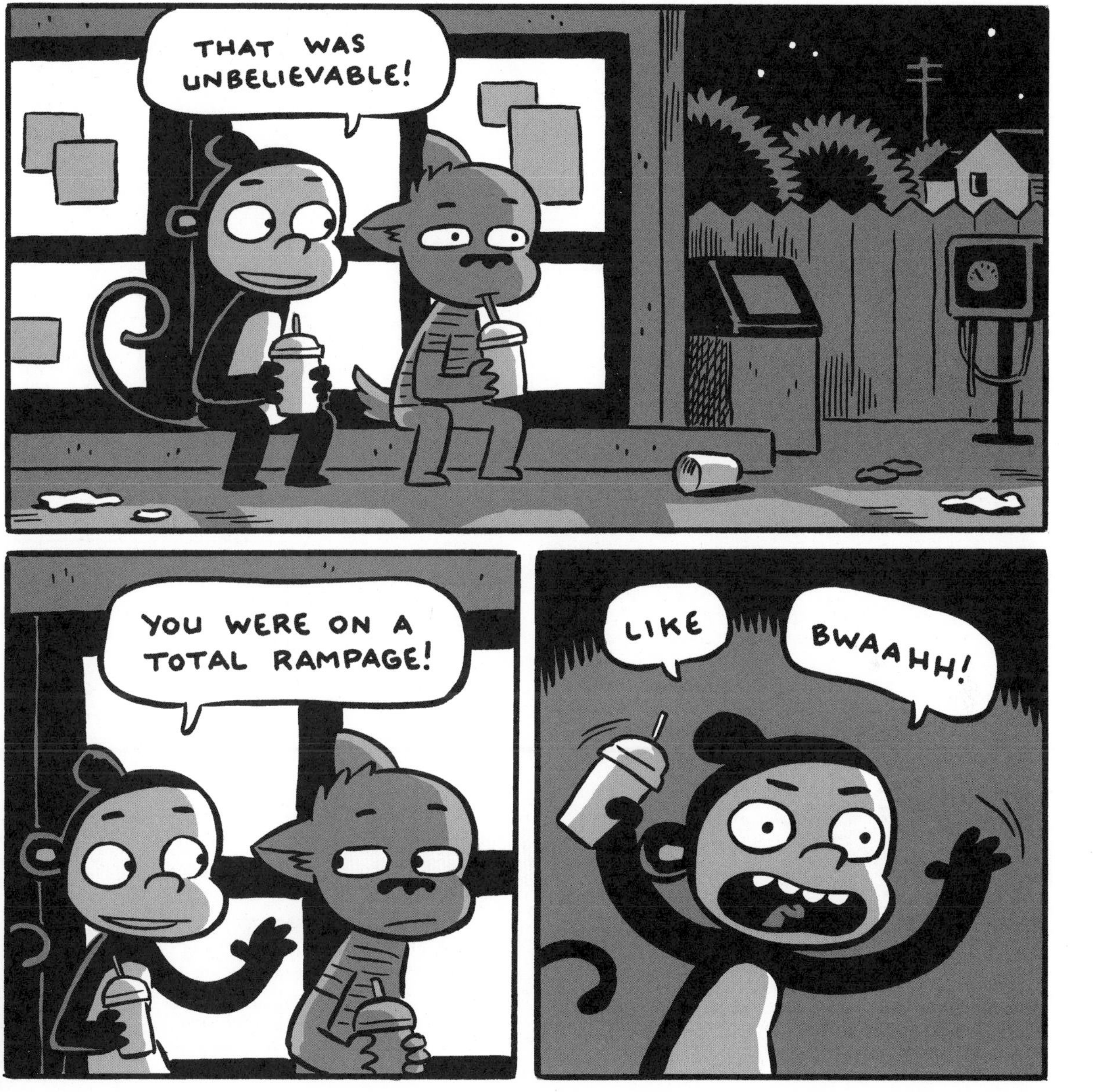
THAT WAS UNBELIEVABLE!
YOU WERE ON A TOTAL RAMPAGE!
LIKE
BWAAHH!

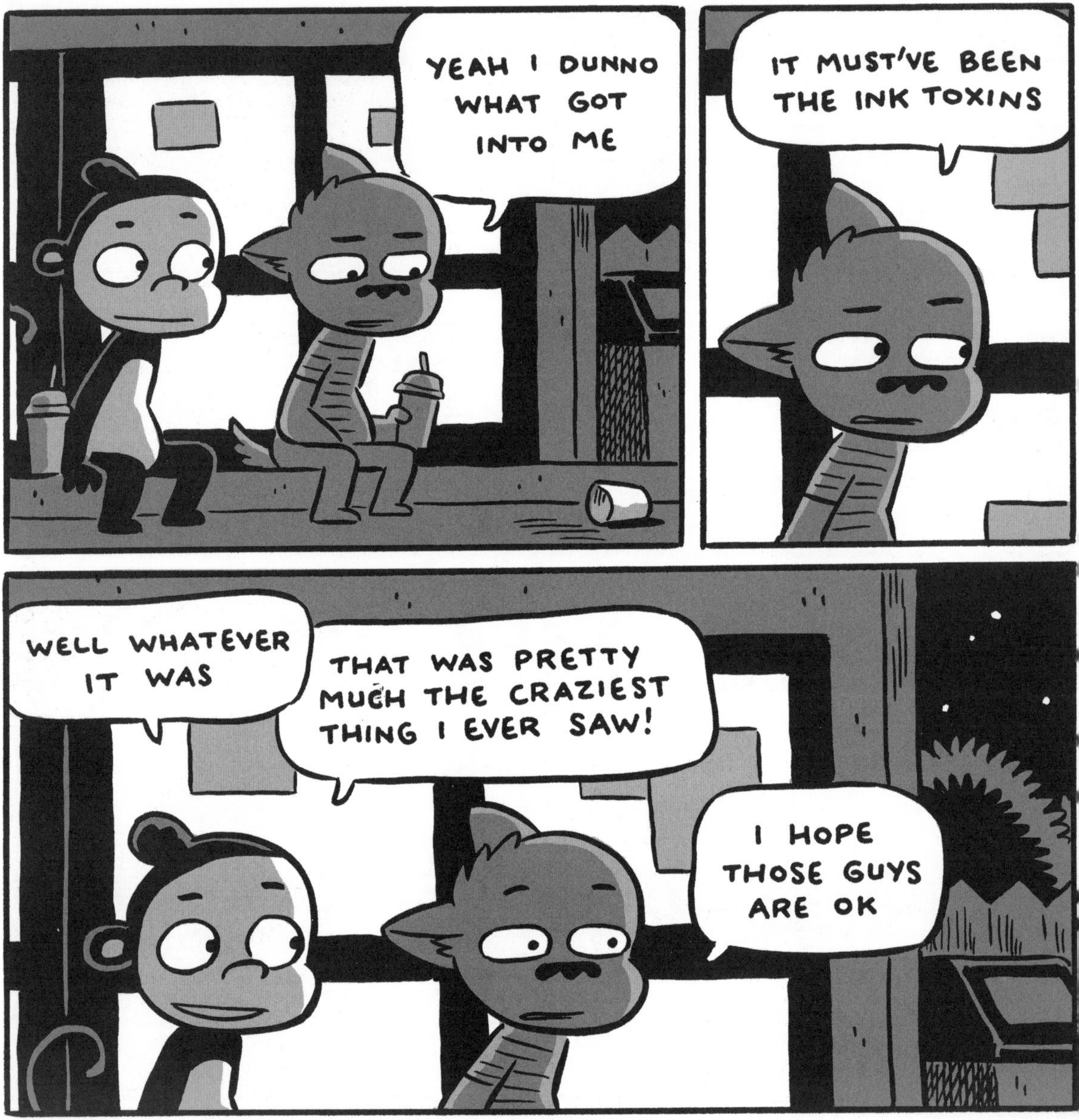
YEAH I DUNNO WHAT GOT INTO ME
IT MUST'VE BEEN THE INK TOXINS
WELL WHATEVER IT WAS
THAT WAS PRETTY MUCH THE CRAZIEST THING I EVER SAW!
I HOPE THOSE GUYS ARE OK

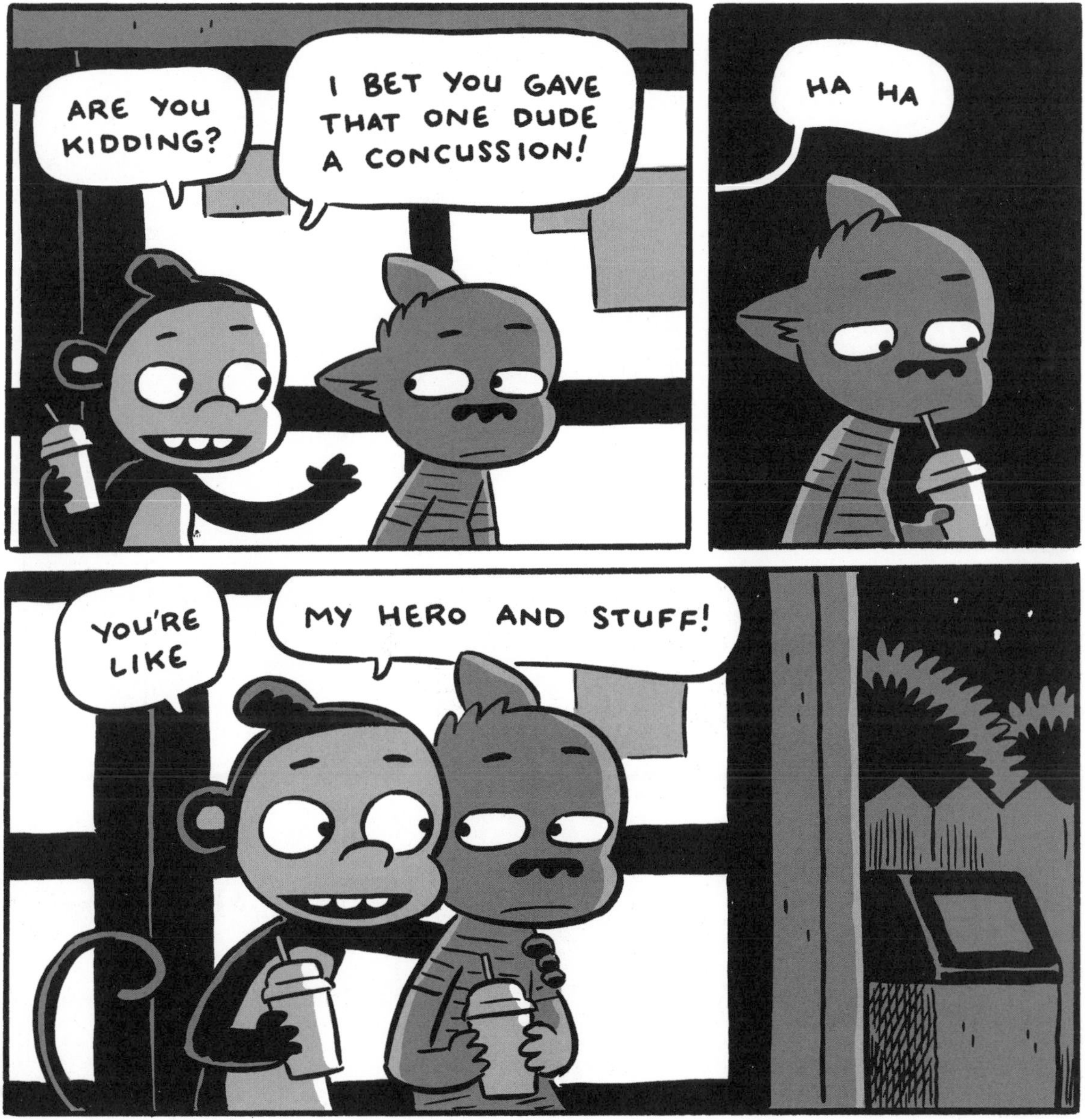
ARE YOU KIDDING?
I BET YOU GAVE THAT ONE DUDE A CONCUSSION!
HA HA
YOU'RE LIKE
MY HERO AND STUFF!

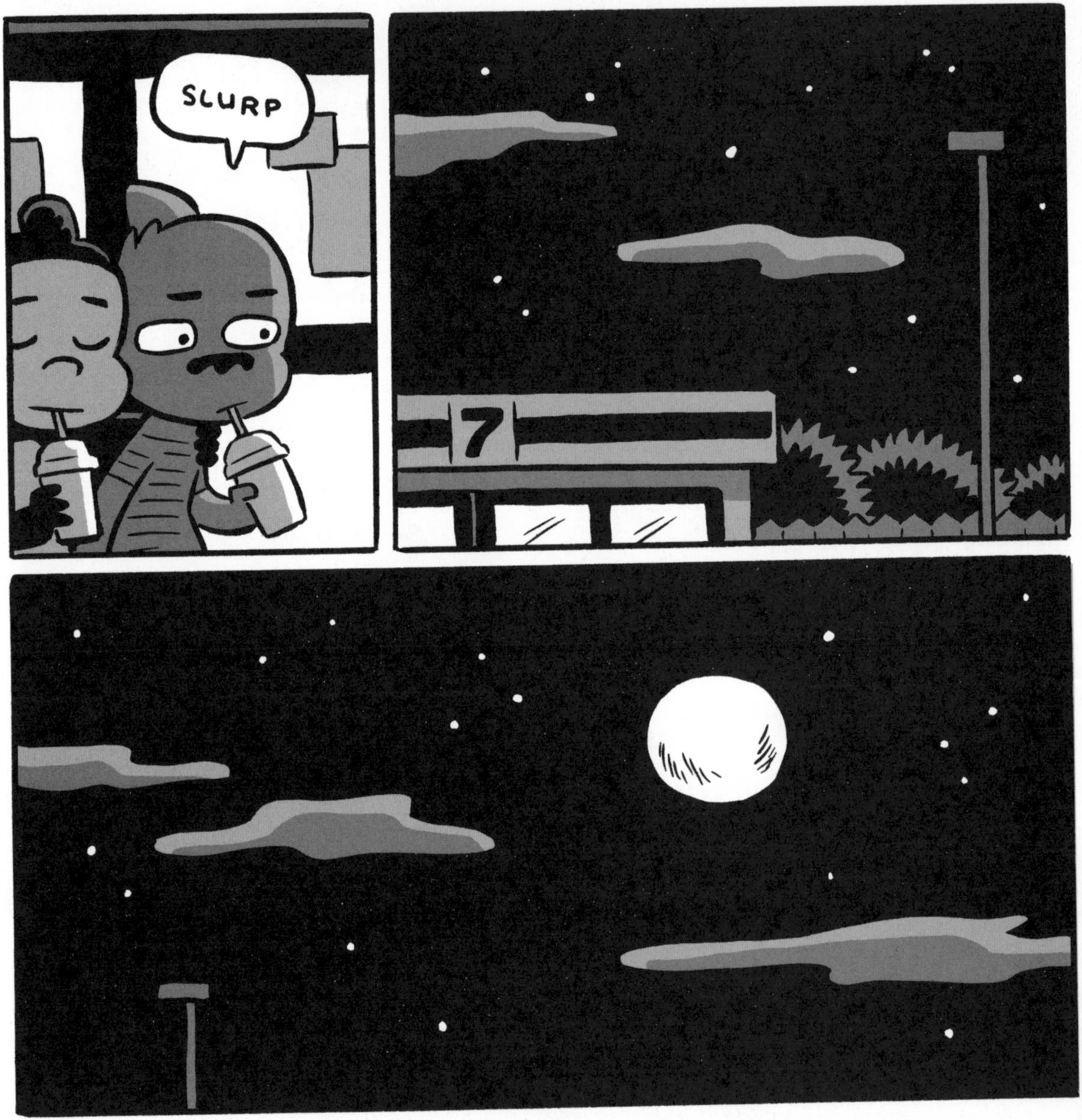
SLURP
7

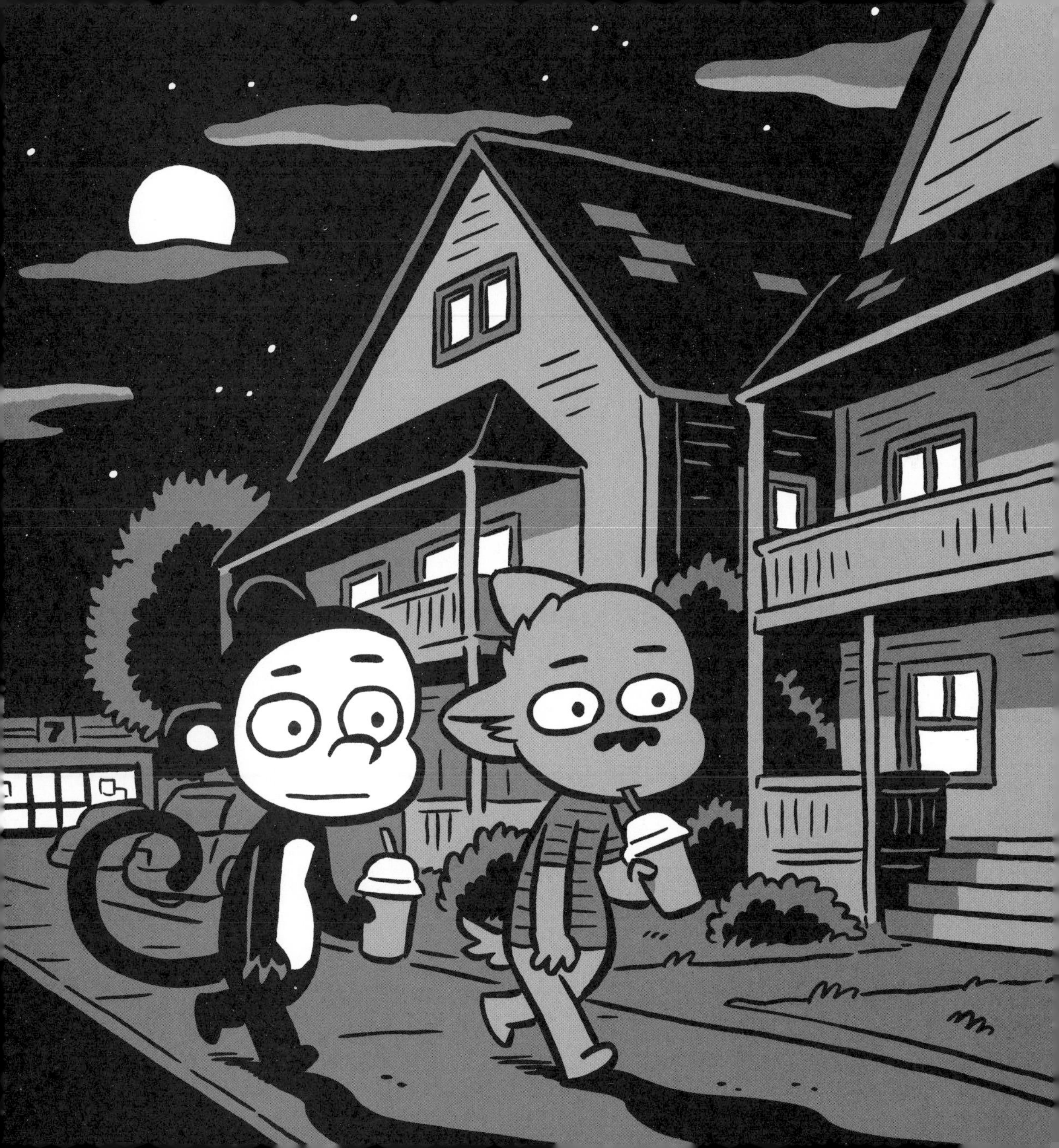
7

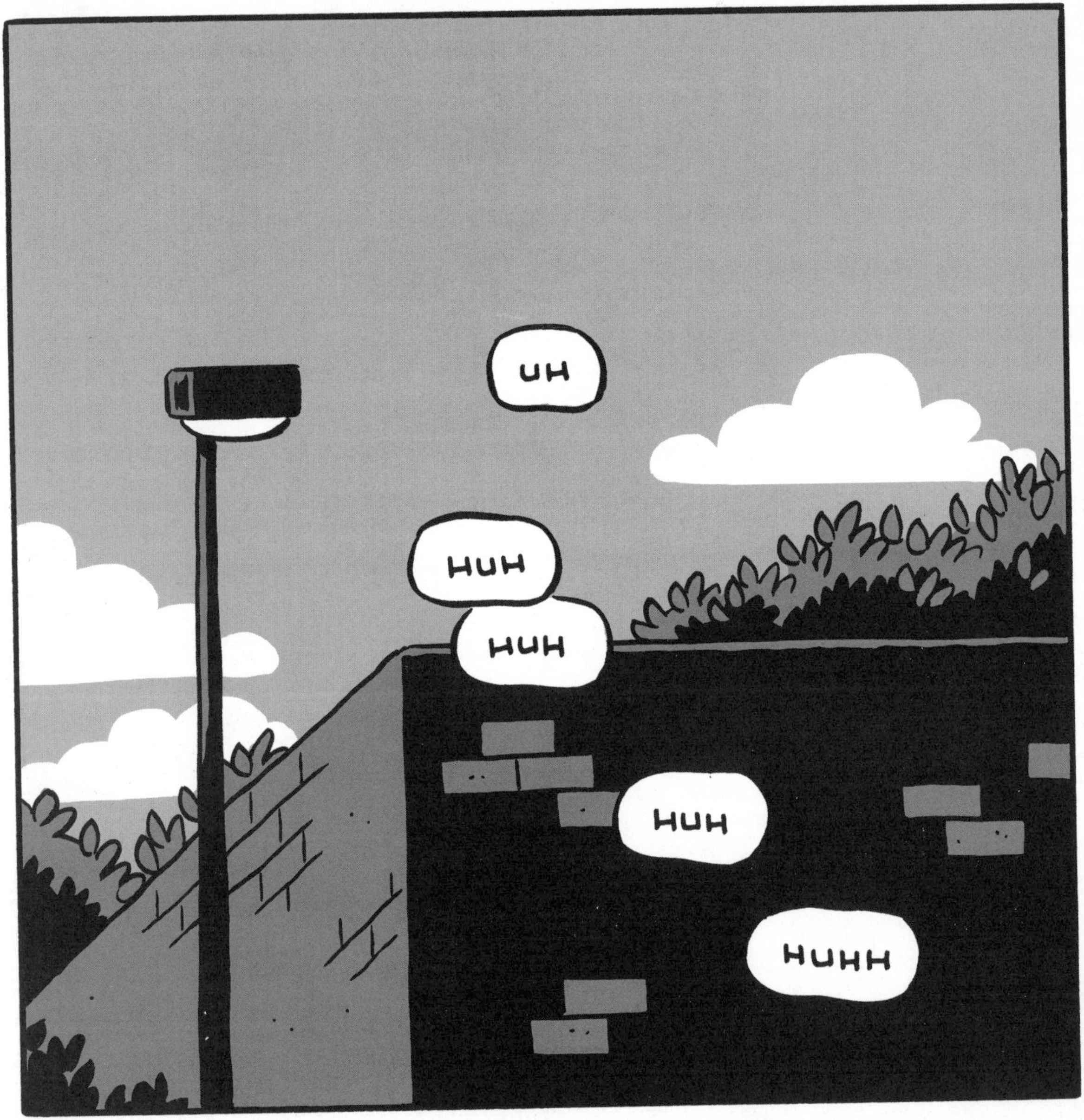
UH
HUH
HUH
HUH
HUHH

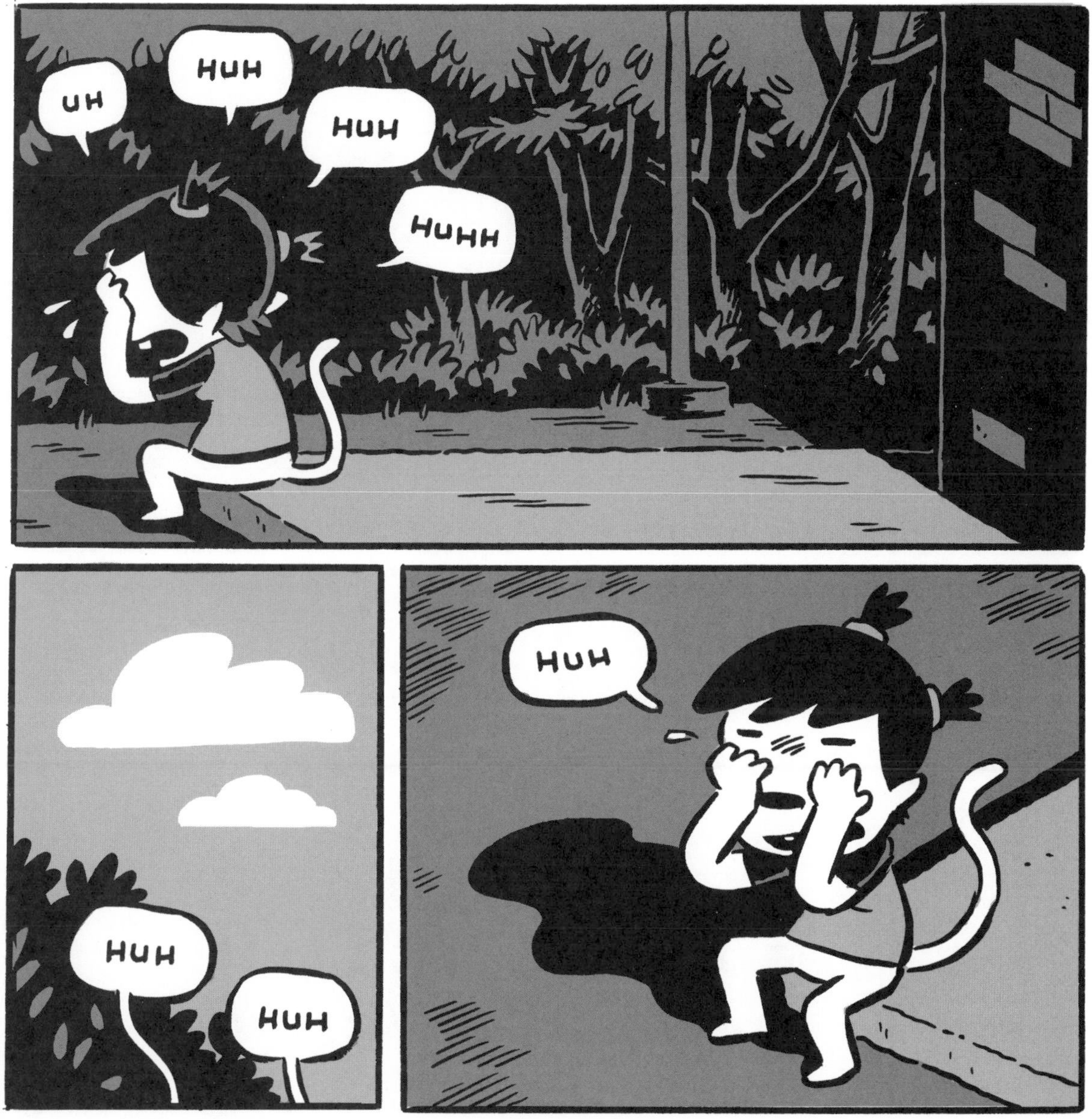
UH
HUH
HUH
HUHH
HUH
HUH
HUH

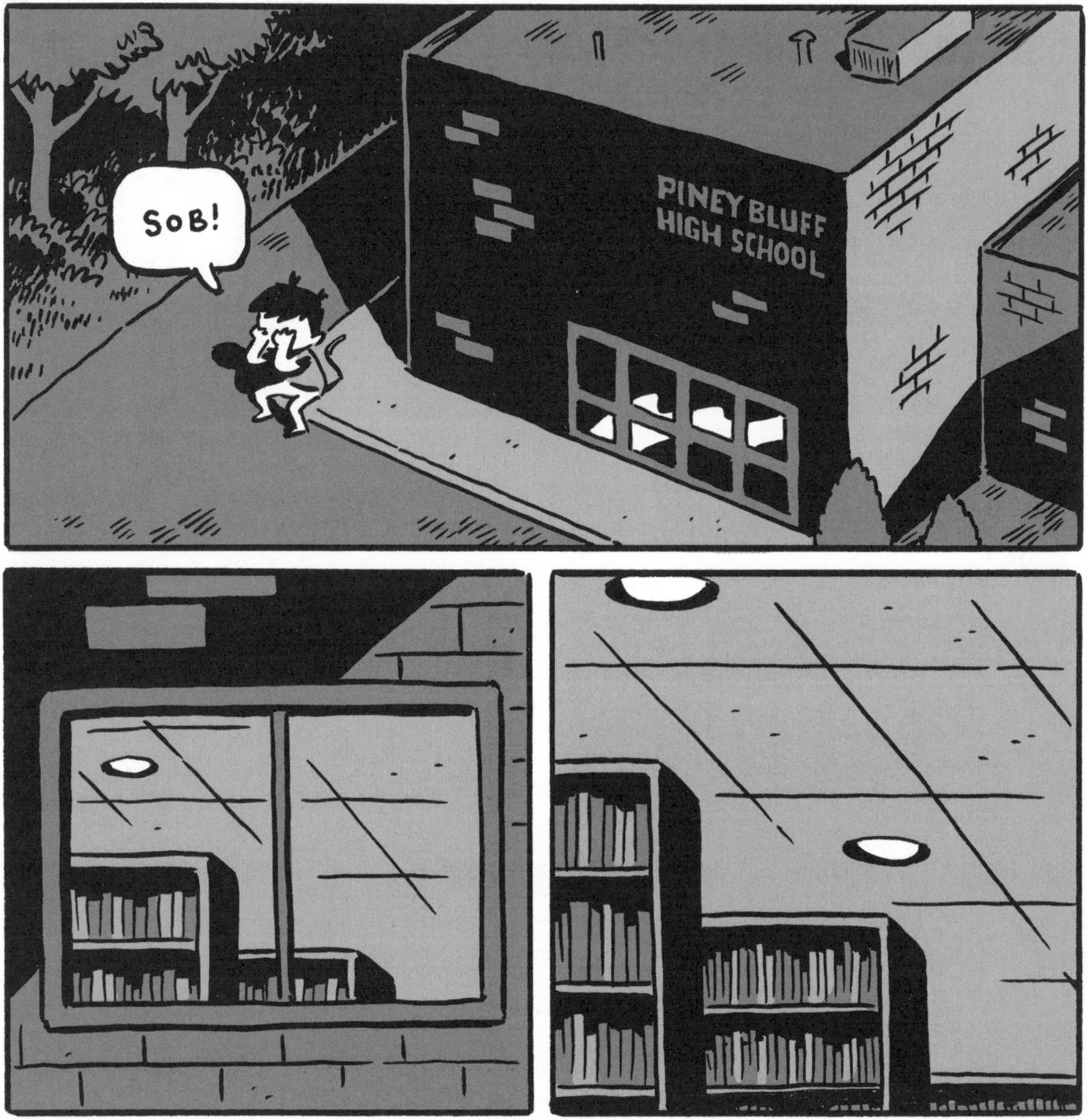
SOB!
PINEY BLUFF
HIGH SCHOOL

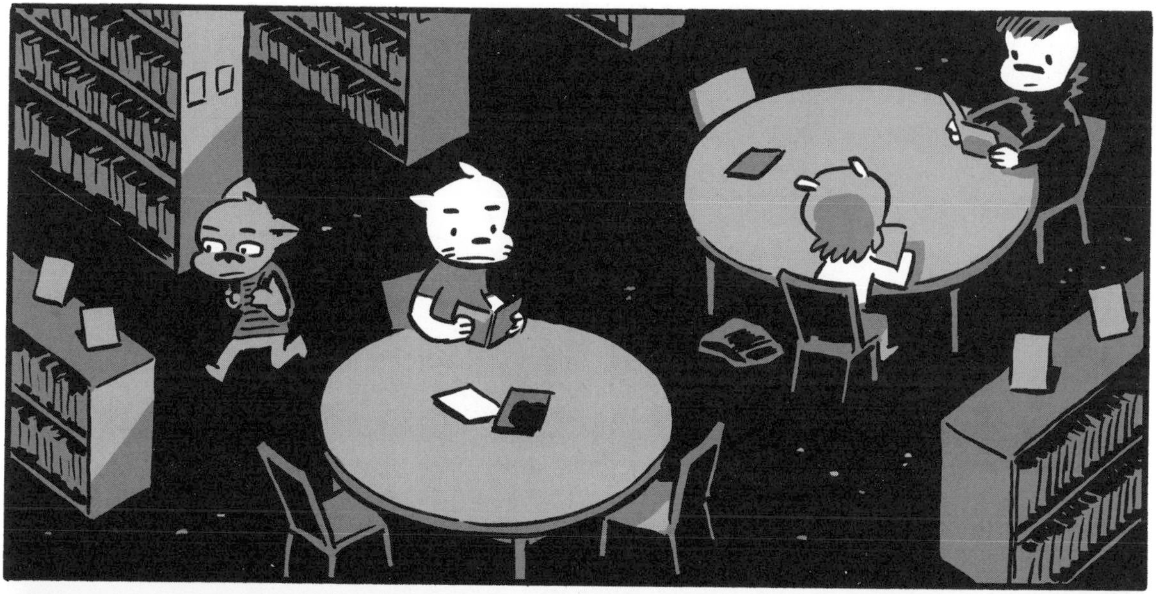

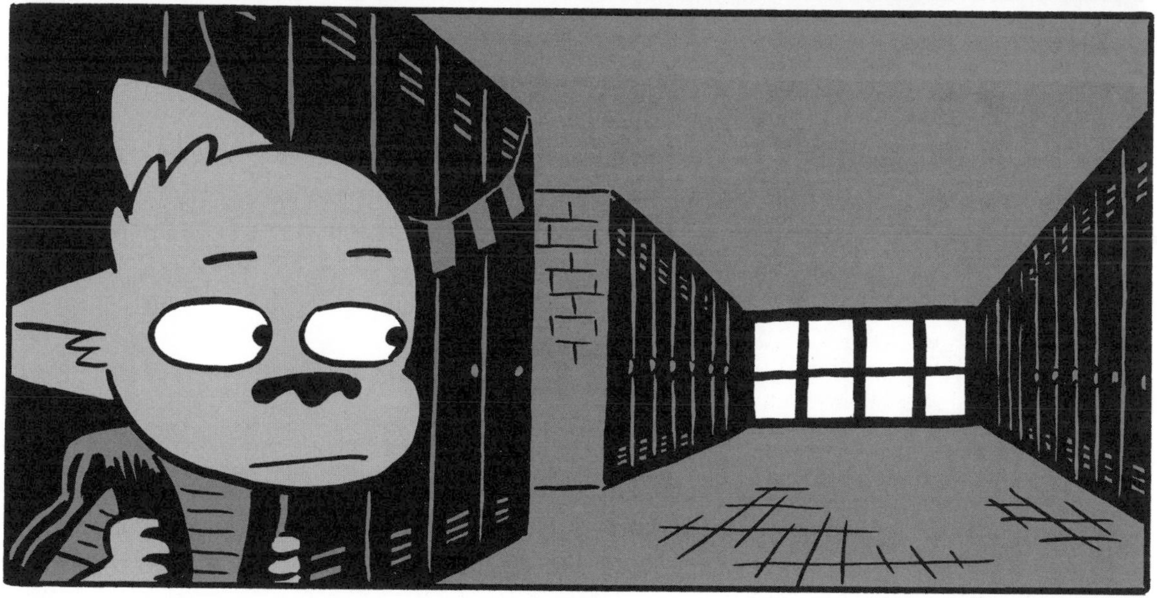

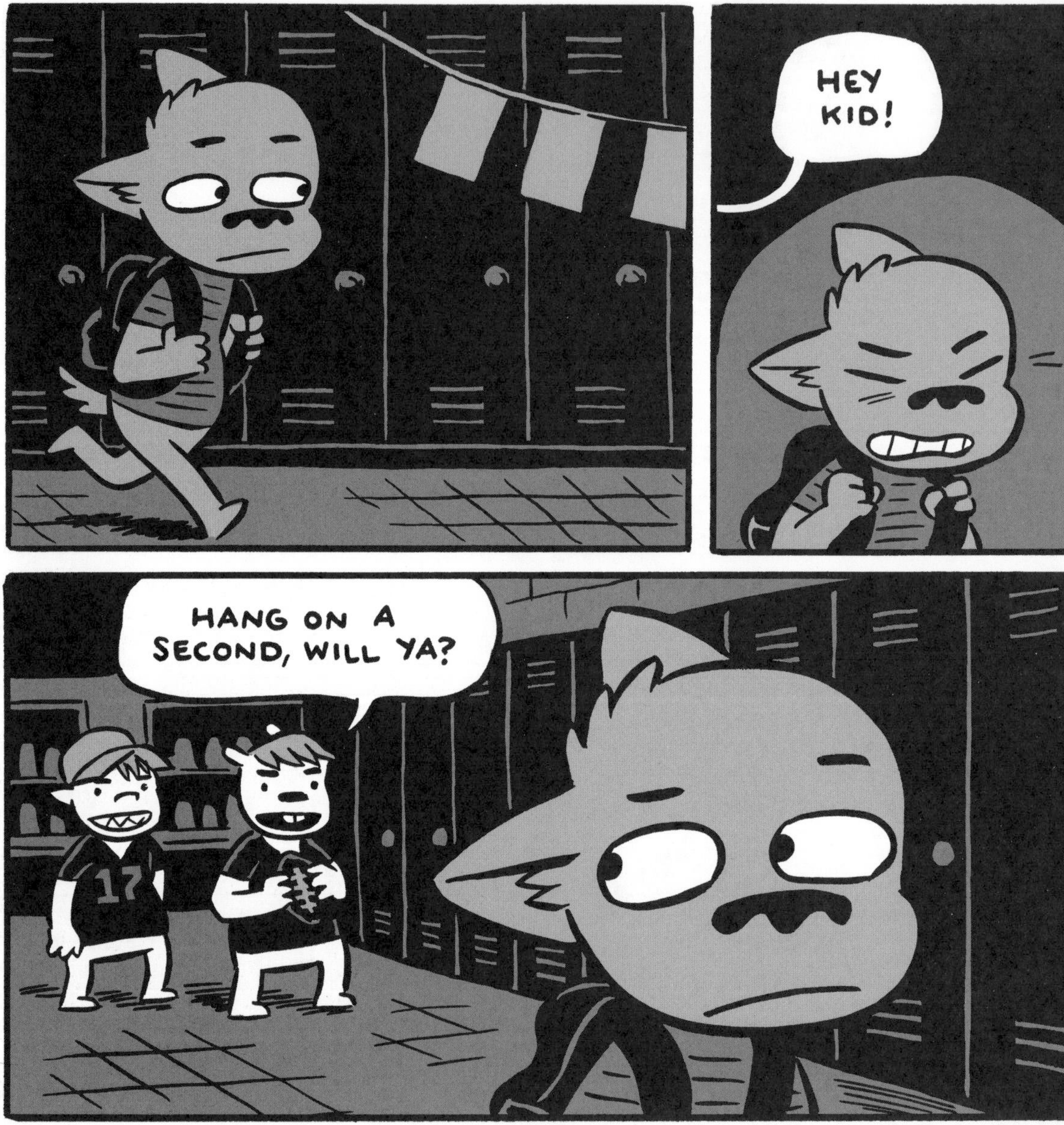
HEY KID!
HANG ON A SECOND, WILL YA?
17

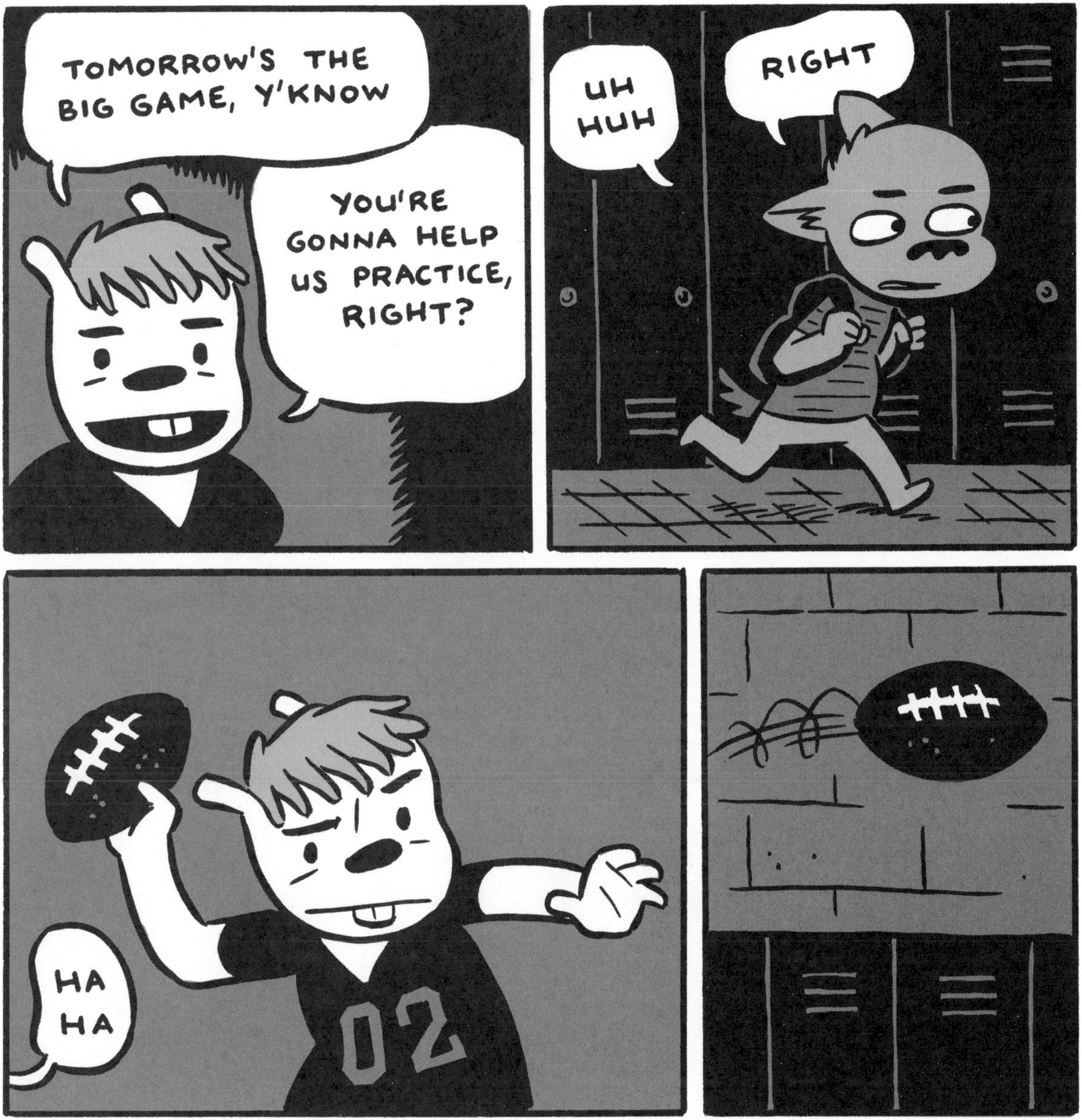
TOMORROW'S THE BIG GAME, Y'KNOW
YOU'RE GONNA HELP US PRACTICE, RIGHT?
UH HUH
RIGHT
HA HA
02

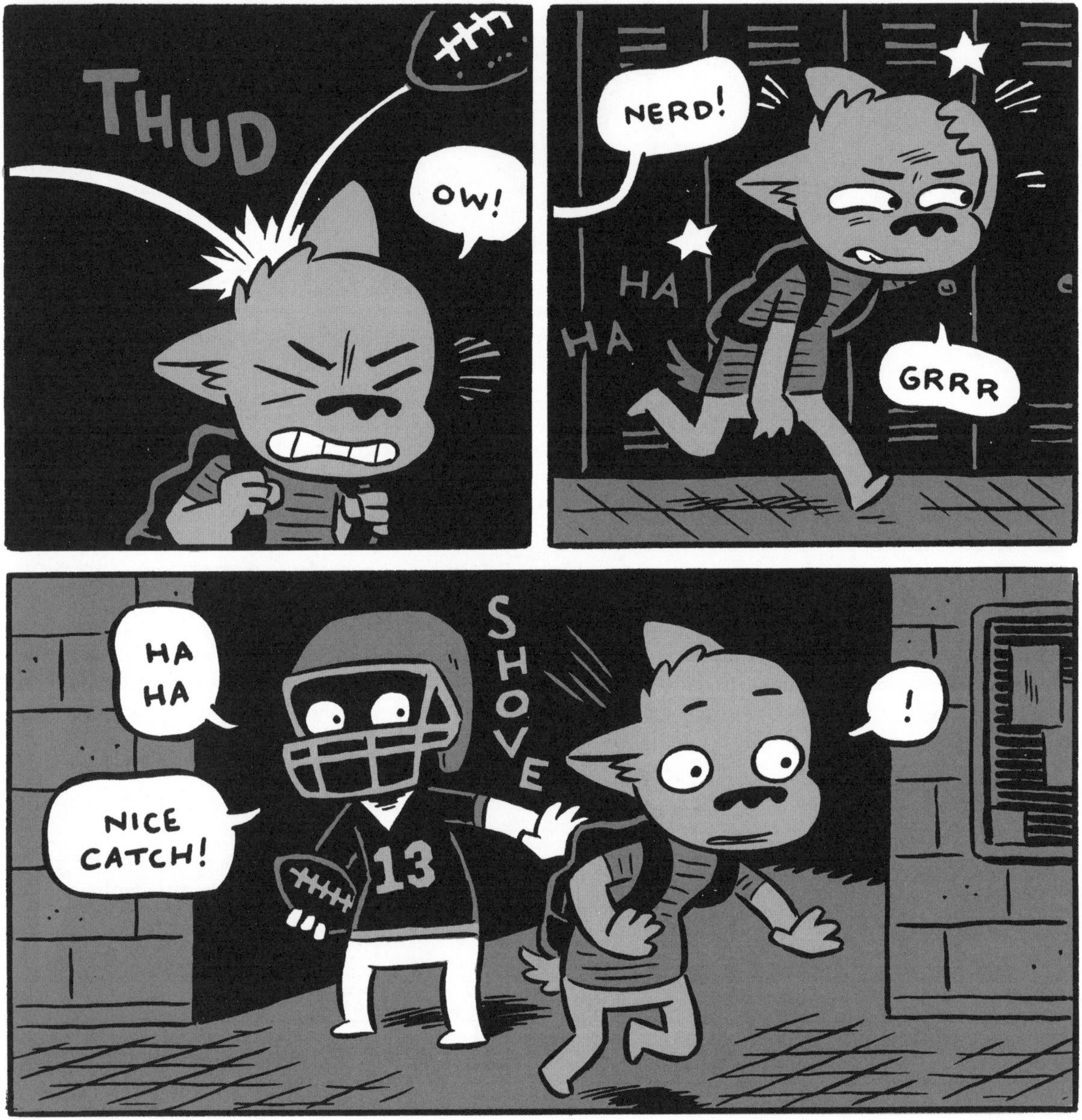
THUD
OW!
NERD!
HA
HA
GRRR
HA
HA
SHOVE
!
NICE
CATCH!
13

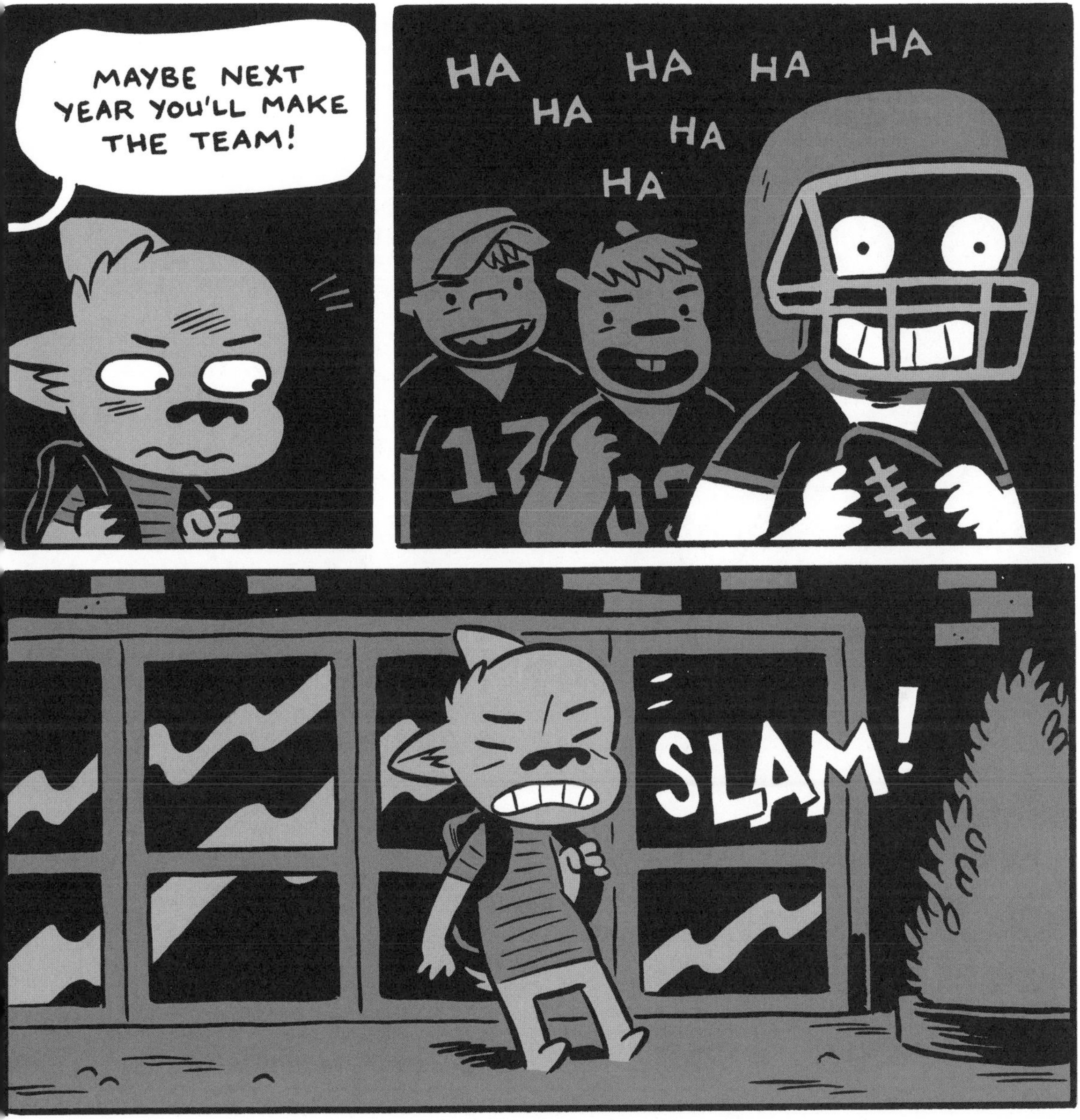
MAYBE NEXT YEAR YOU'LL MAKE THE TEAM!
HA HA HA HA HA HA HA
SLAM!

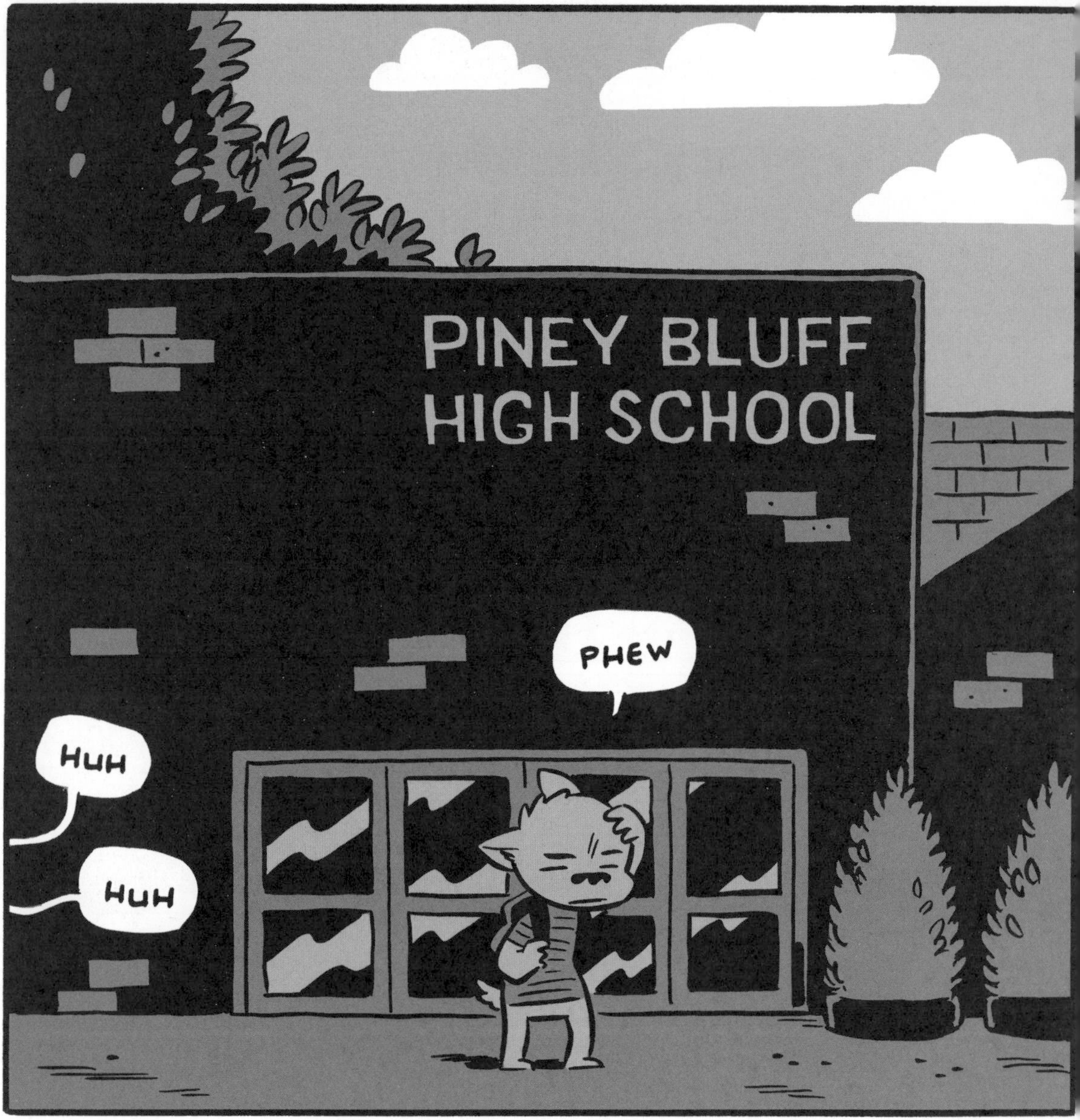
PINEY BLUFF
HIGH SCHOOL
PHEW
HUH
HUH

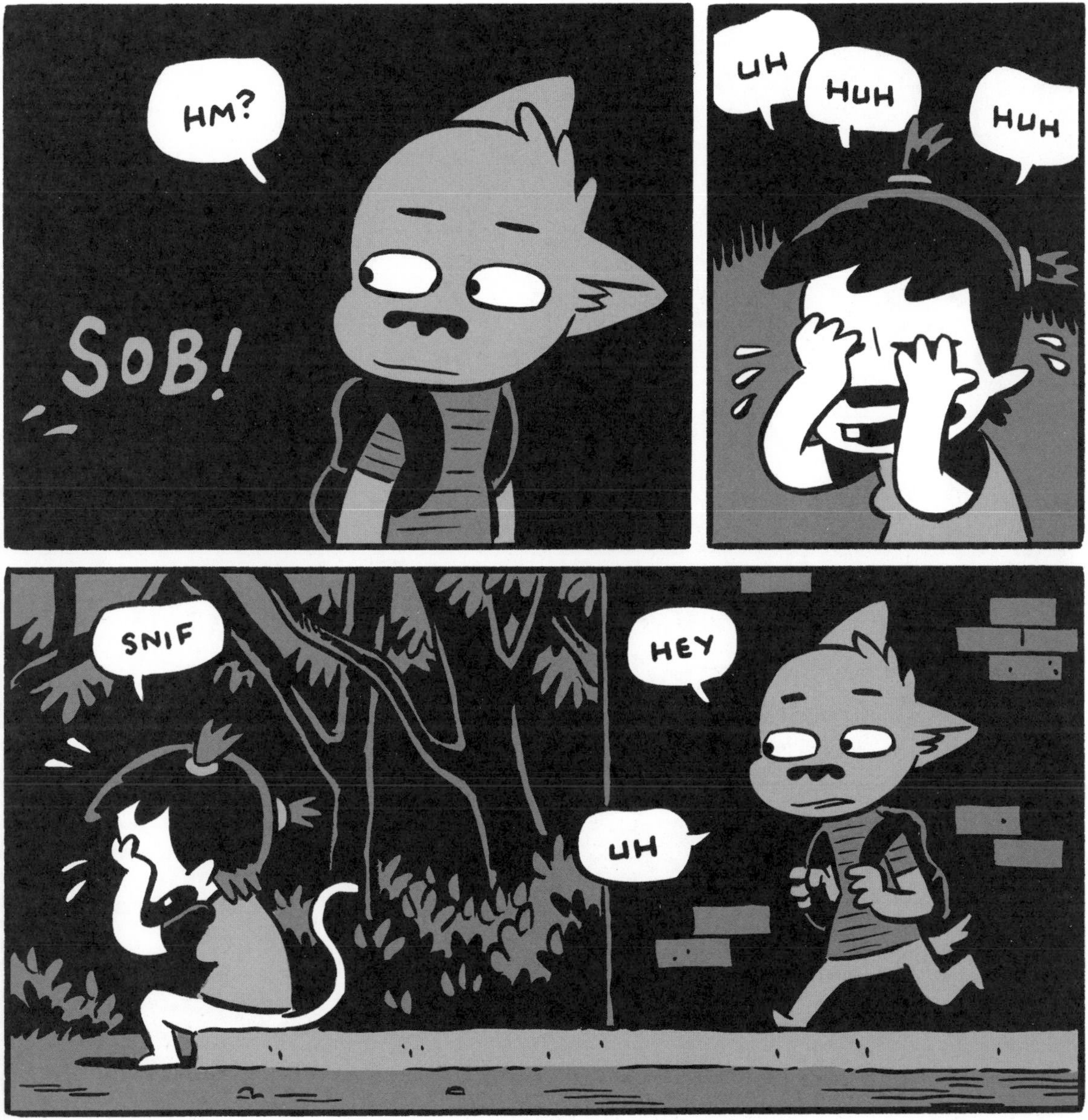
HM?
SOB!
UH
HUH
HUH
SNIF
HEY
UH

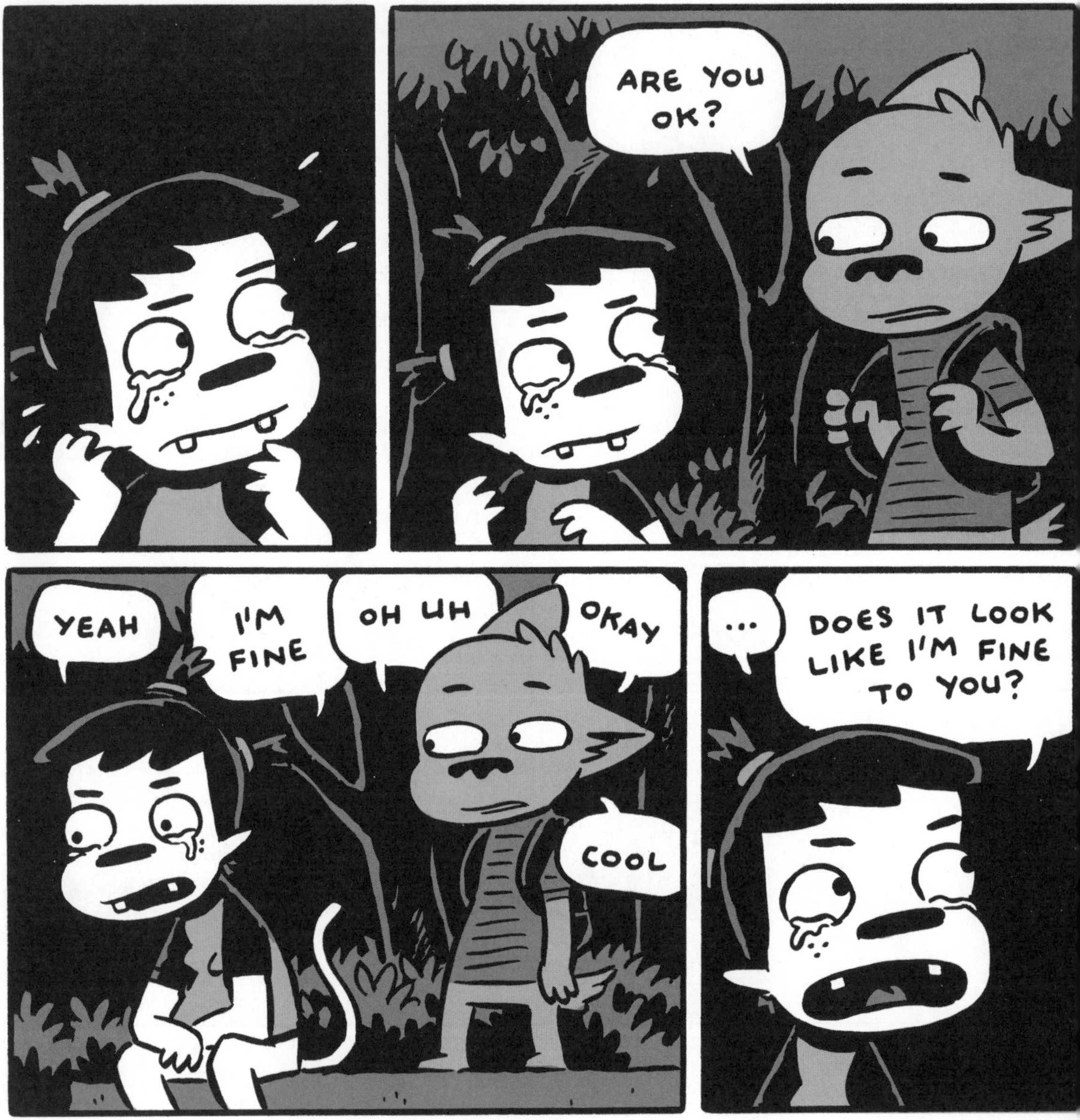
ARE YOU OK?
YEAH
I'M FINE
OH UH
OKAY
COOL
...
DOES IT LOOK LIKE I'M FINE TO YOU?

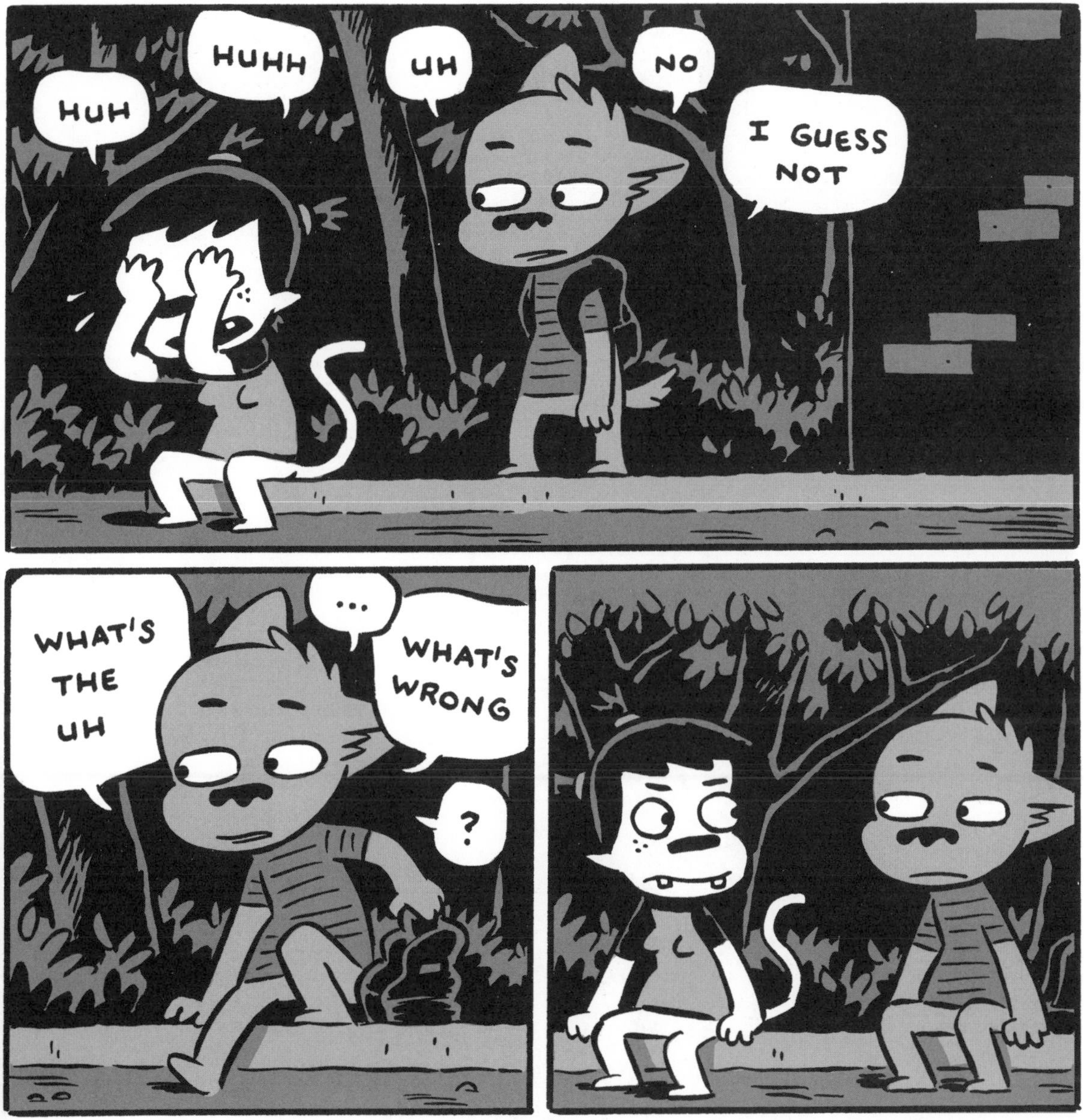
HUH
HUHH
UH
NO
I GUESS NOT
WHAT'S THE UH
...
WHAT'S WRONG
?

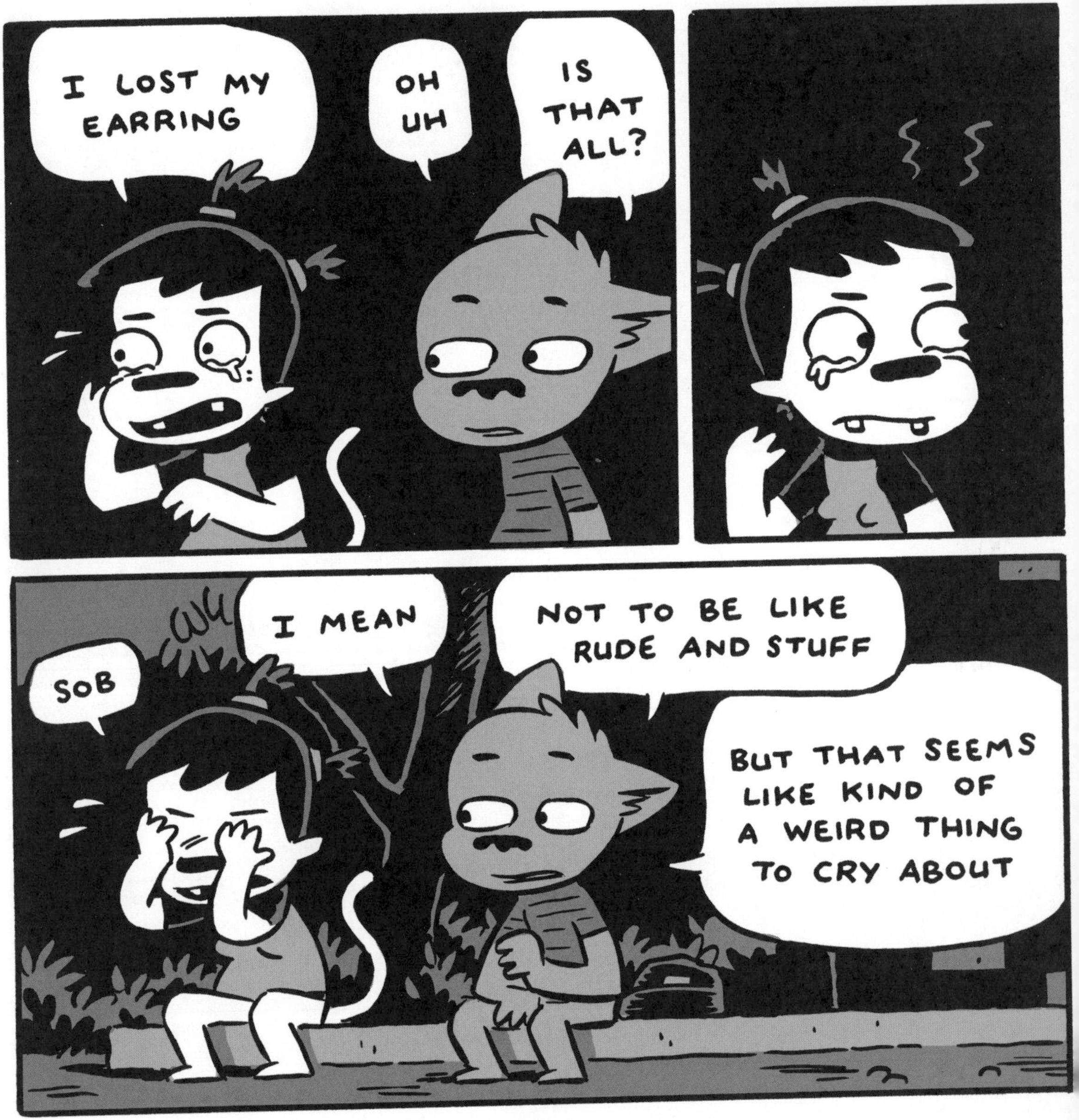
I LOST MY EARRING
OH UH
IS THAT ALL?
SOB
I MEAN
NOT TO BE LIKE RUDE AND STUFF
BUT THAT SEEMS LIKE KIND OF A WEIRD THING TO CRY ABOUT

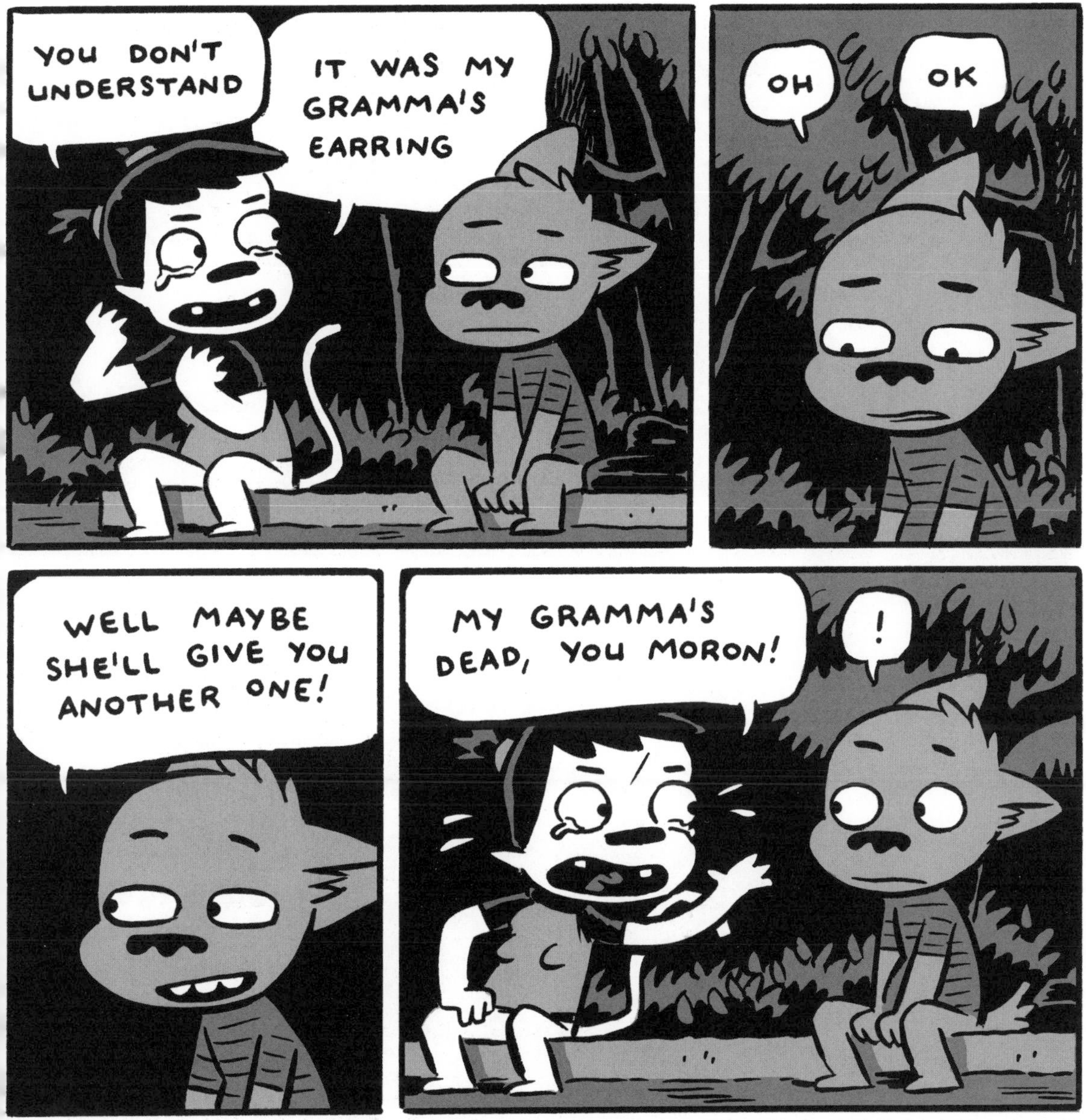
YOU DON'T UNDERSTAND
IT WAS MY GRAMMA'S EARRING
OH
OK
WELL MAYBE SHE'LL GIVE YOU ANOTHER ONE!
MY GRAMMA'S DEAD, YOU MORON!
!

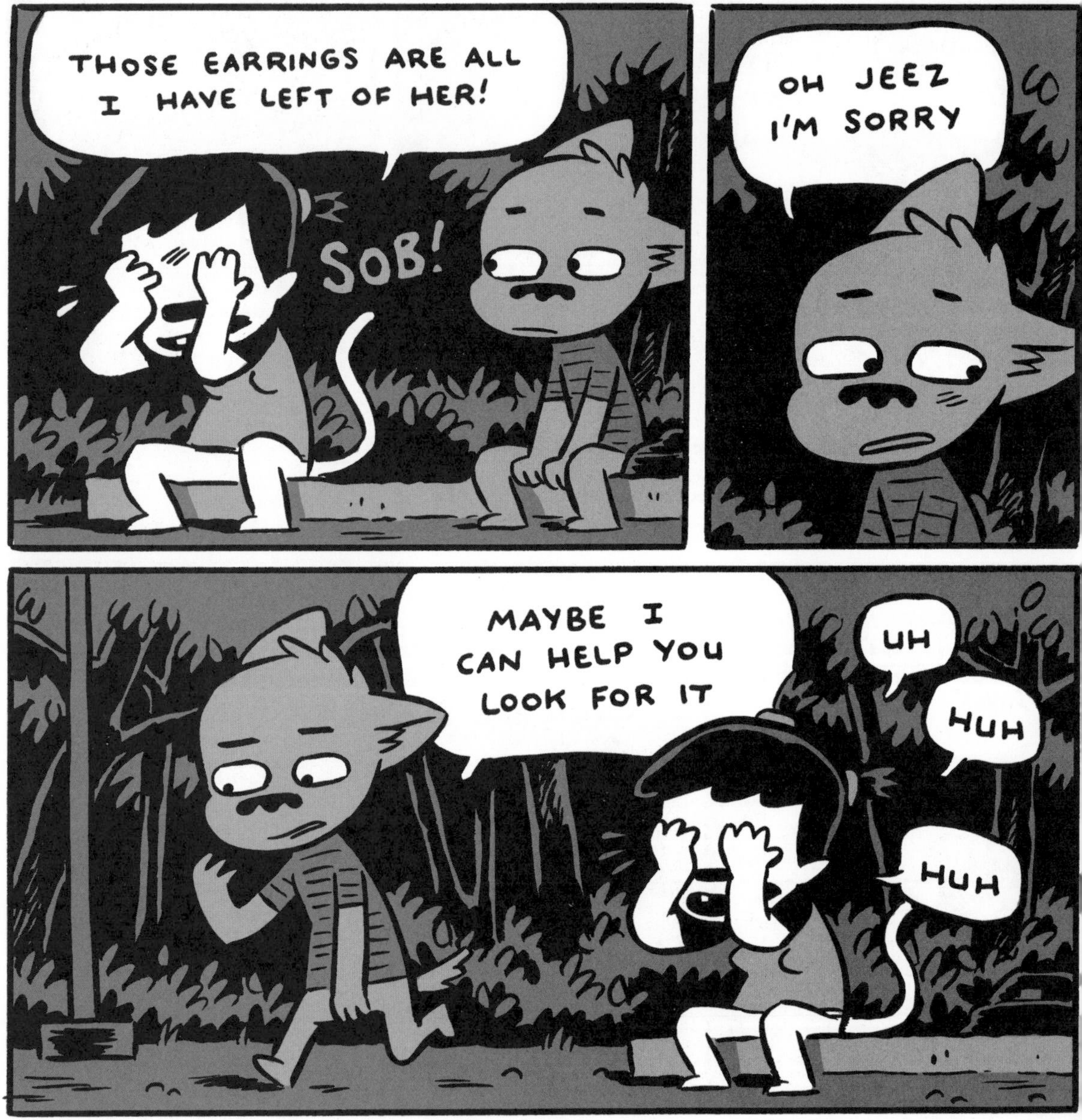
THOSE EARRINGS ARE ALL I HAVE LEFT OF HER!
SOB!
OH JEEZ I'M SORRY
MAYBE I CAN HELP YOU LOOK FOR IT
UH
HUH
HUH

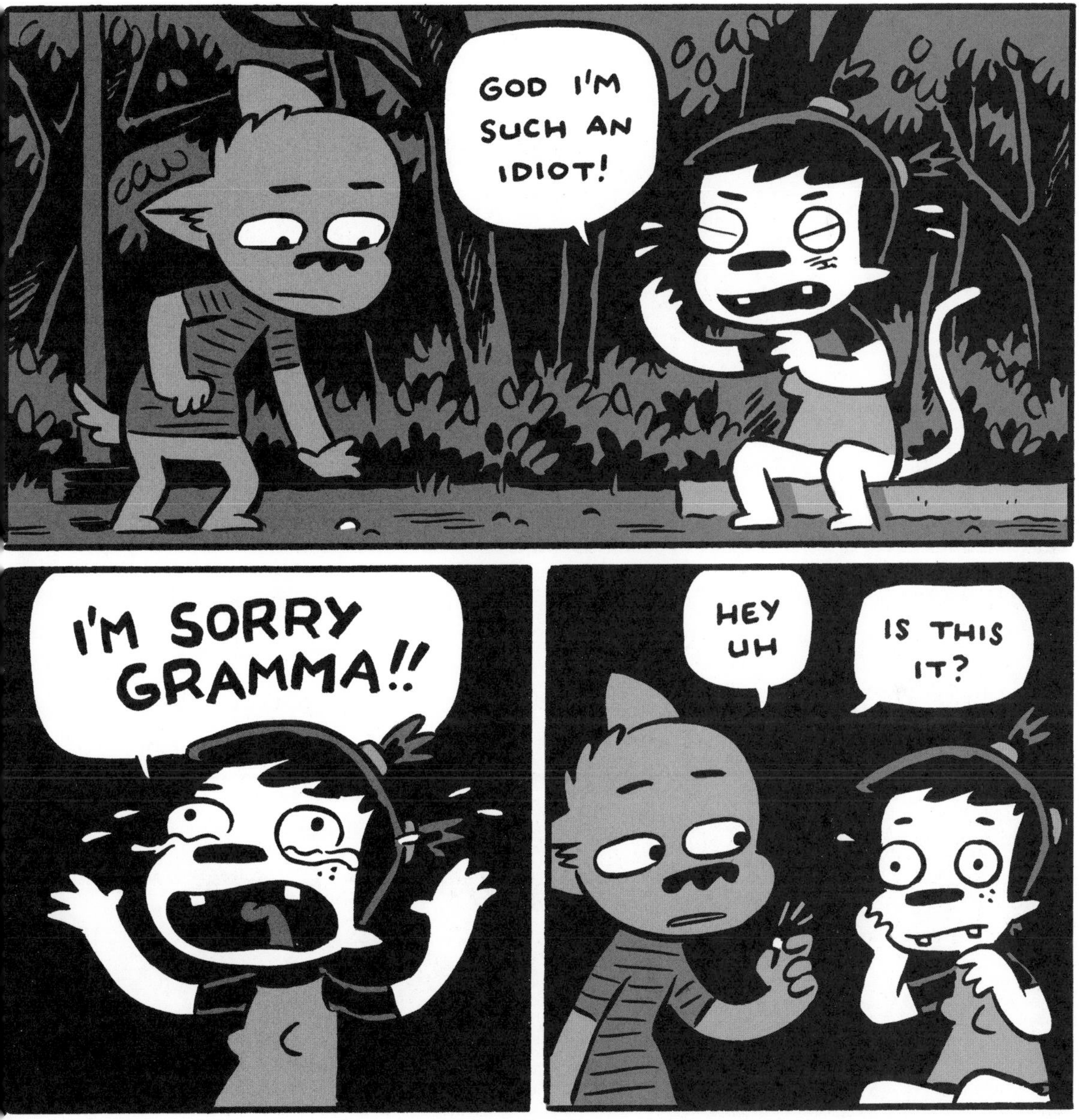
GOD I'M SUCH AN IDIOT!
I'M SORRY GRAMMA!!
HEY UH
IS THIS IT?

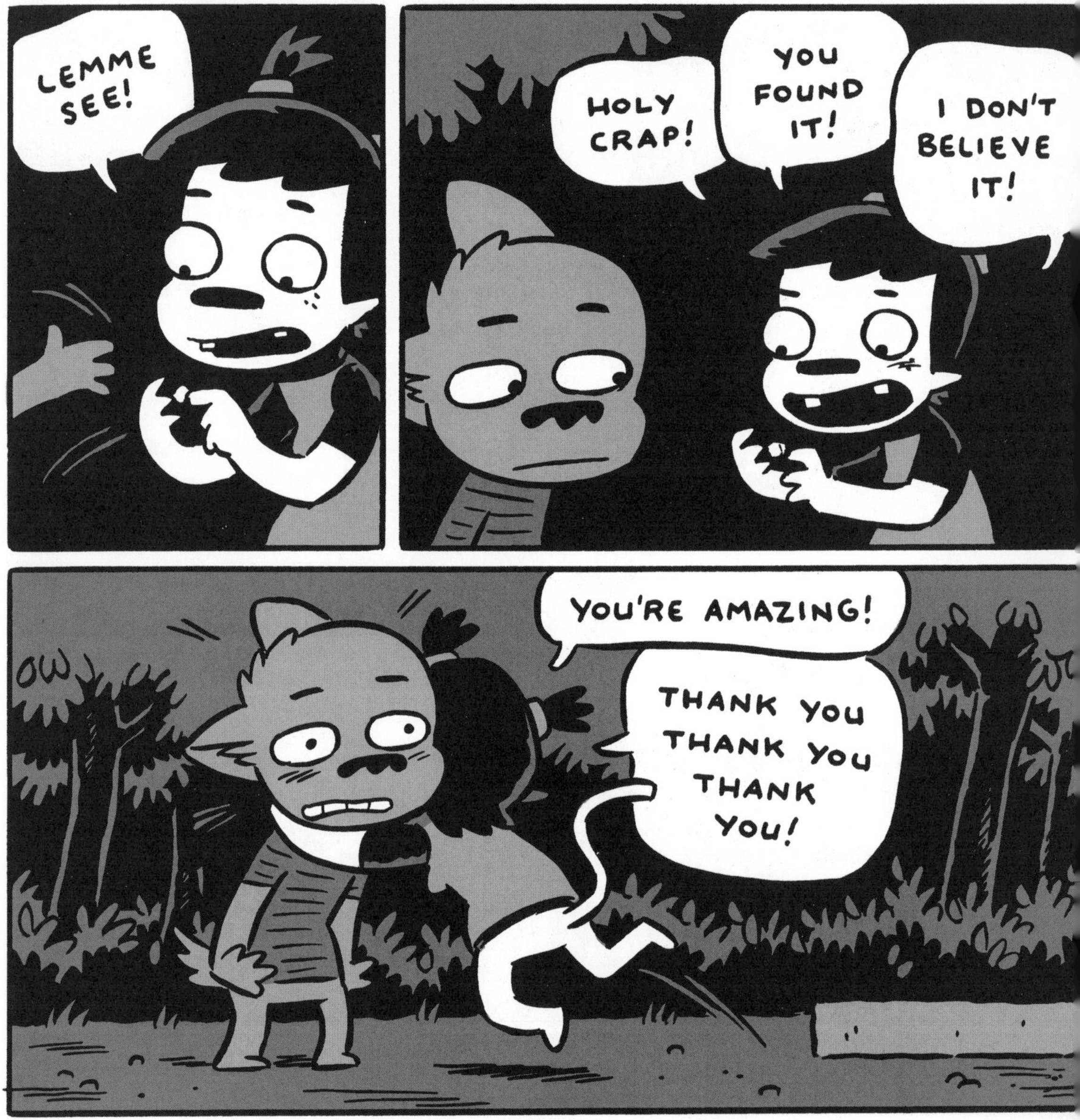
LEMME SEE!
HOLY CRAP!
YOU FOUND IT!
I DON'T BELIEVE IT!
YOU'RE AMAZING!
OW
THANK YOU THANK YOU THANK YOU!

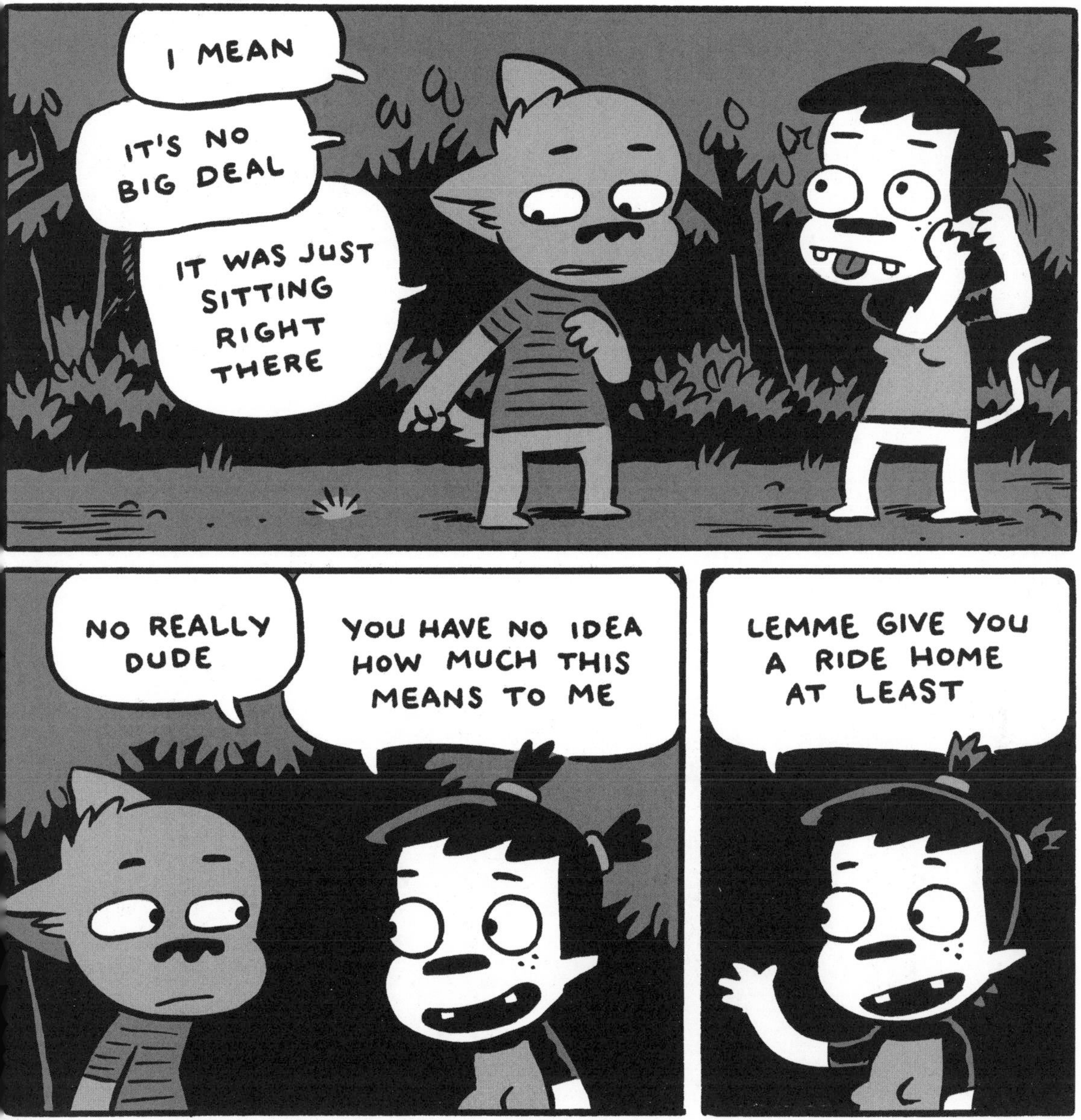
I MEAN
IT'S NO BIG DEAL
IT WAS JUST SITTING RIGHT THERE
NO REALLY DUDE
YOU HAVE NO IDEA HOW MUCH THIS MEANS TO ME
LEMME GIVE YOU A RIDE HOME AT LEAST

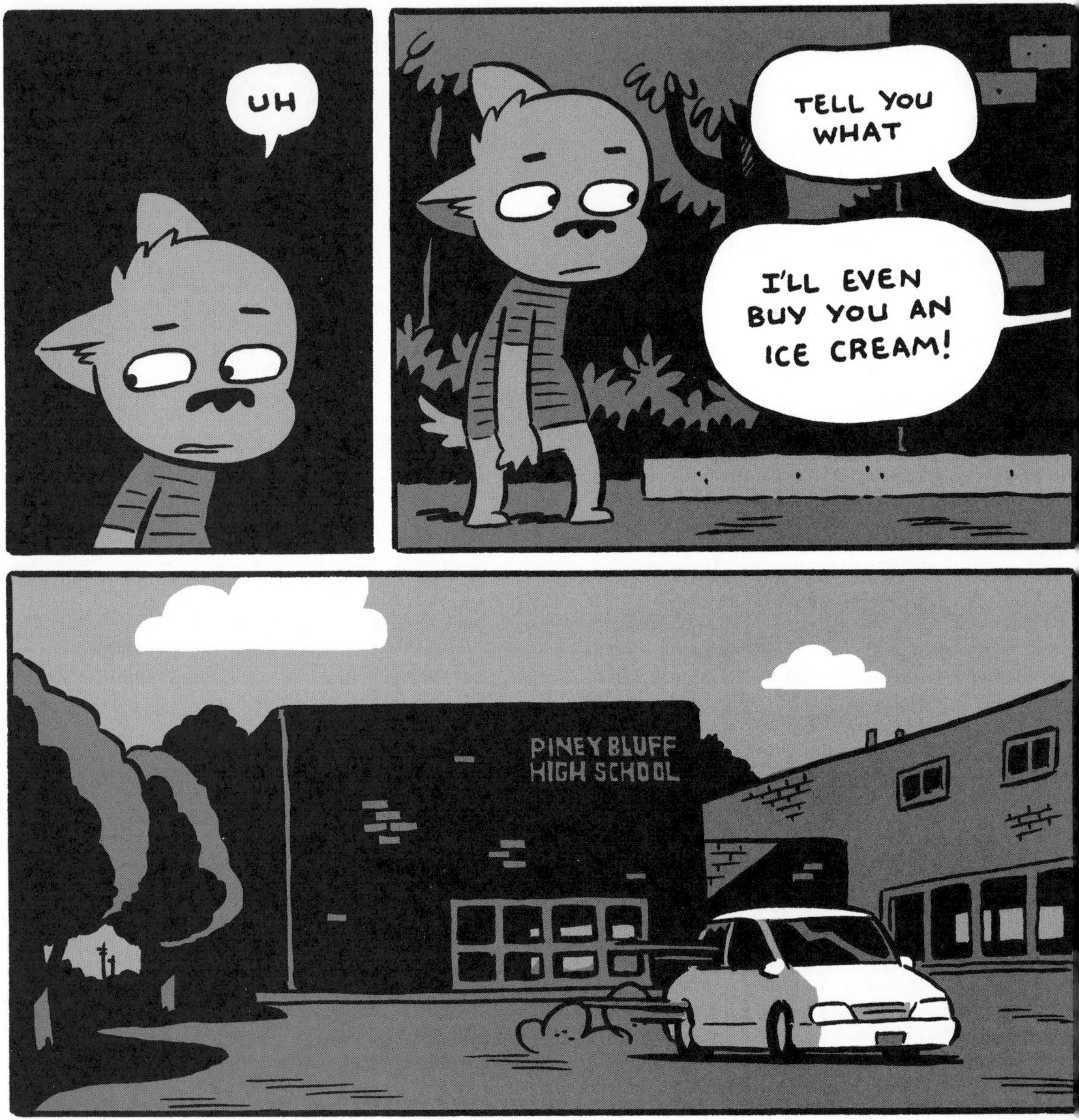
UH
TELL YOU WHAT
I'LL EVEN BUY YOU AN ICE CREAM!
PINEY BLUFF HIGH SCHOOL

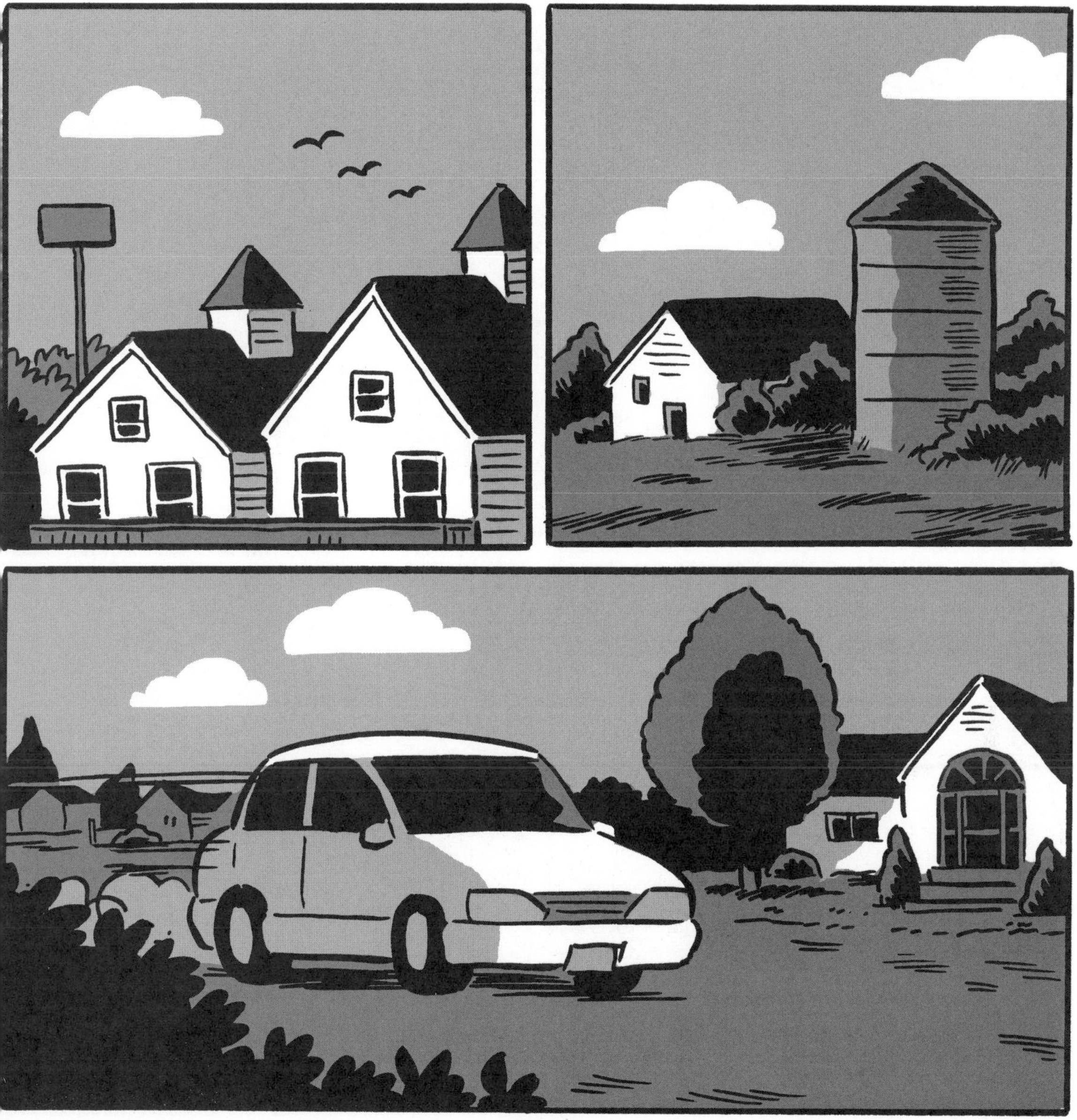

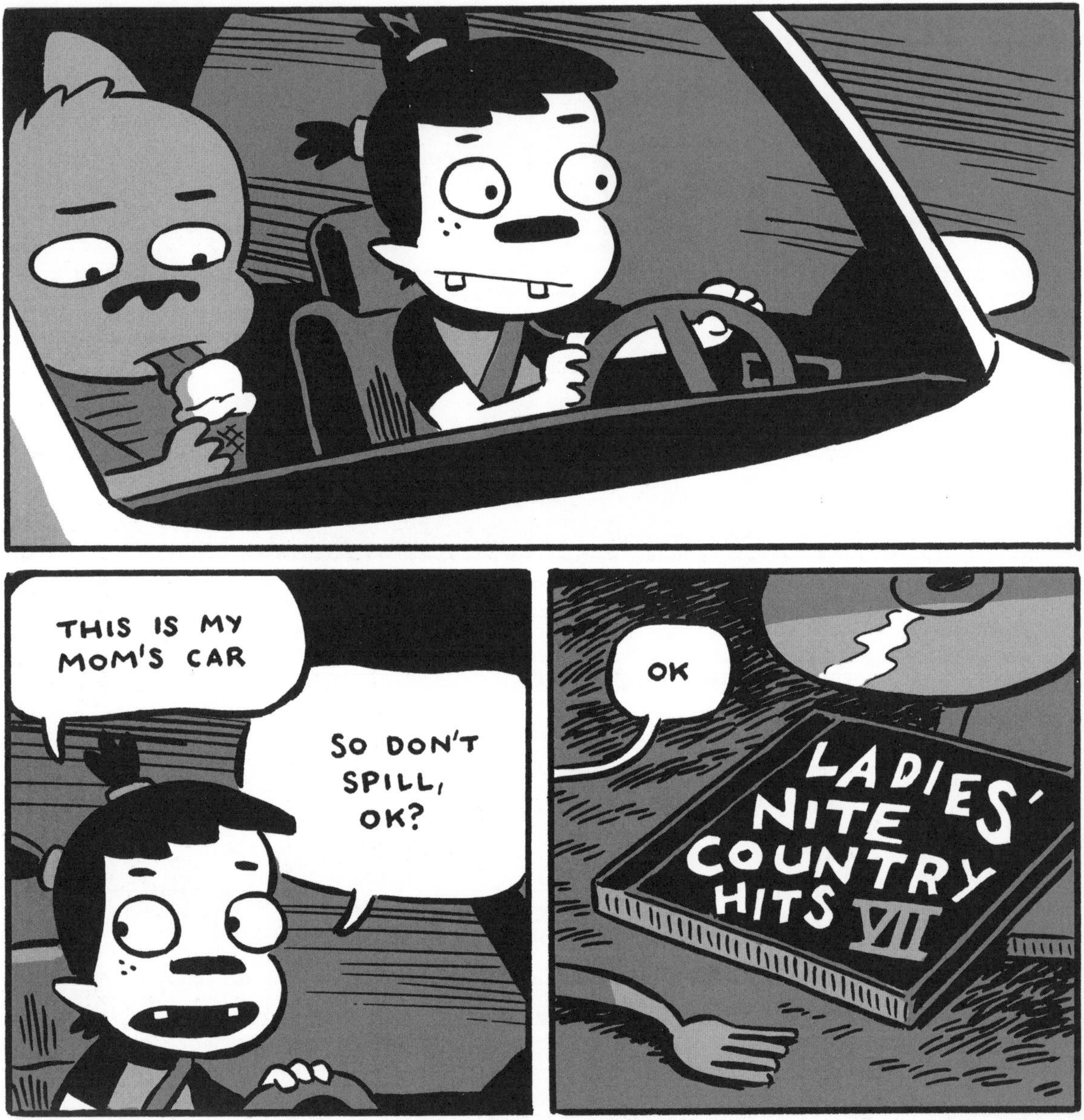
THIS IS MY MOM'S CAR
SO DON'T SPILL, OK?
OK
LADIES' NITE COUNTRY HITS VII

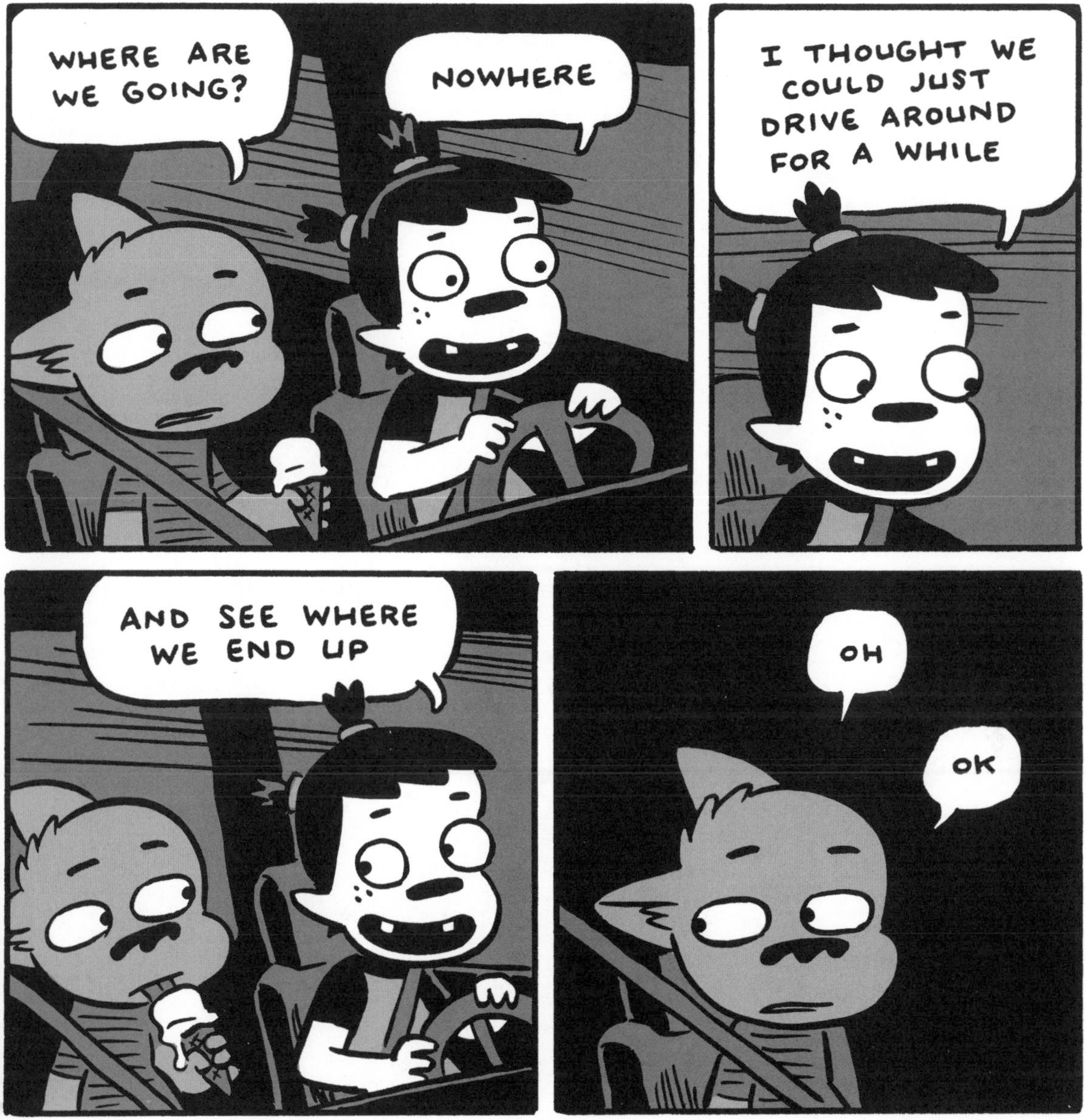
WHERE ARE WE GOING?
NOWHERE
I THOUGHT WE COULD JUST DRIVE AROUND FOR A WHILE
AND SEE WHERE WE END UP
OH
OK

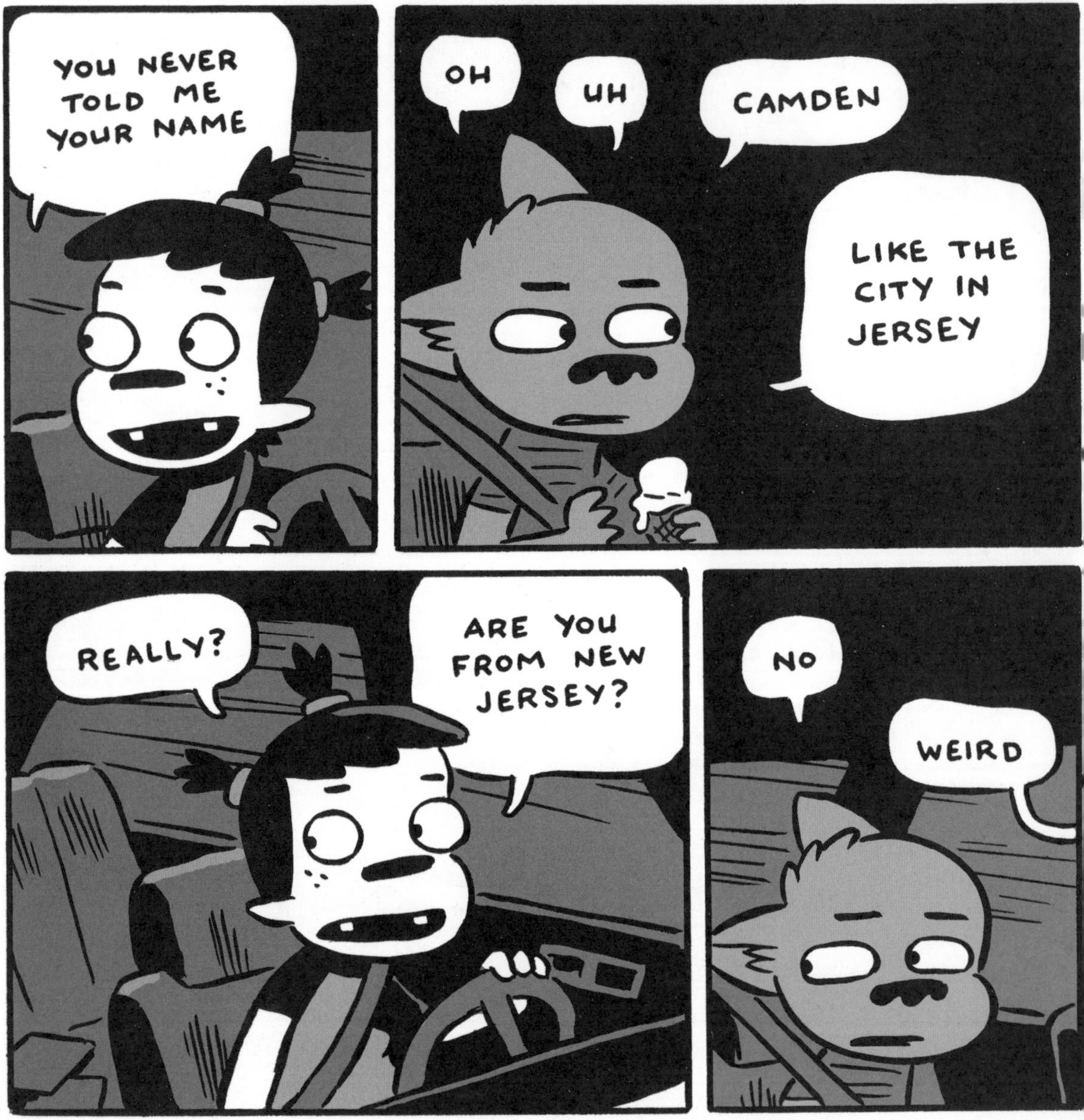
YOU NEVER TOLD ME YOUR NAME
OH
UH
CAMDEN
LIKE THE CITY IN JERSEY
REALLY?
ARE YOU FROM NEW JERSEY?
NO
WEIRD

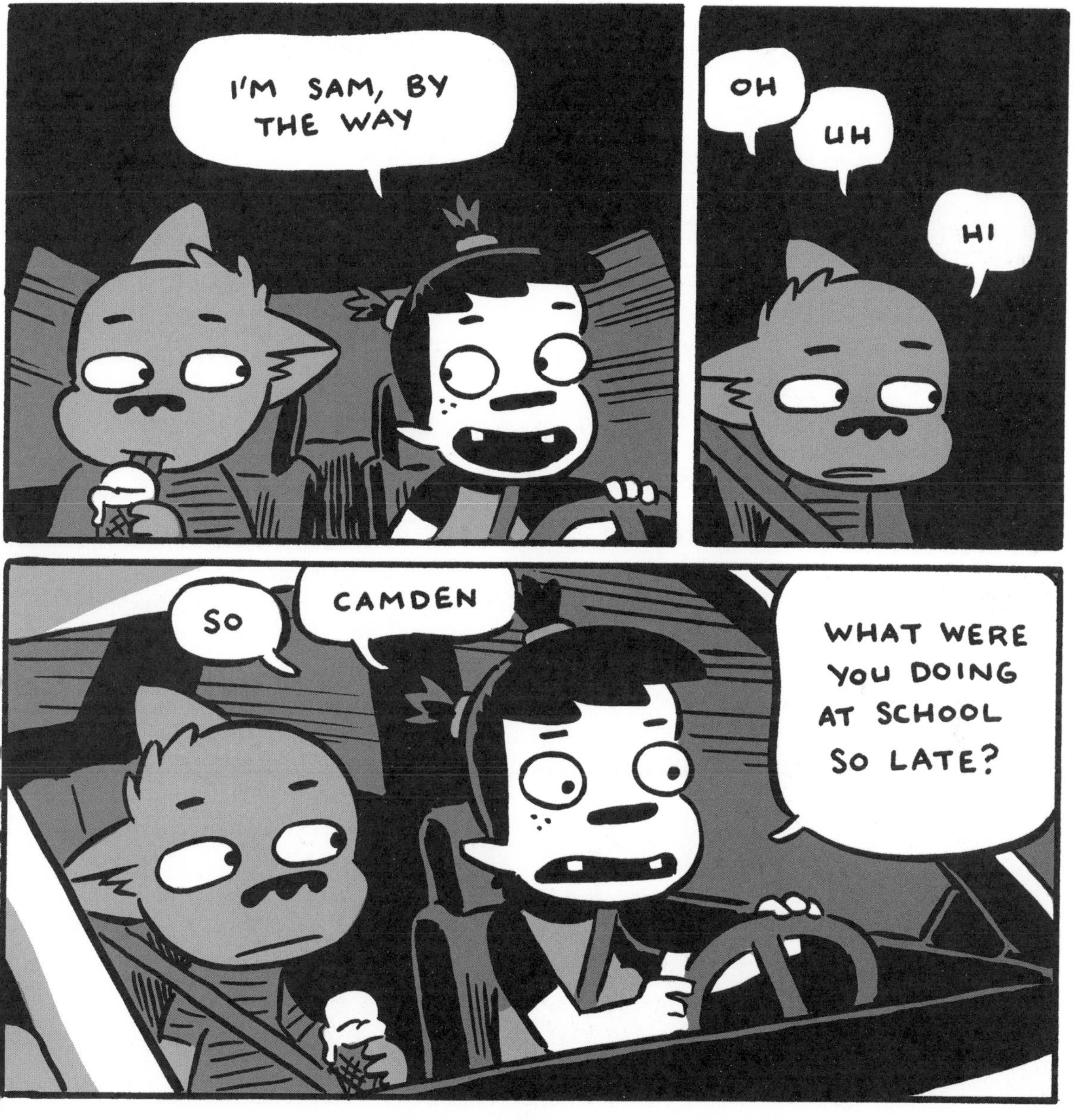
I'M SAM, BY THE WAY
OH
UH
HI
SO
CAMDEN
WHAT WERE YOU DOING AT SCHOOL SO LATE?

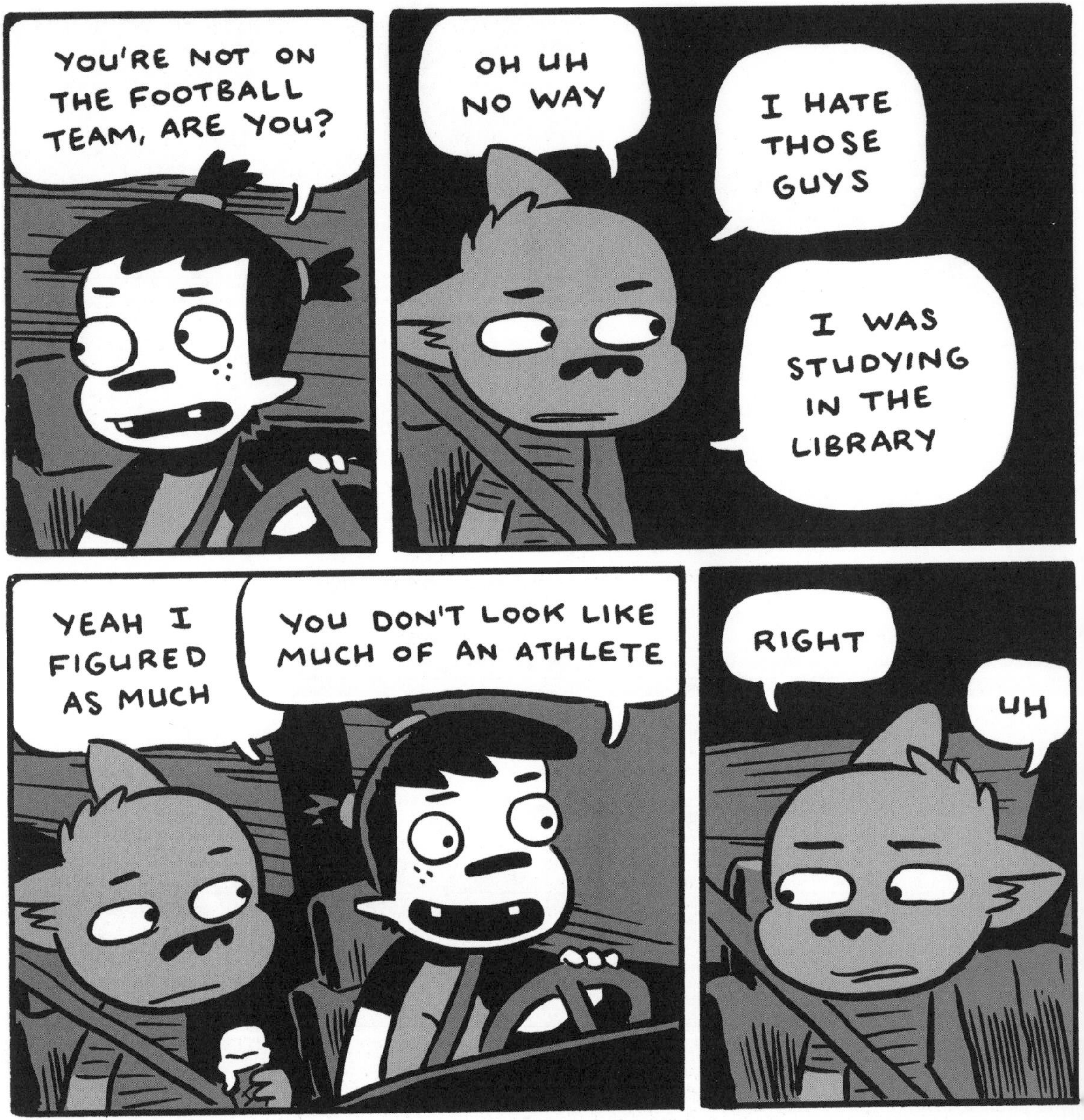
YOU'RE NOT ON THE FOOTBALL TEAM, ARE YOU?
OH UH NO WAY
I HATE THOSE GUYS
I WAS STUDYING IN THE LIBRARY
YEAH I FIGURED AS MUCH
YOU DON'T LOOK LIKE MUCH OF AN ATHLETE
RIGHT
UH

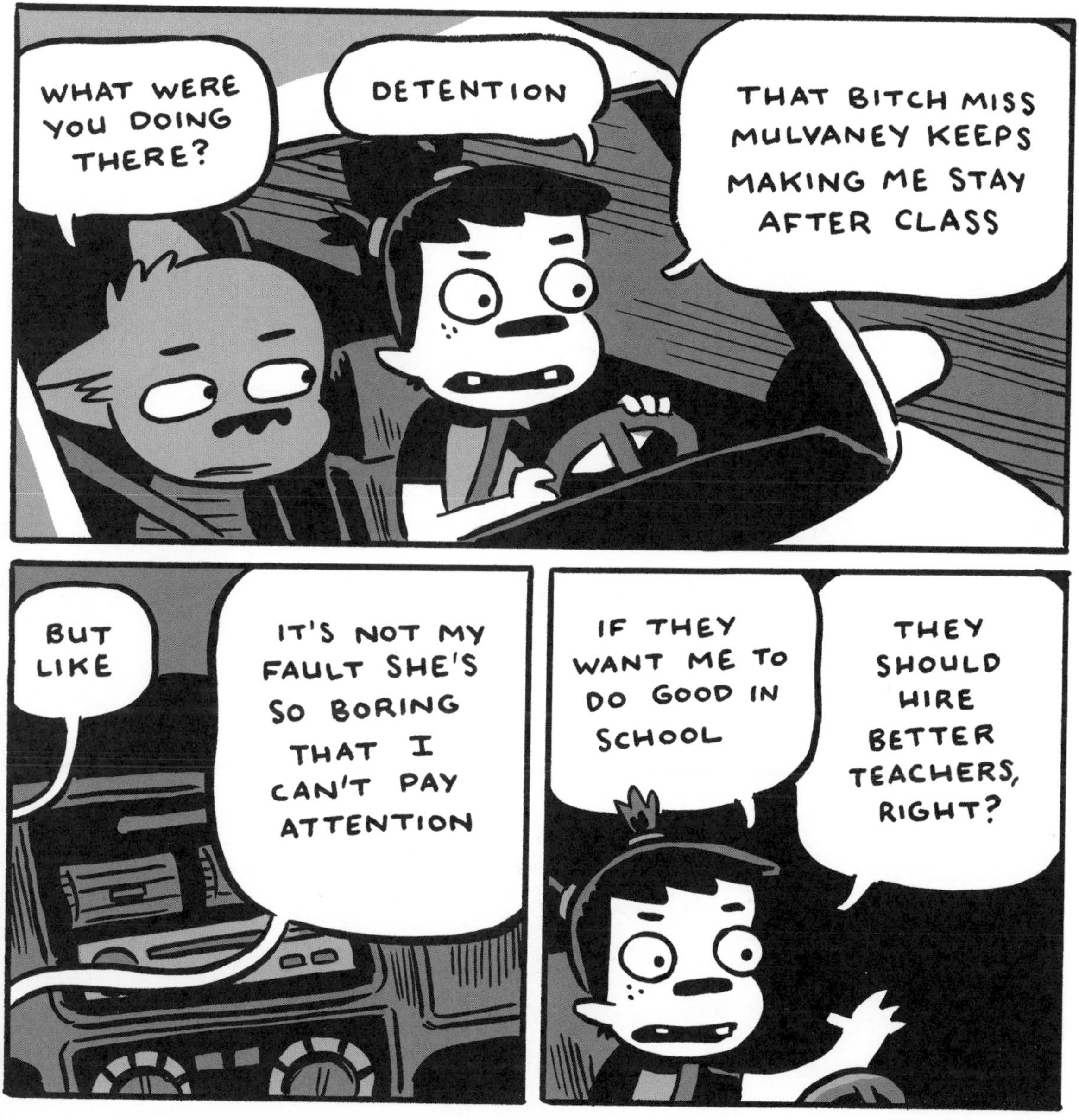
WHAT WERE YOU DOING THERE?
DETENTION
THAT BITCH MISS MULVANEY KEEPS MAKING ME STAY AFTER CLASS
BUT LIKE
IT'S NOT MY FAULT SHE'S SO BORING THAT I CAN'T PAY ATTENTION
IF THEY WANT ME TO DO GOOD IN SCHOOL
THEY SHOULD HIRE BETTER TEACHERS, RIGHT?

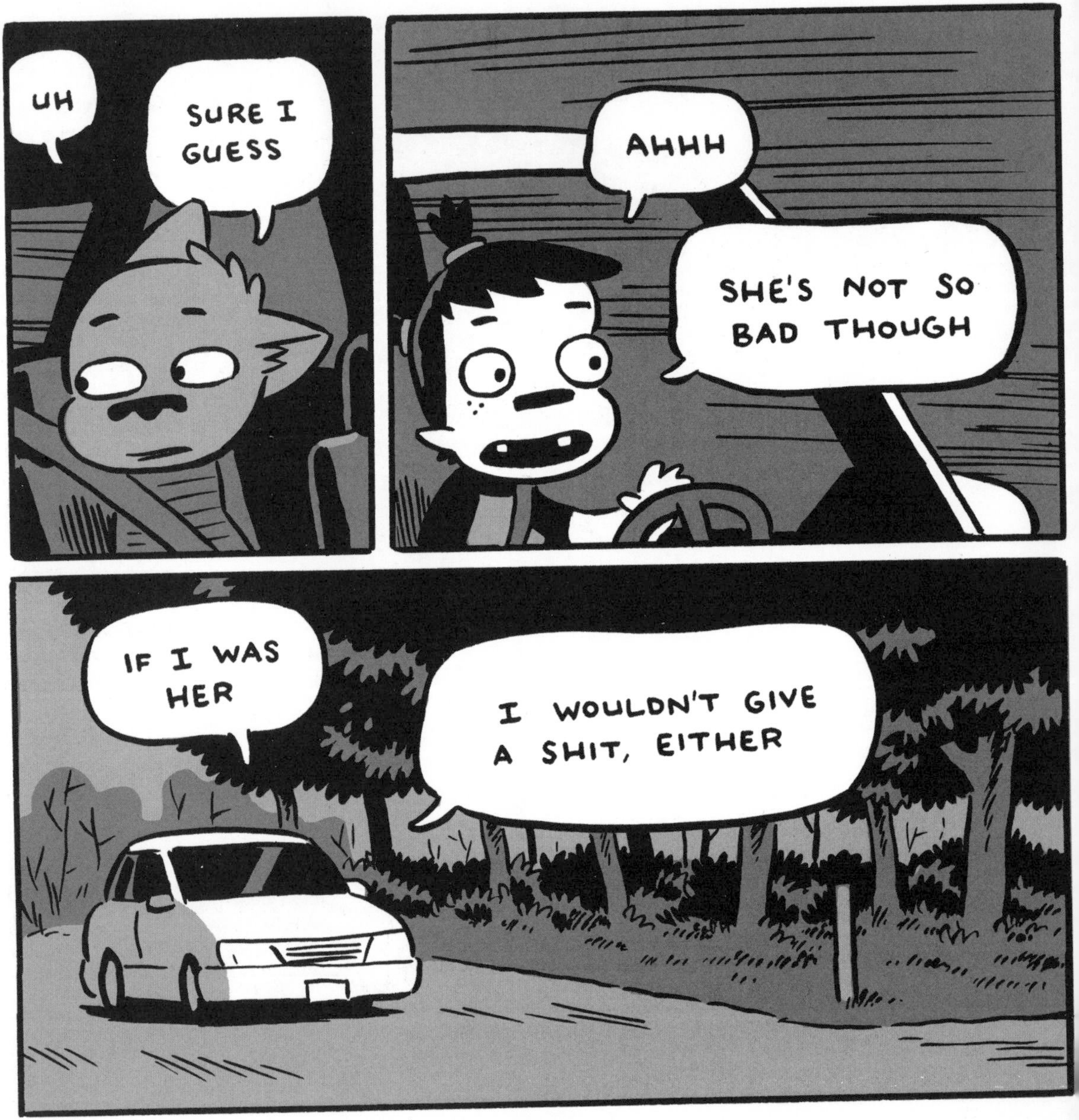
UH
SURE I GUESS
AHHH
SHE'S NOT SO BAD THOUGH
IF I WAS HER
I WOULDN'T GIVE A SHIT, EITHER

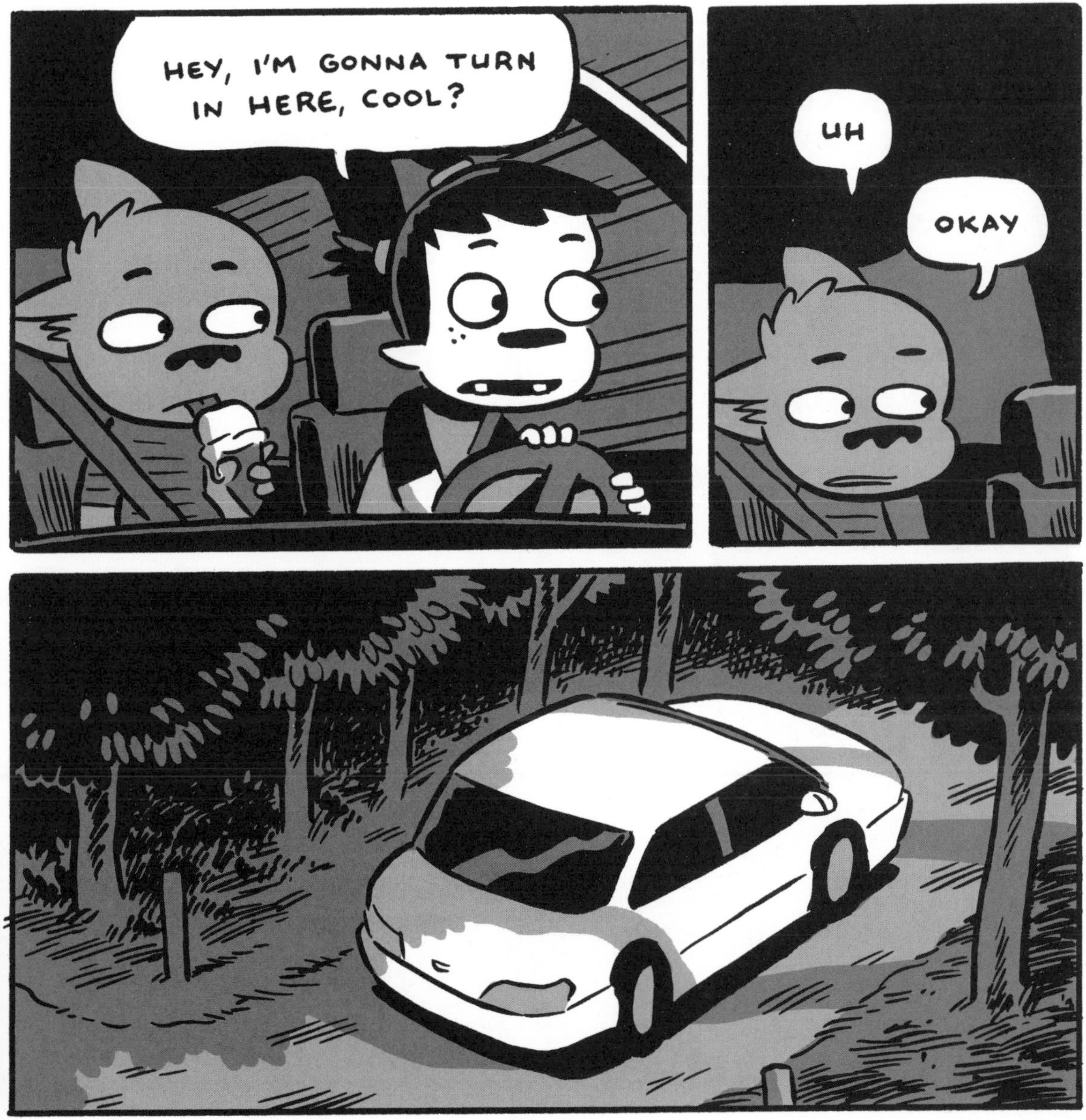
HEY, I'M GONNA TURN IN HERE, COOL?
UH
OKAY

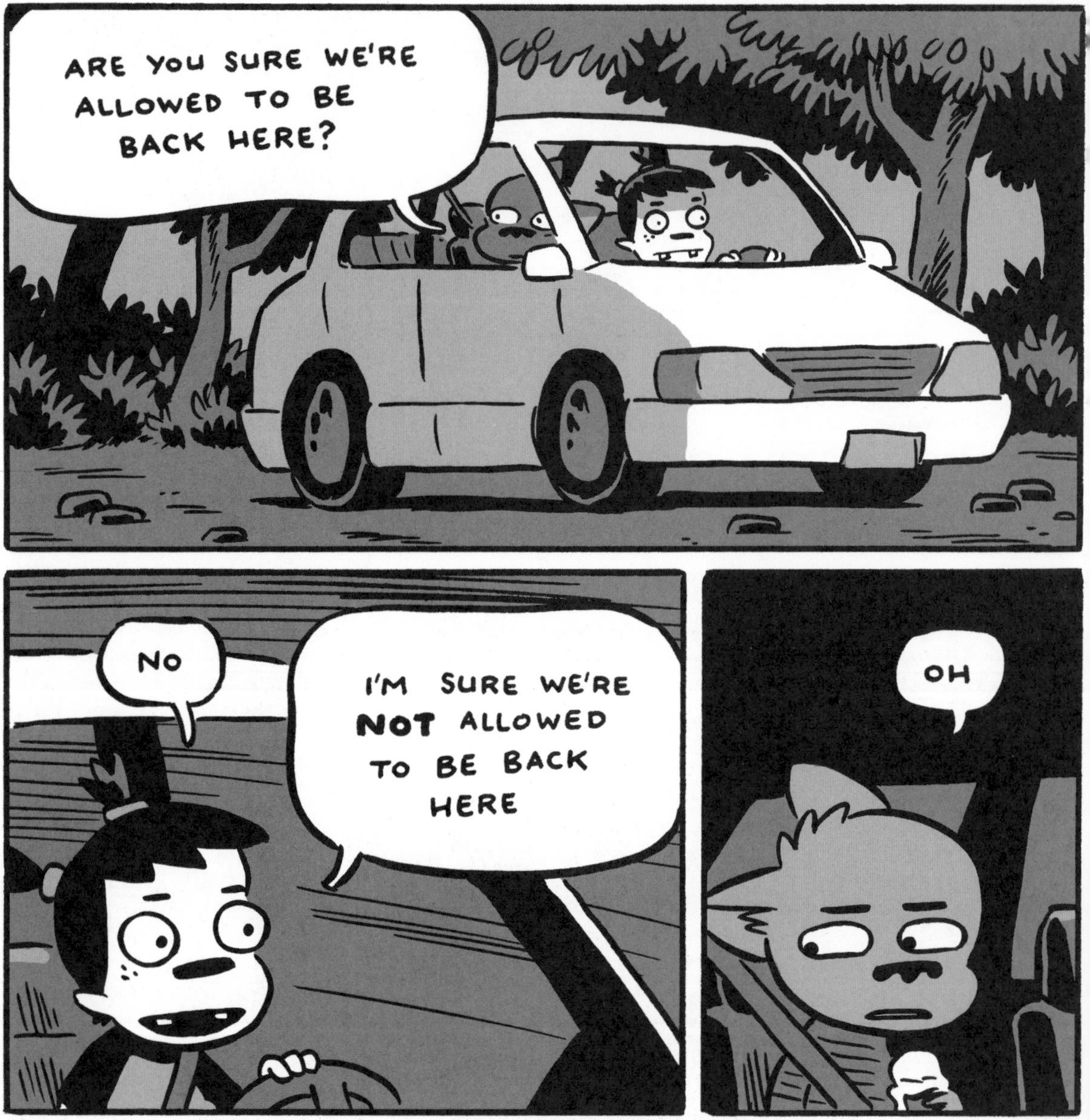
ARE YOU SURE WE'RE ALLOWED TO BE BACK HERE?
NO
I'M SURE WE'RE **NOT** ALLOWED TO BE BACK HERE
OH

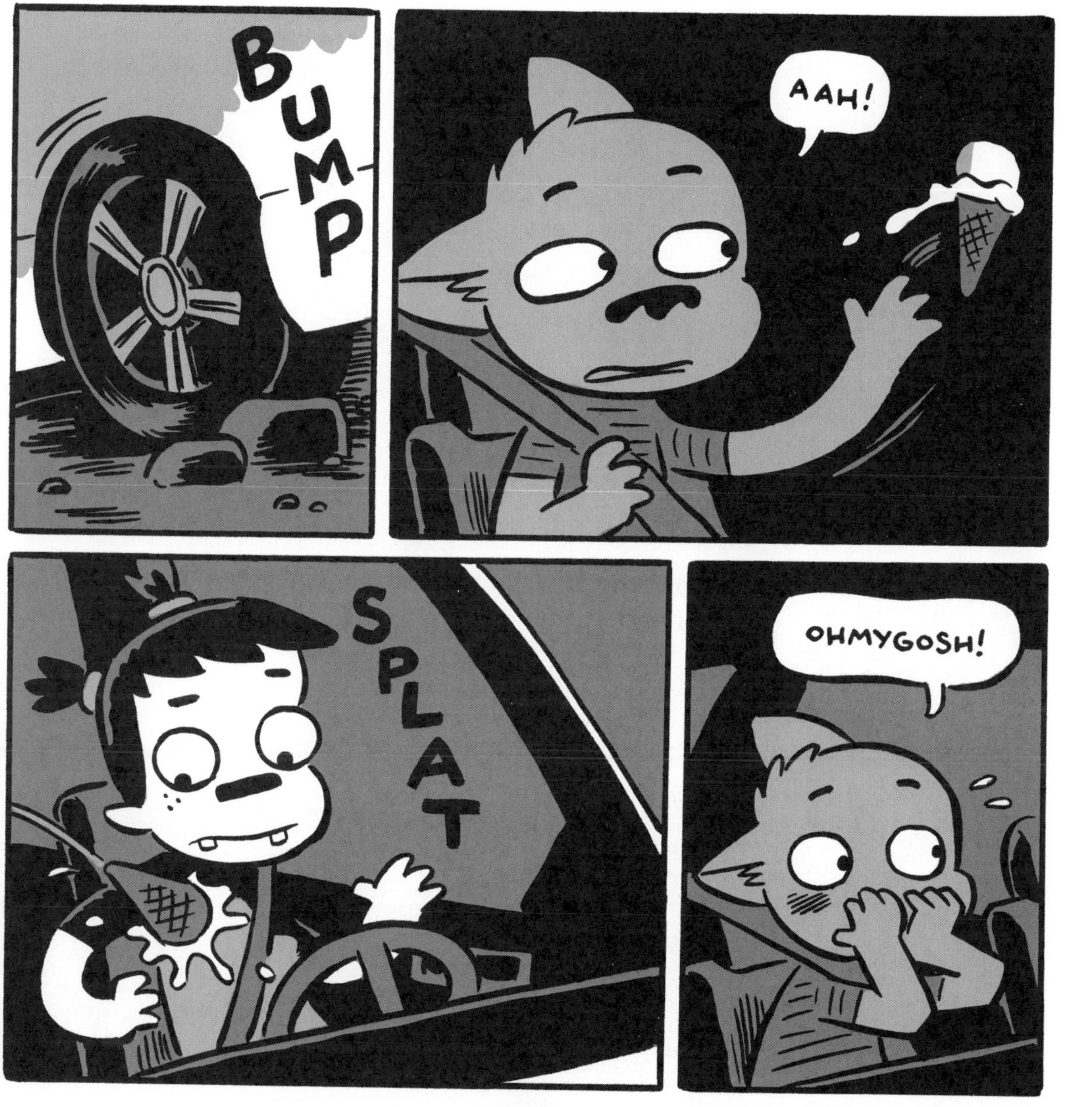
BUMP
AAH!
SPLAT
OHMYGOSH!

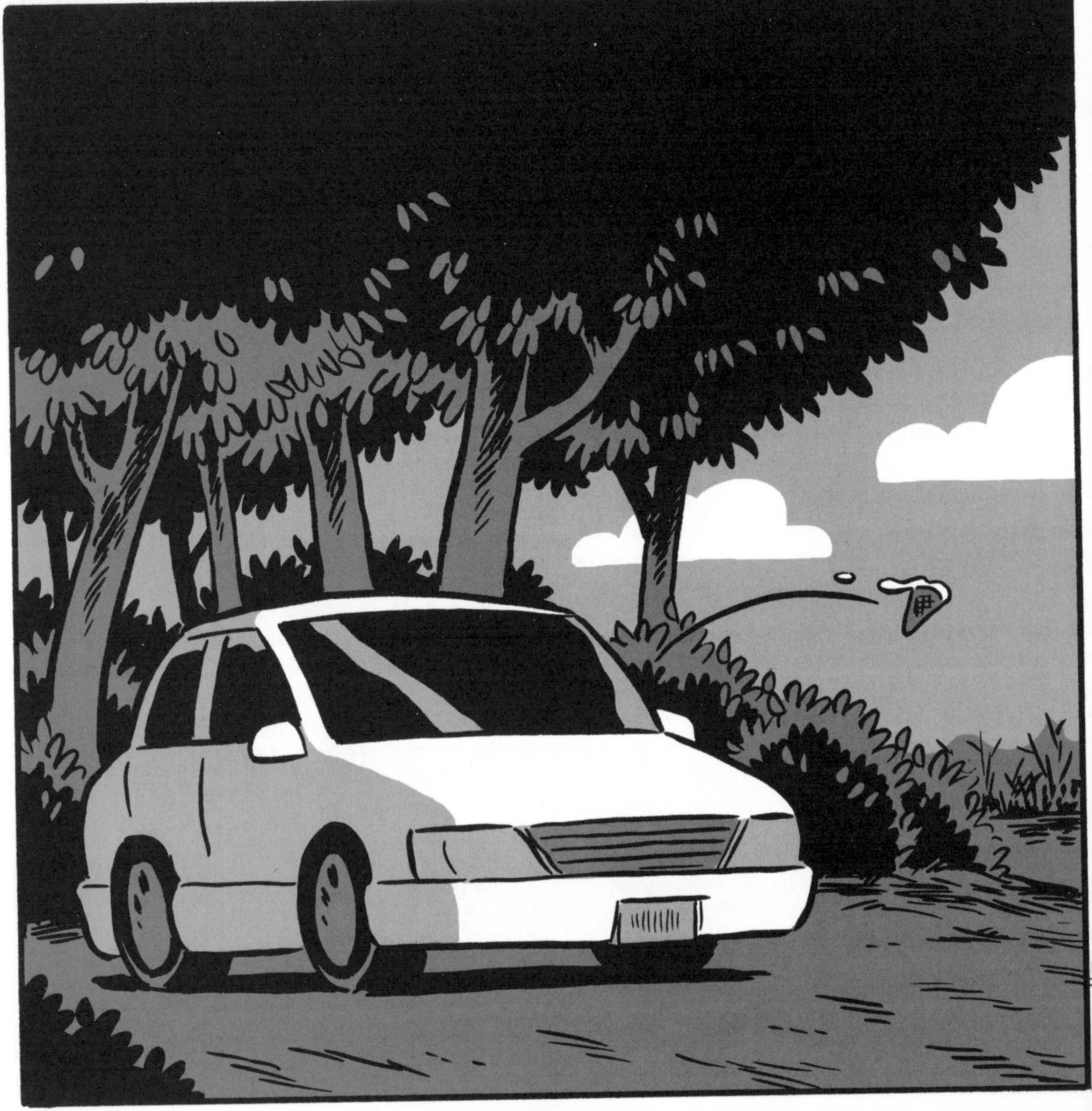

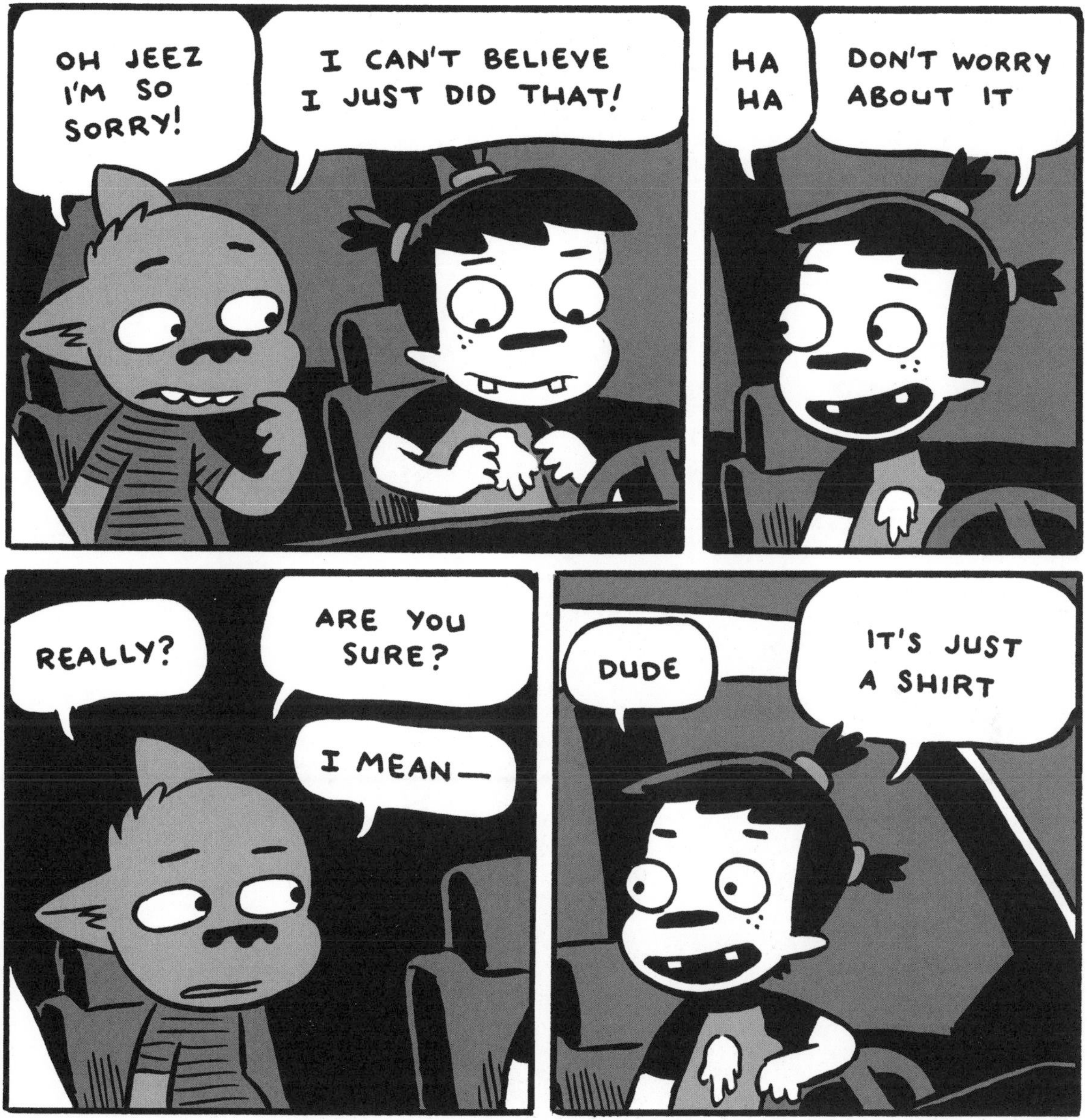
OH JEEZ I'M SO SORRY!
I CAN'T BELIEVE I JUST DID THAT!
HA HA
DON'T WORRY ABOUT IT
REALLY?
ARE YOU SURE?
I MEAN—
DUDE
IT'S JUST A SHIRT

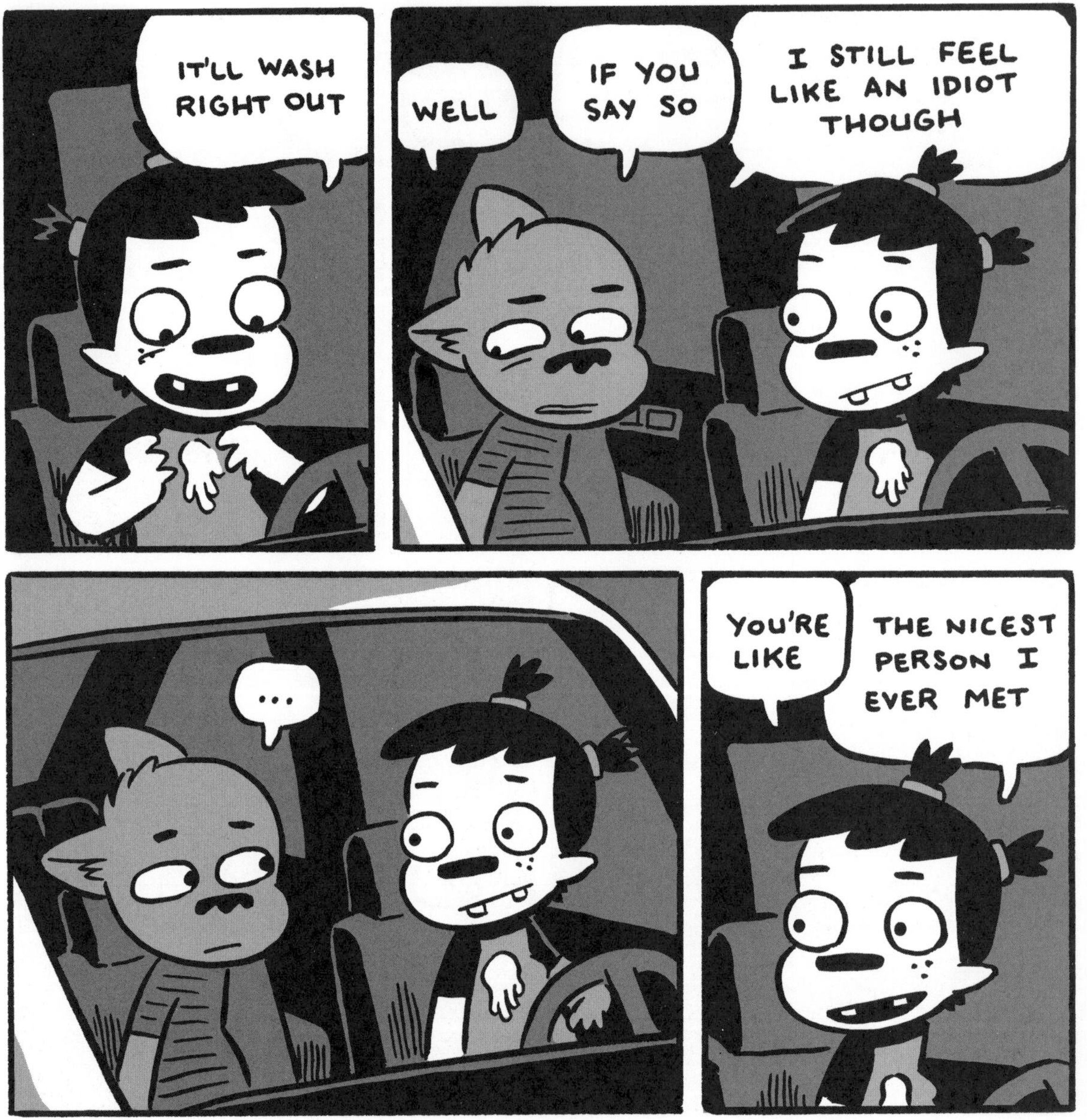
IT'LL WASH RIGHT OUT
WELL
IF YOU SAY SO
I STILL FEEL LIKE AN IDIOT THOUGH
...
YOU'RE LIKE
THE NICEST PERSON I EVER MET

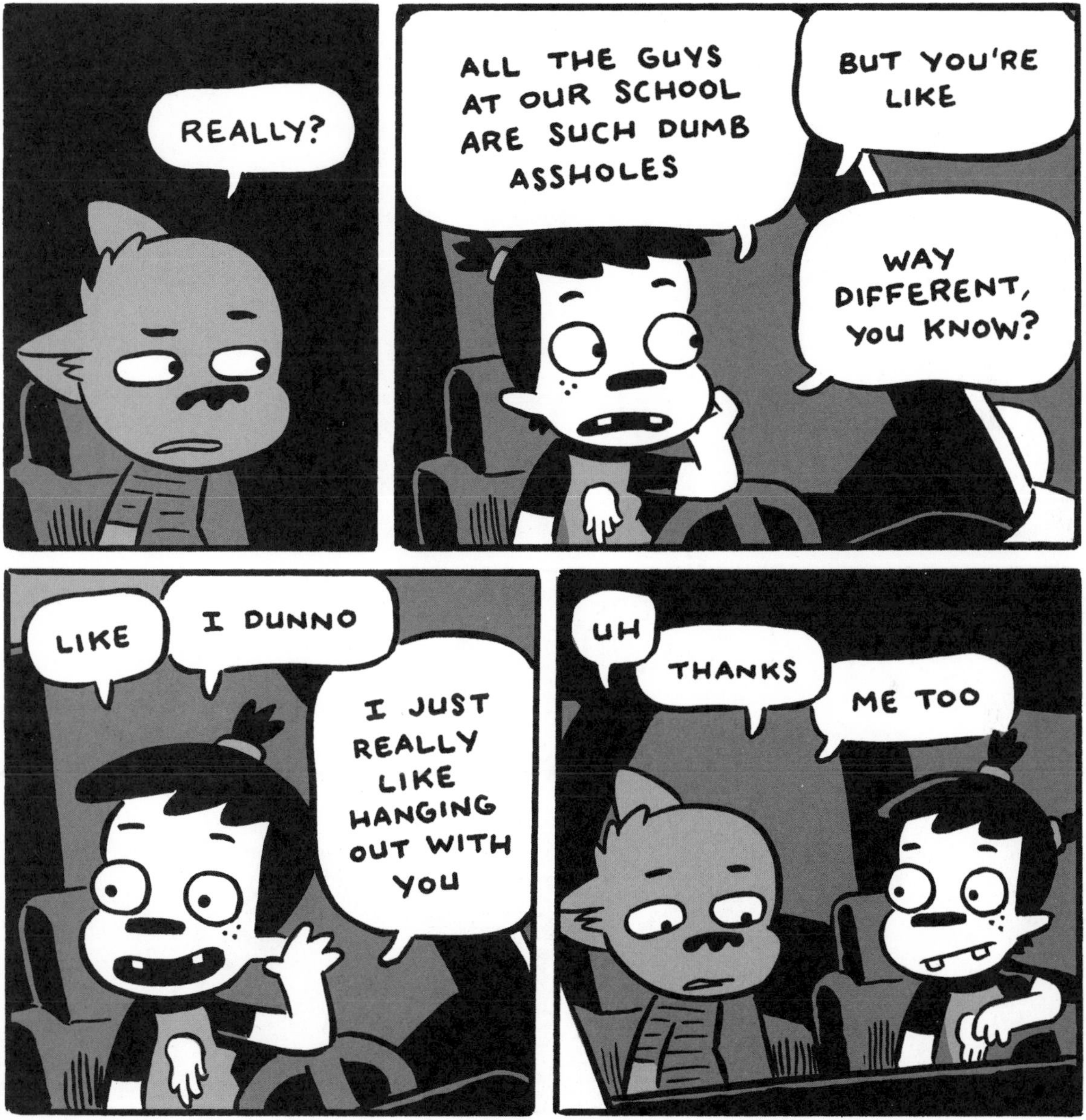
REALLY?
ALL THE GUYS AT OUR SCHOOL ARE SUCH DUMB ASSHOLES
BUT YOU'RE LIKE
WAY DIFFERENT, YOU KNOW?
LIKE
I DUNNO
I JUST REALLY LIKE HANGING OUT WITH YOU
UH
THANKS
ME TOO

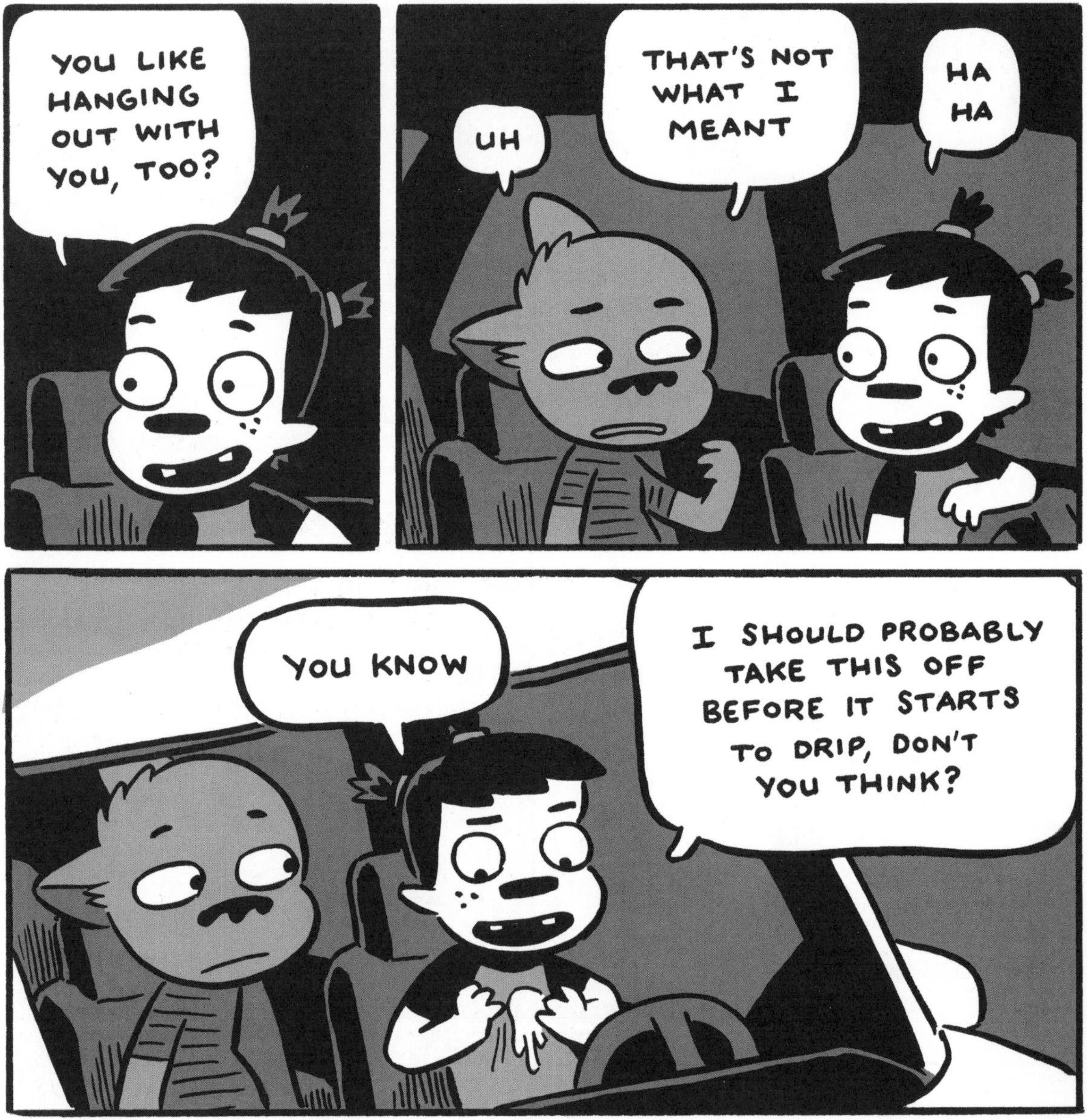
YOU LIKE HANGING OUT WITH YOU, TOO?
UH
THAT'S NOT WHAT I MEANT
HA HA
YOU KNOW
I SHOULD PROBABLY TAKE THIS OFF BEFORE IT STARTS TO DRIP, DON'T YOU THINK?

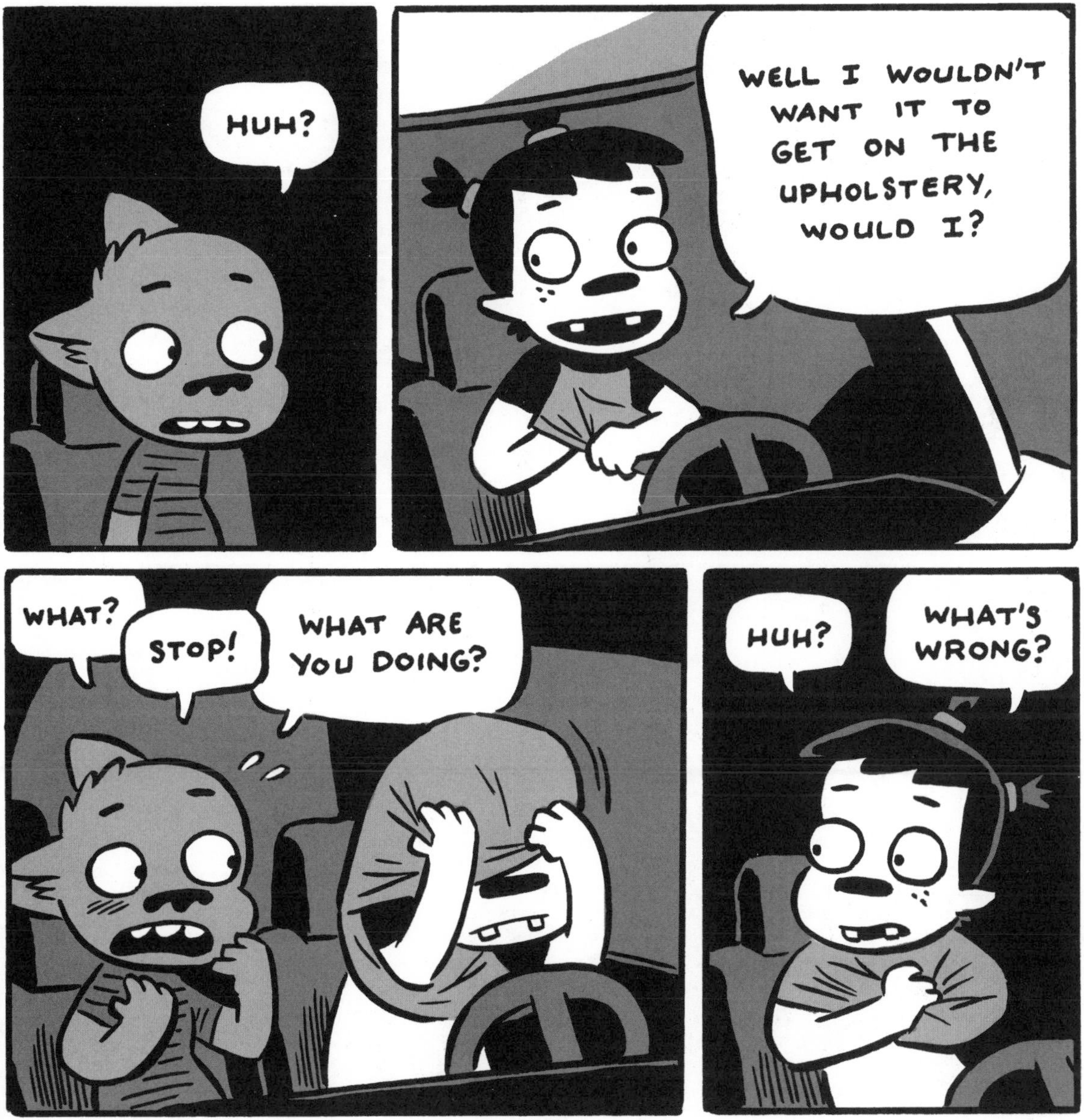
HUH?
WELL I WOULDN'T WANT IT TO GET ON THE UPHOLSTERY, WOULD I?
WHAT?
STOP!
WHAT ARE YOU DOING?
HUH?
WHAT'S WRONG?

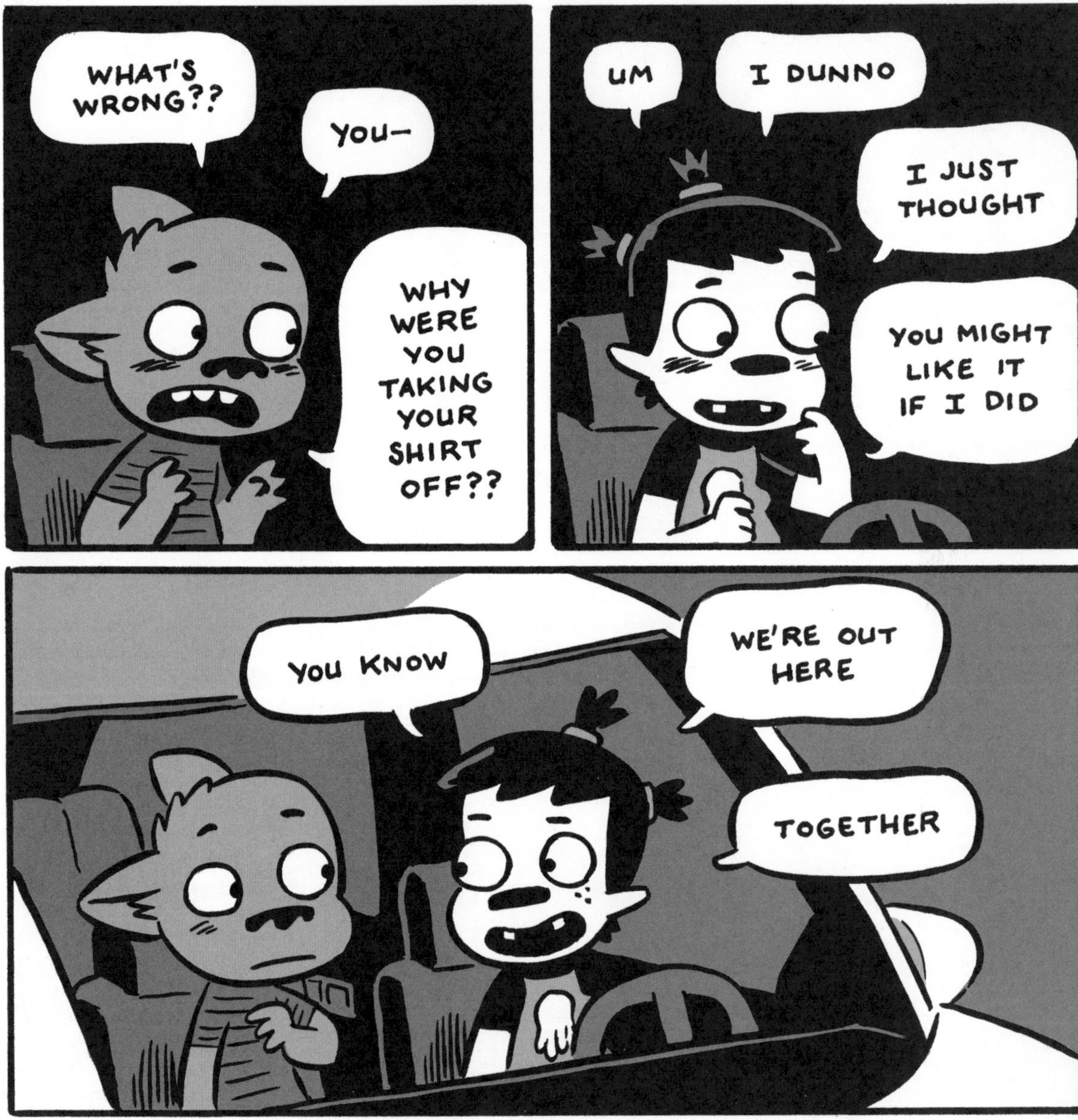
WHAT'S WRONG??
YOU–
WHY WERE YOU TAKING YOUR SHIRT OFF??
UM
I DUNNO
I JUST THOUGHT
YOU MIGHT LIKE IT IF I DID
YOU KNOW
WE'RE OUT HERE
TOGETHER

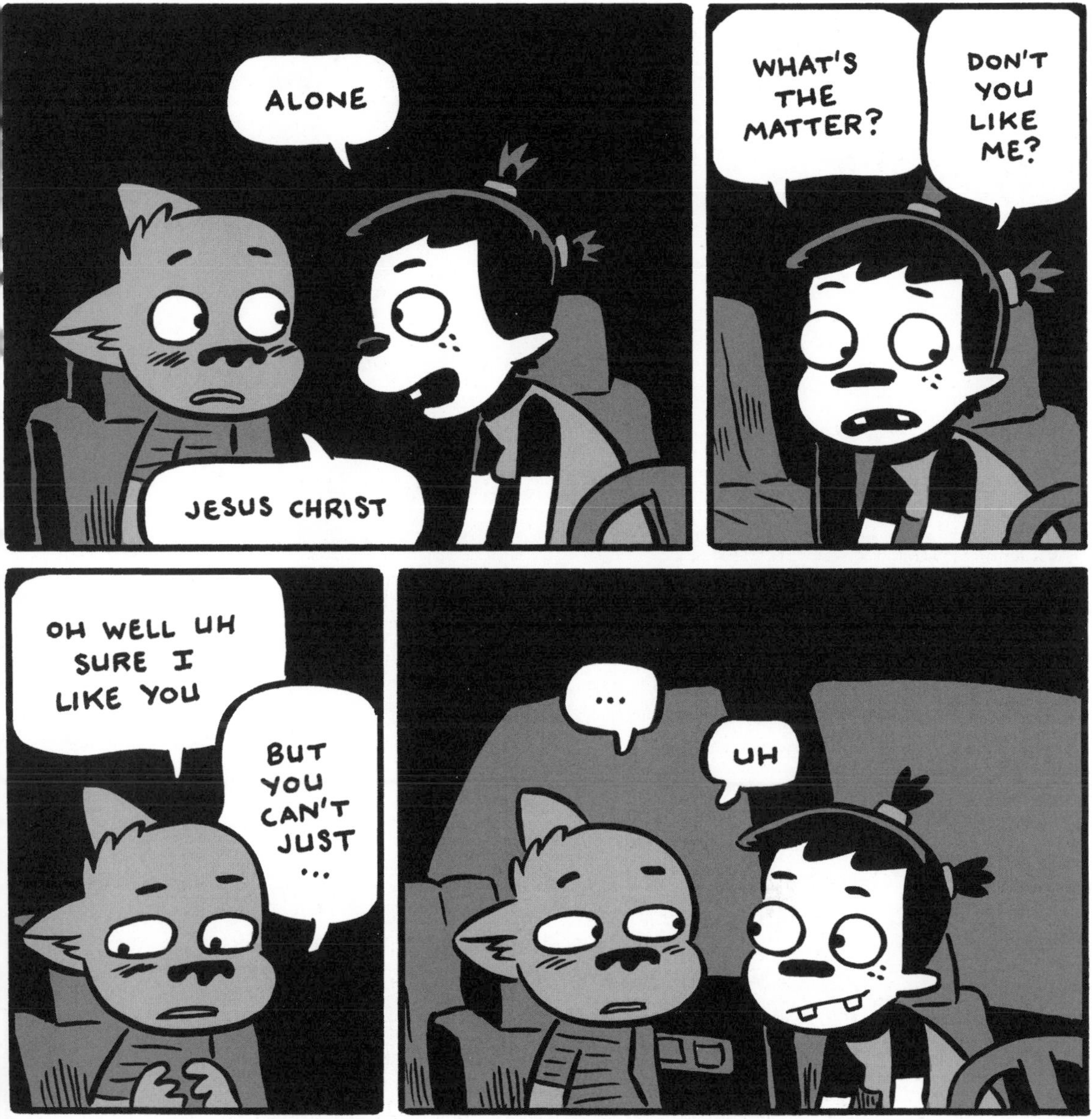
ALONE
JESUS CHRIST
WHAT'S THE MATTER?
DON'T YOU LIKE ME?
OH WELL UH SURE I LIKE YOU
BUT YOU CAN'T JUST ...
...
UH

HEH
HEY
C'MERE
!

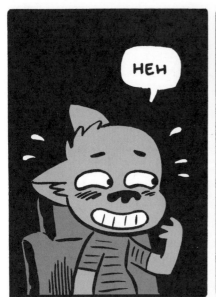

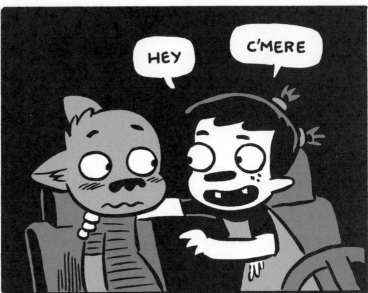

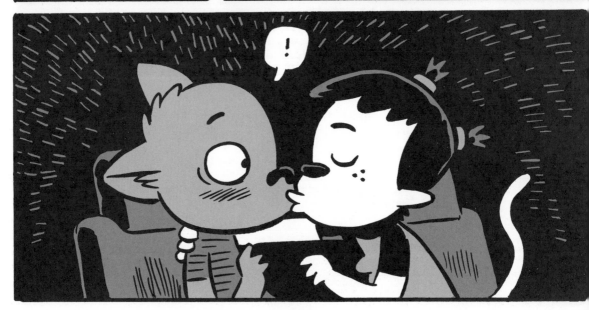

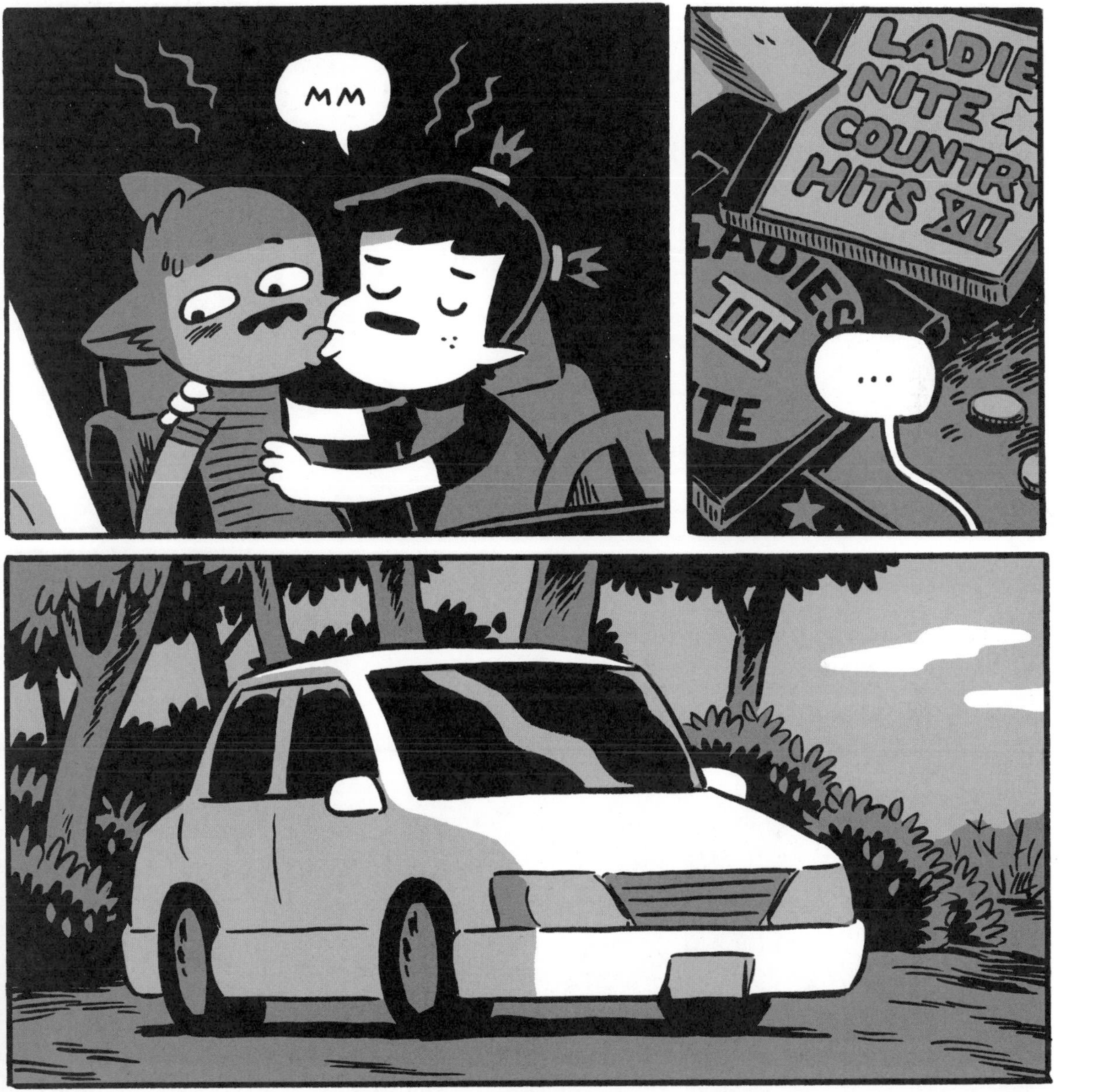
MM
LADIES NITE COUNTRY HITS XII
LADIES III
TE
...

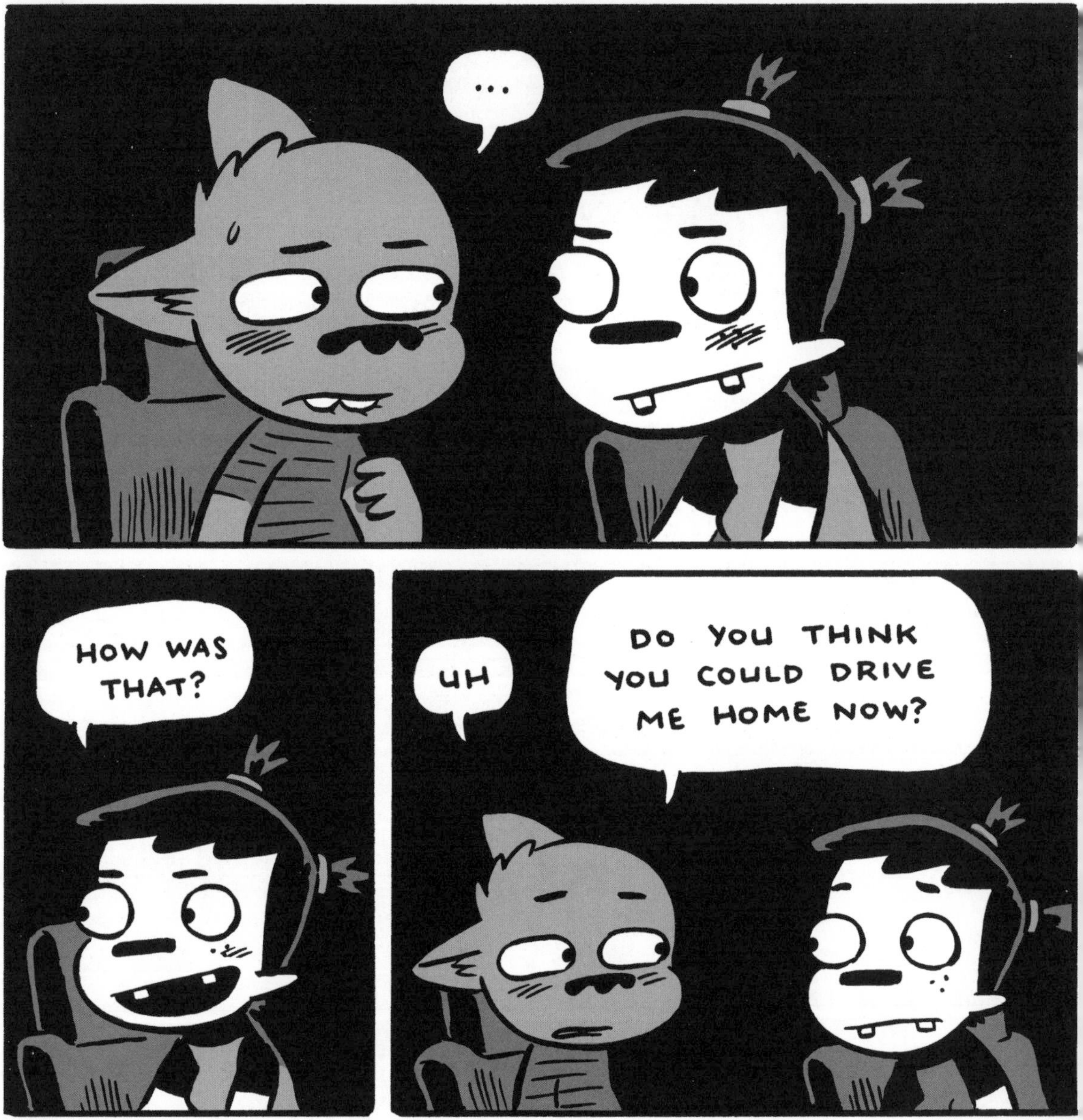
...
HOW WAS THAT?
UH
DO YOU THINK YOU COULD DRIVE ME HOME NOW?

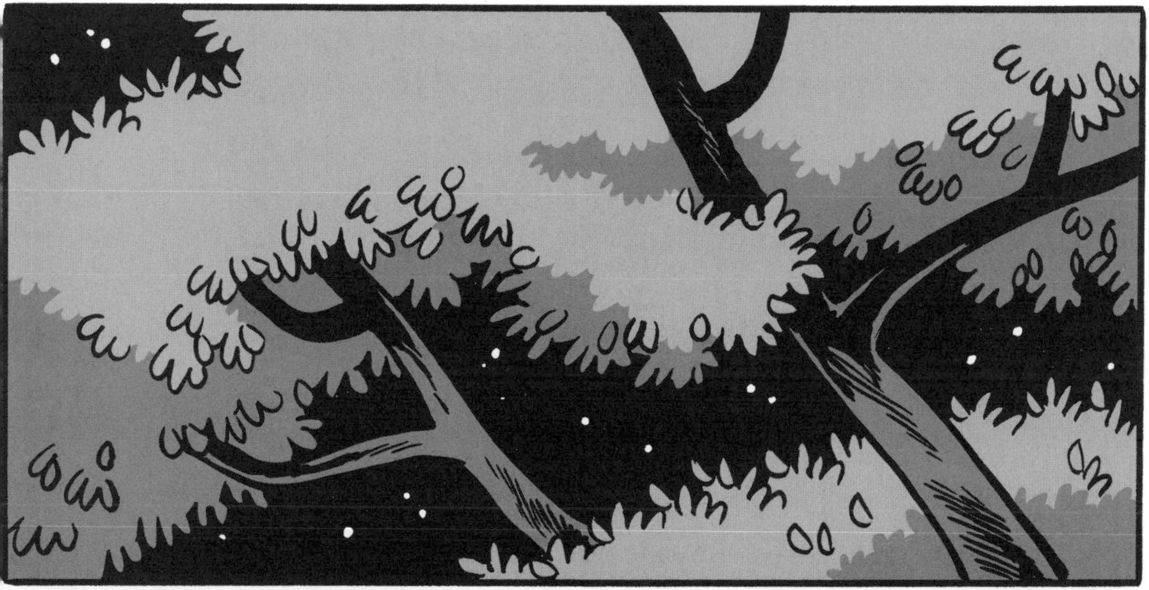

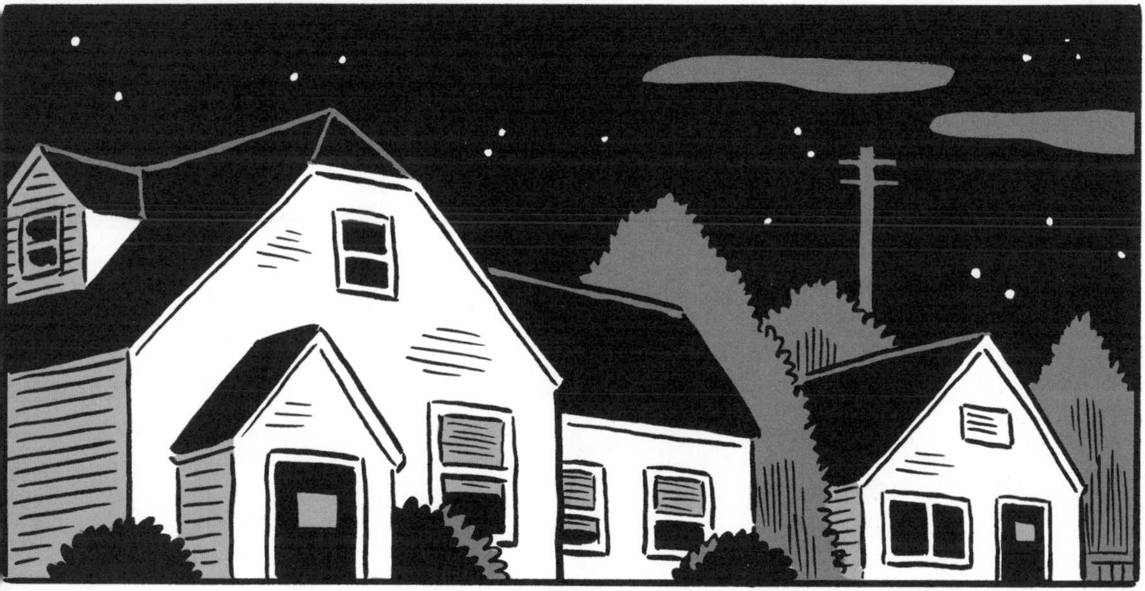

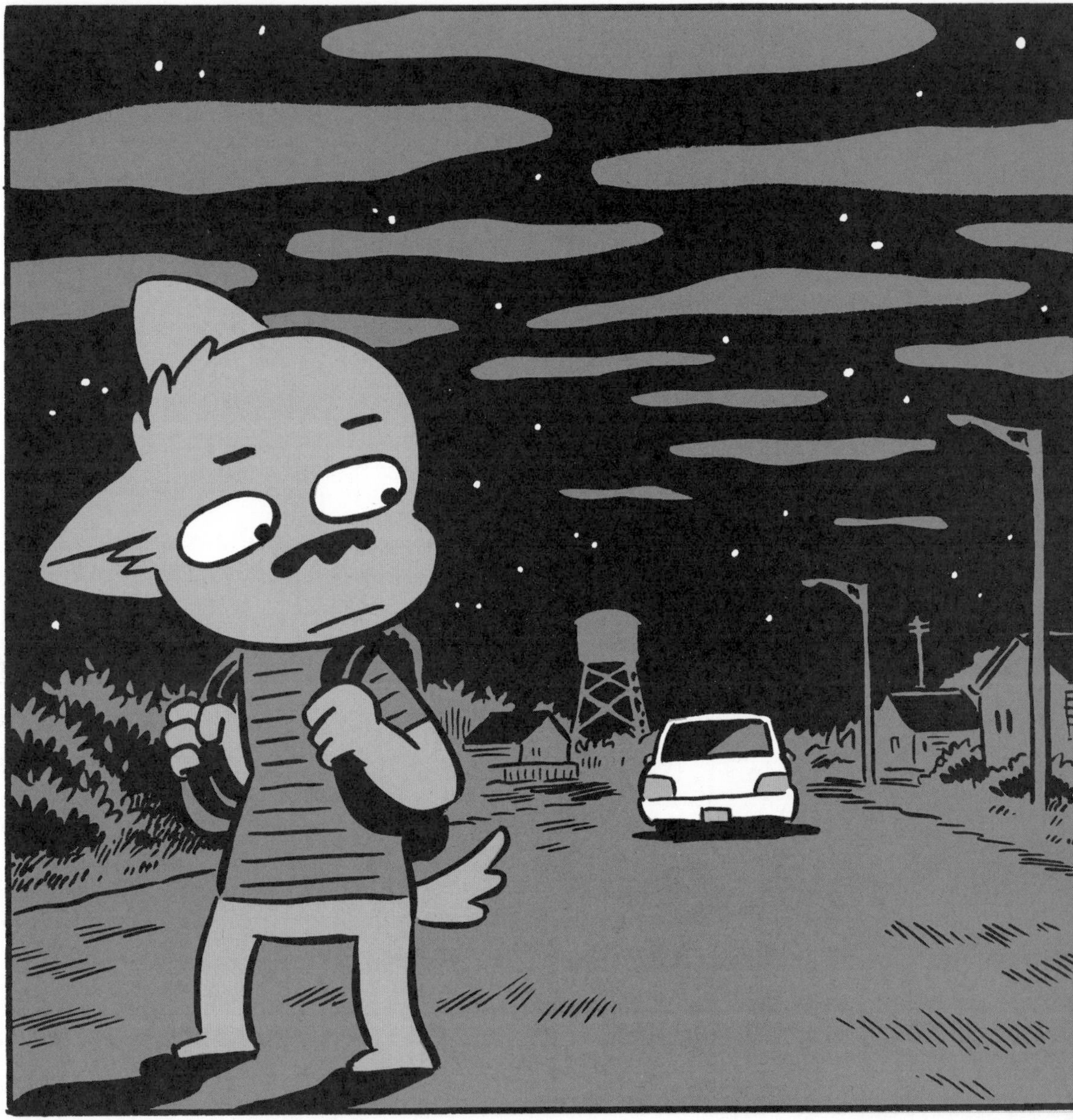

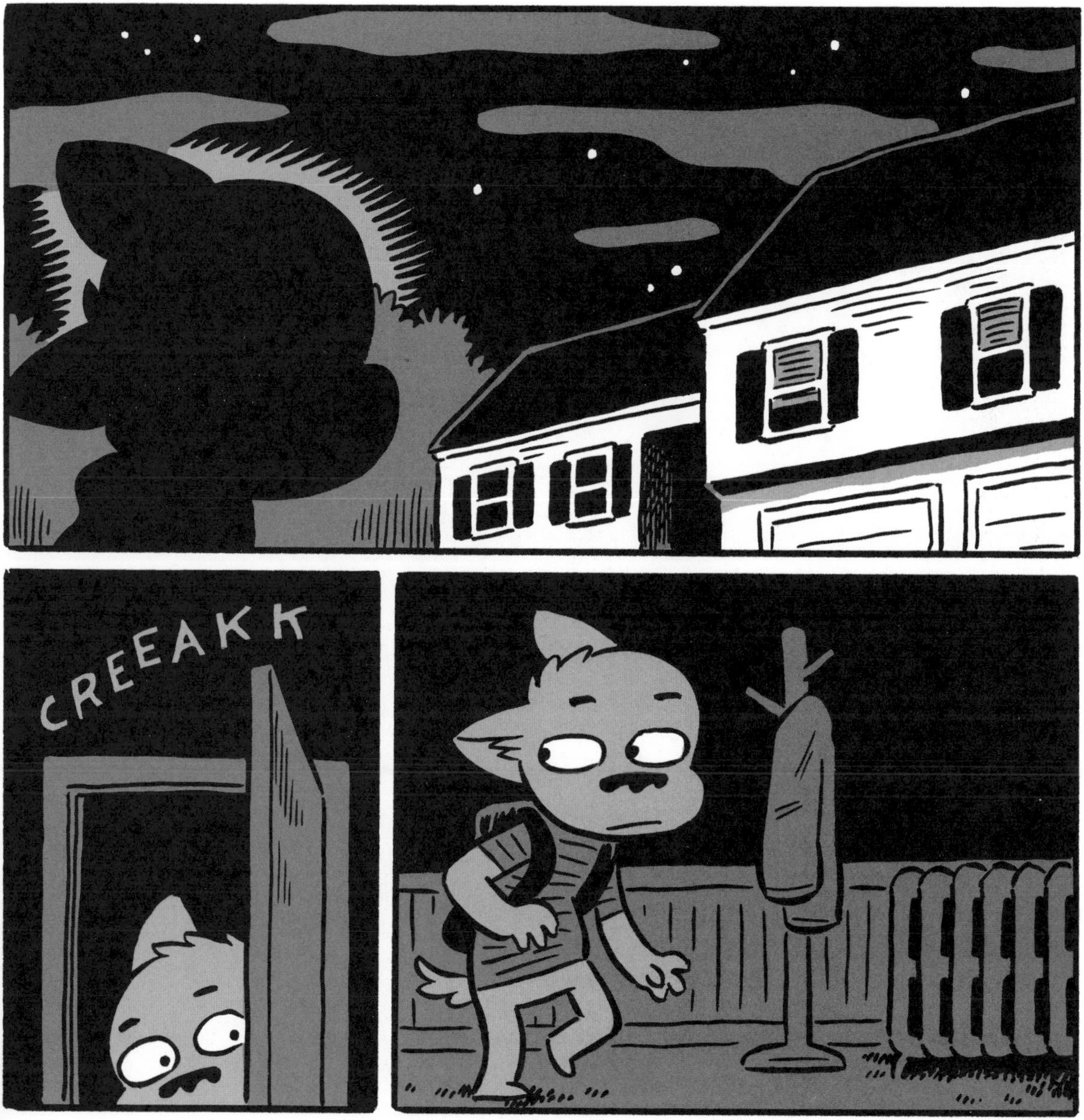
CREEAKK

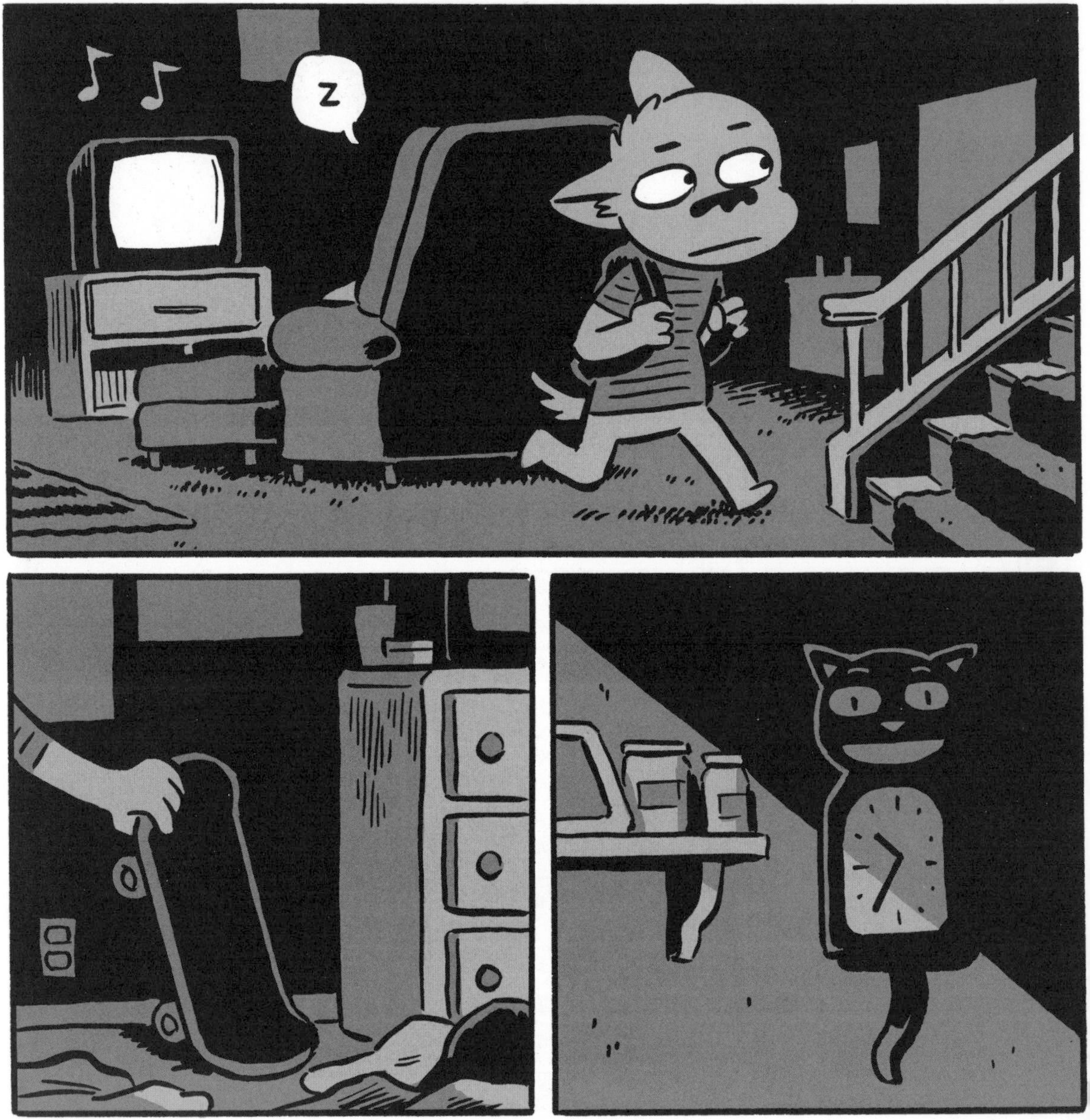
Z

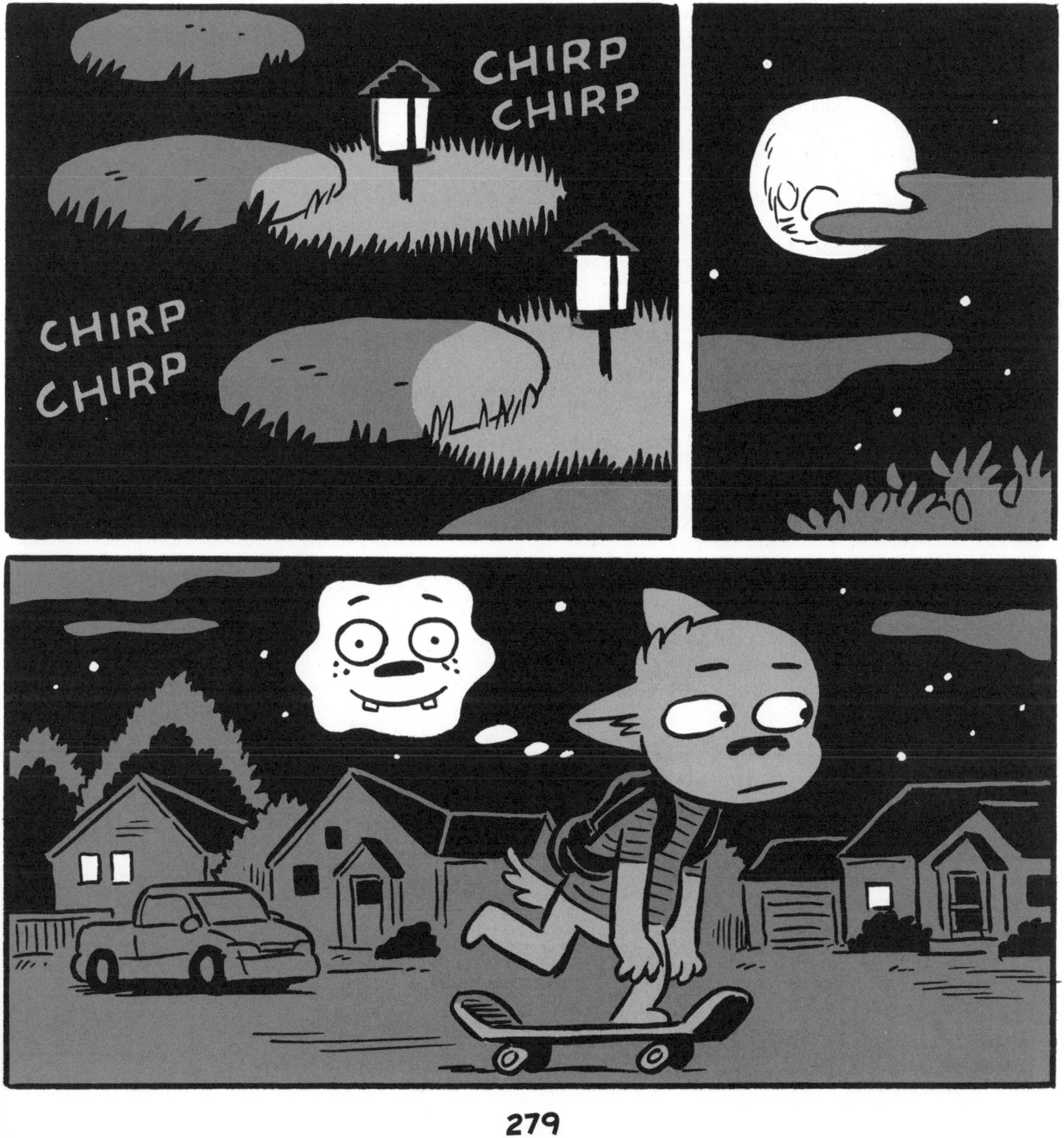
CHIRP
CHIRP
CHIRP
CHIRP

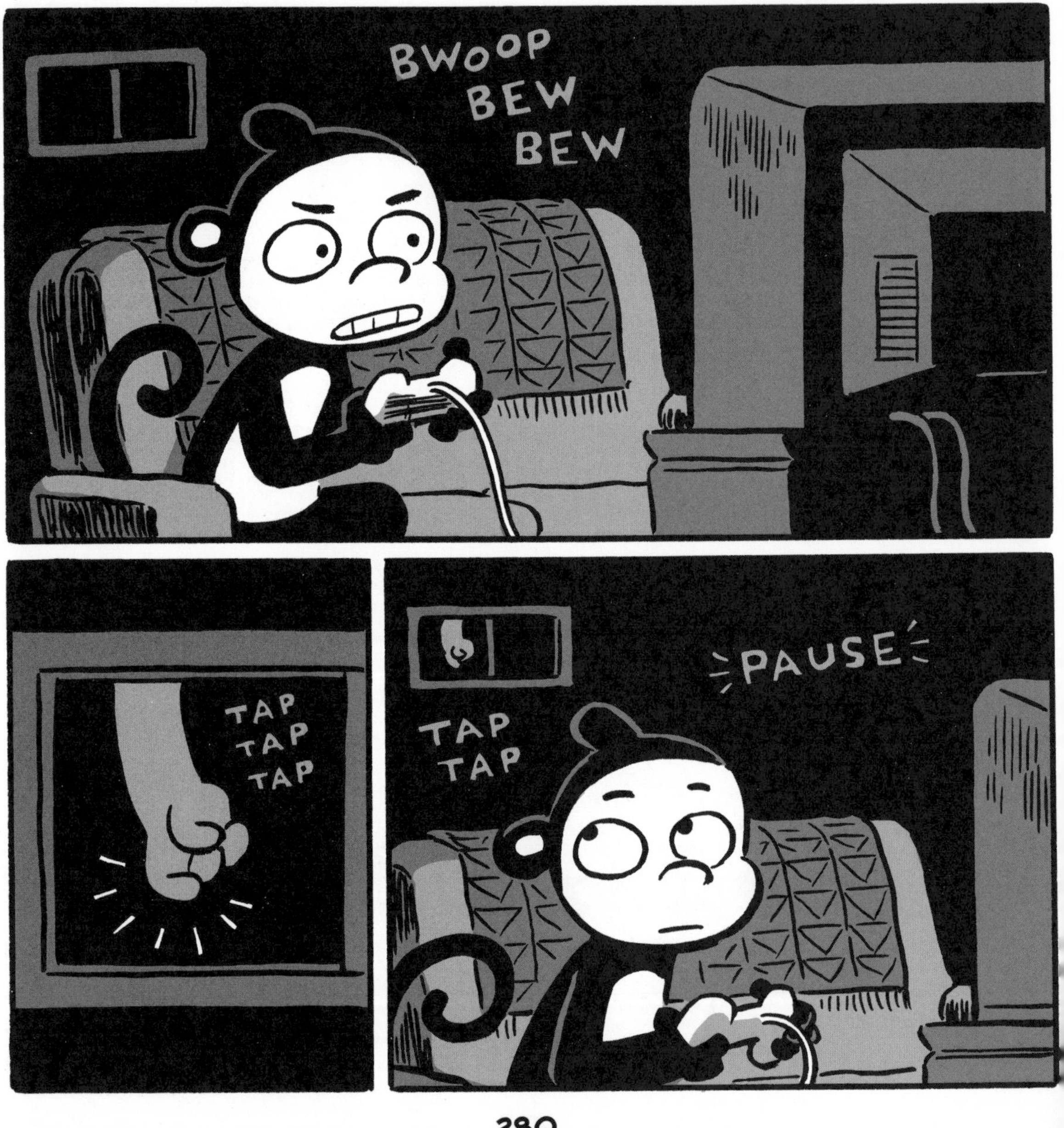
BWOOP
BEW
BEW
TAP
TAP
TAP
TAP
TAP
PAUSE

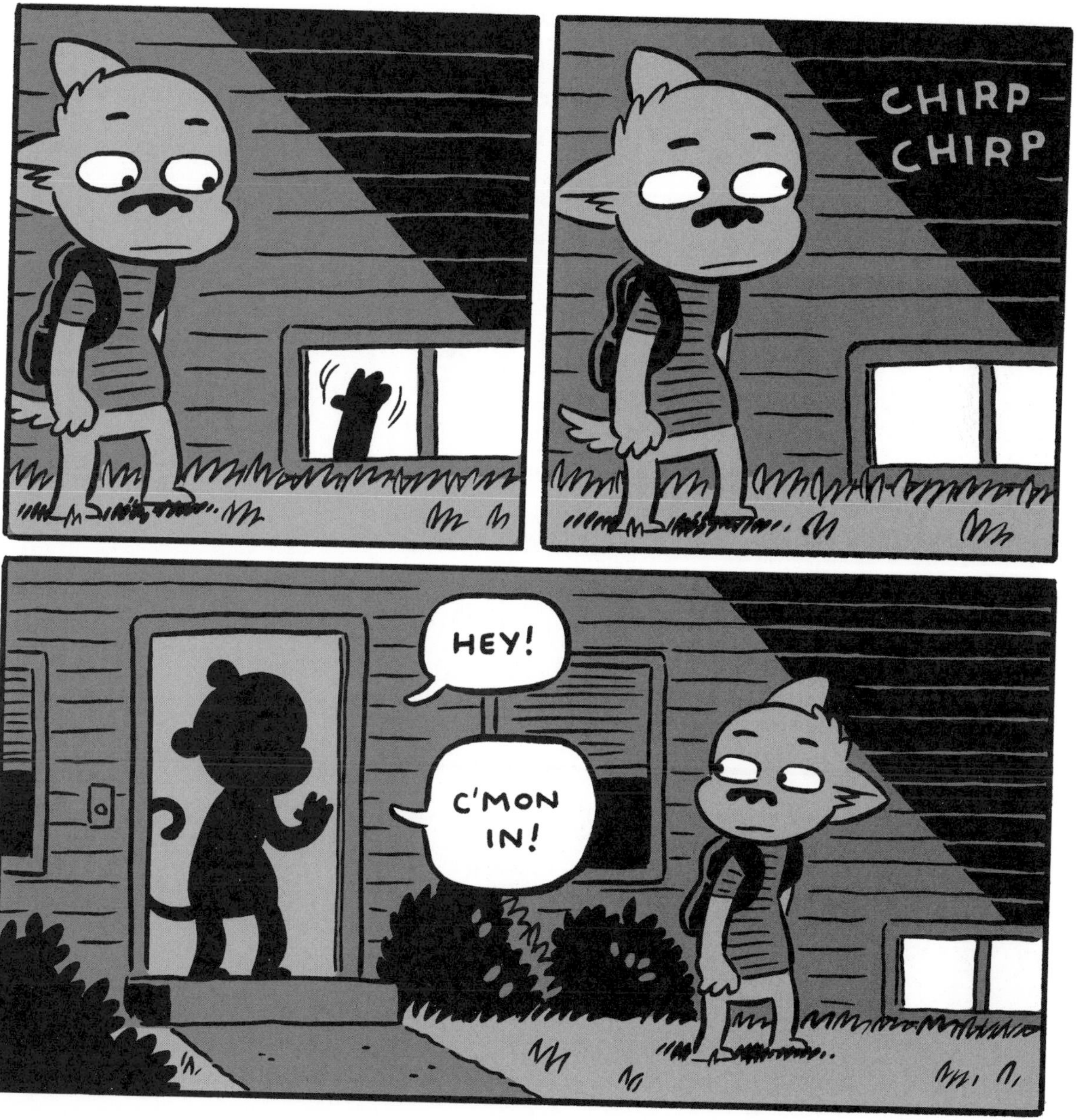
CHIRP
CHIRP
HEY!
C'MON IN!

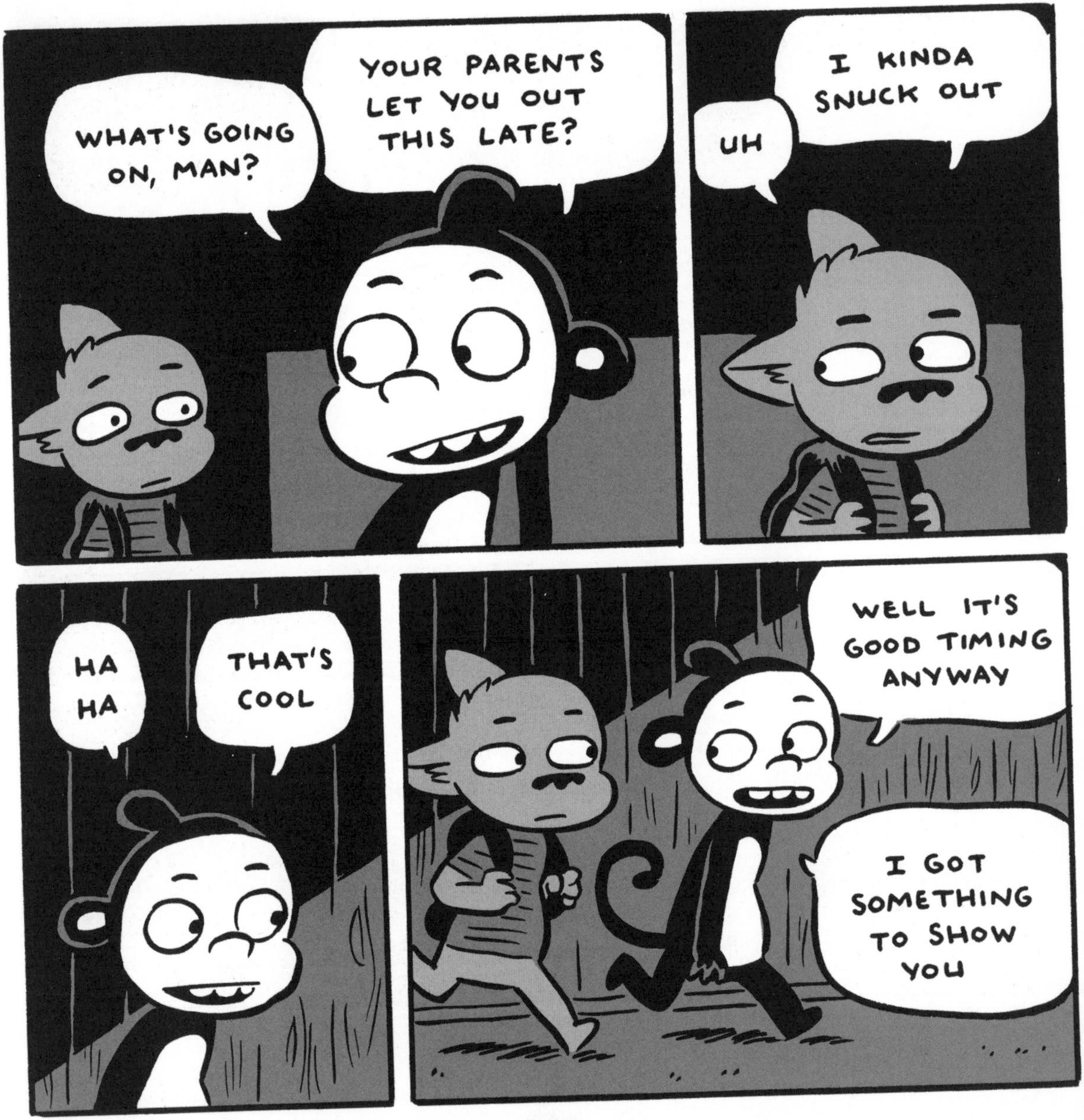
WHAT'S GOING ON, MAN?
YOUR PARENTS LET YOU OUT THIS LATE?
UH
I KINDA SNUCK OUT
HA HA
THAT'S COOL
WELL IT'S GOOD TIMING ANYWAY
I GOT SOMETHING TO SHOW YOU

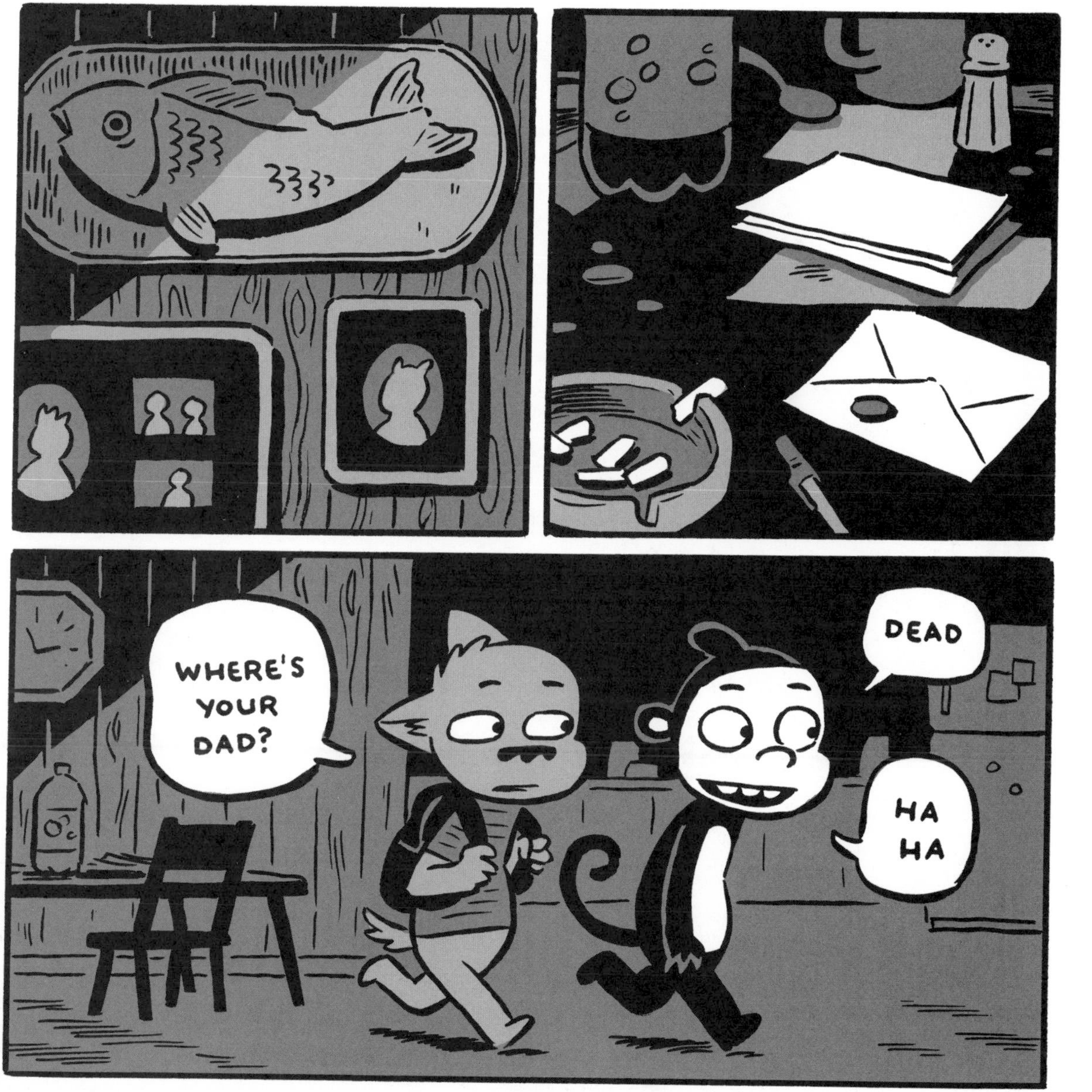
WHERE'S YOUR DAD?
DEAD
HA HA

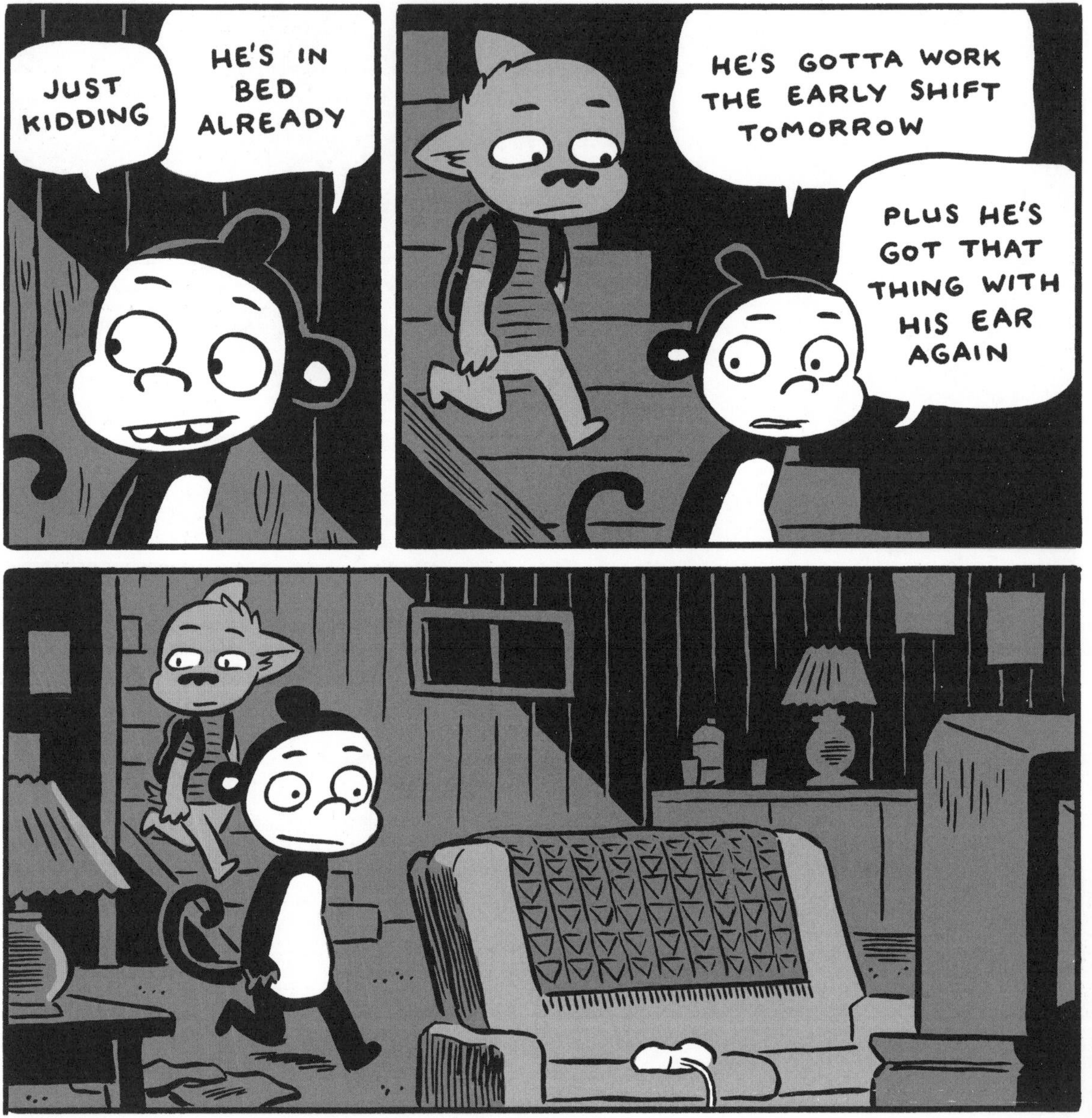
JUST KIDDING
HE'S IN BED ALREADY
HE'S GOTTA WORK THE EARLY SHIFT TOMORROW
PLUS HE'S GOT THAT THING WITH HIS EAR AGAIN

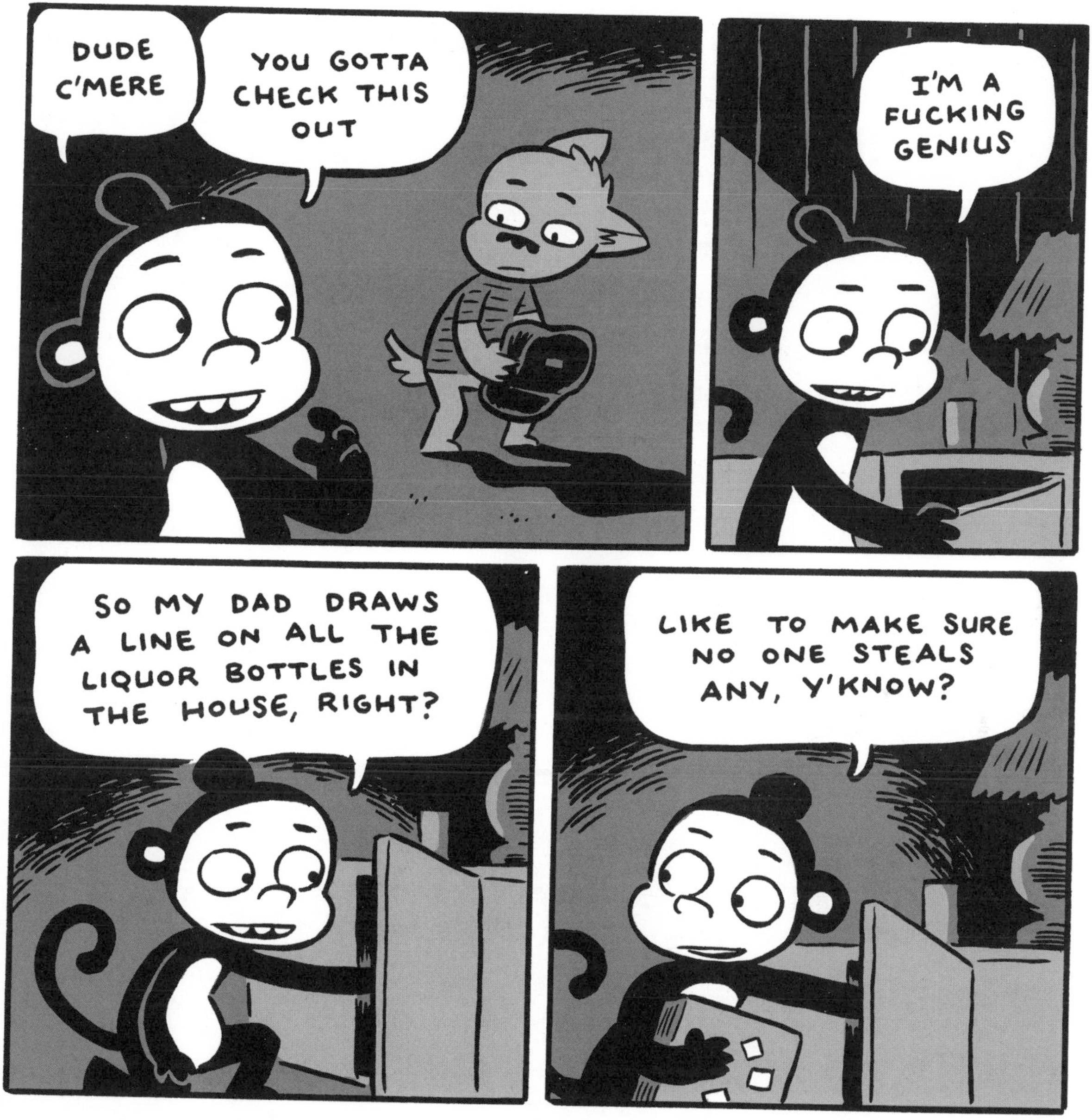
DUDE C'MERE
YOU GOTTA CHECK THIS OUT
I'M A FUCKING GENIUS
SO MY DAD DRAWS A LINE ON ALL THE LIQUOR BOTTLES IN THE HOUSE, RIGHT?
LIKE TO MAKE SURE NO ONE STEALS ANY, Y'KNOW?

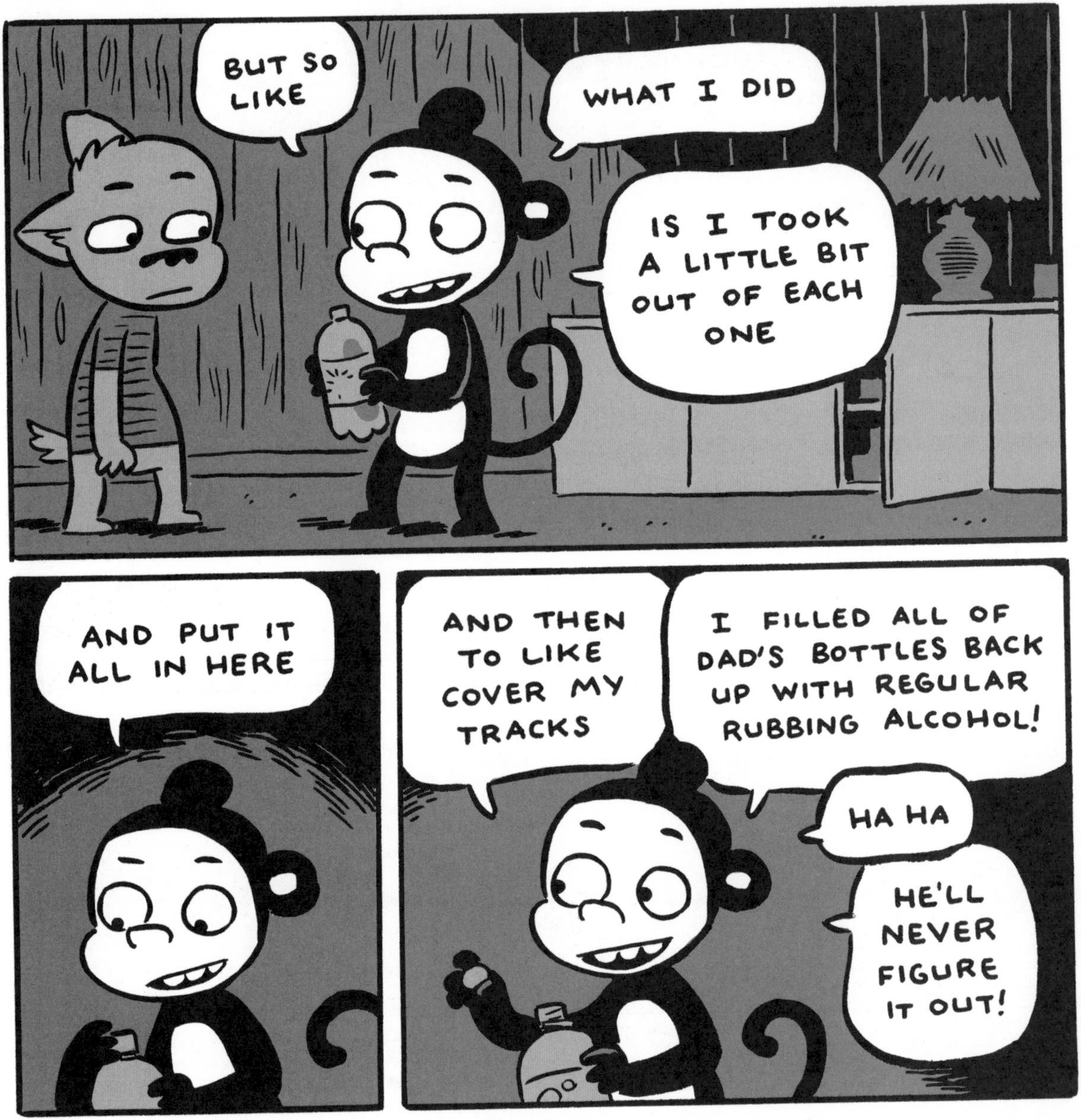
BUT SO LIKE
WHAT I DID
IS I TOOK A LITTLE BIT OUT OF EACH ONE
AND PUT IT ALL IN HERE
AND THEN TO LIKE COVER MY TRACKS
I FILLED ALL OF DAD'S BOTTLES BACK UP WITH REGULAR RUBBING ALCOHOL!
HA HA
HE'LL NEVER FIGURE IT OUT!

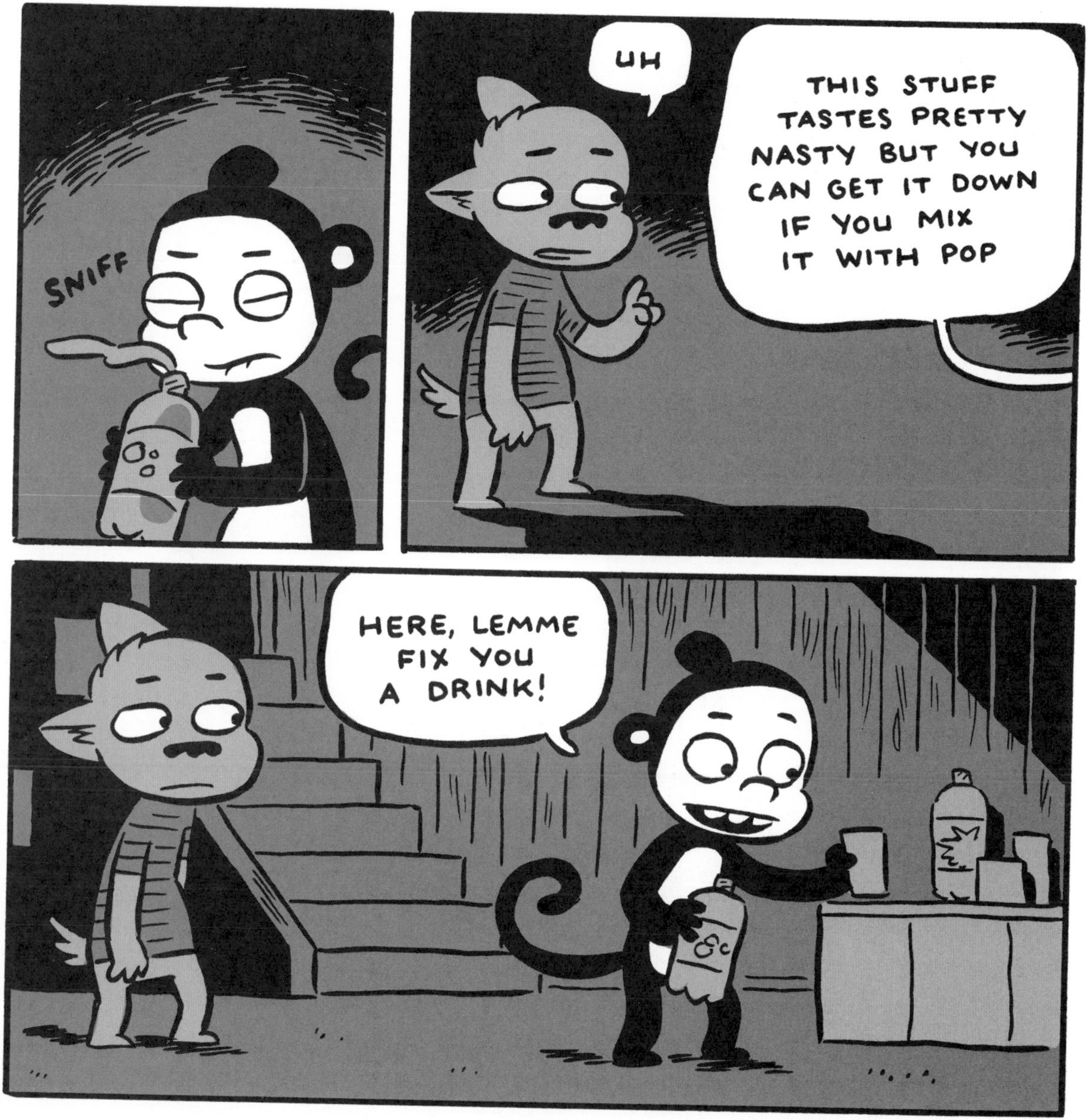
SNIFF
UH
THIS STUFF TASTES PRETTY NASTY BUT YOU CAN GET IT DOWN IF YOU MIX IT WITH POP
HERE, LEMME FIX YOU A DRINK!

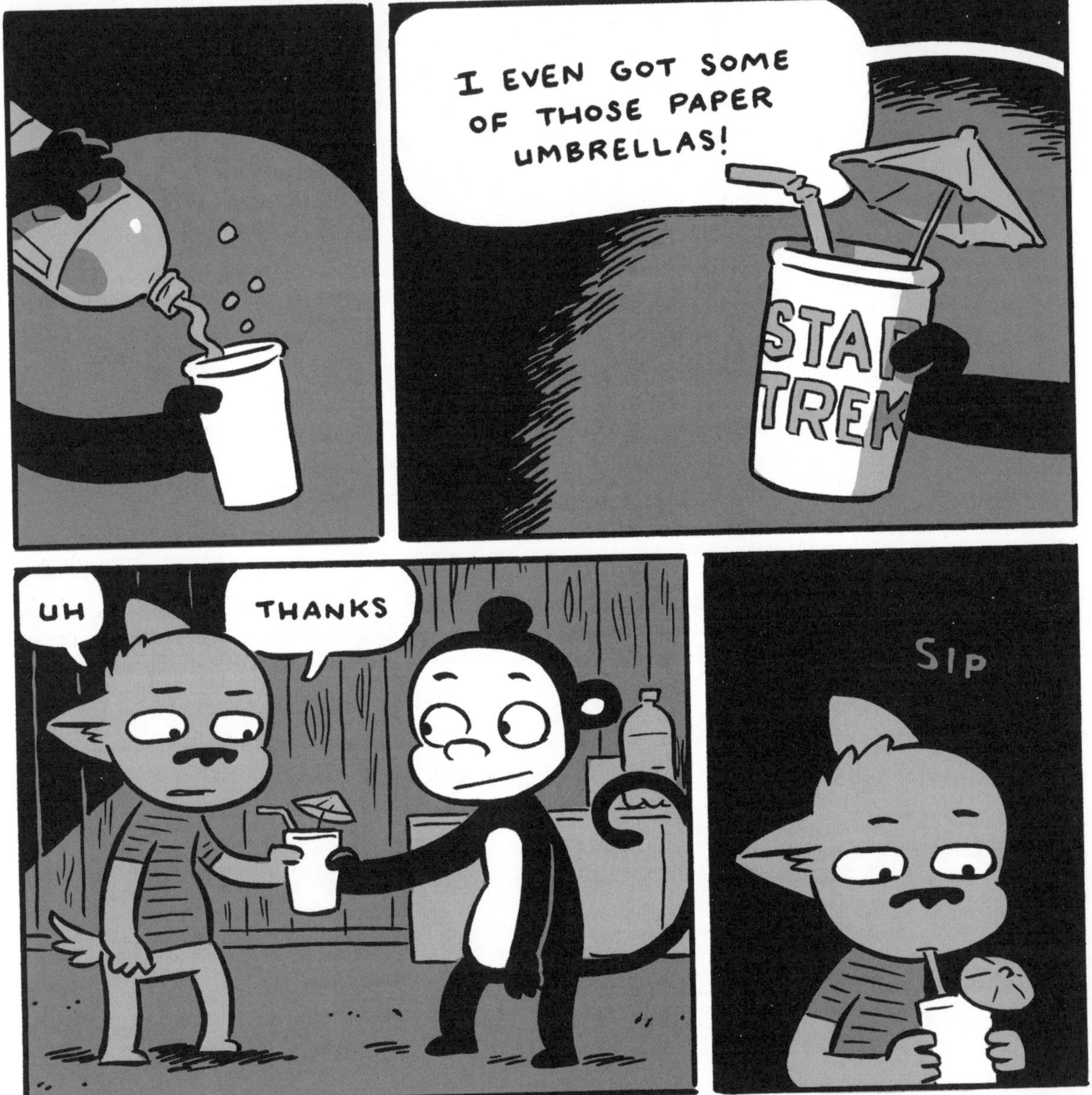
I EVEN GOT SOME OF THOSE PAPER UMBRELLAS!
STAR TREK
UH
THANKS
SIP

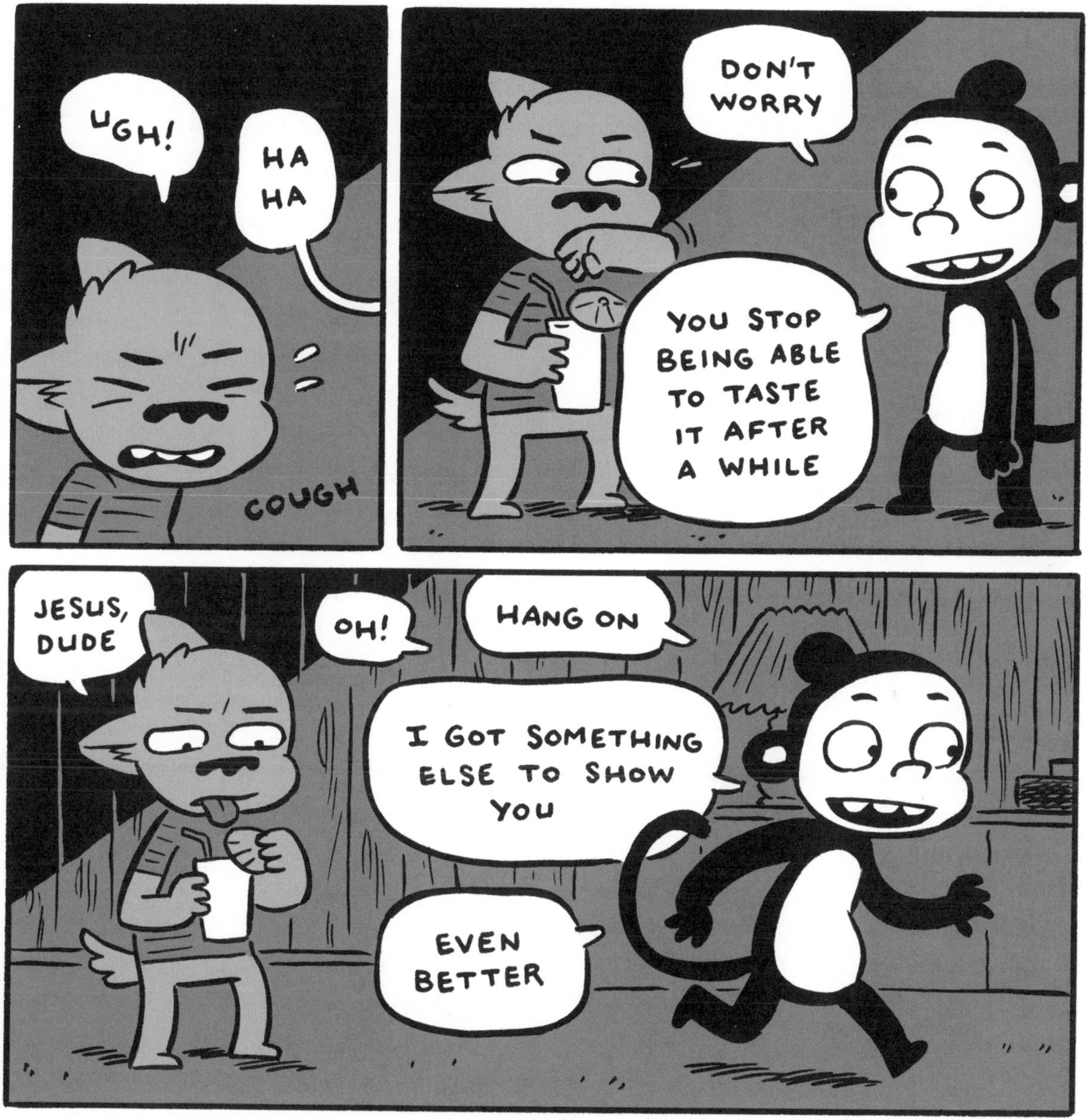
UGH!
HA HA
COUGH
DON'T WORRY
YOU STOP BEING ABLE TO TASTE IT AFTER A WHILE
JESUS, DUDE
OH!
HANG ON
I GOT SOMETHING ELSE TO SHOW YOU
EVEN BETTER

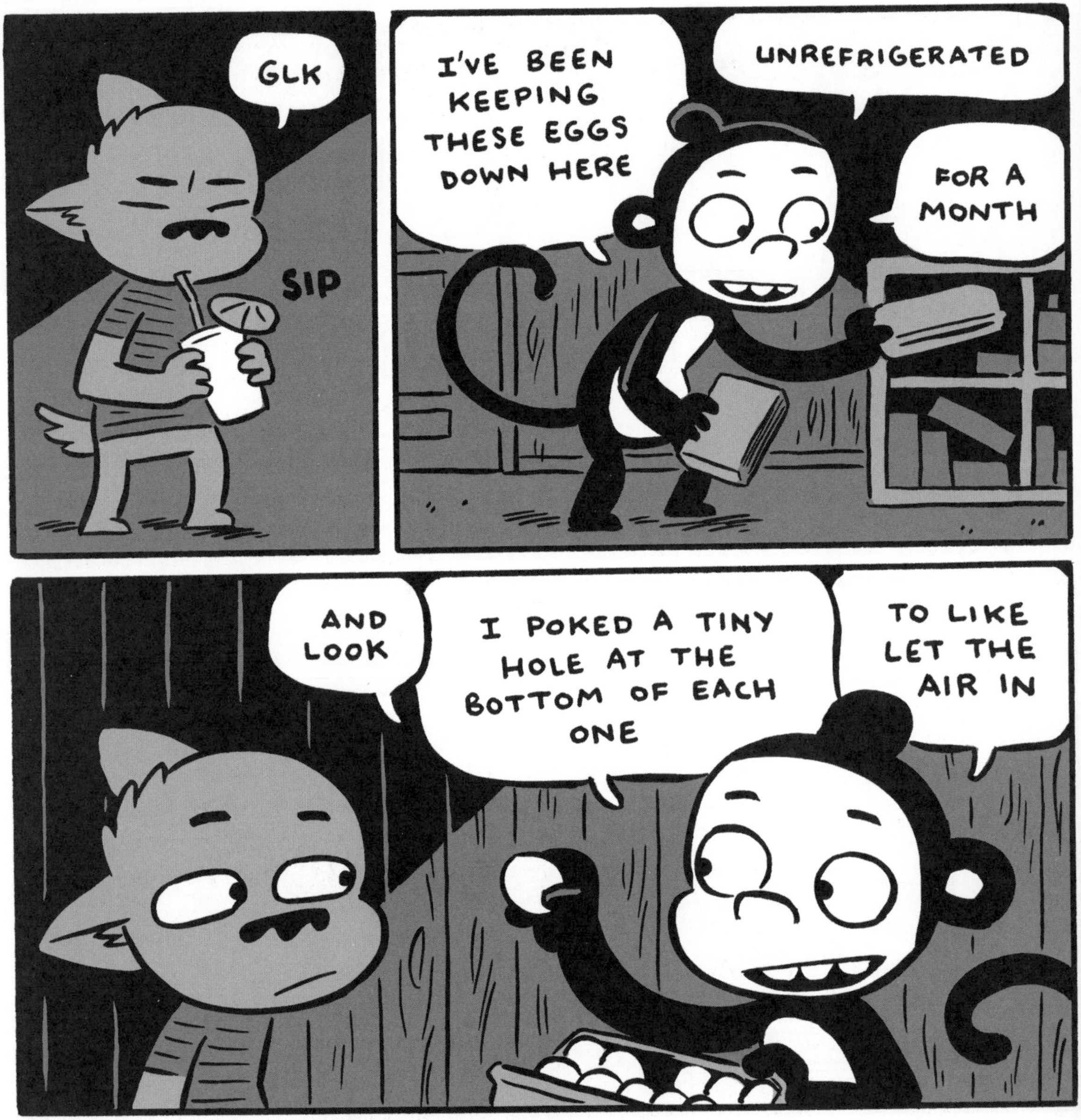
GLK
SIP
I'VE BEEN KEEPING THESE EGGS DOWN HERE
UNREFRIGERATED
FOR A MONTH
AND LOOK
I POKED A TINY HOLE AT THE BOTTOM OF EACH ONE
TO LIKE LET THE AIR IN

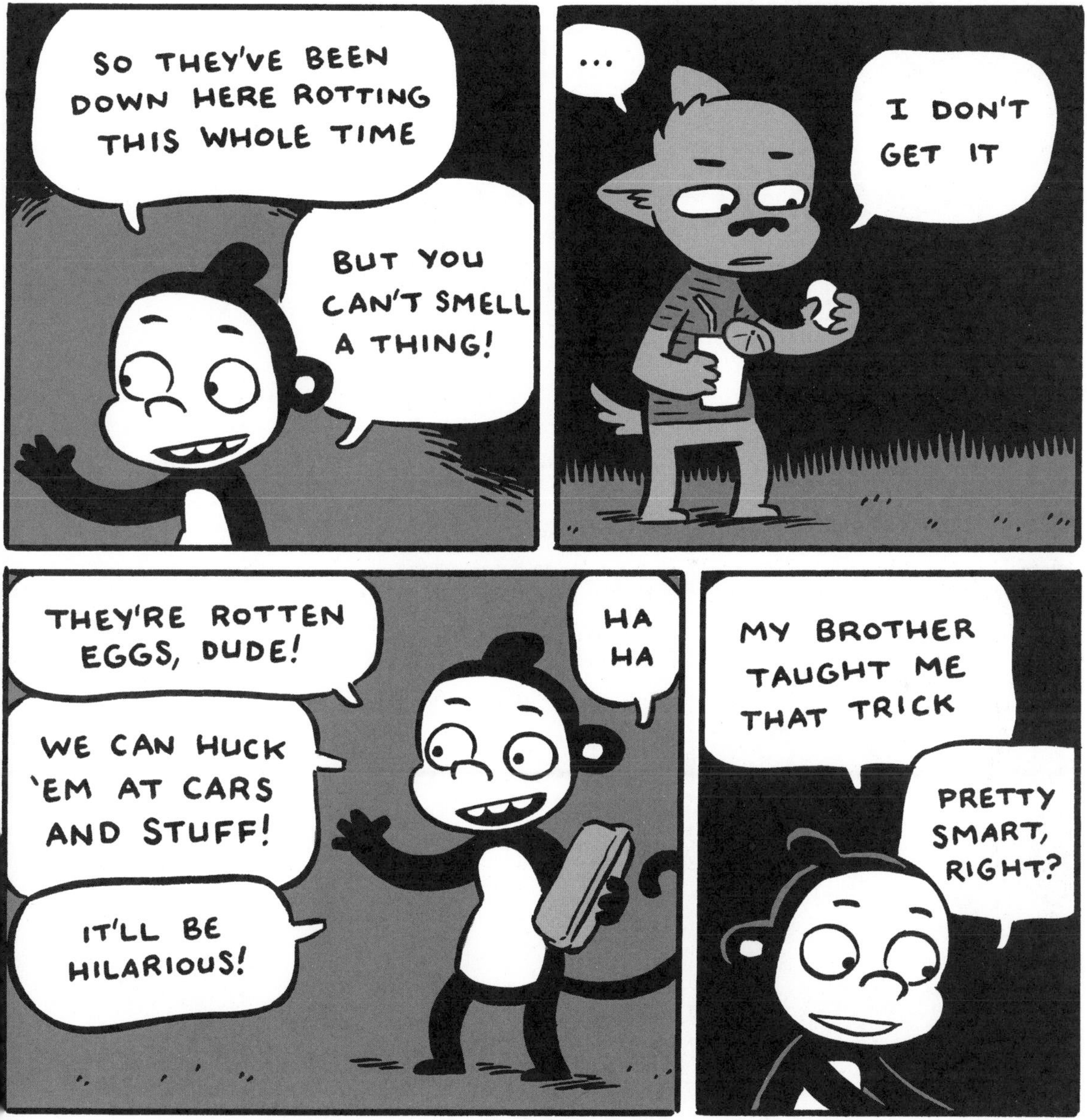
SO THEY'VE BEEN DOWN HERE ROTTING THIS WHOLE TIME
BUT YOU CAN'T SMELL A THING!
...
I DON'T GET IT
THEY'RE ROTTEN EGGS, DUDE!
WE CAN HUCK 'EM AT CARS AND STUFF!
IT'LL BE HILARIOUS!
HA HA
MY BROTHER TAUGHT ME THAT TRICK
PRETTY SMART, RIGHT?

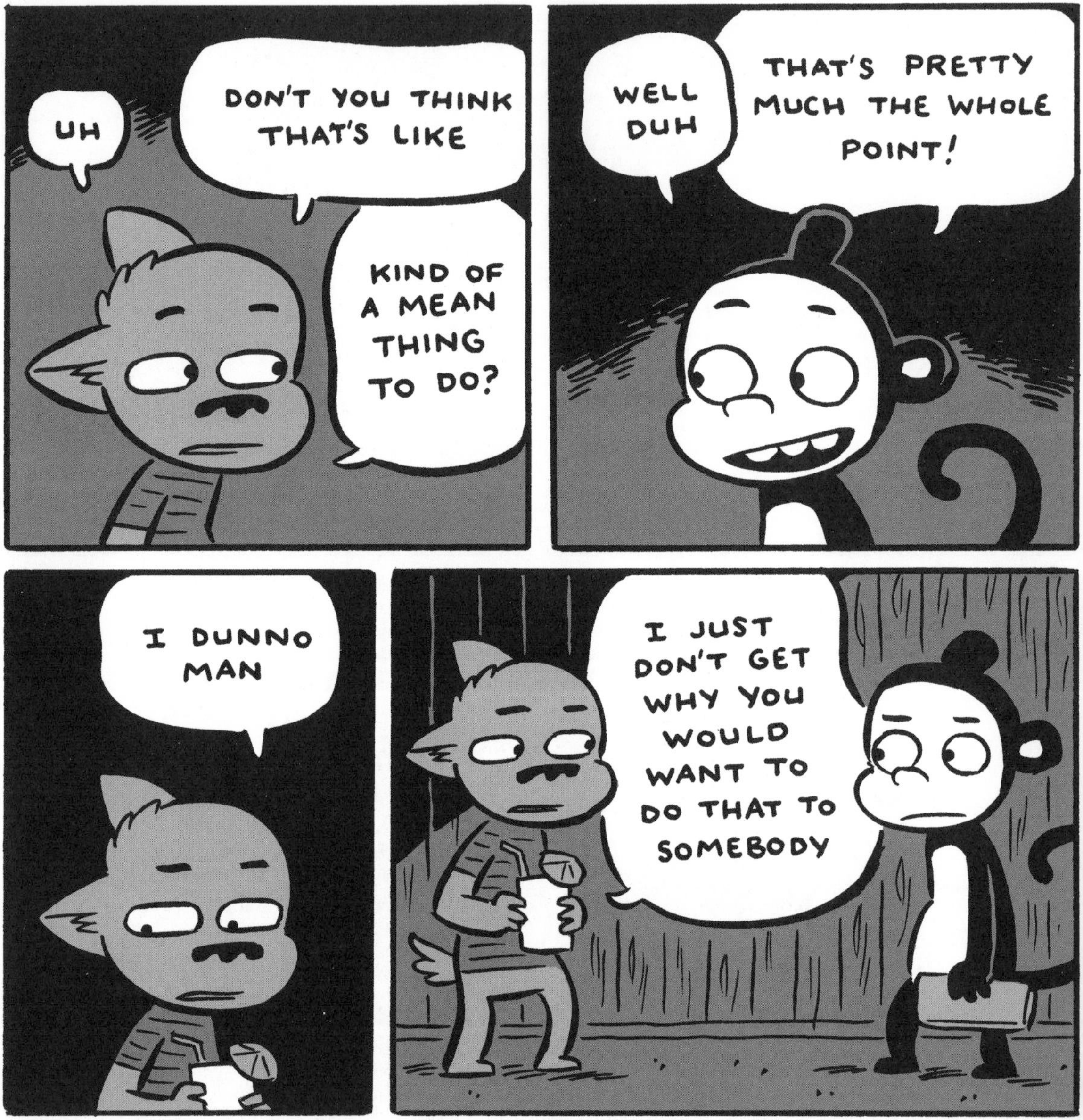
UH
DON'T YOU THINK THAT'S LIKE
KIND OF A MEAN THING TO DO?
WELL DUH
THAT'S PRETTY MUCH THE WHOLE POINT!
I DUNNO MAN
I JUST DON'T GET WHY YOU WOULD WANT TO DO THAT TO SOMEBODY

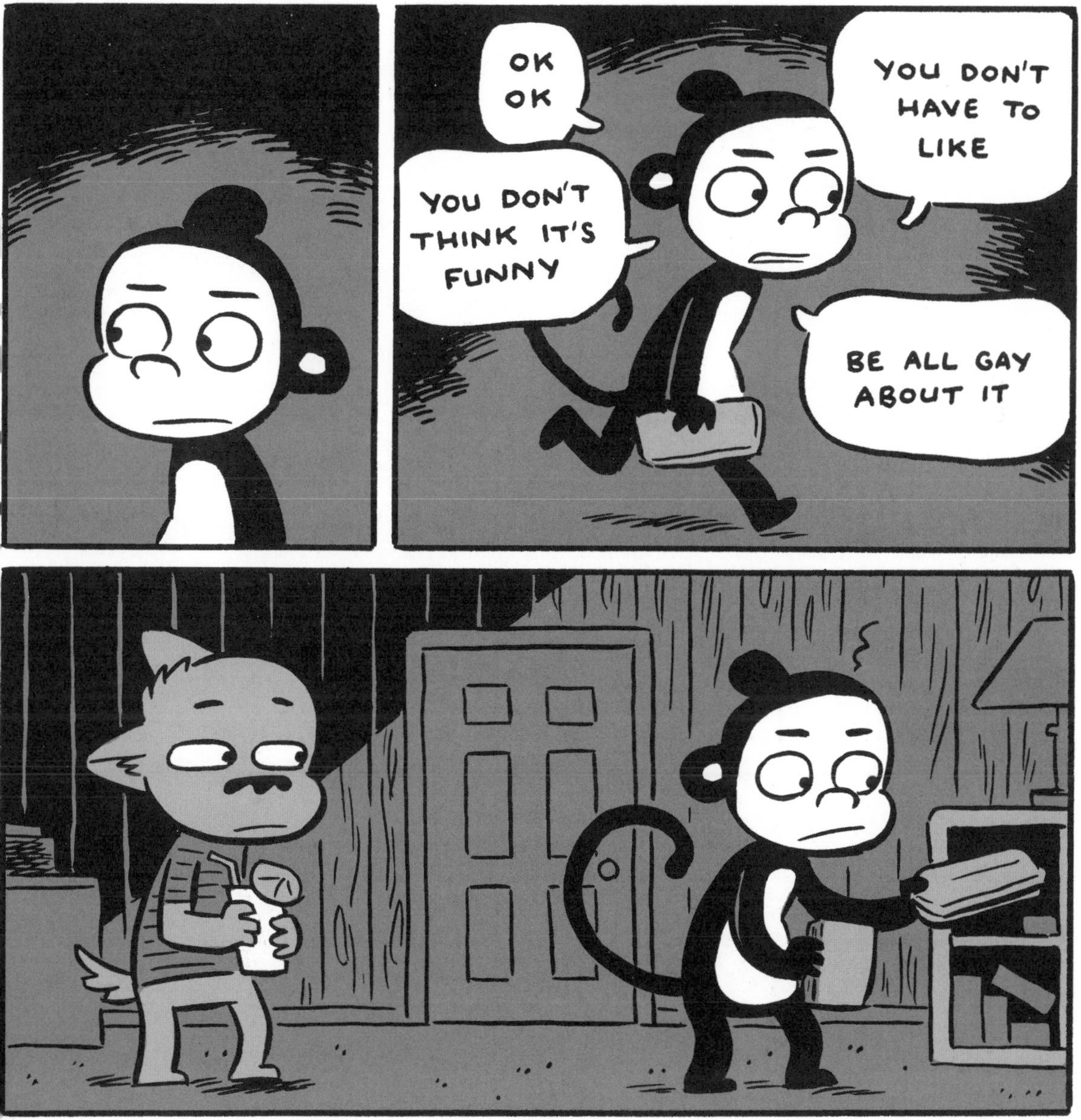
OK
OK
YOU DON'T THINK IT'S FUNNY
YOU DON'T HAVE TO LIKE
BE ALL GAY ABOUT IT

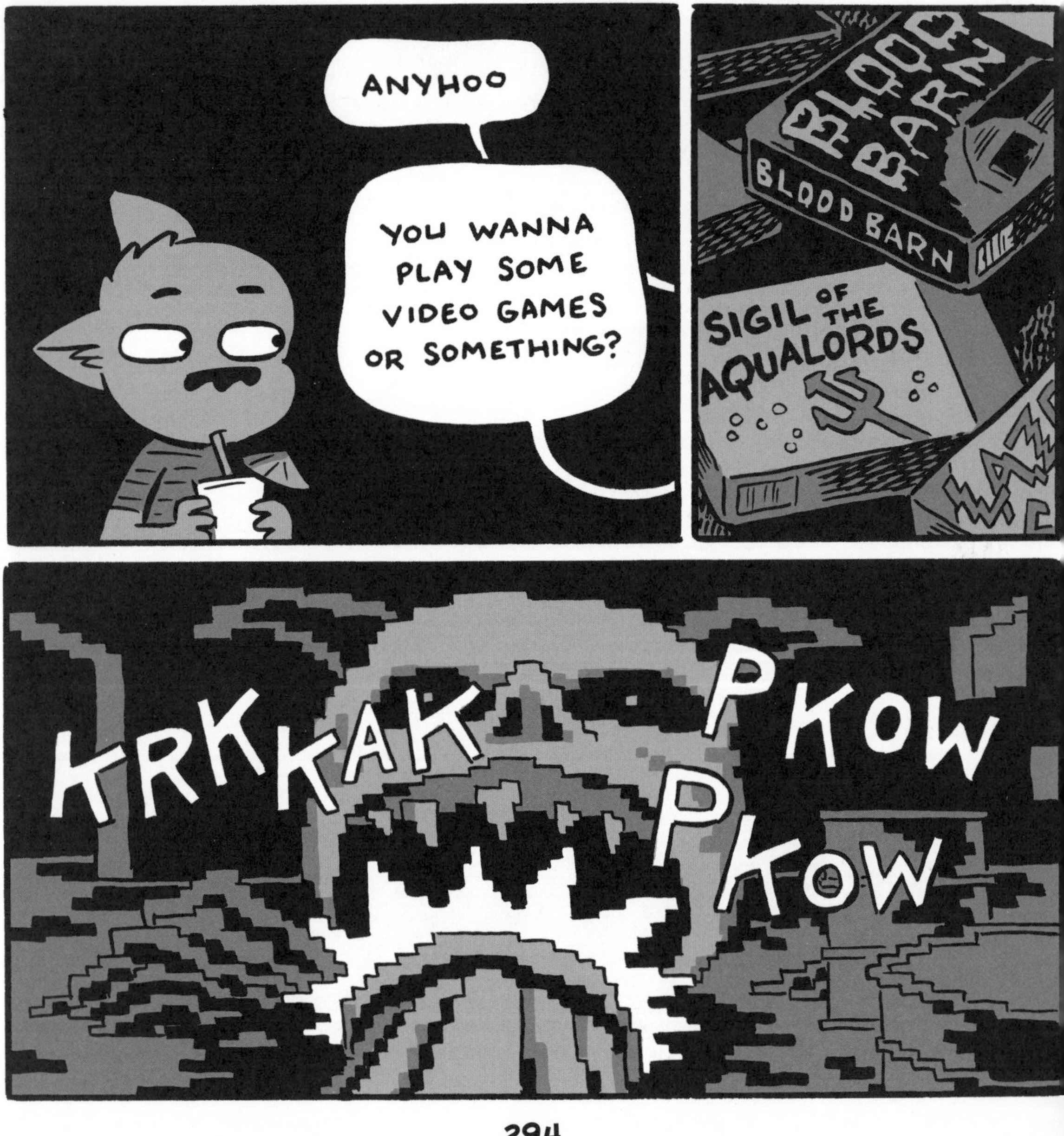
ANYHOO
YOU WANNA PLAY SOME VIDEO GAMES OR SOMETHING?
BLOOD BARN
BLOOD BARN
SIGIL OF THE AQUALORDS
KRKKAK
PKOW
PKOW

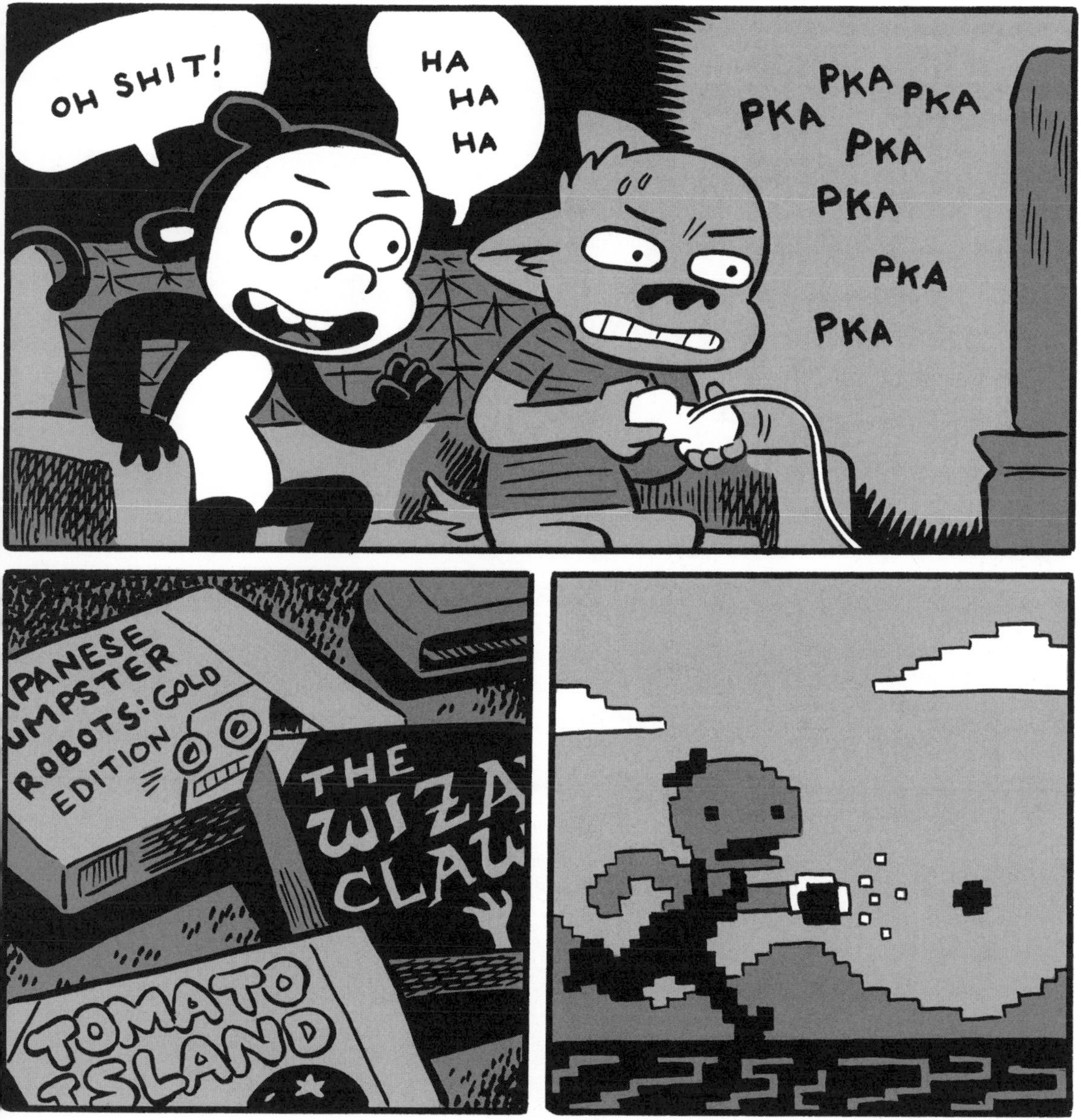
OH SHIT!
HA HA HA
PKA PKA PKA PKA PKA PKA PKA
PANESE UMPSTER ROBOTS: GOLD EDITION
THE WIZA CLAU
TOMATO ISLAND

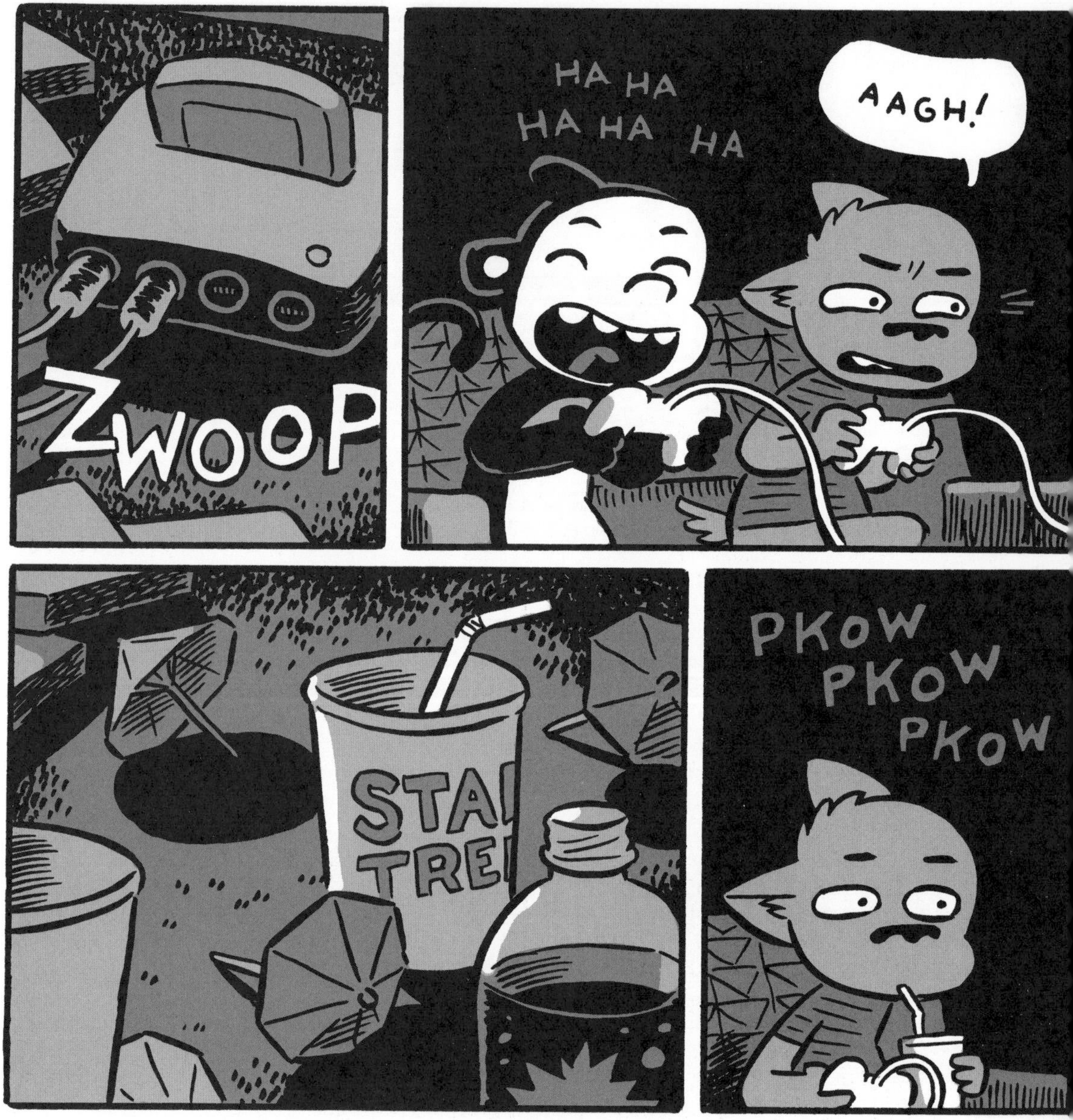
ZWOOP
HA HA
HA HA HA
AAGH!
STAR TREK
PKOW
PKOW
PKOW

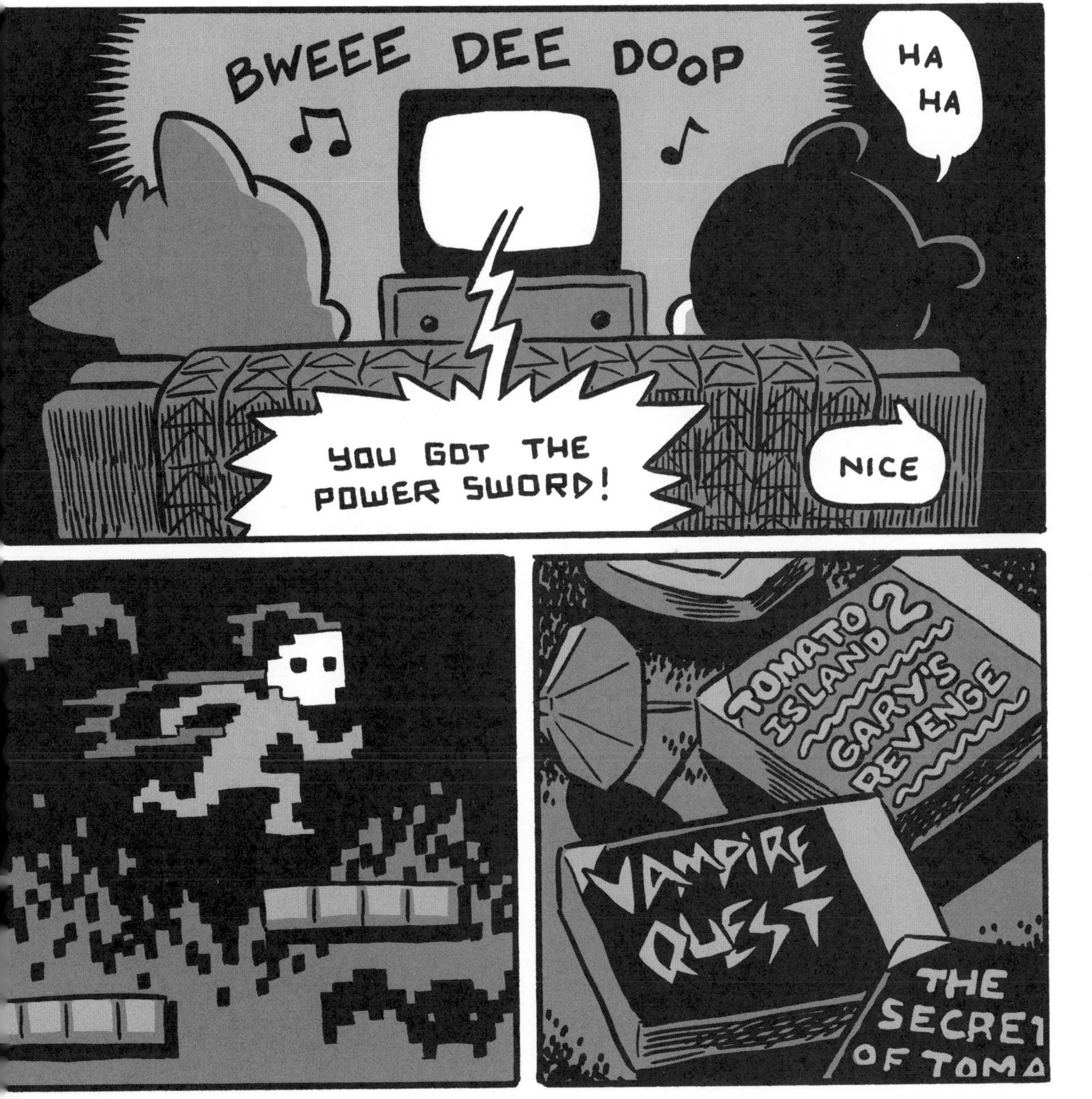
BWEEE DEE DOOP
HA HA
YOU GOT THE POWER SWORD!
NICE
TOMATO ISLAND 2
GARY'S REVENGE
VAMPIRE QUEST
THE SECRET OF TOMA

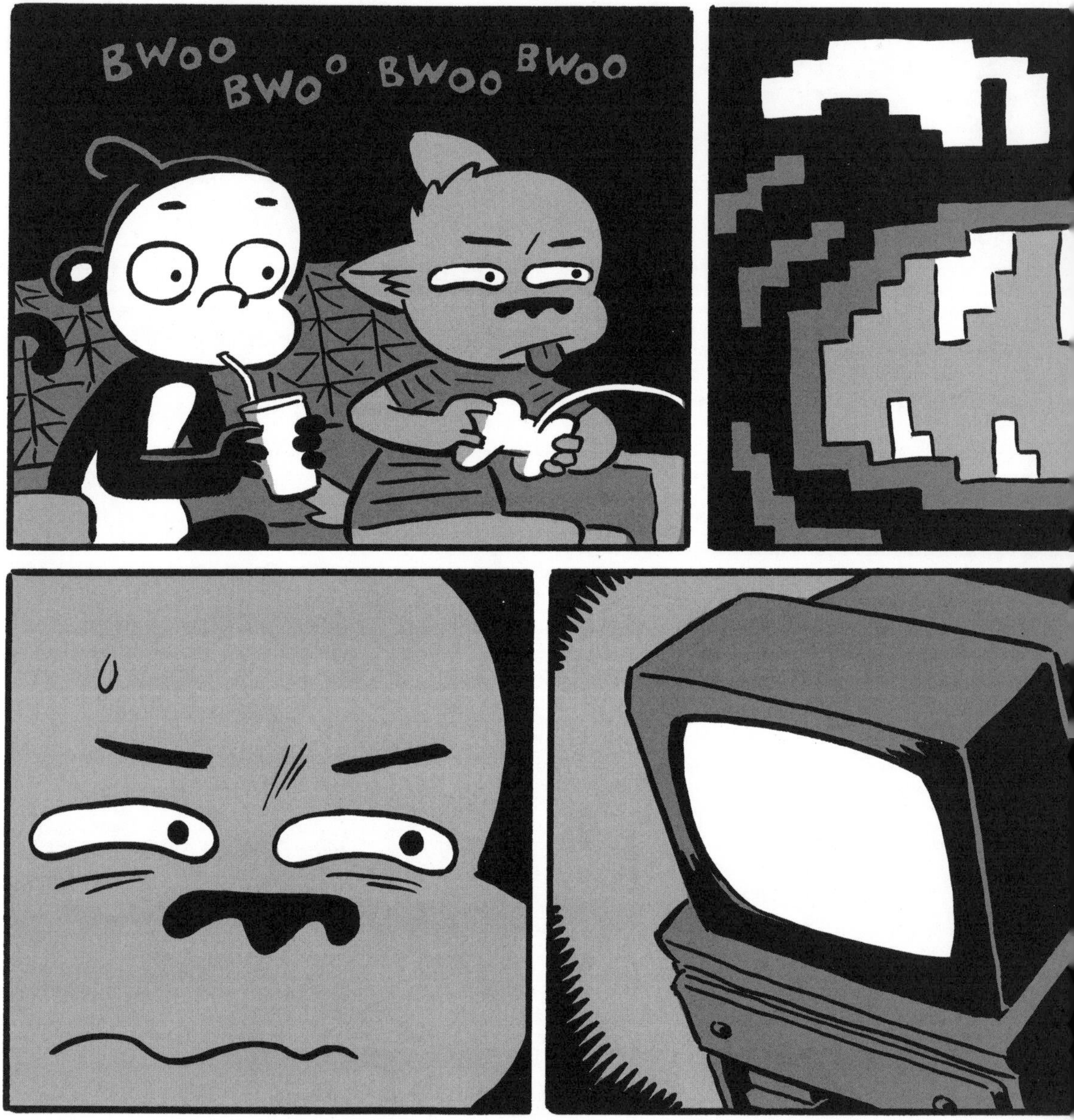
BWOO
BWOO
BWOO
BWOO

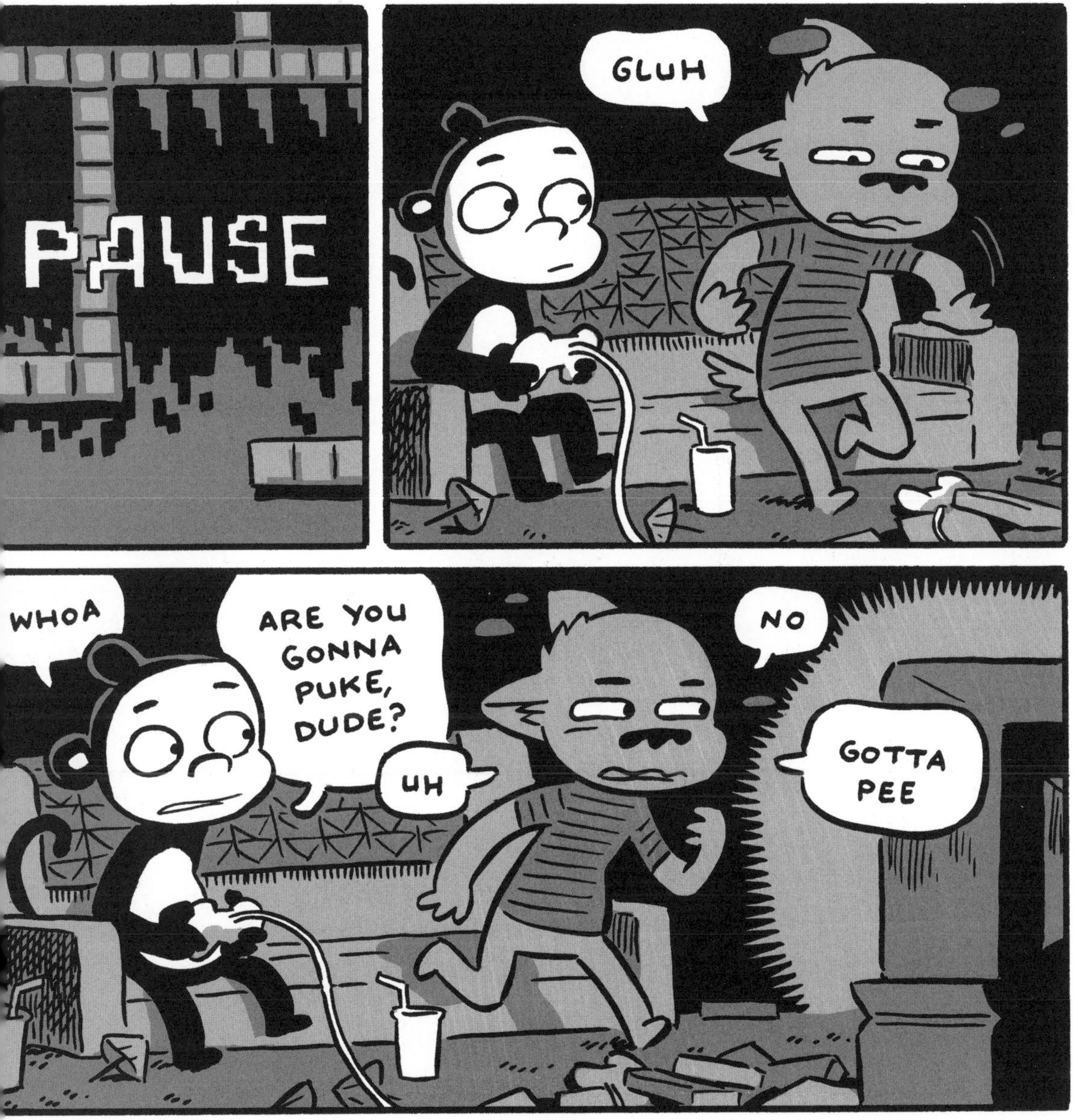
PAUSE
GLUH
WHOA
ARE YOU GONNA PUKE, DUDE?
UH
NO
GOTTA PEE

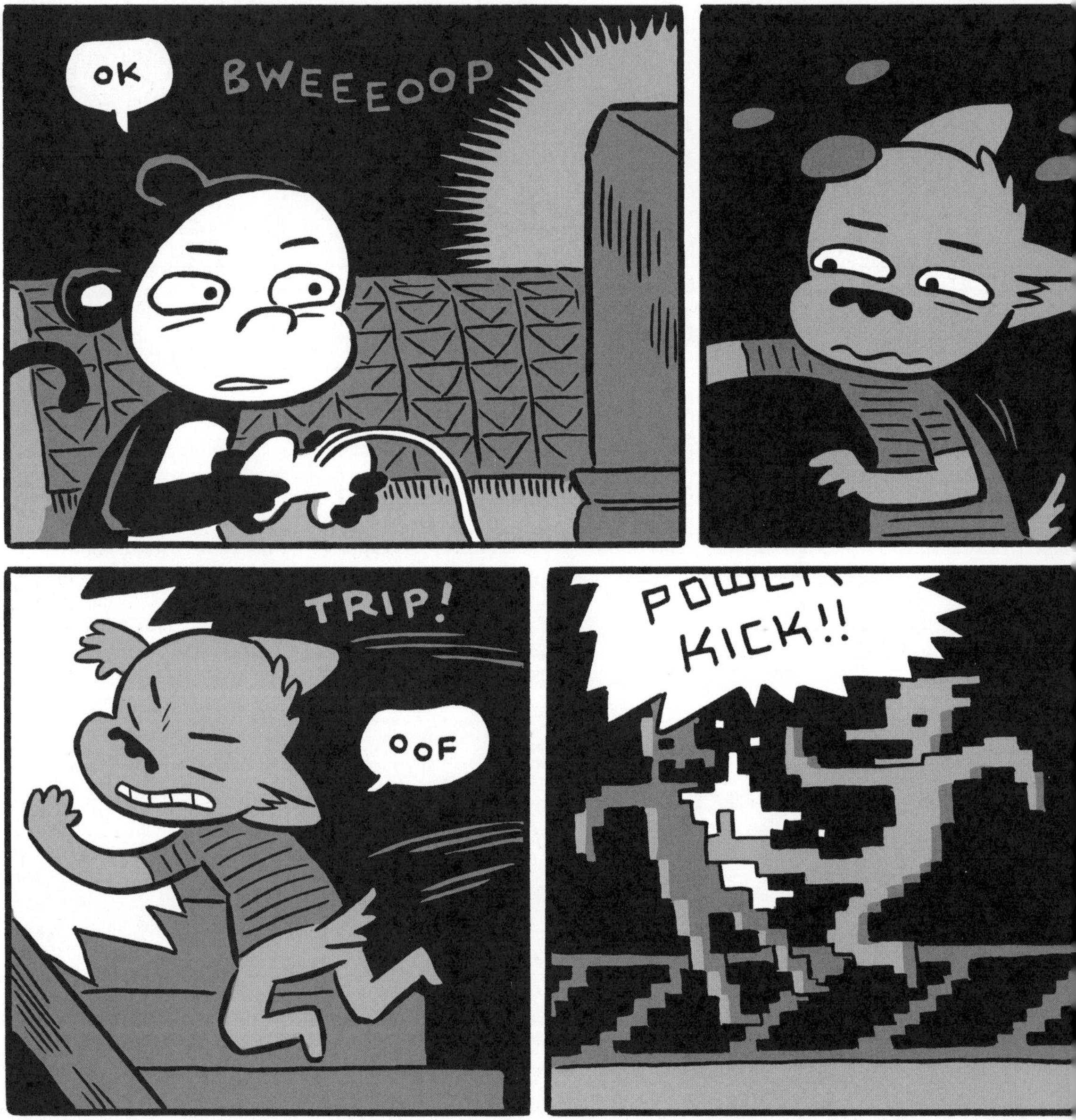
OK
BWEEEEOOP
TRIP!
OOF
POWER
KICK!!

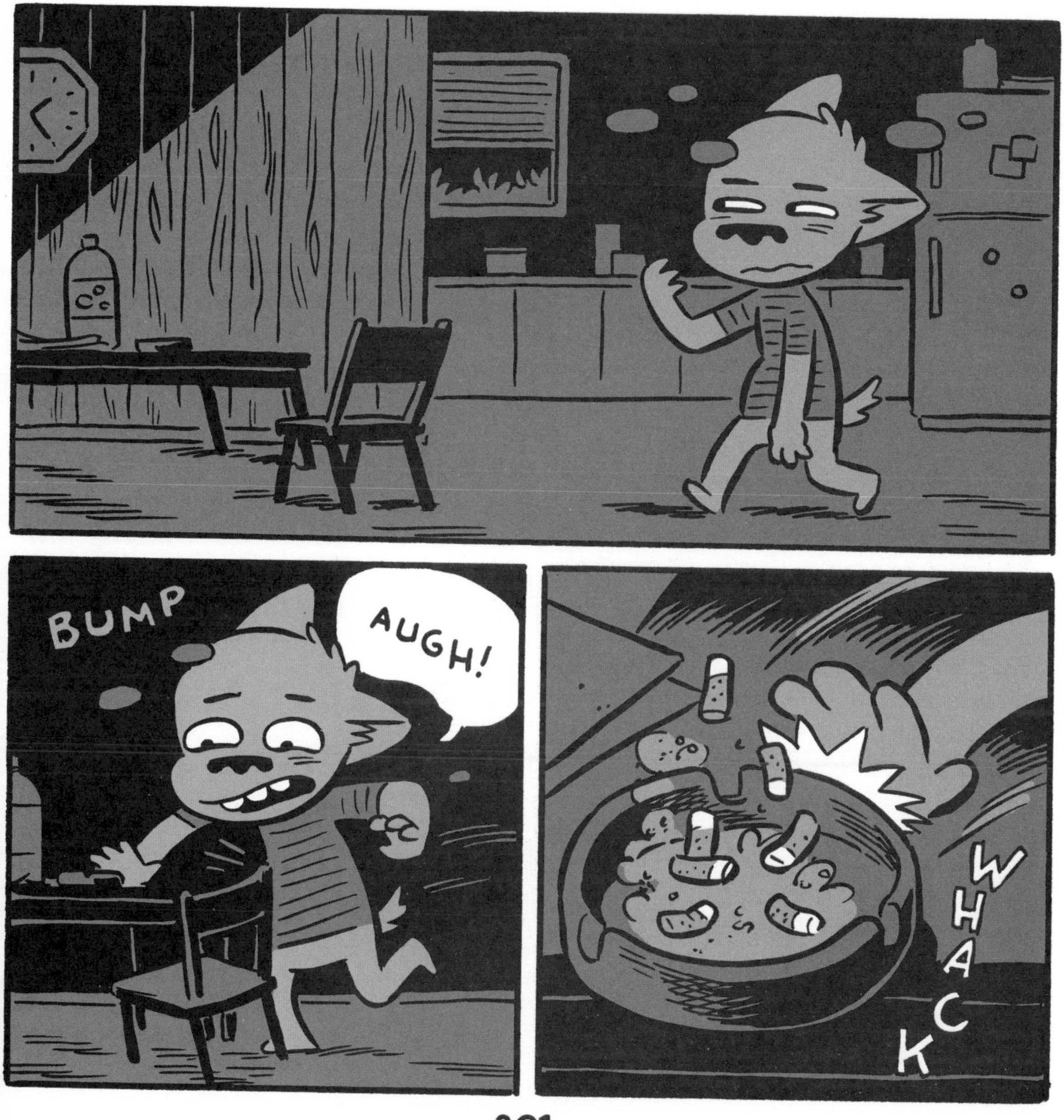
BUMP
AUGH!
WHACK

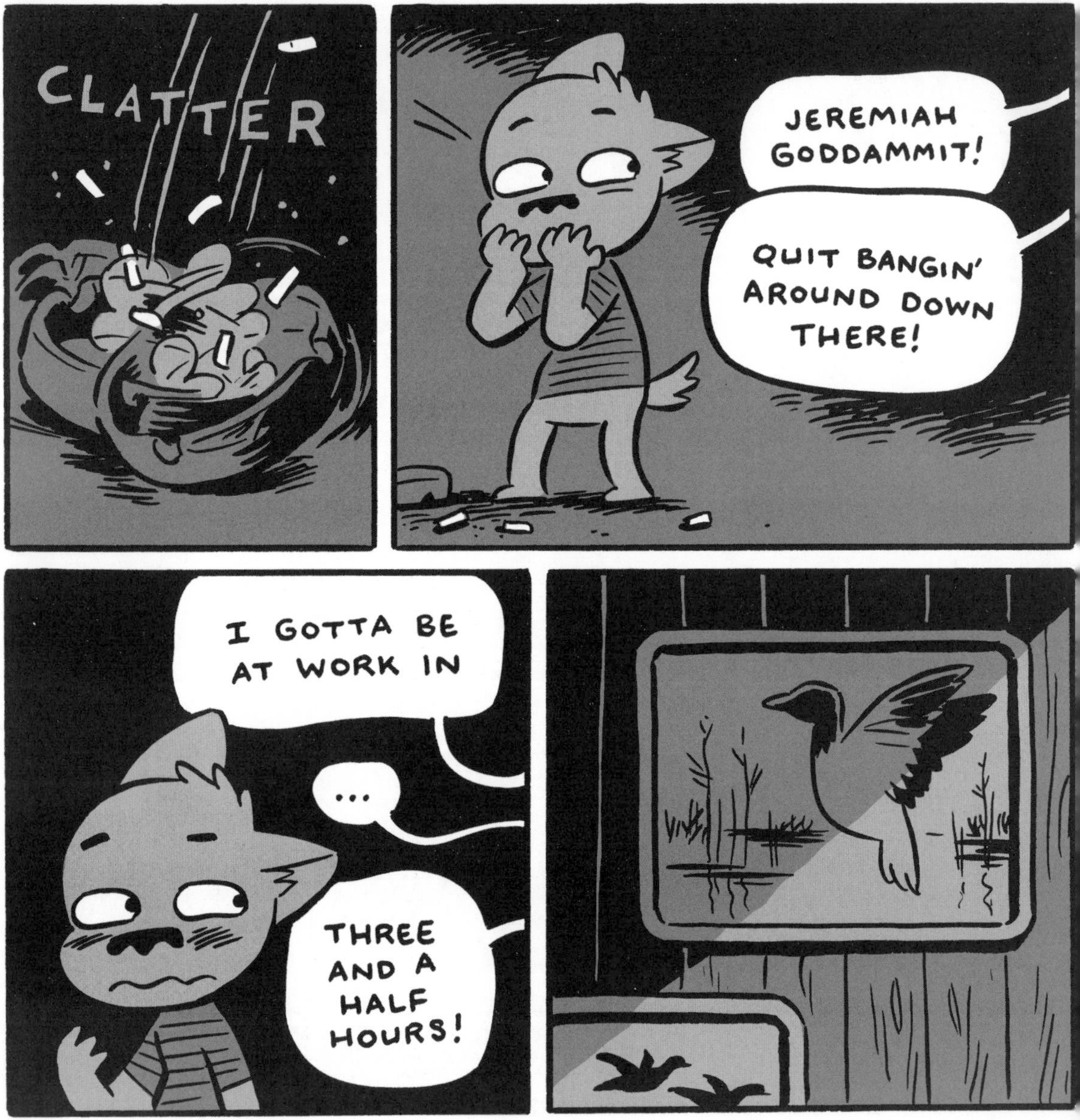
CLATTER
JEREMIAH GODDAMMIT!
QUIT BANGIN' AROUND DOWN THERE!
I GOTTA BE AT WORK IN
...
THREE AND A HALF HOURS!

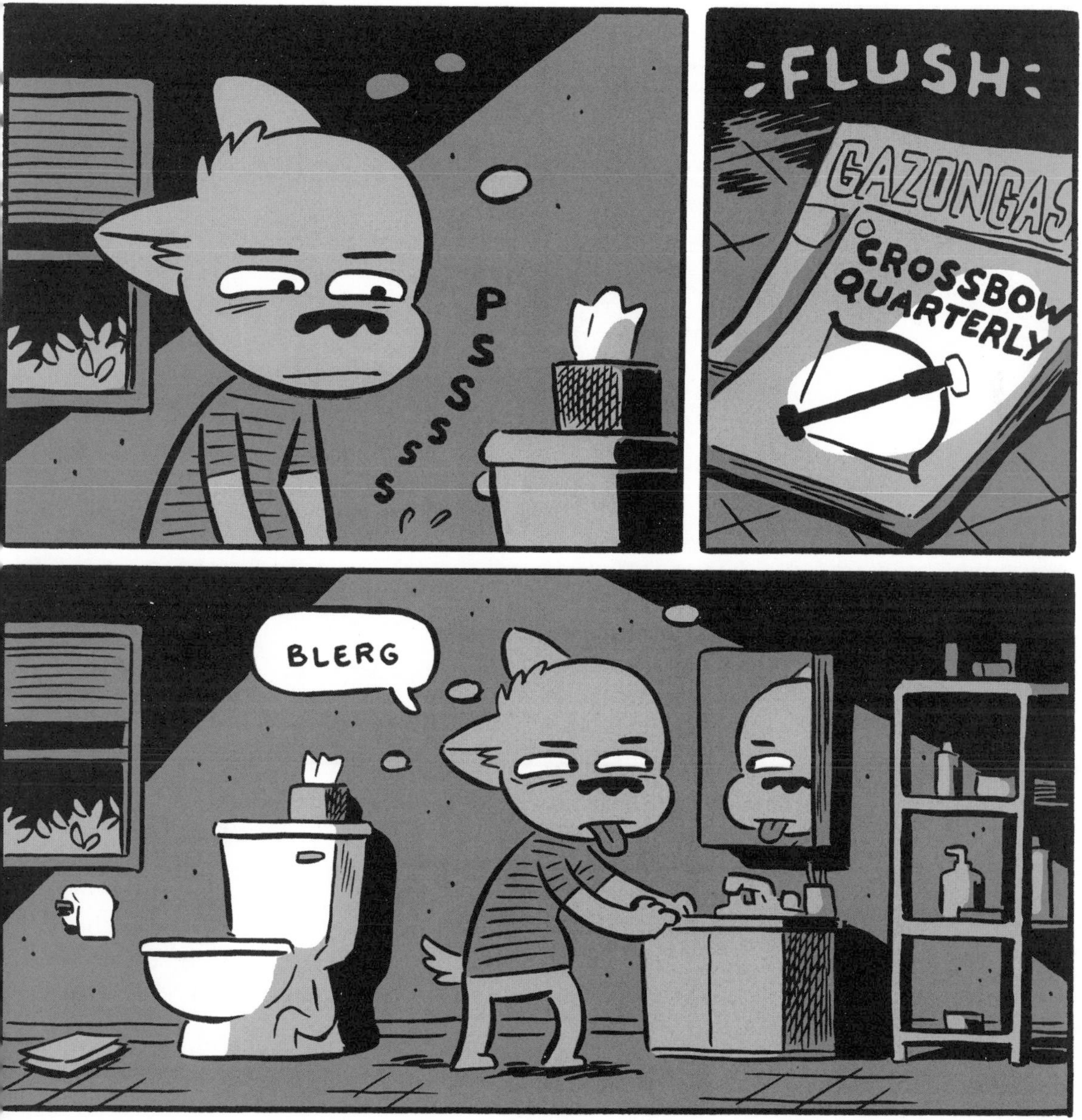
PSSSSSS
FLUSH
GAZONGAS
CROSSBOW QUARTERLY
BLERG

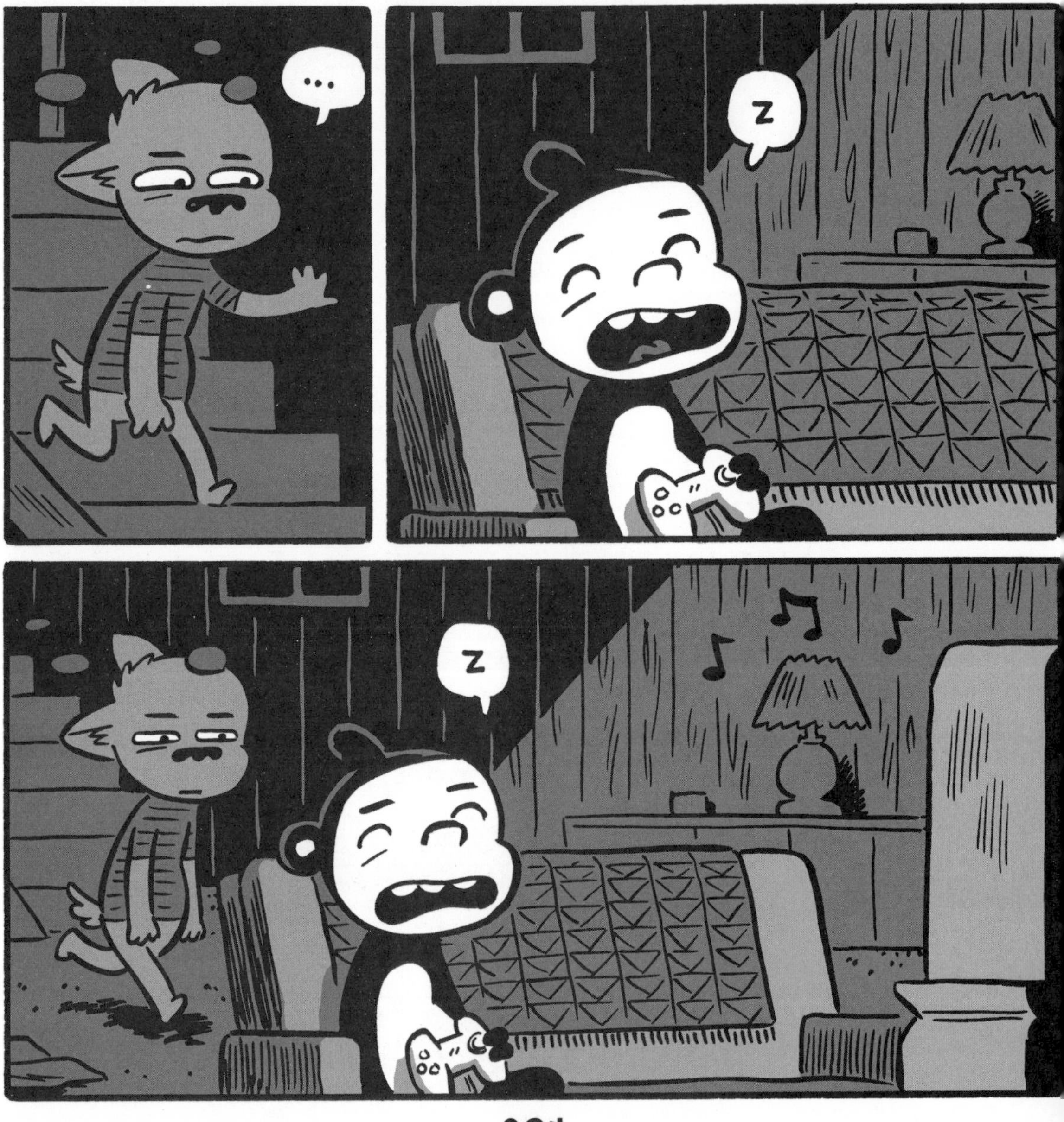
...
z
z

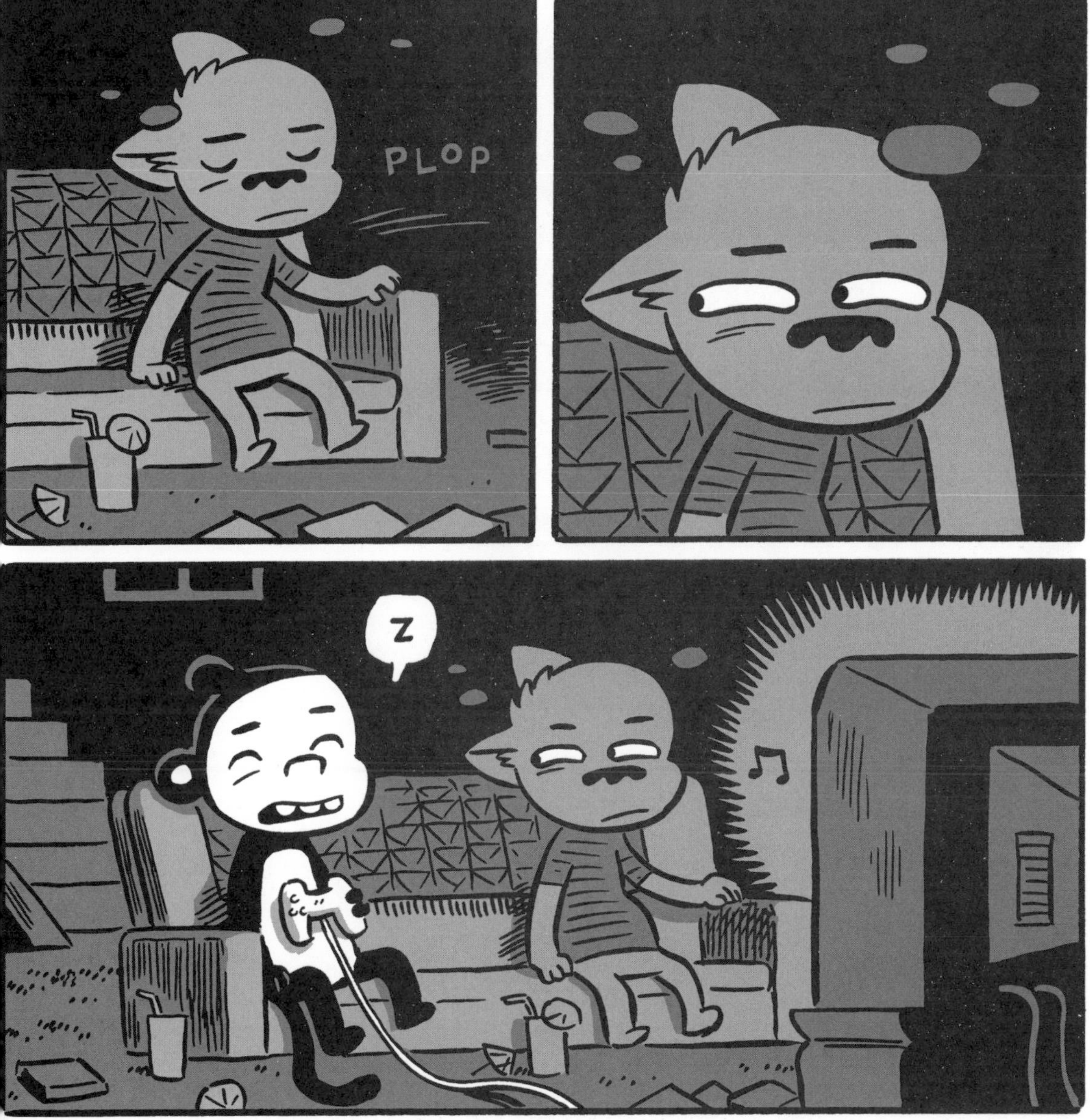
PLOP
Z

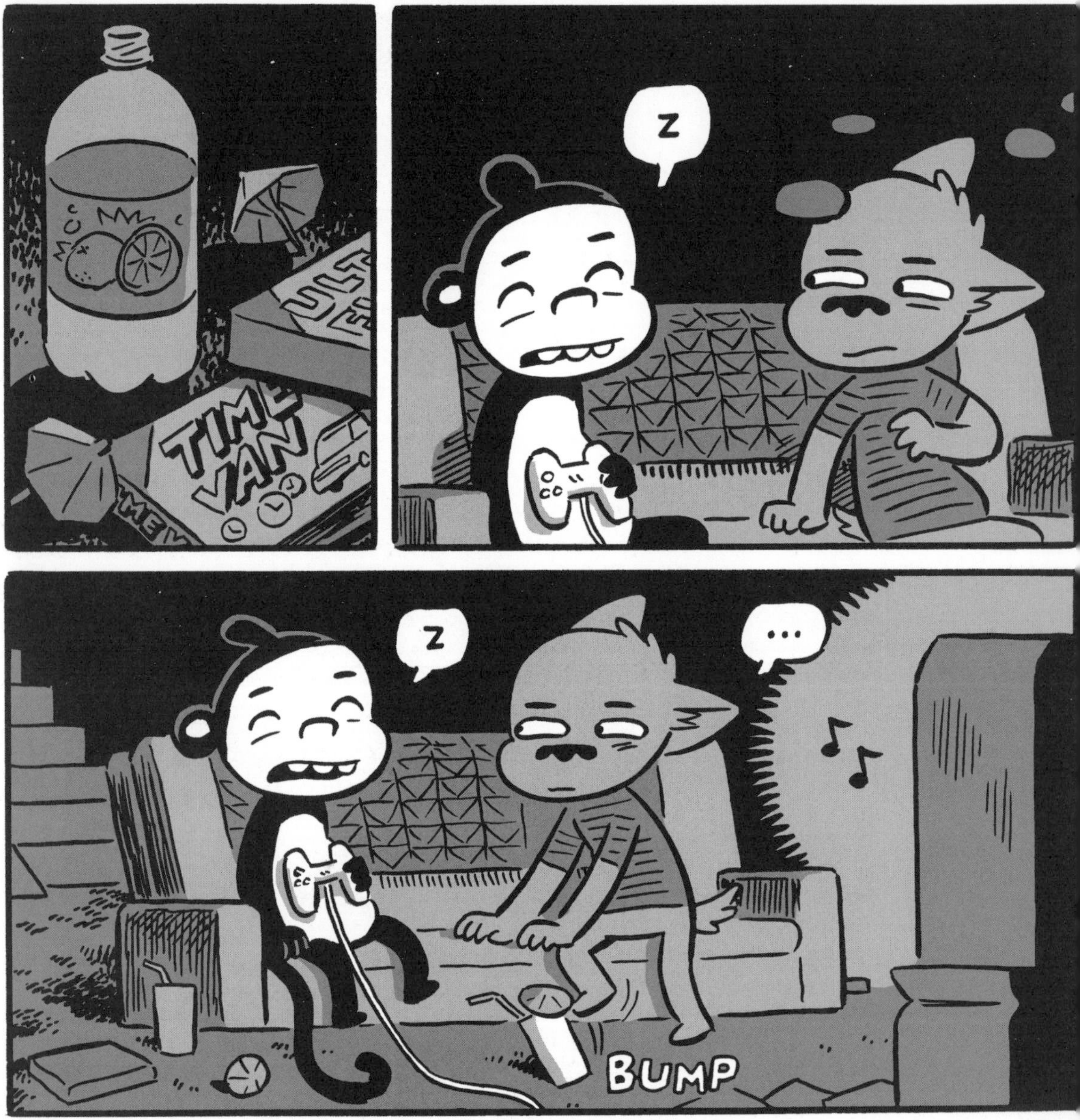
TIME VAN
Z
Z
...
BUMP

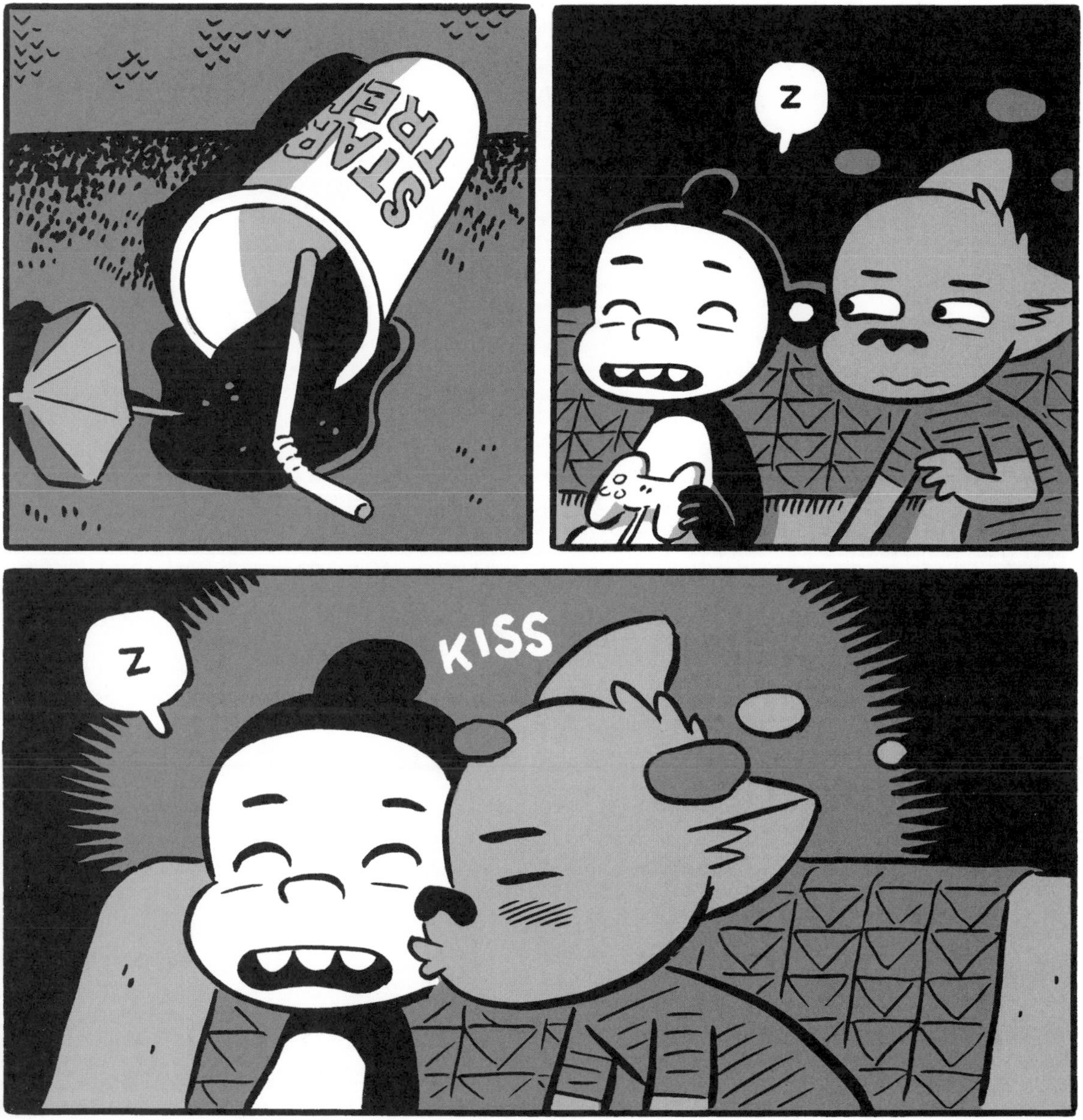
STAR
TRE
Z
Z
KISS

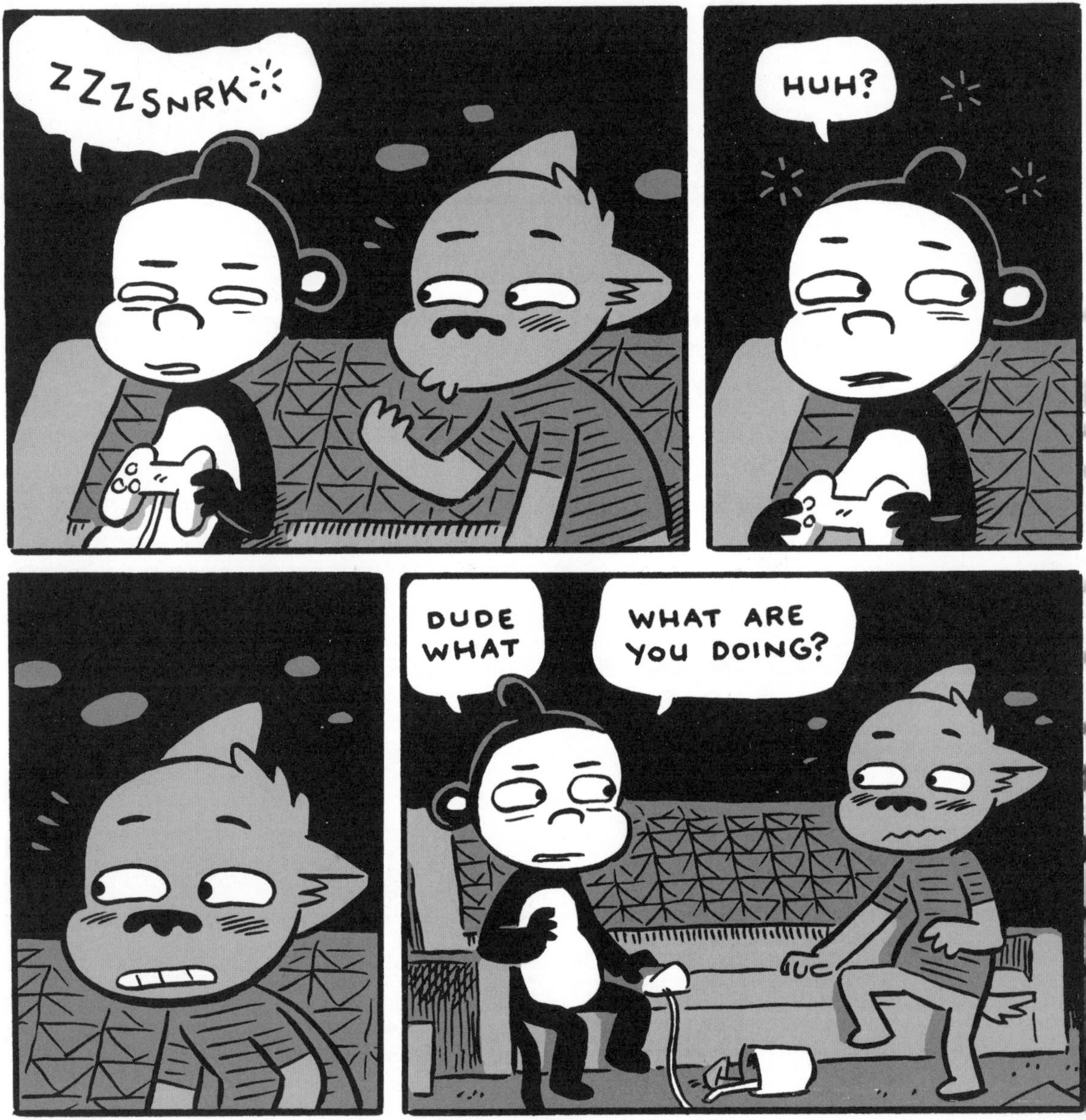
ZZZSNRK
HUH?
DUDE WHAT
WHAT ARE YOU DOING?

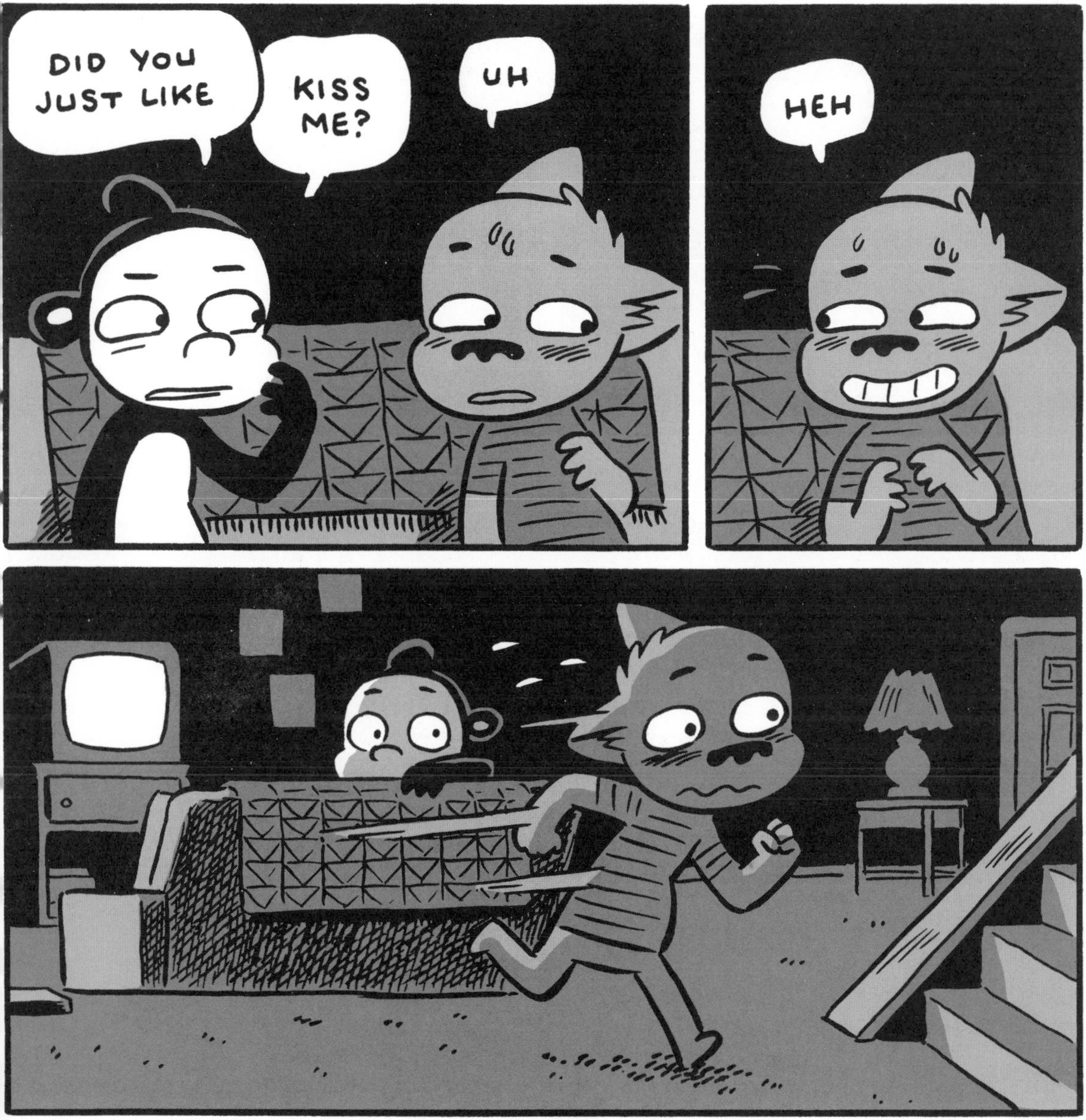
DID YOU JUST LIKE
KISS ME?
UH
HEH

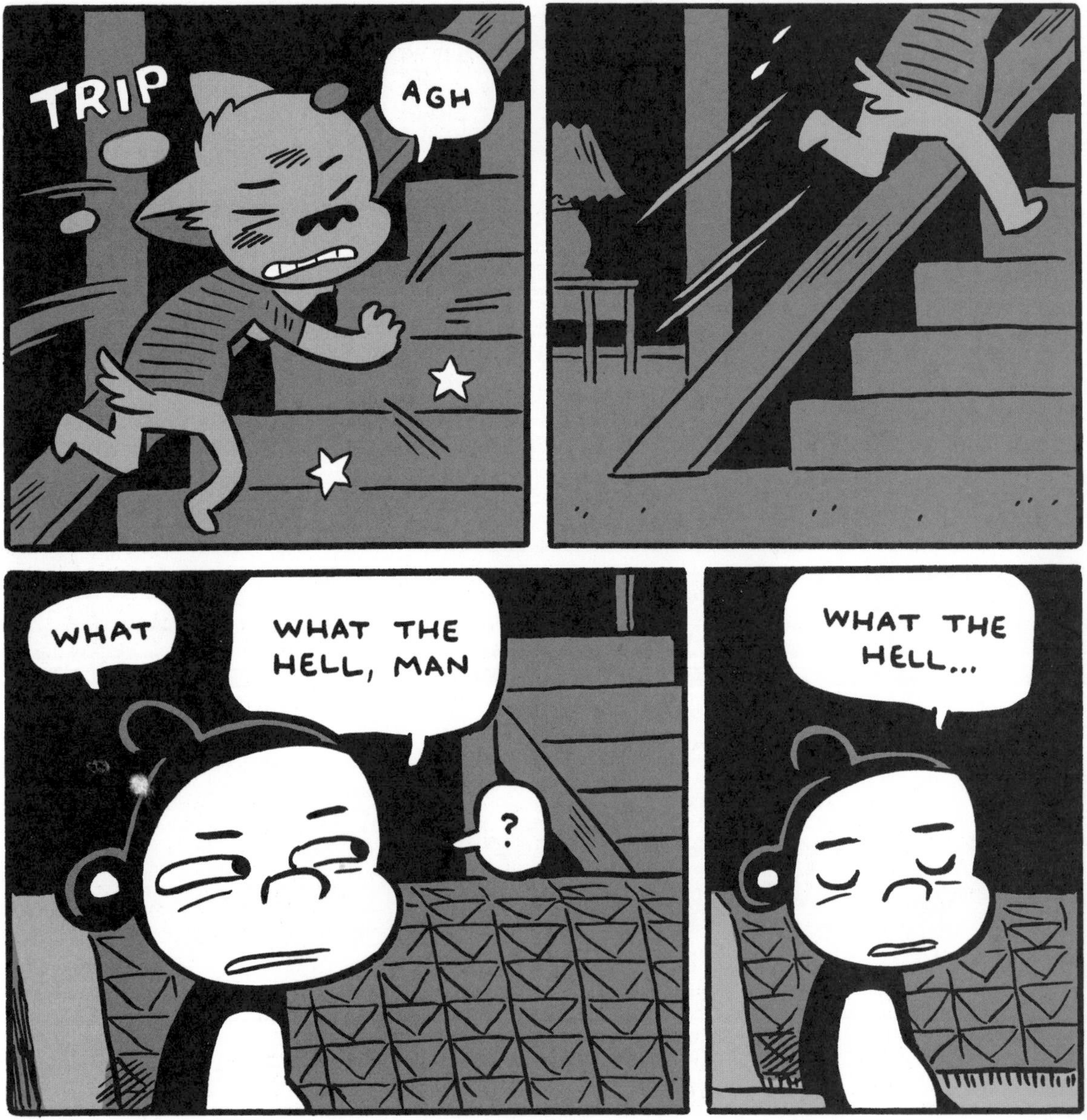
TRIP
AGH
WHAT
WHAT THE HELL, MAN
?
WHAT THE HELL...

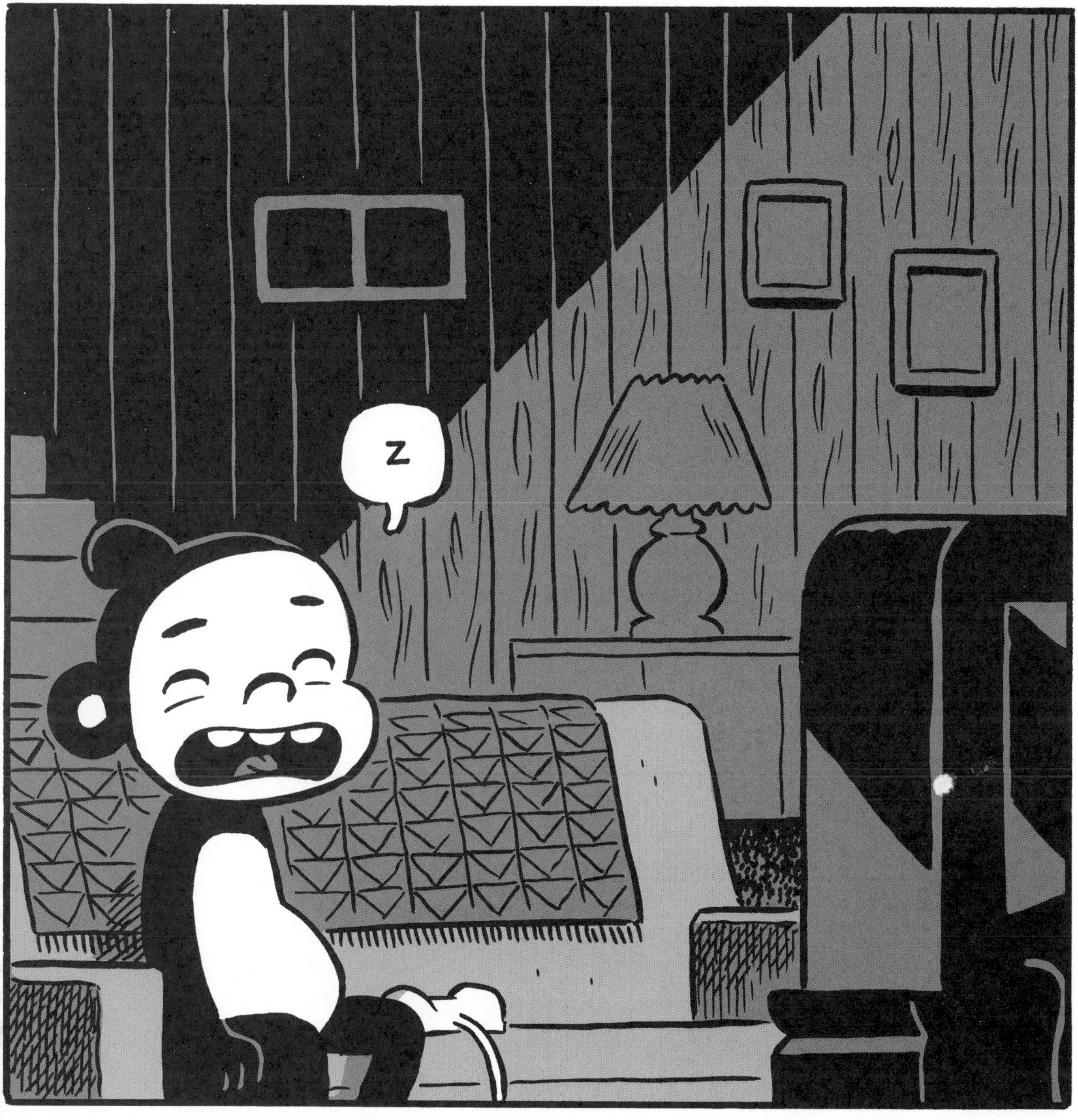
z

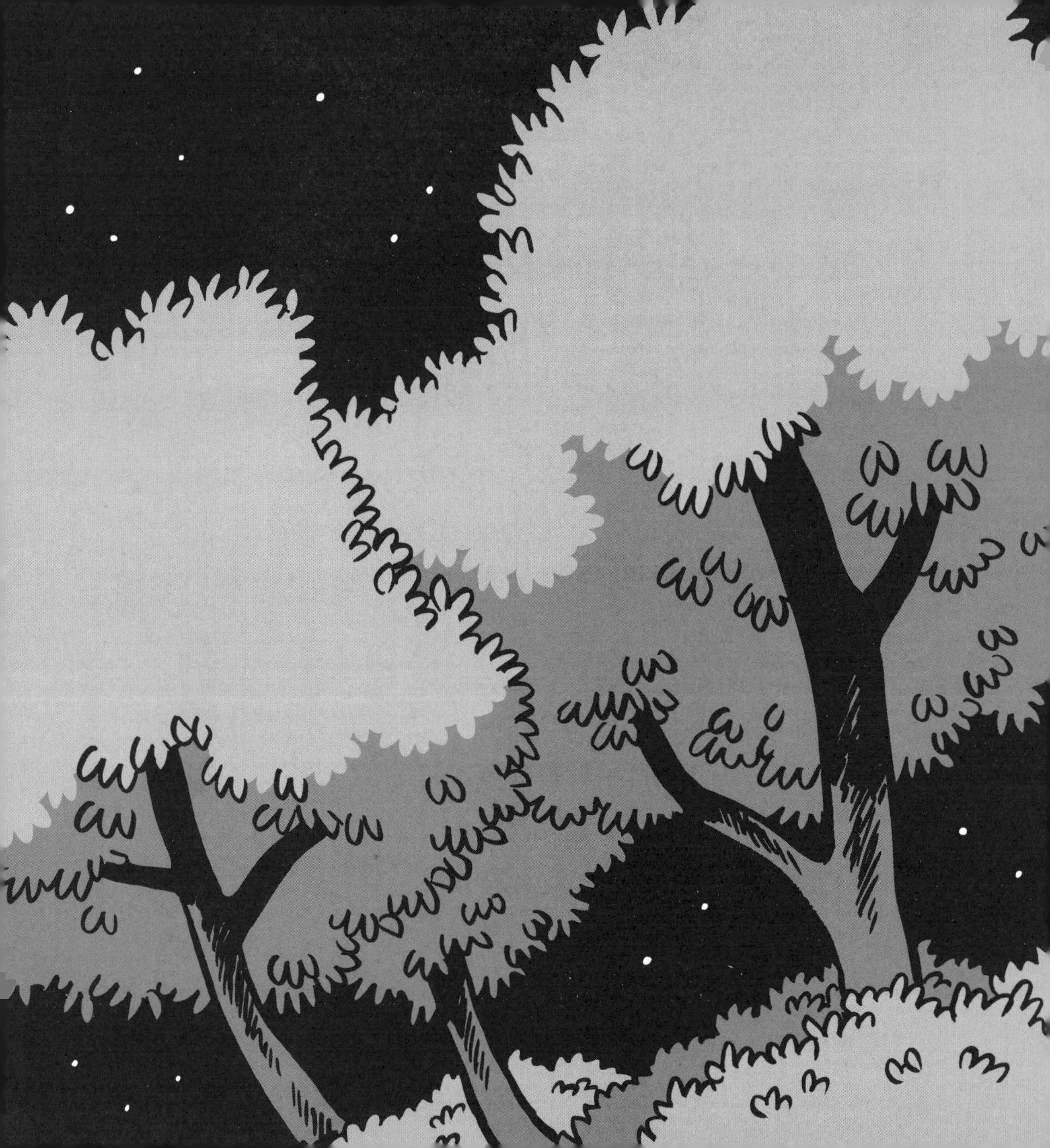

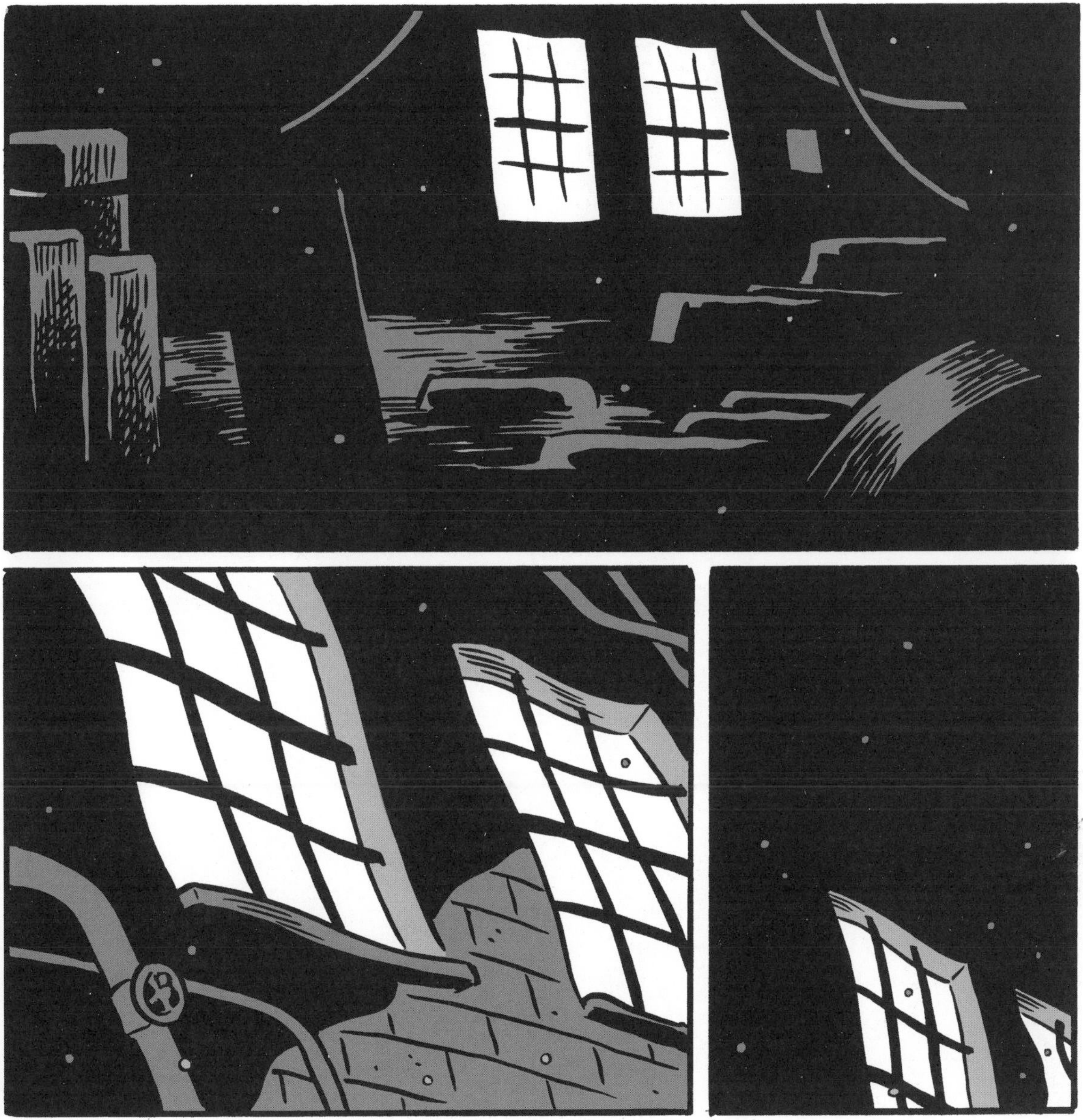

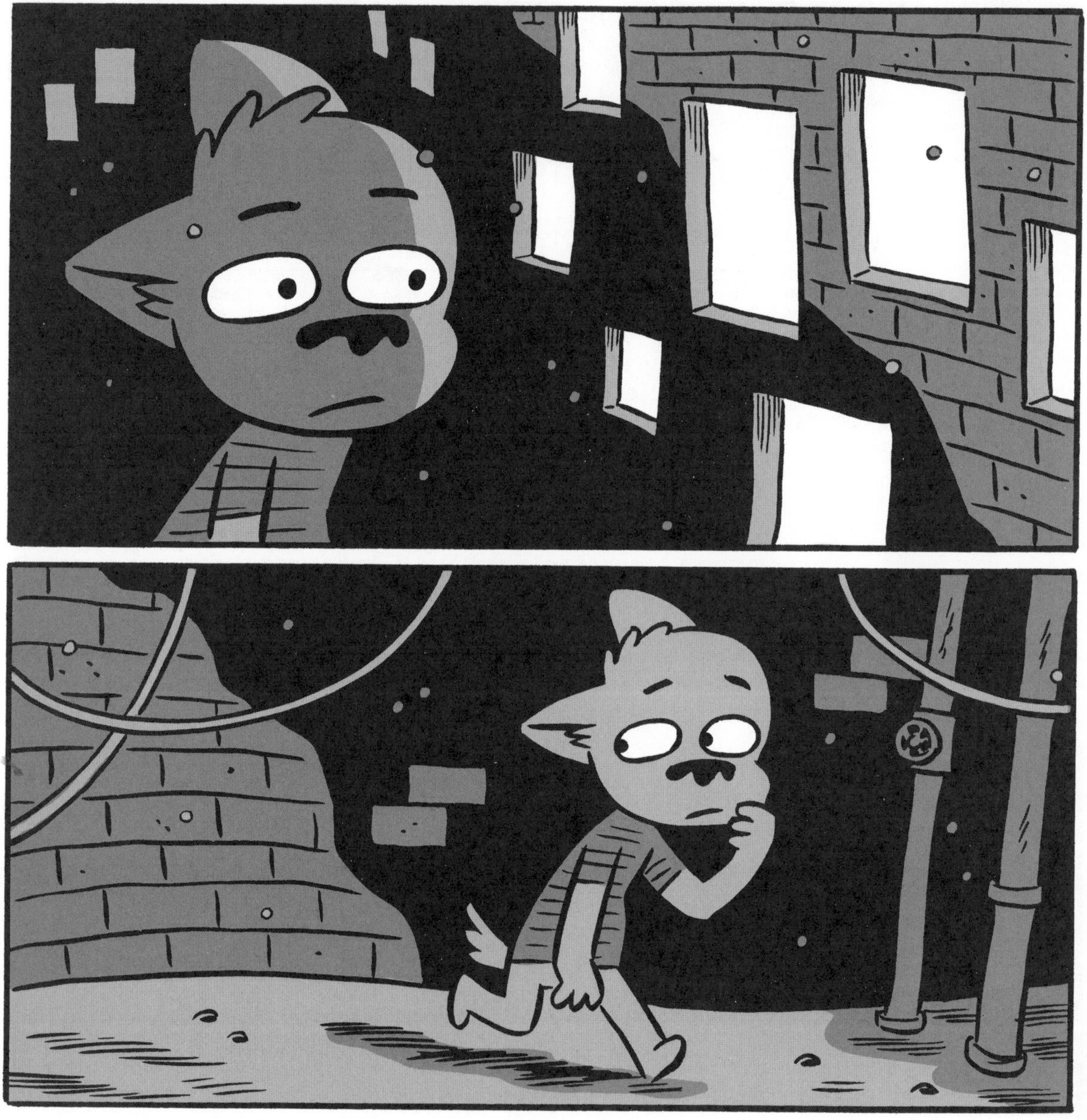

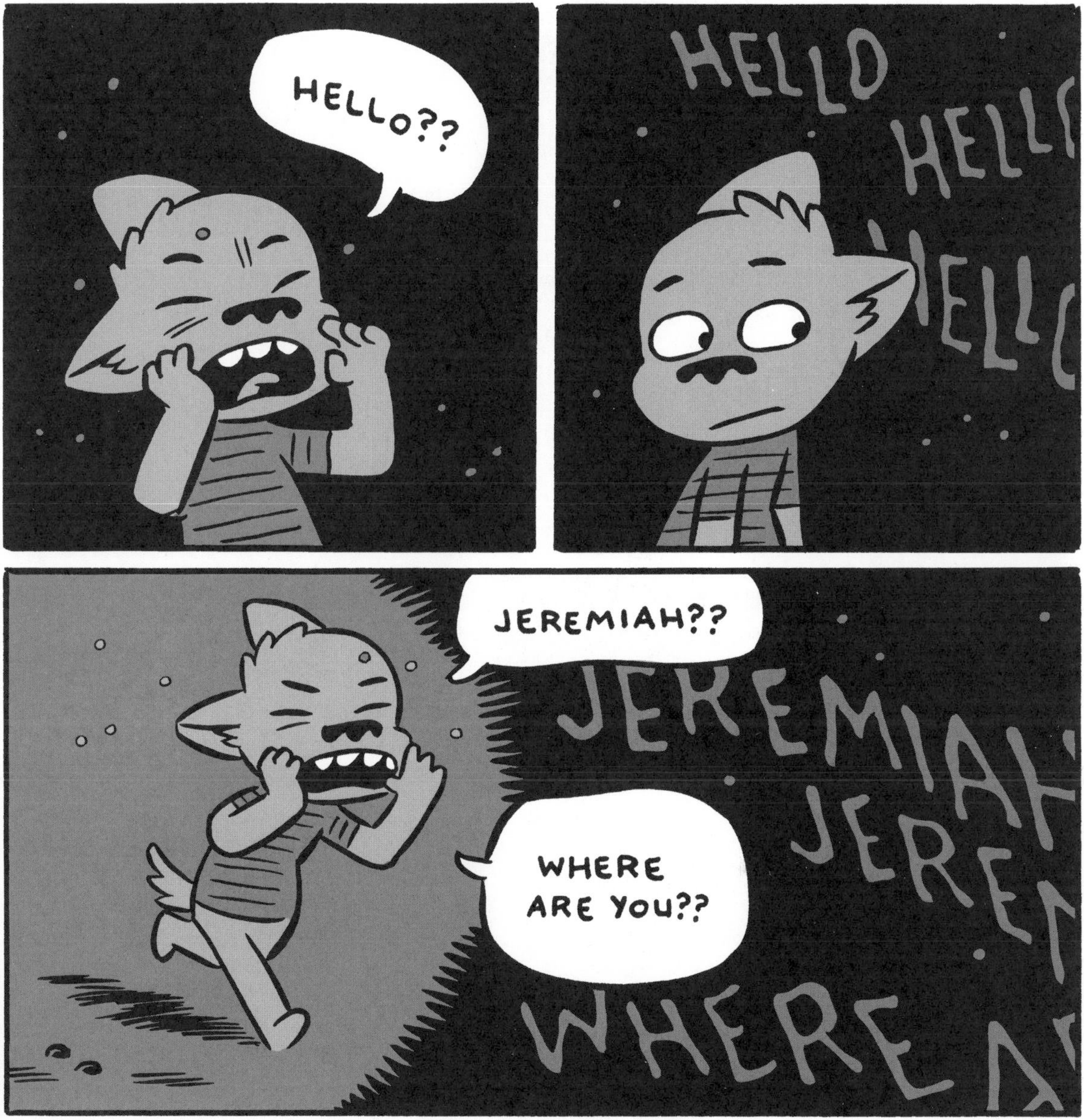
HELLO??
HELLO
JEREMIAH??
JEREMIAH
WHERE ARE YOU??
WHERE

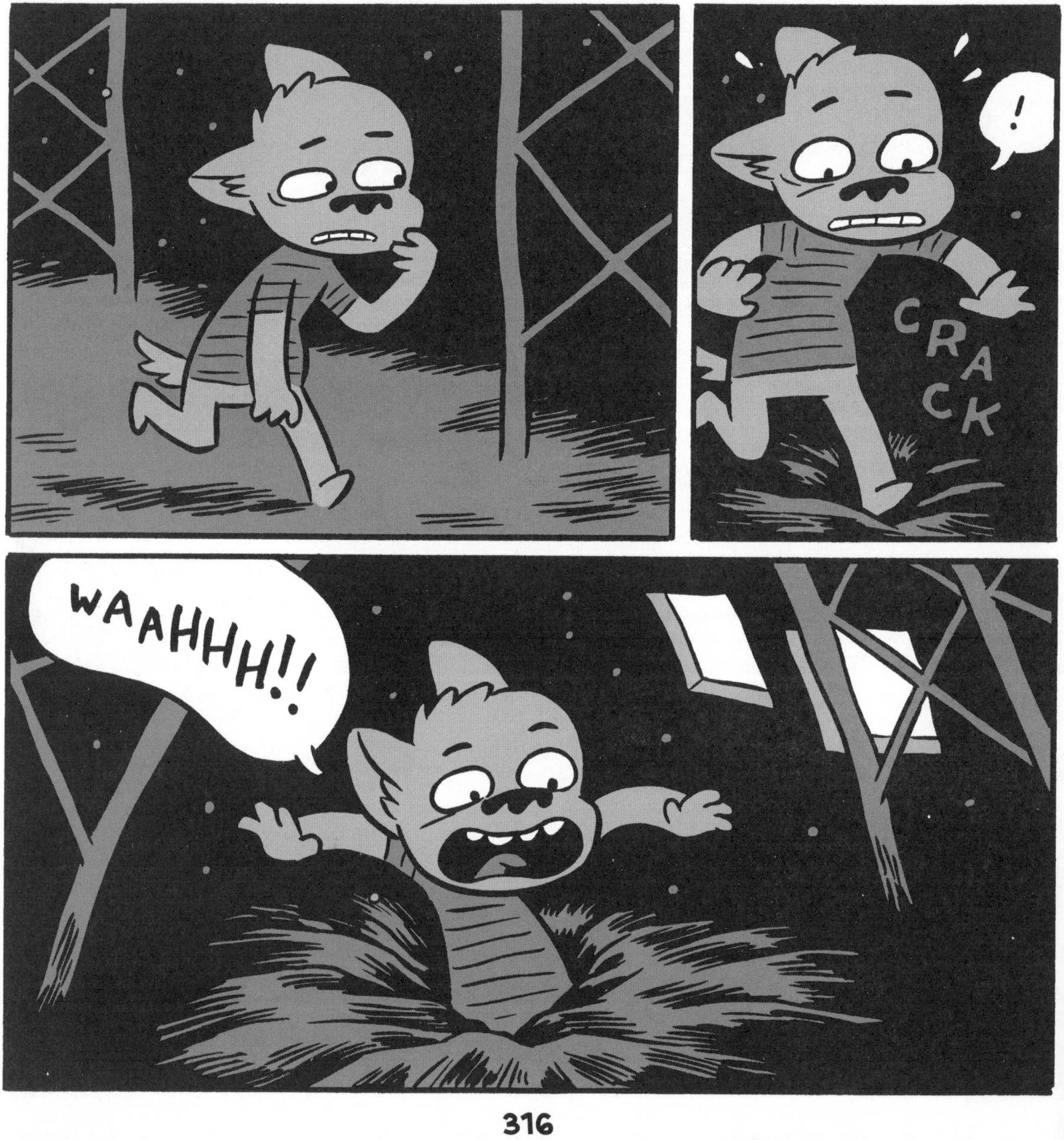
!
CRACK
WAAHHHH!!

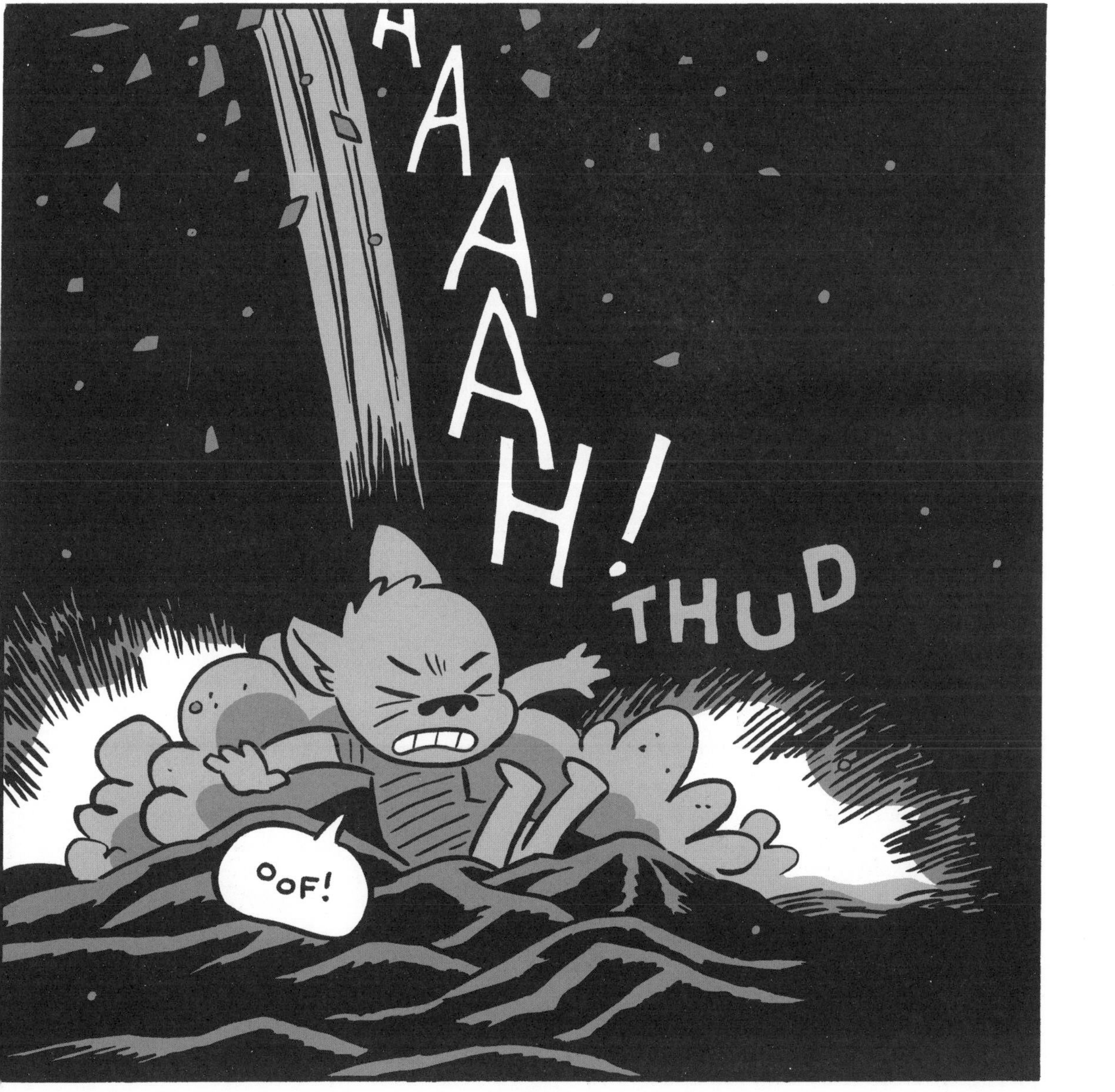
AAAAAH!
THUD
OOF!

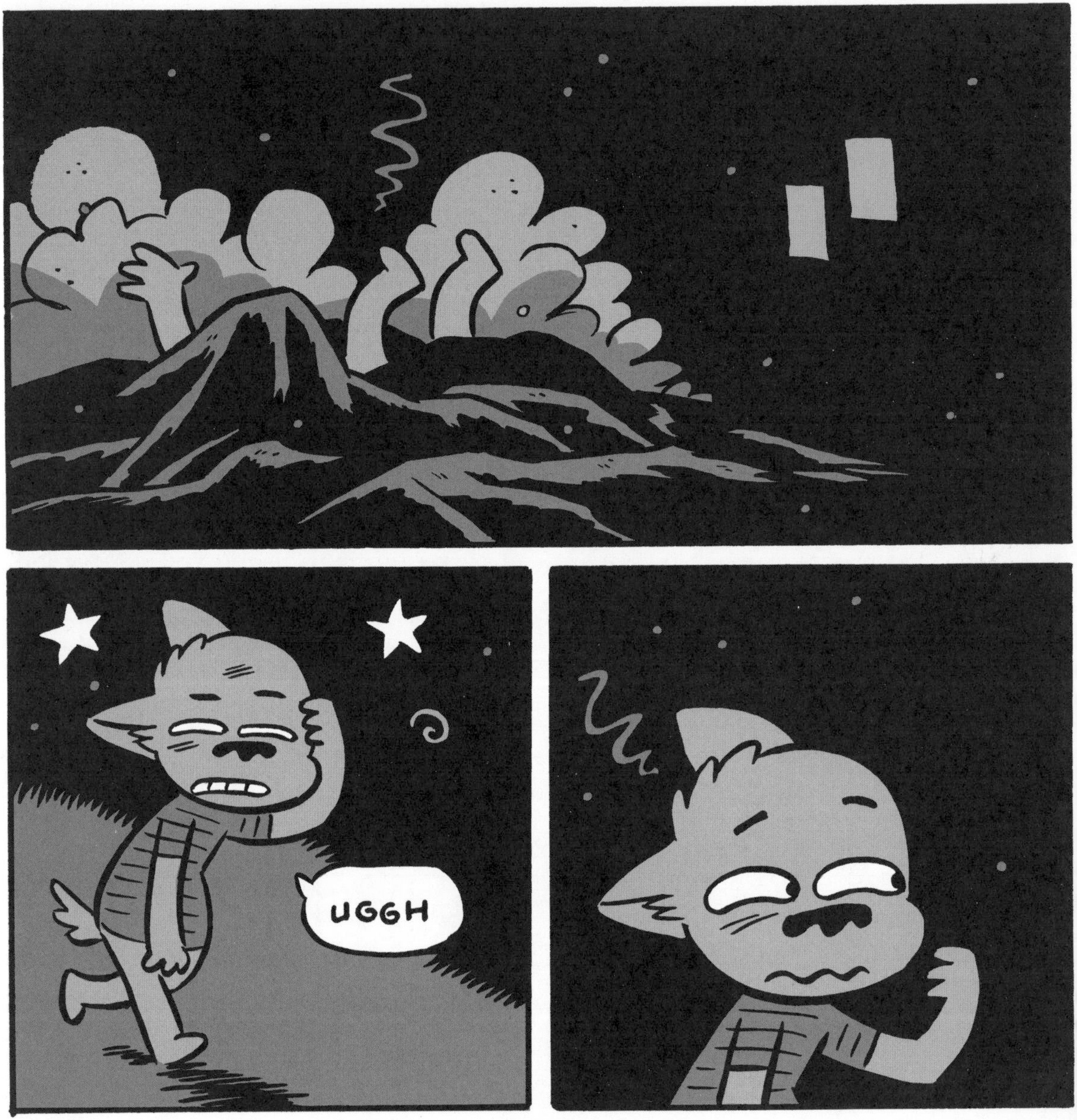
UGGH

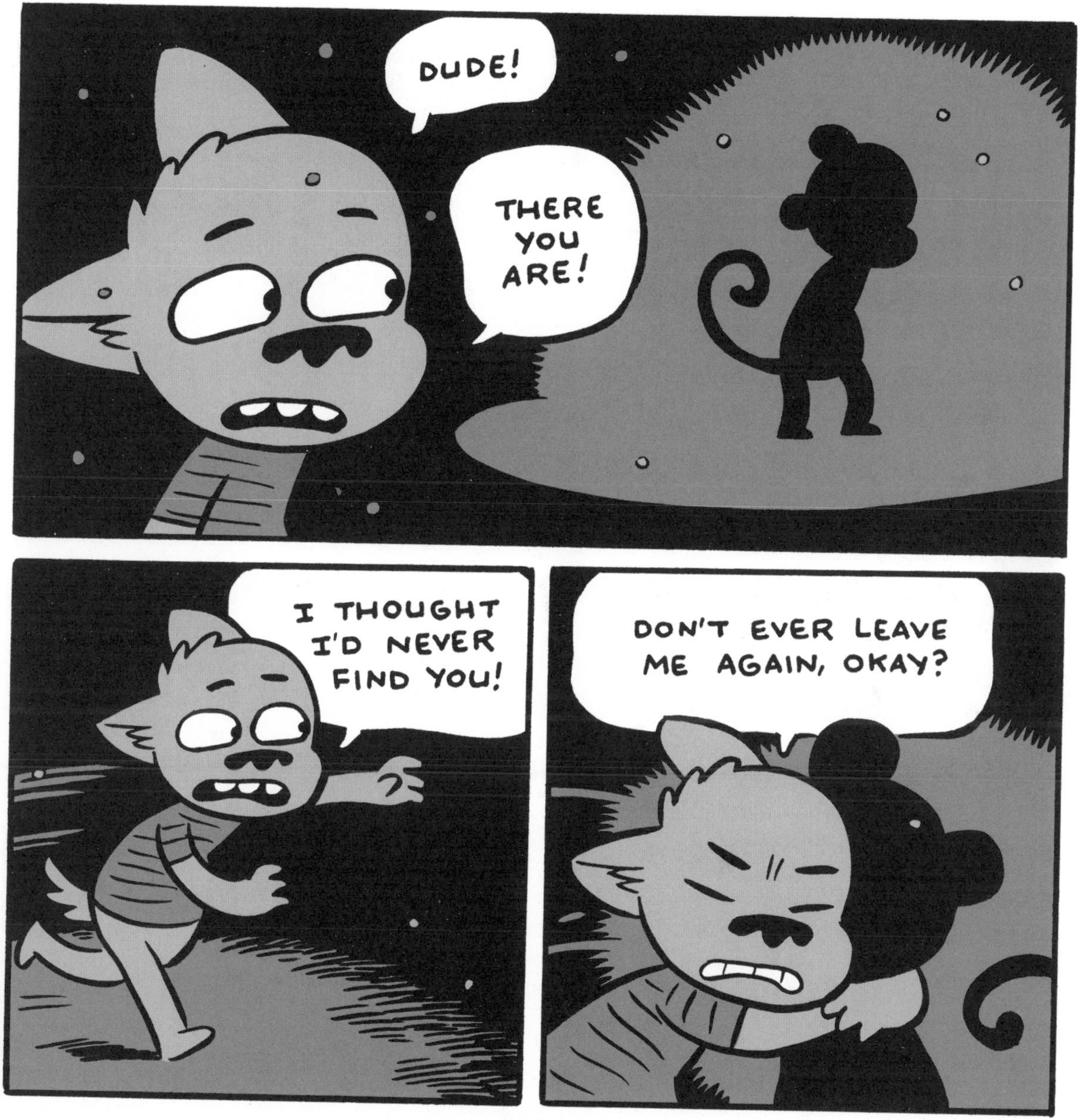
DUDE!
THERE YOU ARE!
I THOUGHT I'D NEVER FIND YOU!
DON'T EVER LEAVE ME AGAIN, OKAY?

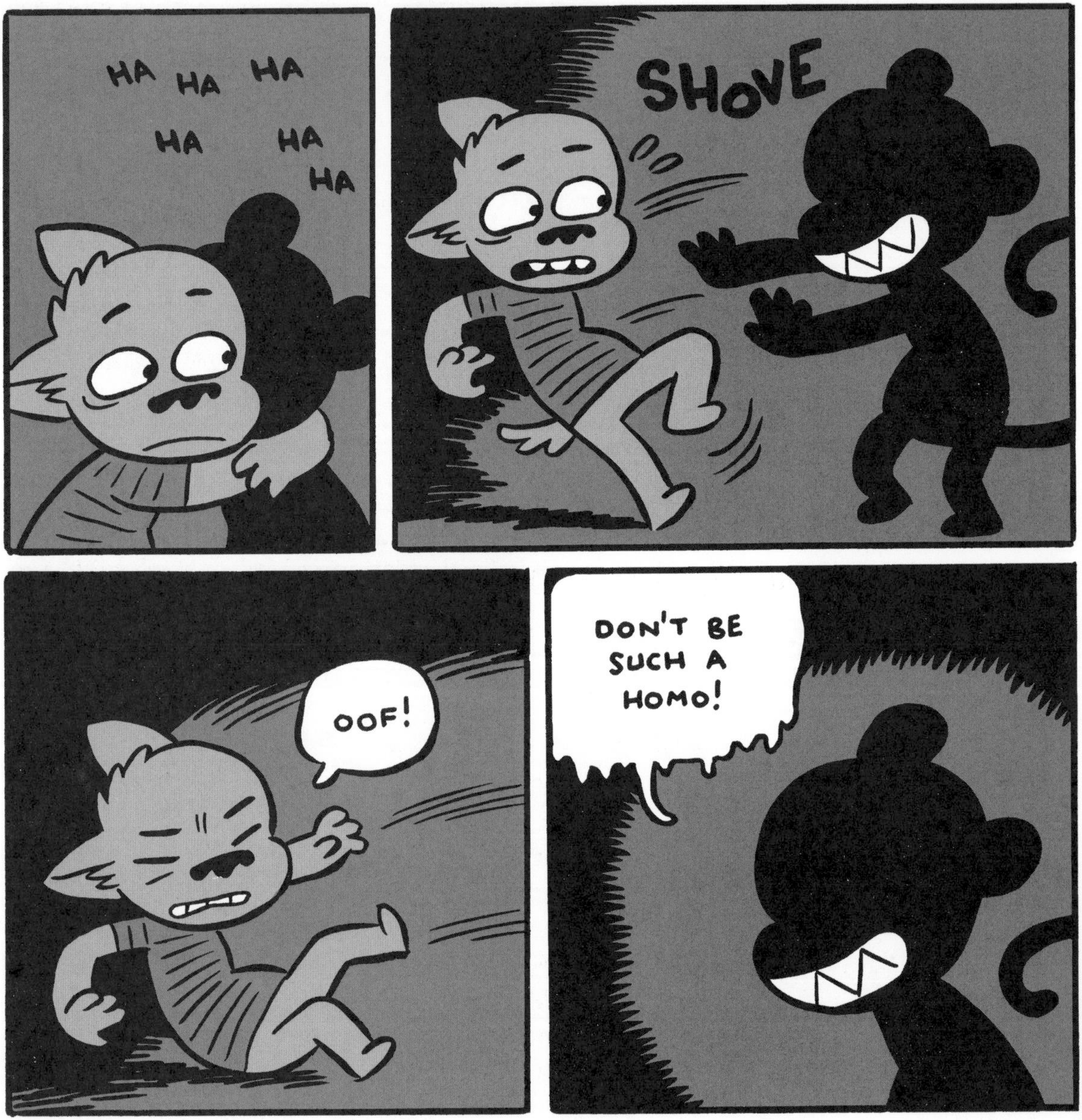
HA HA HA
HA HA
HA
SHOVE
OOF!
DON'T BE SUCH A HOMO!

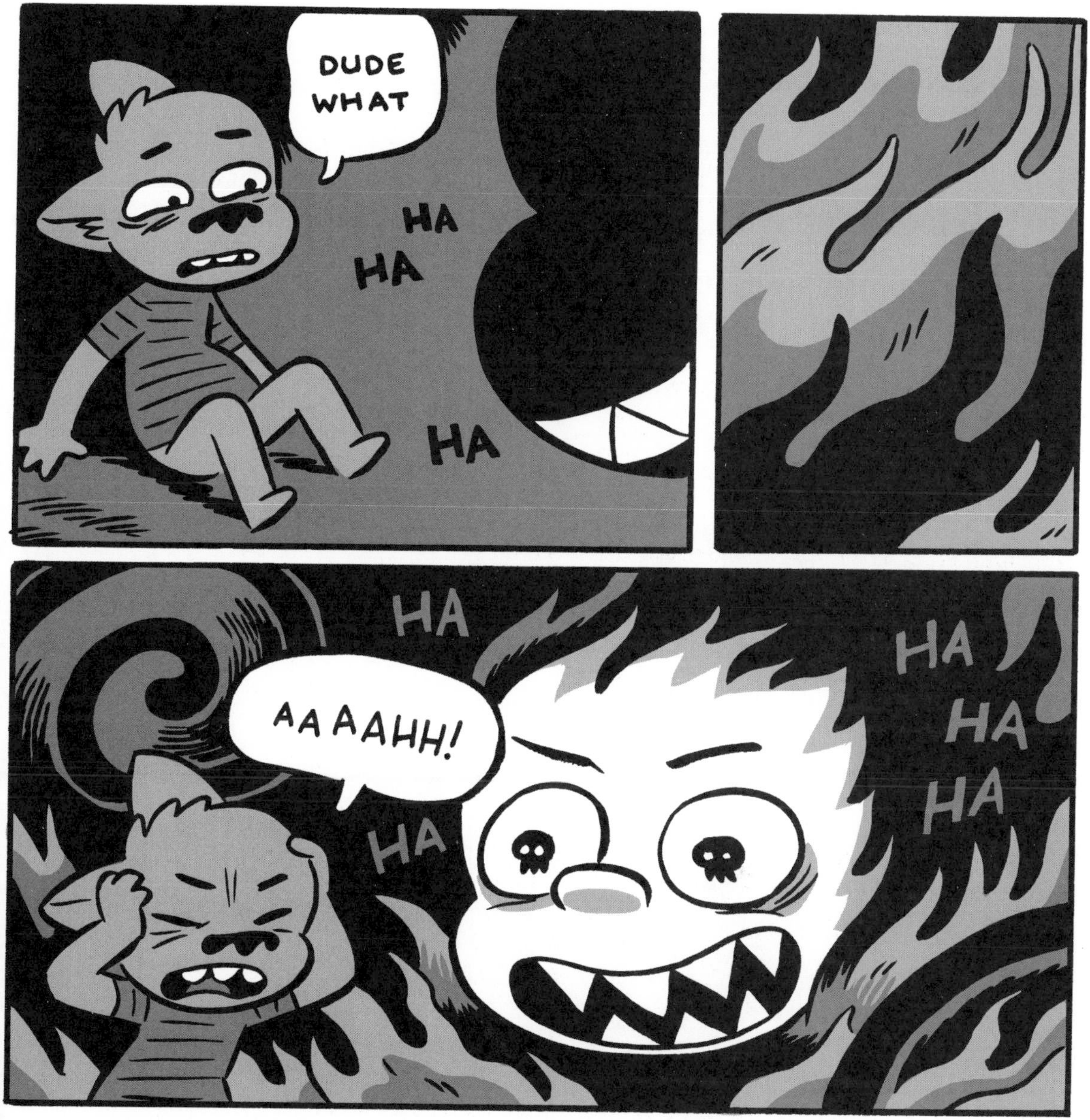
DUDE WHAT
HA
HA
HA
HA
AAAAHH!
HA
HA
HA
HA
HA

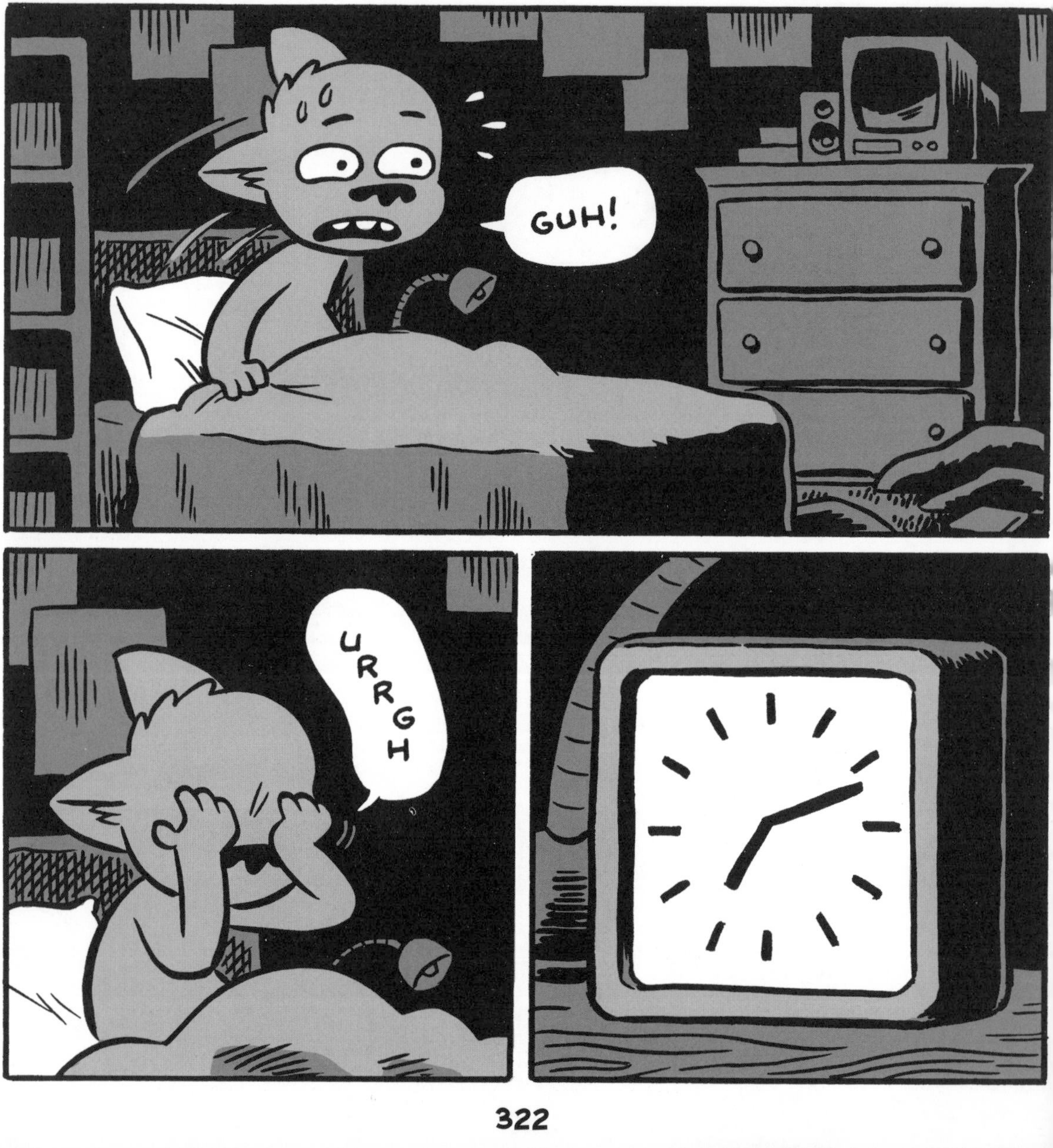
GUH!
URRGH

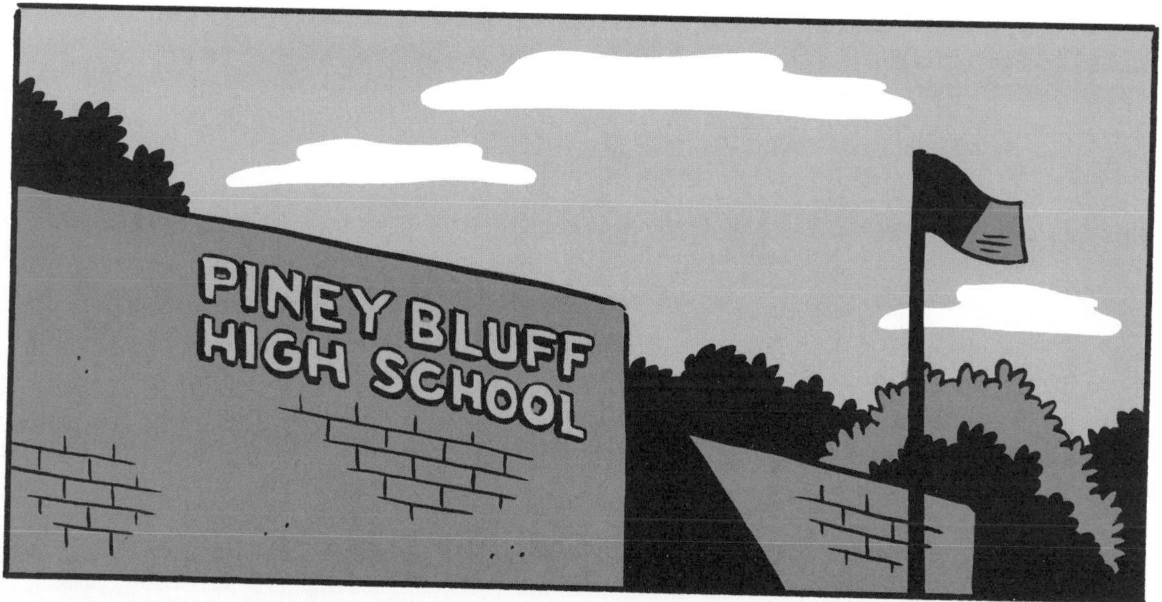
PINEY BLUFF
HIGH SCHOOL
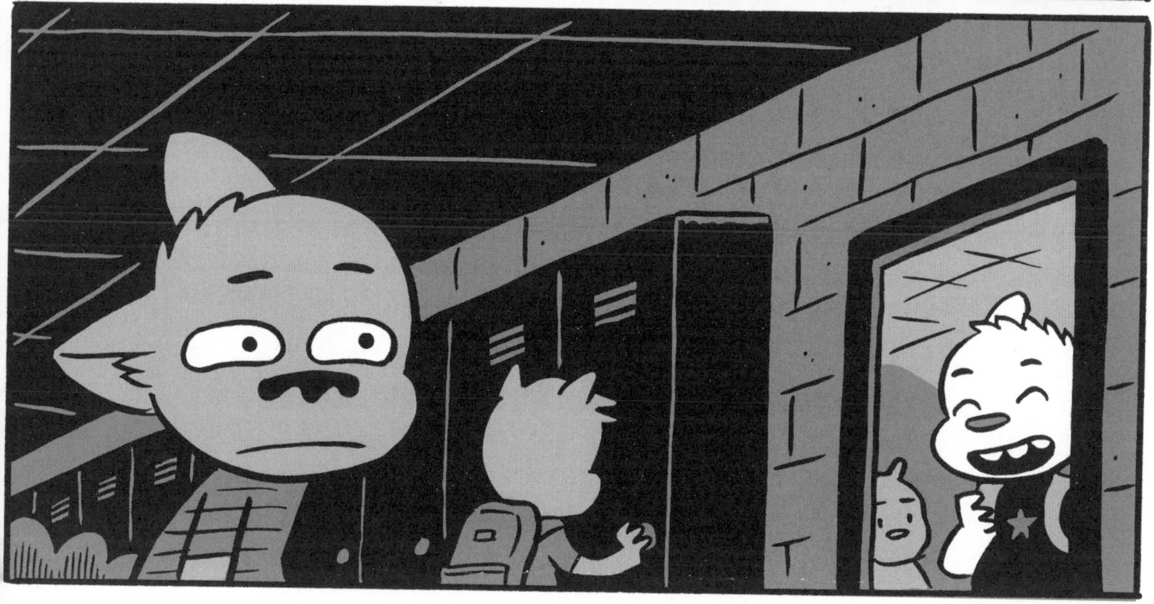

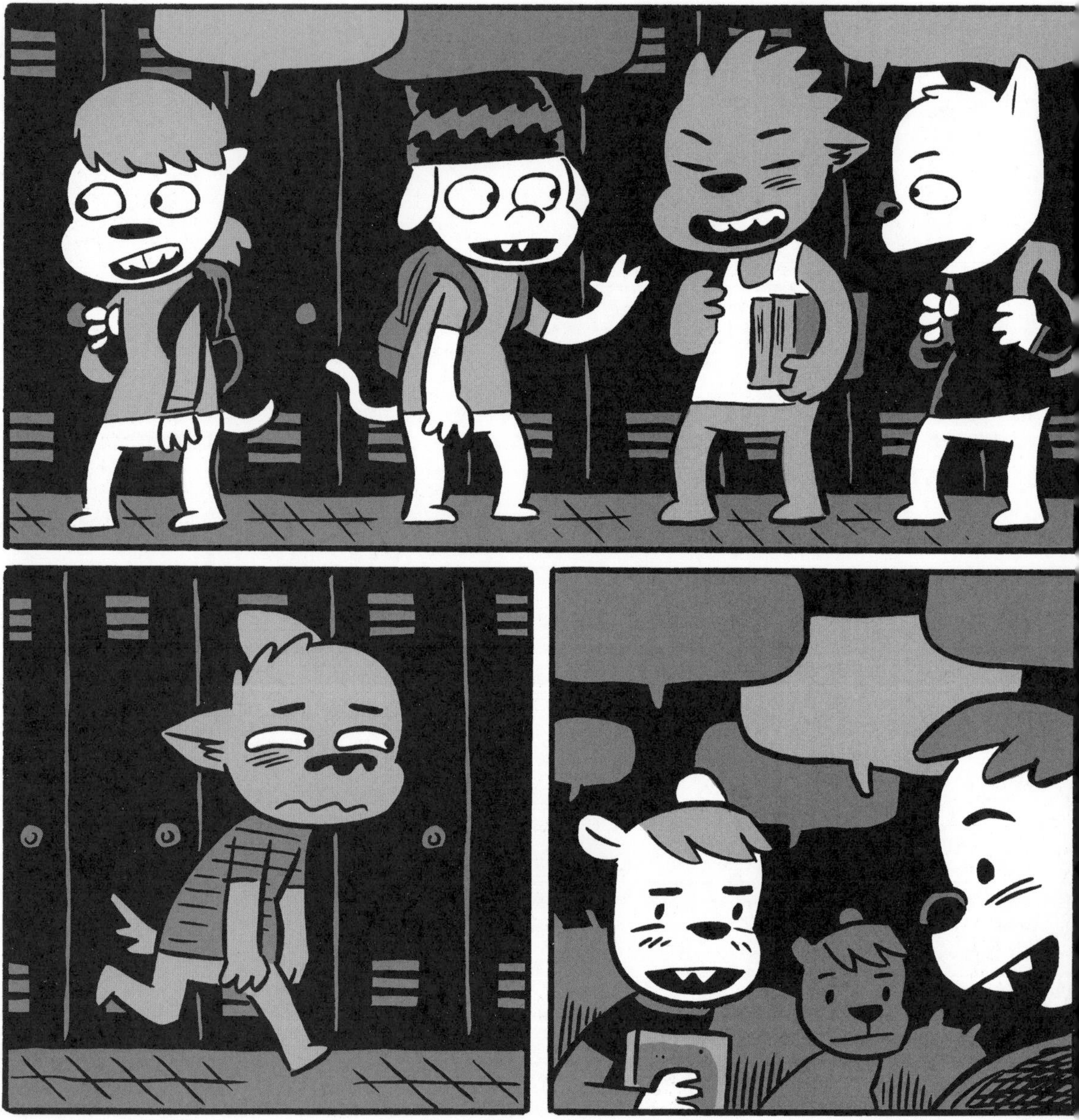

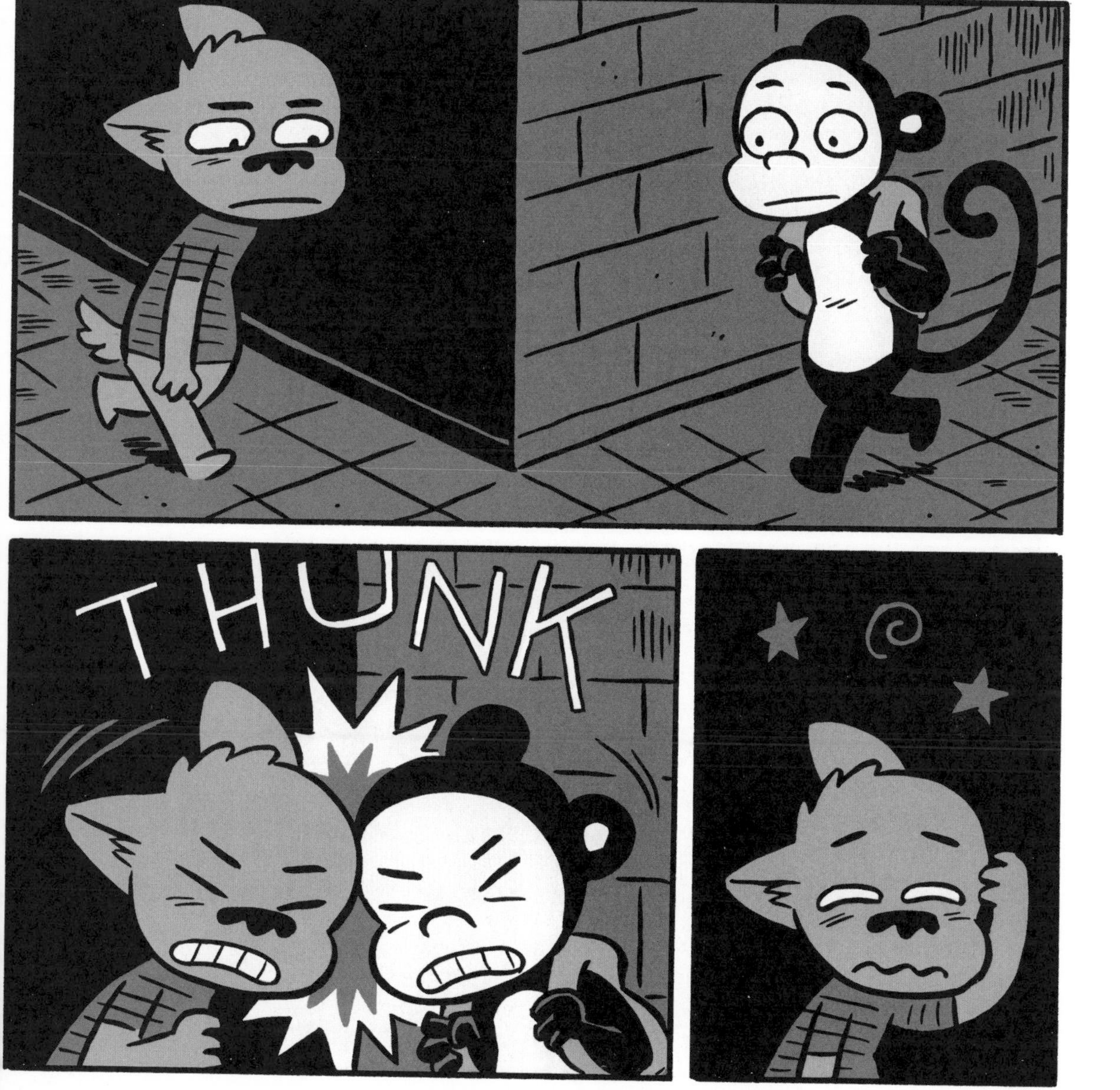
THUNK

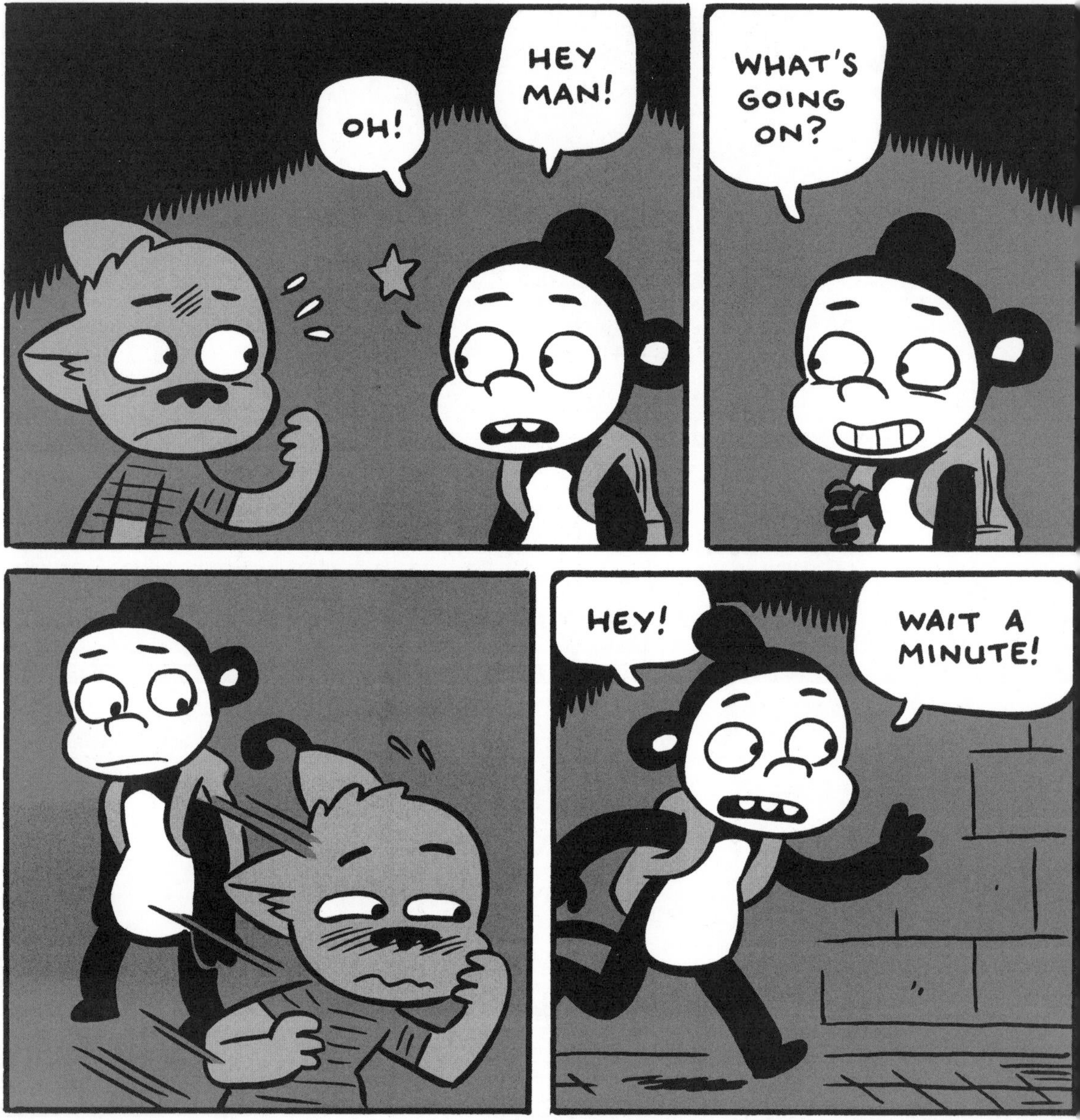
OH!
HEY MAN!
WHAT'S GOING ON?
HEY!
WAIT A MINUTE!

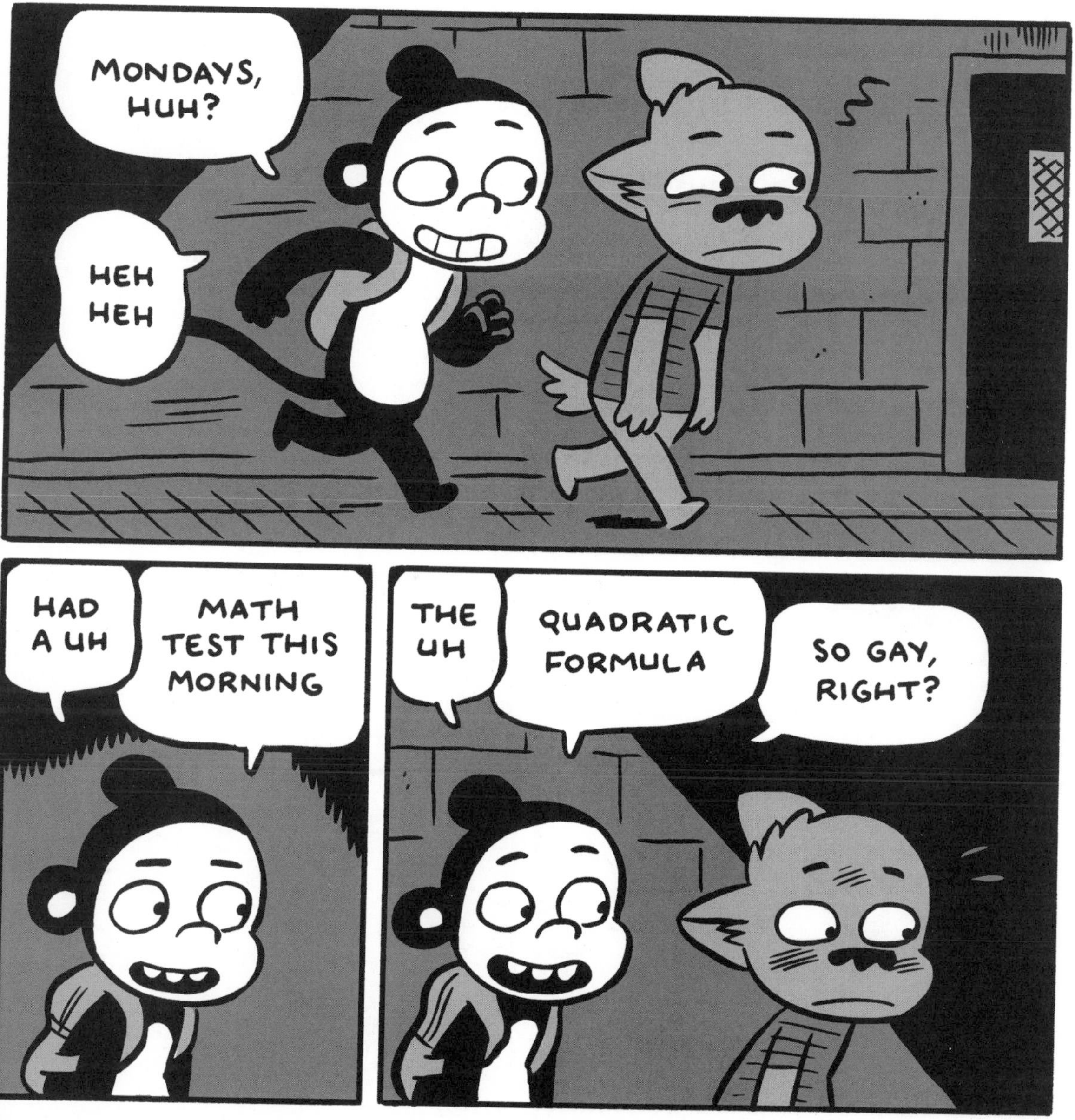
MONDAYS, HUH?
HEH HEH
HAD A UH
MATH TEST THIS MORNING
THE UH
QUADRATIC FORMULA
SO GAY, RIGHT?

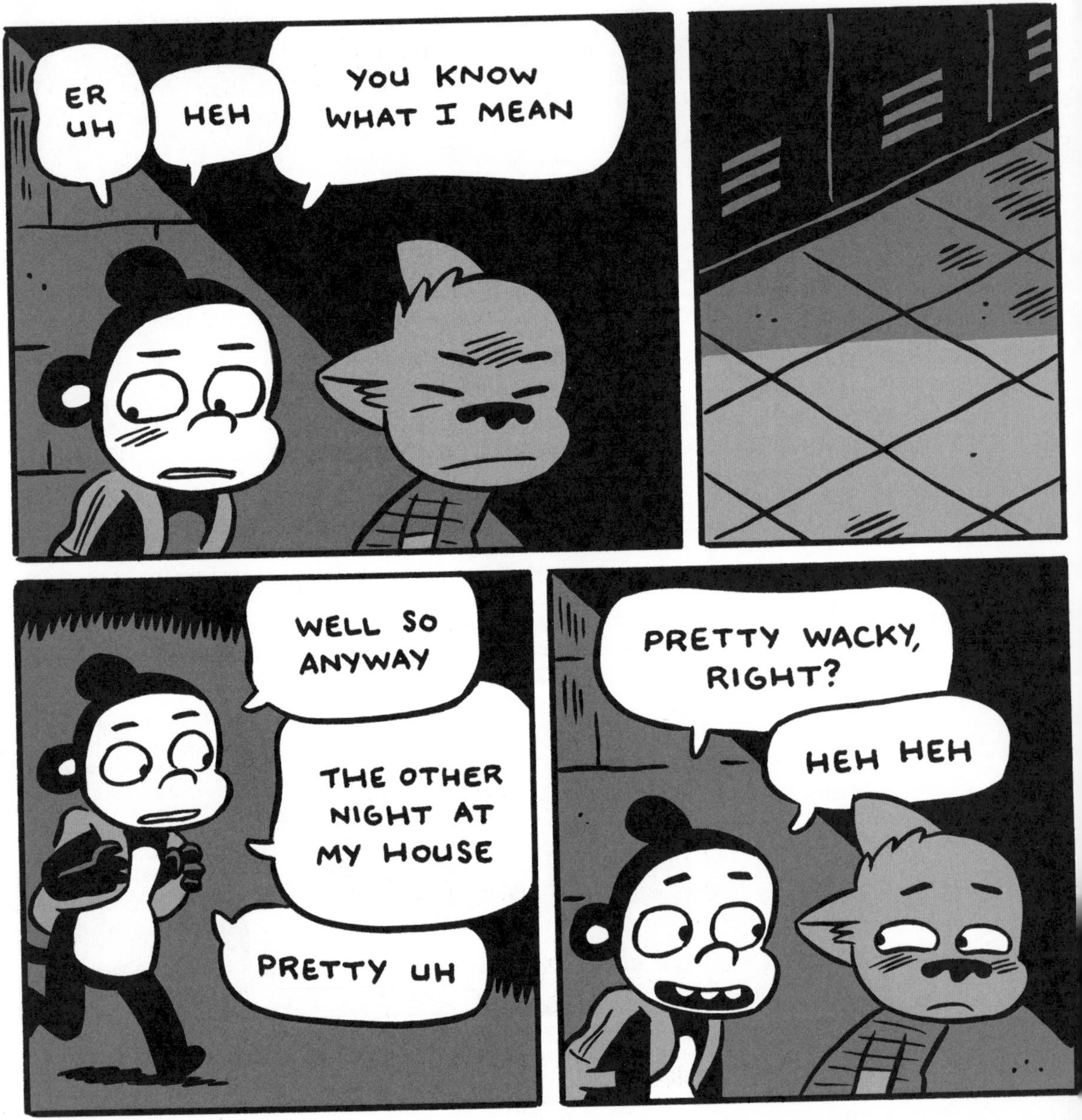
ER
UH
HEH
YOU KNOW WHAT I MEAN
WELL SO ANYWAY
THE OTHER NIGHT AT MY HOUSE
PRETTY UH
PRETTY WACKY, RIGHT?
HEH HEH

MAYBE WACKY ISN'T THE RIGHT WORD
BUT LIKE DEFINITELY SURPRISING
I'LL ADMIT THAT I WAS SURPRISED

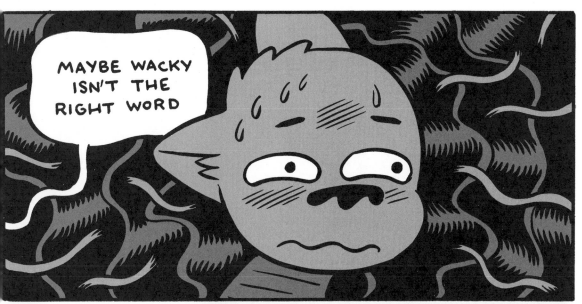

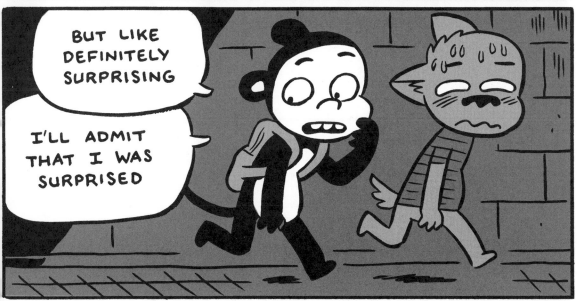

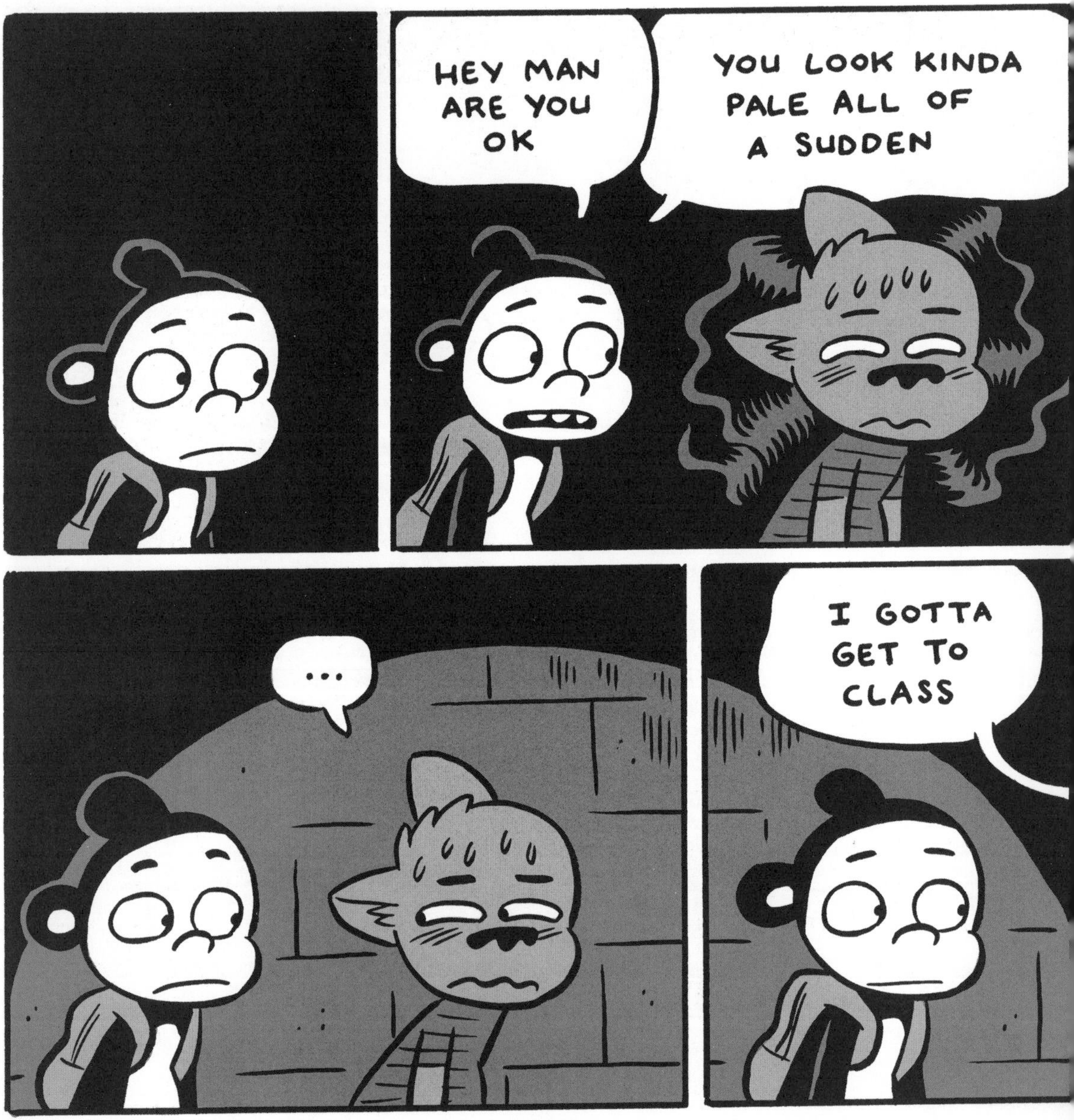
HEY MAN
ARE YOU
OK
YOU LOOK KINDA
PALE ALL OF
A SUDDEN
...
I GOTTA
GET TO
CLASS

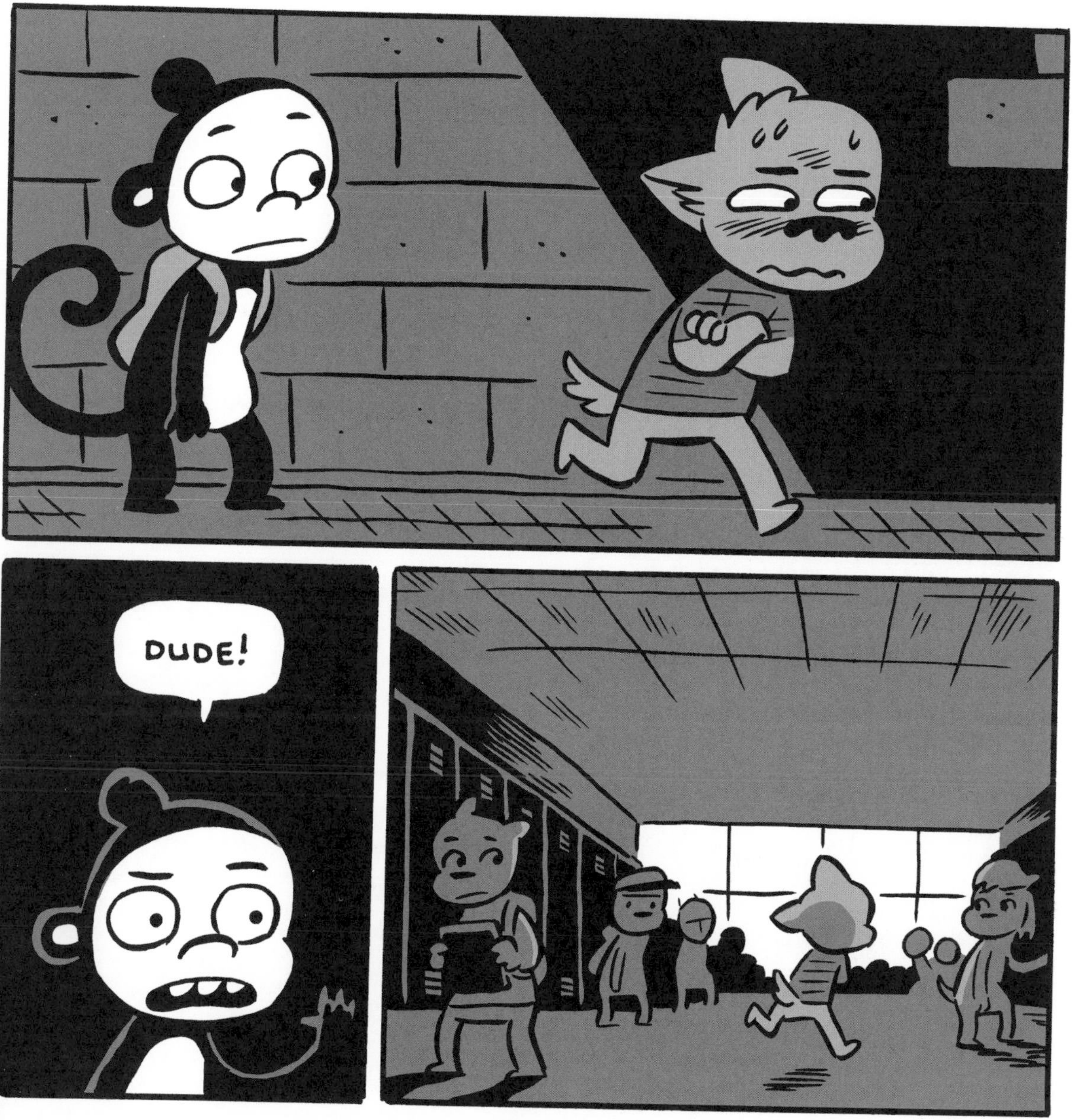
DUDE!

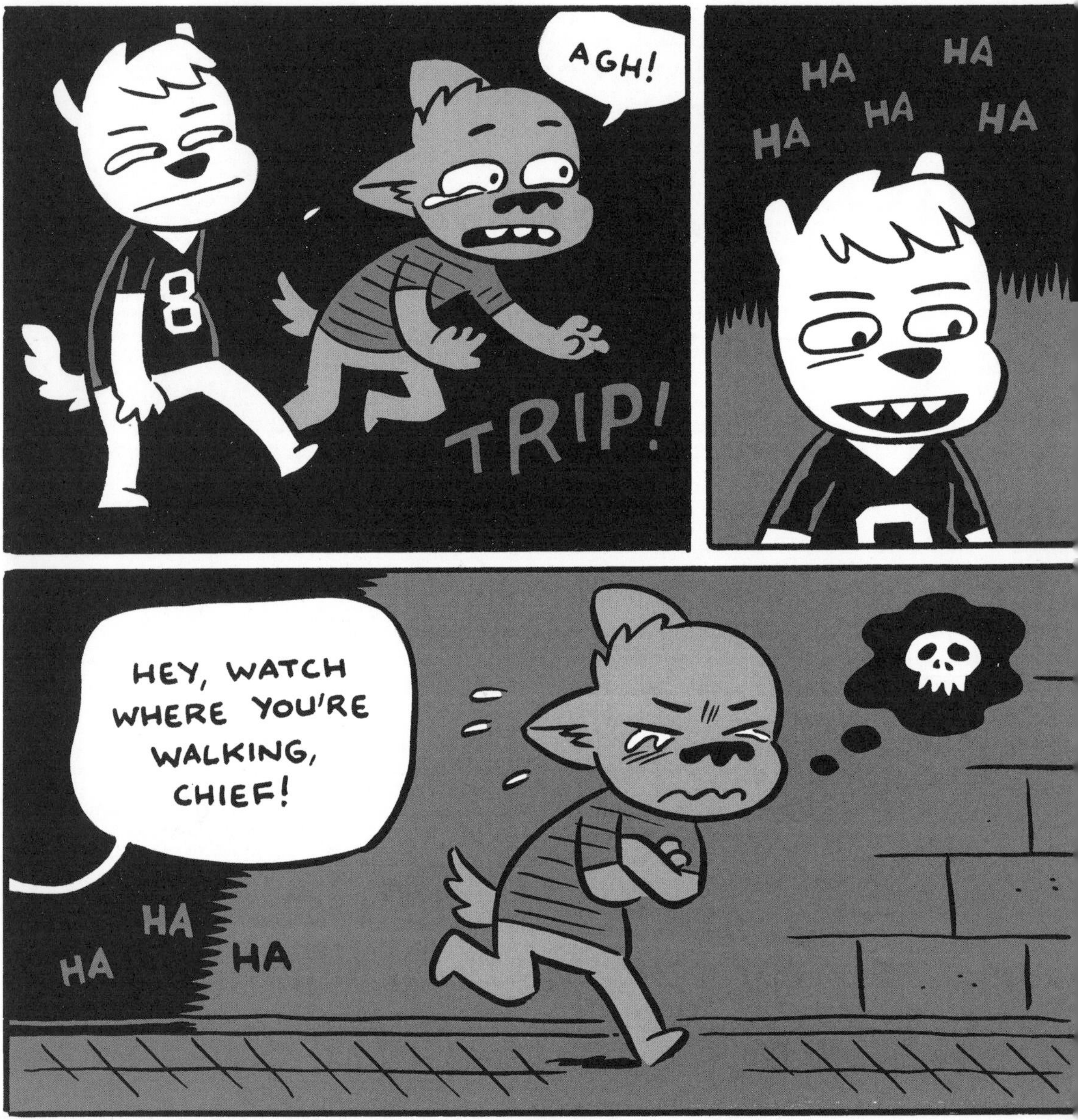
AGH!
TRIP!
HA HA HA HA HA
HEY, WATCH WHERE YOU'RE WALKING, CHIEF!
HA HA HA

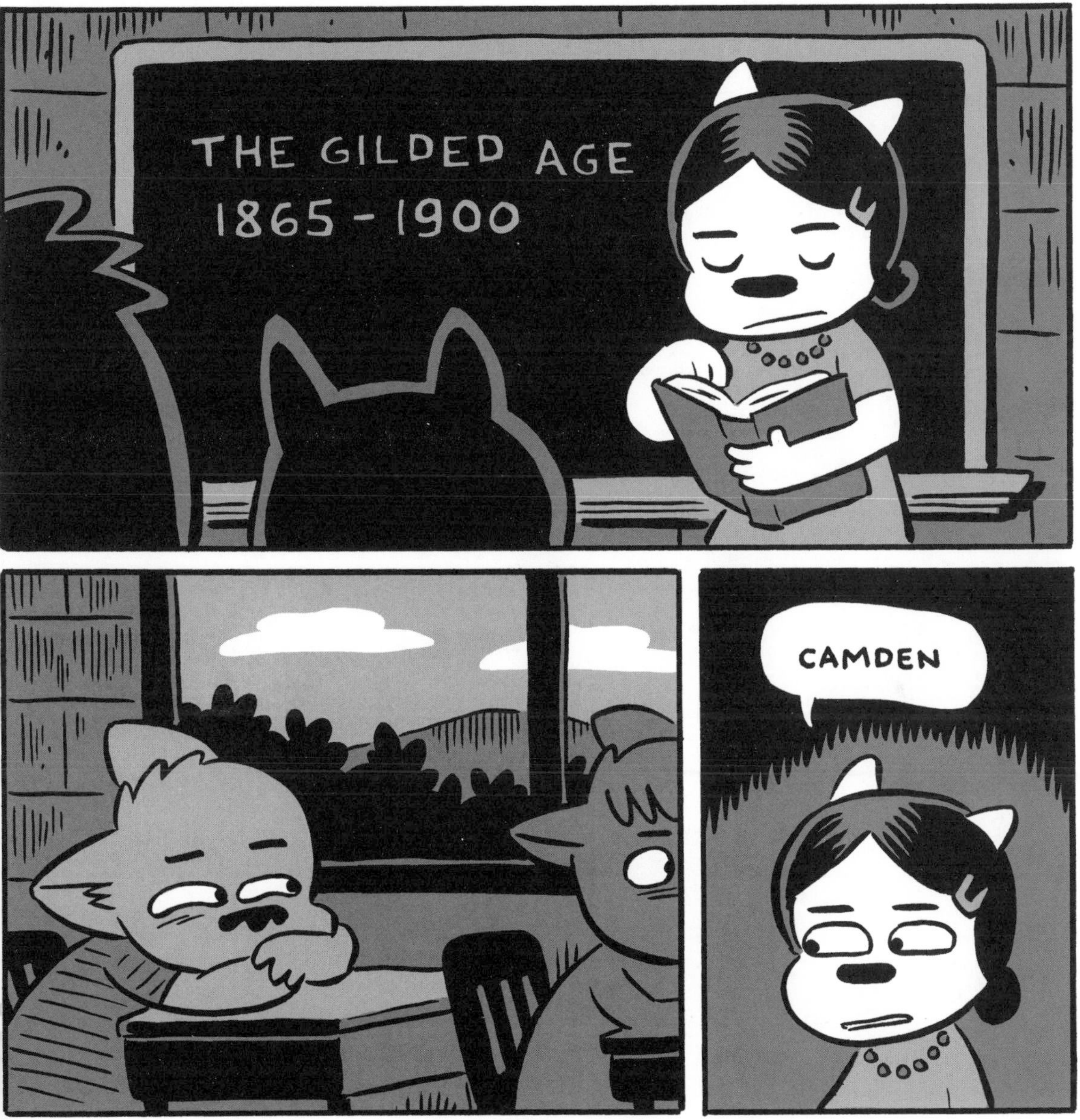
THE GILDED AGE
1865 - 1900
CAMDEN

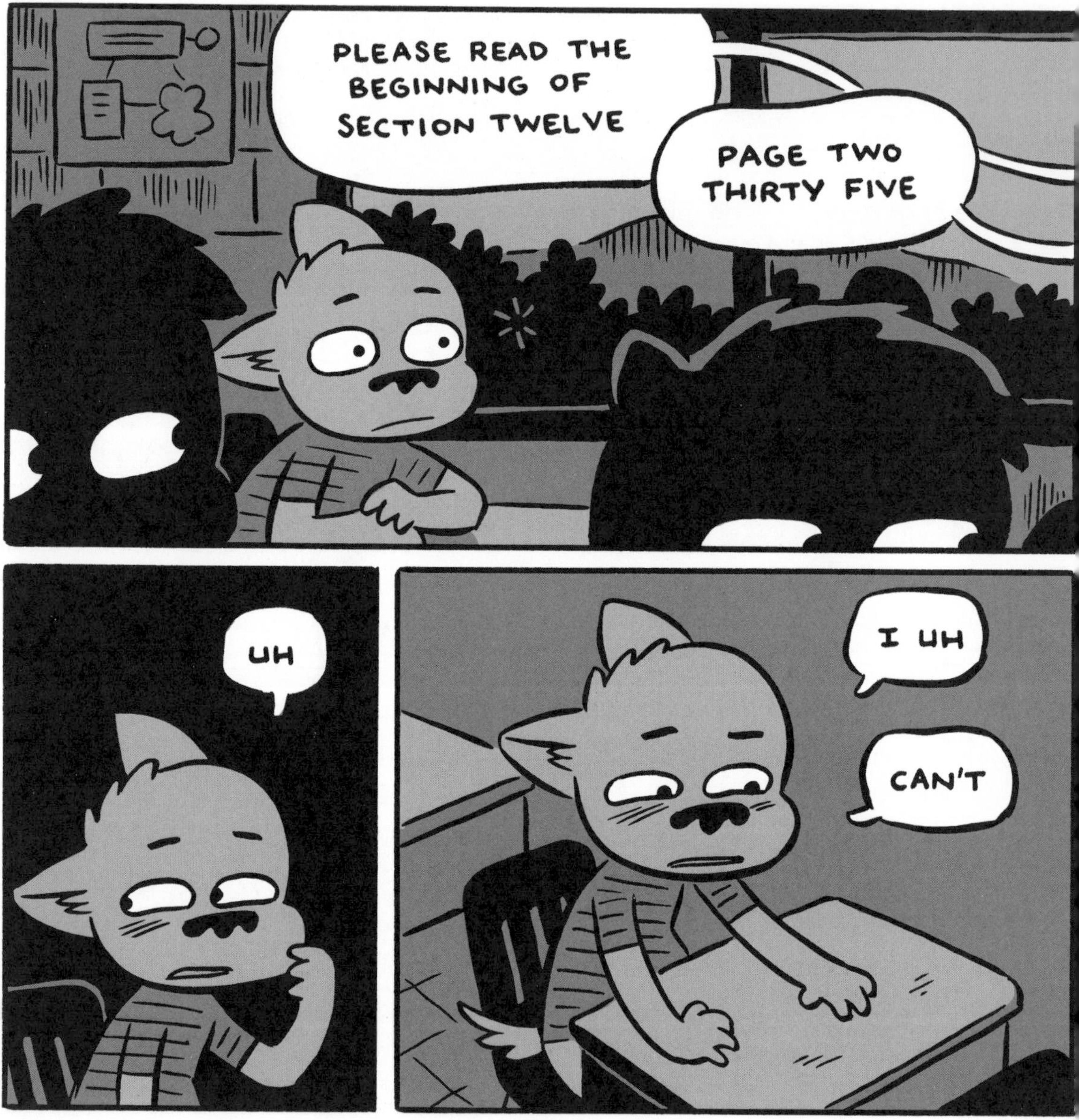
PLEASE READ THE BEGINNING OF SECTION TWELVE
PAGE TWO THIRTY FIVE
UH
I UH
CAN'T

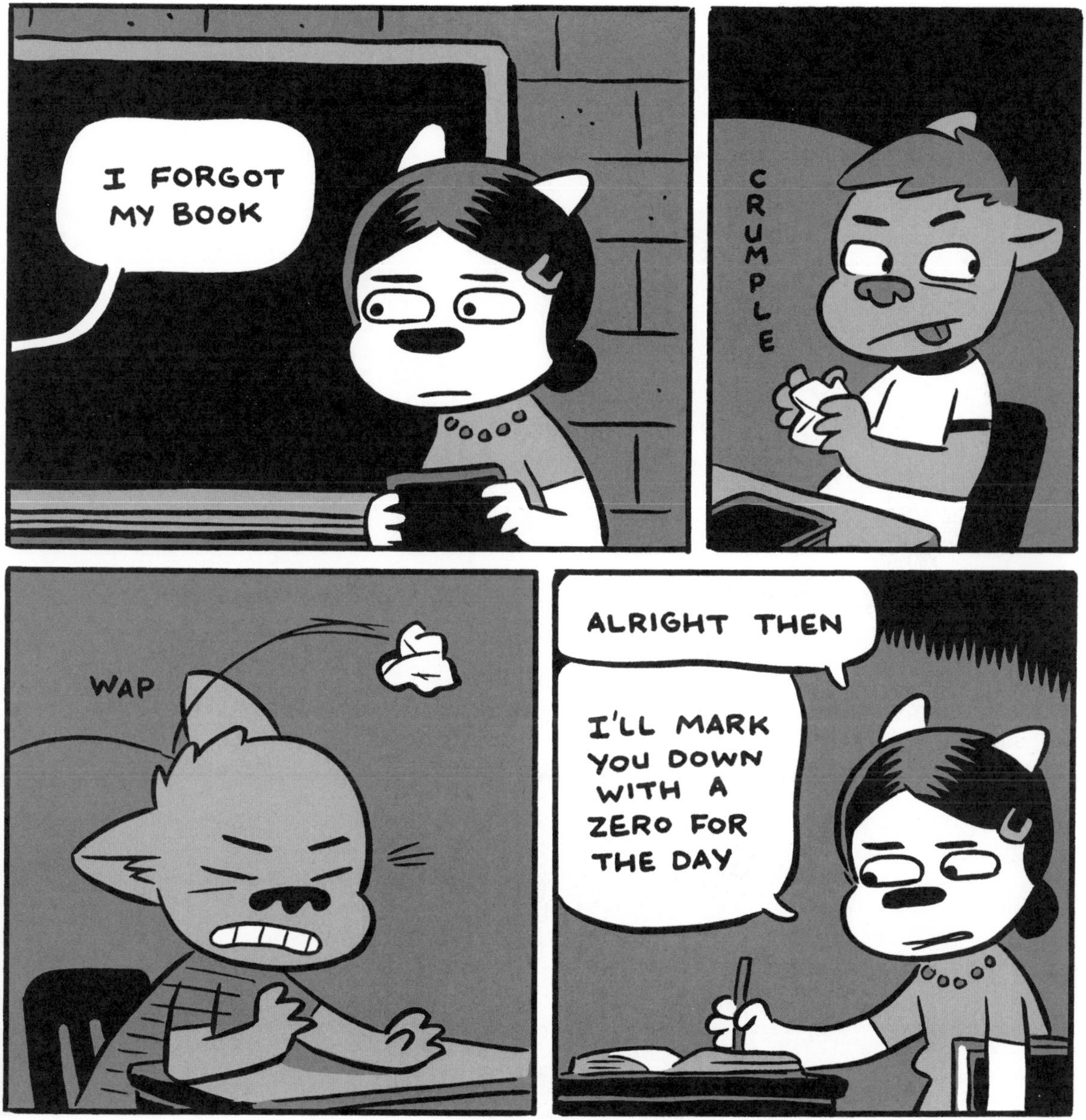
I FORGOT MY BOOK
CRUMPLE
WAP
ALRIGHT THEN
I'LL MARK YOU DOWN WITH A ZERO FOR THE DAY

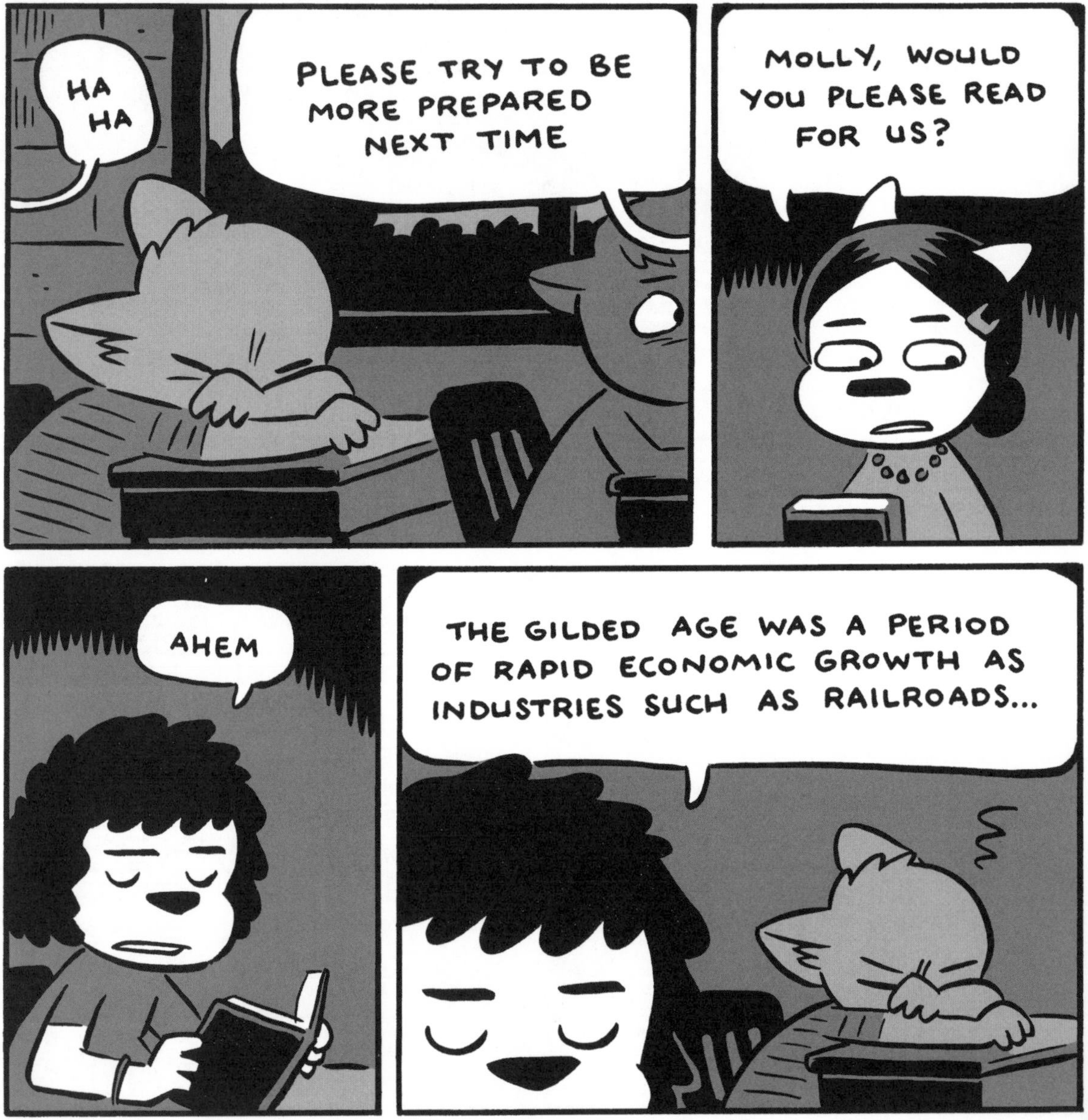
HA HA
PLEASE TRY TO BE MORE PREPARED NEXT TIME
MOLLY, WOULD YOU PLEASE READ FOR US?
AHEM
THE GILDED AGE WAS A PERIOD OF RAPID ECONOMIC GROWTH AS INDUSTRIES SUCH AS RAILROADS...

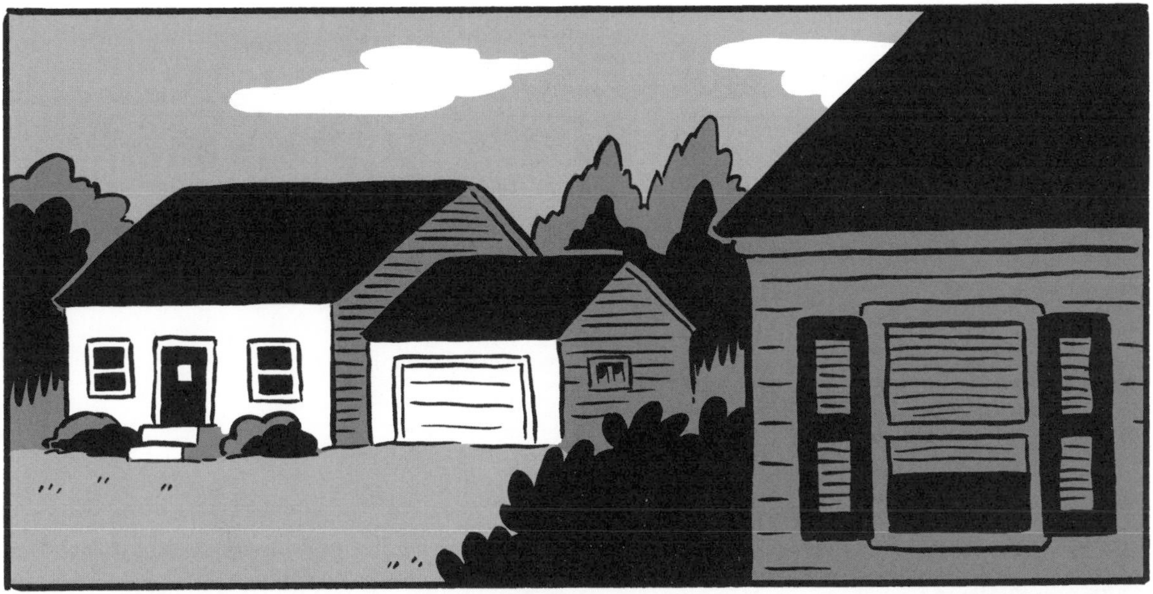

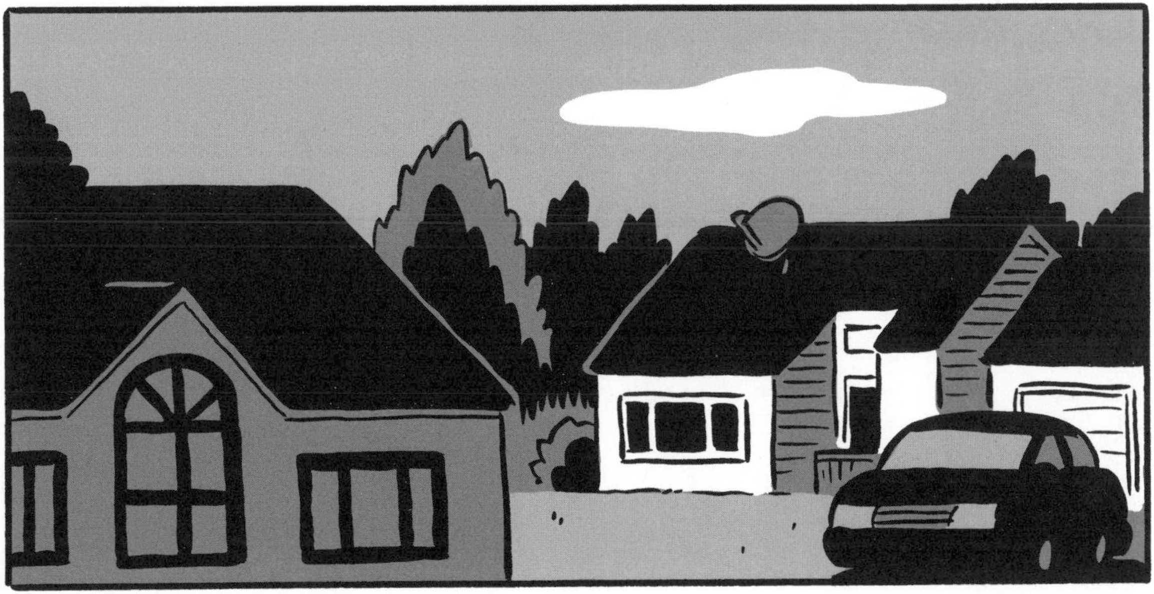

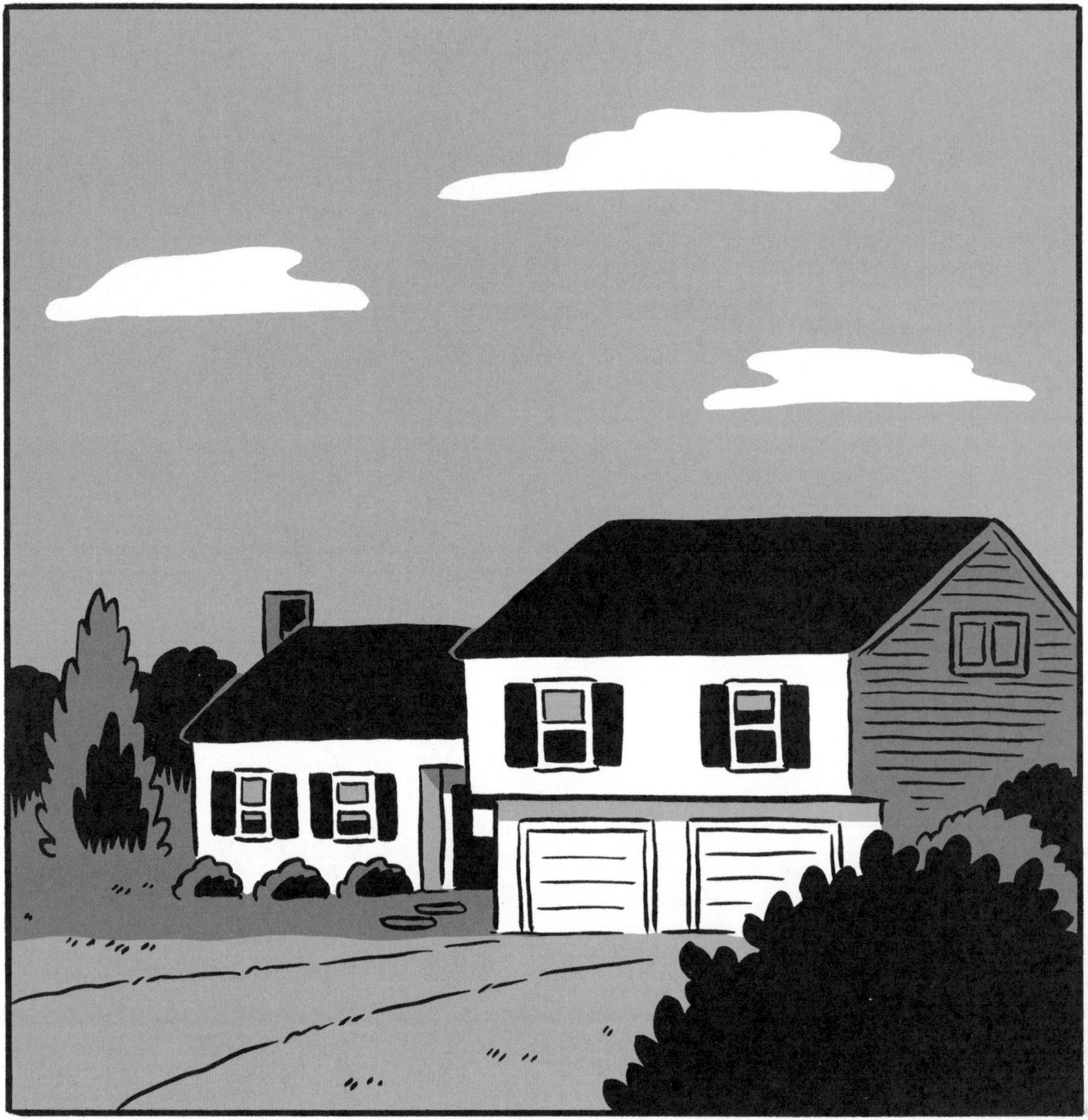

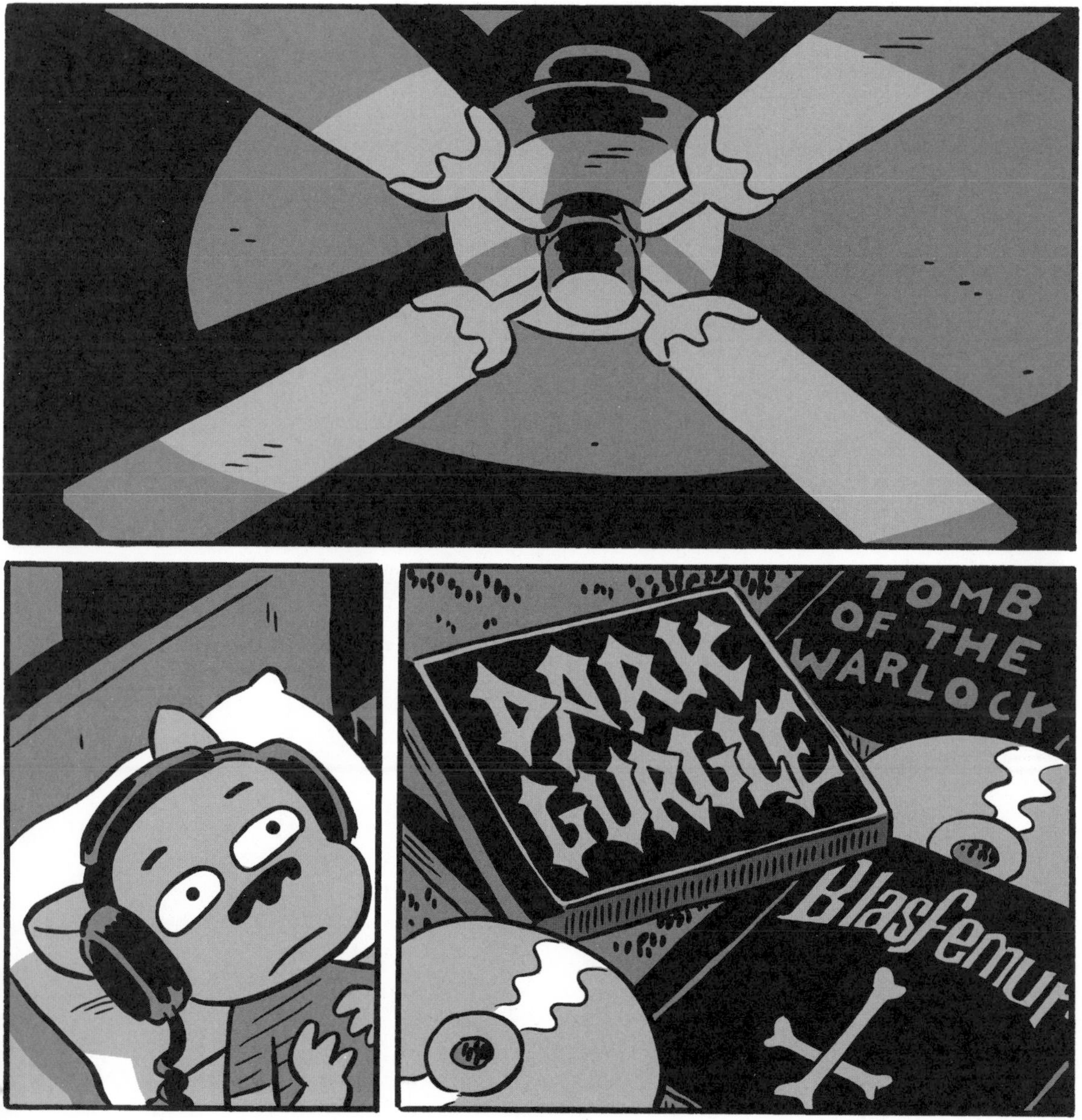
DARK GURGLE
TOMB OF THE WARLOCK
Blasfemur

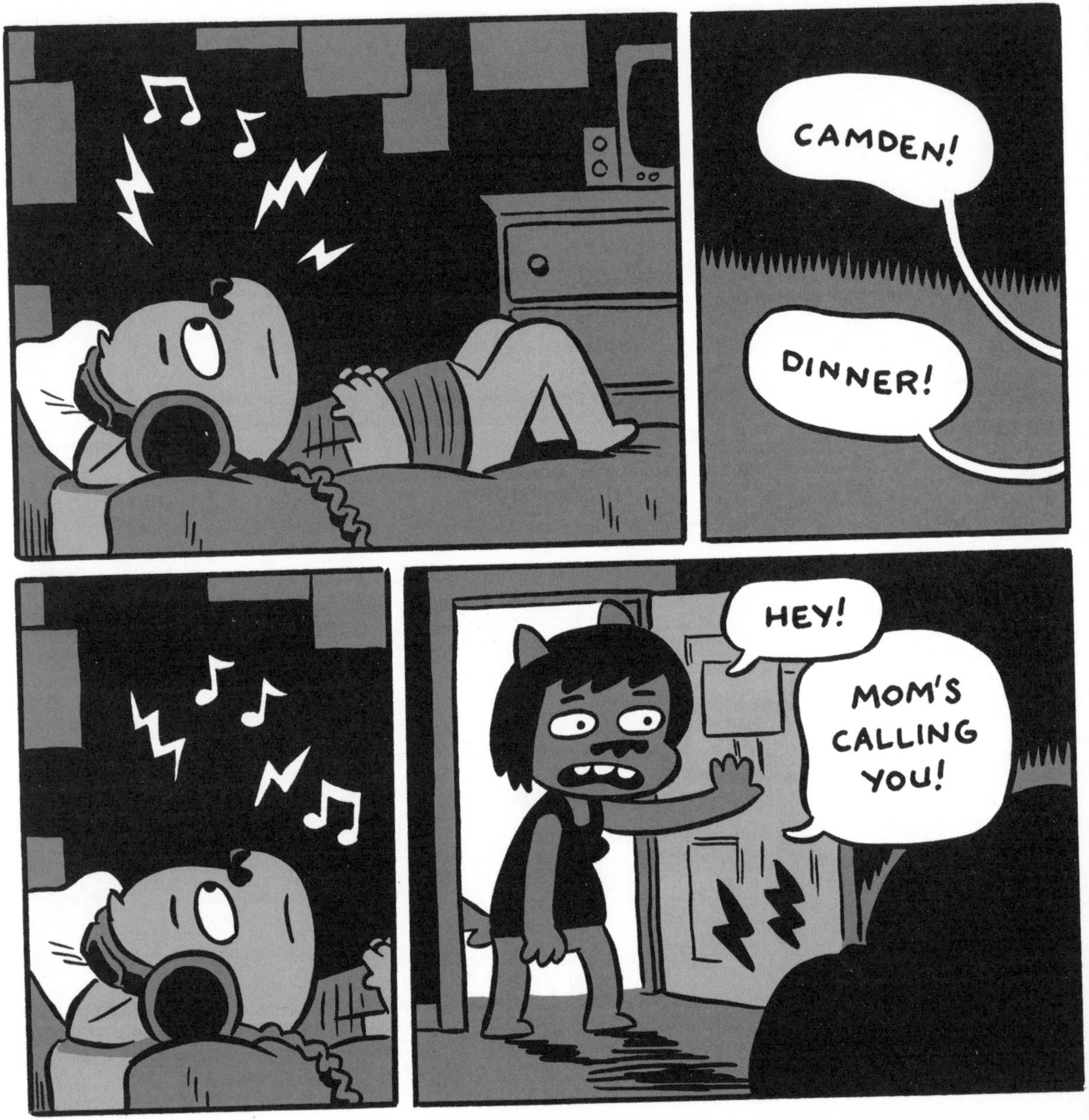
CAMDEN!
DINNER!
HEY!
MOM'S CALLING YOU!

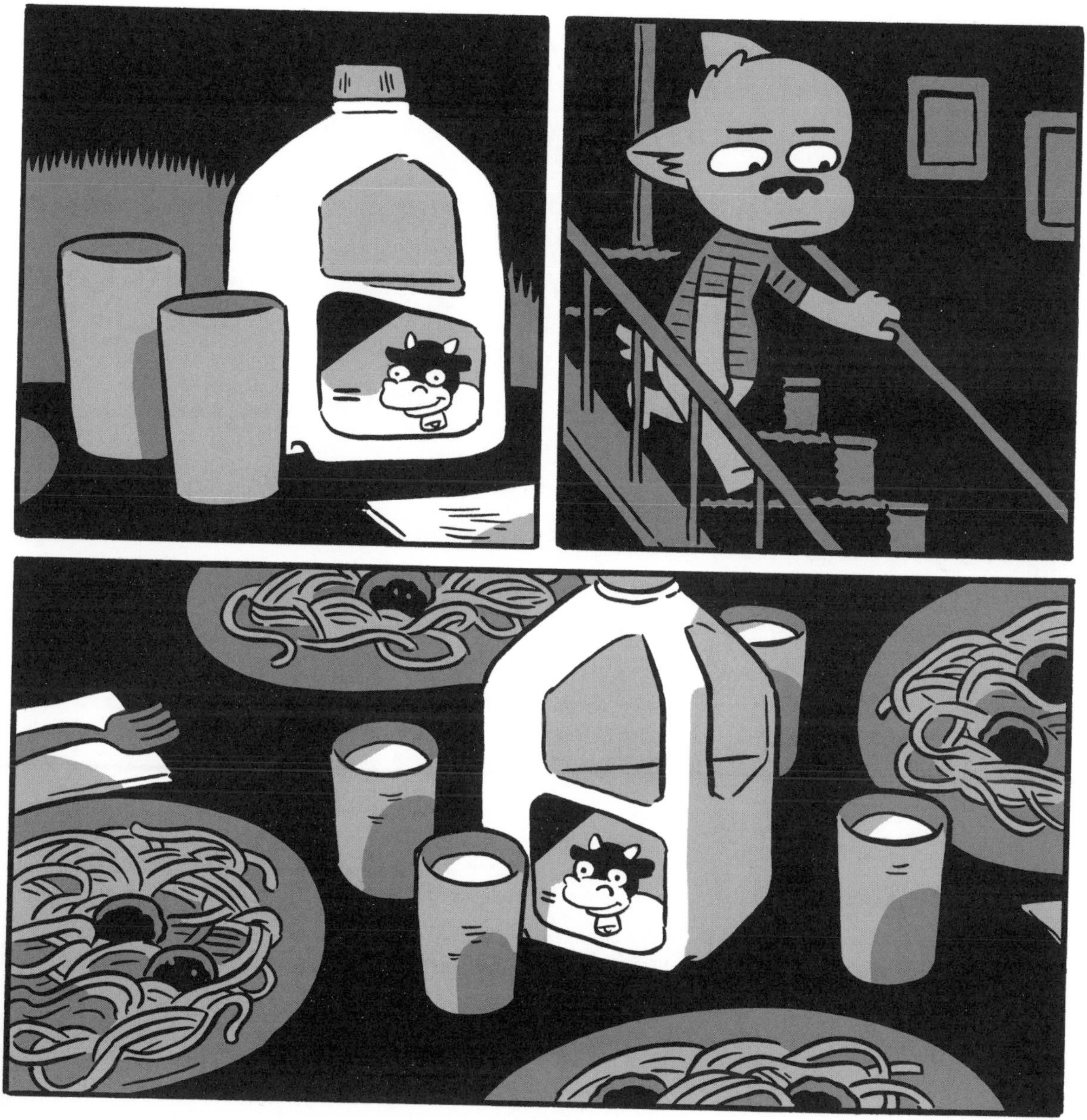

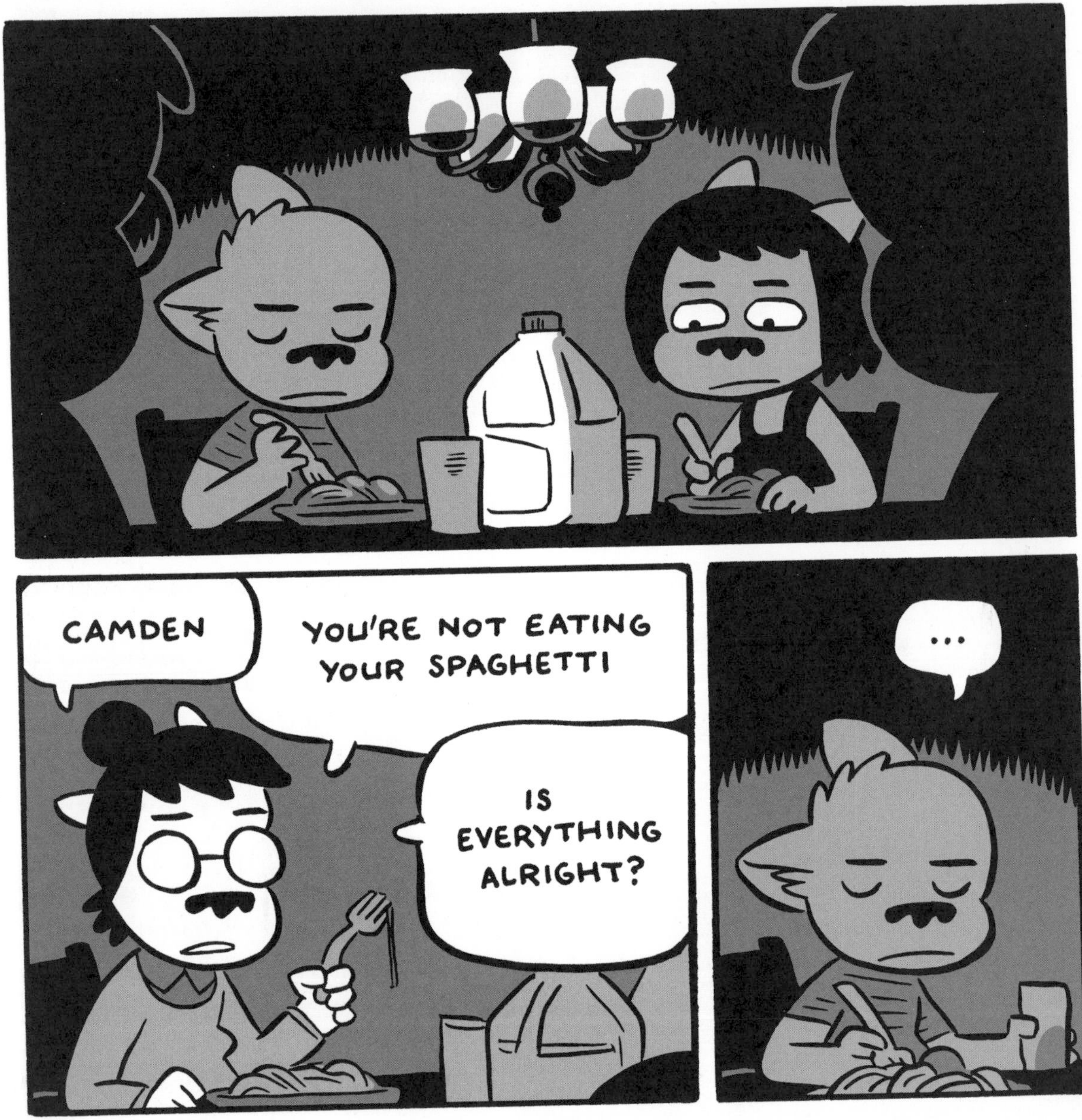
CAMDEN
YOU'RE NOT EATING YOUR SPAGHETTI
IS EVERYTHING ALRIGHT?
...

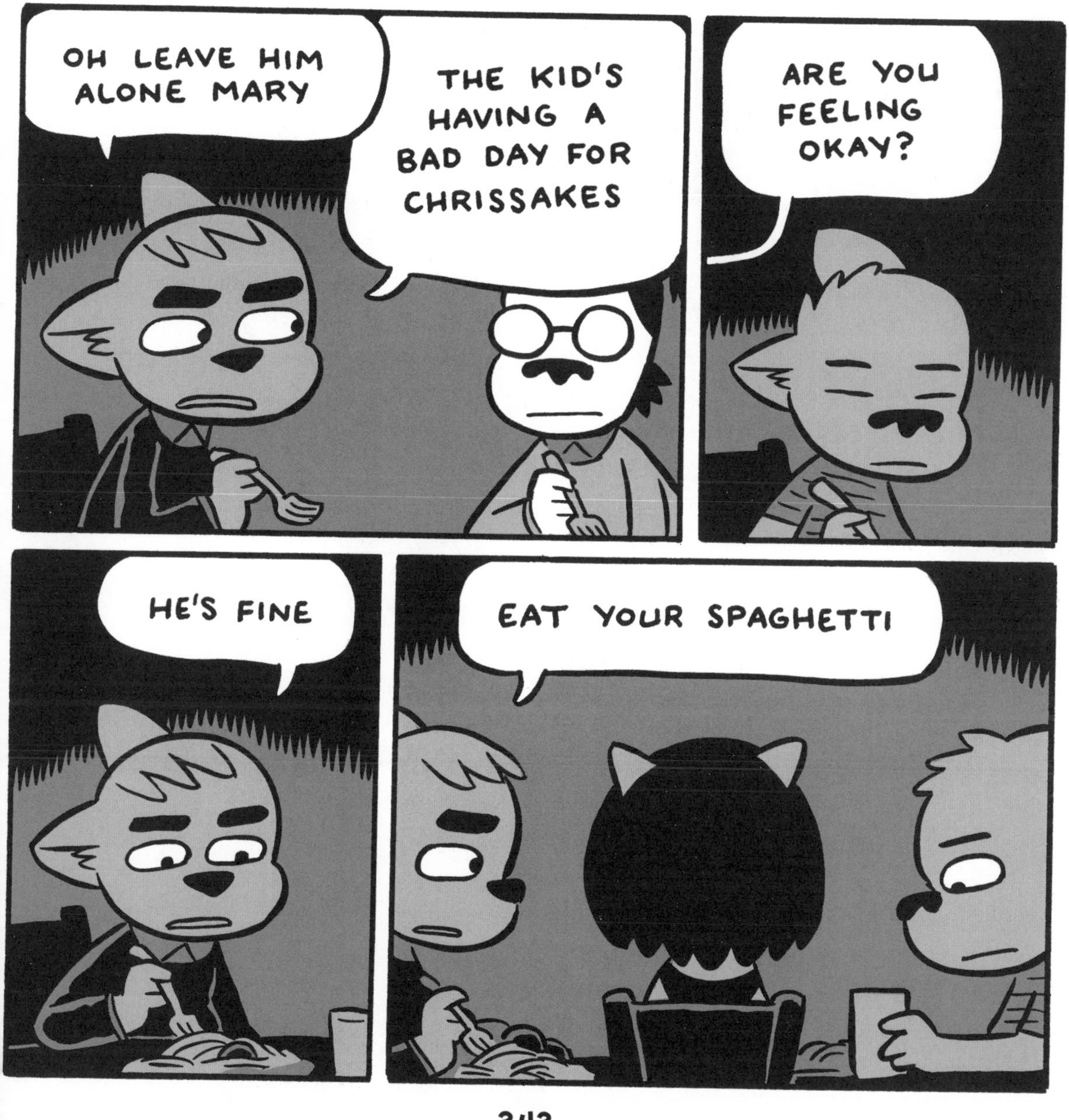
OH LEAVE HIM ALONE MARY
THE KID'S HAVING A BAD DAY FOR CHRISSAKES
ARE YOU FEELING OKAY?
HE'S FINE
EAT YOUR SPAGHETTI

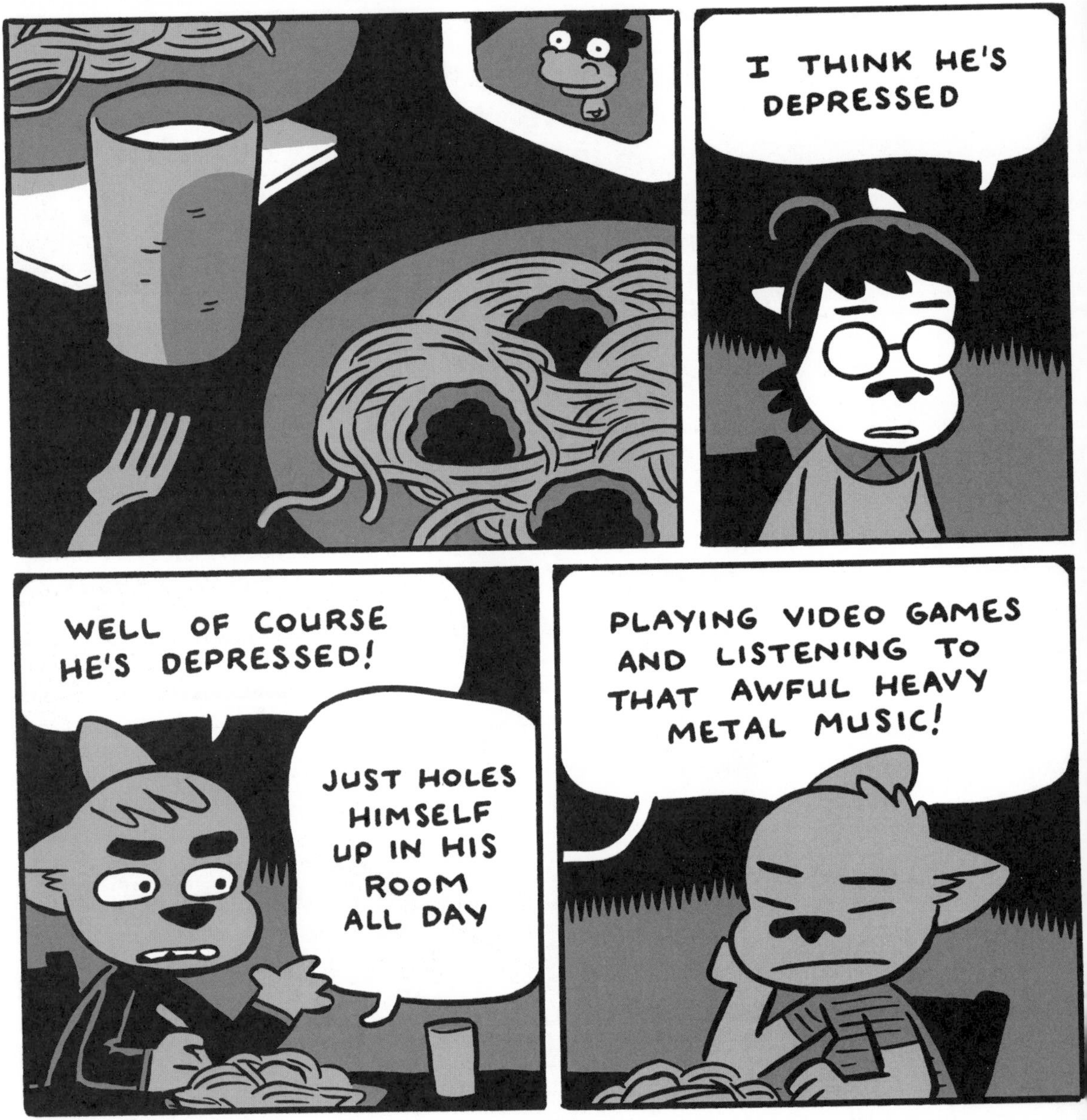
I THINK HE'S DEPRESSED
WELL OF COURSE HE'S DEPRESSED!
JUST HOLES HIMSELF UP IN HIS ROOM ALL DAY
PLAYING VIDEO GAMES AND LISTENING TO THAT AWFUL HEAVY METAL MUSIC!

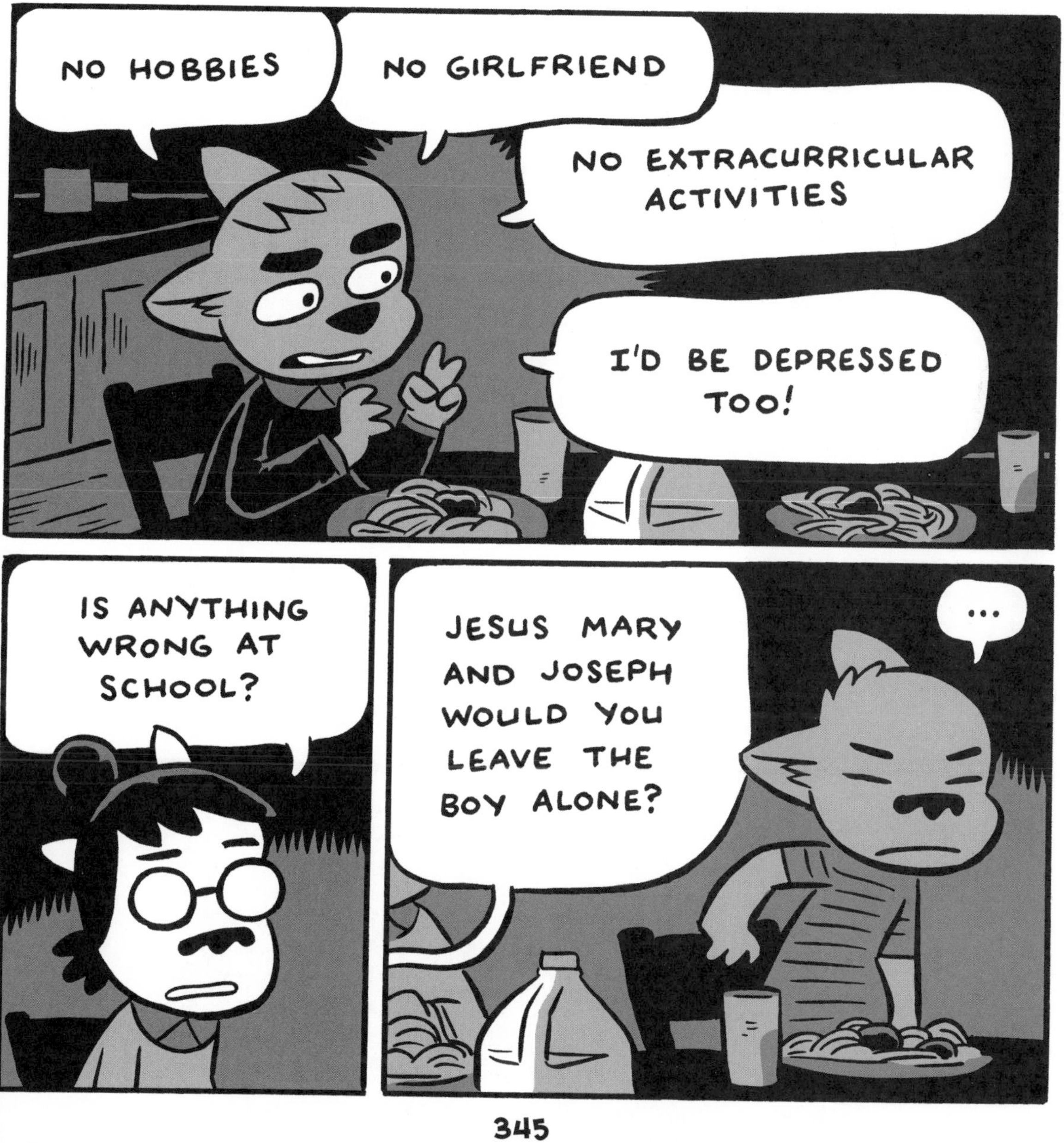
NO HOBBIES
NO GIRLFRIEND
NO EXTRACURRICULAR ACTIVITIES
I'D BE DEPRESSED TOO!
IS ANYTHING WRONG AT SCHOOL?
JESUS MARY AND JOSEPH WOULD YOU LEAVE THE BOY ALONE?
...

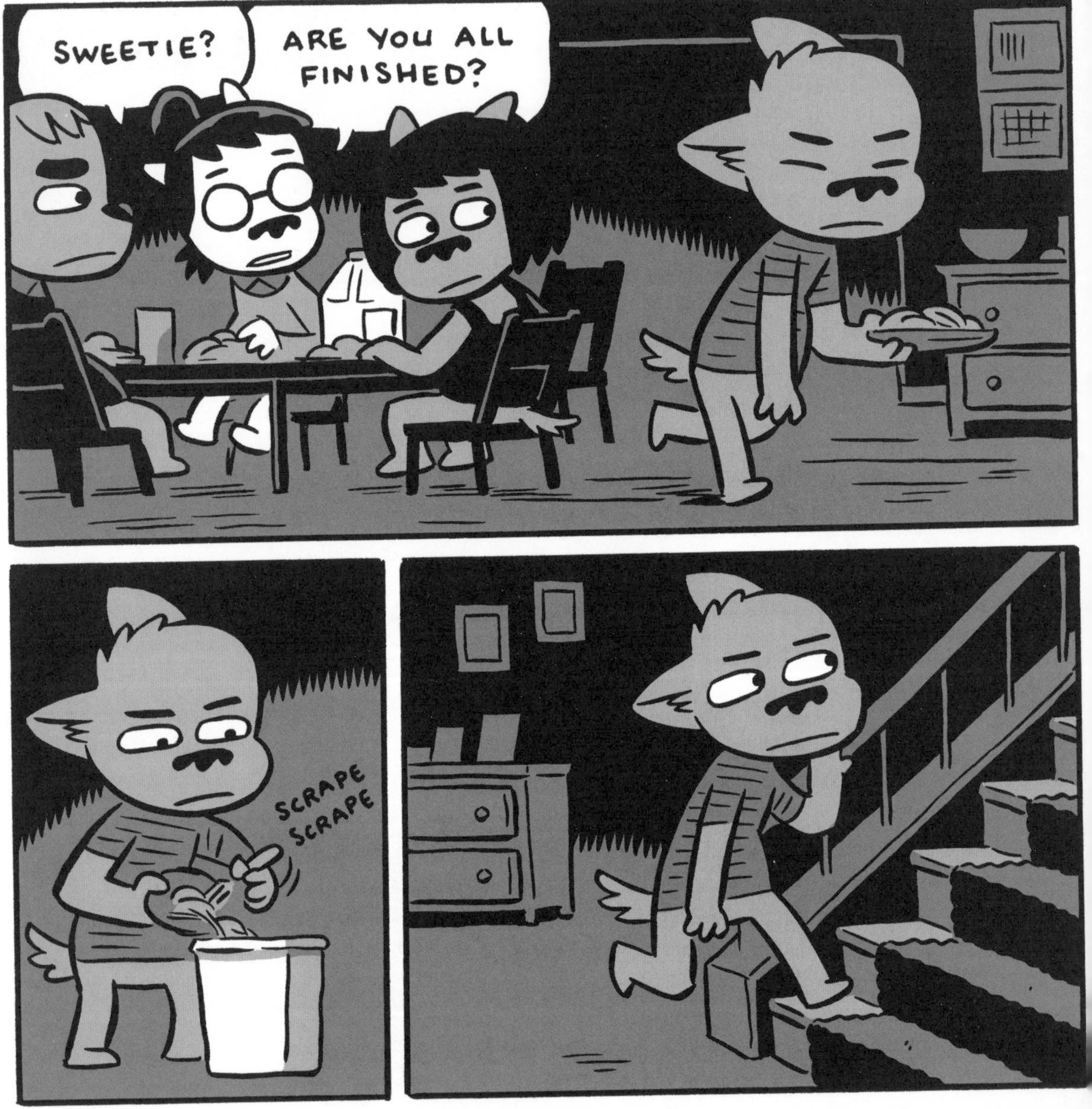
SWEETIE?
ARE YOU ALL FINISHED?
SCRAPE SCRAPE

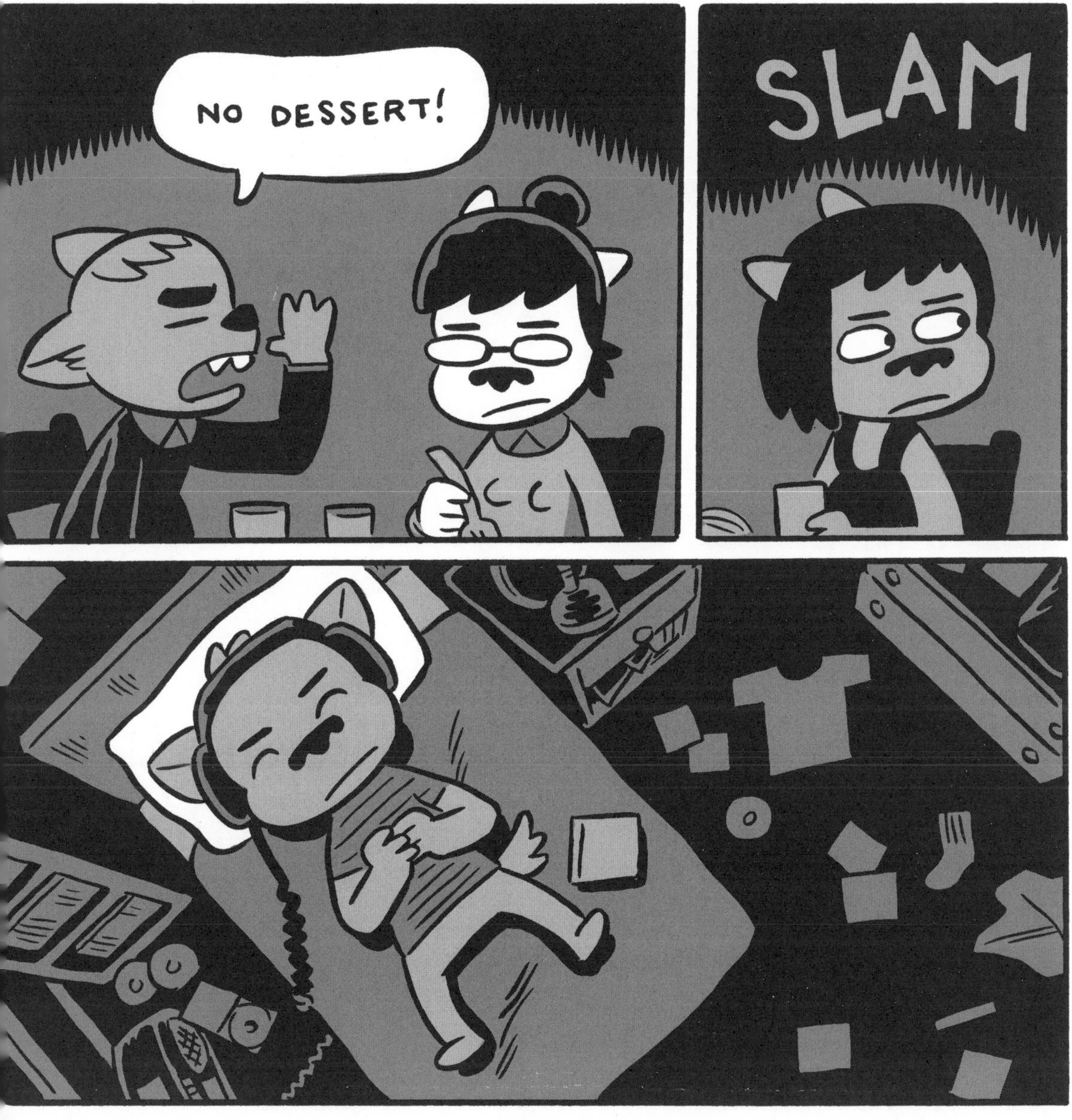
NO DESSERT!
SLAM

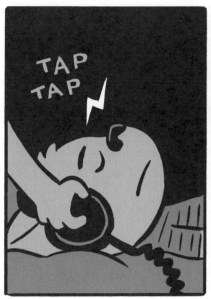

TAP
TAP

AAH!

JESUS! YOU SCARED THE SHIT OUT OF ME!

HA HA

CHILL OUT MAN

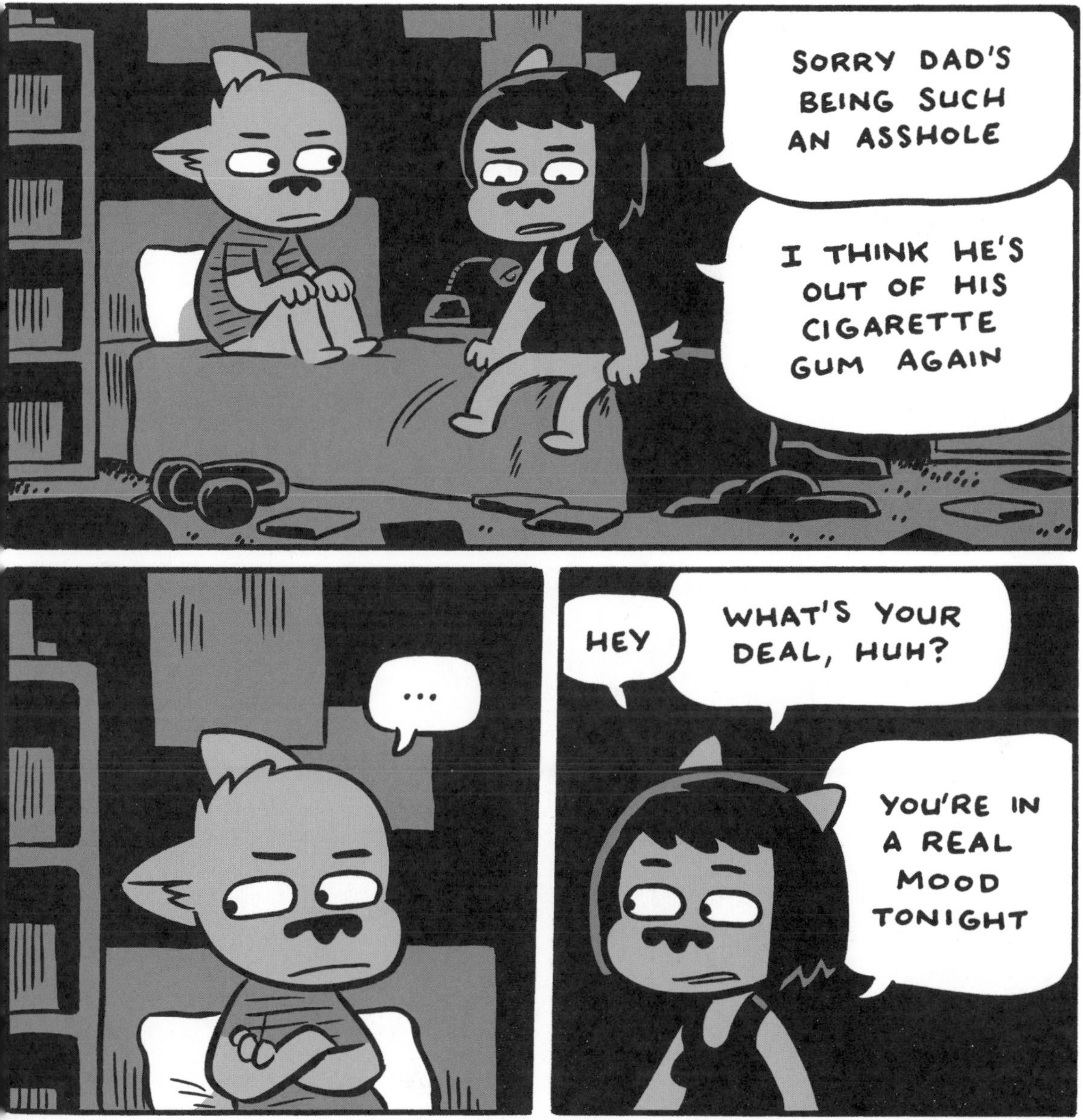
SORRY DAD'S BEING SUCH AN ASSHOLE
I THINK HE'S OUT OF HIS CIGARETTE GUM AGAIN
...
HEY
WHAT'S YOUR DEAL, HUH?
YOU'RE IN A REAL MOOD TONIGHT

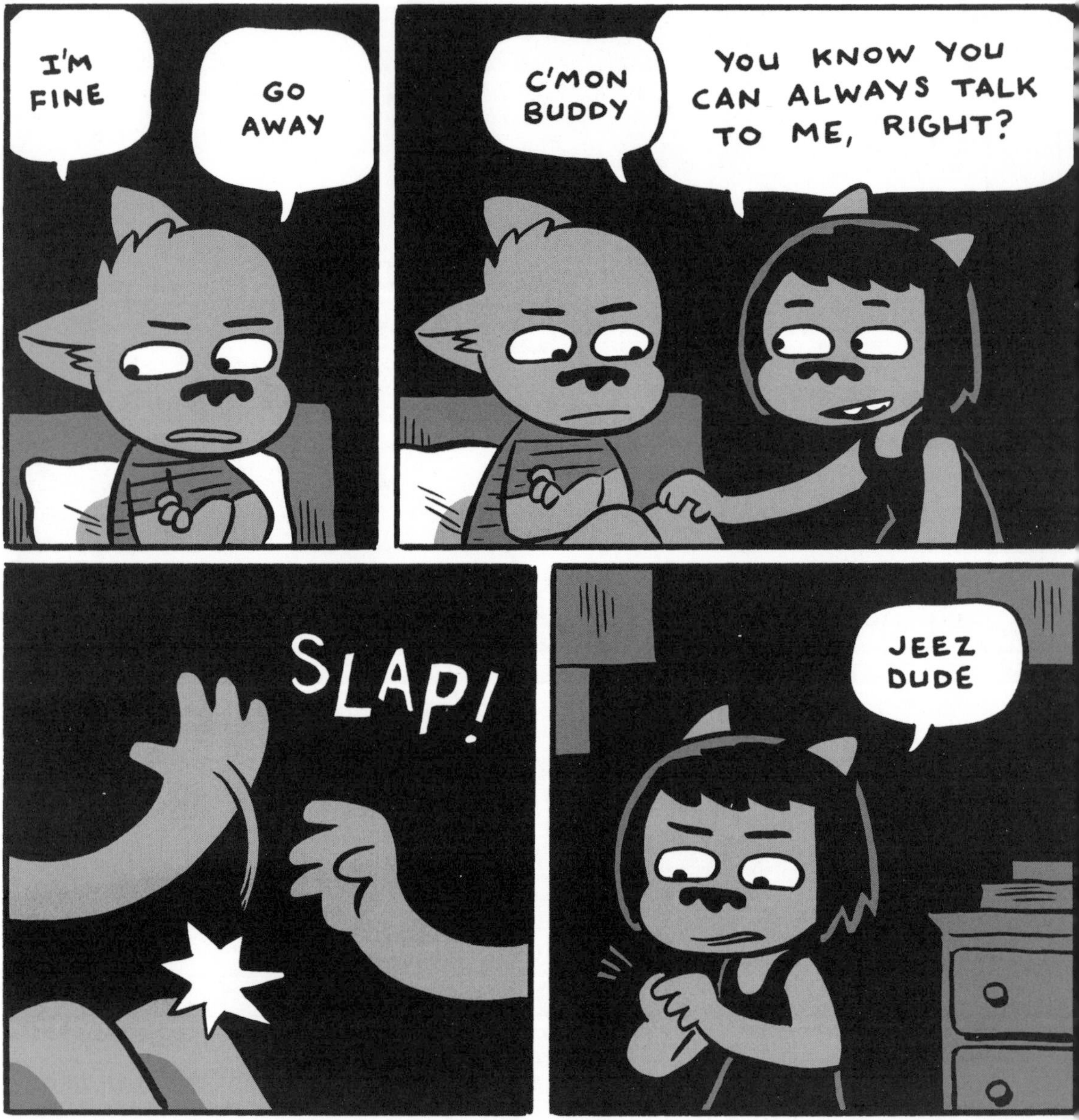
I'M FINE
GO AWAY
C'MON BUDDY
YOU KNOW YOU CAN ALWAYS TALK TO ME, RIGHT?
SLAP!
JEEZ DUDE

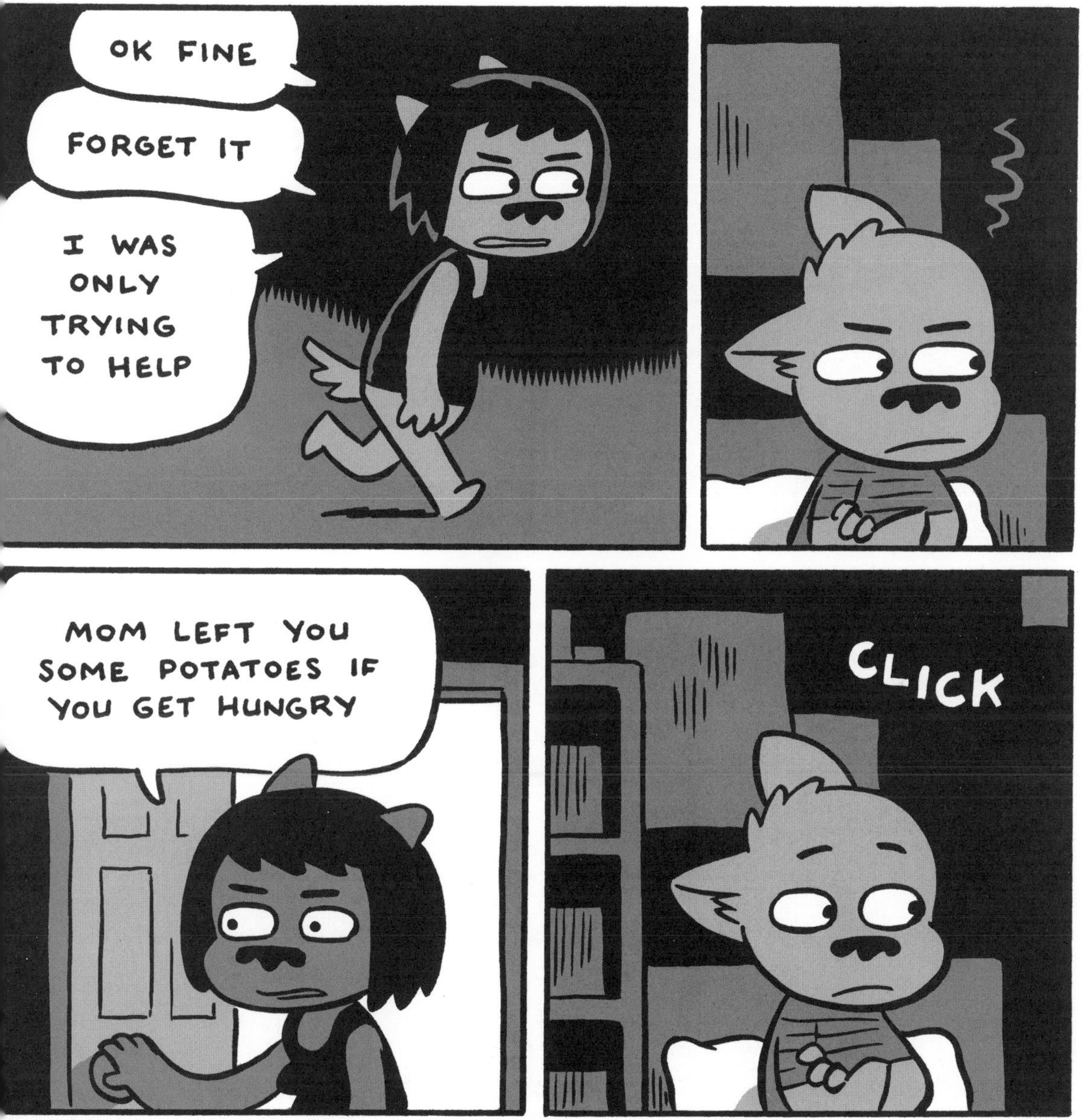
OK FINE
FORGET IT
I WAS ONLY TRYING TO HELP
MOM LEFT YOU SOME POTATOES IF YOU GET HUNGRY
CLICK

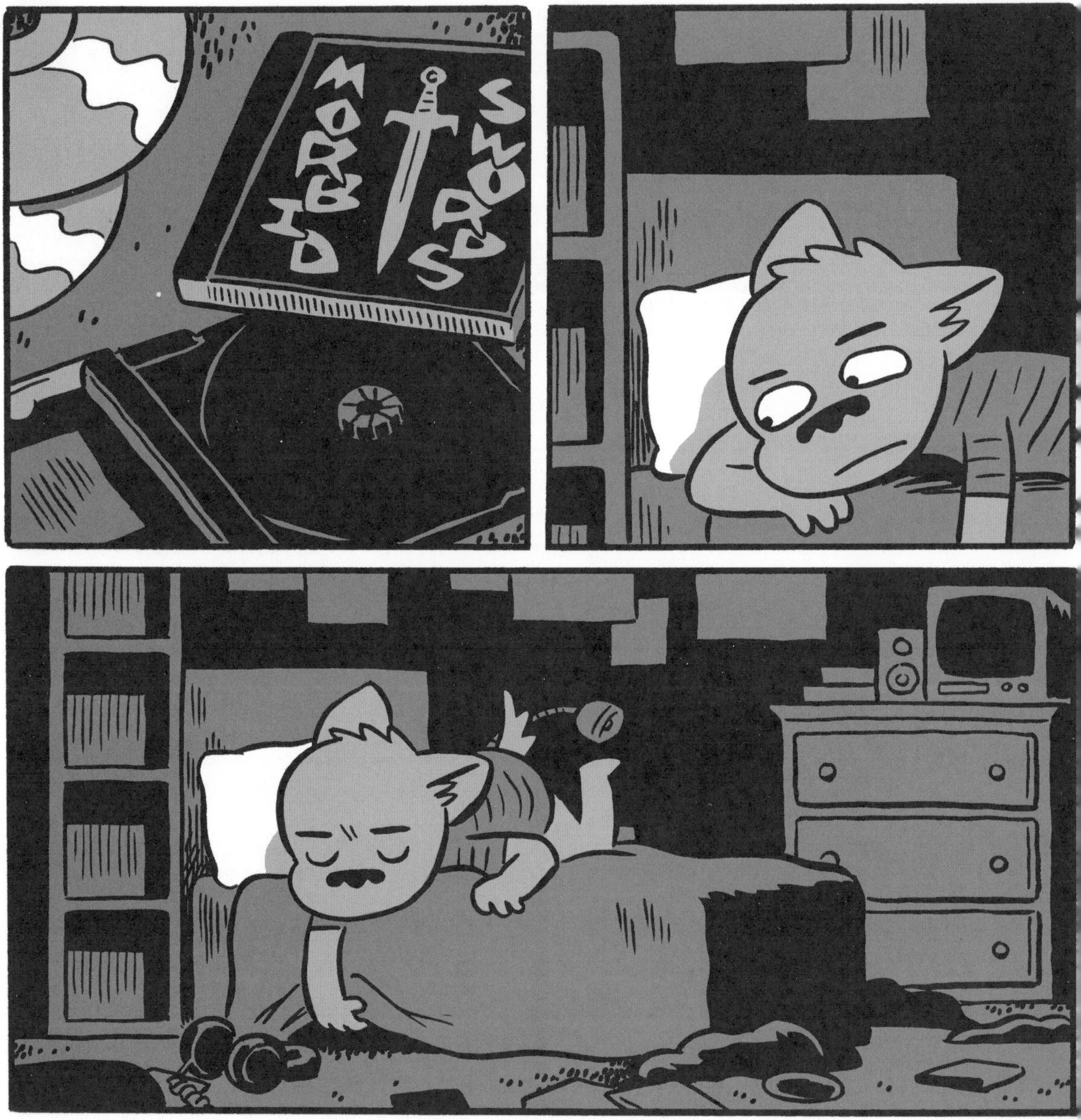
MORBID SWORDS

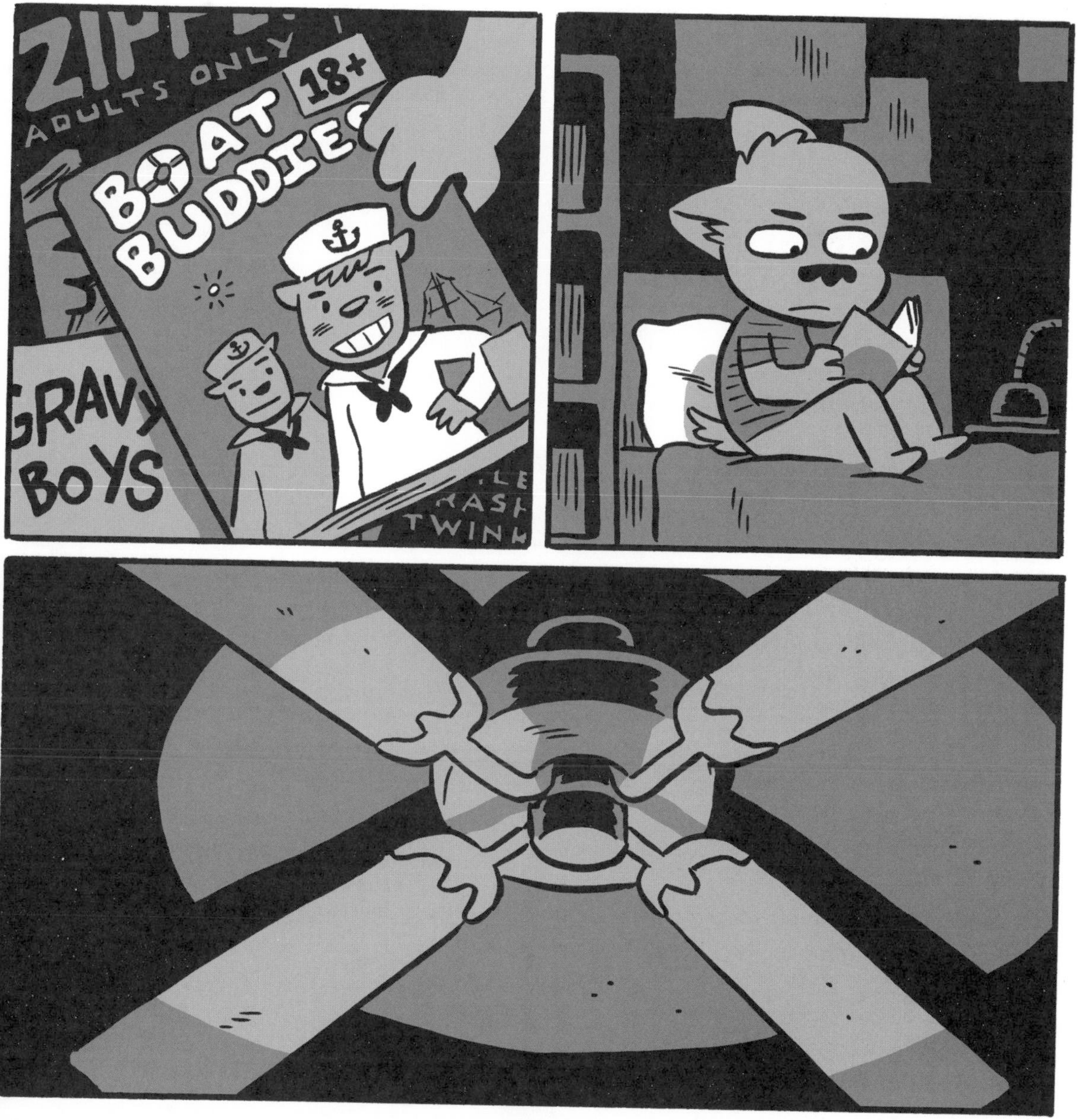
ADULTS ONLY
18+
BOAT
BUDDIES
GRAVY
BOYS
TWINK

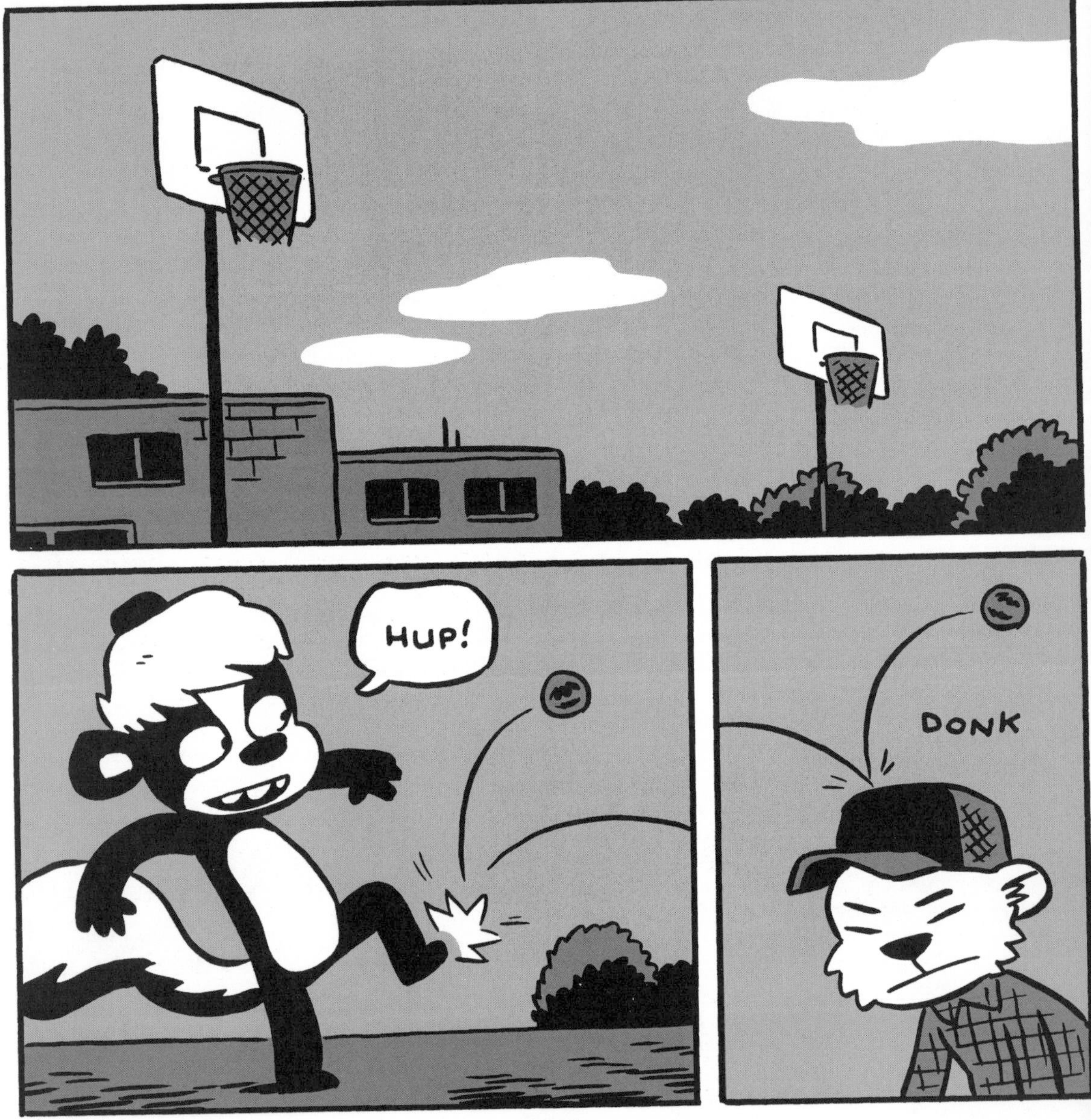
HUP!
DONK

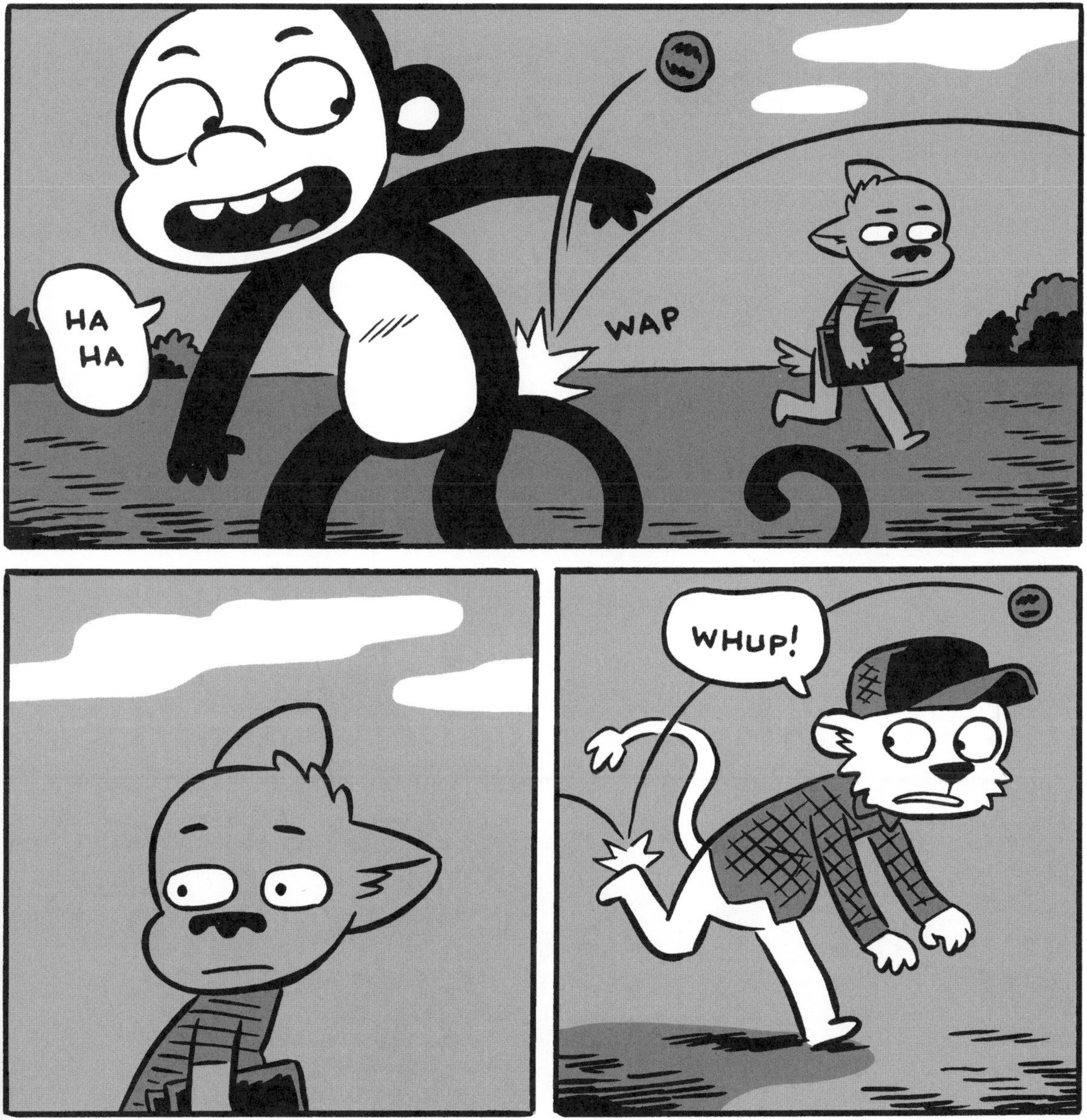
HA HA
WAP
WHUP!

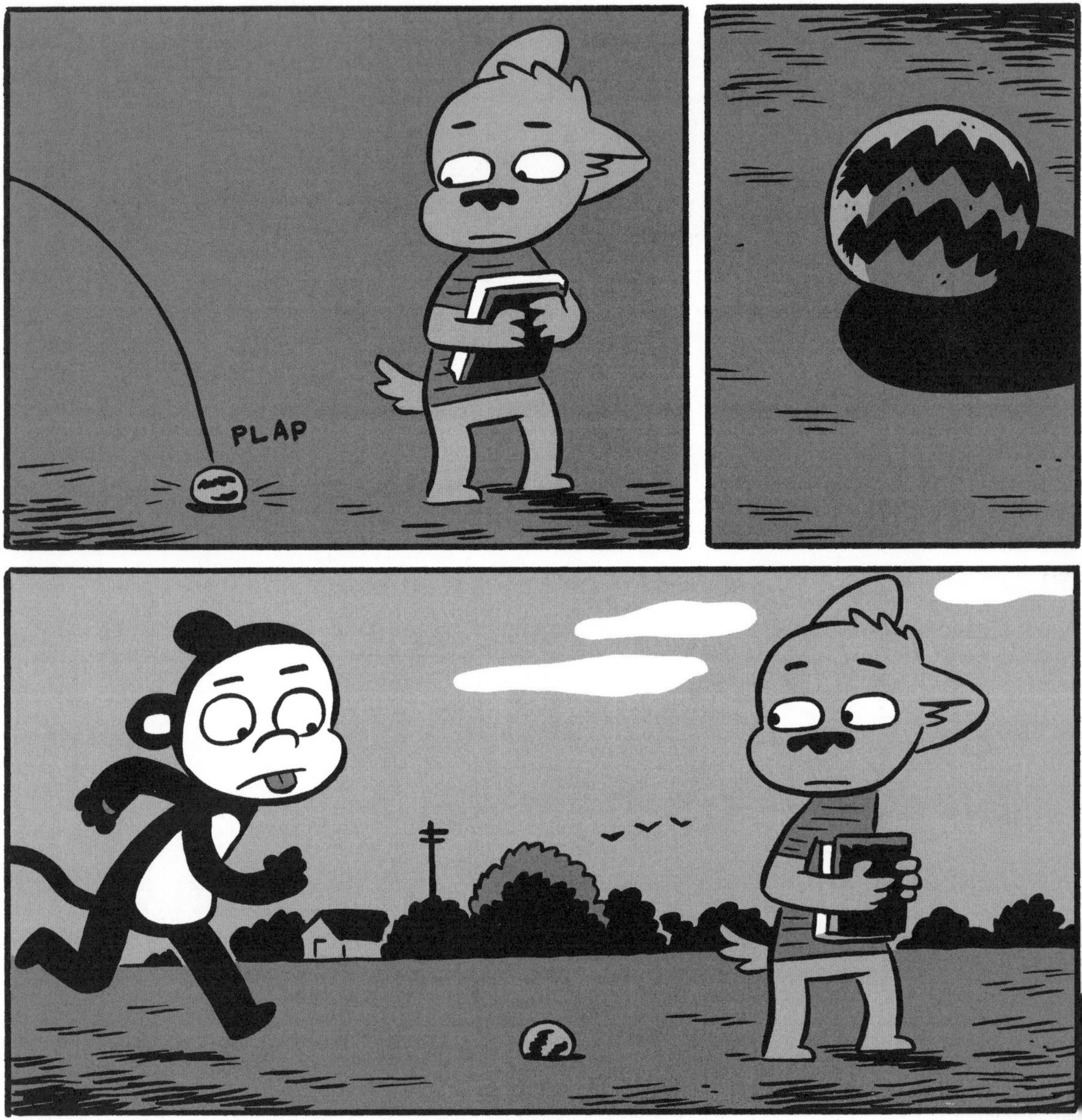
PLAP

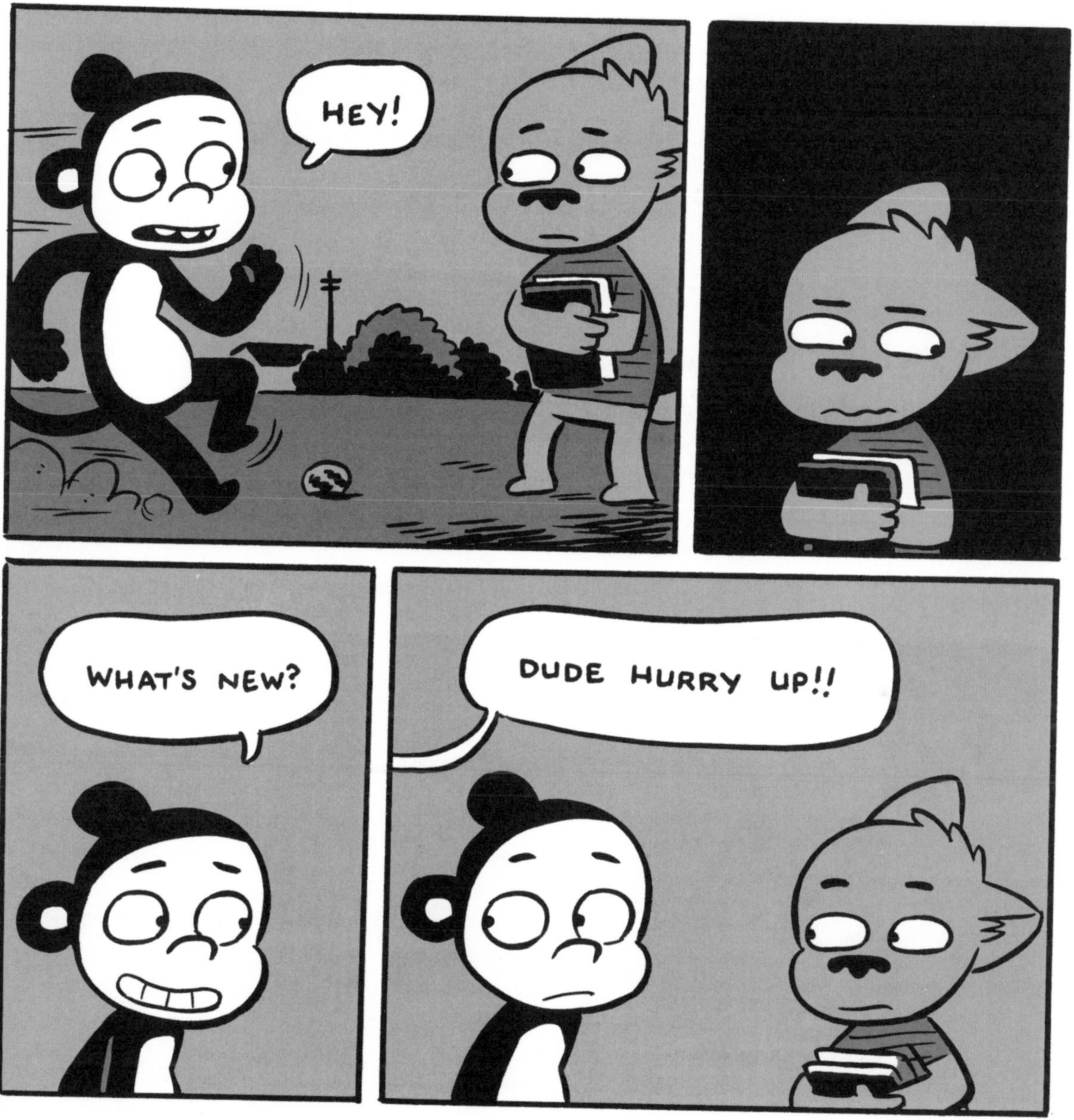
HEY!
WHAT'S NEW?
DUDE HURRY UP!!

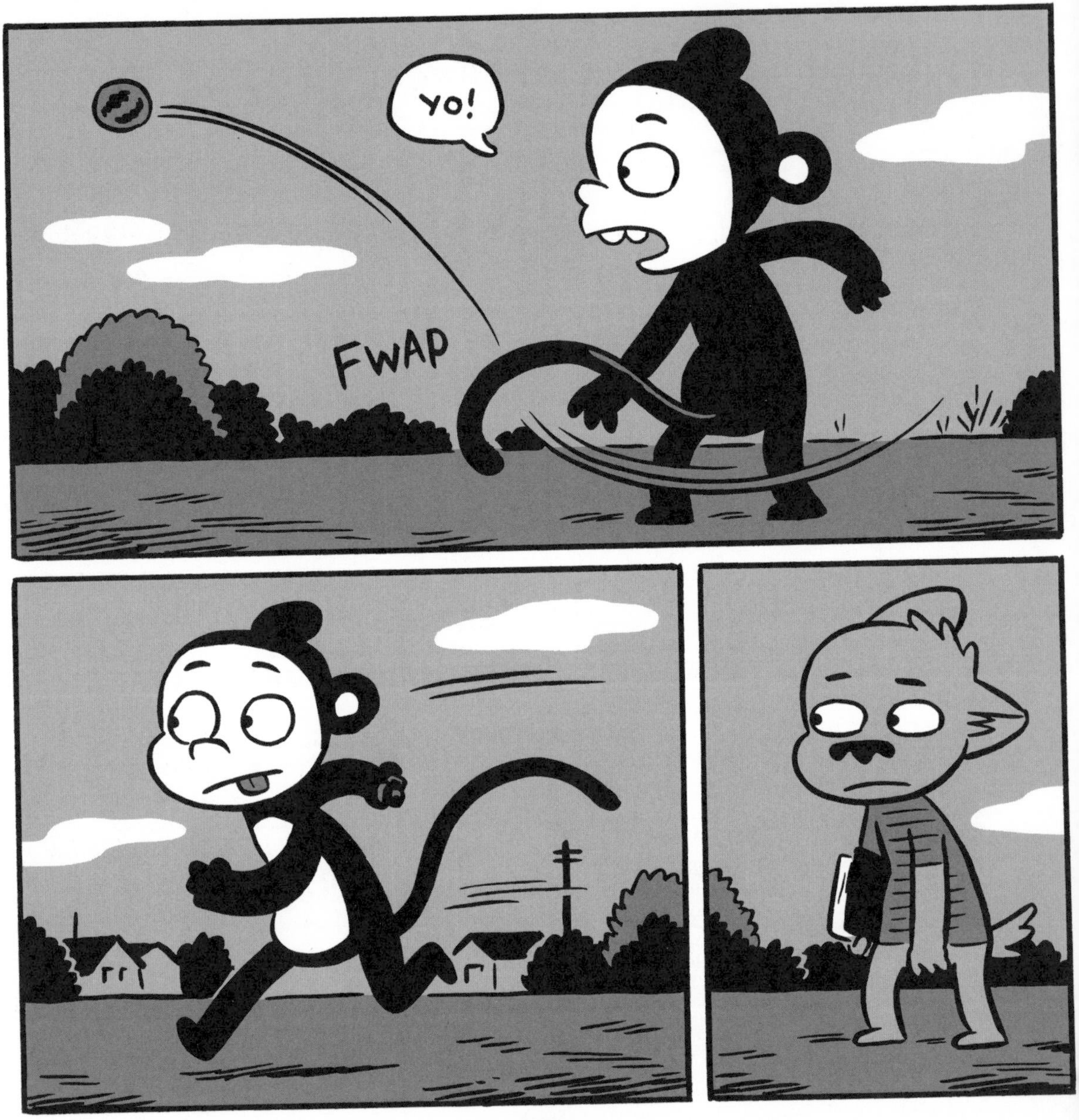
YO!
FWAP

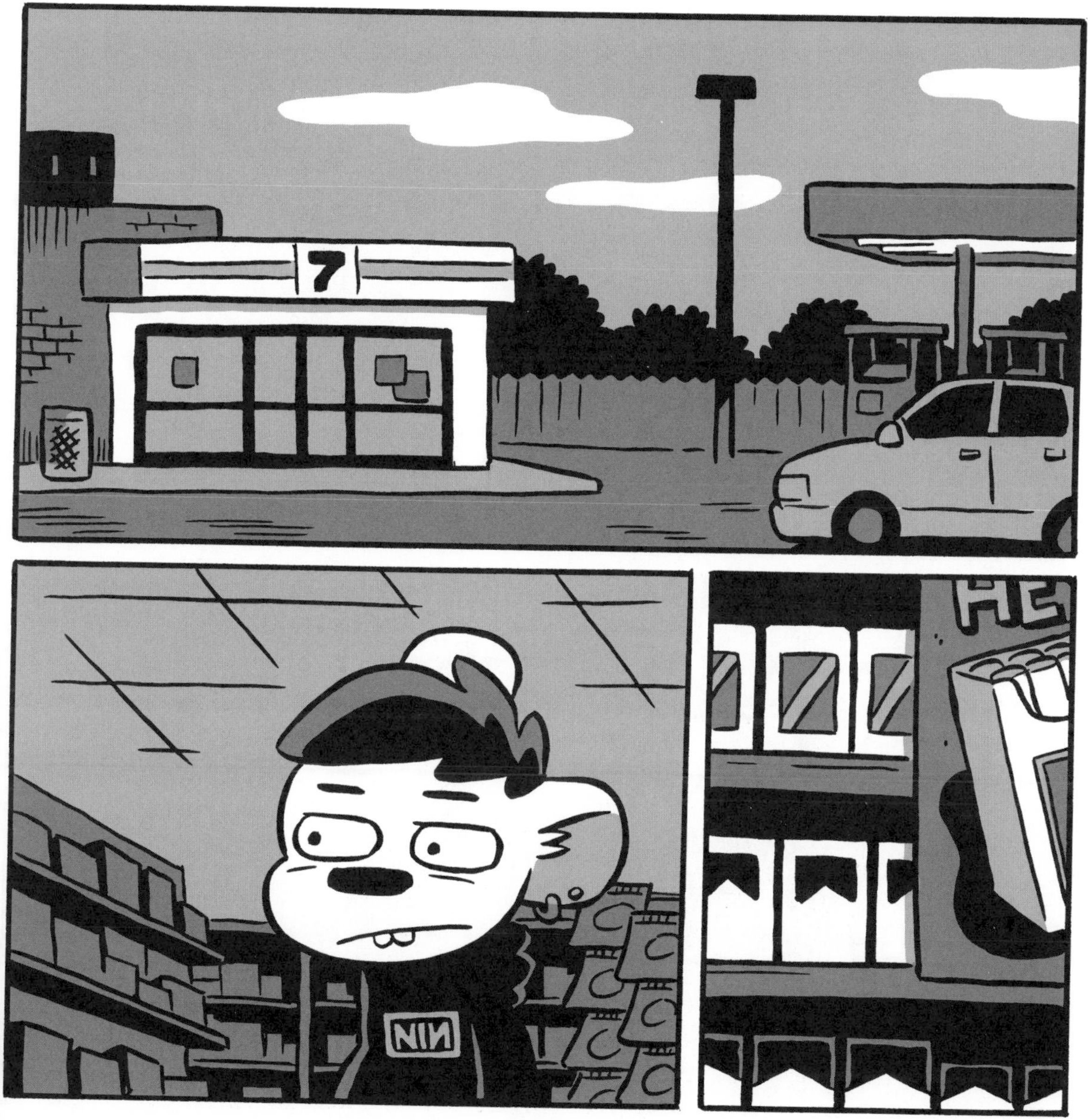
7
NIN

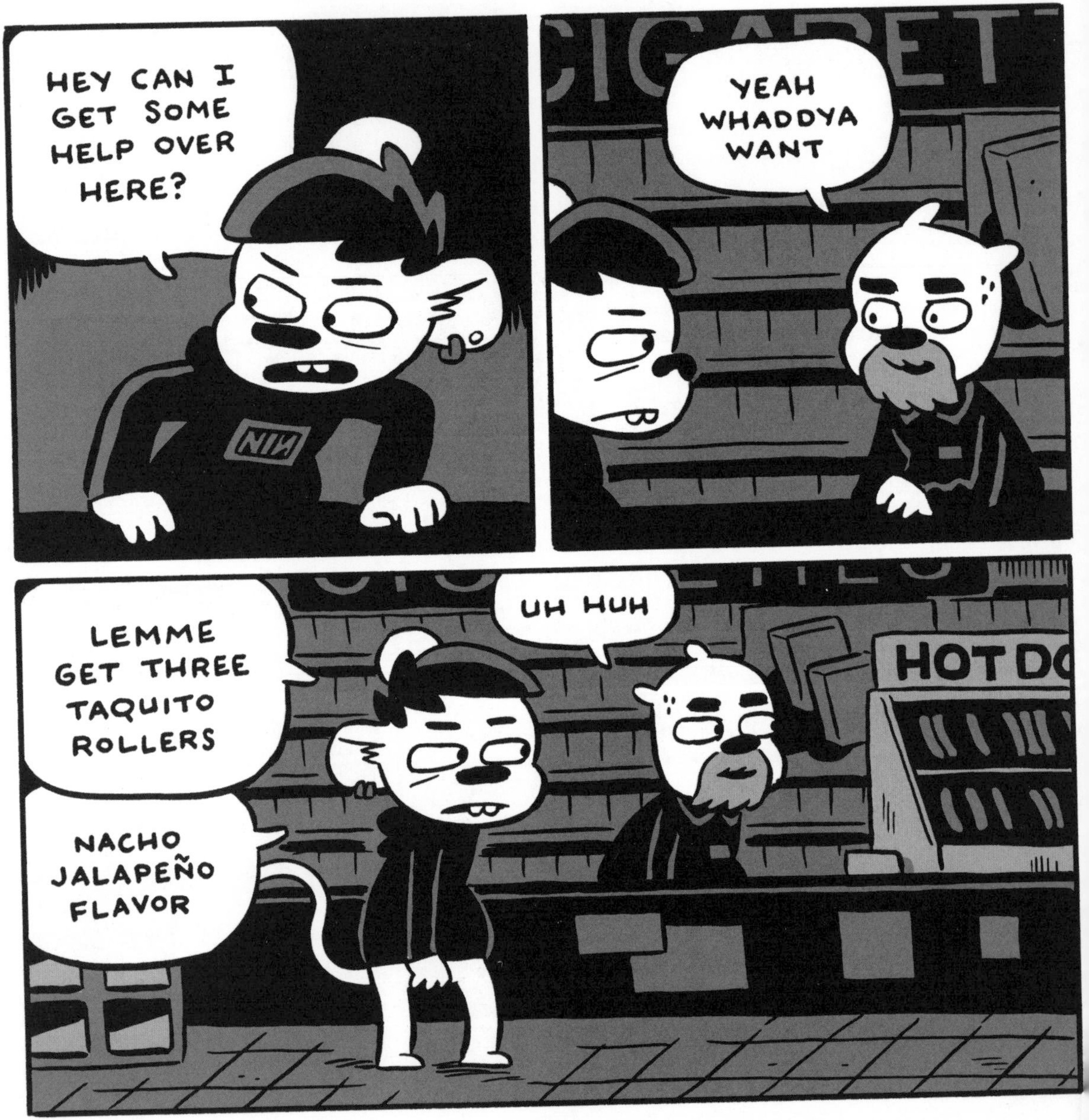
HEY CAN I GET SOME HELP OVER HERE?
CIGARETT
YEAH WHADDYA WANT
LEMME GET THREE TAQUITO ROLLERS
UH HUH
NACHO JALAPEÑO FLAVOR
HOT DO

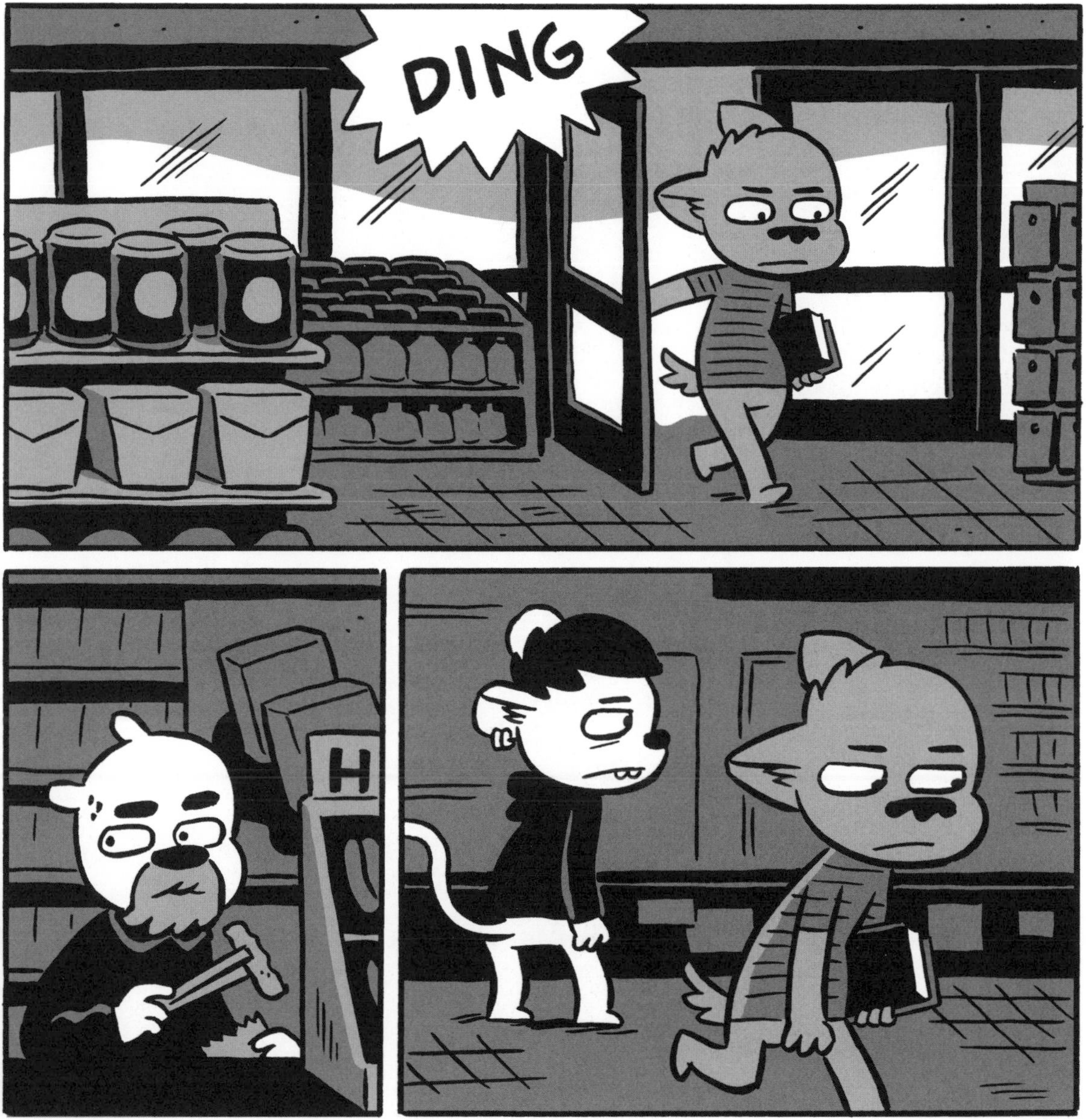
DING
H

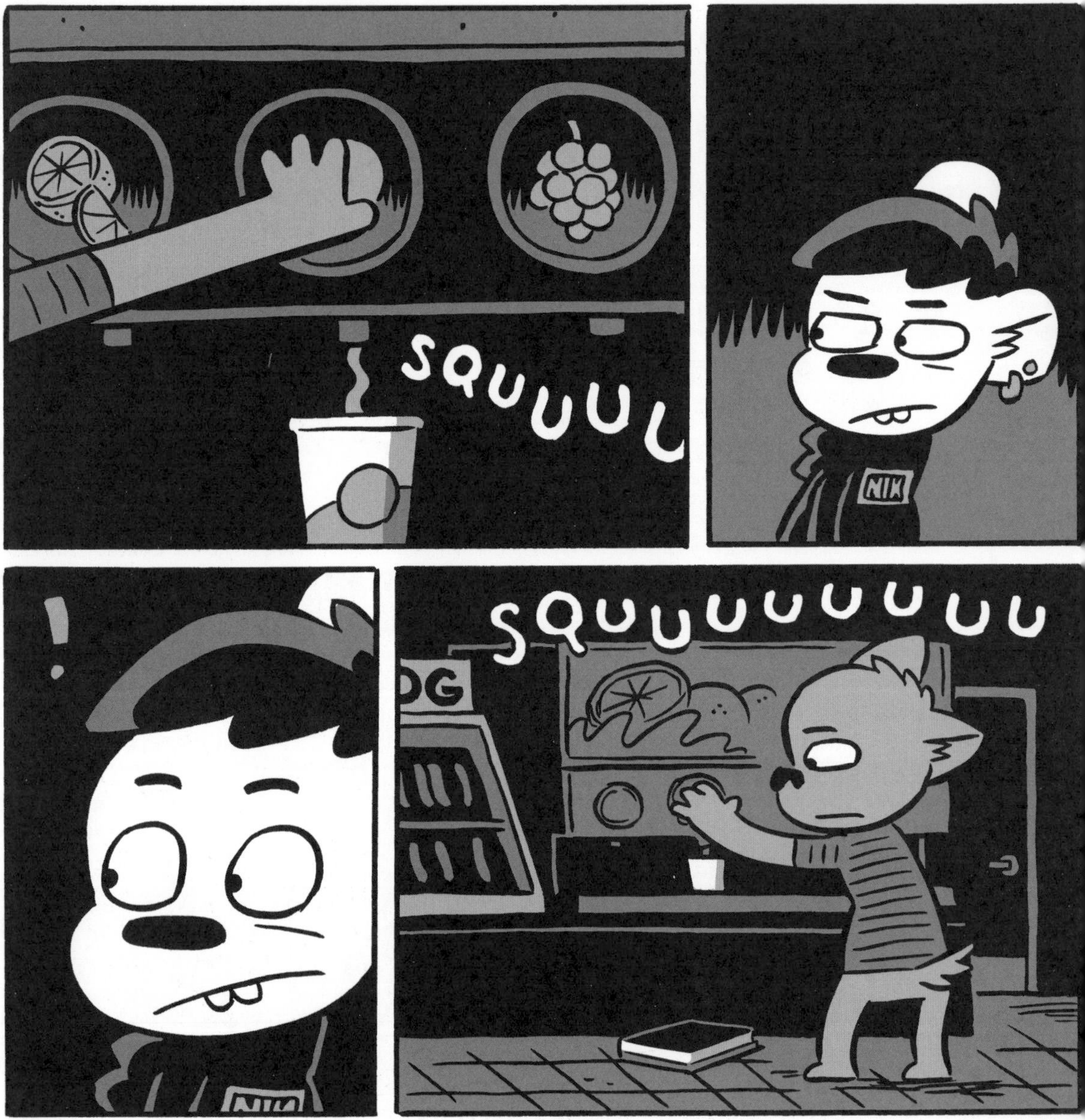
SQUUUU
!
SQUUUUUUUUU
DG
NIK

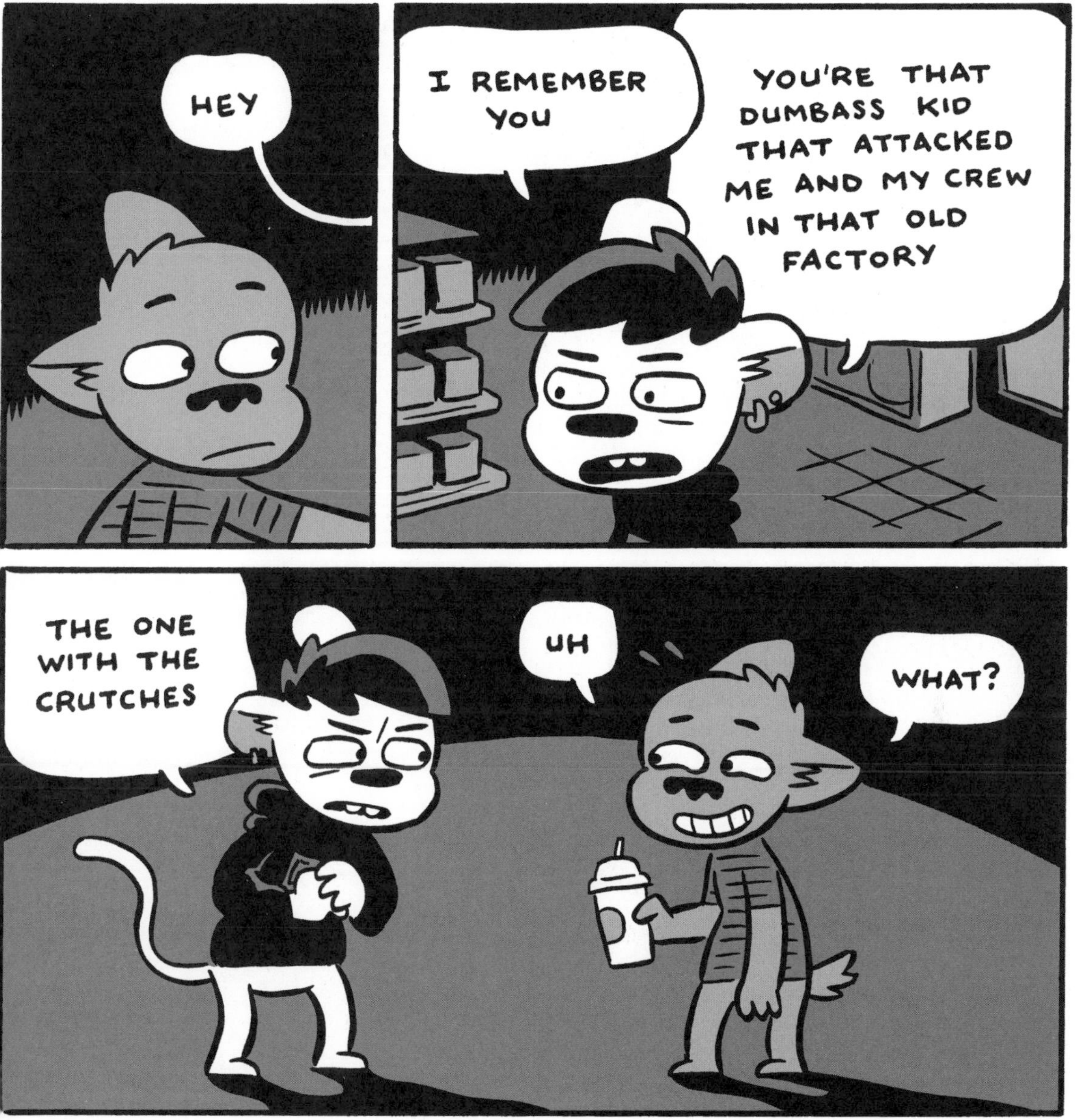
HEY
I REMEMBER YOU
YOU'RE THAT DUMBASS KID THAT ATTACKED ME AND MY CREW IN THAT OLD FACTORY
THE ONE WITH THE CRUTCHES
UH
WHAT?

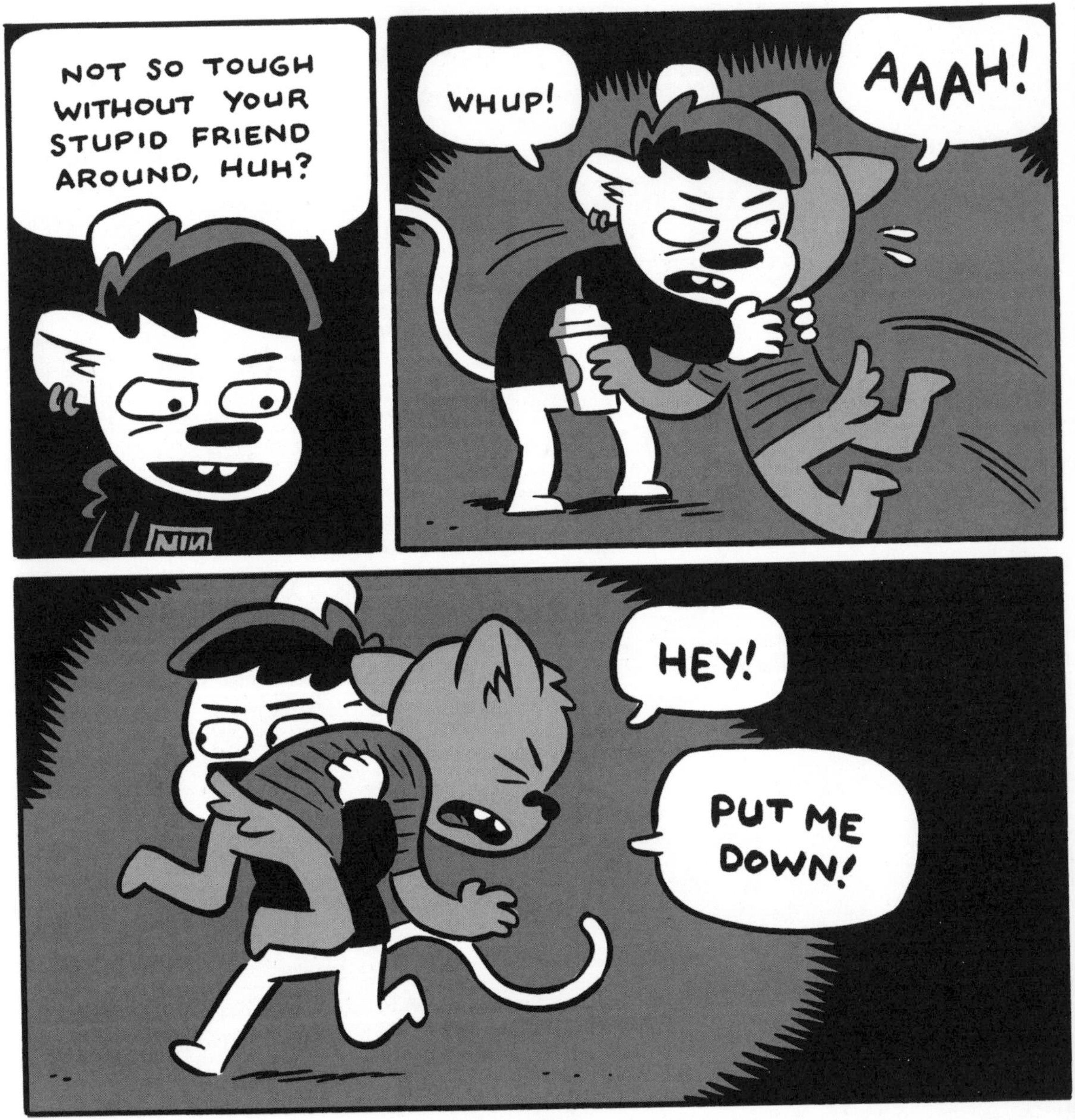
NOT SO TOUGH WITHOUT YOUR STUPID FRIEND AROUND, HUH?
NIN
WHUP!
AAAH!
HEY!
PUT ME DOWN!

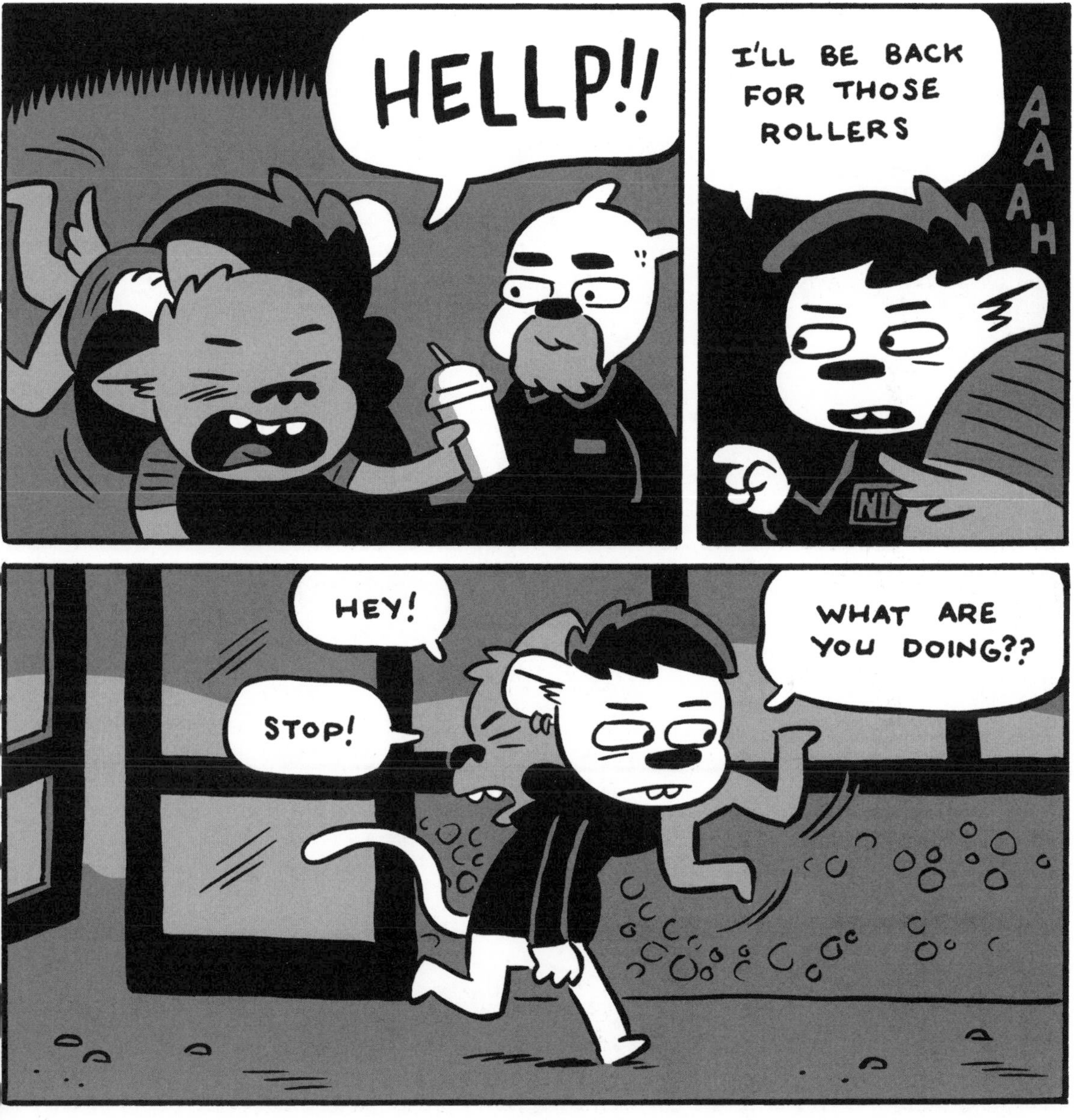
HELLP!!
I'LL BE BACK FOR THOSE ROLLERS
AAAAH
HEY!
STOP!
WHAT ARE YOU DOING??

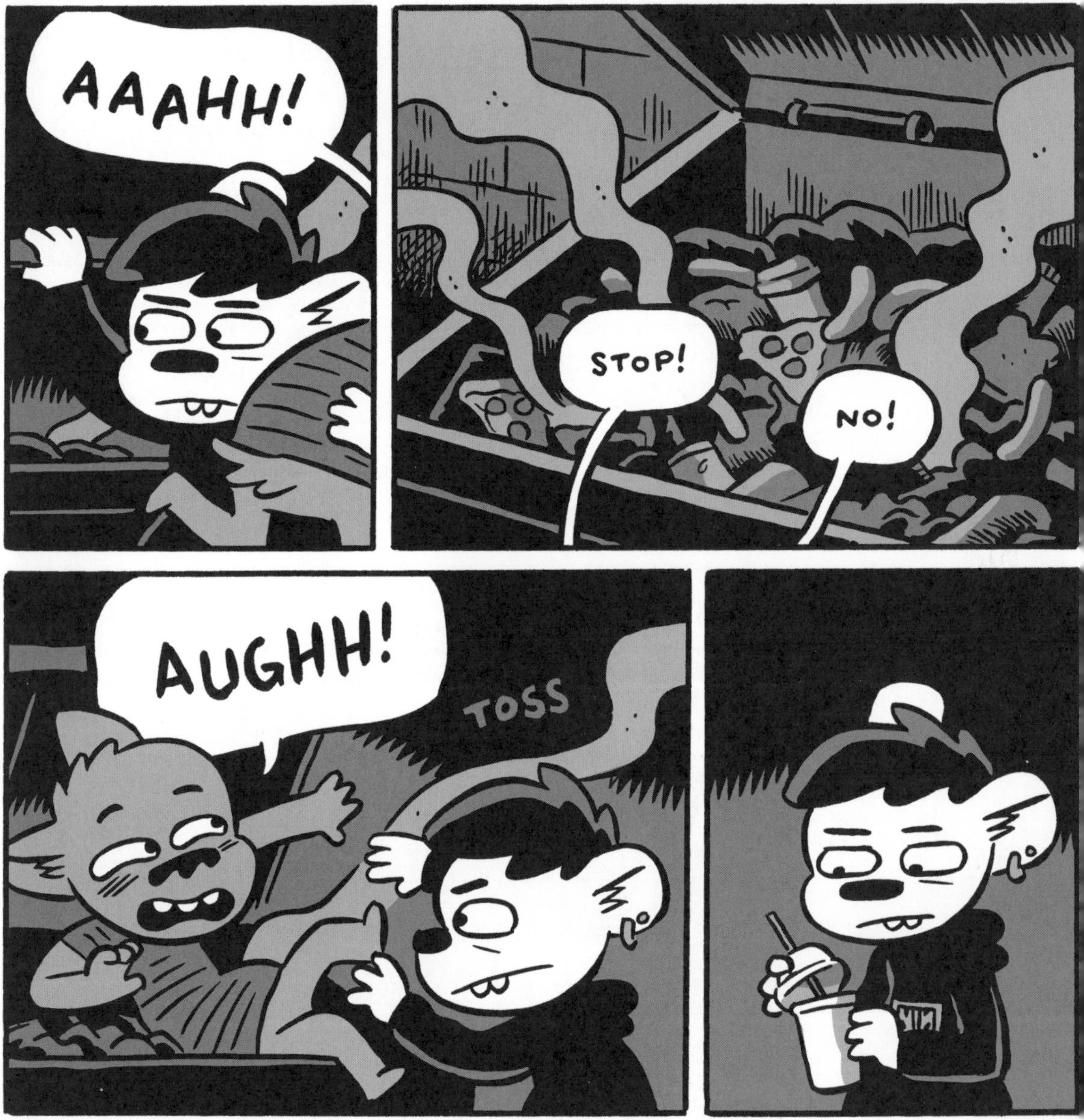
AAAHH!
STOP!
NO!
AUGHH!
TOSS

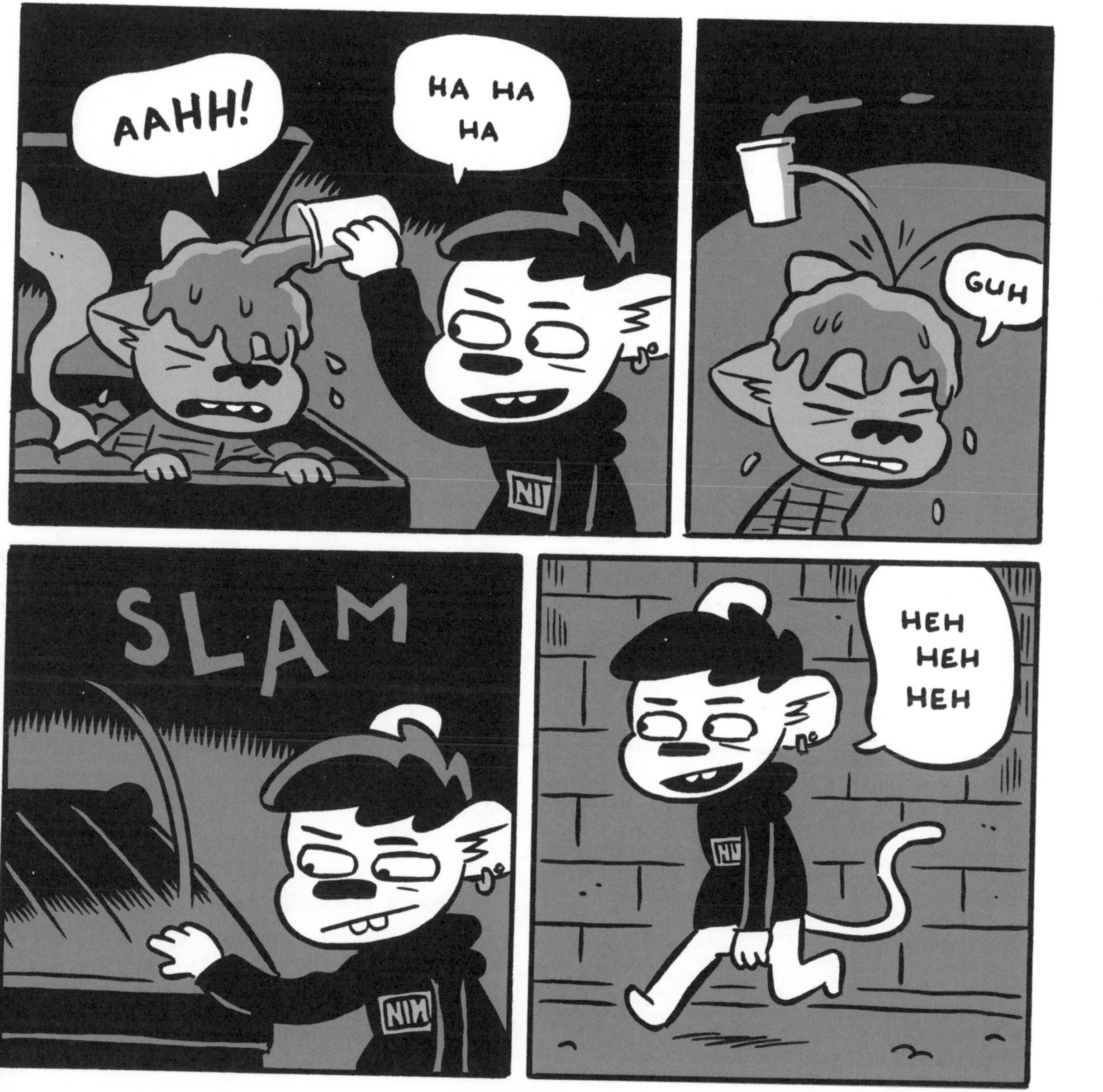
AAHH!
HA HA HA
GUH
SLAM
HEH HEH HEH

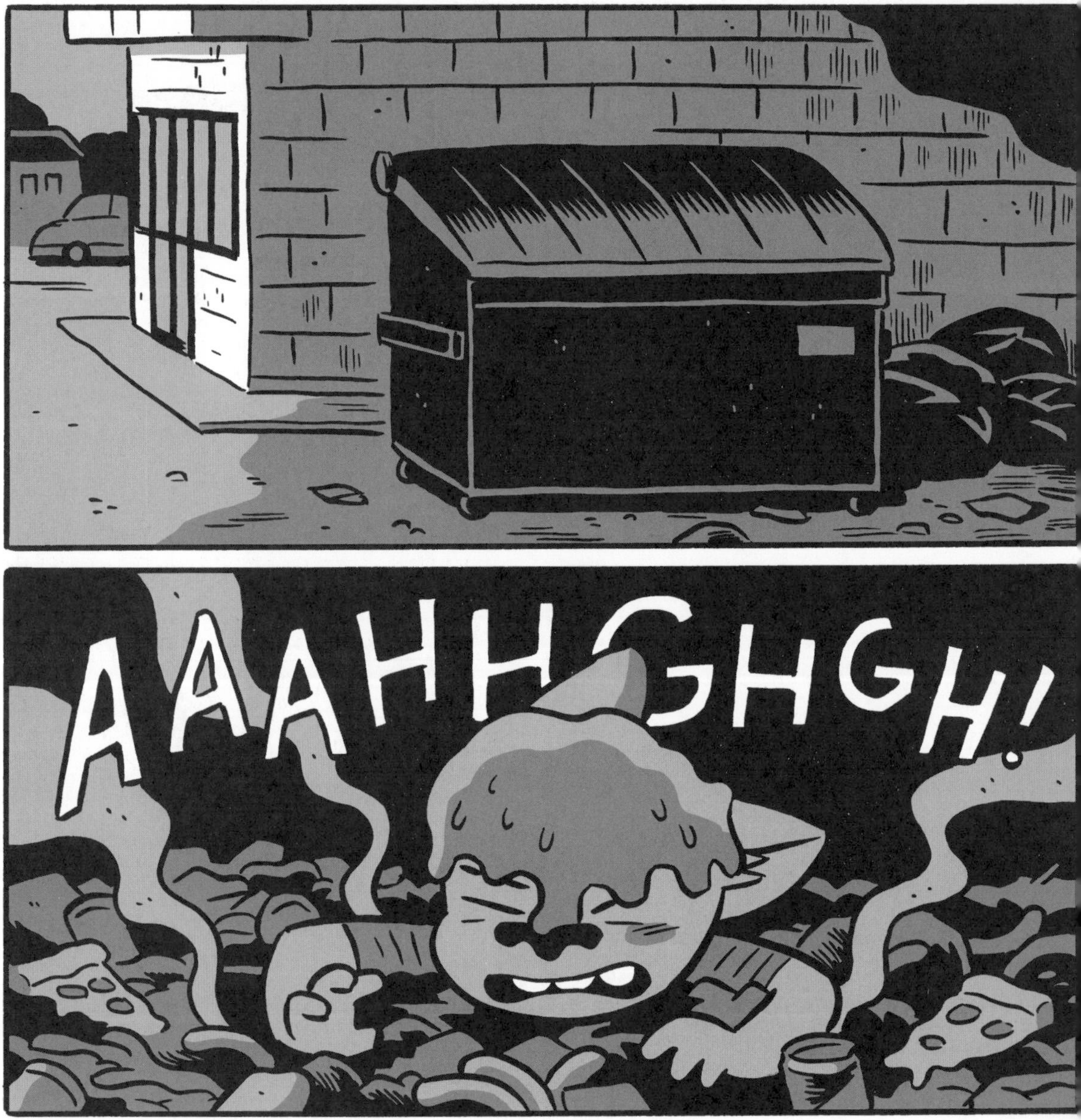
AAAHHGHGH!

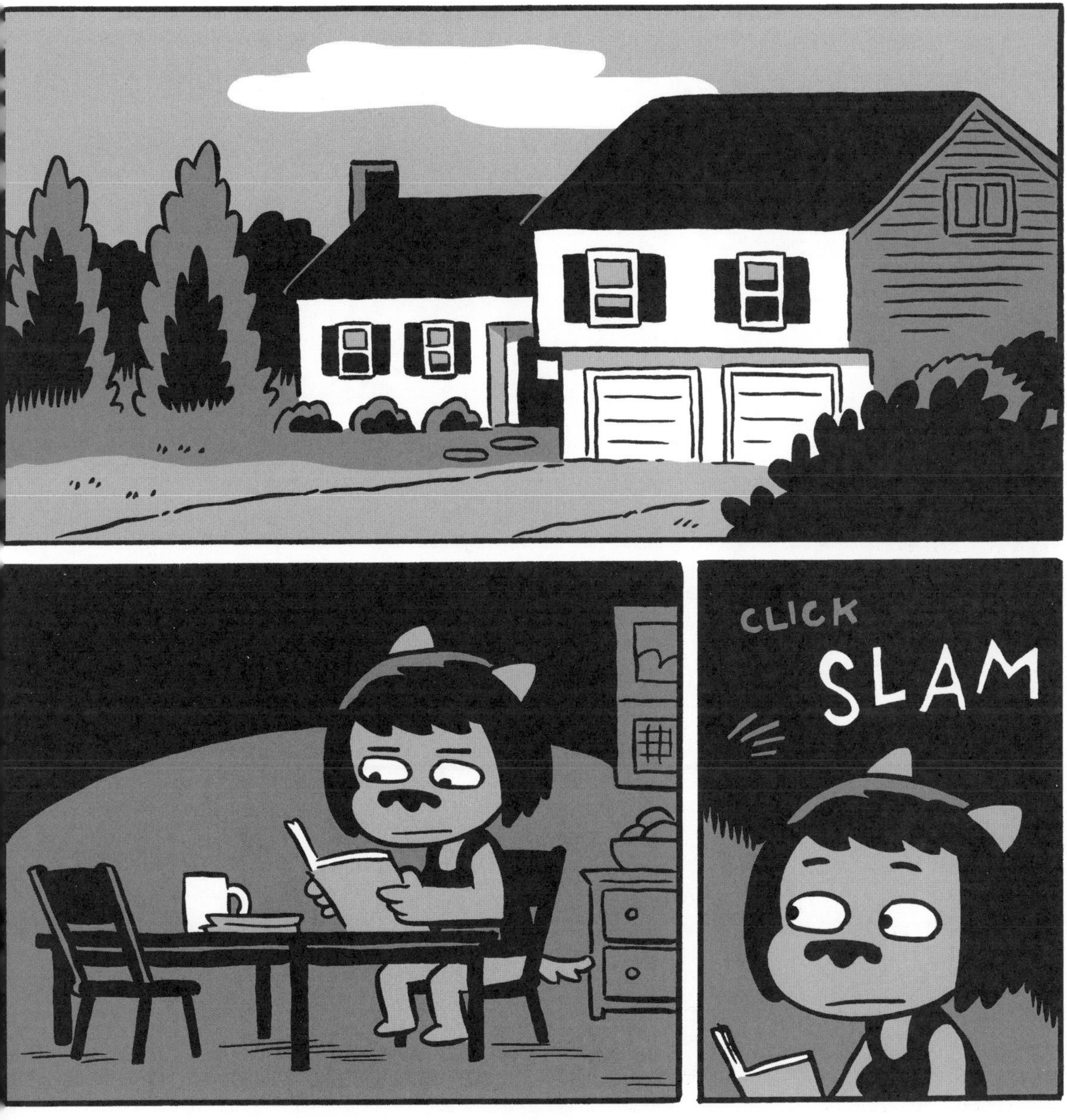
CLICK
SLAM

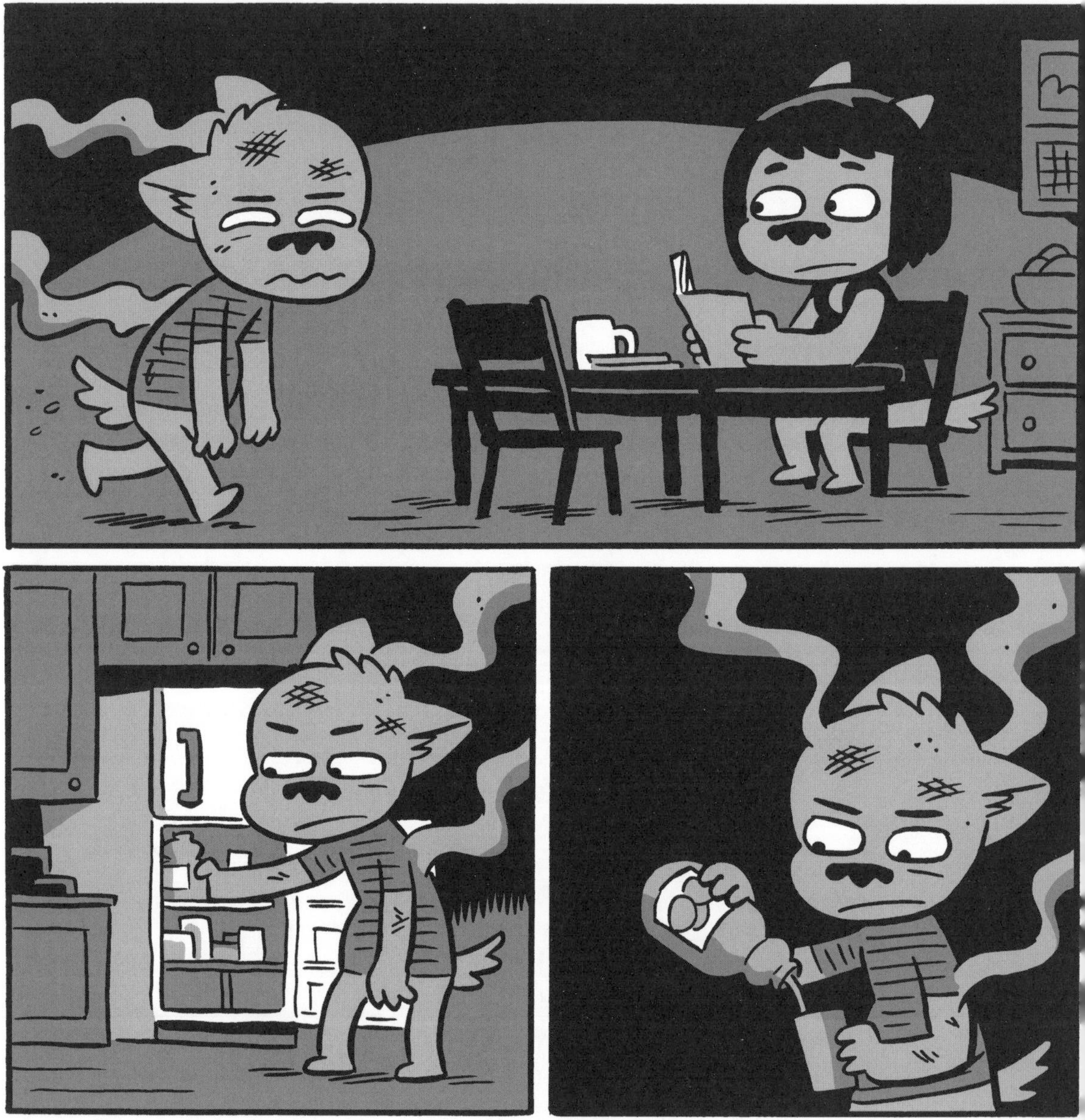

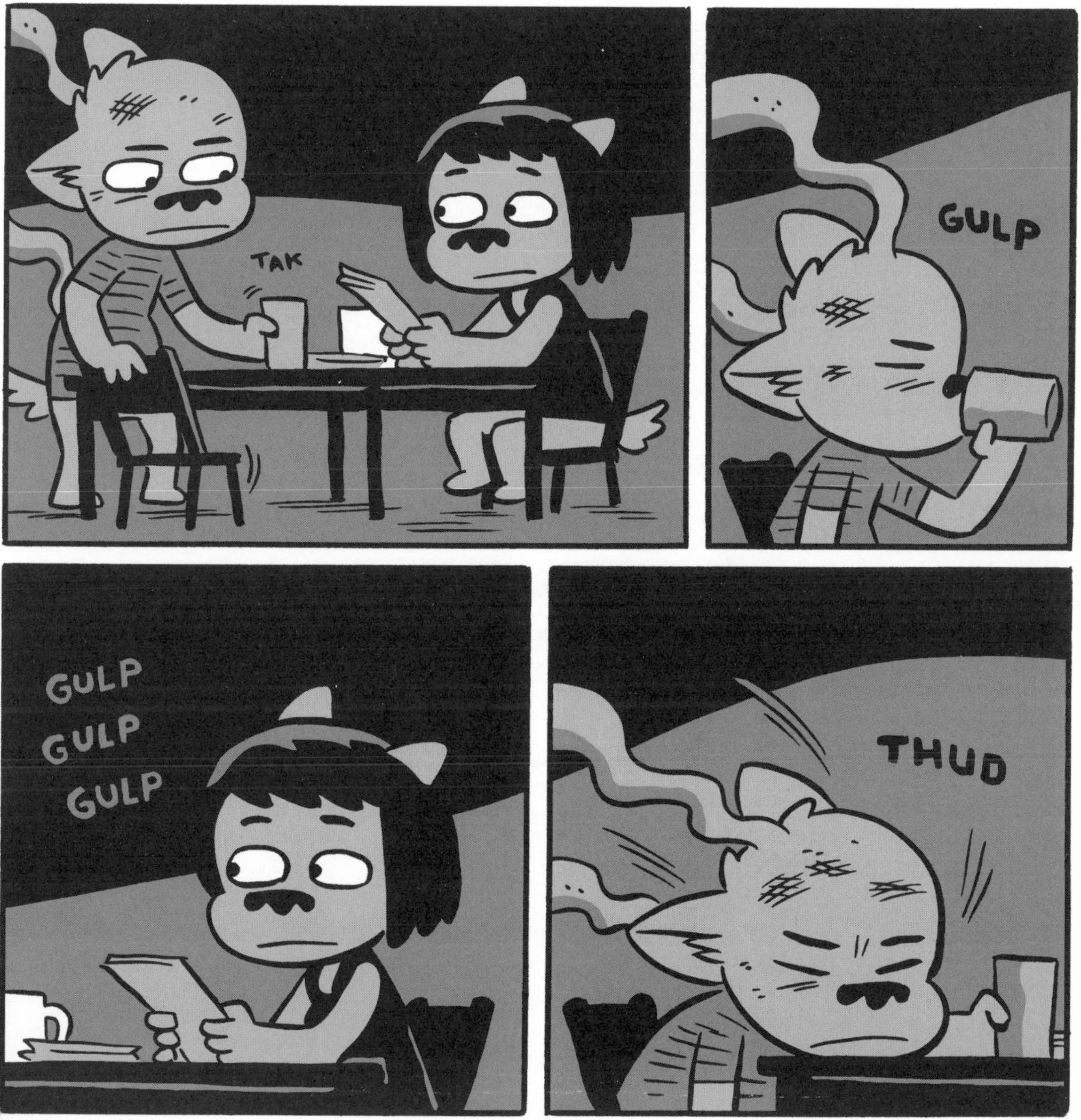
TAK
GULP
GULP
GULP
GULP
THUD

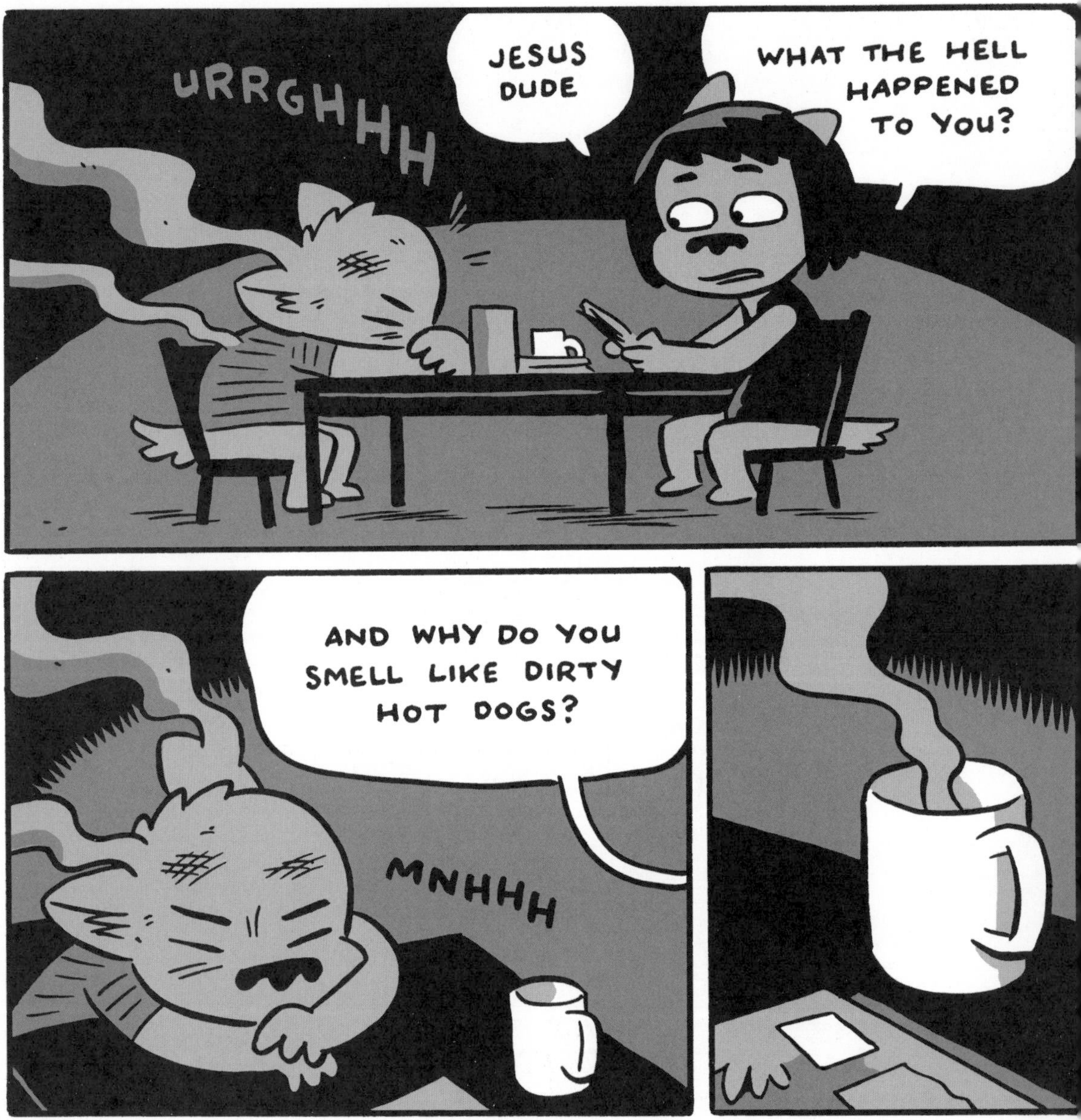
URRGHHHH
JESUS DUDE
WHAT THE HELL HAPPENED TO YOU?
AND WHY DO YOU SMELL LIKE DIRTY HOT DOGS?
MNHHHH

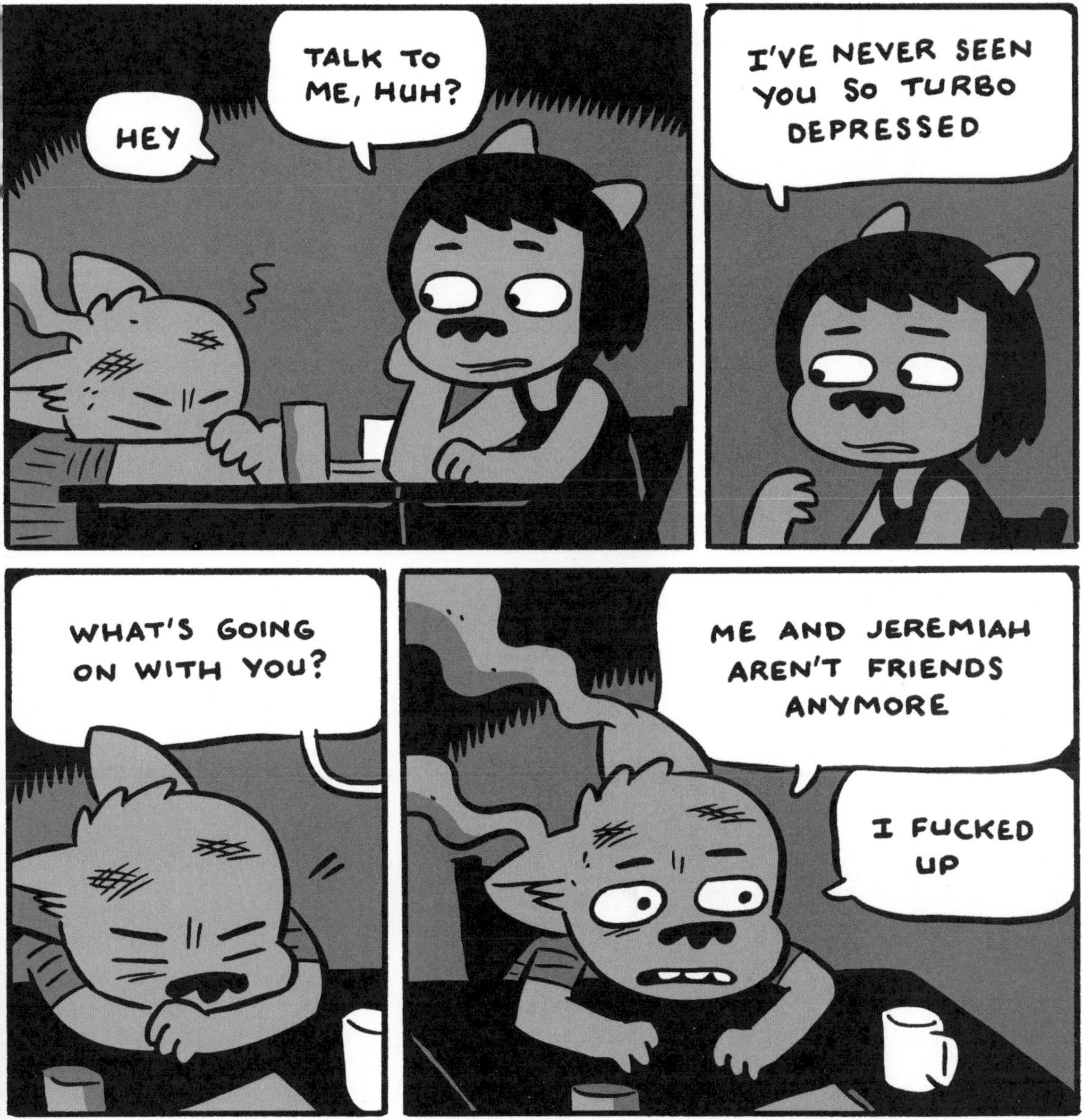
HEY
TALK TO ME, HUH?
I'VE NEVER SEEN YOU SO TURBO DEPRESSED
WHAT'S GOING ON WITH YOU?
ME AND JEREMIAH AREN'T FRIENDS ANYMORE
I FUCKED UP

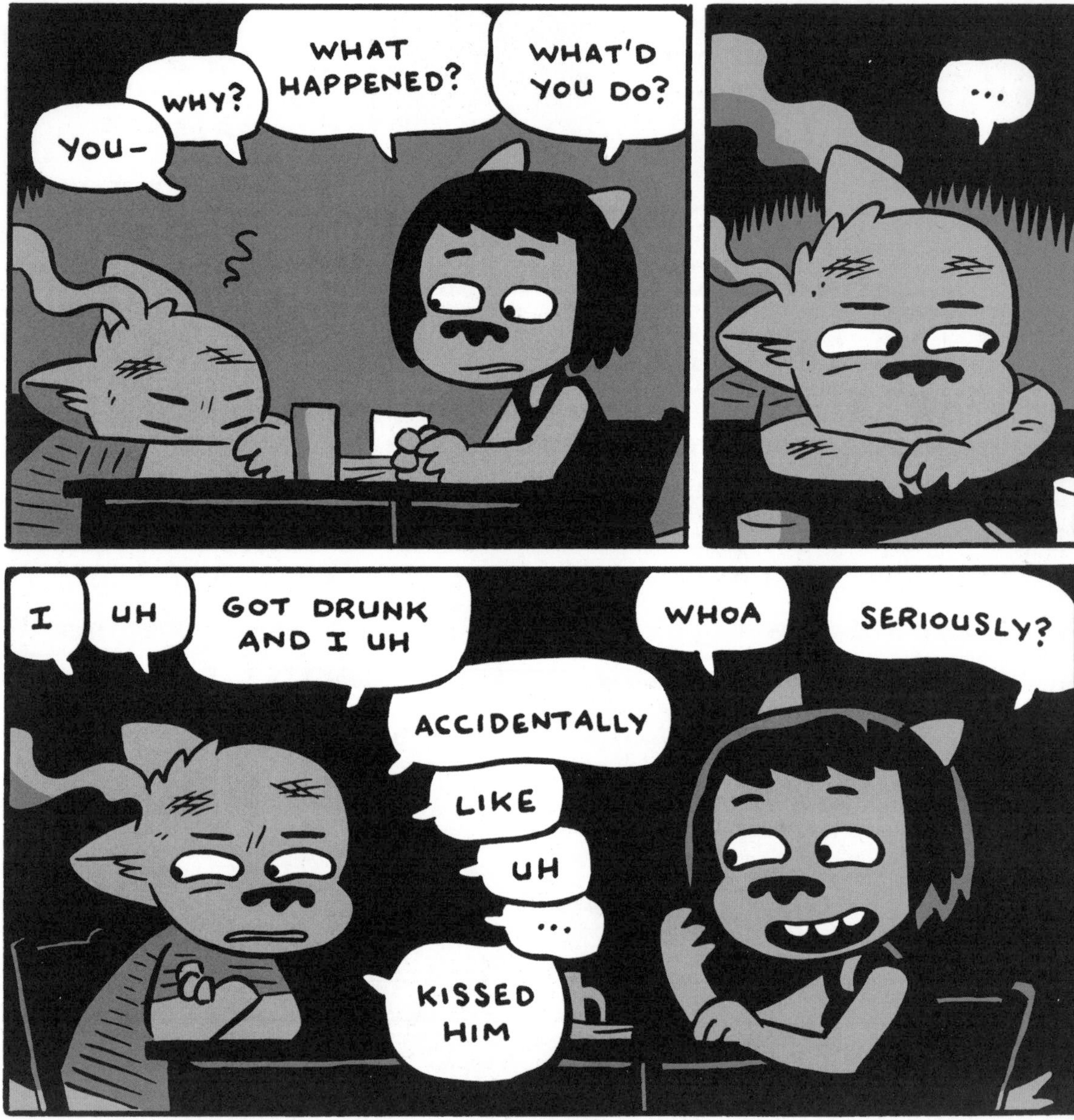
YOU-
WHY?
WHAT HAPPENED?
WHAT'D YOU DO?
...
I
UH
GOT DRUNK AND I UH
ACCIDENTALLY
LIKE
UH
...
KISSED HIM
WHOA
SERIOUSLY?

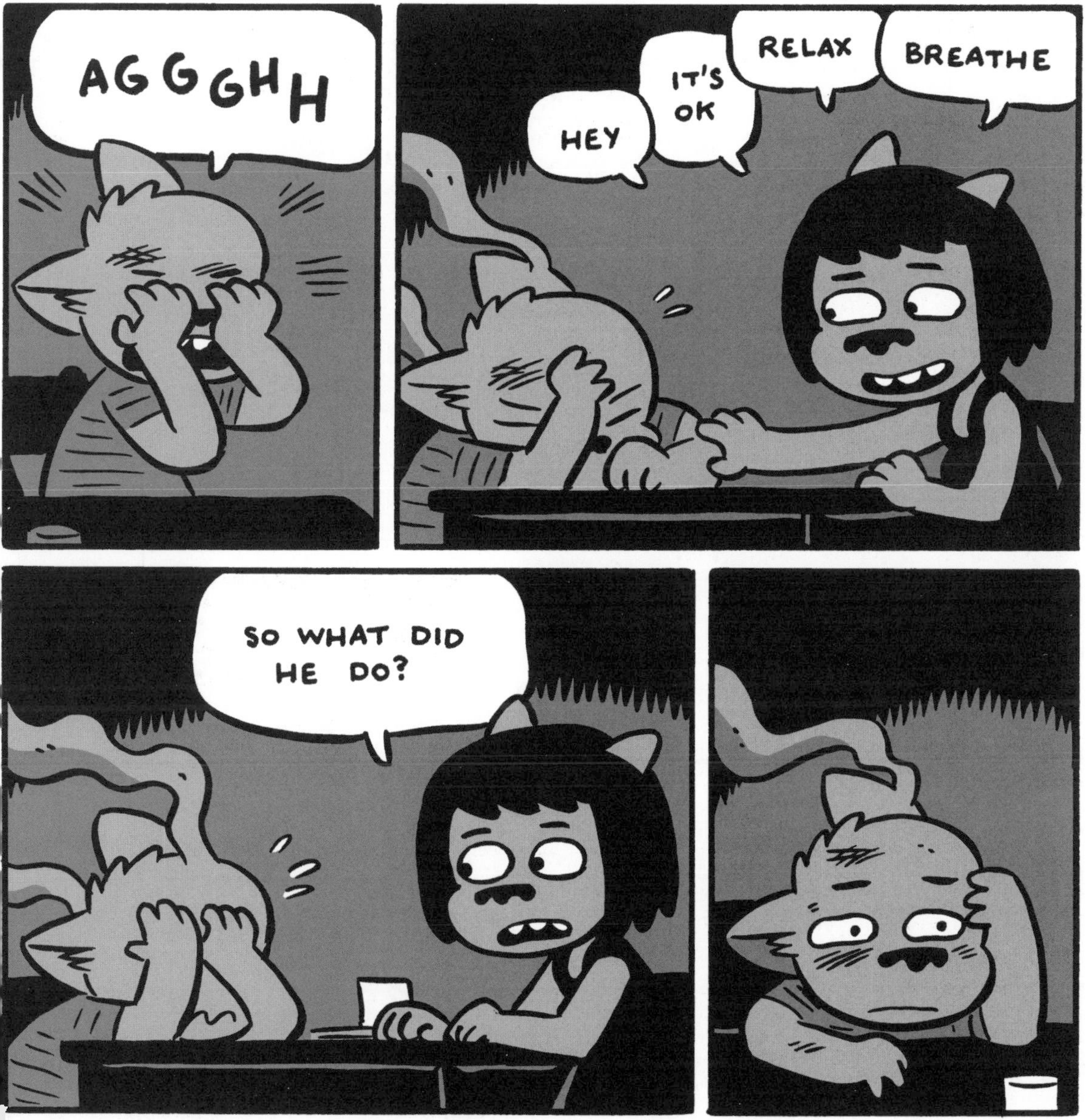
AGGGHHH
HEY
IT'S OK
RELAX
BREATHE
SO WHAT DID HE DO?

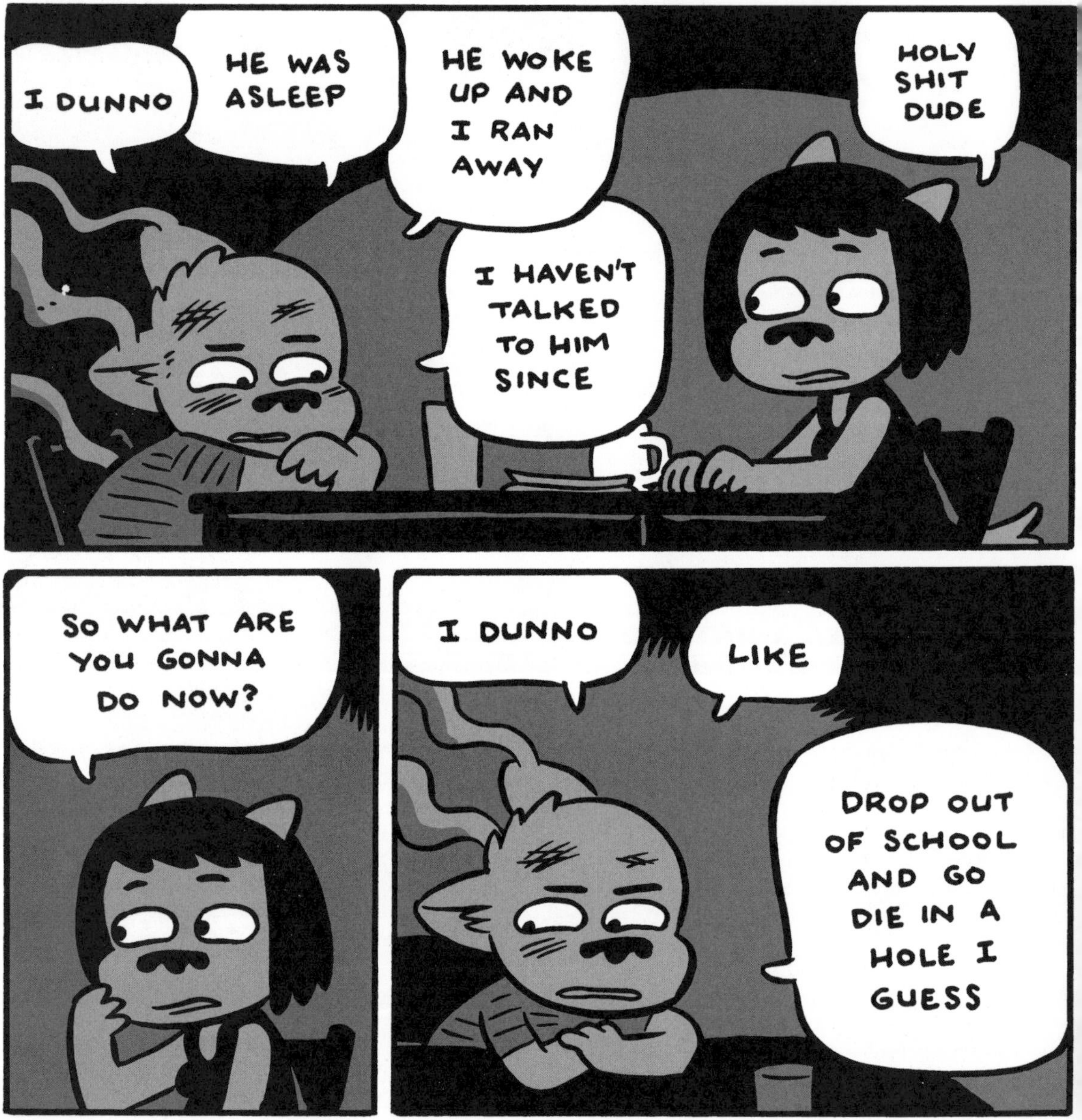
I DUNNO
HE WAS ASLEEP
HE WOKE UP AND I RAN AWAY
HOLY SHIT DUDE
I HAVEN'T TALKED TO HIM SINCE
SO WHAT ARE YOU GONNA DO NOW?
I DUNNO
LIKE
DROP OUT OF SCHOOL AND GO DIE IN A HOLE I GUESS

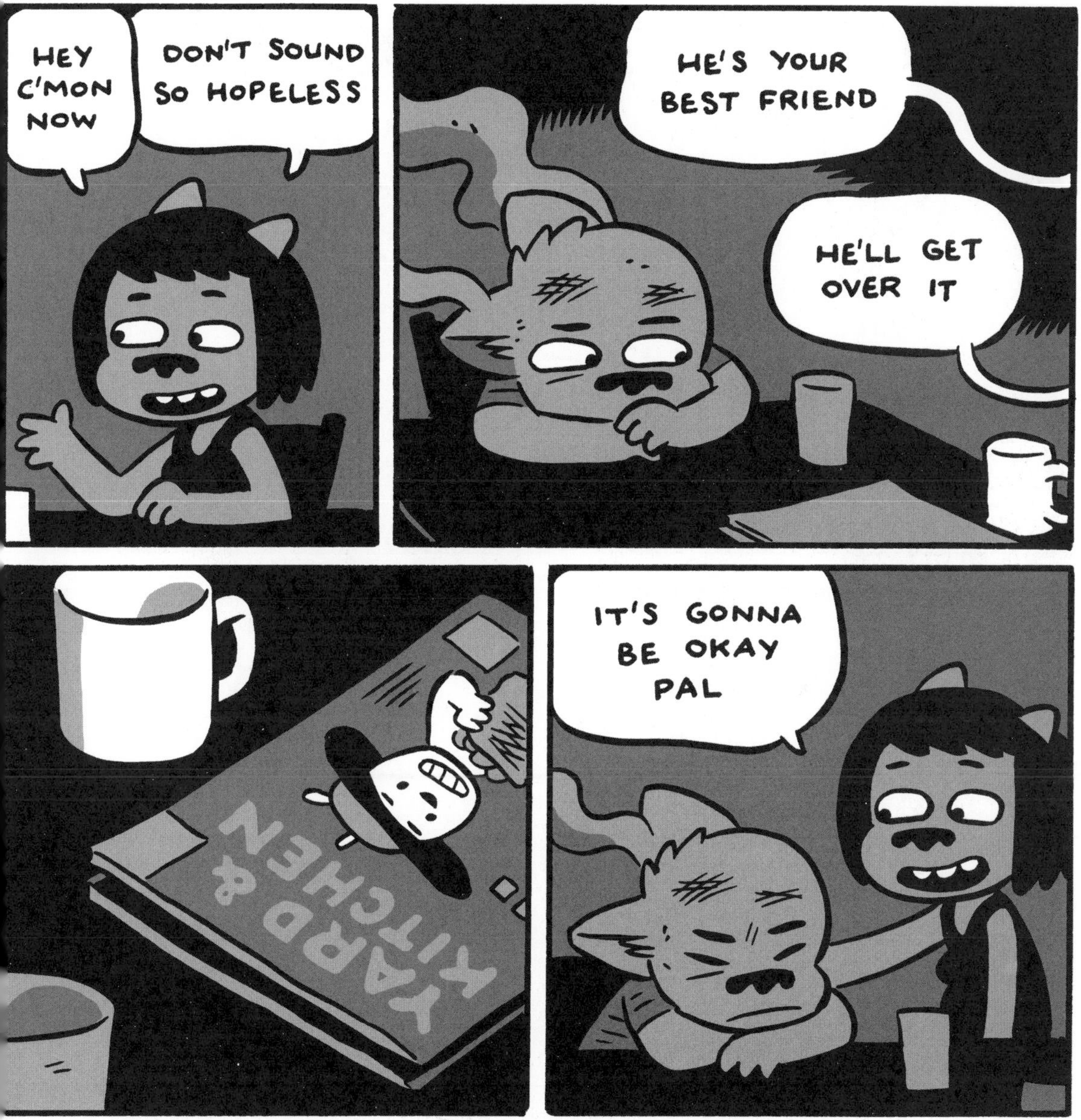
HEY C'MON NOW
DON'T SOUND SO HOPELESS
HE'S YOUR BEST FRIEND
HE'LL GET OVER IT
YARD & KITCHEN
IT'S GONNA BE OKAY PAL

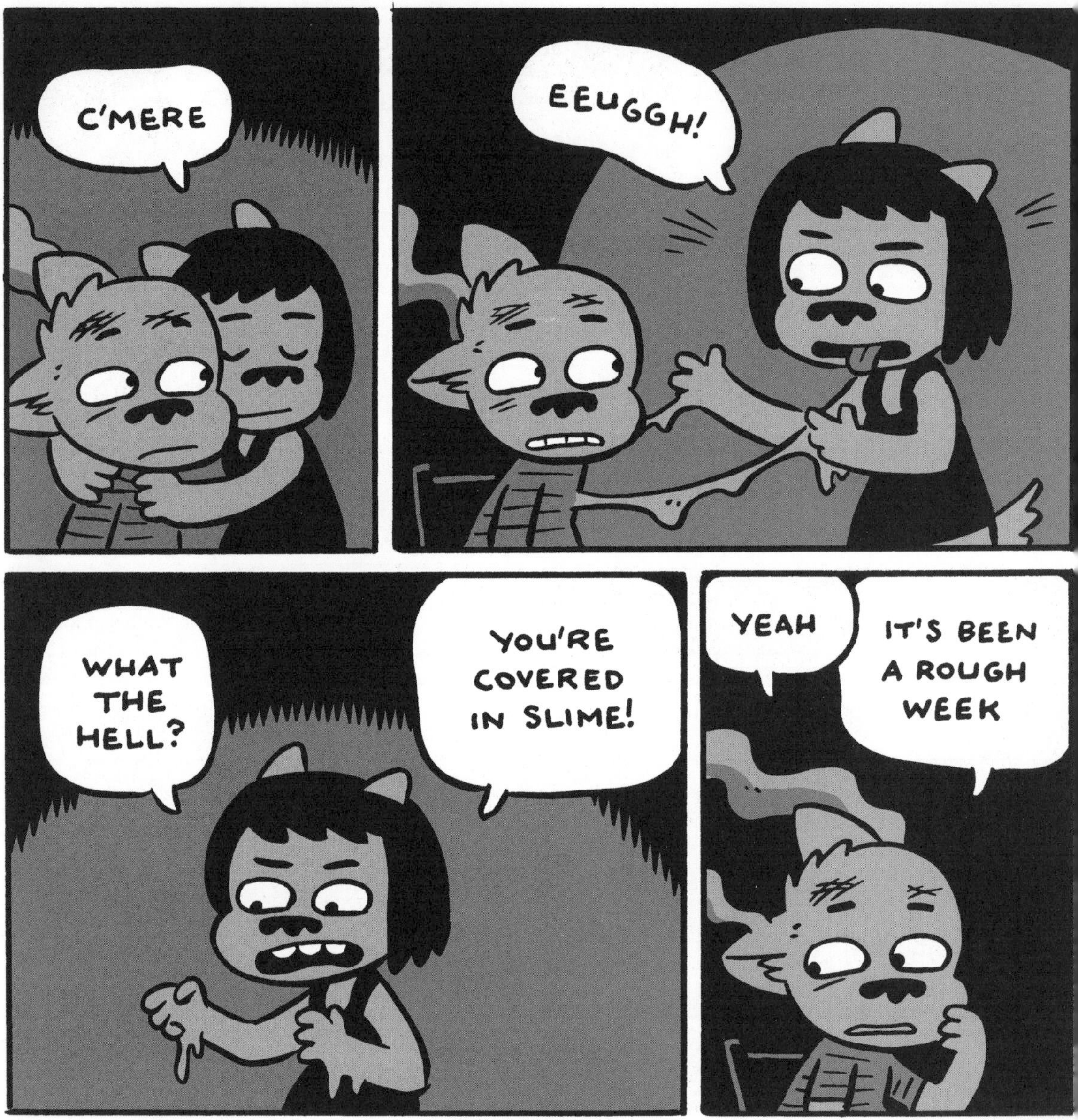
C'MERE
EEUGGH!
WHAT THE HELL?
YOU'RE COVERED IN SLIME!
YEAH
IT'S BEEN A ROUGH WEEK

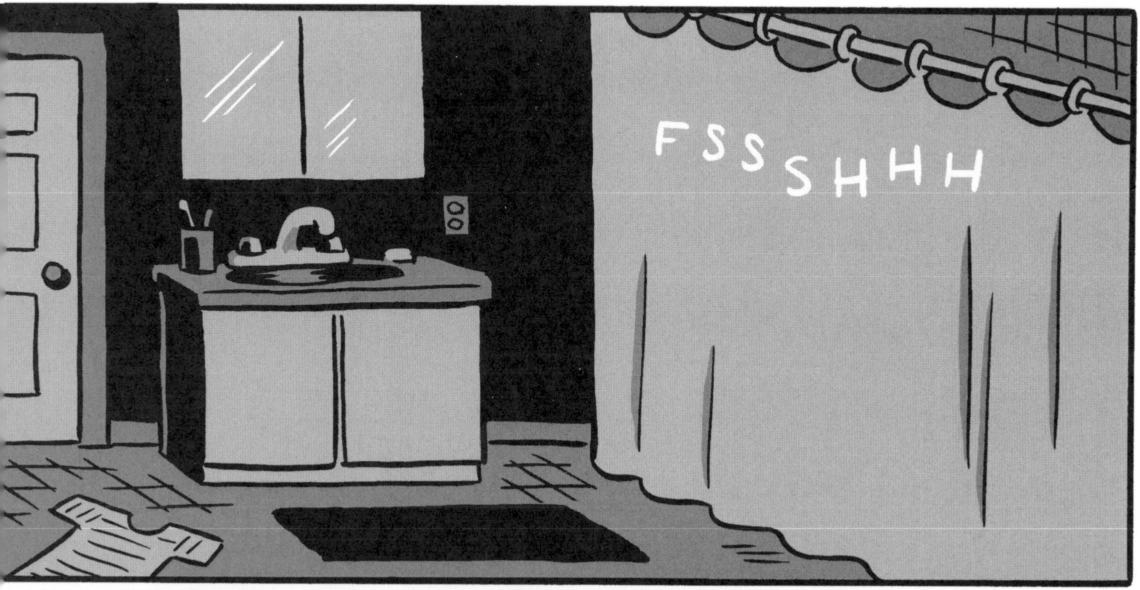
FSSSHHH

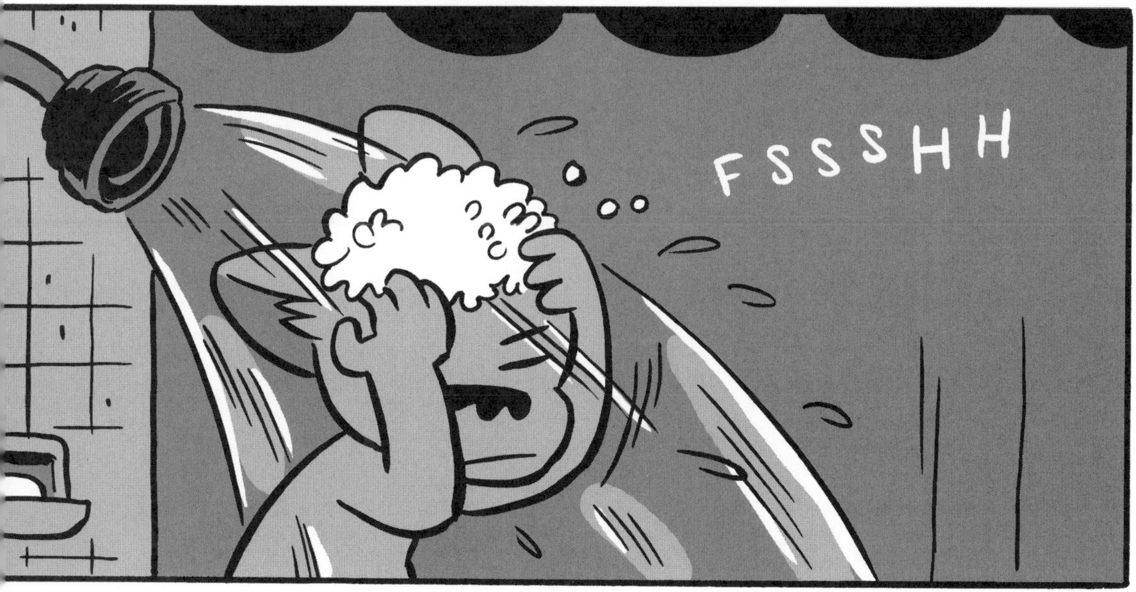
FSSSHH

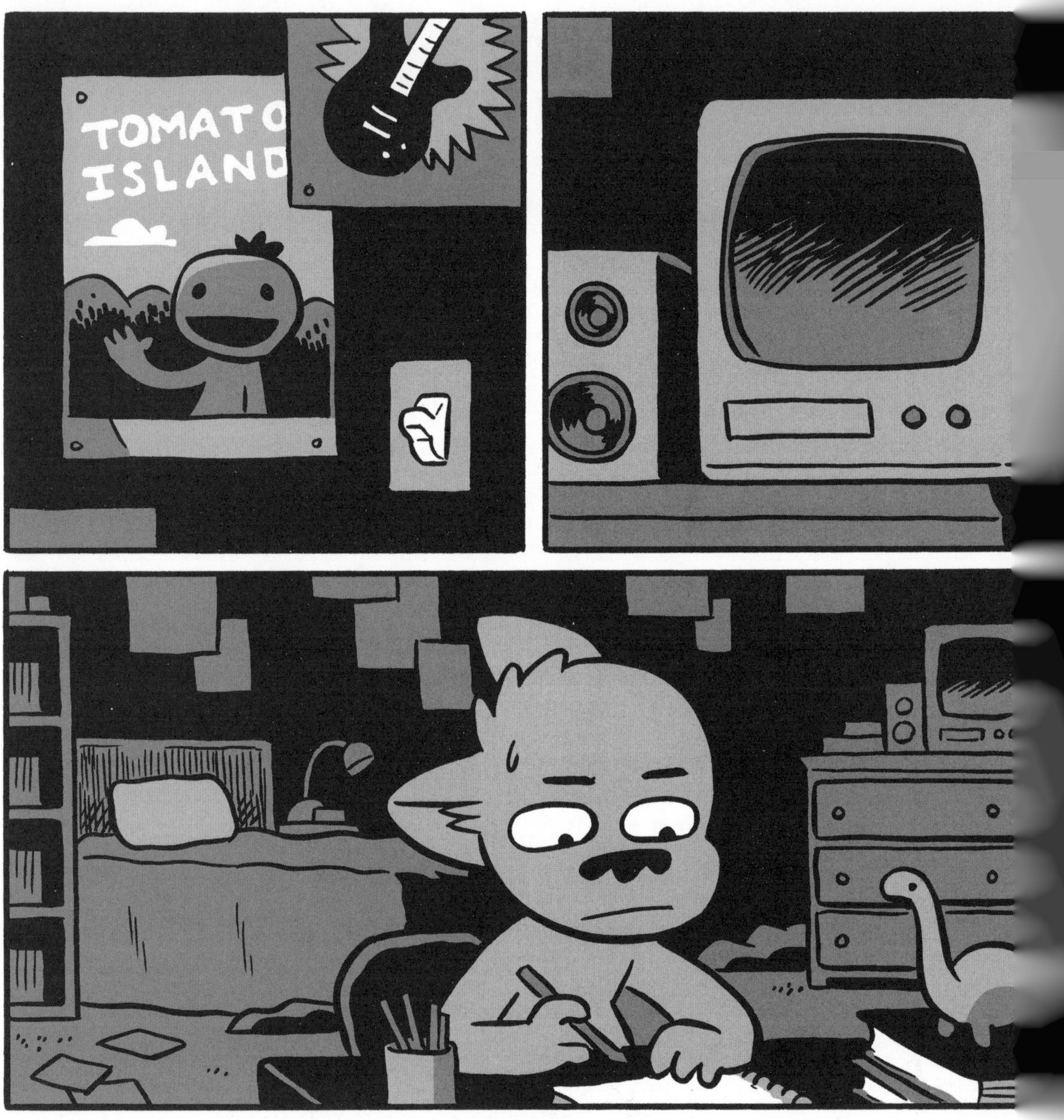
TOMATO
ISLAND

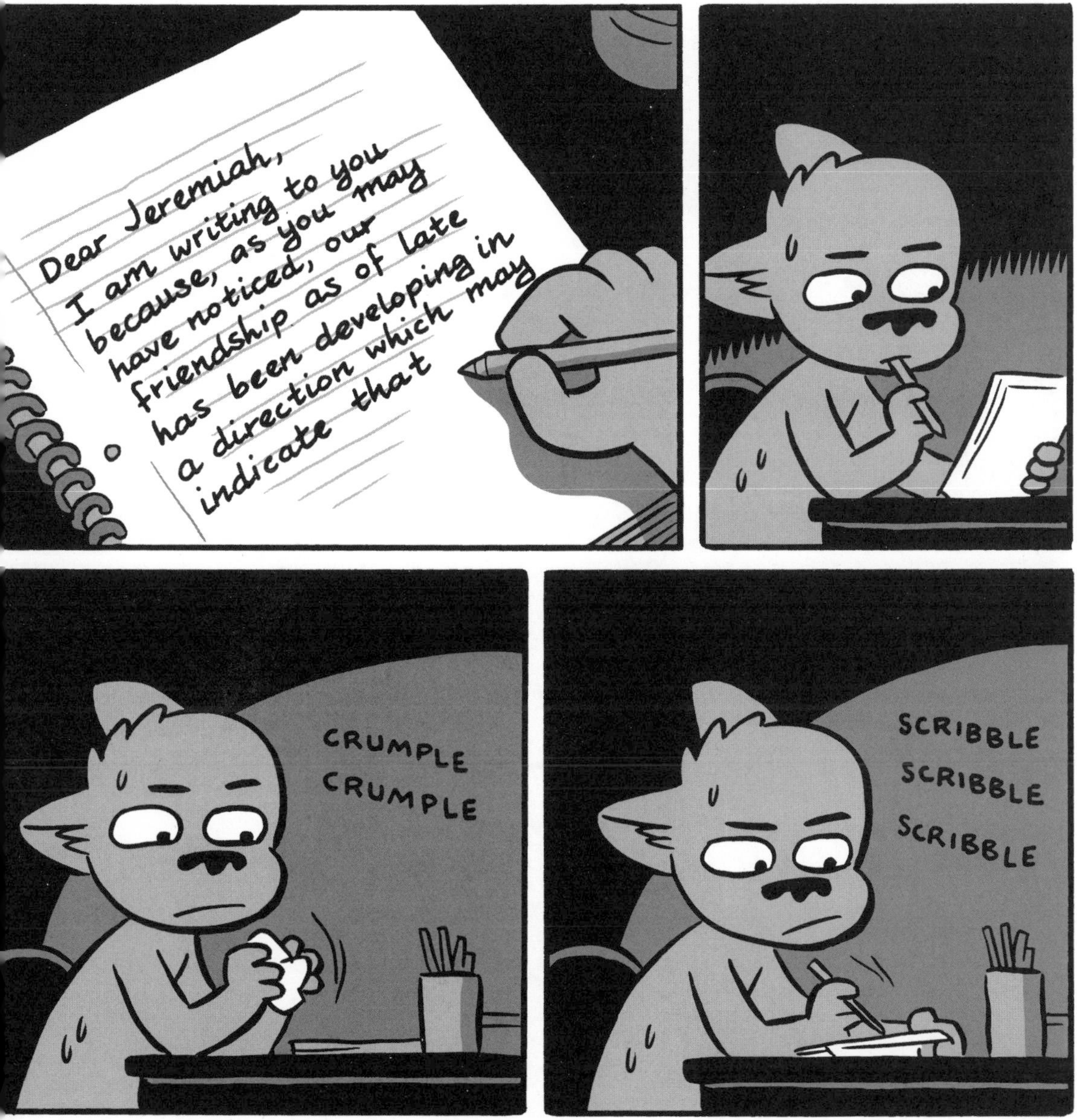
Dear Jeremiah,
I am writing to you because, as you may have noticed, our friendship as of late has been developing in a direction which may indicate that
CRUMPLE
CRUMPLE
SCRIBBLE
SCRIBBLE
SCRIBBLE

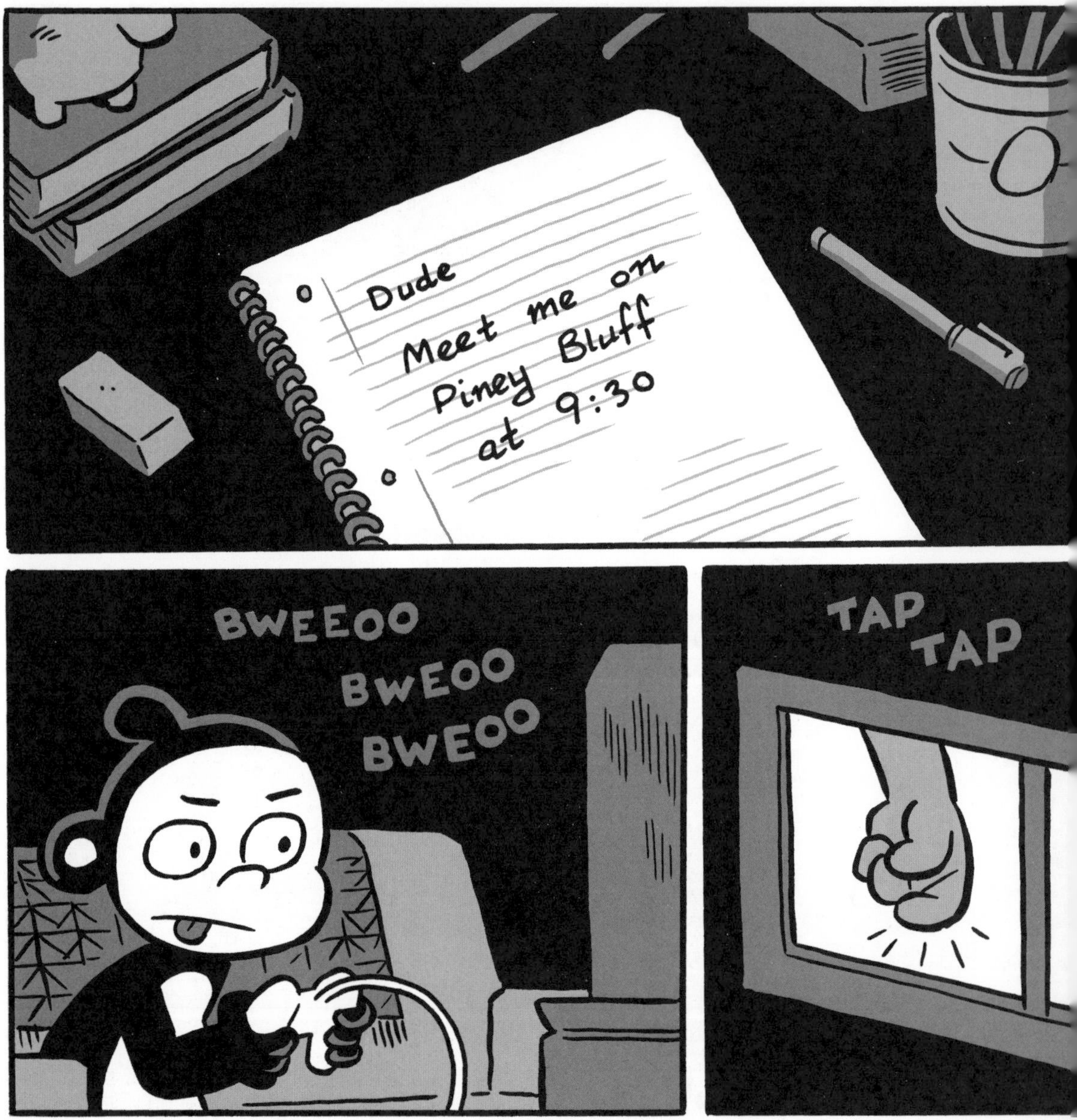
Dude
Meet me on
Piney Bluff
at 9:30
BWEEOO
BWEOO
BWEOO
TAP
TAP

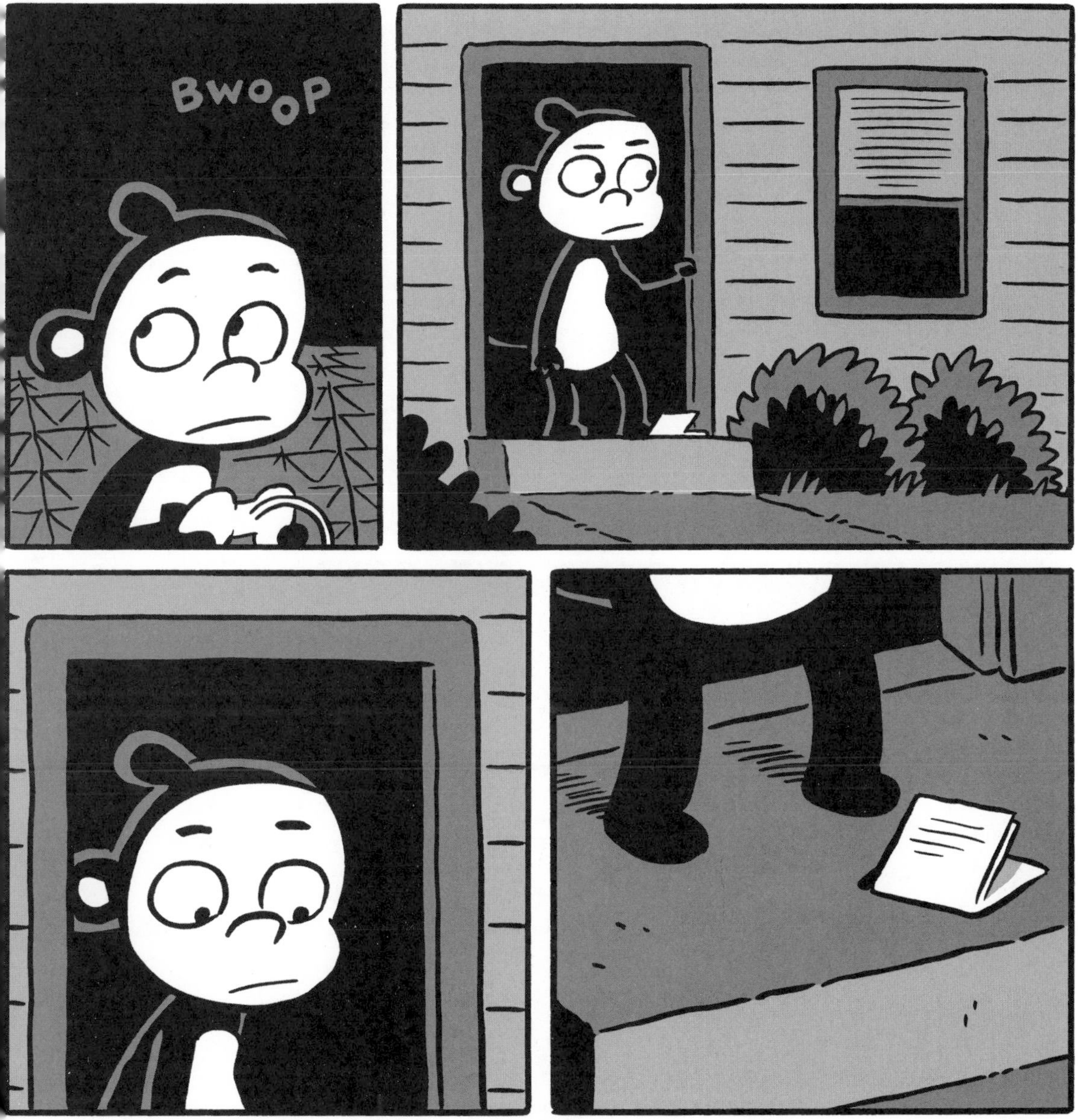
BWOOP

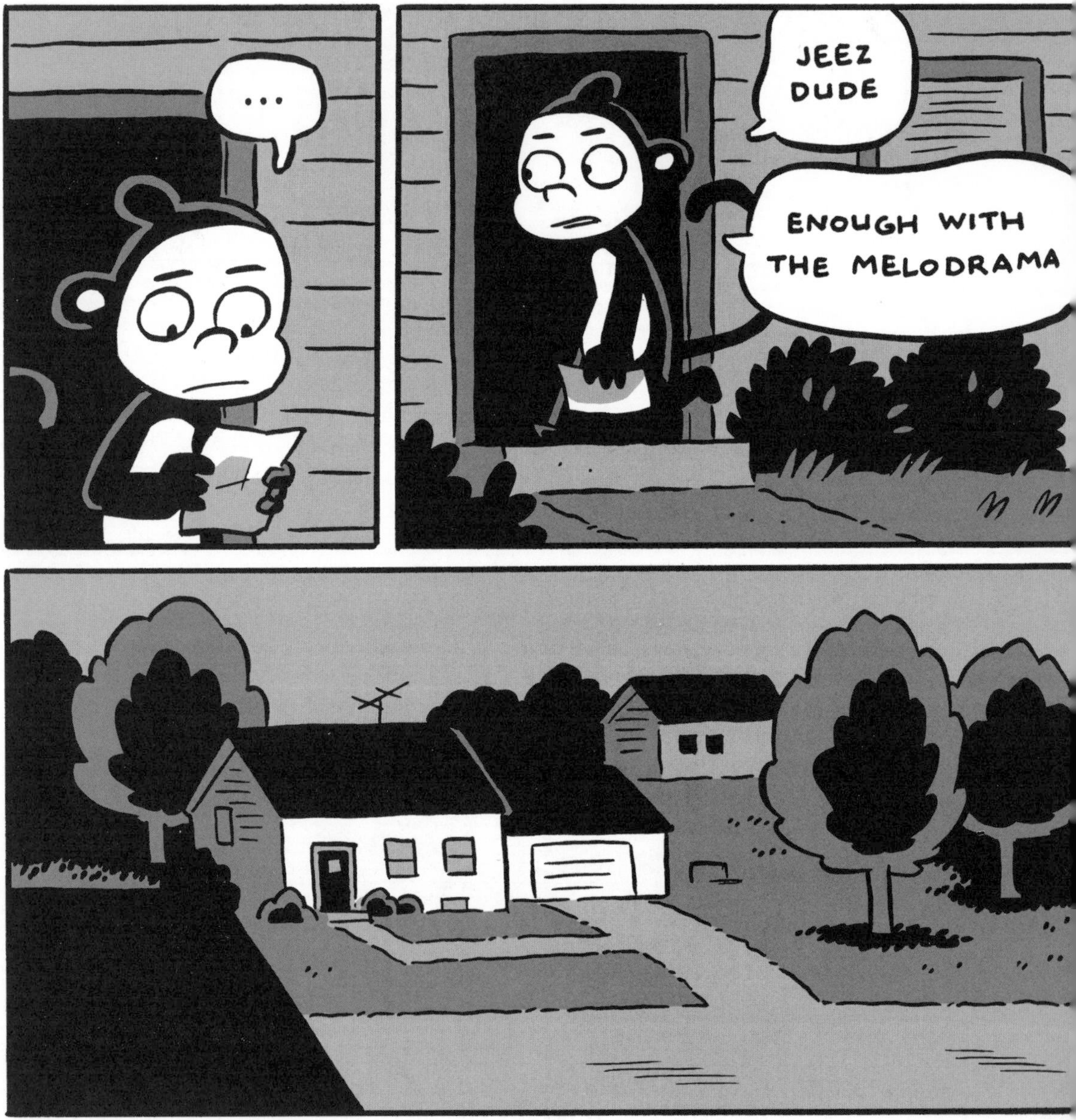
...
JEEZ DUDE
ENOUGH WITH THE MELODRAMA

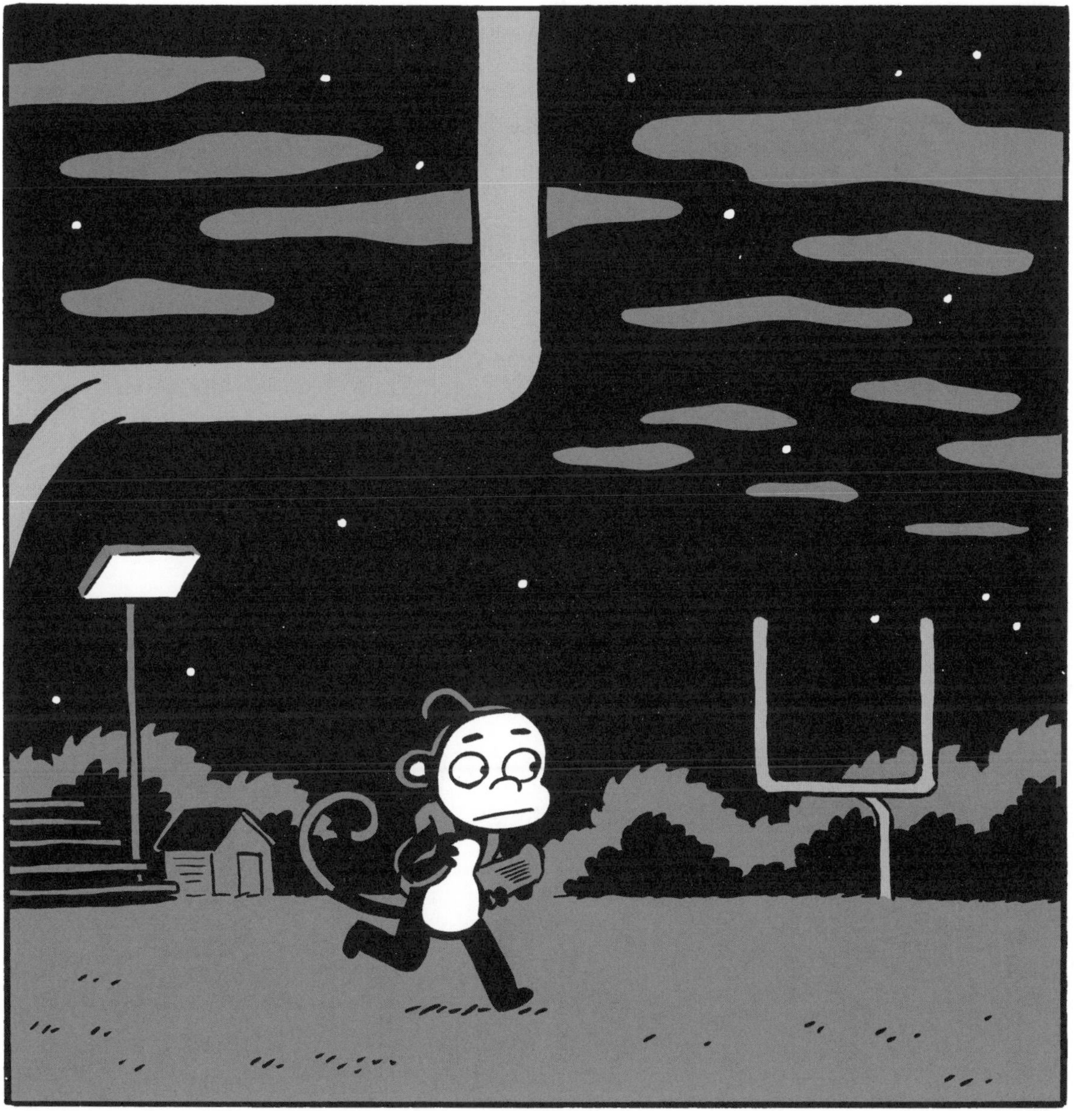

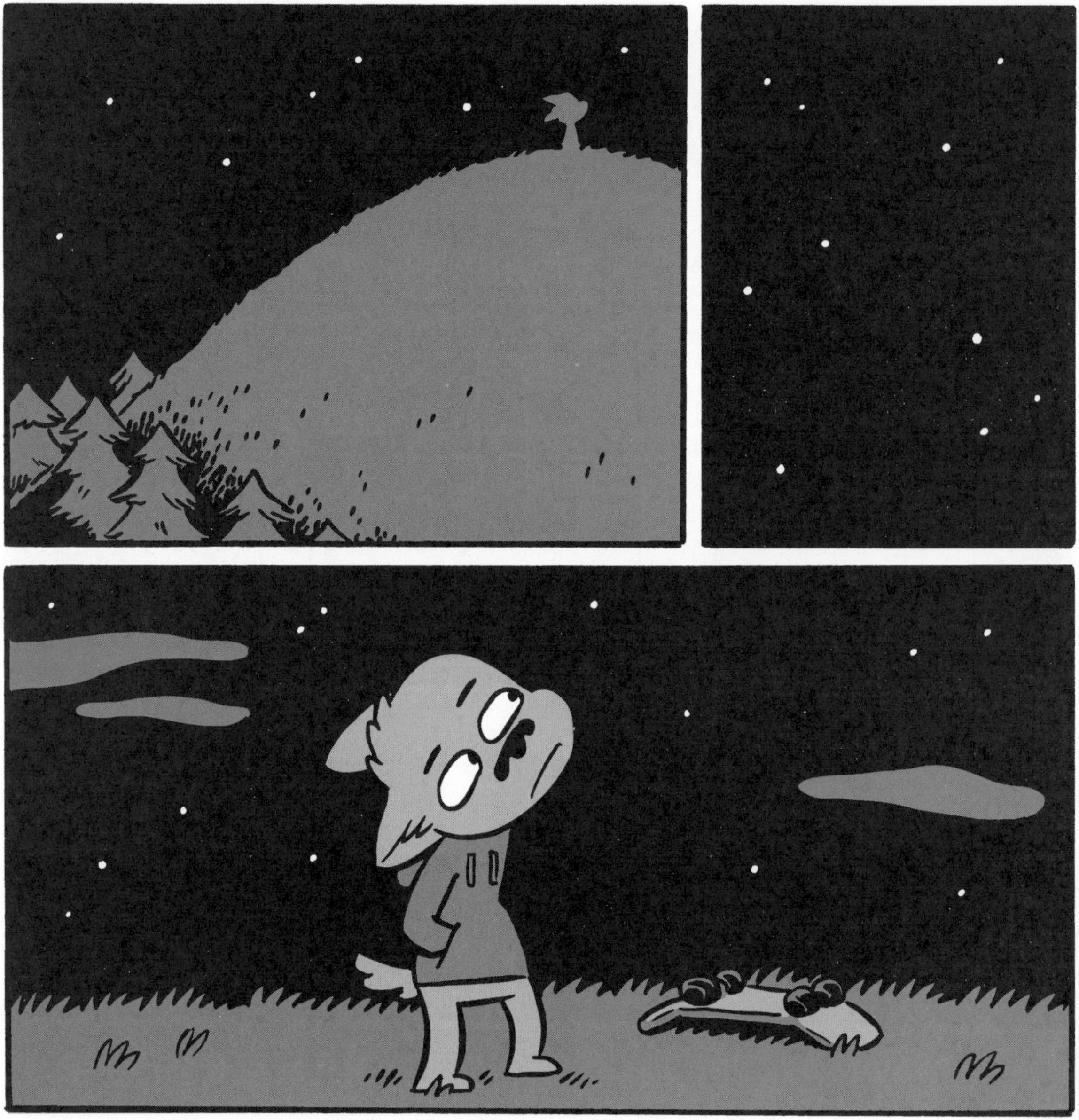

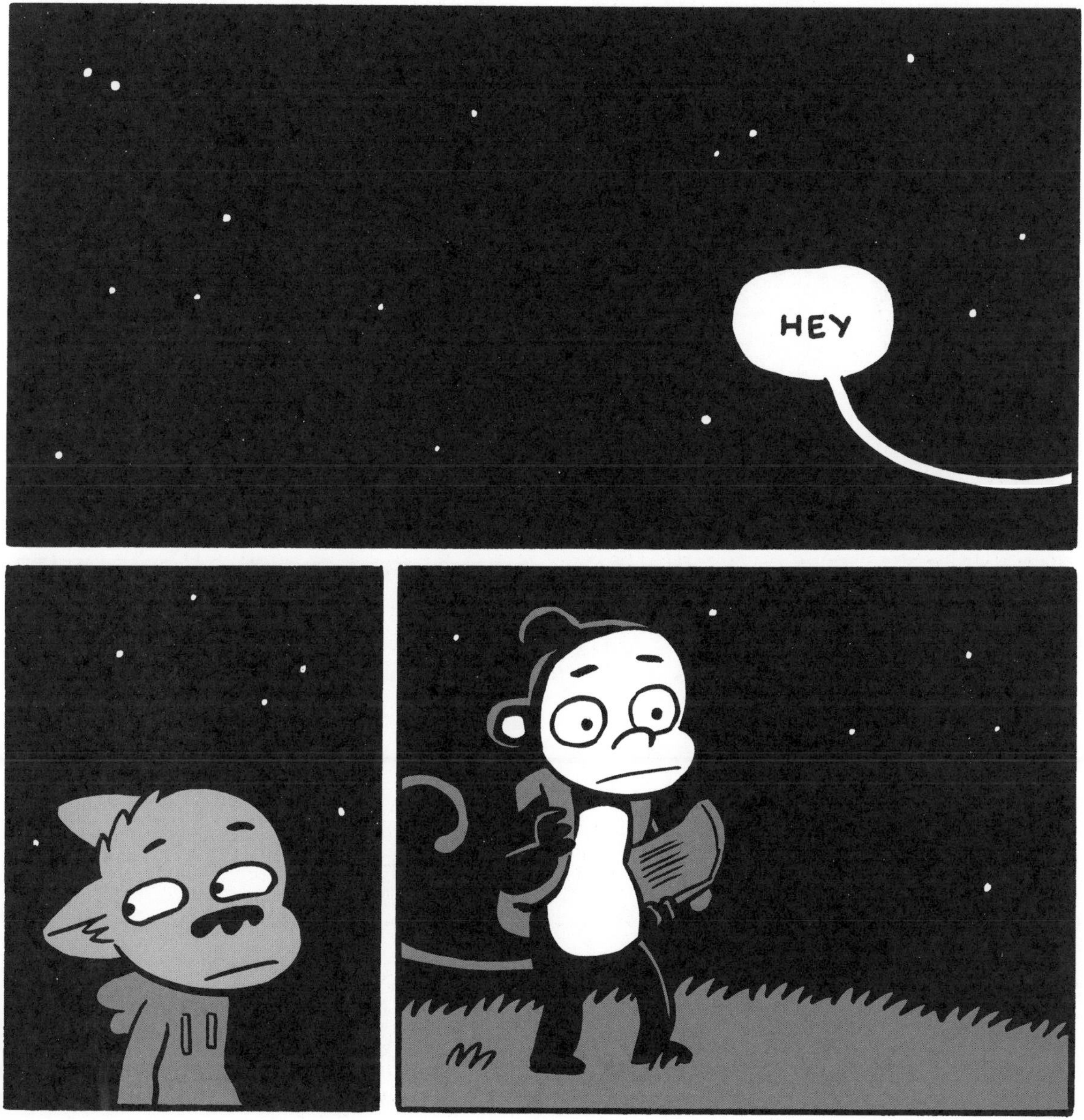
HEY

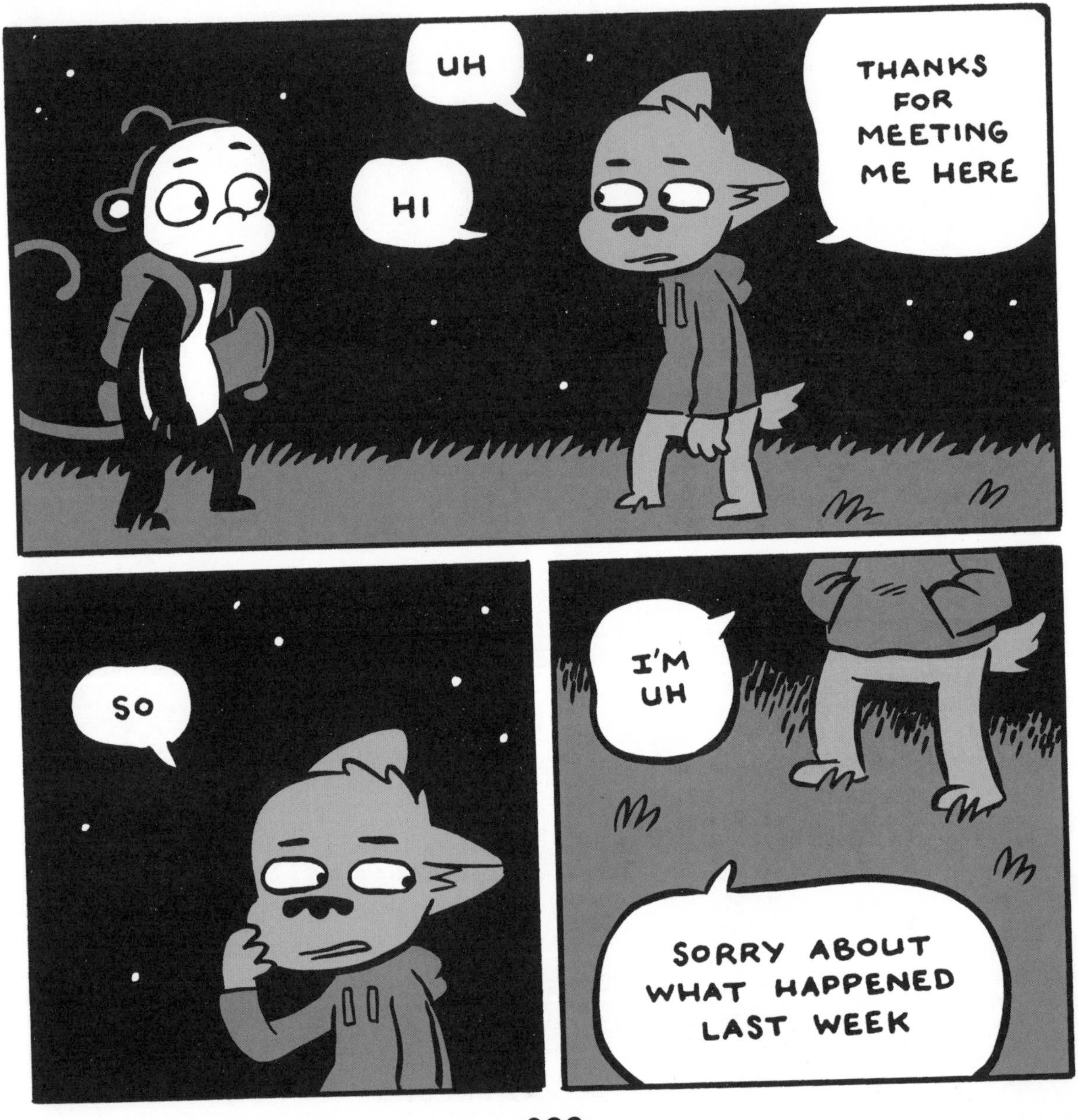
UH
HI
THANKS FOR MEETING ME HERE
SO
I'M UH
SORRY ABOUT WHAT HAPPENED LAST WEEK

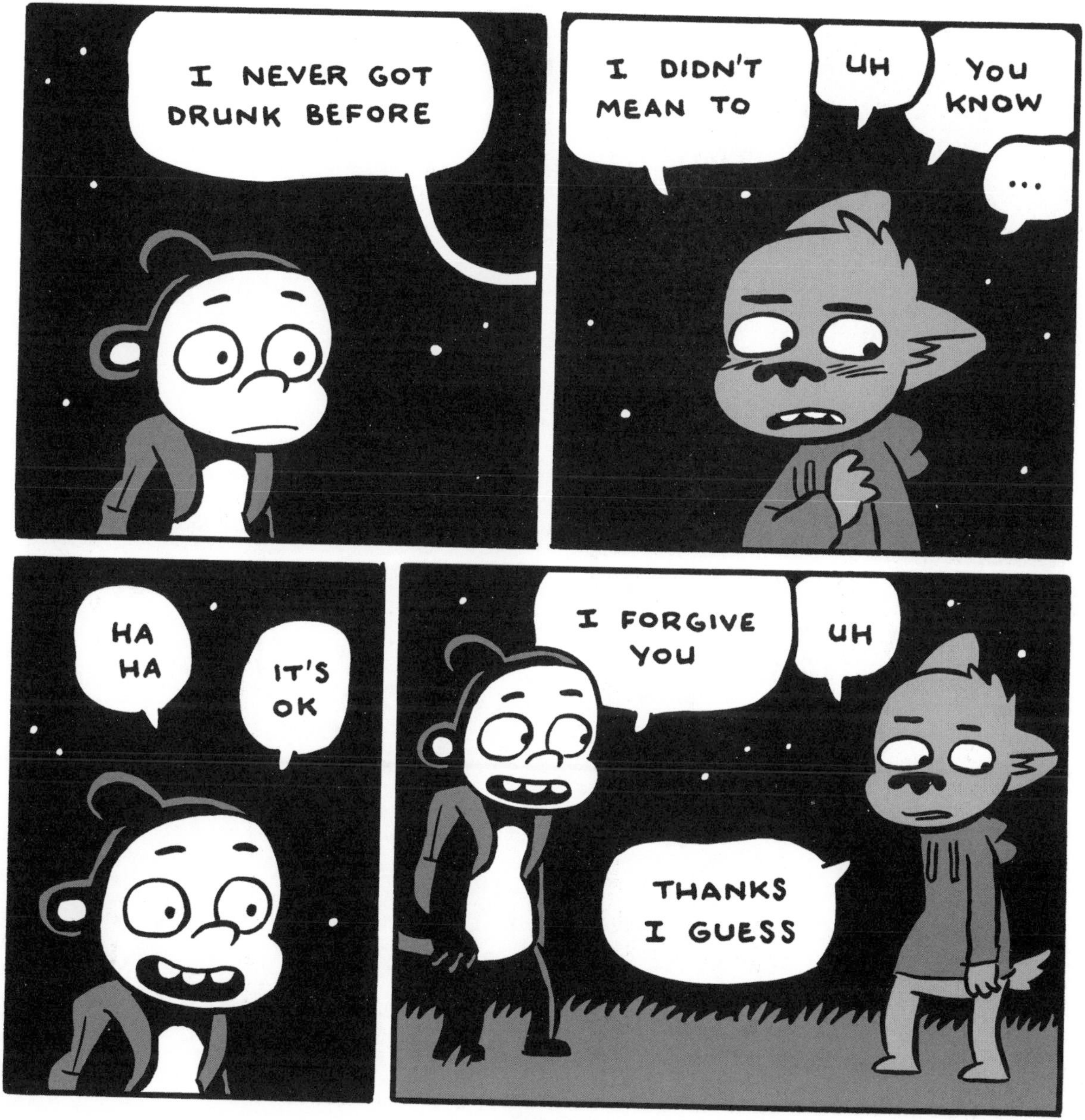
I NEVER GOT DRUNK BEFORE
I DIDN'T MEAN TO
UH
YOU KNOW
...
HA HA
IT'S OK
I FORGIVE YOU
UH
THANKS I GUESS

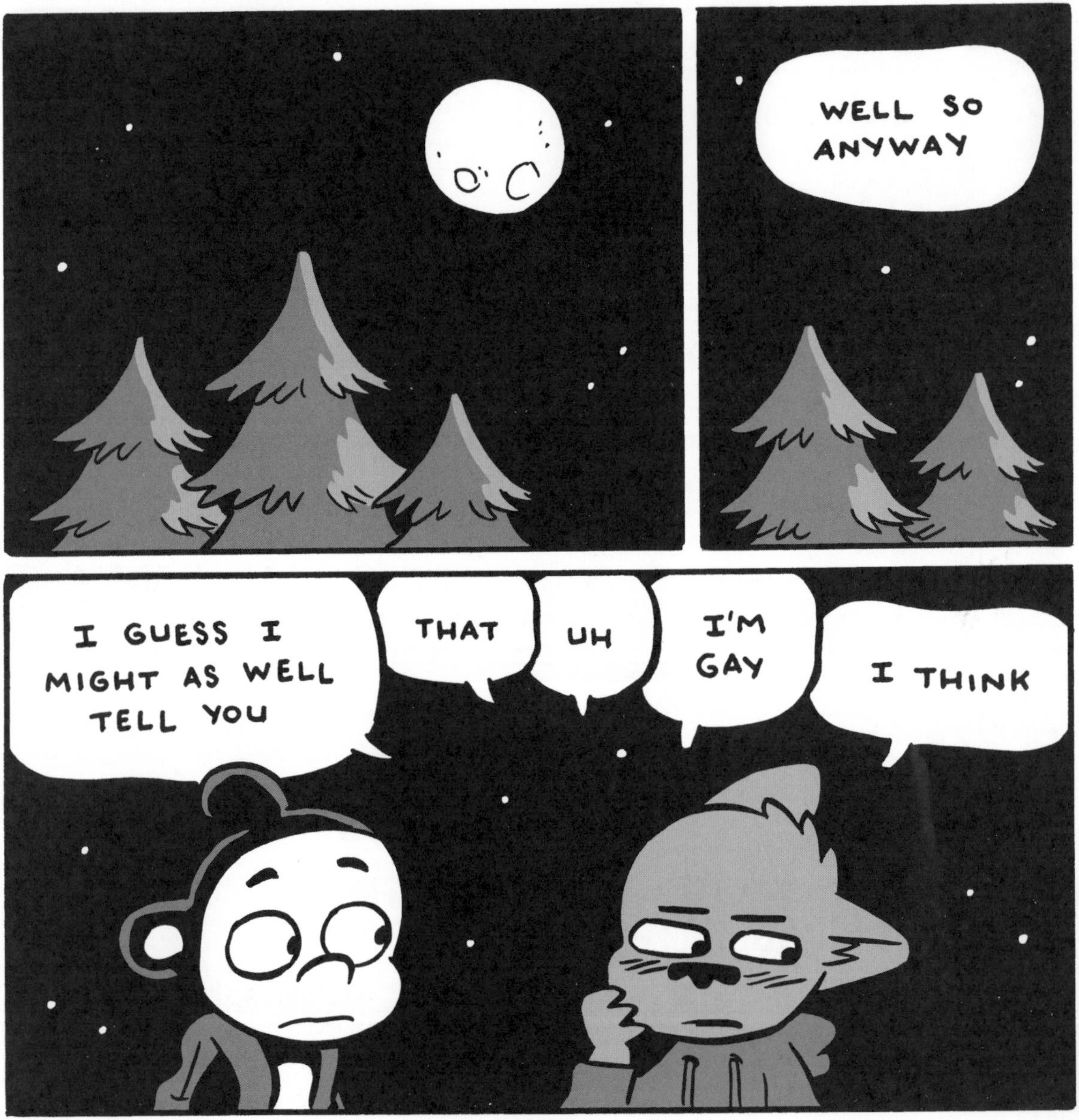
WELL SO ANYWAY
I GUESS I MIGHT AS WELL TELL YOU
THAT
UH
I'M GAY
I THINK

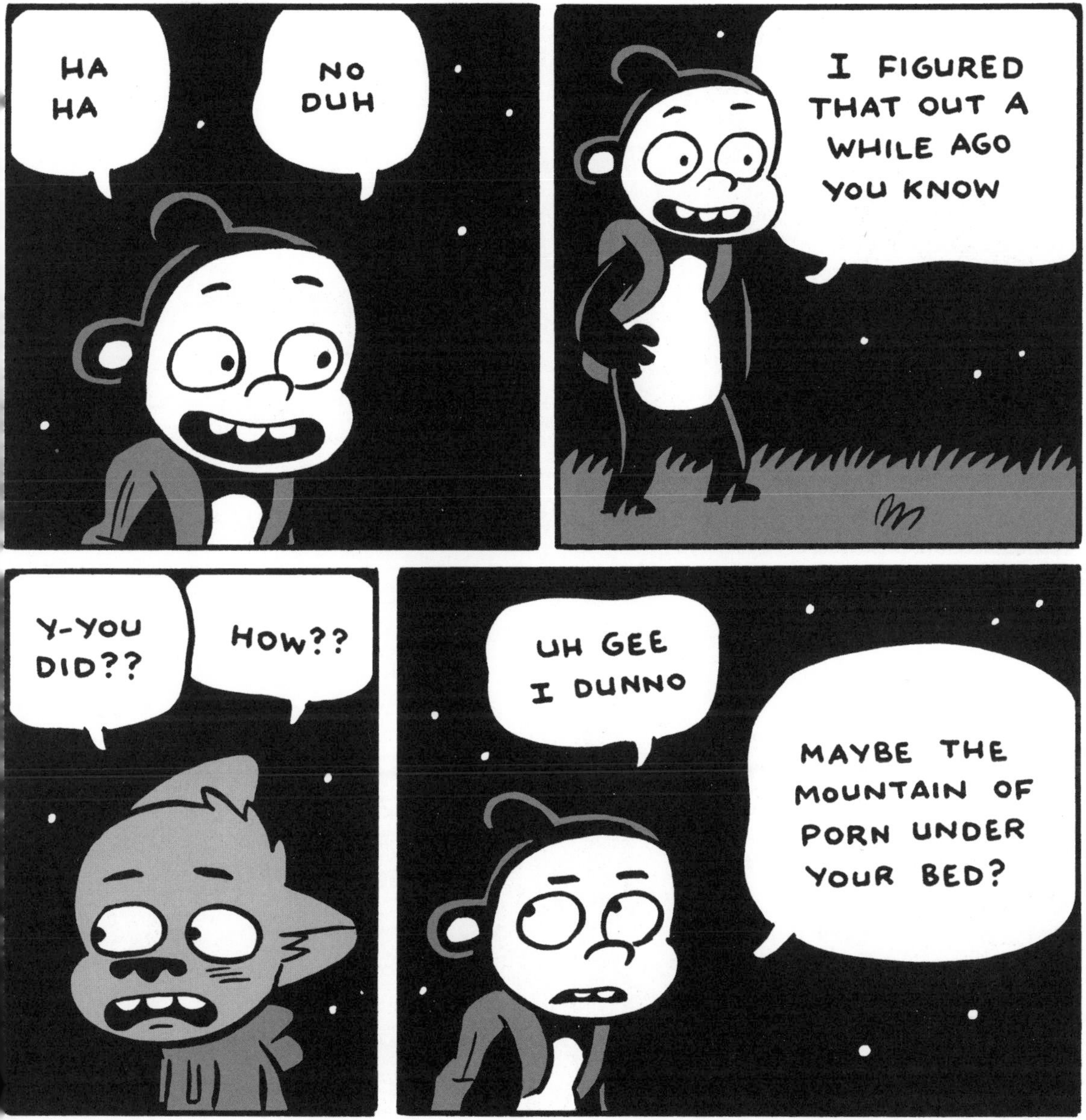
HA HA
NO DUH
I FIGURED THAT OUT A WHILE AGO YOU KNOW
Y-YOU DID??
HOW??
UH GEE I DUNNO
MAYBE THE MOUNTAIN OF PORN UNDER YOUR BED?

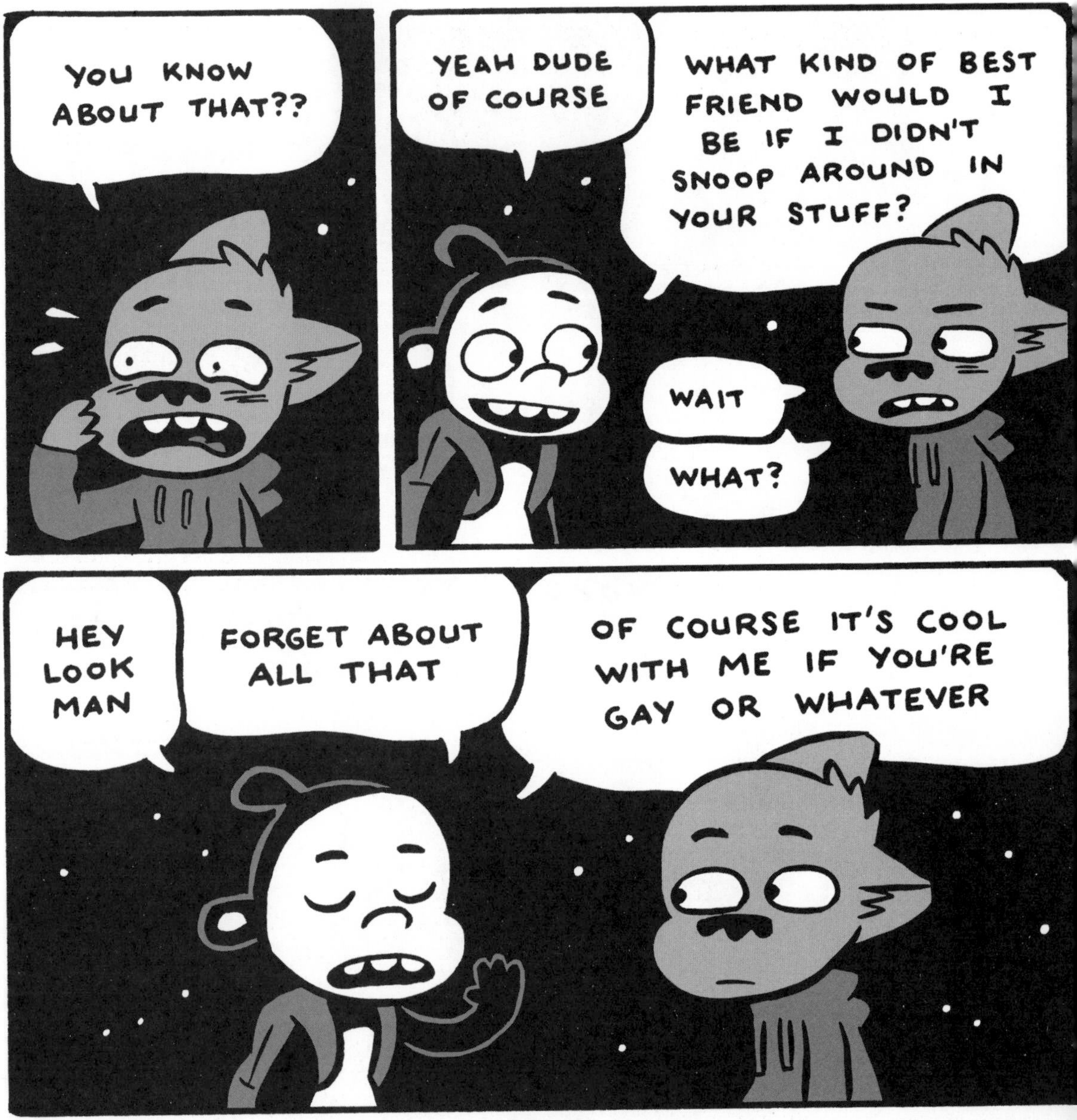
YOU KNOW ABOUT THAT??
YEAH DUDE OF COURSE
WHAT KIND OF BEST FRIEND WOULD I BE IF I DIDN'T SNOOP AROUND IN YOUR STUFF?
WAIT
WHAT?
HEY LOOK MAN
FORGET ABOUT ALL THAT
OF COURSE IT'S COOL WITH ME IF YOU'RE GAY OR WHATEVER

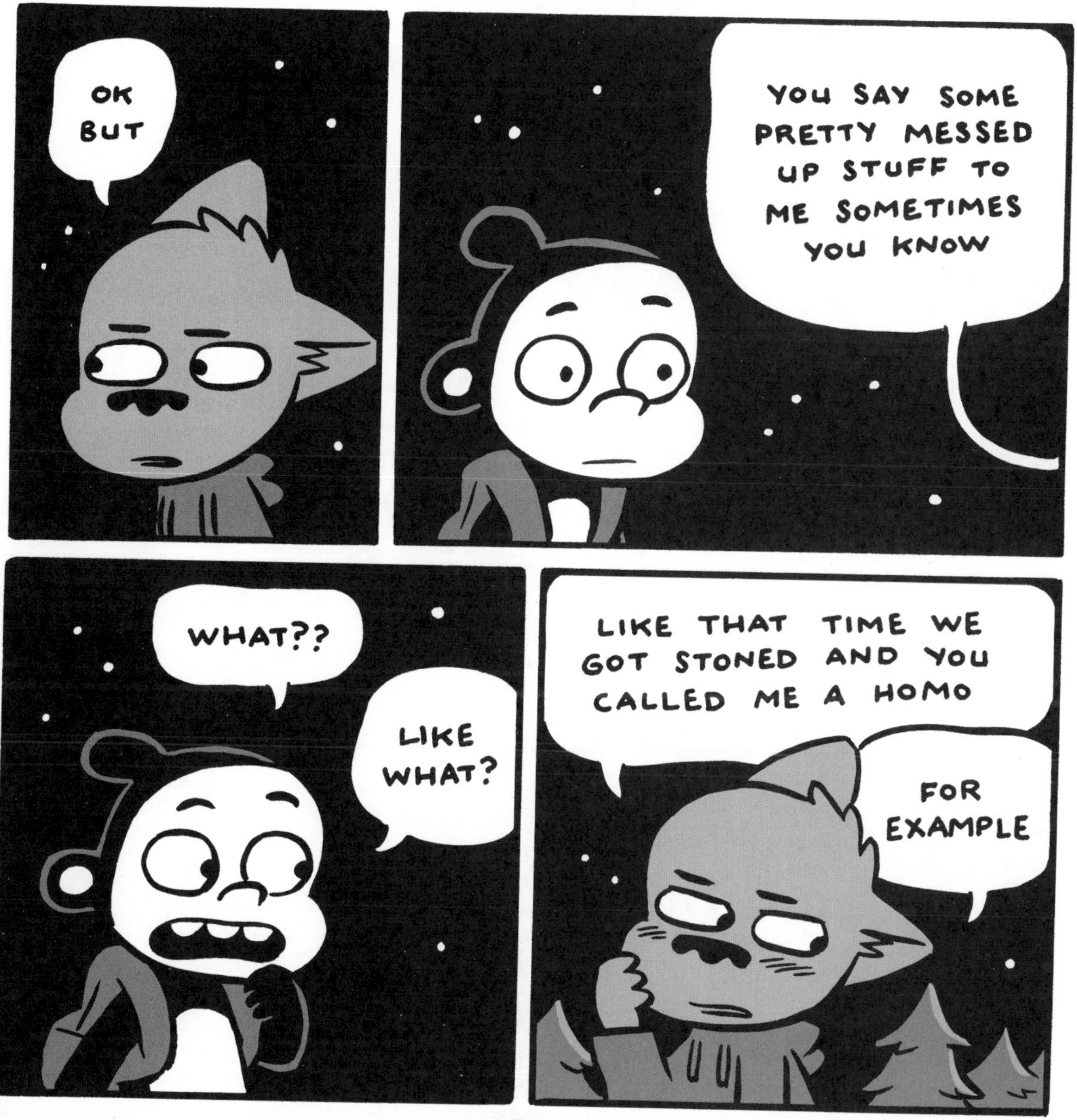
OK BUT
YOU SAY SOME PRETTY MESSED UP STUFF TO ME SOMETIMES YOU KNOW
WHAT??
LIKE WHAT?
LIKE THAT TIME WE GOT STONED AND YOU CALLED ME A HOMO
FOR EXAMPLE

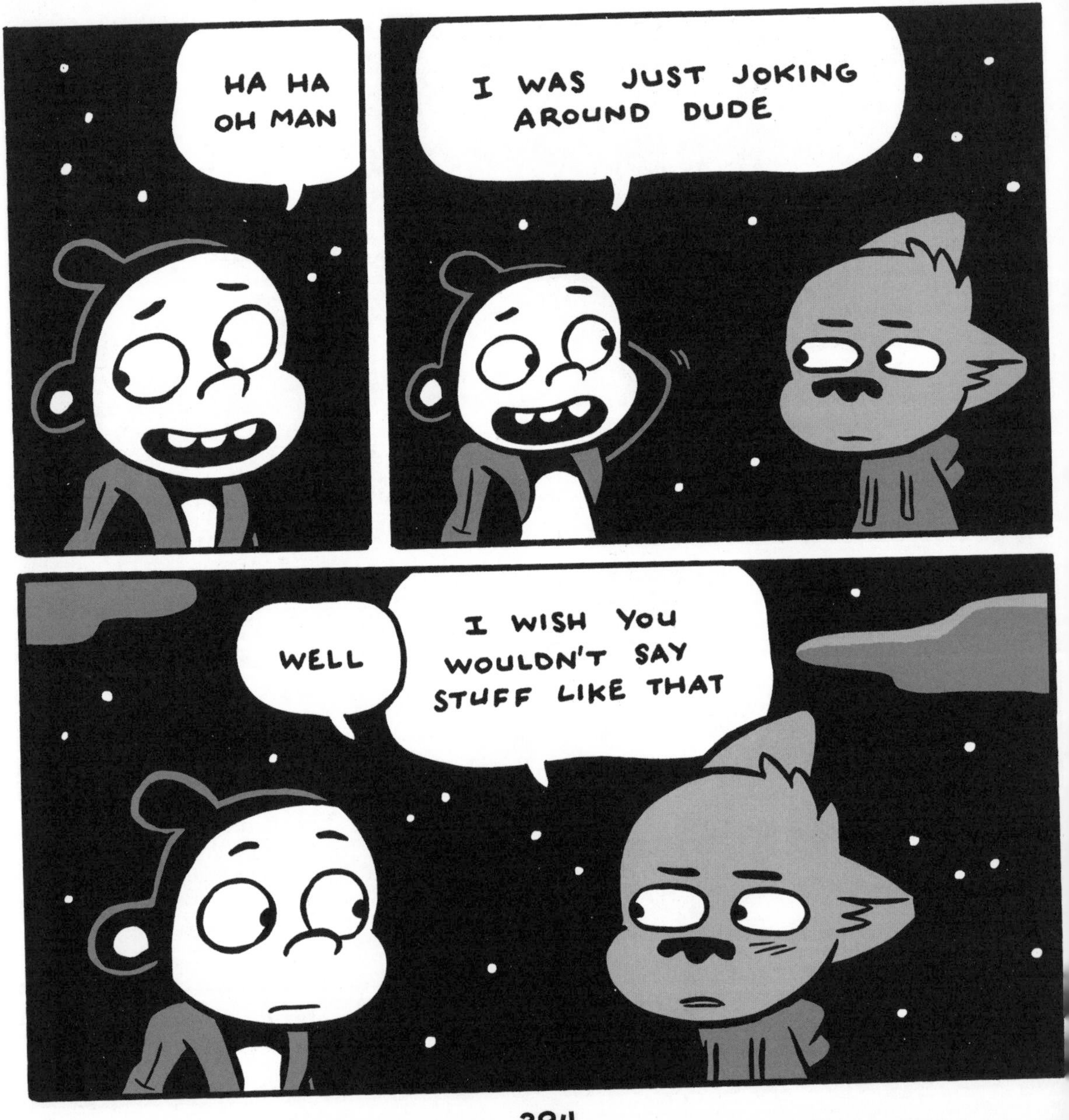
HA HA
OH MAN
I WAS JUST JOKING AROUND DUDE
WELL
I WISH YOU WOULDN'T SAY STUFF LIKE THAT

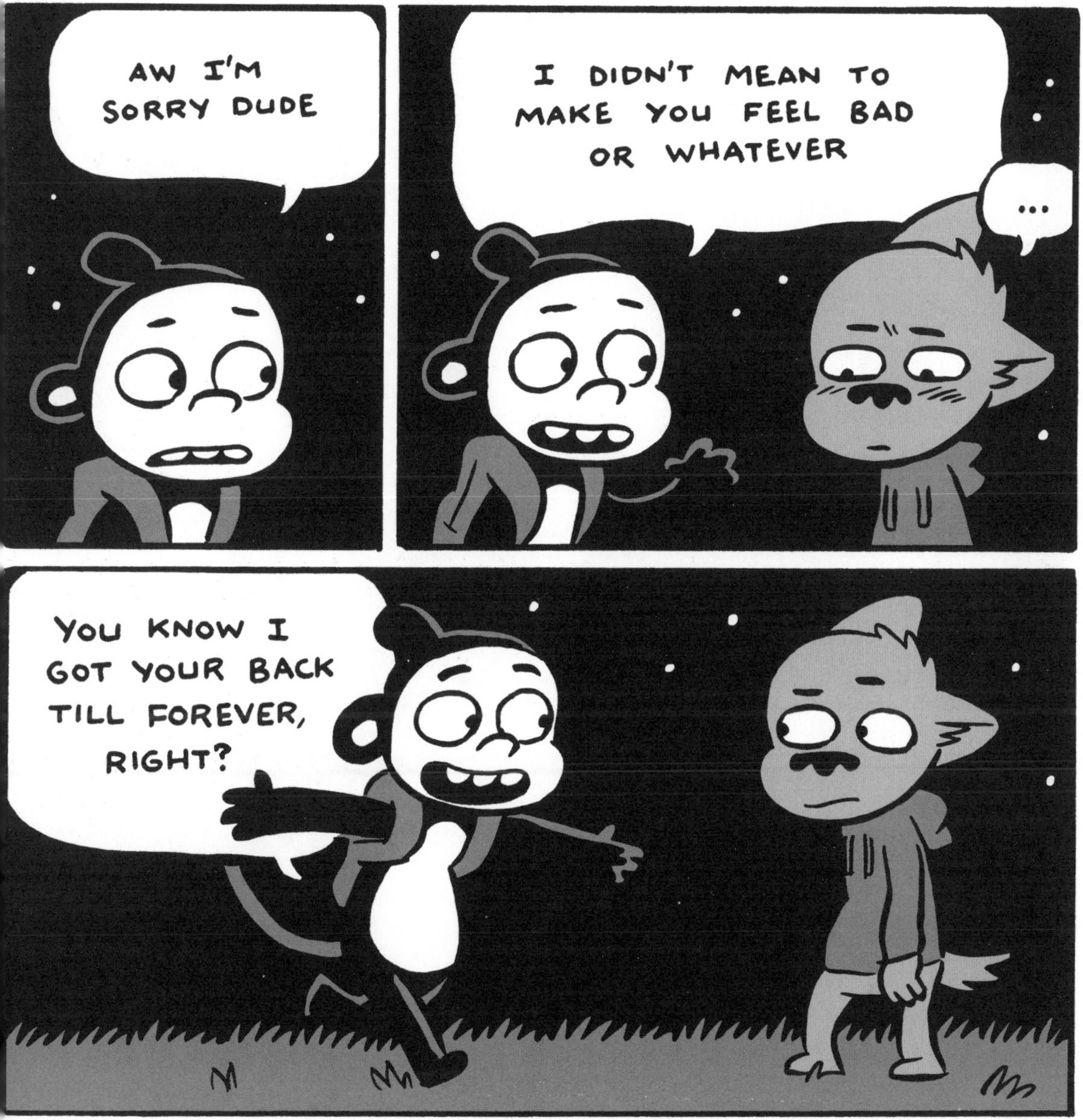
AW I'M SORRY DUDE
I DIDN'T MEAN TO MAKE YOU FEEL BAD OR WHATEVER
...
YOU KNOW I GOT YOUR BACK TILL FOREVER, RIGHT?

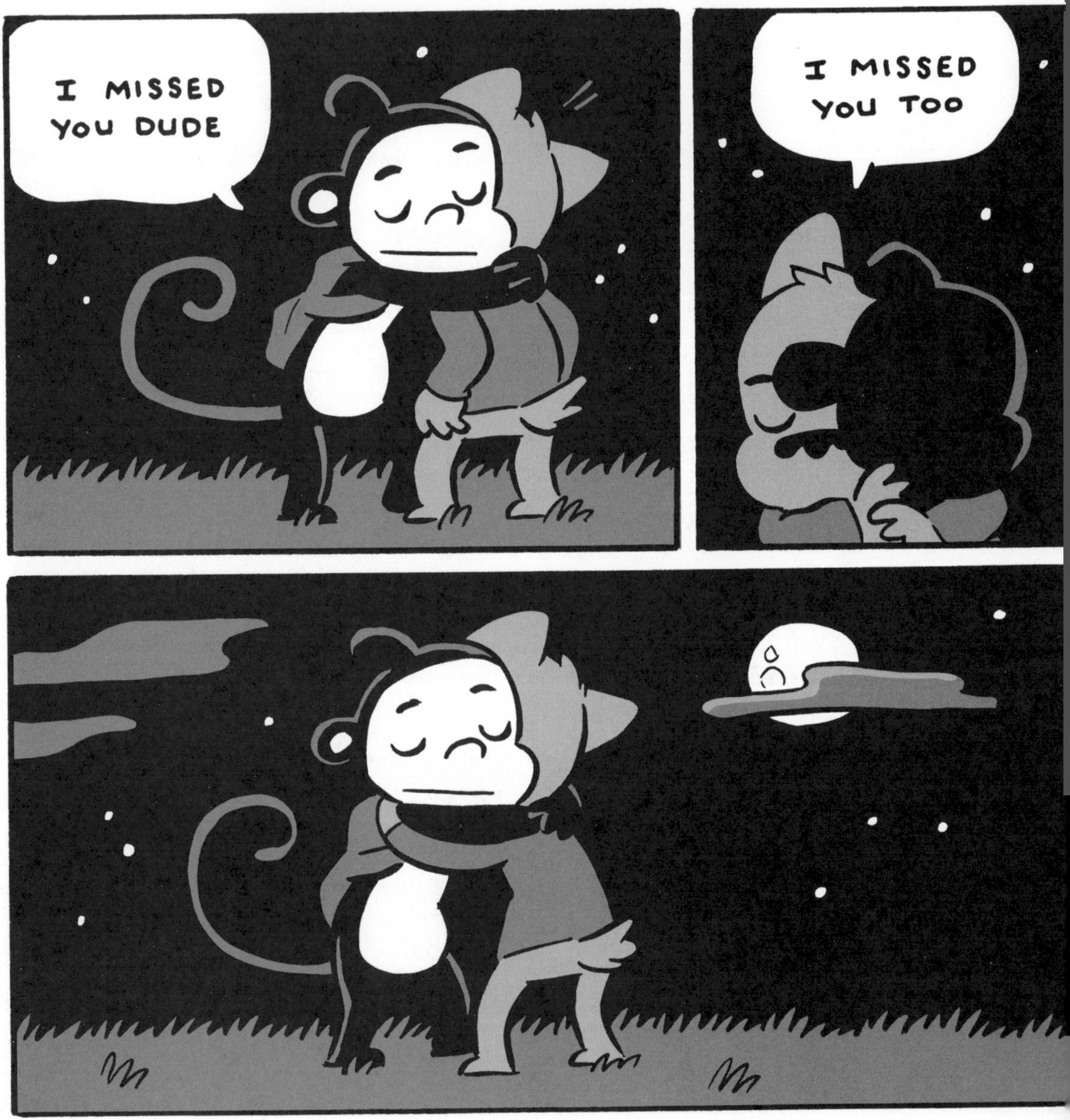
I MISSED YOU DUDE
I MISSED YOU TOO

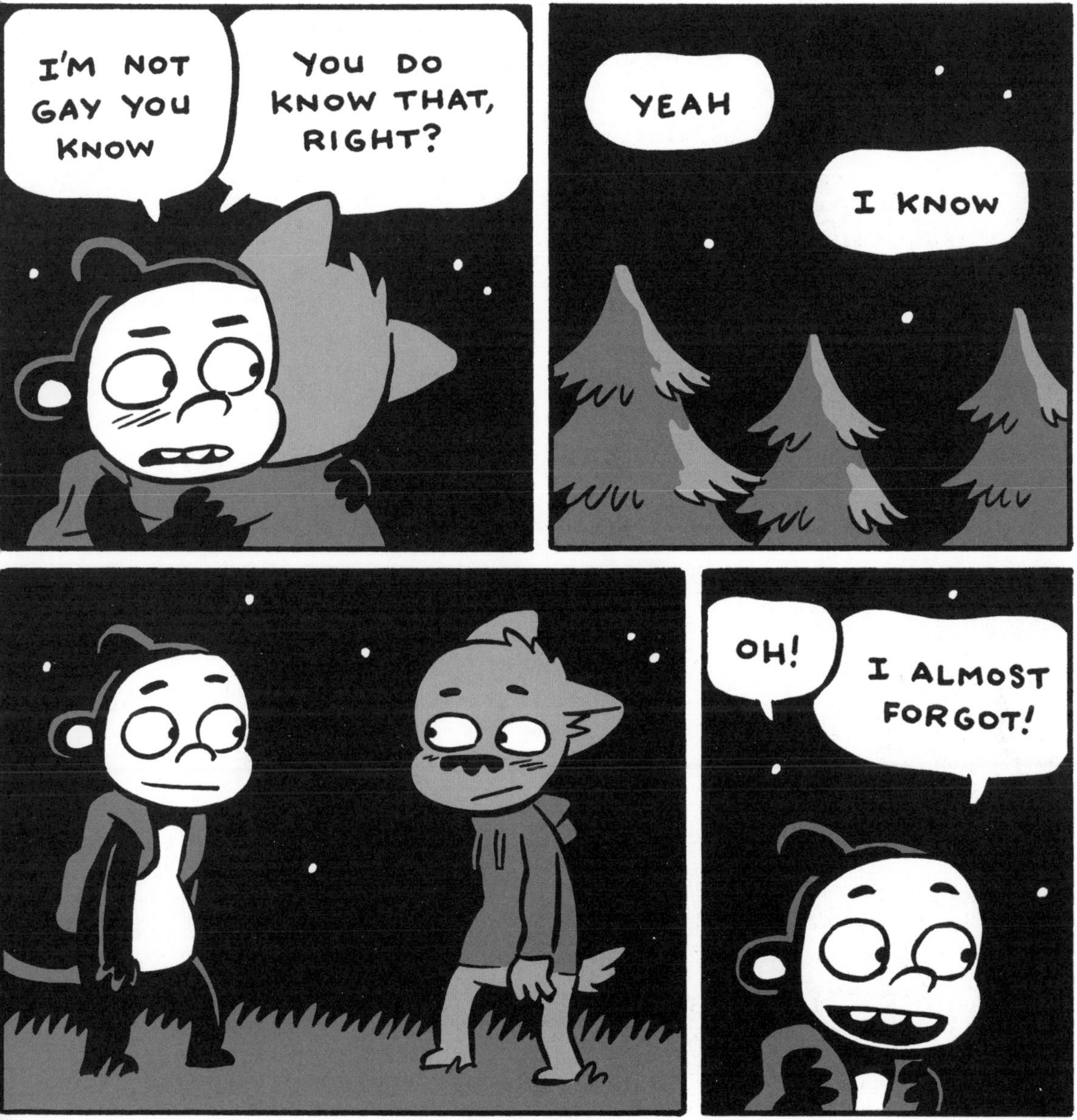
I'M NOT GAY YOU KNOW
YOU DO KNOW THAT, RIGHT?
YEAH
I KNOW
OH!
I ALMOST FORGOT!

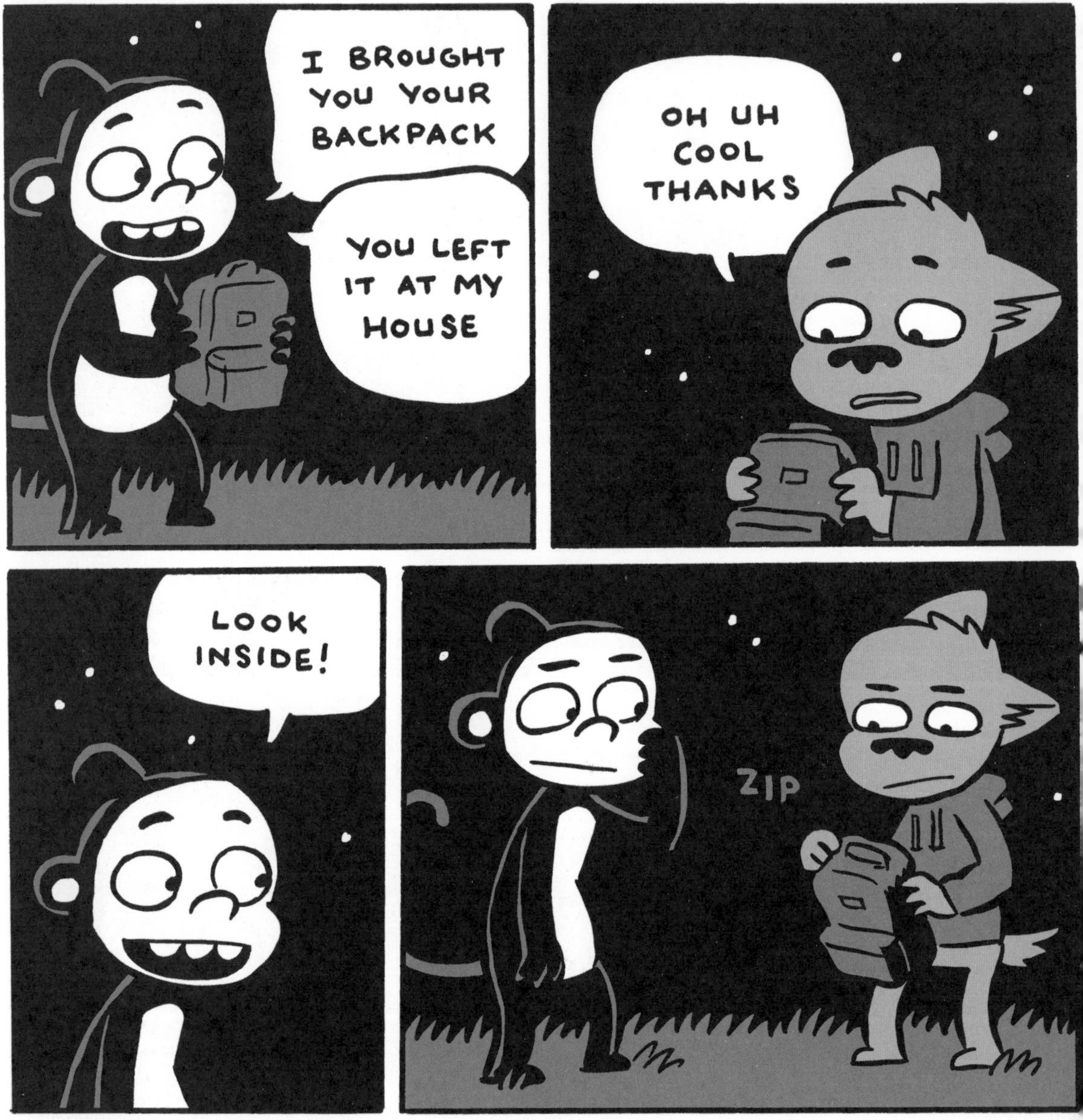
I BROUGHT YOU YOUR BACKPACK
YOU LEFT IT AT MY HOUSE
OH UH COOL THANKS
LOOK INSIDE!
ZIP

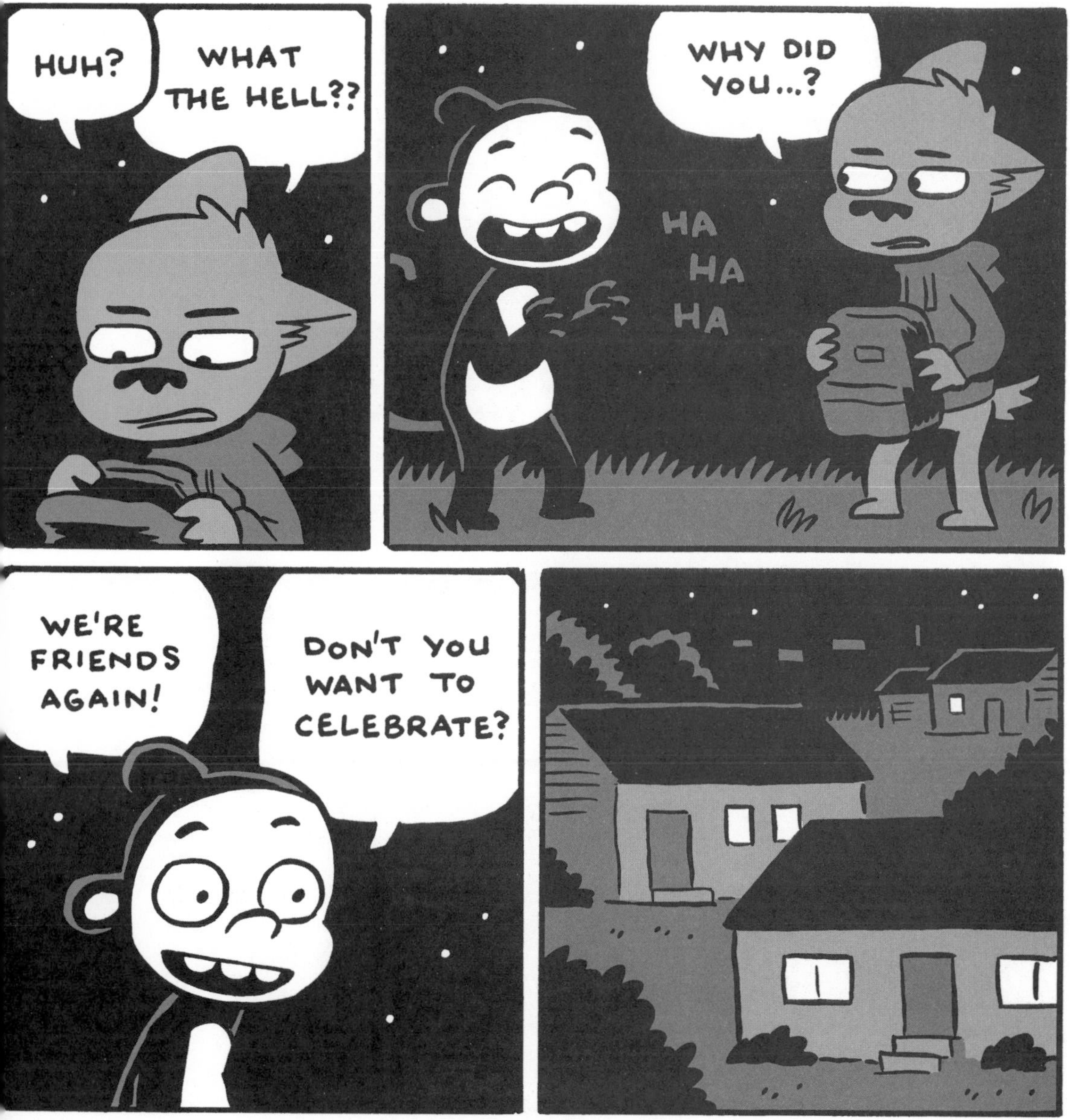
HUH?
WHAT THE HELL??
WHY DID YOU...?
HA HA HA
WE'RE FRIENDS AGAIN!
DON'T YOU WANT TO CELEBRATE?

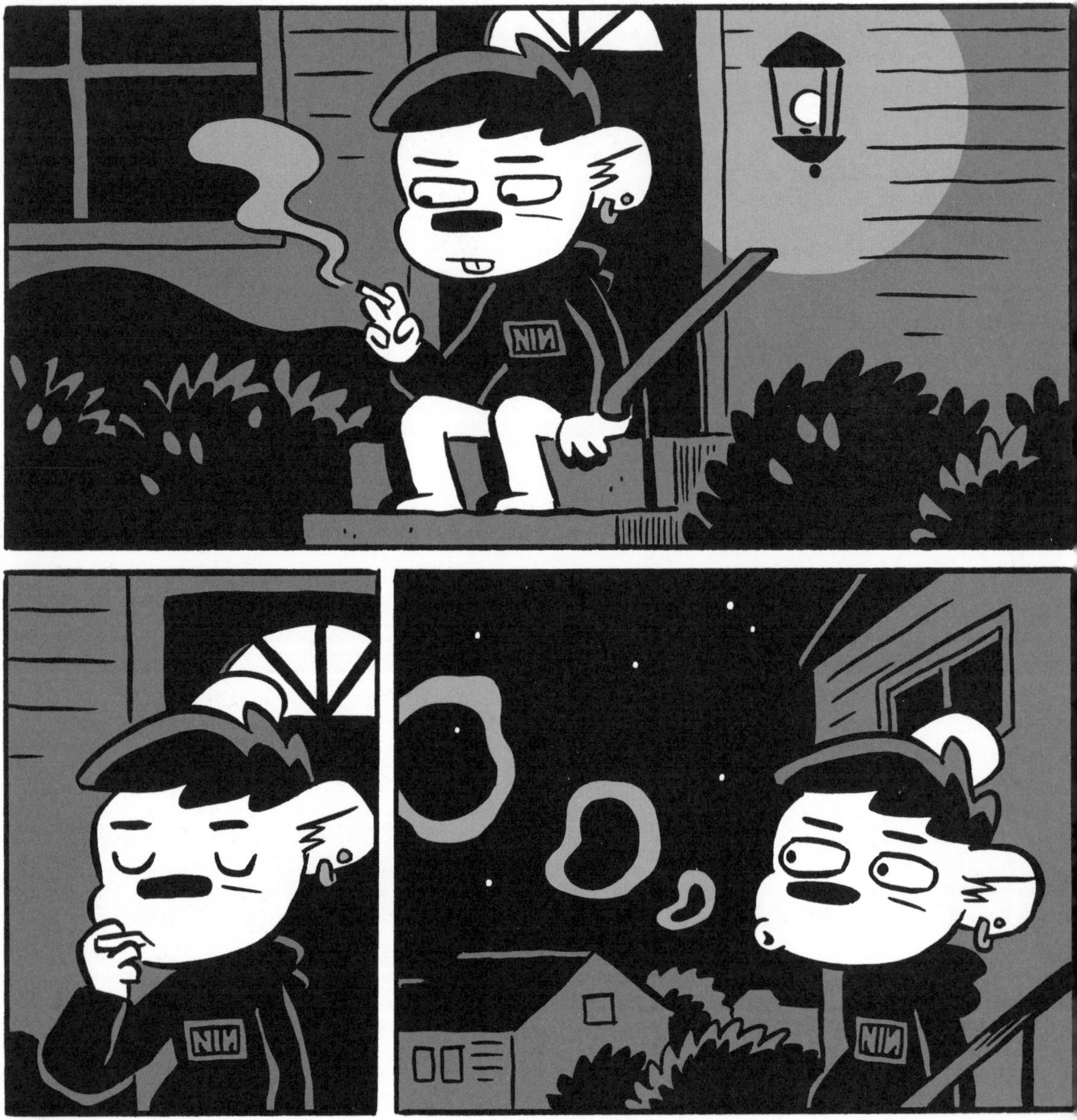
NIN
NIN
NIN

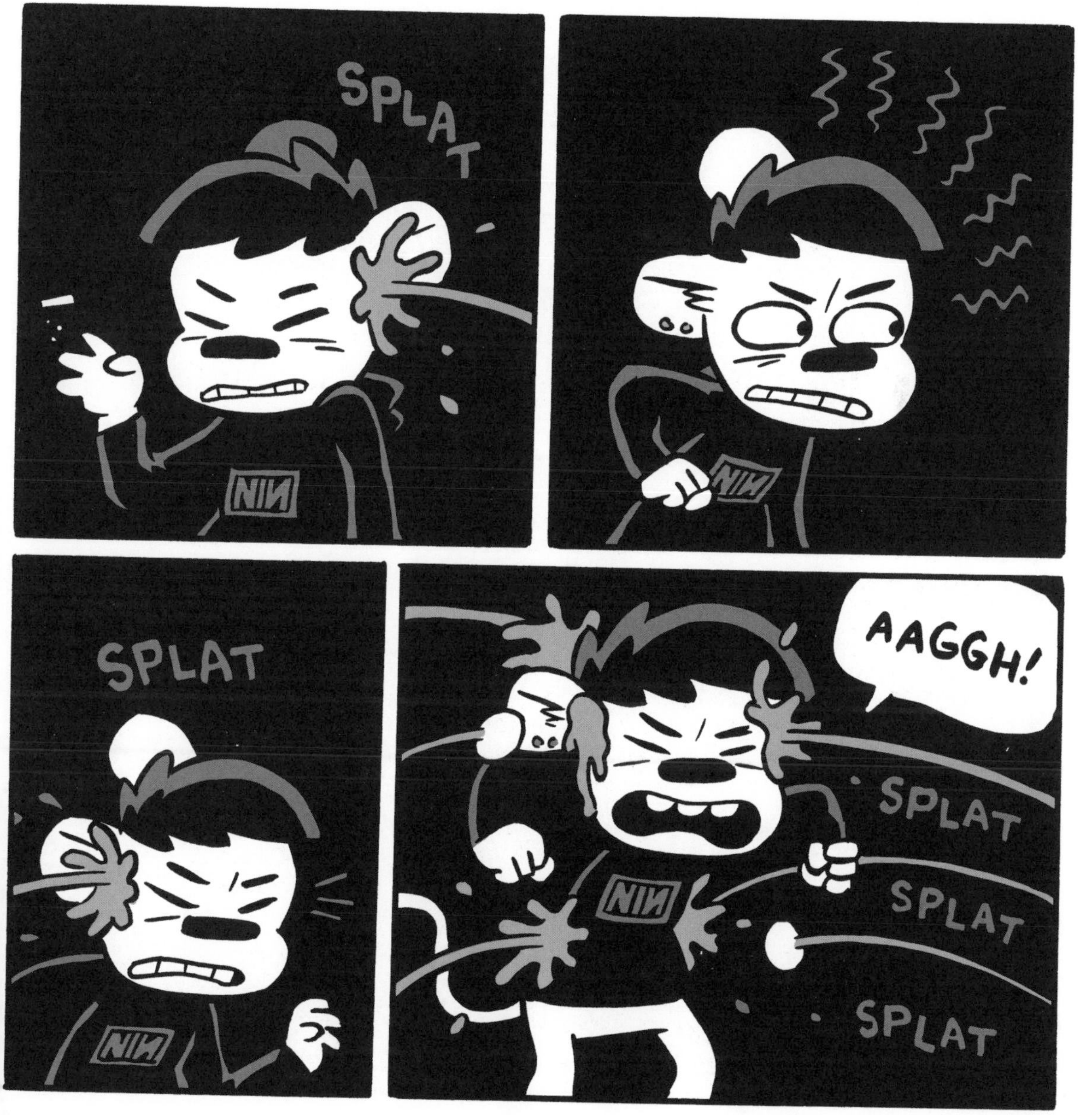
SPLAT
SPLAT
AAGGH!
SPLAT
SPLAT
SPLAT

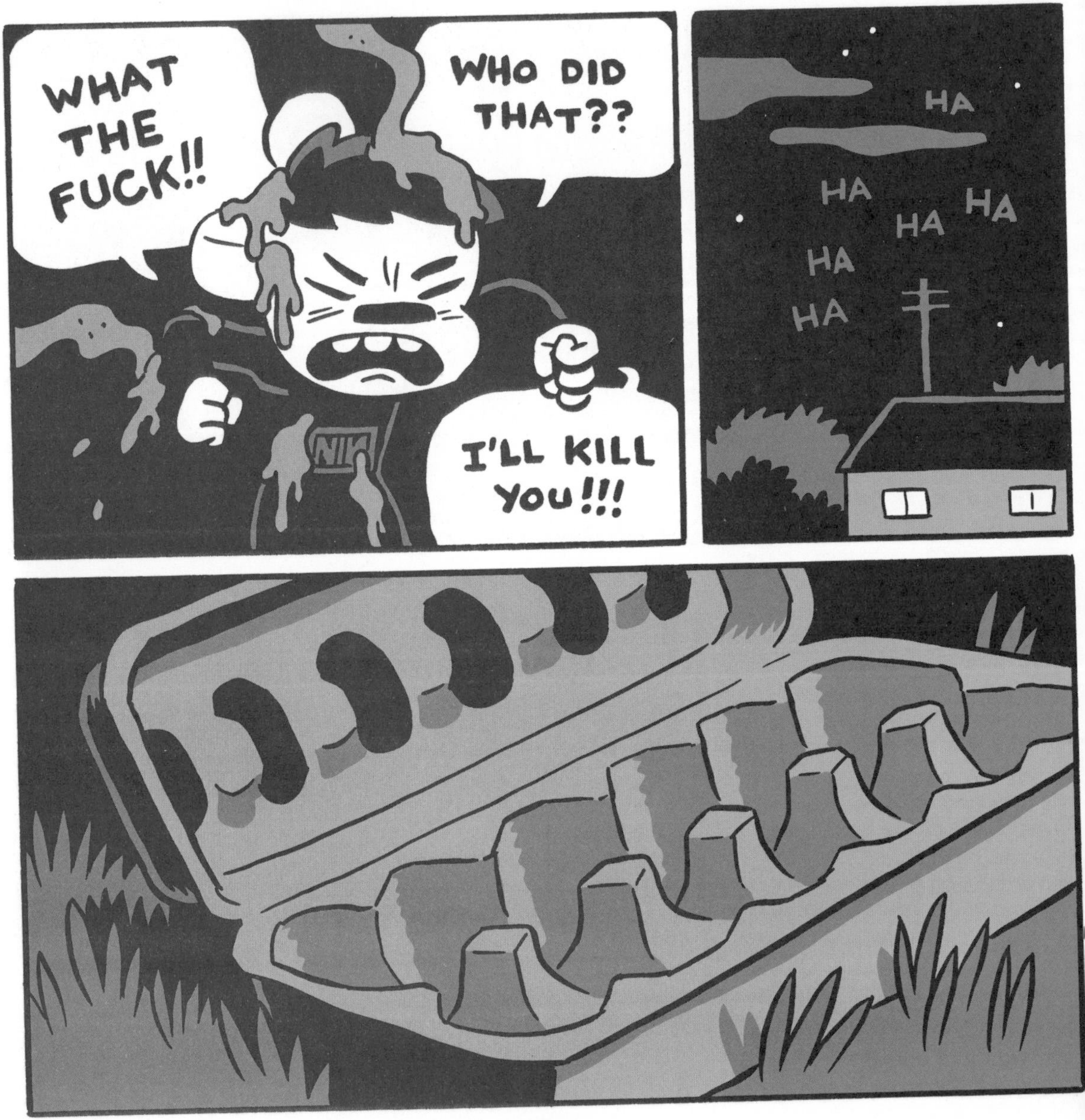
WHAT THE FUCK!!
WHO DID THAT??
I'LL KILL YOU!!!
HA
HA
HA
HA
HA
HA

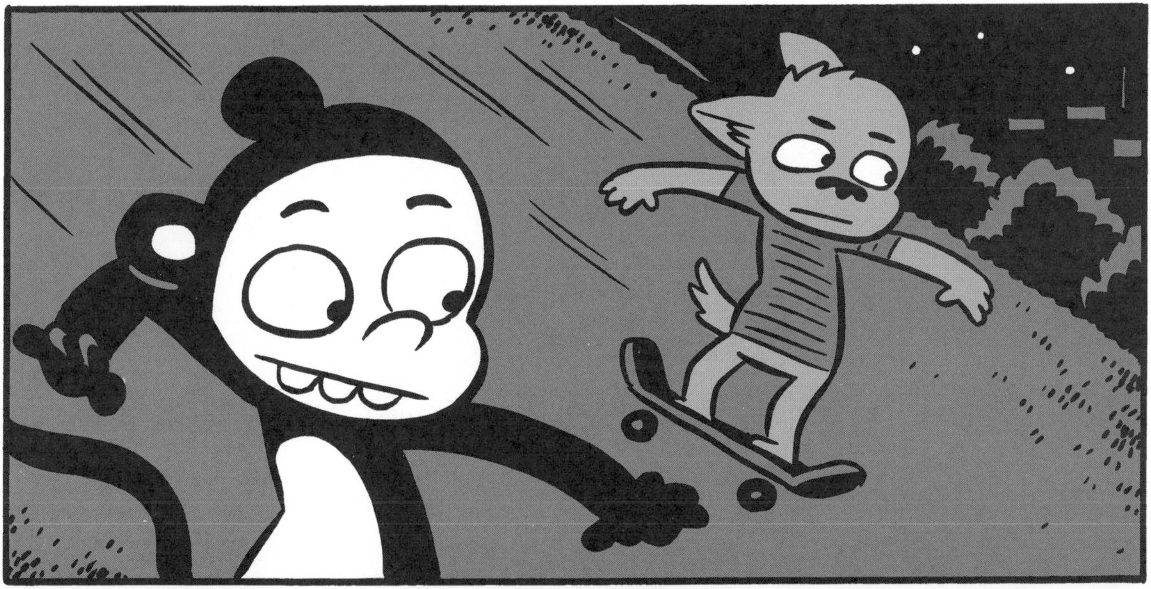

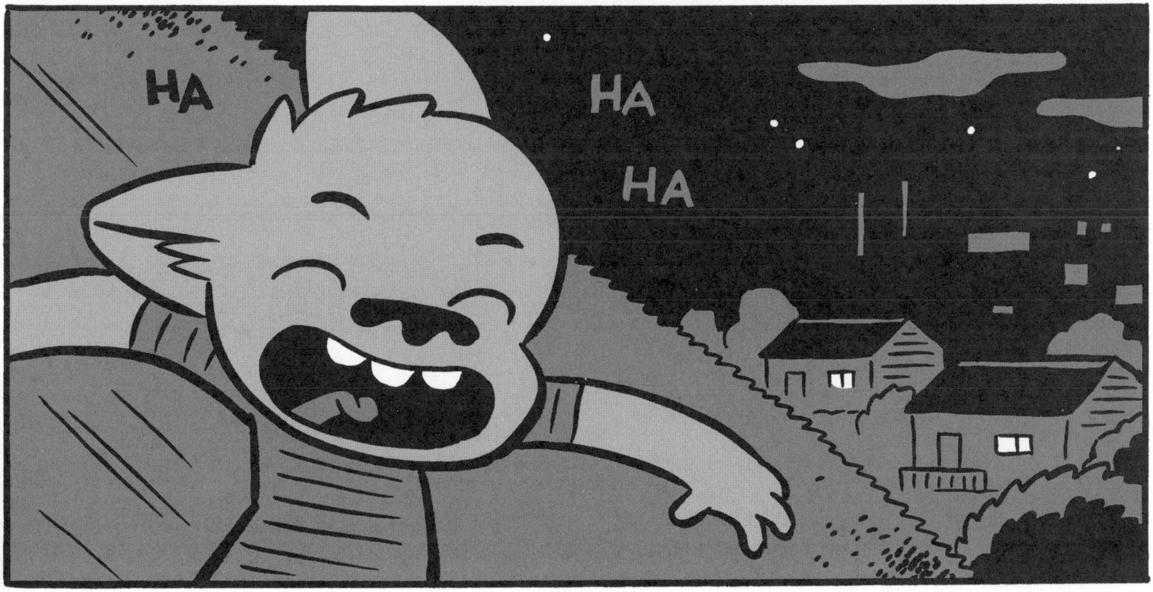
HA
HA
HA

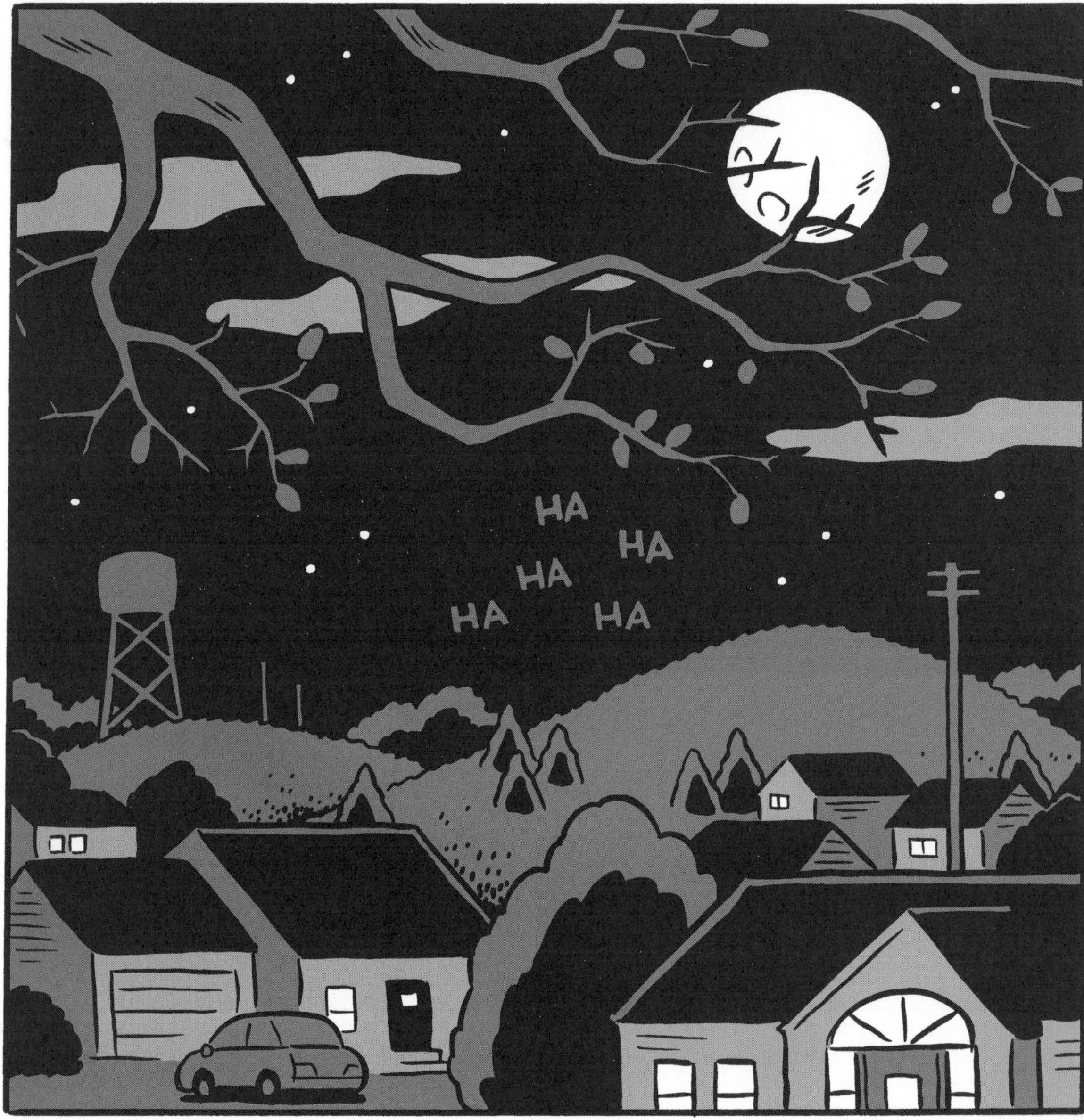
HA
HA
HA
HA
HA

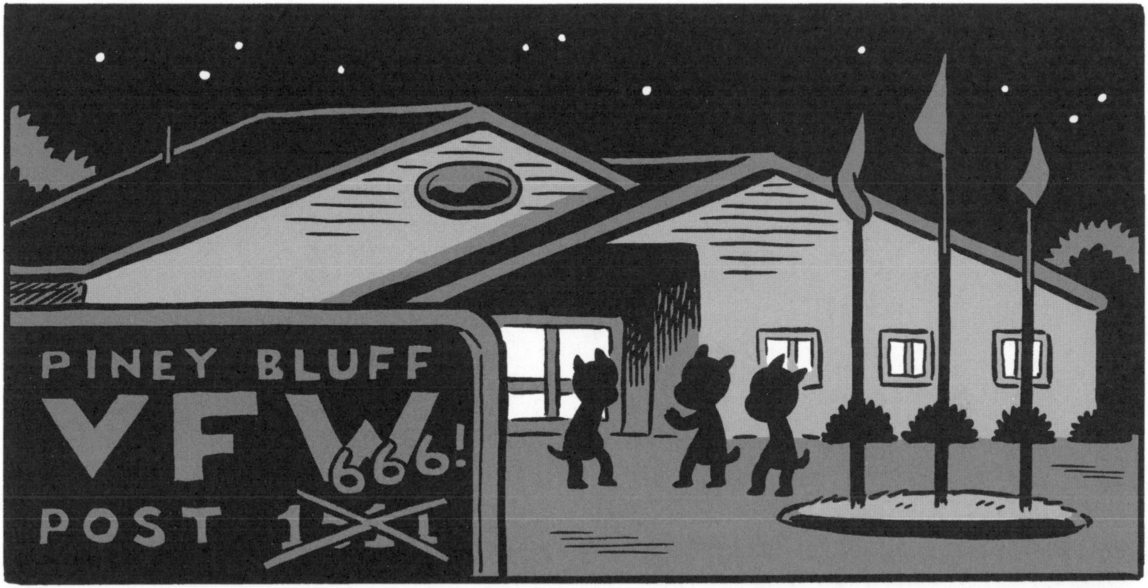
PINEY BLUFF
VFW
666!
POST 1

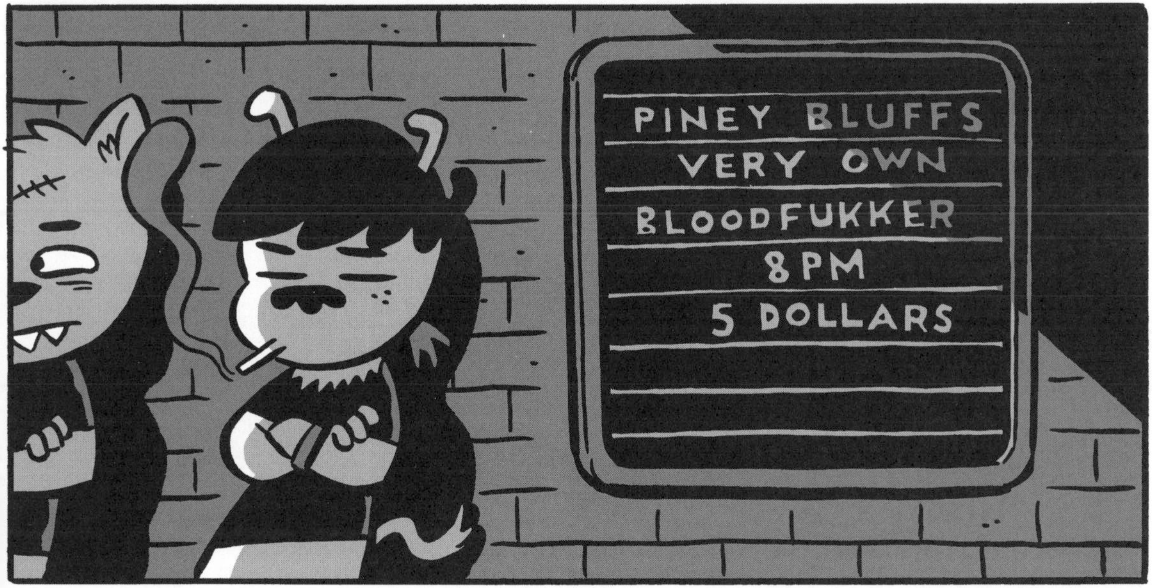
PINEY BLUFFS
VERY OWN
BLOODFUKKER
8PM
5 DOLLARS

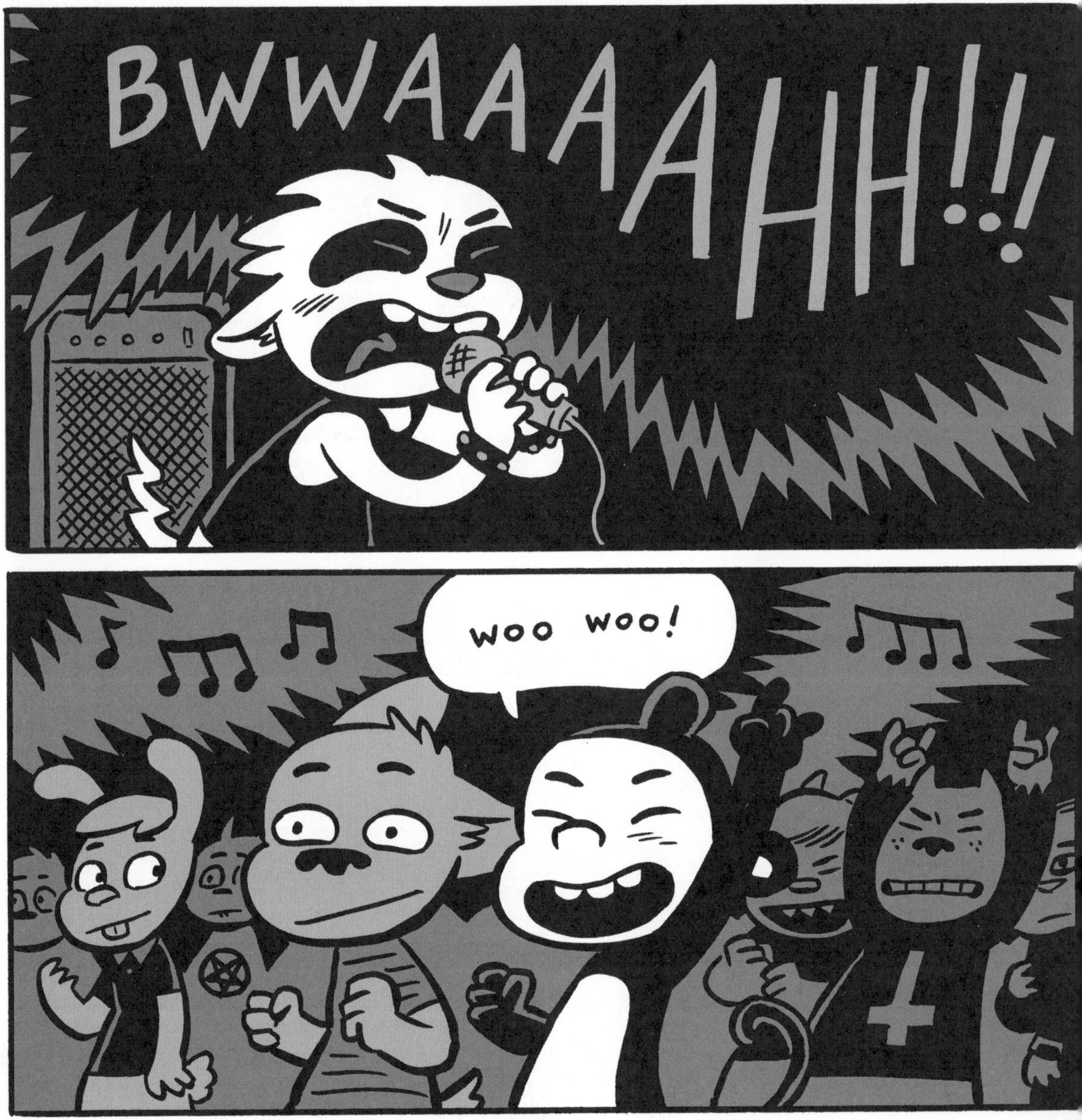
BWWAAAAAHH!!!
WOO WOO!

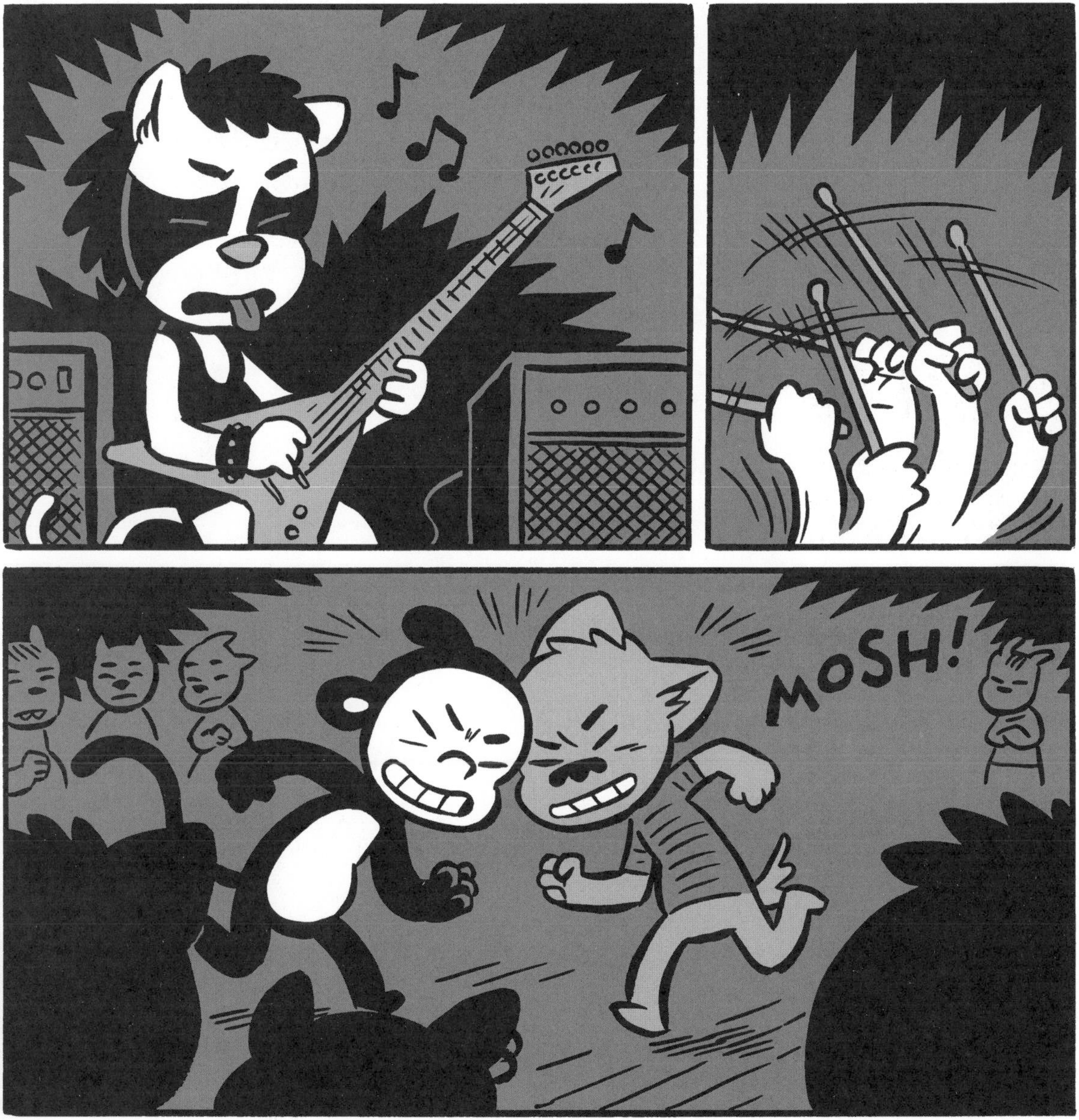
MOSH!

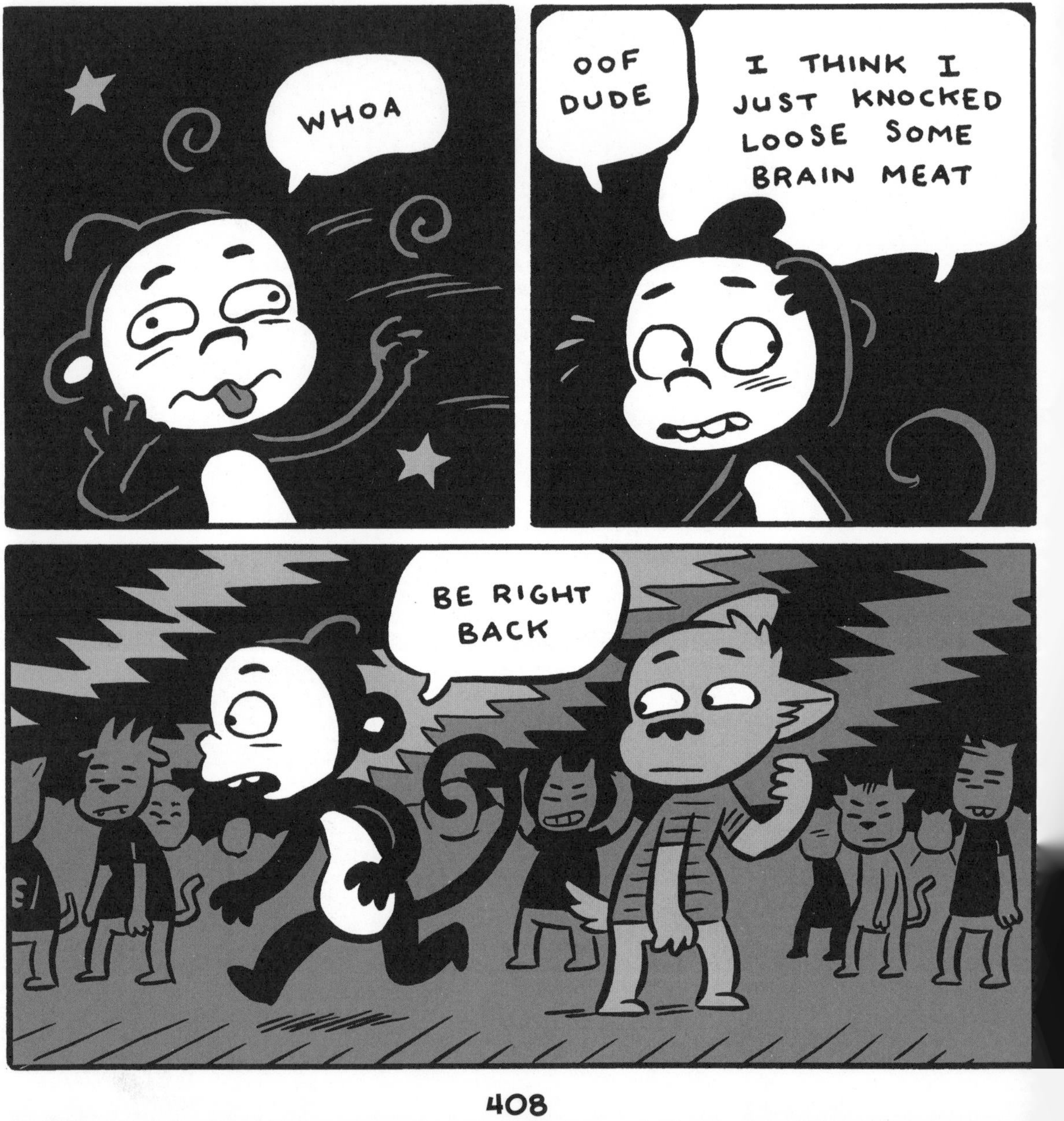
WHOA
OOF DUDE
I THINK I JUST KNOCKED LOOSE SOME BRAIN MEAT
BE RIGHT BACK

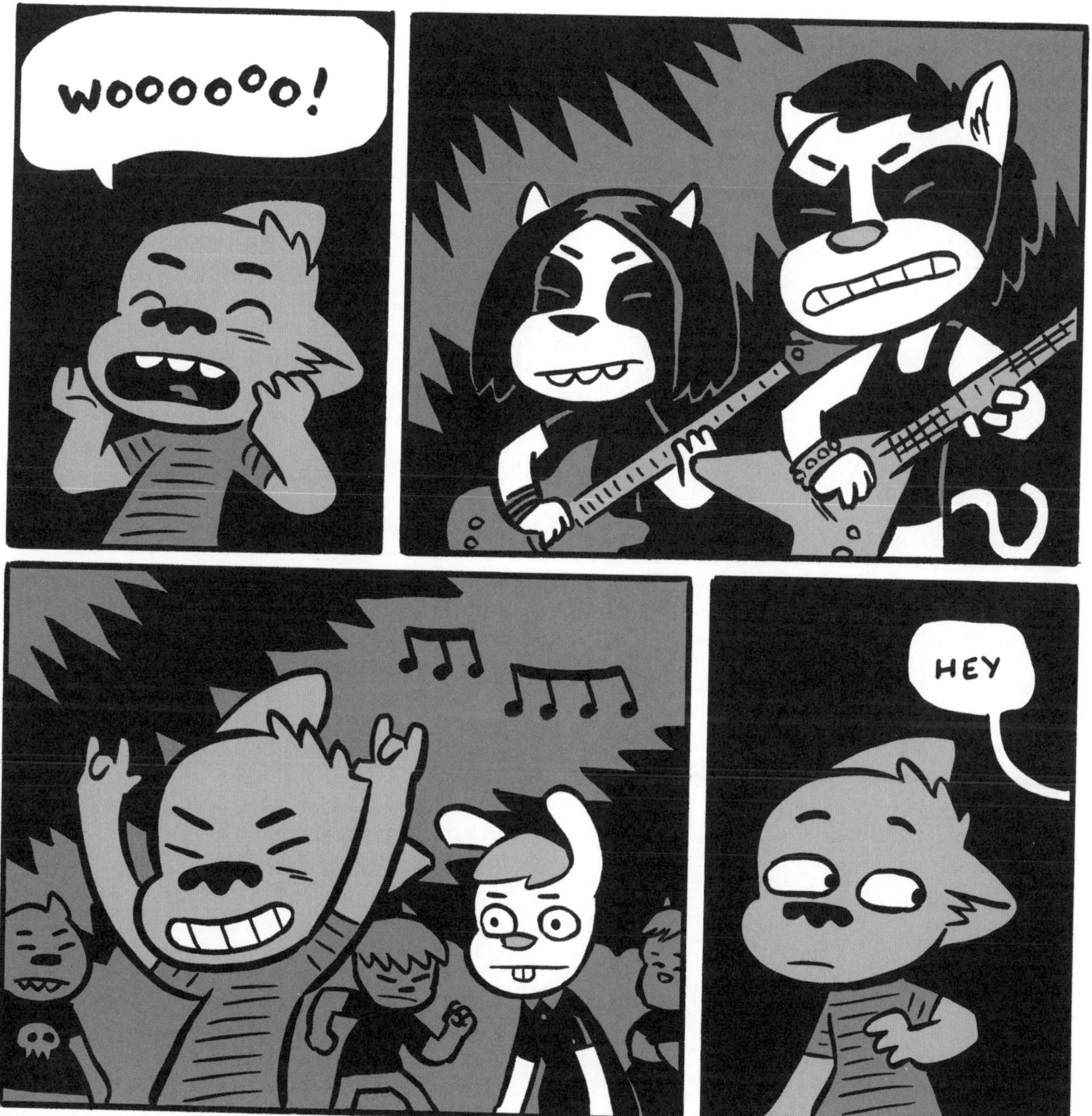
WOOOOOO!
HEY

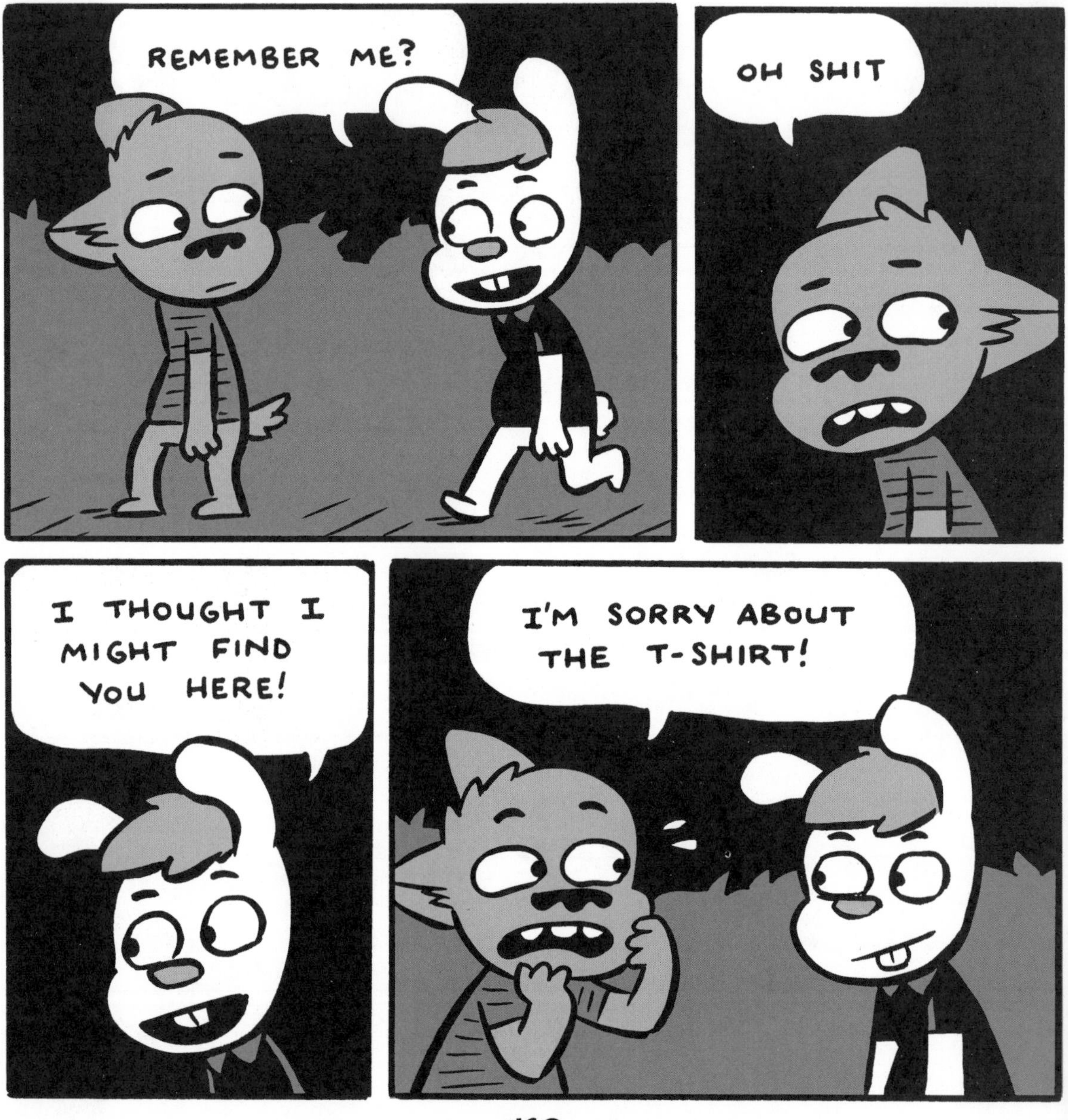
REMEMBER ME?
OH SHIT
I THOUGHT I MIGHT FIND YOU HERE!
I'M SORRY ABOUT THE T-SHIRT!

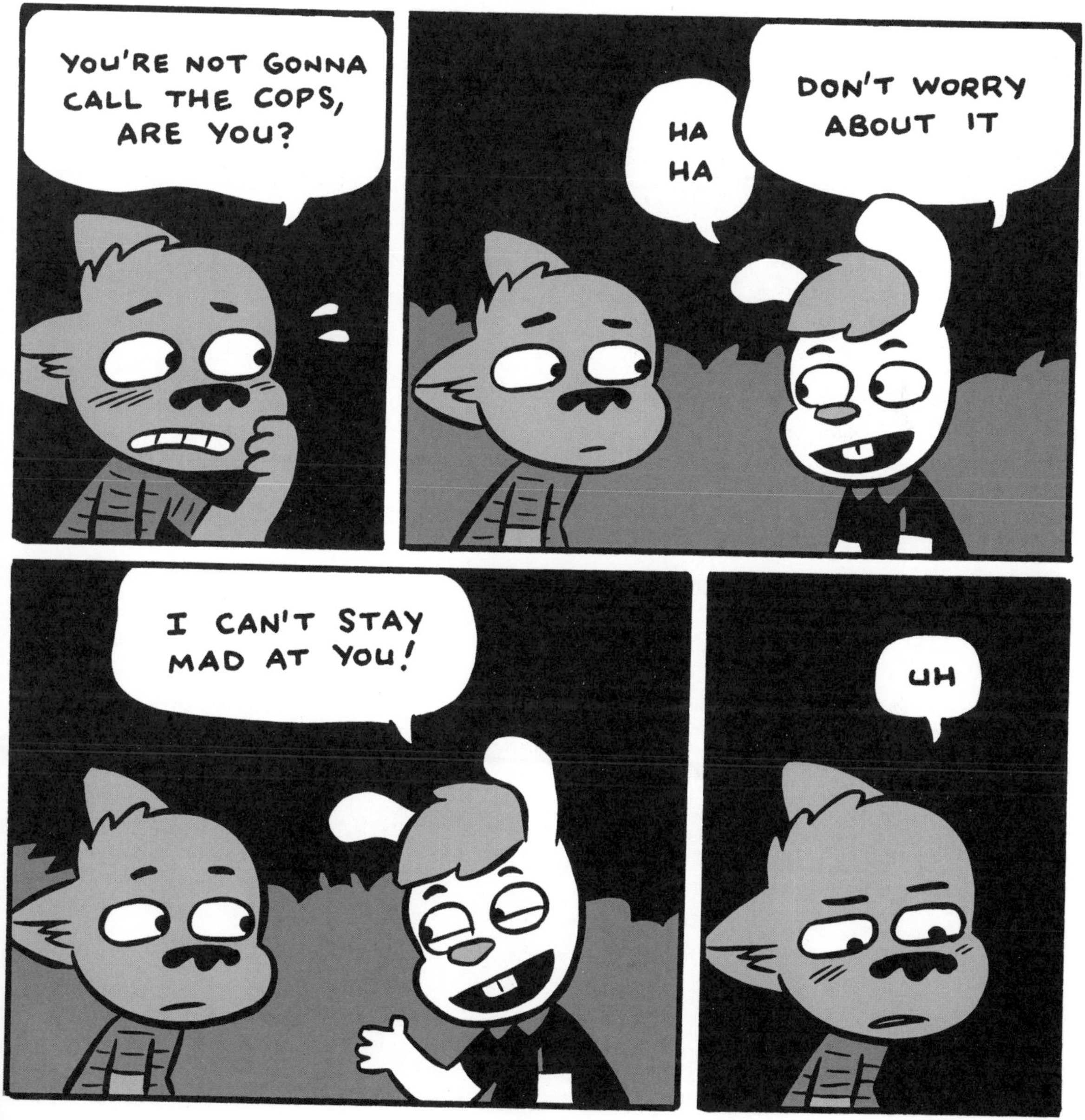
YOU'RE NOT GONNA CALL THE COPS, ARE YOU?
HA HA
DON'T WORRY ABOUT IT
I CAN'T STAY MAD AT YOU!
UH

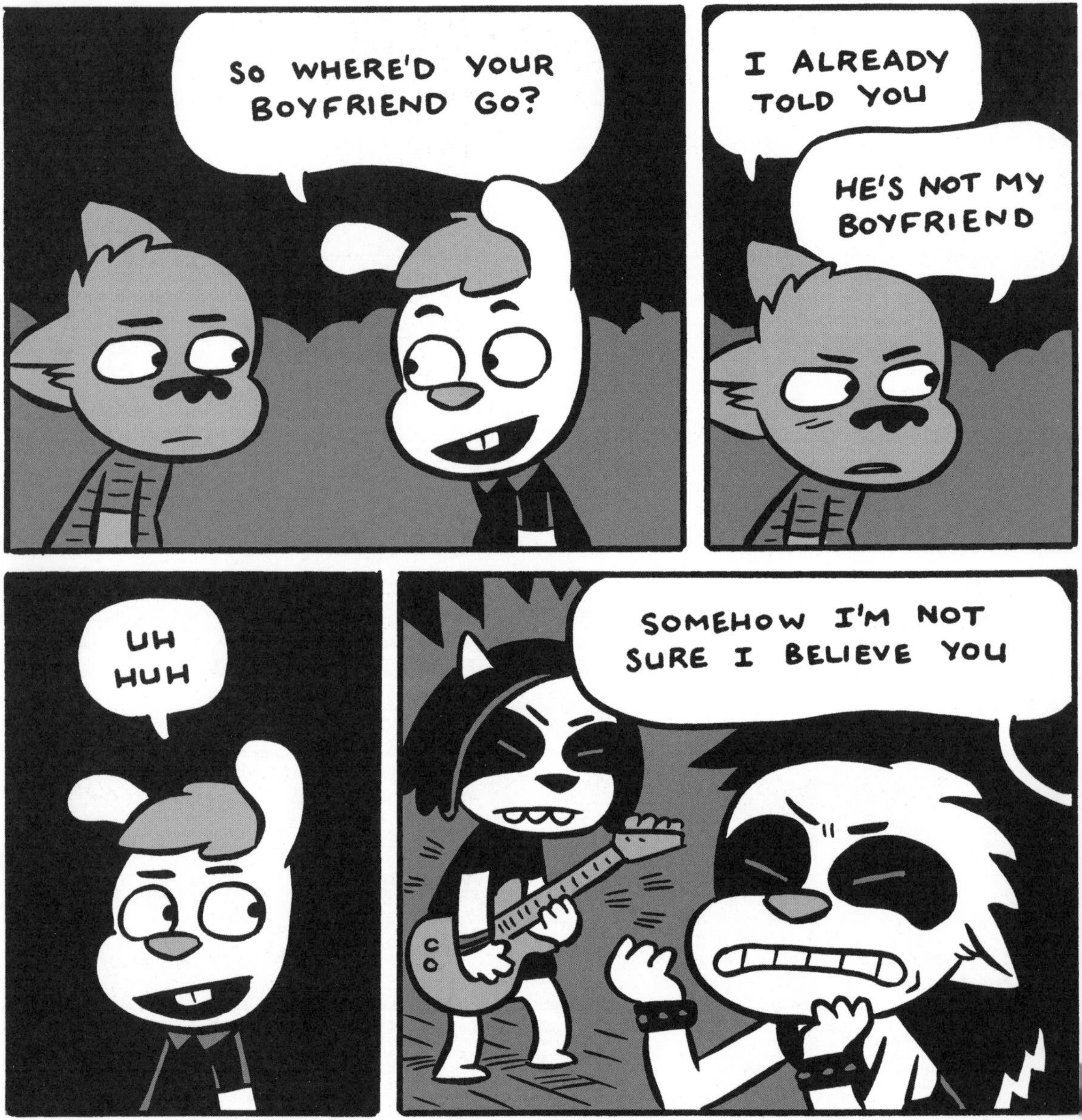
SO WHERE'D YOUR BOYFRIEND GO?
I ALREADY TOLD YOU
HE'S NOT MY BOYFRIEND
UH HUH
SOMEHOW I'M NOT SURE I BELIEVE YOU

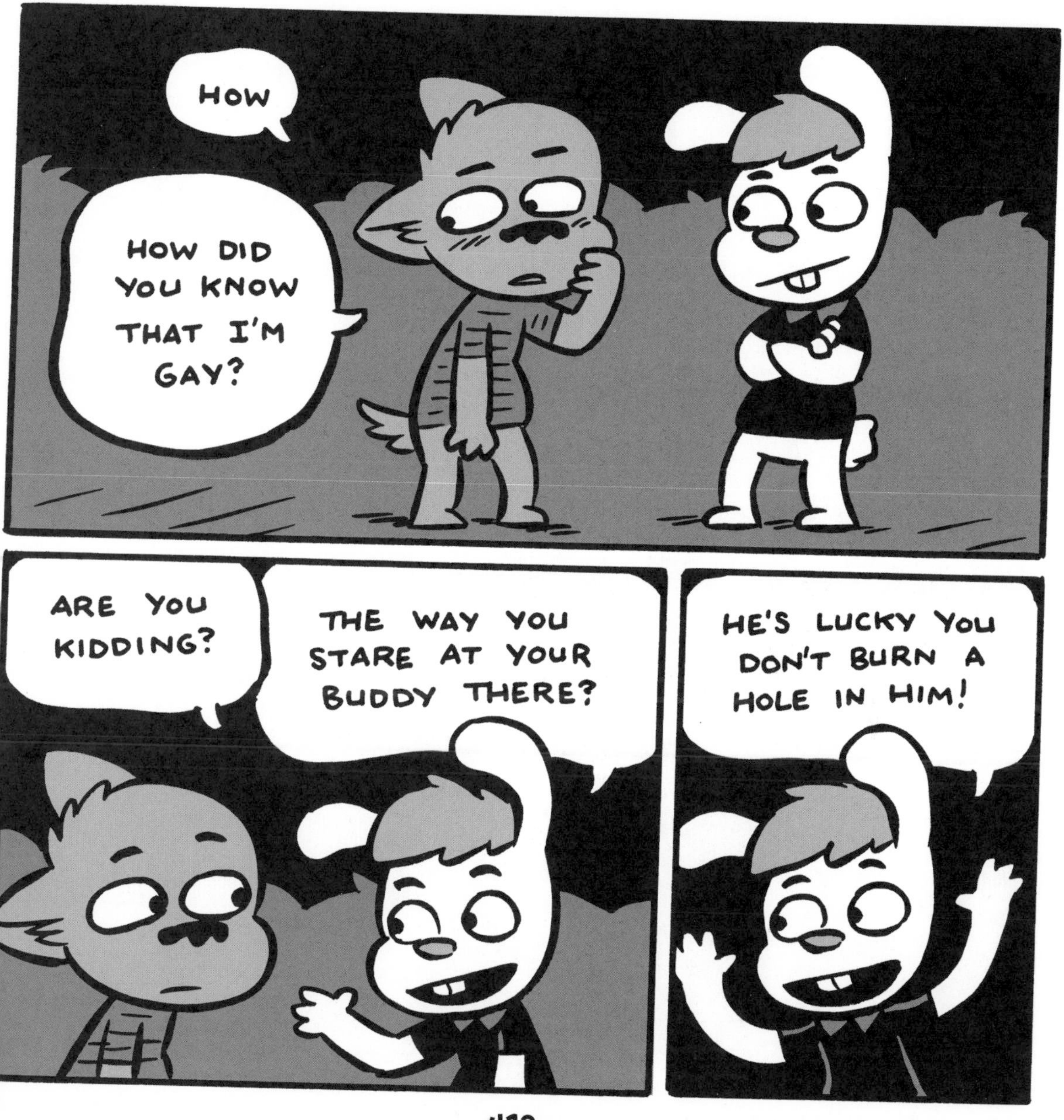
HOW
HOW DID YOU KNOW THAT I'M GAY?
ARE YOU KIDDING?
THE WAY YOU STARE AT YOUR BUDDY THERE?
HE'S LUCKY YOU DON'T BURN A HOLE IN HIM!

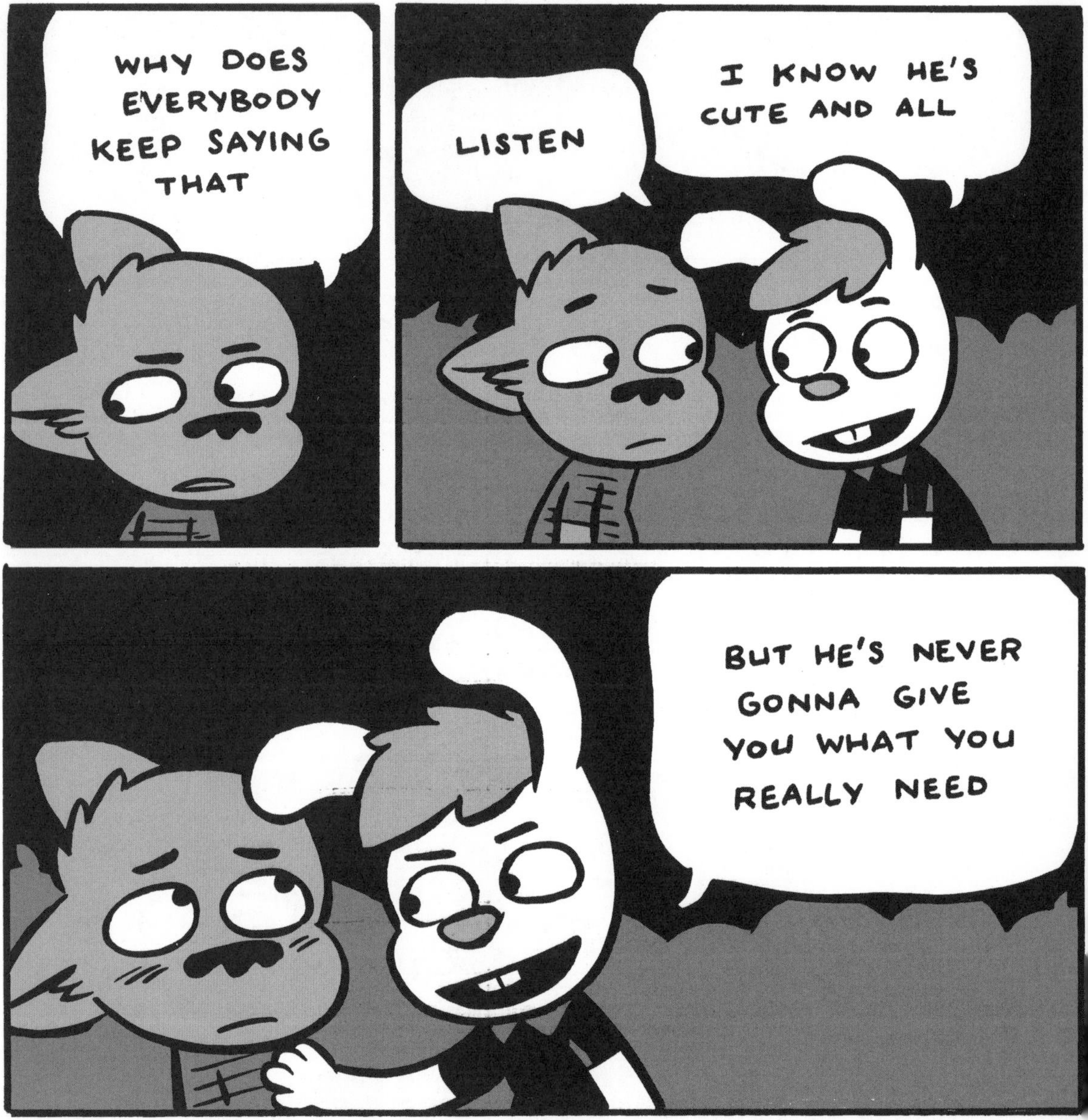
WHY DOES EVERYBODY KEEP SAYING THAT
LISTEN
I KNOW HE'S CUTE AND ALL
BUT HE'S NEVER GONNA GIVE YOU WHAT YOU REALLY NEED

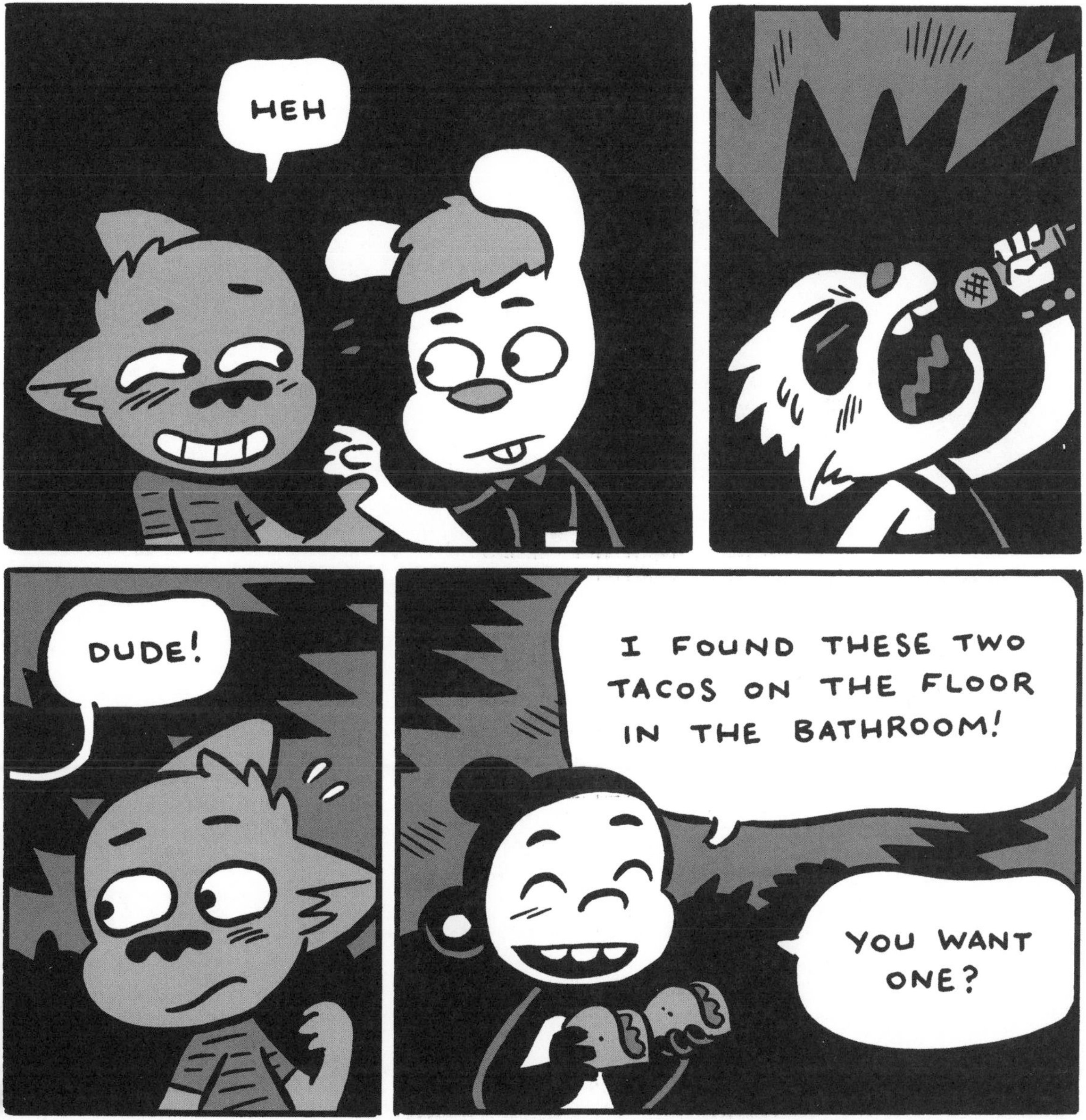
HEH
DUDE!
I FOUND THESE TWO TACOS ON THE FLOOR IN THE BATHROOM!
YOU WANT ONE?

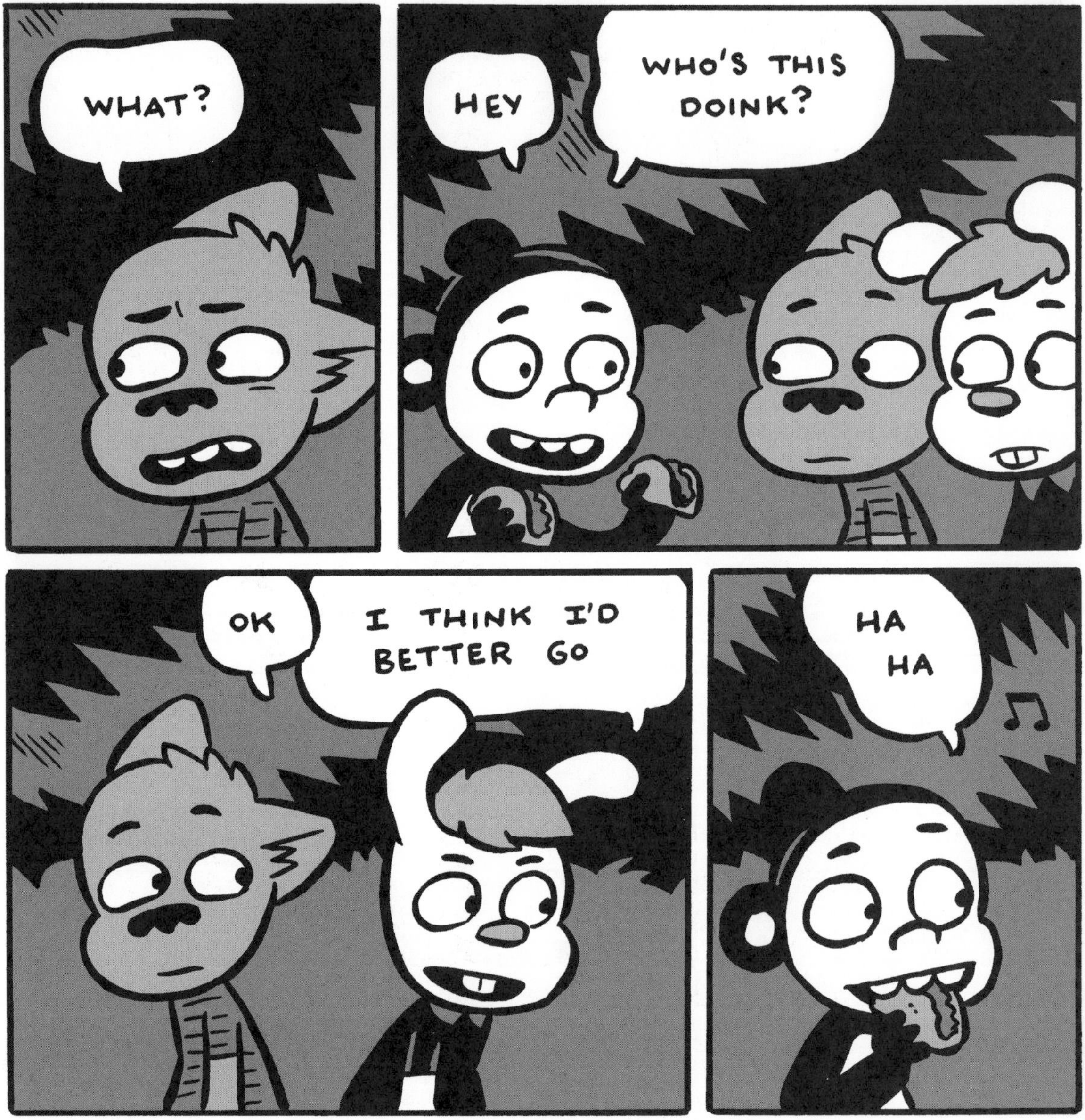
WHAT?
HEY
WHO'S THIS DOINK?
OK
I THINK I'D BETTER GO
HA HA

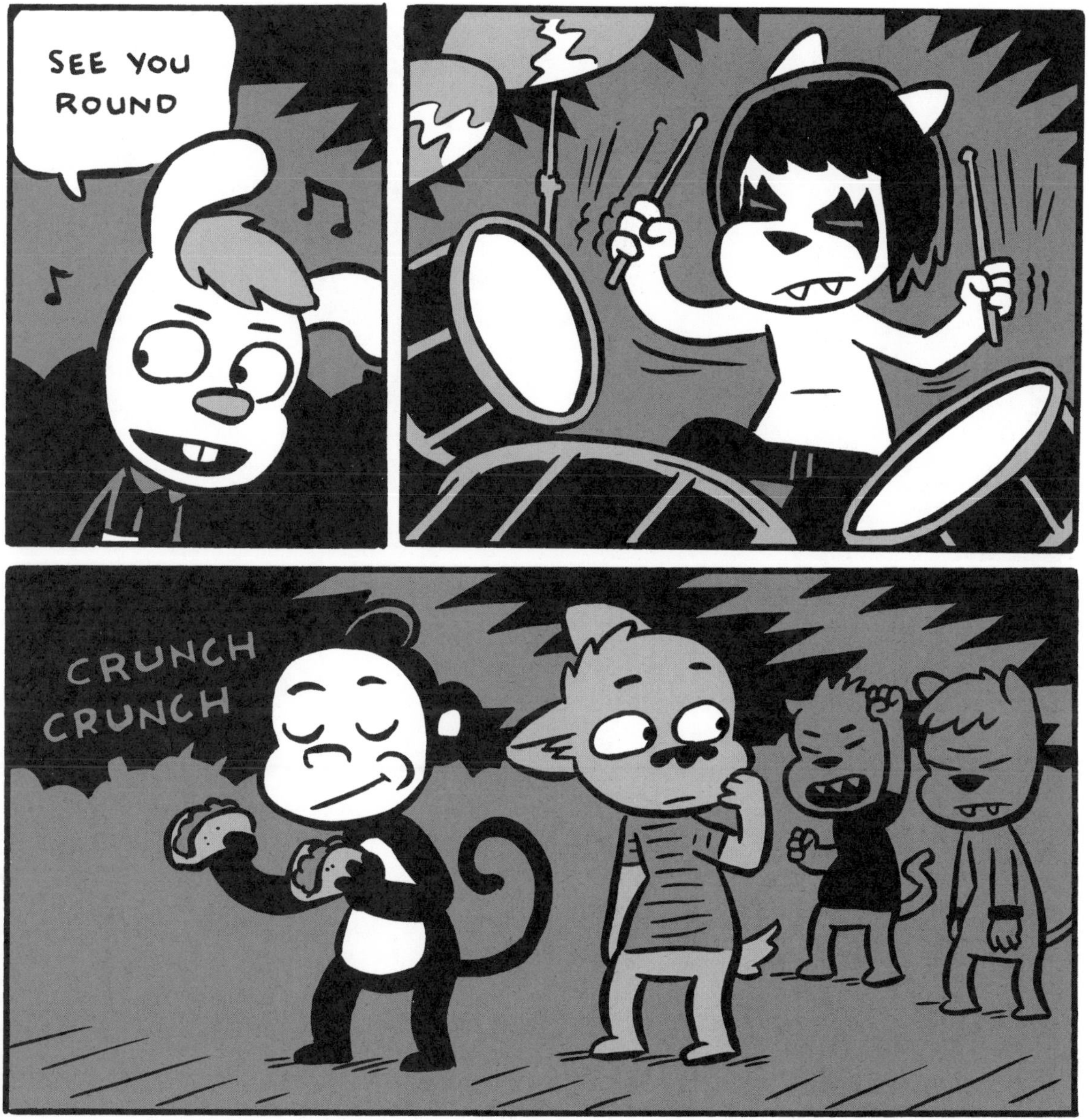
SEE YOU ROUND
CRUNCH
CRUNCH

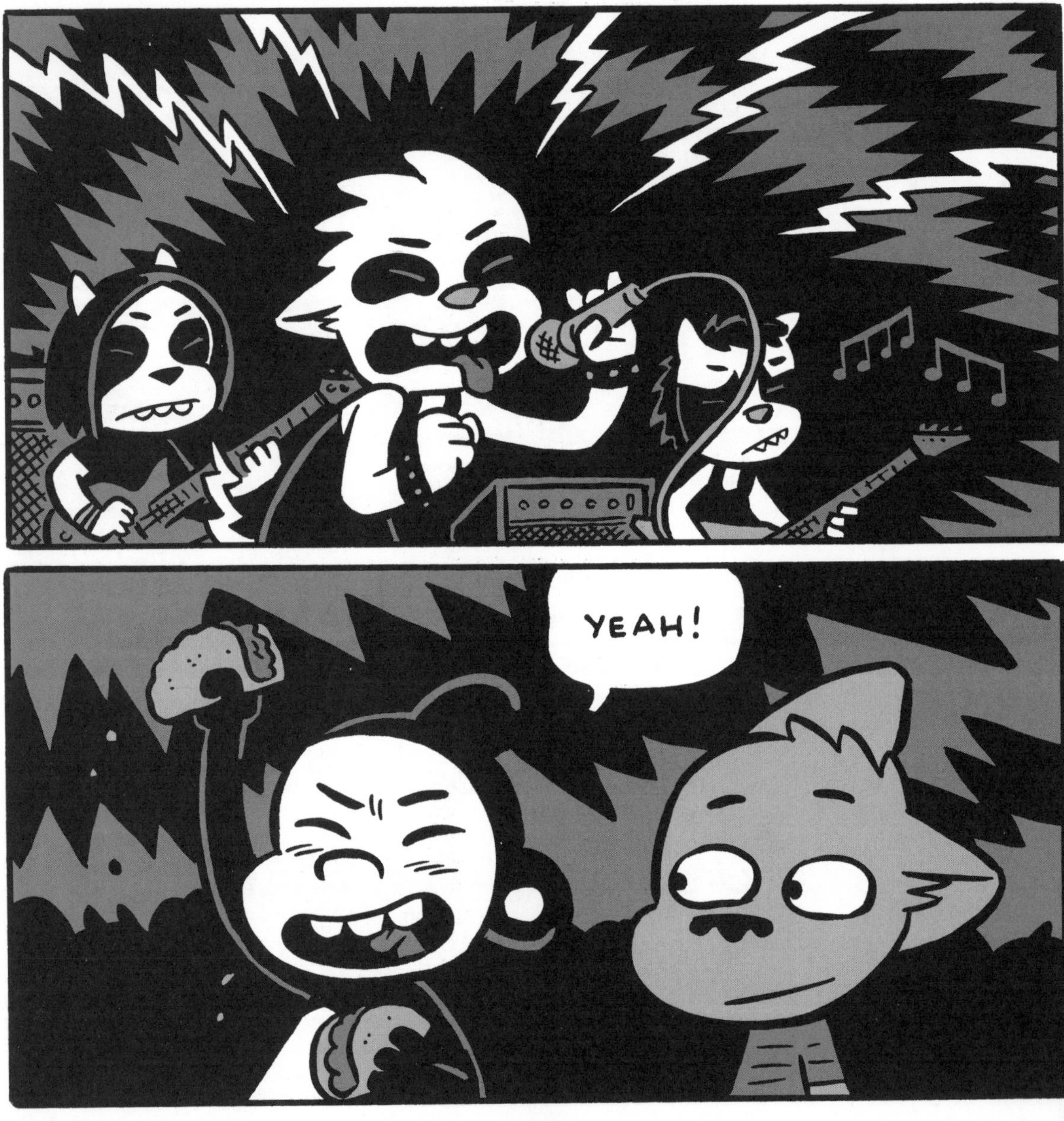
YEAH!

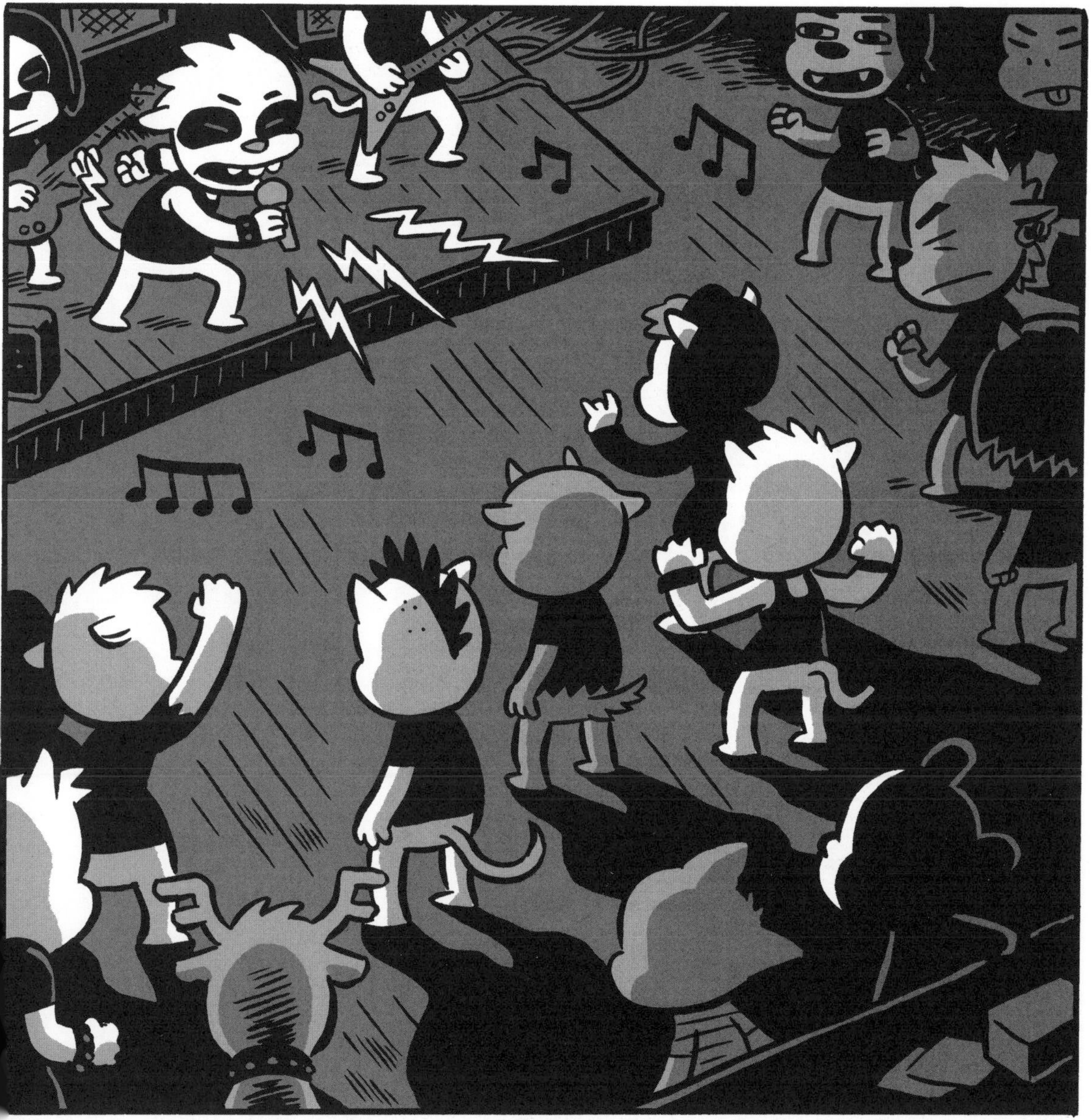

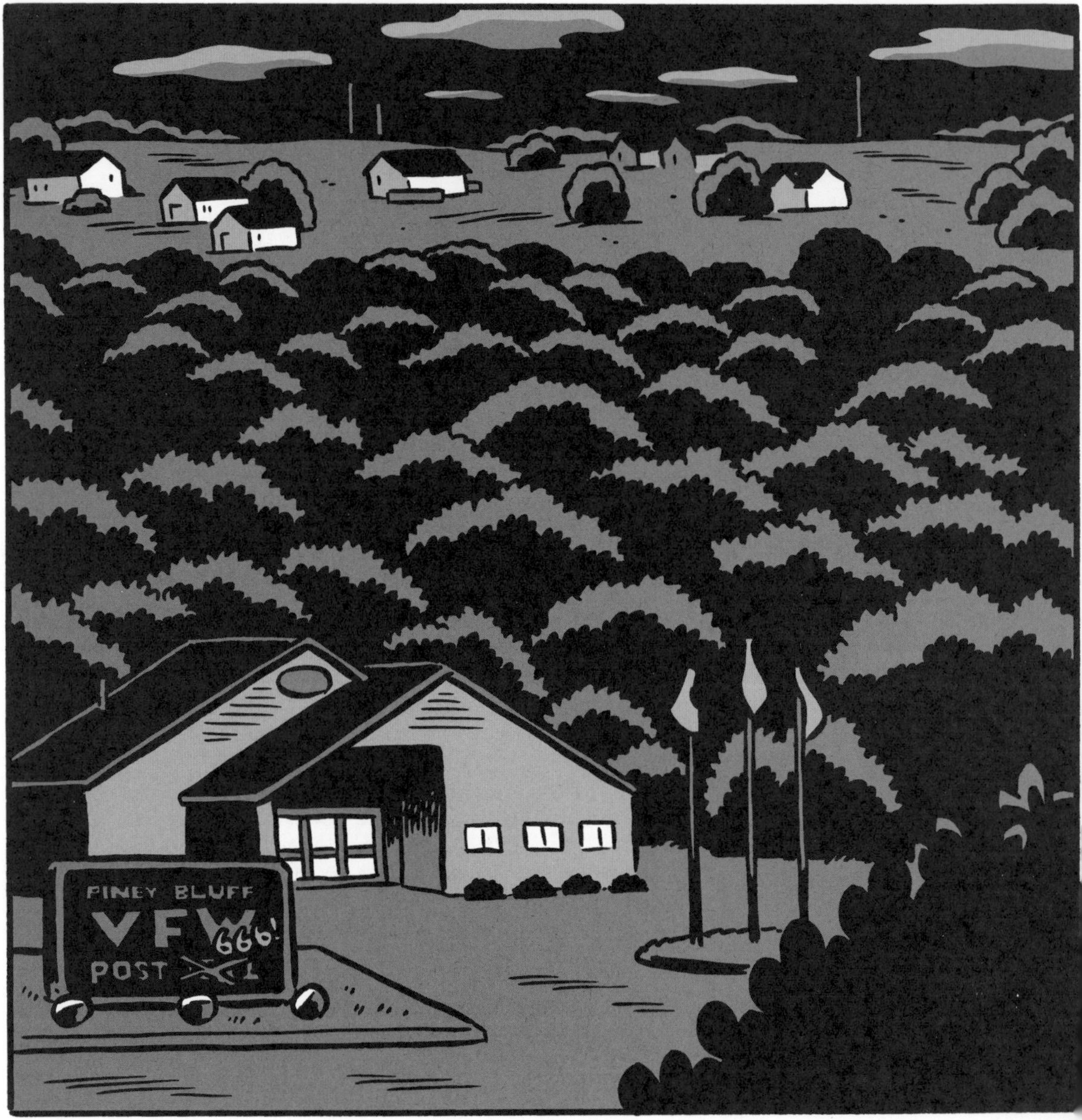
PINEY BLUFF
VFW
666!
POST

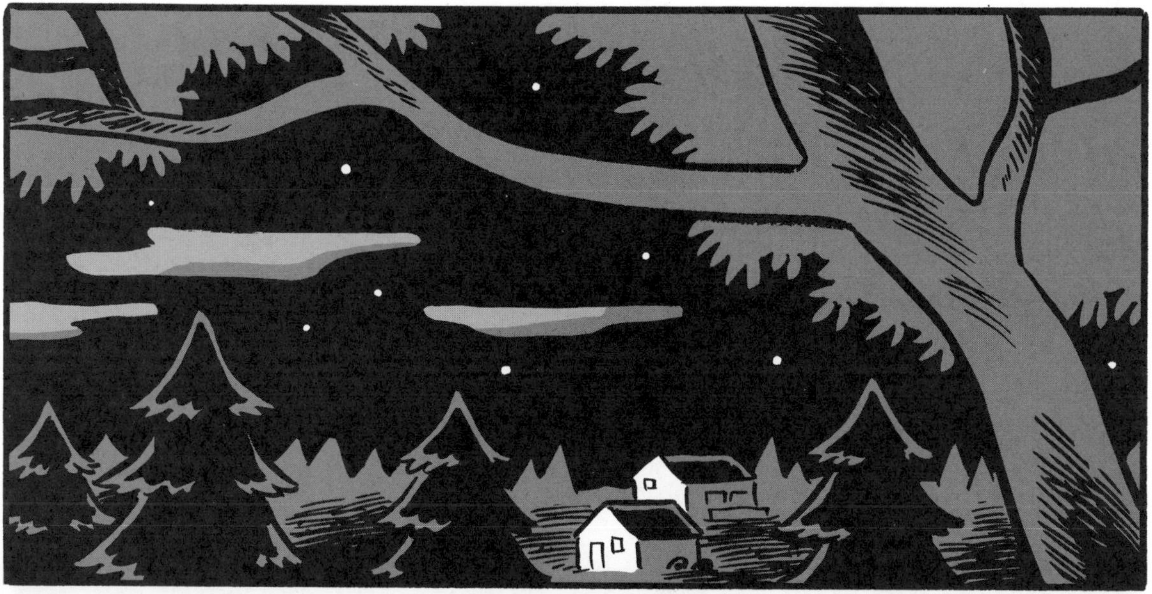

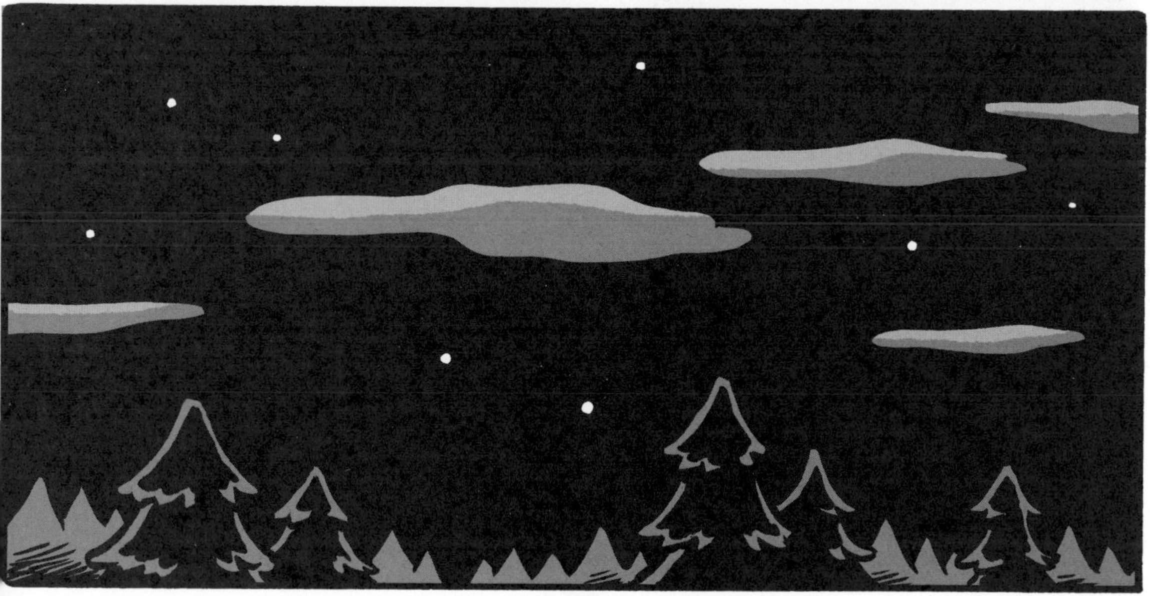

Jon Allen grew up in a small town in Connecticut in the Naugatuck Valley, and he's been drawing comics since he was a kid, initially inspired by reading **Calvin and Hobbes** in the newspaper. He went to school for illustration and got his **MFA** in painting. When he graduated in 2009, he moved to Brooklyn and put all his energy into making comics. Since then, he's worked as a barista, a studio assistant for a handful of painters, a UI/UX designer, and presently, a storyboard and layout artist for a show on **Adult Swim**.

Thanks to...

Nick Abadzis

Gregory Benton

Remy Boydell

Aaron Cockle

Mike Dawson

Sophie Goldstein

Alex Halberstadt

Dean Haspiel

Alex Krokus

Miss Lasko-Gross

Mike Levy

Jeffrey Lewis

Ellen Lindner

Jason Little

Andrea Purcell

C. Spike Trotman

Mom & Dad

& everyone from the studio